ANNAMANDA

A Novel of Courage by Jo Houser Haring

Southeast Missouri State University Press • 2014

Annamanda: A Novel of Courage by Jo Houser Haring

Softcover: $19.00
ISBN: 978-0-9883103-7-7

First published in 2014 by
Southeast Missouri State University Press
One University Plaza, MS 2650
Cape Girardeau, MO 63701
www6.semo.edu/universitypress

Cover Design: Liz Lester

Prologue

Kentucky, 1799

"Heh, heh, heh, pretty lady, heh."

"Step aside, Sir!" said Cyrus.

We was stopped short on the narrow trail, our way blocked by two altogether scruffy looking individuals, their intent questionable.

"Heh, heh, pretty lady," repeated the one, slobbering into his scraggly and matted beard. "Heh, heh, heh," he giggled again and hiked up the greasy buckskins that drooped on his skinny frame. The other said naught, his eyes trying to send out a look of malice that his brain mayhap was too slow to forward. Betwixt the two I would have said that they probably shared no more than half a wit. But that did not make them less dangerous.

"Get behind me, Annamanda," said Cyrus which I, being a thought or two ahead of him, had already done. "Move aside, Sir."

"Heh, heh, we an't want nothin' but to see what ye carry in yer packs," said the one, and with a gesture he removed his cap and run his hand over his thin hair. There was naught about him that was remarkable, save only the grease and dirt and one of his ears which flopped over considerably, the result probably of injury or frostbite.

"What we carry is none of your concern, Sir!"

"Heh. We'll make it our concern," he drooled, the spittle coursing through the shabby beard and onto his shirt. He fingered the knife at his belt. I saw no other weapon. But that still put him one weapon ahead of us, for we carried none, without counting the iron stew pot that my granny had give us upon our wedding and that was wrapped up tight in the parcel which I carried. I tightened my hold on it. Did I have to swing it toward someone's head, I intended to be ready.

"Put 'em down, put 'em down," said the slow one, and the floppy-eared one nodded. I gripped my parcel all the harder, but to my surprise, not to mention vexation, why Cyrus started to putting all his things down.

He unloaded first the heavy pack from his back and let it slide against a tree, then he put down the portmanteau which he carried, and finally with

4

great care, he stooped and slowly—terrible slowly it seemed to me—laid his Bible, which he carried in the other hand, beside the tree next to the portmanteau.

Well, I clung to my parcel. Did anyone reach for it or for me or, for that matter, anything else we owned, I didn't care what Cyrus Pritchard did, I for fair intended to split wide some heads with my granny's cooking pot before either of them rascals touched what we owned—pitiful little though it was.

But I had misjudged Cyrus's intent, for when he come up from his Bible, he held in his hand a right hefty tree branch, fallen so long from the tree that it was dry and without leaves and made a most effective cudgel. And by the time he had done swinging it, why the floppy-eared one was making through the brush in a high hurry, and the other'n lay on the path before us, looking dumb, blood gushing from his forehead.

Cyrus bent over him, examining the wound.

"Is he dead?"

"Naw. This kind don't kill easily. He'll sport a sore head and mayhap will think more than once of stopping travelers with a view toward robbing them. We'll leave him. His companion will probably return for him." He retrieved his parcels and I helped load him up, handing him his Bible the last thing.

"We'd best step lively and find shelter before dark, Annamanda. I would not like to be caught in the shadows once them two has regrouped."

Nor I.

I stepped along behind Cyrus as lively as I could, but truth to tell, six months gone with child, I did not step as lively as I had when we begun our journey.

Cyrus was following the Call of the Lord and I was following Cyrus.

We had followed from near to Carolina, across Kentucky, carrying what little bit we owned in our two hands. The Lord would provide Cyrus had insisted, and so far He had. Or somebody had, anyway.

We had walked and we had rode with diverse travelers by wagon and horseback and we had even caught a raft or two headed down this or that river, so long as it was westerly. We was headed to the far western edge of Kentucky where Cyrus had been called to preach, but what had started as high adventure had bogged down considerable, and it was not enough that we walk or ride with strangers, be rained on and cold, miss meals and home comforts, but now we was reduced to beating off rascals with sticks, too far gone to turn back.

But Cyrus had faith in the Lord. And I had faith in Cyrus.

Chapter 1

George Washington Pritchard

"Now, push, push again, Mistress Pritchard. Push on an' hold it."

"Yes, Ma'am."

I endeavored to follow the instructions, but though the pushing did seem to come natural, the holding was most hard.

"It'll come, it'll come." Mistress Hankens said that with the firm conviction of one who knew from experience. But I was not at that moment inclined to learn, only to endure. "Next time, it'll be easier," she said and she wiped my brow with a cool cloth. "An' by the time ye've birthed ten to twelve, why it'll be like the old cow a-calvin'. How old are ye? Seventeen ye said? Wal, that's not old to be in first partruition, nor so young neither, though I've always held it's best fer first births that yer mother an' other kinswomen be the ones to bring ye through it. An' don't ye think that's true?"

I nodded, but that only to be amiable, for it was not my mother at that moment or anything else on earth that I desired so much as I desired relief. At another time I might have been put off to have been compared to a cow a-calvin', but as the torment twisted my lower body, I would not have been surprised to have truly brought forth a calf at any moment, possibly a two-headed one at that. I could not speak, as I was not capable of anything save clutching at the ticking and endeavoring to keep from shrieking.

"I have never questioned the Almighty in His Wisdom or His Plan, ye know," continued Mistress Hankens, "but now an' then it's hard not to wonder if He were female, would He not make the birthin' process some easier, at least to limit it to daylight hours in warm weather." Though she did not say that last comment with unusual force, Cyrus looked up from his Bible, reached for the stack of wood at his side and poked two or three logs onto the fire against the cold outside and the deepening evening gloom inside, proving that he had been paying more attention than his posture might admit.

My father's house had been possessed of window light and I missed it. Most particularly did I notice that lack when Cyrus even during daylight hours struggled by light of the bark to make out the Word. For it was of such importance to him that he could not lay it by until the weather was warm enough that he might take it out of doors, to read it with more ease.

I felt another spasm approaching and prepared myself for it but not quickly enough to prevent a moan from escaping my lips. And at that (I did but dimly perceive) Cyrus rose and put the Book aside, grasped his axe from the corner and quitted the room, without I think, a backward glance. I might have pondered upon the fact that there was wood enough to carry us through two or three winters already split, as Cyrus was wont to go to the wood pile whenever he was troubled or vexed or simply unoccupied. I might have pondered that, I say, had not the anticipated spasm o'ertaken me.

"Push, girl, push. Now, n'en, it'll be along anon," comforted Mistress Hankens. She wiped my brow once more and we both heard the steady striking of Cyrus's axe beyond the house. I was quite breathless from my ordeal.

"I don't hold with his doctrine, ye know," said Mistress Hankens jerking her head in the direction of the sound of Cyrus's axe. "I don't hold with it atall."

I did not answer, being still out of breath and myself preoccupied. This was not a complaint that was new to me or to Cyrus or to others of the Faith.

"It's a narrow and hard doctrine. I don't hold with it atall," she repeated. "The elect and predetermination. Why, that would cut off salvation fer but a few, and we was put here to save our own souls and the souls of others. And he's such a young and comely man to espouse such a hard doctrine," she went on, "an' you, too, if ye do indeed follow the precept of yer husband, which of course the Lord insists that the good wife do." And she laid upon me such a stern expression of disapproval that I would have answered, but my concentration was otherwise employed and I was praying fervently that the Lord would hasten the progress of this dilatory infant and so ease my suffering.

"An' don't fergit to push and hold," admonished the midwife as I groaned and stretched and finally relaxed. "There's lots hereabouts that don't hold with it, that take it quite amiss," she continued. "Depraved? Certain we come into this world depraved, depraved from Adam and the Fall, an' we got to do somethin' about it, not set on our hind ends and expect to be saved or no accordin' to the whim a' God before ever He established the world. We've all got as fightin' a chance as anyone, and it's up to us whether we be saved or no. Grace or predestation or elect. I don't hold with it, don't hold with it atall."

Had I not been working up to another spasm, they coming it seemed to me closer and closer now, I might have been tempted to have pointed out that she was not alone in either her contempt of the doctrine or in her unwillingness to face Cyrus Pritchard directly with that contempt, he already having earned a just and sound reputation, even in his youth, for uncommon strength of argument and firmness of purpose. Perhaps it was as well, being preoccupied as I was, for it would not sit well with me to dispute an older person, particularly not one so kindly and helpful as Mistress Hankens had been to us, and us near strangers, and in her view doctrinally unsound.

"It's almost time," I whispered, surprised that my voice was so weak.

"Yes," murmured Mistress Hankens. "Now just push and hold, remember. It'll come, it'll come. Ye'll know it when it does."

The door opened. I could not see it for my eyes was closed, but I could feel the rush of cold air, which was nicely refreshing.

"It's time," I heard Mistress Hankens say, and the door closed and Cyrus stood outside and waited. I would that he could a' waited indoors, as it was passing cold and working toward weather outside, but as we had only one room to eat and sleep us, he must stay without. It would not do a man in the room where birthing was in progress.

For a moment, between them fearsome pains, I thought upon the loneliness of my condition. My first birthing attended by a stranger, with neither kith nor kin—none but Cyrus—near. The form of my dear mother flashed across my mind's eye and my sister Martha Elen, just younger. How eager would she have been over this first niece or nephew, eager in her own sassy manner. Ah, mayhap she had already got Joseph McCade—that hopeless wanderer—to stay still long enough to wed and was herself great with child.

Then my homesick thoughts was jarred by the reality of where I was. I was rattled clean to my ear lobes, I thought, by a fierce pain. It passed at last, and I relaxed into the ticking, huffing and puffing with the strain of it.

"I don't hold with it," growled Mistress Hankens again, more I think at the closed door than at me. Through the mist of pain and exhaustion, I could hear Mistress Hankens continue her diatribe, quoting Scriptures and presenting those arguments so familiar and at once as puny to those of the Old School Baptists. I could not make out her particular persuasion, be it New Style or Methodist, Methodist most likely, as the country was fair to bein' overrun by those of that persuasion, though it was obvious that she held with the false Armenian doctrine of free will. As Armenianism had crept into an assortment of doctrines, it was often difficult to tell one from the other. But the woman was well-spoke in her faith and I might have discussed our differences at length—for I could dispute right well—had I not been otherwise occupied.

"I might like a sip of water," I murmured.

"No, no. Not now. Soon, but not now fer ye'd only just puke it up an' ye got more pressin' work than pukin' up water."

Her words were then lost to me as was my thirst in a mighty thrust of pain that fair shriveled my innards and twisted my extremities, and I thought that I ne'er could hold that shout of suffering that was building in me.

"Push, push, push!" I pushed, I strained, I prayed and just when I thought I was spent entirely and could do no more I felt a pop and a loosening and an instant relief.

"Ah," sighed Mistress Hankens, "a boy." And as I struggled to my elbows to look, I heard a sharp slap and a howl of life, perhaps I thought that same howl that I had suppressed so many times in favor of this young one. Mis-

8

tress Hankens propped him up for me to see as well as hear, and I viewed my son, a new-born sinner, depraved and defiled in original sin, but I could only hope born in Grace, redeemed from corruption before the world began.

He might've been protesting his corrupted state for he howled and kicked and waved his puny extremities to such extent that Mistress Hankens laughed aloud and said proudly, "Oh, he's fine, he's fine."

"Cyrus," I whispered.

"Anon," replied the midwife. "Let us finish what we've to do here." I knowed that to be true. A man must neither preside at nor even be made aware of the birthing process. It be women's business only. We would present him the child only after we was both cleaned up and order brought to the proceedings. Until then Cyrus would have to shiver outside.

Mistress Hankens took pity, opened the door, poked her head without and said, "It's a boy," and slammed the door shut again. In good humor she dispatched the afterbirth and cleaned the mess, wrapping and binding the babe with no more comment on doctrine, for there's nothing like the birth of a sinner to gladden the heart.

Mistress Hankens might have been thinking that one day he would needs be born again, this first time only a rehearsal for that more important birth. But I felt glad in my heart, certain that so perfect a little creature must surely have been born in Grace. I knew Cyrus would chide me if he knew I had such a thought for we can none of us ever be truly certain of Grace, so I vowed to myself not to say nothing of that sort to Cyrus.

Mistress Hankens brought the babe to me and showed me how to suckle him, though I did not need so much lesson as she seemed to think, I being my mother's oldest daughter and having helped to preside at many of her later births as well as those of kinswomen and neighbors. The proceeding from that point of view was not new to me and now that my torment was eased, everything else came easy.

"Now," said Mistress Hankens, "I'll give ye this advice," and I prepared my mind for more disputation of doctrine, but she had else in mind, for she continued. "This advice, as ye have neither mother here nor kinswomen to do it fer ye. He'll be at you in short order," she said jerking her head toward the closed door behind which Cyrus waited. "He'll be right at ye again, it's not his fault a' course. It's just the way they are. They can't help it as it was Eve brought it all down on us that first time. So be sure ye suckle this babe as long as ye can an' it'll help to keep from gettin' another'n right on. I don't know why t'is but t'is. Them wives as get tired of suckling a toddling young one and give it up has got another'n to suckle fair to nine months on. Mind that. Suckle that babe 'til it's two or three years gone. An' don't worry yourself; it won't thwart God's Plan none. Ye'll still manage to have a house full ere yer quit, fer yer a strong and healthy girl with lots a' babes in ye. No need to be burdened with too many little ones all at once. Ye got the time."

With that she swung wide the door, catching Cyrus who was standing in front of it in some surprise. She motioned him in and he came, walking carefully as if on egg shells. He peered down at the babe for a long moment, trying to maintain that serious composure and dignity of men that the moment demanded. But his eyes, like the lock of hair that was given to falling across his face at inopportune moments, gave away his excitement.

"We must pray, Annamanda, dear wife," he said soberly at last. "We must thank God and offer praises unto Him for fulfillment of that which was ordained before the beginning of time."

I agreed. I would thank God for having pre-ordained this tiny sinner and also for having pre-ordained his perfect little fingers and toes and the obvious strength of his constitution.

And thus we prayed, even Mistress Hankens. She bowed her head, for I peeked to see, and but for furrowed frown when Cyrus spoke of this moment as pre-destined before the world began, she seemed as caught up in the spirit of the moment as Cyrus and I was.

Cyrus prayed his prayer and, lifting his eyes after the final Amen, announced, "We will call him George."

"George?" In truth we had not talked of names, though I had taken my own counsel in the matter many times previous. George was not one of those names that had come to my mind.

"It is my father's name," said Cyrus, "and it is the name of General Washington without whose leadership these free states might ne'er have come to pass. We'll call our son George Washington Pritchard."

For just a moment I felt a little pique that he had made such a decision without consulting me, and after all had I not gone to no small trouble in behalf of this babe? I almost spoke up but caught myself in time. Both Cyrus and Mistress Hankens was quite content with the name and in truth I had no great misgivings, though it did seem some cumbersome for such a tiny creature to be burdened with. Anyway, wasn't this Cyrus Pritchard's firstborn son and a most momentous occasion for him? We would not bicker over so insignificant thing as a name.

"George is a good name," Mistress Hankens was saying. "I've knowed a sight of Georges and, but fer that King from England, they was to a man decent and God-fearin'."

"George, George Washington Pritchard," I tried the name on my tongue and it instantly found its way to my heart.

Mistress Hankens reached for her cloak, which was folded in the corner, murmuring again that George was an excellent choice of names. She flung the cloak about her shoulders, and Cyrus rose from his knees in some haste.

"Why you're not going yet, not tonight, for it's almost dark to go so far. But I will walk you if you must," he added.

"Naw, naw, naw," she waved him aside. "I an't about to go home until the daylight hours. I'm only goin' out to take my comforts before it gets darker or colder. I don't cotton to barin' my backside to the northwind."

At which Cyrus flushed, for such kinds of flippancy was very hard on him.

"Do you suppose," I murmured after she had quitted the room, "that the Lord has pre-ordained supper for us this night?" I found myself with uncommon appetite which I blamed on the day's work I had accomplished.

"Well, if the Lord an't," he said, "Mistress Hankens has." And he frowned again possibly at the lightness of his own tone. Old School Baptists an't necessarily stern, without humor or frivolity, but because of his years, Cyrus in attempting to appear older and wiser demanded more sternness of himself than the other Elders demanded of theirselves. But sometimes he could not help himself his youthfulness. "She has prepared a stew for us from the squirrel I brought in last night. It's on the fire."

And certain enough when Mistress Hankens returned with a rush of cold air through the open door, she set about immediately stirring up the meal.

We ate then in mostly silence. One time the baby, George—such a well-defined name for an infant yet so ill-defined in personality and form—fretted and stirred in his sleep and all the three of us started as if we had forgotten his presence.

"This is a nice and tight air-free cabin, Mister Pritchard," said Mistress Hankens as she cleared the table. "Do ye then plan to settle here and clear this land?"

"That was not our intent," Cyrus replied. "We only stopped here because the winter slowed us and I found this cabin which with some work has been satisfactory to our limited needs. We have been headed toward the far western edge of the country."

"Ah, an' then, ere ye goin' only to the river or will ye go beyond?"

"Beyond the river is Spanish and French," said Cyrus.

"That an't stopped too many set on goin' ther I noticed. Anyway, ther's land enough that the French and Spaniards'd have a hard time locatin' ye, did ye not want to be located. Spaniards, I hear," she added, "is even willin' to encourage settlin' in ther lands in exchange, a' course, fer yer loyalty to them and ther cause."

"I have kin on the Kentucky side, two or three days from the river. We think to stop there. But I will heed the Lord's Will"

"Well, I don't mean nothin' amiss but it's prob'ly just as well that ye travel on, fer the truth is we got about as many denominations as one county can rightly hold now without addin' yet another'n, an' that not by most so prized anyway."

Cyrus said nothing for he never cared to get into an argument on Scriptures to no real purpose.

"Anyway," Mistress Hankens went on amiably enough, "we got us here some Methodist an' some New Style Baptist as well as some Seventh Day Baptist an' Presbyterian an' Quaker an' Congregationalist an' Lutheran an' Universalist an' a Deist or two. We'd be hard put to accomodate nothin' more. The county fair rocks a-Sunday with hymns as it is."

"Well," said Cyrus slowly and deliberately, "if you got all those things only, but none that teaches the true Word of the Elect by Grace, then you are certain in need of one more, for you are spiritually poverished."

"Now that, the elect and predestination, them are the old faith, certain to pass away, fer the new faith, they ere a-clearin' of the brush, so to speak, in many new an' modern ways."

Cyrus answered her softly as I had known he would. "This is Armenianism and Pelagerism, free will doctrines is all, and they an't so new as the one goes back to Pelagius in the fifth century and the other to Brother Arminius in the sixteenth. These new style folks, Armenians, wh'ere they call theirselves Methodist or Seventh Day or Duty Free, these folk think strangely enough to prune the trunk so that the branches would flourish. That is the only new idea and it most certainly false."

"Well, I don't hold with that a' course. Truth is there's been other Hard-shell Calvinists through here on ther way west but never 'lected to stay. It is a sight," she said then as if to change the subject, "the variety of doctrines that have passed west from here. Fer them that stayed, ther's twice that went on. Sometimes a body'd get the idea that we are here perched on the highroad to Judgment, the saints of all persuasions as do pass us determinedly by, flowing toward the river, as it was the Jordan not just the Mississippi that they would cross."

"Well," said Cyrus, "not only just Saints, I fear, for we have encountered already a goodly number of persons who would never so qualify."

"That's true. That's true. Fer they, too, pass us by, but that's not always quickly enough. Only last month someone came into Master Enos Will's house where only his elderly father was an' busted open that old feller's head and left him fer dead an' took with them his timepiece that he had had since before the Revolution an' likewise took two or three guns that they found there."

"Ah," Cyrus shook his head slowly and sadly from side to side.

"Well, they tried to make it like it was Indians that done it, but none was fooled. Was most certain some of them godless an' merciless ones as lives near an' on the river so that when trouble approaches, they can skim acrost that river in amongst the Papists an' unregenerates an' so be safe."

"And is that territory yet Spanish? I had heard that it was French, that Napoleon had got a hold on it from his strength and Spain's weaknesses."

"It's hard to say. Ye hear first the one an' the other. Not that it makes a difference. French or Spanish, one's about as bad as the other. Ye'd be wise to be on the look out fer the river scum, Mister Pritchard," Mistress Hankens added with a most solemn look at Cyrus. "They may not count so many as the Indians an' the French an' Spanish, but to my way a thinkin', ther far more dangerous, fer ther's no treaty to hold 'em, nor ere they bound by any of God's laws an' they strike fer no reason, as it pleases 'em."

Cyrus acknowledged her words with a nod. I could have told her that we had already met with that kind once on our journey and that good soul might have been most surprised at the strength with which Elder Cyrus Pritchard dispelled that attack, though I did wonder me myself about that situation. Had it not been for that big stick lying so handy we might have been in serious straits, me being big with child and Cyrus armed only with the Word of God. I do still wonder that that stick lay there so close by where Cyrus laid his Bible, but I would not ever speculate on it to Cyrus, for he would never entertain any argument that God might dabble in the everyday affairs of man.

We rose in the morning to a bright day, some warmer than anticipated and Cyrus set out almost at once a-hunting. "I can find a fat rabbit, I think, feeding," he said.

"A fat deer might better suit," suggested Mistress Hankens.

"We live on small game," said Cyrus, "for we would move on soon and I'd not waste meat that I have neither the time nor the means to preserve."

"Well, then," said Mistress Hankens, "think ye could dig some sassafras roots and strip some bark? It's nigh that season and a tonic made of it t'would go a long way toward bringin back the strength of yer wife."

Cyrus only nodded as he left.

Mistress Hankens with few words set about ordering the cabin, pausing to deliver small George Washington to me for suckling and loving.

"Well," she said at last, "I think yer on yer way an' I think to be on mine." And so saying she secured her cloak and tossed it about her shoulders.

"Why, Mistress Hankens, you'll not go yet. Wait until Cyrus returns and he will walk you safely home."

"Naw, naw, I can walk myself. I'll go only so far as Bryan Newhope's an' Master Newhope or one of his sons will saddle a mount an' carry me on. They're most accommodatin', the Newhopes, in such manner."

"But, Mistress Hankens, it's not entirely safe to walk so far by yourself. An't you afraid?"

As soon as I had said it, I repented it, for the look she turned on me I knowed well and I knowed the answer to expect in return, for it was the answer common to the folk that walk the lonely border.

"I am not afraid, Missy," she said, vexed and apparently forgetting that despite my years, I was not a child, but a wife and mother. "I have lived on the border for all the years I can remember. My father followed the border westward, for he both wanted the fertile land an' to be shut of people ever pressin' in upon him." She give me a stern look. "I am not afraid. Nor am I careless. I have respect for the dangers from man and beast. I know them well. Though I have always lived side a' side with the Injun, I know to respect what he can do, fer I have seen it an' what I an't seen I've heard about. I seen with my own eyes betimes them scalped an' them roasted over slow fires an' skinned an' otherwise tormented. An' I've heard of the babes with ther heads smashed open agin' rock or tree trunk an' living, beating hearts torn from dying bosoms. Oh, I could indeed go on all day with stories of such carnage," she said somewhat cheerfully seemed to me, considering the subject.

"A' course ther savages an' infidels an' much of what they do is right by ther own lights, but ye'd certainly ne'er expect such from God-fearing Christians." She paused at that point and frowned, "Except may some Papists. I've heard fearsome stories about them Jesuits that rides the river, particularly south from here," she added. "I have seen the French an' the English an' the Spanish, too, that would drive us out an' set the red man agin' us. Likewise, the river scum an' others like them have always followed them same borders.

"It an't a easy land, Miss, not the people in it nor the beast nor the seasons, but we here have survived because we know all that an' take nothing for granted. I'm ne'er a fine lady in bonnet an' bustle. I know what's to be done an' I do it. And if yer afraid, Missy, ye've no business bein' here."

I only bowed my head, a little 'shamed to have said what I knowed better. I, too, with my father and my people had lived close to the border as long as I could recall, and those same words she spoke were the ones my father spoke and my mother and everyone I had knowed who lived regularly far out from the settled lands. And though my mother and her sisters had expressed some reservations when Cyrus decided to follow his Call to the far western border, they had at last wished us well, for they trusted that we both understood what was involved. And Mistress Hankens was right that fear had no place in the wilderness. Those afraid needed to stay close to civilization and protection, for they was a danger to themselves and to others also.

"No," I said, "I understand and I'm not afraid. But it is cold and there are dangerous people abroad. I only thought that no one should travel alone."

"Well, it's not so far, Mistress Pritchard, an' you an' yer pretty babe have need of protectin' now a far sight more than I, fer yer in no condition to protect yerself at this moment, much less yer baby."

She drew her cloak about her and smiled her cheerful smile. "I'll see ye again ere ye move on toward the river, I suppose. But should I not, I just wish ye an' yer comely man good fortune even in yer faith—though I don't hold with it. But I understand and respect that ye both must cling to the faith of yer baptism."

"Oh, I an't baptized in the faith yet," I said. She shot me a sharp look and I realized that for the second time, I had said that which was better kept to myself.

"I will be soon, I know," I said. "My people have all been, my mother and father and aunts and uncles and even some of my younger brothers and sisters. I have only been dilatory."

She did not ask further, for which I was grateful. I could not explain to her or to Cyrus or to anyone else the annoyance I felt in not being able to go before the community of the church and its fellowship and announce my deep depravity and the vileness of the flesh, for certain I was that it existed, for we are born in sin, defiled and pitiful in the sight of God. I had but to experience that and announce it to those I would join to be accepted into the fellowship of sinners, hopeful but not certain of eventual salvation.

The truth was, embarrassing to admit, that I had not yet had that experience, that deep recognition of depravity and the hateful repugnance of it. Others in that fellowship most certainly had, and expounded upon the horrors of that experience and piteously begged inclusion into that small but mighty band of hopeful. But wait as I might, personal evidence of depravity had not become evident to me. And I did some days so envy those who could recall with such clarity the anguish that came with such revelation. I wondered if it would ever be mine.

Cyrus did not press, nor any of the others, for they knowed that it was a personal thing, that only I could ever experience the depth of degradation necessary to understand the nature of that which was most abhorrent to God in man. I would have to come to it of myself. And I did envy those who had traveled through that valley and now dwelt within the community of the hopeful. But not the saved, not necessarily the saved, as those of Mistress Hankens' mistaken persuasion might like to believe.

"Well, anyway," said Mistress Hankens, "I am convinced that, wrongheaded as ye may be in these matters, yer both sound of heart an' hopeful of redemption. That much, in my own mind, is all that counts, though of course there's many as holds that only baptism in the true faith an' bein' born again will warrant heavenly eternal life. But I suppose we shall see?"

I nodded at that.

"Well, again, take care of that young one, fer saved or damned, we need all the sturdy young blood that we can get along these troubled borders. An'," she added as she drew open the door, "don't fret none about me, fer I travel in the path of the Lord an' I have faith that He will see me safe."

Cyrus was most vexed when he come home not so very long after and found that Mistress Hankens had left alone, and he made mention of going after her. I only told him that I did not think she would welcome his company, which was true, for she had struck me as being of a stubborn turn of mind and independent.

"And, anyway, she said that you belonged here for the protection of your family." That last had a strange sound, but indeed we were now a family and not simply a couple. And Cyrus looking back and forth between me and young George, nodded with a bemused look about him, as if he, too, had found it startling to have gone from single to couple to family in so brief a span of time. He sighed at last, more in perplexity than vexation.

"Cyrus, she's traveled these woods and paths for all her years, and from the look of her that would not be a few. I would not worry for she has experience of the territory."

"I suppose." He waited for a minute. "But the border is in a turmoil now, no one knowin' whether it's French or Spanish beyond or what to expect of either or the British for that matter. And it's unsettled times that creates the turmoil with no effective laws to speak of. We are not the only travelers that have been set upon in recent times I've been told. It's common enough, and not all of those set upon have escaped injury."

He looked so solemn that I kept still, though I did think to point out to him that our encounter had not been without its casualties. Then young George began to fuss, and our attention was immediately drawn in that direction.

It was some several days on that Myron Wills, the oldest boy of Master Enos Wills, knocked upon our door and sought admittance against the cold, diffidently with his hat in his hand.

He was most certainly welcome, for though I was up and about, I was not recovered enough to travel about, and it had been some time since that I had seen any but Cyrus and Mistress Hankens. And after young Wills had warmed himself at the fire and had accepted a cup of warmth, I said as much to him.

"Ah, an' was it here that Mistress Hankens was comin' from on that day?"

The way he said it made me catch my breath, for it was too serious to be but ordinary conversation.

"That day?" Cyrus said and I knew that he had made the same observation that I had.

"Ye've not heard, then?" said the young man.

"Mistress Hankens?" My heart was in my throat.

"Well," said the young man with the solemnity of one given the opportunity of being first with news of dramatic events, "not exactly with Mistress Hankens. She is to my knowledge safe at home. But young Billy Newhope that give her a ride from his father's house to her own, was set upon on his way back by some unknown persons, an' had his head bashed in an' his horse stolen an', I guess, left for dead."

"Dead?"

"Aye, but he'll survive, fer he's a tough young one, but he'll carry about a sore head fer a time, as well as a arm in a sling."

"And did he know who was responsible?" asked Cyrus.

"Why, no. They was strangers, though he did mark that one had a most noticeable floppy ear. They was ruffians of the sort that are seen a lot between here an' the river."

After the young man had departed, assuring us that he would be most cautious on his route home, Cyrus sat for a long while before the fire, his Bible unopened on his knee, and seemed to ponder the fire as if it held some message for him.

"I am glad," he spoke at last, "that Mistress Hankens did make it safe. I would have been most grieved had she not."

16

"Well, she did say that she did not worry, for she traveled the path of the Lord," I said and immediately encountered the slow frown that was Cyrus's manner of suggesting that my comment had not been doctrinally sound.

"And was young Billy Newhope, then, guilty of straying from the path of the Lord and as a result had his head bashed in?" he chided me with the gentle grin that usually accompanied his observation of such lapses.

"It was only an expression," I said, a little provoked, for sometimes it did seem to me that it was unnecessary to carry doctrine over into every little thing.

"If the Lord was responsible fer keepin everyone out of harm's way, then we certainly would have to give him poor marks in that area, now wouldn't we?" he went on.

"I know that very well!" I snapped, and he grinned again. "It is not always necessary to beat a dead horse in order to show theological superiority," I said in what I hoped was an effectively haughty manner.

He grinned again, but then lapsed once more into a thoughtful study of the flames leaping in the fireplace.

"My dear wife," he said at last and I knew that he was being most serious, for only in high seriousness did he address me, "I have to give some thought to our further removal and the Call I have received. For now I have a family that needs protection. Before we advance, I must be as certain as is possible that that is the course that the Lord has so ordained. It is terrible hard to be certain sometimes just what the Lord wants."

Well, I for one certainly knew that to be the truth.

Chapter 2

Patsy Bradene

Little George stood before the fire, staring into the flames, his hands clasped behind his back in most solemn imitation of his father. I suppressed as best I could the smile that was in my heart, for he had just asked in high seriousness, "Mama, d'ye think that I shall be among the everlasting chosen?"

We was, the two of us, waiting for Cyrus to return, I no less than George anxious, for he had been gone several days to an Association beyond the river.

I answered George that all we could do was live as if we was and strive to build the Kingdom of Heaven on earth, at which he had frowned and become silent.

This was not his first venture into doctrine, and we were most careful always to take his questions seriously, though it was hard not to smile at that small suppliant, for he was most serious and thoughtful for someone who had not quite passed his fourth year.

I actually was not anxious that he be so serious. I supposed that his personality was the result of too much exposure to adult conversation and too little exposure to things childish, for there had been few children for him to see and become acquainted with in his short life. Though that, I thought pleasantly, was about to change, and I patted the growing roundness of my stomach with something like anticipation.

I had at first feared having one babe upon another, but old Mistress Hankens' advice had proved sound. I had nursed George until I felt sufficiently ready for another babe and then that one had been visited upon me almost immediately, though, alas that babe had not survived his birth. And now the third was on the way and we could only pray that it was a part of the Lord's Plan that this babe be strong enough to make successfully that rigorous journey into life. Then George might have a chance to be a child ere he become an adult.

George was a strong child, uncommon bright we thought, his natural serious inclinations abetted by the constant flow of visitors who come to confer and discuss the Gospels and doctrine with Cyrus, whose fame as a thoughtful and careful renderer of the Scriptures had spread amongst all practicing Old School Baptists and Calvinists and Predestinarians, not to mention a few of the others—Armenians of one art or another who came with a mind to dispute and left, often enough, confused and shaken in their own doctrine.

This, young George Washington Pritchard had been exposed to for all of his young life and it was no wonder that he thought more like an ancient little man than the three-year-old child that he was.

Mayhap it was because I was a proud mother that I saw in the boy depths that it seemed other small children did not have, yea even many adults did not have. He questioned beyond the questions that little children question. He did not ask where the sun come from or why the grass was green or such things as that intended only to keep your attention and for the enjoyment of the sound of their own voices. His questions was more probing and seemed sprung from some mysterious source, sometimes so uncanny that you'd spend days a-wonderin' where they'd come from. And he could so fix his eyes upon your face that betimes it seemed he was looking clean down into your own dark soul.

Though such did not happen often, still when it did, it could be unsettling. Such an occasion had rose not a month gone when we was all out of doors at various chores, and every time I had thought since of it, why it troubled me in some ill-defined way.

Busy at my wash pot, I had heard a small sound from Cyrus who was nearby sharpening his tools, and I had looked up. Cyrus had stopped what he was doing. I had followed his gaze to the edge of the clearing, and with a quick start, made out the figure of a man so still that he might have been naught but a slender sapling on a tree breezeless day.

Alarmed, I had pulled George near to me.

But Cyrus had only frowned and watched and all at once raised his hand as in greeting. The figure had remained poised for a moment and then returned the salute, ducked his head and vanished, just that quickly.

Well.

"Who was that, Daddy?" George had asked.

"It was a solitary, son."

Ah. So indeed perhaps it had been. "How could you be sure, Cyrus?" I had asked. "How could you know at a glance that it was one of them solitary persons and not one of the scum of the river or a bandit?"

"It's hard to say, Annamanda," he had replied. "There is just about the solitary a sense of the woods, a shyness, almost as a wild animal is shy and skitterish, a nervous tension, the way that a deer paused at morning feeding is tensed."

"Daddy," asked George, "what is a solitary?" He had stumbled some over the word, but considering his age and the state of his speech, I thought he said that new word quite creditably.

"Well," Cyrus answered, "a solitary is just a man that wants to be alone. He travels the woods all by himself. Lives on berries and roots when they're available, or bear grease and corn meal when they an't—and whiskey when he can get it—hunts a little, mayhap sells some pelts for what little he needs. He's as close, I suppose, to a wild animal as a modern man can become."

"Ain't he lonely?" asked the boy.

"Lonely? I don't know. Seems that if he was lonely, he would seek company, don't it? I truly don't know. What I do know," he said after a pause, "is that the solitary goes on before the rest of us, that he leads civilization where it would go. The solitaries seem to go first, followed by single families and then the groups. In betwixt and between come the rowdies and the ruffians, the scum and the wicked, those that would benefit being far removed from the law of the settled lands."

"An' where does the solitary go, then? Or does he stay?"

"No," Cyrus had answered, "no, the solitary betimes keeps moving away from the crowd."

Dear little George had frowned a small frown and weighed what seemed to me to be more explanation than such a little sort could be expected to understand. At last he looked at his father and asked, "And God, when does the Lord come? Does He wait 'til all else is there and then He comes?"

Cyrus had sighed and frowned. I knowed that he wanted to give a serious answer, for what in another child would be only a senseless question seemed from George to be perched on the edge of the profound.

"Why, George," answered Cyrus at length, "indeed God goes ahead with the solitary, and yet He stays behind with us. How does He do that? Well, His ways are strange and wondrous, you know that, don't you?"

George had nodded gravely. He was most preoccupied for a while and then he had announced, "I will be a solitary some day."

"Why, whatever for, George?" I had asked.

"Well, because God will go alone to a solitary, but we have to share Him."

That memory come back to me at times as now when George stood so straight asking his solemn questions. But apparently spiritual thoughts had deserted him, for his next question was more in keeping with his age.

"An' when will my father be home?" he asked suddenly. "Why has he been so long?"

"Well," I said, "I wouldn't think he'd be much longer, a day or two at most. The Association he visited should be over and done, and he on his way home."

He spoke a little petulantly, for he was not a perfect child by any means. "He's been gone too long and I want him back."

I said nothing, but I did agree. Usually George and I was able to accompany Cyrus to these Associations and listen to the several days of preaching and enjoy the fellowship of others of our persuasion that we otherwise did not often get to see. But I was at that unwell and uncomfortable stage of childbearing and so felt it best to stay home. And George with me.

We was never afraid, of course. We had arrived at our destination after George's birth and found a nicely secure settlement, though Cyrus's kin that we had been seeking had gone on—no one could say whether back the way they had come or on toward the far western frontier.

The Indians was always a threat, of course, but they always had been, just as the weather was and the wild animals and the wilderness in general.

Kentucky had been a bloody battleground in the past, and north into Ohio and Indiana Territory the Indians remained restless and threatening, so that the settler who would be secure and retain his scalp was always on the alert.

We had a nice cabin, with window light, and two tight rooms set upon land cleared by Cyrus, and we had neighbors near. There was a small congregation that Cyrus ministered to and a school kept at odd times during the winter not so very distant at the Old Shawnee Ford. I could not see that we could ever want for much as the land was fertile, and Cyrus a willing and industrious worker. And I could see that we might add to the cabin as our family grew as I was certain it would. I was a content housewife, a far cry from that thoughtless girl I had been when I first followed Cyrus into the wilderness.

Though still not baptized.

That was the most serious disaffection that I could find with my life. I waited in vain, it seemed, for that sense of shame to descend upon me, that sorrowful remorse that showed me my own corrupted state. How many had I watched fall on their knees, wailing and moaning before the blessed Saints, pleading in their supremely sinful state to be admitted to that band, asking and receiving admittance.

And still it had not come upon me. I knowed myself to be every bit as degraded as any of those, and yet I could not announce it; I did not feel the intensity of it. It was most provoking.

Even small George could say, "I am a poor, pitiful vessel, Mama." And I could do naught but sigh.

"George," I said, "the time has come for sleep. Get to bed, and by tomorrow I'll bet your father will be home, and he'll have wonderful things to tell us of happenings elsewhere."

He objected that he was not yet sleepy and he could wait for his father and he stamped his little foot in some vexation, at which I took him up by his suspenders, aimed him toward the out of doors, and directed him to relieve himself thoroughly. He was not a perfect child, as I have said, and upon occasion had been known to defile his straw tick. I stood by the door and made sure that he followed my directions before I let him back in, wrapped him for bed, listened to his prayers, and at last tucked him away. As I had suspected he would be, he was asleep almost before I had turned my back.

Cyrus indeed was there when he awakened the next morning, having slipped late into the cabin and thence into our bed. "We'll talk tomorrow," his only greeting, and his tired sigh discouraged any further attempt at conversation.

Cyrus might have slept longer, but George was atop him as soon as he woke up, and Cyrus, good naturedly grumbling, allowed himself to be pulled from the warm bed. And he sat at the table, the boy leaning against him, as I prepared a meal for us.

"And was the meeting successful?" asked the boy.

"Aye, very." Cyrus turned to me as he spoke. "There was such an outpouring of faith in the Lord and prayers for help and upwards two dozen came forth to announce their sinful state and beg inclusion into that band of hopeful. There were tears enough I think to raise the river Jordan to flood stage."

"What!" said George, his eyes quite wide.

Cyrus laughed and pinched the boy playfully. "It is only an expression, Son. There was no flood of actual water."

I had to wait until George had sufficiently stuffed his mouth with mush and gravy that he could no longer ask questions before I could put my own to Cyrus. Who was present that I knowed and who had married and who had new babies and who had asked after us, as well as a few necessary questions concerning the various preachers who spoke and how they was received.

Cyrus, as he answered those questions in turn, did not look at me but stared steadfastly at his plate, which was unusual, for when he started talking of such things, he usually became so animated and excited that he ceased all else and waved his hands and spoke rapidly and peered hard at whoever he was addressing. It was a little strange. It come to me that he had something weighty on his mind that he was loathe to share with me.

Cyrus went about his chores that day—restocking the woodstack by the door and tending the garden—small George hard upon his heels with questions and observations, more of the latter than of the former, for truth was, he could indulge himself in those pointless questions of childhood and often did. It was not until George eventually collapsed into a tired heap by the fire and fell fast asleep that I was able to question Cyrus, for I knowed by then that he had something grave upon his mind.

"Tell me more about the Association," I said, "for I am hungry for news." I had the feeling that whatever concerned Cyrus resulted from that meeting.

"It was," here he paused and frowned and from his eyes glinted that light that now and then signaled a beautiful agitation of spirit, "a soul-revealing experience. I have heard others speak of such experience and even thought that perhaps I myself had occasionally briefly experienced it, but now I know that not to have been true."

He stared hard into the fire and I waited patiently.

"There beneath that heavy shade, for there was no building to hold us and only a lean-to for cooking, not far off from the banks of that great river,

I felt such an outpouring of hope and love of righteousness and peace with God, that I all but floated off above the river. But, alas, in the eventual parting both heart and feet were heavy."

"And were the petitioners and the brethern of so righteous and sanctimonious disposition?" I asked, for it seemed to me that such experience as my husband described must have come from some outward source.

"I know not. I cannot say from whence the Spirit came, only that it did come. It filled my heart with such amazing peace and my mouth with such words and phrases and appeal that when I spoke, the tears of rejoicing and the wailing of joy spread throughout the group, and I spoke not for one or two or three hours, but upwards of six, ceasing at last as my voice give way. Had not that puny instrument failed, I might yet be speaking and they listening."

He sat staring still into the fire, and I could not be sure which burned brightest, the light from the fire or the light from his eyes.

At last I asked, "And what does this mean?" I ought to have fallen on my knees and rejoiced with him, I knowed, but truth was I had a sinking and anxious feeling that this discourse was only prelude to that which would profoundly affect us, and I was apprehensive.

Cyrus did not look directly at me. Instead he poked at the fire with a stick and seemed to be carefully considering what he would say.

"There is a need," he said at last, "in those western lands. There is a need for the Word, the Truth. If you could only have seen the signs, those frightened and hopeful souls, clinging to the words that God sent me. I had a vision, I know, Annamanda. God came into my heart. I felt His Plan as clearly as if He had writ it in block letters."

"He told you to go west."

I did not ask it as a question for I already knowed the answer. And there was a numb hollowness in my innards, for I knowed that where'er God sent Cyrus, I and mine would go also. God might be particular about who He directed to go, but He was not so particular about who might have to go along.

Cyrus nodded, still avoiding my eyes.

"To the river?"

"Beyond."

I could not catch the sigh that escaped my lips, though I tried, for I didn't want to seem to question God's Will, though I might question Cyrus's interpretation of His Will.

"Beyond the river? But that's dangerous."

"Oh, no, not so dangerous, for it's rapidly settling. And, Annamanda, there's lovely, fertile land there, to be had almost for the asking."

"There's lovely, fertile land right here and no need to ask for it. And safe too."

"Well, that's not necessarily, for ye've heard yourself the stories of the restless savages north in the Indiana Territory. We are too far from civilization out here to be particularly safe anywhere. This one place is not very much safer from one sixty miles hence."

When I did not say anything, he went on. "The brethren out there spoke with me and begged me to consider, for I did not tell them how strong had been God's presence at that meeting, though I think they must have sensed it. They have offered me land, help in clearing the land and building a cabin, and a singing school from which I can realize enough profit to see me through until sufficient land is cleared to make a crop."

I looked out at the tidy, little farm, the corn crop not yet laid by, and the peaceful hills beyond.

"We must get on," he said gently, following my gaze. "Before winter sets in and before you are far gone in your confinement."

"It is a long way to go and perhaps not safe," I said again, being unable to think of any more potent argument. I recalled before George was born, when we owned only what we could conveniently carry in our hands, being set upon by river ruffians. We owned not a great deal yet, it was true, but still far more than we could carry ourselves.

"The deacons have provided," Cyrus said. "They are most eager, for as I said they sensed the Lord's presence at the meeting, and they feel as I do that this is of His Plan. They are sending a wagon and ox, and several are coming themselves to help us pack and to make the journey with us."

"When?"

"They are on their way."

Thus they came in three days time, by which time we had sewed our slight affairs, the land returned, with little compensation for the corn crop and the cabin, to the neighbor we had arranged to take title from, that title not yet taken.

Cyrus hastened to meet the group that approached the cabin, for he recognized them. There were four afoot and two in the wagon, and the one handling the oxen, a woman, but such a woman as I had hardly ever seen in my life, three ax-handles tall and a barrel wide at least. Beside her sat a man as large as she, the two easily a match for the yoke of oxen that pulled the wagon.

Cyrus led one of the group to me, as the others climbed down and otherwise accommodated themselves. The man who followed Cyrus wore a flat crowned hat and a serious and solemn expression, which I noted Cyrus's expression suddenly exactly matched. They were joined by George, who took his father's hand, mumbled a shy response to the deacon's greeting, and matched his stance and expression exactly to those of the two men. And there they stood, the three of them—looking solemn together.

"This is Brother Kencaid, Elias Kencaid," said Cyrus to me. "He is an elder of the Salt Creek Association. And this, Brother Kencaid, is my wife. Her name is Annamanda."

"Ah, Sister Pritchard," said Elder Kencaid, and he bowed slightly at the waist, putting some strain there I noted on the buttons of his vest. Elder Kencaid had about him that air of authority that, had I not already knowed it, would have warned me that he was a pastor of some sort. I responded only with a smile, not bothering to correct him. I was used to being addressed as Sister, even though, were the laws of the church specifically followed, I should not have been so addressed.

The others in the group immediately came forth and were called by name: "Brother Thomas Lease, Brother Amiable Simpson, Brother John Cuthcart," and the last, "Brother Reuben Bradene and his wife, Mistress Patsy Bradene."

I could not help noting that Mistress Patsy Bradene, the remarkably over-sized wagoneer, was not accorded a "Sister," and I wondered if that was an oversight. The woman was not only immense, but she was also as remarkably untidy as she was big. Her hair was matted, as was that of Brother Bradene, and they were both dirty, patched, and generally ill got-out. Not only that. I noticed that Patsy Bradene scratched herself immoderately, even in those places I had been taught that a modest woman did never itch.

I was relieved that the others of the party, deacons and elders in the church, was very much of the sort that I was accustomed to, clean and gentle spoke.

But, ah, the Bradenes. Especially the wife, for an overgrown man is not so strange, an overgrown and rough man. But everything about Patsy Bradene was outsized—her figure, her voice, her manner—and when she announced loudly, "I need to piss," and strode off toward the trees, I did my best to keep my own manner unruffled.

"Mistress Bradene," said Brother Cuthcart when Reuben Bradene had quitted the group to see to the oxen, "is of a rough and hearty texture, but inside she is as soft as potash soap. As is her husband Brother Reuben."

"Is Mistress Bradene not a sister in the church, then?" The naming of Reuben "Brother" and his wife "Mistress" for a second time seemed to me more than just an oversight.

The deacons looked at one another, shuffled, and looked uncomfortable. Finally, Brother Amiable Simpson said, "Patsy Bradene has been a member of the Lost River Church but has just recently been churched. Her husband remains a member in good standing, and Patsy, though her letter has been removed, remains a friend in the hearts of most of the flock."

"She is," added Elder Kencaid, "difficult to deal with, is all, fer she's given to strong drink, and upon occasion turns unruly fer that reason. She's un-common strong, y'see fer a woman, and few is a match fer her when it comes to handling oxen and ass, though the Bradenes have recently give over cul-tivating the land and returned to the river, both being brought up on it and right knowledgable of it. They did try for some time to live upon the land, but somehow lacked the knack fer it."

"Well," said Cyrus, "it's good that she and her husband is so uncomplain-ing about the matter."

"They're good folk—no doubt about it—but rough textured, very rough textured."

"Why was she churched?" asked George who was standing nearby taking in more than he probably ought. I give him a stern look, though I was itching myself to know the answer to the question.

"It's all right," said Brother Kencaid. "Naught a child couldn't hear about. Brother Ullyses Kern did bring a distress against her fer she got drunk and in a fit of rage inflicted copious and severe wounds upon Brother Kern's jackass that she had been turning his garden ground with."

"Severe wounds upon a jack?" said Cyrus.

"Brother Kern brought the beast before the assembly himself, that all could examine the damage. And it did appear that he had been sore put upon for he bore welts and one ear was cockeyed, his tail appeared to have been mishandled, and, truth is, there was evidence that he had been bit upon the face."

"Bit!" I said.

"Well, Brother Kern so claimed and Patsy could not recall enough of the event to defend herself. Truth is, fer many years we all overlooked certain of Patsy Bradene's flaws of character as they was more than balanced by her integrity and willingness to be of help in any cause. She is kind to children," he added.

I most certainly did hope so, and I looked toward George with the intention of suggesting to him that he comport himself in such manner as not to anger Mistress Patsy Bradene, as the poor mule had done. Although, contrary as those beasts can become, I am sure there are those who would sympathize with Mistress Bradene's fit.

When it come time to feed the group, Patsy Bradene rose to help and much as I tried, I could not keep her hands, which appeared to have been quite some time between washings, entirely out of the foodstuff. She put the corn dodger she had formed from wet dough into the oven—her hands being after the mixing of the corn meal some cleaner than before—and heaped the red coals high upon it, heat enough I hoped to purify the grime which had washed from her hands into that mixture.

Later, as there was not room at the dinner table for all of us, Patsy Bradene and I, along with George, waited until the men had finished their meal.

The men spoke of those things closest to their hearts, of course, of Grace and the Kingdom of Heaven on earth and reported to each other of encounters with various Armenians, Methodist mostly.

"A Methodist weed," said one, "a little sprinkle and it's saved." And they all laughed.

Reuben Bradene having silently gobbled plate upon plate of victuals, at last sighed loudly, comforted himself with a large expulsion of air, and once again filled his plate to heaping. However, this time he rose and carried the plate to his wife, and she accepted it without a word. Thereupon he took his spoon, wiped it diligently on the tail of his blouse, handed it to her, and returned to his seat at the table as she greedily attacked the victuals. George, wide-eyed, shot me a look, for he knowed that he would have been roundly chastised for any similar action. Cyrus and Elder Kencaid, apparently noting themselves Brother Reuben's act, removed theirselves quickly from the table, and the other men followed, leaving ample space for Patsy, George, and me. And listening to the men converse as we ate, I realized that Reuben Bradene had yet to speak, though he nodded with enthusiasm and generally smiled a great deal.

Elder Kencaid said, "This Armenianism, save yourself business, it appeals to them without patience. Can't wait. They needs must go out and rustle about and stir things up and so convince theirselves and others like them that they are bound by their works to be among the saved."

"Well," said Cyrus, "I don't suppose it hurts them none."

"No, but they can become that contrary, all the same, when questioned closely," said Brother Cuthcart. "I mind the time a few months back that I was set upon by one such—a blacksmith who was working on my horse—during a discourse on salvation that so angered him that he attacked my very horse, with blows and kicks."

I did not say nothing, but I did wonder to myself at going off to a place where the taking out of anger on horses and jacks seemed to be commonplace.

"I would hate to think that the salvation of my soul depended on how hard I worked to save it. My, I am an industrious enough man," said Brother Lease, who had been uncommon quiet up to that point, "but did my soul depend on it, I would feel bound to go at it not than twenty-four hours each day."

The men laughed and agreed, and the conversation moved on toward more immediate and practical matters, it having already been agreed on the need for haste. "We need to get you settled and secure in a cabin before winter. And I would get beyond the river as soon as possible," said Elder Kencaid, "for there's talk of Indians and where there's any unrest of any kind you can always count on finding the river scum, too."

This would not, of course, frighten anyone unduly, for there was always talk of Indians. It had been years since any general uprising, only now and then isolated incidents of violence. Still, where the savages was concerned, caution was advised. Some was to be trusted and some not. But there was always talk of unrest along the border.

"The Injun that wants my scalp," spoke up Patsy Bradene, "had best be 'pared to part with some of his own."

Looking at her, I thought that was surely true.

"Will we see Indians, Mama?" asked George.

"Might, mightn't," said Patsy Bradene with a wide, gapped grin, and she scratched here and there at herself. I had been remarking the scratching she had been doing and was becoming some concerned, for it seemed to me that there followed little welts after her scratching. I was becoming fairly well convinced that the woman harbored fleas, though I could not actually yet prove that.

"Anyway, boy, ye can ride with me on that 'ere wagon, and I garntee that ye'll be safe as in yer mama's womb."

I made up my mind then that I would satisfy myself in the matter of fleas before George set foot upon that wagon.

We did not get started west still as quickly as we'd have liked for there was too many who would wish us well. It was three days gone before we had managed to be fed by all those who would feed us and then to make our goodbyes and then to get our goods packed and loaded on the wagon. I noted, too, that it was Patsy and Reuben and Cyrus who did most of the loading and packing of the wagon, those deacons being too long gone on various disputations and consideration apparently to pause for so slight a thing as hefting loads of items into the wagon. Brother Amiable Simpson did lift a hand with the loading of a few things. Truth was, Patsy and Reuben Bradene exhibited such strength and energy that none else seemed really to be needed.

Through it all, Reuben had said naught, but only grunted now and then, and I did wonder if the man was actually mute. Nor did his mate have a great deal more to say, even though she did seem in charge of the family communications and gave Reuben directions and when necessary spoke to one or another of the deacons in his behalf. She spoke mostly in casual conversation—when she spoke—to George, which worried me for she was not always moderate in her speech. But she had George's ear, and he followed her around like a puppy.

"Mistress Bradene," he asked at one point, speaking the way children do and coming out with what you would rather they didn't, but so quickly and surprisingly that you haven't a chance to stop them. "Mistress Bradene, an' why is it that you and Brother Bradene haven't got no children of your own?"

"Why," answered Patsy Bradene before I could manage to interrupt the conversation and steer it in a more seemly direction, "I dunno why t'is, but t'is the Lord's Will, I guess." And she hoisted the large black cooking pot up to her shoulder and with a frown seemed to consider in all seriousness what the child had said. "We seem t' lack that what it takes to put a young'un together. Mayhap," she said with a most sorrowful glance toward Reuben who was not paying attention to the conversation, "if we had more of the necessary paste we could make 'un."

"Paste?" said George but before he could say more, I collared him and sent him toward the garden to see had we missed any implements around there.

It was well on into the morning by the time we was loaded, the hens tied and tossed into the wagon and the mulch cow attached to the back. And then we was off. I had insisted that George and I could walk.

Mindful of Lot's Wife, I did not look back.

"Is it a long way?" asked George, hardly before we had got started. "When will we get there?" And then, "I'm tired." He was already eyeing the space beside Patsy Bradene on the wagon.

"Why, not far," answered Patsy Bradene. She had been singing, or rather she had been attacking a melody with more vigor than success. She gave up that activity to answer George. "Don't fret it, my man," she went on. "It's only a matter of putting one foot a'fore t'other enough times 'til yer there."

My will was not as strong as I had thought it, for before long, George was indeed perched on the wagon seat chatting amiably with Patsy Bradene. The walk was slow and passing pleasant and in truth it was an even trade. Patsy kept George from whining and fretting, and George kept Patsy from singing. I should perhaps 'a felt a little guilty, for what Patsy sang were those wondrous old hymns. I was certain that the Lord would not take amiss that the singer and supplicant might not 'a been able to found the tune had she a divining rod for it. But then the Lord had other things to distract Him from the racket, and I did not. I would confront the matter of fleas should the time come that it needed confronting.

We camped that night by the side of a clear little creek, not far from a small settlement of houses. There was some argument amongst our group as to whether the creek would flow toward the Ohio or the Mississippi. I did not enter into the dispute, friendly though it was, because I had no mind for that sort of thing. Anything I said would be little more than a simple guess. But George was not so shy and announced to all that it did indeed run into the Mississippi River. And George proved to be right, for the next day someone inquired of the settlers nearby and they affirmed it.

Cyrus was always most proud of this ability of George, though young and completely inexperienced, to always know the direction. I would never have said anything to Cyrus that might dampen his pride, but truth was that this was an ability that the child had probably inherited from my side of the family, though I myself did not possess it. My own dear father was possessed of that ability to an uncanny degree. He could tell the direction on a cloudy day or dark night as accurately as he could when the sun or stars shone bright. He needed but the stir of a leaf, or some said not even that much, to know the direction to go. And he'd only laugh when asked how he did it, as if it were some kind of magic, which it was not. He did not know himself how he knew, only that he did and he praised God that it was so.

So it was with George, though he had not been severely tested in the matter, of course. But he did have that same uncanny sense of direction and to be most self-confident of it, as was my father.

We had planned a week's journey to the river, and instead of becoming tired as I had feared, I felt myself becoming stronger. Both the weakness and the illness that I had been feeling subsided with the fresh air and the exercise.

The sky remained clear and the breeze pleasant. I remarked on that, and Brother Kencaid replied that it was the Lord's Will and that while He would visit hardship and grief upon His children, He was fair in the matter and would mete out like amounts of sunshine and pleasure.

At one settler's house we passed, the woman who come out to talk warned, "Ye'd best take care fer ther's been sighted some squirrely kinds in and about the woods 'twixt here and the river."

I could tell from the way she said it that squirrely kinds was not the kinds we wanted to encounter.

When we encamped that night, there was some conversation about what the woman had said. Cyrus as was his wont went directly to the matter. "We are going across the river and into them new lands. I feel that it is God's Will that we go, yet I do wonder about the laws and lawmen. T'would seem that lands so new to the United States would yet be unmanaged."

"Well," said Brother John Cuthcart, "that's very much as it is. There remains a wild element, and there is always a question of safety in such situations."

"But," announced Brother Kencaid, "yer gain' into the land of Eremus Lodi." He said it as if we should understand that the name made a difference.

"Eremus Lodi?" said Cyrus.

"Eremus Lodi," said Brother Kencaid with a peculiar frown settled between his eyes, "is the holder of large tracts of land west of the river, lands which he has had since long before the French, that he claimed during the Spanish occupation. Don't ask how, fer none knows how."

"What manner of man is he?" asked Cyrus and, had he not, I surely would have.

"It is enough to say that he has controlled his land through Spanish, French, and American rule, and that those who might trouble others do not trouble Eremus Lodi."

"He is just," said Brother Thomas Lease. "Just."

But the way he pronounced the word "just" made me wonder, for I could not but link it with the word "Terrible." It seemed to me that, as it had been pronounced, the two went together. Terrible and Just.

"And of what persuasion is Eremus Lodi?" asked Cyrus.

"No one knows," answered Brother Kencaid. "I have heard it said that he is a Deist, but I know not with any certainty. He has certainly made no claim to predestination of any sort that I know of."

I did not hear the rest of the conversation, for by that time George had begun to nod, and I needed to get him bedded, so I went about that task. I only heard certain murmurings that I did not try to make out and returned from tucking George to sleep in time to hear Brother Kencaid say with a nod, "What is to be, will be." And the others, even Patsy, stared quietly into the dwindling fire.

The next evening we camped hard upon the river, figuring that we had more hours ahead of us than we could make before nightfall. We walked to the bluff overlooking the river and stared beyond. I had seen bodies of water. They was not new to me, but this river was such a sight that it caught my vision and held it hard. The rushing, tumbling water, whirling and grasping at the bank, catching and tossing large logs as easily as the lesser debris, was magnificent, I thought, as must be an army marching forward in full color, and every bit as menacing.

"How do we cross?" I asked, and from the tightness with which George held to my hand, he must have had the same thought.

"Oh," laughed Brother Cuthcart, "it is not so impassible as it looks. It's high, fer we've had copious amounts of spring rain, but the rivermen who pole the rafts knows how to navigate it. Never fear."

I took in a deep breath. Cyrus give me a gentle look and reached for my free hand as if to assure me that, was it the Lord's Will that we pass the river, we would pass. It was not really my concern.

While we set up our camp and put the pot on to boil, Cyrus and Reuben took rifles and went off to find a rabbit or a squirrel for our supper, and Brother Kencaid and Brother Lease took their pails and went down along the nearby creek which drifted into the river to see if they could likewise catch us something to fry.

Patsy and I led ourselves, getting ready what we could whilst Brother Amiable Simpson and Brother John Cuthcart sat on a log and carried on a disputation. I have noticed that if there is gathered together more than one old Style Baptist, you will have a dispute. It will likely be friendly and there will mostly be points of agreement, but they are not capable of carrying on a discussion of doctrine, I think, without finding some manner of disagreement and enjoying theirselves no end in arguing it.

They was so engaged and not paying no attention, and Patsy had gone on down toward the creek to fill a bucket, when George made a strange noise and tugged at my skirt. Right behind us, hardly five feet away stood two men, the one tall and heavy and the other passing slight. They did not have a good look about them. I turned to speak up to the deacons who was too furiously talking and gesturing to have noticed the arrival of the two, but the lesser of the two took a couple of steps and caught George up in his arms.

"Put him down!" I said and that so emphaticially that the doctrinal disputation come to a sudden halt, but it was too late, for the larger of the two held a rifle up and grinned at the two deacons with less humor than most people exhibit when they smile. Through his matted beard, his open mouth showed as many holes as it did working teeth. Those that were left ill-stained and unsightly.

I reached for George, but the little man only backed off and giggled, holding the boy aloft. "Quiet, girl," snapped the bigger, but I ignored that command. "Put him down!" I was not in no mood to be polite.

The little man giggled again, snorted, and spat. George was wide-eyed and stiff as a board, and the little man lowered him slowly, for George was not a slight child, and proved quickly to be more of a burden than the little fellow was willing to sustain. But having put George on the ground, he still held the boy by the collar. I moved toward him, but the little man tugged George hard against him, pulled his knife from his belt, and held it to the boy's throat. I stopped short.

All of this had happened so fast that the two deacons had not managed even to get to their feet, and sat at the mercy of the grinning ruffian with the rifle.

"Heh, heh, heh. We only want to look around and see what ye got we could use," giggled the little one again, a thin stream of dark spittle coursing from his lips and into his scraggly beard.

"Let my boy go," I said this thus less furiously, for I was afraid for George.

"In a minute, maybe, Missy, I feel like it."

It was then that I noted that the villain sported a floppy ear, and though there was nothing else particularly familiar about him, I could not expect that every river scum in the country had a frostbit ear.

"We got others comin'," said Brother Cuthcart, right fiercely I thought, considering that he was looking into the barrel of that rifle. "Ye'd better be off afore they come or ye'll be in fer it."

"Yea, yea, fer sartin, fer sartin," said the big one, emphasizing his point by waving the rifle barrel up and down.

"I allow," said the floppy-eared one, sticking the knife up close to George's face, "that I'll leave a mark 'er two fer this young'un to 'member me by." He pricked the skin on George's cheek, and as the child cried out, I sprang for him, surprising the rascal so that he fell back a bit, still hanging onto the child with one hand and the knife with the other. But 'ere I reached him, I stopped, for towering over that slight ruffian, her shadow enveloping him, one arm upraised, an iron skillet in hand, stood Patsy Bradene. And as she slowly brought down the skillet, there was upon her face such a beatific expression as ever I had seen and with greatest ease, effortless almost, the skillet come down hard enough upon the unsuspecting villain's head that the echo of it might well 'a been heard in Orleans. And he, soundless save a grunt, slid slowly to the ground.

Patsy Bradene stood over him, and George leaped into my arms. The rifle toting scum was so startled that he let his guard down, and it was Brother Amiable Simpson who jumped him and wrested the gun from him with such ferocity as to belie his Christian name.

The floppy-eared one tried to rise and for his efforts got banged again, this time on his good ear, with Patsy Bradene's skillet. "Move," said Patsy Bradene most placidly, "an' I'll squeeze ye in the middle 'til the shit runs out one end and the snot out the other." He must 'a believed her for he lay still, whimpering and nursing his battered ear. I thought that with such a blow he must surely go through life ears flopping on either side.

And that was how Brother Kencaid and Brother Lease found us, and shortly Cyrus and then Reuben, each one hearing the tale from start to finish as he come up.

There was some considerable discussion about what was to be done with 'em, as we had not the means really to hold them and yet did not feel safe with 'em abroad. Patsy Bradene had several suggestions, all quite colorful, which was rejected.

At last, Reuben, Cyrus, and the deacons accompanied the two ruffians to the river, divested them of all their weapons, as well as all their clothes, and set them adrift in the river on the skiff that they had apparently arrived on.

And as they drifted toward the current in the middle of the river, Patsy Bradene joined the men, for she was ne'er so modest as most would be, particular in that sort of situation, and yelled out careful instructions on how they could be expected to be greeted were they foolish enough to accost us anymore.

The men of our party took turns by twos that night in keeping watch, but it proved not to be necessary. We broke camp and started south along the river without more incident.

If Cyrus noted the floppy ear of that river scum, he did not remark upon it. Nor did I. But that bent ear attached to that ill-kept and sorry head did make an impression on my mind that would not go away.

It was near to noon-day when Patsy Bradene give a sudden "whoop" and pointed toward the river where a boat struggled in the churning current. At first I thought Patsy was calling our attention to the boat's distress, but that proved not to be true. For it turned out that the boat was headed our direction and that for the purpose of transporting us across the river.

The boat or raft—whatever it was, for it was an ill-made and gangly thing that seemed unable to make up its mind whe'r to be a raft or a flatboat—was manned by two sturdy rivermen, front and back, the one at the oars, the other at the tiller. The front-most one waved his hat and whooped back at Patsy and grinned a broad grin.

"Why, it's the Deiterbecks, Jacob and Otto, come to fetch us," cried Patsy, and she waved again. And in short order the craft was pulled to the shore, the front-most Deiterbeck—who proved to be Jacob, the other his brother Otto—wading ashore to tie it to a sturdy sapling that seemed to have been placed at the river's edge for that very purpose. Introductions was then forthcoming.

I had ne'er seen two more dissimilar brothers in my life. The only characteristic they shared was their length which like the Bradenes' was considerable. Jacob, grinning and noisy, was perfectly balanced by his brother Otto, silent and grim.

I looked from the wide and rowdy river to the two rivermen, the one grinning broadly, exposing several gaps in his smile, and the other still and stony silent. I looked back at the river and then at the wide raft tied to the tree and then at the rivermen again. I did not voice my lack of enthusiasm, for I seemed to be the only one of our group to question either the reliability of the craft or the skill of the oarsmen.

"D'ye need to make a trip to hell an' back," Patsy was saying, "why Jacob an' Otto will git ye ther an' return ye, an' that without much as a singed whisker."

"Aw, Pat," announced the gap-toothed Jacob, "only if you an' Reuben crew us." And then he chuckled at that thought and winked broadly at George whose wide gaze had not left the riverman's face.

"We was set upon by scoundrels," announced Patsy, for all the world as if the riverman had asked how our journey had been—but he hadn't.

"Scoundrels?"

"The one with the floppy ear," said Reuben. I couldn't keep from giving him a sharp look, for he spoke seldom.

"Ah," said Jacob, sending out a stream of darkened spittle through one of the convenient gaps in his smile, "that'd be Drooly, huh?"

Patsy Bradene nodded.

"Wal, fer Drooly, an' that other'n, his name's Skeet, ye got no worry a' long's ye keep yer face to 'em. Neither one's got the sense 'er the courage to do nothin' but molest ye from the back." He thought about it for another moment and then added, "They'll be one day food fer the fishies, both of 'em, fer that's the way of the river scum. Drooly, now, he's prize example, too, of that scum, not human seed, him, but 'pregnated by the slime along the riverbank and borned from no woman but from a dark hole at the edge a' the river." Then he winked broadly at George, who was staring hard at him the way children will do. The surly Otto only continued to frown.

In spite of my reluctance, we was shortly packed and boarded upon the Deiterbeck vessel, and hardly before I could send some hasty prayers skyward, we was shoved off and riding the river. It proved to be as lively a ride as e're I'd had in my life. And though I'd ne'er rode an unbroke horse, I did think that the two trips would be some alike. I braced myself in the middle of the raft, for I had no mind to stand as Patsy did at the edge, and held George tight by the hand. That busy ride did not do my easily unsettled stomach much good, and I was relieved when it was ended and we had put to on the western side of the river, some miles down from where we had started.

Through the entire trip, Jacob talked. Sometimes Patsy interrupted, and they jonered one another and teased, but it was Jacob the riverman who held forth the most. It was obvious that he was one of them gifted talkers who in spite of hogging all conversations was entertaining, that you could not hold it against him.

He and George had took something of a fancy to one another, and once we landed on firm ground again, why, George tagged after the riverman, much as he had been tagging after Patsy and Reuben Bradene.

I was surprised at how quickly our goods was transferred once more to dry ground, the oxen, which had been unyoked for the voyage, yoked once again and ready to go.

"Wal, boy," I heard Jacob say to George, "just ask me a question, fer I know all that's to know, fer the river brings it to me on the spring flood."

"Is there wild things upon this side of the river?" George ready to accommodate the riverman apparently.

"Wild things?"

"Animals, wild beasts?" said George.

"Ere ye afeared?" asked the riverman in mock seriousness.

"No," said George. "I only wondered." But he did have a strangely thoughtful look about him.

"Wal," said the riverman, "ther's the usual—bears an' snakes an' painter-lions. Ere ye feared of painter-lions?"

George solemnly shook his head from side to side.

"Wal, ere ye afeared then of The Beast?" Jacob said that last with a fearsome frown upon his face, though there was a twinkle just behind the frown.

"The Beast?" said the boy.

"Aye, The Beast. Ye know it not, n'en? Wal, it's a fearsome thing, I hear, though I've ne'er seen it myself. But they say," and here he leaned toward George and went on in a bed whisper, "they say that it's tall like a man, but most wild, an' that it hides and pounces out upon the unwary an' eats ther hearts out!"

"Oh," I said, "now that's no thing to be telling a little boy."

"Jacob," said Patsy with something of a frown upon her usually placid face, "no, Jacob, none a' that."

"Wal," he grumbled cheerfully, "naw, I guess it an't a right good bed-night story, now, is it?"

George, however, instead of looking frightened, frowned as if he was worrying an idea around. And knowing the way that little mind worked sometimes, I was not surprised when he come right back with another question.

"Is he a solitary?"

"What?" answered Jacob. He had stirred up more, I thought, than he had reckoned on.

"A solitary. Is The Beast one of them solitaries?" The boy asked his question most seriously, and he probably had a deeper intent behind the question than the riverman could e're expect of one so little.

"Wal," pondered Jacob, "I dunno. A solitary? Wal, yes, now I s'pose that's possible, that's just what he is."

With a lengthy, frowning stare toward the heavy undergrowth and woods nearby, George started to speak, but was stilled by a sudden gesture from Otto, who was pointing in the distance.

On a high bluff, quite some distance beyond, sat a rider upon a horse. The reins was loose and the rider sat casually with his hands crossed upon the pommel, while the horse, its long neck bent, nudged through the grass and leaves as horses will do. It was too far away to make out much about the rider except that the horse upon which he sat was black and the rider, a white man, was uncommonly tall I had to wonder if Baptists was the only normal-sized people on this side of the river, for almost everyone else we'd come upon was uncommonly over-sized.

"Ah," said the riverman raising his hand in salute, "that's Eremus Lodi yonder."

That name was familiar. I recalled it from the earlier conversation of Brother Kencaid. I watched that figure then with some curiosity, waiting for him to move toward us, but he did not. At last, almost reluctantly, he lifted his own hand in something like a returning salute and, pausing, at length turned his mount the opposite direction and guided it, stepping slowly, out of sight.

Well! Such thing was almost unheard of. Travelers was not so common a sight that you did not stop to visit and converse. Indeed, what would have been a simple courtesy in a city was on the frontier almost an unwrit law. And here this man being offered a friendly greeting all but spurned it. Now that was arrogance.

The riverman Jacob, perhaps sensing what I was thinking, shrugged and with a slight grin muttered, "Ye ne'er know about 'im, wh'er he's froze er thawed. Froze today, looks like." He shrugged.

George tugged upon Jacob's fringed blouse. "Does it smell of death?" he asked.

"What?"

"The Beast? Does it smell of death?"

The riverman was apparently some perplexed at the question. He looked down at the boy who was staring hard at the riverman's face the way he could do when he was intent upon something, as if he would reach himself into that man's skull and bring forth the answer.

"Wal," said the riverman a little uncomfortably, perhaps sorry that he had brought the subject up at all, "wal, I dunno, mayhap, yes, it prob'ly does smell like somethin' dead."

"No," said George, "not like something dead, like death."

The riverman looked around in confusion, and I interrupted, "Now, George, enough of that. It's just a scary tale. You'll not sleep if you dwell on it. There's no such thing as The Beast," I added, giving the riverman Jacob a dark look.

"Ah, but, Mama," said George with a deep frown, "something smells of death." He paused and stared hard into the deep woods beyond.

I followed his glance. Did I detect a shadow then, there and gone in the dark woods? Or was it mayhap only a cloud passing quickly over the sun? I looked up, but could not tell, for the sun had fallen behind the tall trees upon a distant hill.

"I smell death," murmured George, staring into the distance.

Chapter 3

Sarah Elizabeth

We was not long in getting settled, at least temporarily. Though all of the deacons had offered us shelter, it had been John Cuthcart's invitation that we had finally accepted. George and I found ourselves in that lively household, while Cyrus and several of the congregation searched out a place for us to settle and build.

Clara Cuthcart—for Clara was Mistress Cuthcart's Christian name, and I thought it a most pretty one—was an amiable hostess, friendly and full of information. "It's probably as well," she said in her friendly but forthright manner, "that ye did not choose to stay with Brother Bradene and Patsy. I doubt that ye'd taken to it. They being much upon the river, that cabin is only shelter. Ye can't say no more of it."

She had reference to Patsy Bradene's insistence that we take shelter with her and Reuben. I was fair alarmed at that prospect, for Patsy still did itch herself considerably, and the idea of fleas was still much in my mind. Apparently Brother Reuben was likewise distressed at the prospect, for that man who spoke so rarely was moved to ask his wife, "Pat, d'ye think we got the room?" His voice was low, the sounds rubbing together like a handful of creek gravel. "We got but 'un room," he finished lamely, looking distressed, first at Patsy and then at me.

"Aw, we kin make the room," said Patsy. "We'll lay a big pallet on the floor and make us a good, old Baptist bed."

At that Brother Cuthcart had interrupted with the offer of board at his cabin, "Which is large, with a loft and more located where ye needs must look to settling."

I was grateful to Brother Cuthcart and anxious to accept his offer, even when Patsy Bradene included in her objections the fact that Brother and Sister Cuthcart had already "a house full of young'uns." But then as quickly she amended, "Ah, but that's all right maybe now, an't it, George? Young'uns fer ye to play with?" At which the boy's eyes did light up considerable. I wondered that maybe Patsy Bradene might be a little put out, but she wasn't. She did seem to understand that the idea of playmates his own age would likely appeal more to a boy even than the company of a fascinating adult, for so George did view Patsy Bradene, she being the sort of adult that he had never been near to before, strong as an ox, but in many ways no more grown up than he was.

Clara Cuthcart was eternally cheerful and eternally busy, for her children stepped in stairs from the largest about eleven down to the youngest, not yet crawling to any extent. And I who had had the care of only one for upwards of four years stood in awe of the way in which this good woman managed her brood, usually with only one hand, the other occupied as it was with stirring or wiping or scrubbing.

There did seem to be at any time a young'un on her hip and one at her elbow with some need or grievance. I looked out at one point to see if the Cuthcart children did indeed line up outside the cabin door, waiting each a turn at its mother, but it did not seem to be the case. By some instinct or other, one would break away from the others as if at an appointed time, dash to where his mother stood, just in time to take the place of one returning to play.

I even looked out to count the Cuthcart children and came away with seven, decided that was not a proper total, so counted again and came away with eight. Nine, the proper total Sister Clara later affirmed.

Through all of that, Sister Cuthcart kept up a constant discourse, giving me advice, offering gossip that I hardly understood, and asking questions, which she was not at all shy of. In the course of answering some of those, I chanced to mention the sighting of Eremus Lodi, offering as I did my opinion of his ill-mannered behavior.

Clara Cuthcart perked up. "Ye seen him?" she asked.

"Only from quite a distance. I could make nothing out of his features."

"Ah," she sighed. "Ah, I would give the world to see him up clost, fer I've heard of him ever since we fetched acrost the river. He appears and disappears, like a spirit himself, indeed ther's folks I've heard that are actually afeared of him, that claims evil follows his footsteps. Truth, there is a great variety of stories concerning him, both good and bad, though," she added, "I'd not be quick to b'lieve all that I hear on that account, for ther's always those given to tellin' more than ther actually privy to."

"Ah," I laughed, "the tale tellers do abound, don't they?" And then I told her of the riverman Jacob's fanciful tales, particularly the one about The Beast.

When I had done with it, she give me a sharp look and then said, "Wal, that story is right common and ther's them, too, that do believe it, the story of The Beast. Ther's those that claim to have seen it, though I'd be more inclined to think some such stories is more the result of too much spiritous liquors or a dark night encounter with a bear—or both. Still, it an't the kind of story to scare the young'uns with, there bein' no need to scare 'em with make-believe when ther's terrors enough that's real."

George joined the Cuthcart children at first timidly, for he was passing shy with children, as he was not with adults, he having had more experience of the one than the other. But in short order he was accepted, assigned a chore, for each of the children old enough to receive orders got them, his being to gather dry branches and sticks to keep the kindling stack piled high. I was proud of the industrious way in which he went about his chore.

Fortunate for Mistress Cuthcart, her oldest two was girls, and they carried a large share of the burden. It seemed to me that the black wash pot in the yard was forever boiling. One child was at all times responsible for it, and they took turns and was most serious.

"A pot of boiling water untended is more dangerous to a bunch of young'uns than a tribe of Injuns," Sister Clara announced. I knowed that of course, but with only one little one to watch, it had slipped my mind.

"I do too much warshing, I know," said Clara cheerfully. "Ther's plenty others that sew ther young'uns into ther clothes early October and leave 'em ther fer the whole winter long. I do not know," she sighed, "how they tolerate the smell, fer a room full of young'uns crowded together on a winter day is fair odorous, no matter what."

"An'," she added, "I will boil my clothes. Never mind the ones that is content to just pound thers out with creek rocks. I want mine boiled; it's the Dutch in me, I guess. So that boiling pot," she ended, "has to be watched."

All but the youngest, including George, understood the danger of the boiling pot and they stayed clear of it. Still, the precaution was very wise.

Sister Cuthcart was nearer to my own age than most of the women I had recently met, though of course a little older and considerably more experienced of child rearing. She was nearly as wide as she was high, a merry, round little ball, bouncing the long day through from chore to child, chattering all the while, managing to carry on a conversation that had little to do with the wiping or the fixing or the scrubbing she might be attending to.

"I go to the door an' tot 'em up ever once in a while to make sure I still have as many as I started the day with," she nodded from her scrub pot toward the group of playing children. Rachel, her oldest, was seated on a log bench peeling sweet potatoes, while I cut the tops from turnips, separating them into two piles to be carried to the ring for washing.

"They get away from ye, if yer not careful," she added. "No matter how ye threaten, sooner or later ye'll have to go after a wanderer. The boys is worst."

I glanced over my shoulder at the group of playing children to assure myself that George was among them. I need not have worried. So happy was George to have so many playmates that there was no danger of his leaving them.

"Not so long ago," Clara went on, "two to three years gone, Brother and Sister Bates—they've since left the country—lost 'un, a small boy, that simply wandered off on a fine fall day. They looked and searched, and ever'one in the country, too, fer days thereafter with nary a sign. Some opined that the Injuns might've got him, others that he might've stumbled into the creek or even wandered so far as the river."

Mistress Cuthcart sighed. "They found him late in the winter, someone, I don't recall who, found him, his bones anyway, already picked clean by the varmints—or somethin'—though his clothes was fairly well intact. Poor tad was hid under some brush, too fearful mayhap to come when he was called, not so very far indeed from his home. It was sad."

I thought so, too.

"Ther was considerable commotion. Ever'one had an opinion, the way ever'one always has an opinion. Some blamed poor Mistress Bates that he got away from her, but I don't call that fair, particularly in view of the Lord's Plan, that what is to be, will be.

"The Bateses moved away over it. Some got to worryin' whether the tyke had reached the age of accountability, wh'er he was one a' the elect er not, and the argument—fer he was close on that age that most thinks marks the difference—got so heated that it reached into two or three pulpits. And then at Lost River meeting one night Mistress Bates took the floor and fair to lambasted 'em all an' said to her thinkin' the Lord would ne'er condemn a guiltless child, an' then someone else took the floor an' said that what Mistress Bates said smacked seriously of Armenianism 'cause we was all born in sin, an' Mistress Bates stood up an' told 'em all to go to hell, an' shortly after that they left the country."

Sister Clara took a breath, shifted the baby from one hip to the other in order to inspect a scratch presented her by one of her littler girls, and then commenced her recitation again before I had time to collect my thoughts and add any comment.

"Well, me," said Clara, "I can't say as I blame her, but I did keep my mouth shut, which John Cuthcart said later was a good thing, though he was surprised that I could do it. I an't one to question the Lord's Plan nor Heaven forbid try to explain it," she said. Then she went ahead and did that very thing. "I've been guilty of that myself. Sometimes it's right hard not to try to take a peek at God's Plan and try to make sense of it, even though it an't rightly none of our business.

"I knowed that the losin' of babes is part of God's Plan, else it would never happen, but it does, to most ever'one sooner or later. There's hardly a family that hasn't lost some at one stage or another. Though I haven't," she said somewhat fiercely it seemed to me, "I haven't and I don't intend to."

I knowed that she no more than I could read God's Plan to that degree, yet I wished her well. I thought of the one that I had already lost and of the one yet a-comin', but I did not make mention of either.

In ten day's time, Cyrus and the deacons had got cleared a space for a cabin and got it up and roofed, though not yet chinked. The acres that they had chosen lay they said near to Lost River about six miles distant from the Cuthcarts, though a little closer to the Leases, and within the circle that made up the area of the Lost River Meeting House.

"We don't plan to take title," said Cyrus. "For one reason, no one seems to know who we would take that title from, wh'er the land belongs to the United States or is still owned by those who hold the large Spanish tracts. For another reason, it is likely that we will not stay long here, but remove ourselves to a newer congregation as the settling proceeds."

That last was not happy news to me. I did not long to be forever following the sunset, as some people seemed so eager to do. I did hope in my heart that the Lord's Plan would include a more permanent residence for us, but of course I did not say that to Cyrus. He was most pleased and excited and was clearing land from daylight to dark, his Bible usually open on a stump nearby, where when he needed to rest, he would take himself and so pursue the Scriptures as he needed to during daylight hours.

In such manner he used his time and was eventually able to break a small area of ground that had never in this world before been broken. He borrowed Brother Ullyses Kern's jack for the job, and I could not keep from inspecting the beast with a view toward ascertaining the damage at the hands of Patsy Bradene. But no such damage was in evidence, though he did seem uncommon placid and cooperative for such an animal. And though it was late for planting, Cyrus did manage to get in a crop of sweet potatoes.

In between times, we all worked at chinking the house with mud from the river bank, which was not so gravelly as most such banks.

"I do not know," Brother Kencaid had said, "just how the maps may mark this river, probably with some Spanish name, but it is here called Lost River because it rises and then loses itself here and there for some time before it finally gathers itself together and flows into the Mississippi."

And the river did indeed do just that. You could follow it awhile, gurgling and placid as a just-fed babe, shiny, silvery pools here and there, and then suddenly it was gone, only to surface several yards and on. There was fish, but not many, being unable to get to each other and forced to make their livelihood in a very small area. Some of the pools was passing deep, they said, and in truth there was a place well south of our cabin where the river widened into a pool, almost the size of a lake, and there stretched across it a rope bridge.

"A foolish idea," said Brother Kencaid, "fer ye have but to go a few hundred yards to practically dry ground where the river is lost again. I do not know who made the bridge, nor why, fer it's a useless thing."

And it was a ragged thing, not used, nor likely to be, for it didn't look safe.

"Possibly," said Cyrus peering at the thing, "it was built by travelers when the river was high and running full and did not sink below the ground?"

"Well, that'd be an explanation," said Brother Kencaid. And we passed on.

George was not long in proclaiming himself lonesome and announcing his unhappiness in no small manner. I knowed just how he felt. I had myself enjoyed the company at the Cuthcarts, though it was indeed lively and crowded. But being summer, many of the children were content to sleep outside the door, where a small fire kept both the bugs and the night terrors away. I could imagine that being confined on cold winter days with many would not be quite so pleasant. And I hoped to myself that perhaps the Lord's Plan did not include quite so many children for me as it had for Clara Cuthcart. That was an ignoble thought, and I immediately told myself so and apologized to the Lord for it.

"I do not see why I can't go play with the boys," George would pout, for that was what he called the three young Cuthcart boys—Arthur, James, and Jeremy—who were closest his age, though in truth he played with them all, oldest to youngest. He did as a matter of fact dote on the smallest Cuthcart and carried her about as if she were his own special toy, and now and then he would get into a proprietary argument with one or another of the other Cuthcart children over it.

He was some mollified when I at last told him that I thought "the Lord willing" we would anon be blessed with a babe of our very own that he would certainly need to help me care for. He was very excited until he understood that it would be past Christmas time before that happened. And he began to sulk again, for to him, as to all children, Christmas always seemed impossibly distant. And he whined again that he wanted to play with "the boys."

"In time," I said. "Meeting time and you'll see them again."

That did not suit him. "An' how can I play when I have to sit still and listen?" he complained.

"Well," I reminded him, "the boys have to sit still and listen, too." He only glared at me a moment and then stomped away.

One day in early fall, Patsy and Reuben Bradene made their appearance. They did not explain why they were there and I would never have asked. And in truth, I was pleased to see them, although I had to admit to myself ashamedly that I was just as glad that the weather was warm and we could sit outside, for Patsy still scratched herself, and it was always a little better to be able to position yourself upwind of both the Bradenes.

Reuben and Patsy was given to dropping by at odd times. You never knowed when to expect them, though they rarely stayed long, sometimes with views to offer and sometimes not. George was delighted—as always—to see them, and certainly Patsy to see him. Reuben as was his wont said nothing, though his expression was friendly.

"We are goin' to have a baby after Christmastime," George announced. And though Patsy give me a happy smile, I thought I did detect a sad look in Reuben Bradene's direction. In truth George's announcement, though he delivered it to the few who passed our way, was not necessary, for I was far enough gone with child that a blind man almost could 'a told it. I was not like some that carried their babes inconspicuously.

"We ere a-goin' to pole up the river to the salt works," Patsy at last announced. "Up at the Saline Creek near to Ste. Genevieve. We'll bring ye back whatever load a' salt ye need," she offered.

I thanked her for that and then asked by way of conversation what all kinds of goods they transported.

"Why, anything," answered Patsy. "Salt mainly, for ther's always need of that. Sometimes lead from the lead mines or simply travelers, fer the river fer all its contrary ways is still the safest way to travel, particular would ye go to the south."

"How is it, Sister Bradene, that you and Brother Bradene do prefer the life upon the river?" I asked, though the information was truly not none of my business.

Patsy frowned, looked at Reuben, and then began an answer, "Wal, the river, it's that we're familiar with it, I s'pose, that we know what dangers to expect. We could not seem to get right with the land," she added, frowning a little deeper still, and I could not keep from thinking of Brother Kern's jack. "We did think when we took up residence upon the land that one day we would have young'uns that would need shoes an' mayhap to learn to write ther names an' to cipher an' all that t'would seem to come easier upon the land. But . . ." and here her voice dwindled off into silence.

"The river," said Reuben, startling me some, for he seldom spoke and that usually only in answer, "the river, why h'it's the end of the old and the beginnin' of the new, fer h'it splits them down the middle, yet Wit binds them both together and provides fer both at the same time. An'," he added slowly, "ther needs be someone to mind the river as ther's those that mind the land."

Well, awkward-put though it was, I thought that I understood what Reuben was saying, though it was a new idea to me. I had only thought of the river, when I thought of it at all, as something that needed to be got across.

Shortly after that, the Bradenes took their leave, though in passing I heard Patsy admonish George to be careful. "The woods," she said with a quick look behind her toward the trees, "the woods is filled with strange things. Don't go amongst them 'ithout yer maw or yer paw." It was wise counsel of course, yet it struck my heart with some apprehension.

After they was gone, I thought on them for a long time and wondered how it was that they had got to be such serious Baptists. Well, come a time when I felt like asking questions again that was none of my business, I'd ask them that.

I had nearly come to that time when I would need stay at home and wait out my confinement. Yet I decided to take in one meeting more, for the weather come meeting day was bright and lovely, the way it can be on a late fall day sometimes, that I could not resist the temptation to go out and about.

Cyrus preached a stirring sermon that day, too. We was able to take the benches and sit outside which was always a blessing, for the cold would too soon drive us all inside for several months.

There was some strangers amongst us that day, nor was that so unusual. It did seem that new settlers was continuously streaming into the district, and we was happy to accommodate any Christians—or infidels for that matter—that cared to worship with us and many did seek our fellowship. Of course, there was others that would have braved hell's fires before they would have taken fellowship with predestinarians, but that was their loss, I thought, and none of ours.

At the close of services, one of them strangers approached and introduced himself to Cyrus. "Ah, Brother Pritchard, my name is Lemuel Stephenson an' I've oft heard of your superior way with the Holy texts an' now have satisfied myself that such was no exaggeration." And he enthusiastically pumped Cyrus's hand.

"Why, Master Stephenson, I do thank you for those kind words. Where, pray, d'ye come from that you've heard such remarks?"

"I heard them most from the folk at Old Shawnee Ford, I fear," he said gravely, shaking his head. "I guess the Lord knowed what he was doin' when he moved you on," he added.

"I don't think I understand," said Cyrus.

"Why, an' haven't ye heard of the massacre at the Old Shawnee Ford some months gone?"

He did not have to have an answer, for from our startled expressions he could surmise what that answer would be.

"Ah," he sighed, "ah, indeed I'm sorry to be the one to carry that news. It was terrible, they said, terrible. I was never present but only heard of it from those that was."

My heart sank. I had that terrible feeling in my innards that comes with painful distress.

"They left not one living in that entire outpost. Caught them sleeping in the early morning, going from house to house, burning and killing. Apparently young braves that done it, fer they took no prisoners, but left corpses burned or hacked and mutilated.

"It is not certain that any died quickly, but it is hoped that was the case. There was apparently no sign of the tortures that sometimes do accompany them kinds of raids."

Master Stephenson did not spare us of the details neither, and not only did no one ask him to soften them, indeed mothers gathered their young ones about and bade them listen.

As Clara Cuthcart had one time said, make-believe stories such as them that did abound of The Beast was to be discouraged, for the young'uns needed to understand the real danger. Though such stories as Master Stephenson told might unsettle some young'uns' sleep, it was still necessary that each child and each adult understand the real dangers from fire or Indian or wild animal or even the climate itself.

Even so, my heart was near broken to think of all them folk that we had knowed and left behind, to think of how they had perished, and how we likewise would have perished had we not gone on. Truly, the Lord's Plan was more than I for one could comprehend. Them people at the Old Shawnee Ford had been, almost to a person, decent and God-fearing. There was certainly others abroad that the world could have more readily spared.

It was late fall by the time Cyrus's promised singing school could be got together, and by that time my own condition was as pronounced that I could not go along with him to it and enjoy myself. I had to be content with his recital of the events.

Cyrus was truly blessed with a strong and proud voice, and to a true and perfect pitch he added the wondrous knowledge of hymns I sometimes thought by the hundreds, hymns that his pupils at the singing school, mostly women and youngsters, was anxious to learn, all the verses as well as the chorus. And to be truthful, such singing schools also provided a chance for socializing and entertainment beyond meetings once or twice a month. There was then young women in attendance and accordingly young men, who probably was not so interested in learning singing as they was in gathering in the presence of the young women. I would love to have gone each time.

The pupils paid what they could, mostly in goods—yam, salt, eggs, and whatnot. The eggs that Cyrus brought home was indeed welcome, our own hens not having survived the trip. We had jist as well left them behind in Kentucky with friends, for the only ones that prospered as far as the chickens was concerned was the assortment of varmints along the way that had welcome meals of fat hen.

Cyrus returned from his singing school one afternoon obviously glum and displeased. George, who had accompanied him, announced, "Patsy Bradene come to singing school today." I needed no further information for I had heard Patsy Bradene sing.

"D'ye think you can teach Patsy to sing?" I inquired in all innocence.

He give me a forlorn look and said finally, "I could teach a brown spotted hog to sing before I could teach Patsy Bradene to sing. She comes no nearer the tune of a song than a catfish to a tree stump."

Still he thought that perhaps he might put together a reasonable Christmas sing, he said, adding, "Though I might have to face Patsy Bradene the opposite direction from the rest of the class, with her head out the winder or in a bucket."

It was near to Christmastime and Cyrus had one last lesson with his singing school before he presented the Christmas sing. George was anxious to accompany Cyrus, as he usually did, but this time his head was stuffed up and his throat was sore and we both forbade it, as there was the first light snowfall of winter on the ground. "There's a hint of weather in the air," said Cyrus, "and I'd not be surprised if the wind did not pick up out of the north."

George, generally a reasonable child, give vent to quite a fit of temper at that, and Cyrus held him up and give him a matching scoldin' for it.

"There's times," Cyrus said, "that we cannot do that which we would do. You are not well. You may not go."

"But the boys will be there," sniffed George. "The boys will be there to play and I won't get to."

"I don't know about that," said Cyrus, for sometimes Clara Cuthcart did indeed come to the singing school, usually with several of her older children along. "I do know you will not be there," he added firmly.

And so it was. I did feel sorry for the forlorn little creature, for he was very lonesome and did not get much chance to visit with his friends. But I also had myself to feel sorry for, for I was swollen and uncomfortable and too far gone with child to be able to see anyone. I fixed us each some brown sugared tea, and I said to him, "We'll drink our drink and then we'll both take a nap and so feel much better. For you certainly want to be well by Christmas to be able to go with Daddy to the Christmas Sing."

He nodded, but without spirit, and drank his tea in silence. "Now lie on your pallet," I said, "and close your eyes and before you know it, Daddy will be back."

I thought that such good advice that I lay back on my own ticking, though I was not comfortable, but my breathing which had been so terrible hard did seem some easier, and I thought I might be able to rest.

And indeed I drifted away, neither conscious nor quite unconscious, addled thoughts, not quite dreams, and in them dreams I seemed to feel a breeze and wondered where the chinking had come loose or if the wind had come up so hard that it whistled through the logs as it sometimes did. I know not how long I lay thus, but it was the cold that finally brought me out of it. It was a moment before I adjusted enough to note that the wind was indeed whistling through the cabin and it come from the door which stood wide open. I sat up in bed shivering and looked around, coming at last to complete consciousness with the sudden discovery that George's bed was empty, and he was nowhere in the room.

I sighed. He had gone out, most like to relieve himself, and left the door wide. I glanced at the fire and realized that I had slept longer than I thought and probably more soundly, since I wasn't aware that George had gone out. The fire needed restoking that was sure or we'd freeze ere we got it started again. I poked several sticks into the thing and stirred it, the blaze lifting significantly, and then I stoked it with another two or three sticks. I was at that task several minutes before it satisfied me. Still, George had not returned, which was strange, as it was really too cold to stay outside for long.

I stepped out and called but got no answer. I went around the cabin, looked and called again. Still no answer. Nothing as a matter of fact, not bird call nor rattling of ancient oak leaves. It was terrible still and I felt a hollow in my stomach.

"George!" I shouted. I was shivering and cold, and I thought to myself that if that young'un was hiding or playing a trick on me, he'd feel a switch across his legs that'd settle him good.

George was a reasonably well-behaved child, the beloved and only child of two loving parents, and as such he did not often feel the wrath that other children in more crowded conditions are made to feel.

At that moment I myself did not feel so well, and all I wanted was to lie down again near a warm fire.

"George!" I rounded the other side of the house and looking down noticed the small footprints that followed the path of the larger footprints that Cyrus had made earlier as he walked off toward the meeting house and his singing school. I felt the muscle of my throat constrict in either anger or fear, possibly both. I did not know how long the child had been gone, if he was dressed warmly. Then Clara Cuthcart's story of the little lost Bates boy came back to me and such a heat of fear washed over me that it might 'a been mid-July. But it was not.

I rushed back into the cabin and began to pull on warm clothes. I put on extra wool socks and boots, a sweater beneath my cloak and a heavy woolen shawl around my head and woolen mittens on my hands, and then I hurried out into the cold.

The wind had picked up, as Cyrus had predicted it would, and was shifting to the north. The clouds promised early darkness, if not more snow. And that thought had no sooner crossed my mind but the snowflakes began to descend as they do, first singly, and then in twos and threes and then in groups. I realized in horror that did I not find the child soon, the footprints would be gone under the fresh snow. Fortunately, the little footprints kept step with the big ones and those could be seen long after the little ones was gone.

I alternately cursed myself for a fool and promised myself what I would do to George once I caught up with him. It was of course possible that he had got all the way to the meeting house, and I would meet Cyrus and him on their way back.

It was also possible that he would get hopelessly lost, that we would not find him until spring, when the varmints would have stripped his bones of flesh and naught would be left of him but his little clothes. I was breathing hard and I had to stop. I had lost sight of the tracks, for it was an open space where the powdery snow was beginning to blow. I looked around in panic, remembered in some comfort that George had my own father's uncanny sense of direction, and then remembered, in some less comfort, that I did not and must take care not to lose myself in the process. I ignored a sharp pain in my back as I searched the space for signs of tracks, finding them a few yards beyond.

48

These I followed, but they was beginning to fade with the ever increasing snowfall. If only I knowed how long he had been gone, had he been gone long enough to have made his way to his father, or was he as like as I to be lost once the snow covered the tracks he was following?

I realized finally that the tracks was leading toward Lost River, which name suddenly frightened me, and it should not have. It was not a dangerous river, and going either up it or down it, you was bound to find a settlement or at least a house. And it was a shorter way I remembered to the meeting house, at least in winter time, when the branches was bare and the high brush was laid low by the frost. So that Cyrus most likely had followed that path, and George also.

I was wetted through, I suddenly realized. I had on too many clothes. I hardly thought that possible that one could sweat profusely on so cold a day. It was the activity, I thought, and then I felt another sharp pain across my back, so sharp it almost felled me. I leaned against a tree until it passed and realized then what was happening and why my clothes was suddenly wetted through.

"God in Heaven," I cried. I was genuinely angry. "What are You doing!"

"George!" I screamed in a panic again. "George! George! George!"

Then I stopped and thought. There was no need to be so anxious. When you live and survive on the border, you make each step a careful one, you do not go thrashing wildly about. There was at this pain nothing I could do but go on and quickly. I would follow the path along the stream and either discover George there or he would have already made it to the meeting house. There are worse places perhaps to give birth than a meeting house.

There was no need for panic. George, the little wretch, was quite capable of making that trip safely. If, I thought, he did not run into a wild animal or an Indian or a ruffian of one sort or another. He could lose his way. I had no guarantee that he was as safe in the woods as my father; I only thought so.

"George!" I called. "George!" And then I stopped and held my breath briefly. If there was dangerous things abroad, they most certainly would find me, the noise I was making. I slipped to the edge of the river and another pain caught me, these last two being far too close for comfort. I clung to a small sapling until the pain passed and I looked out on the river, which was already covered with a thin layer of ice, the snow collecting on top of that. Not two weeks earlier I had been by and there had been no sign of ice. How quickly winter come in.

I had lost sight of the tracks, but I knowed which direction to go. Once I made that decision, the river would lead the rest of the way. I cut through the brush hardly bothering to try to go around the denser spots. It was clear that I had to make it to help as quickly as possible. I had no time to search for George but only to hope that he was already safe, or else to get as quickly as I could to safety myself and leave others to search for the child. I was between pains for several minutes and commenced to hope that they had only been premature and would subside entirely, but that was not to be, for in a rush come two or three together, so close that I could not be certain how many. I sunk to my knees and then to all fours and waited their passing.

I was almost to the spot where the old rope bridge hung, I thought, which would put me near to halfway to the nearest house. I had got to my feet once more and was struggling ahead looking to find the bridge where I thought it ought to be, but though it was yet light enough to see, I could not make it out crossing the width of the river, which was some curious. I knew it ought to be in sight, but it wasn't. I scanned the area first across the river and then along the far bank and then the near bank, and at last caught sight of one end of the bridge attached as it should have been to a pair of strong trees, but dangling down instead of crossing the river. Well, at least I knew where I was and that I was on the right path.

I paused and then pushed myself ahead, for I had no time to dawdle and consider what might have happened to the bridge. I needed to concentrate, for at that point the bank was steep and treacherous. I gathered up my skirts and started around the remains of the rope bridge, and as I passed heard a sound. I listened, holding my breath. The wind had died once more and it was still, the light snowflakes making no sound as they drifted earthward.

"Mama." It was a whimper, soft and tired.

"George! George! Where are you, son?" I clung to the tree and looked frantically around me.

"Mama. Out here."

I followed the sound, and it was the same path that the dangling rope bridge took. Out a few feet from the bank, the rope dropped toward the water and that was where I saw my baby, clinging to the end of the rope, half in and half out of the water, surrounded by the ice he had broken through.

Frantically I looked around. A long stick, but there was none that long. I looked up, but the rope was attached so high that had I not been heavy with child, I still would not have been able to climb to it.

My child was in the water and he would freeze ere I could get help, and as I considered the situation, I was wracked with yet another pain.

"This can't be," I said aloud. I considered screaming but stopped myself before I started. There was no help about. I was between that rock and that hard place for certain.

"Hang tight," I called softly to George. "Hang tight. Mama will come for you." I grasped up as long a stick as I could readily find and lowered myself to hands and knees, for to spread my weight more evenly and crawled down the embankment and carefully onto the ice, relying on the ice to be solider close to the bank, and slowly I stretched out as far as I could and inched—more slid slowly across the slick and cold surface, pushing myself on my side with one leg and one arm, the stick stuck as far in front of me as it would go.

Sister Cuthcart's words came back to me. "I an't lost 'un and I don't intend to lose 'un!" And then as I moved ever so slowly across the ice, I muttered aloud, I think, "What is to be will be. It an't mine to question God's Will." And then I thought grimly to myself, "Whether 'tis or not, God helps them that helps therselves." And I knowed that it wasn't proper doctrine and that the deacons would chastise me for it, but at that moment I did not have the time to reason it through. It was Sister Cuthcart's words that gave me heart. "I don't intend to lose 'un!"

Had I give myself time to think about it, I might have sat upon the bank and moaned and cried and so lost my little son. But I did not, nor did I think it foolhardy to risk two more to save one. I did not intend to lose 'un! God's Will or no! I would just take it up with Him when I had the leisure to do it.

George did not move, struggle or cry. He just hung on grimly, for he was a wise and brave lad for his age and understood the peril of the situation. I did not call to him or anything, but just worked myself patiently and slowly, not pausing on the ice lest the warmth of my body thaw it. A pain overtook me, and I just gritted my teeth and grunted and kept moving, kicking myself along like a little fishy.

"Lord," I whispered, "just keep the ice secure and I'll do the rest." It seemed little enough to ask, even if it meant a slight adjustment of His Plan.

The child was not far out, though it seemed miles at the rate I traversed it. But I was at last within reach with the stick, and I lay on my side as much as I could and stretched the branch toward George. I did not have to give him instructions for which I thanked God. He reached carefully, not jarring the ice or rippling the cold water, and grasped the stick with one hand and as I commenced to tug him toward me, he let go the rope and grasped the stick with the other hand and still without struggle allowed me to tug him until his small body was slowly pulled up on the ice. I commenced scooting backward until he was up far enough on the ice that he could scoot himself.

"Just slide along the ice, Son," I said, terribly winded. "Don't struggle lest you crack it." And thus we slowly inched back the few yards to the shore. I gathered his little body to me and stifled the sob of relief that rose in my throat, for we was a long way yet from safety.

Miraculously, George remained dry from his waist up, and I pulled him and myself up under the bank. I did not have the strength to go higher, and this was a protected spot, dry with leaves, where no snow had yet collected. I would have give almost anything for a fire at that moment, but it was not to be had.

Instead I stripped George's wet clothes from his bottom half, wrapped his trembling body in the woolen shawl and pulled him within my cloak and hard against my warm body where he trembled and shivered but did not cry.

"I'm sorry, Mama," was all he said when he finally stopped shivering violently and could talk.

"What was you doing on the rope, George?" I asked. I was not angry only curious.

"It's a shorter way to meeting house, Mama," he said. "I was afraid I would be too late to find the boys, so I thought to take a shortcut across."

I did not realize that it would be shorter that way, for the stream bed meandered so, I hardly knowed what direction it was taking, but George explained it so confidently that I was certain that he knowed what he was saying.

"I'm sorry," he whispered again.

"Shush," was all I said. And then I gasped and rocked with a right hard pain holding my breath and biting my lip to keep from crying out.

"Mama?"

"I cannot move, George," I said quietly. "I am in need of help. Can you go for help, George?" I had felt his limbs and they were warm. I was comfortable that he must not have been in the water long enough to have done himself serious harm.

"Where, Mama?" he said, his eyes wide.

"I'll wrap you warm, George," I said after a wave of pain had come and gone, "and you must find your way to the nearest house for help. It's not so far. Can you do it while there's yet daylight?"

"Yes, Mama," he said resolutely.

I stripped off my own boots and one pair of stockings, grateful that some kind Providence had warned me to overdress, for I did have extra clothes that I could spare. I pulled the stockings upon on George's short legs and then with more strength than I thought I yet had in me, I pulled and tore until I managed to get one of my loose petticoats tore off me and I ripped it into strips as best I could and those I wound round and round the stockings on George's legs and up around his crotch and round and round, until he was made into a snug bundle, and I took my own boots and stuffed cloth into the toes, tugged them on his tiny feet and then wrapped those with cloth from my petticoat to keep them secure. His own upper clothing including the cap, but no mittens, was dry, but for the tail of his jacket which was wet, but froze stiff; I did not think it would chill him. I pulled my own mittens off and with an extra length of petticoat secured those around his small fist so they would not come off.

All got out, he was most peculiar looking, but I was satisfied that he was warm enough to make the trip.

"Now, go, George and do not dawdle. But take care. I would not have you lost or drownded. Take no short cuts, only go the way that you're sure and find whoever you can and send them back. Just be sure to tell them by the rope bridge. That's all it needs, by the rope bridge. Can you remember?"

He said that he could. He clambered up the side of the embankment and turned the proper direction, and I was left by myself, at least temporarily. For it was obvious that I would be joined by whatever young'un the Lord had willed and that soon.

I hardly had time between pains to consider my plight. Had I been able to, I might have speculated upon the fact that it was George's misdemeanor that had brought us to this pass. But I did not. I only thanked God that he was not drownded and that help would soon be on its way. For when circumstances is altered from good to worse, you take comfort not in what might have been but what is hopeful in the new situation.

It did occur briefly to me that Cyrus ought soon to be making his way home and pass by. And then just as quickly I remembered that this being a shortcut, he was more likely in snowy weather to make his way back the longer but more secure path and not pass this way at all.

It was growing dark more quickly than I expected or else the time was passing faster than I thought. I was being twisted within so frequently now and so roughly that I did not think that help would arrive in time to see this babe arrive. So between pains with what strength I could muster, I scratched the leaves about and made myself as snug a nest as I could against the river bank and wrapped myself in my cloak and shawl and waited.

That this babe could come so quickly, with so little warning, surprised but did not amaze me. I knowed that it happened. That sometimes labor stretched into hours and days, and other times it was practically over in minutes. This babe I hoped was as strong as it was precipitate.

I could not have said how the time passed for I was in no mood to try to count the minutes. All I knowed was that from time to time I was shook with pains, each coming that much more severe.

Coming out from under one of them pains, I noted that of a sudden the wind had died down, and I was relieved for it become that much warmer. I took a breath and glanced up. Over me a sudden shadow seemed to pass, and I frowned at it. Then I heard a crack as if something moving in stealth, but so slight a sound that I could not be certain that I had heard it. And then in the still air, I detected an odor, strong and unpleasant, a stench almost, that I could not recognize. I lifted my head and strained at the dark.

Then the wind, as if politely paused for something, come on again and the noise of the rattling leaves drowneded out any sound, and the breeze pushed that strange odor away and spread it wide over the frozen water. Nor did I have time to consider, for I was wracked back by another hard pain and then another and another one on top the other, 'til I was not quite certain where one left off and the other began, and then, just as suddenly, as I writhed and stifled my screams, I felt the telltale pop and loosening and relief. I reached my hand in under my skirt and, gripping the small head, helped to guide the little figure into the world. I tore at the cord and worried it and twisted it about until I felt it snap, and I pulled the little one close to me, fearful to expose it to the elements.

I struggled clumsily with it yet under my skirts and finally gave it a little pinch and such a howl of anger rent the air that I could not myself keep from laughing out loud. "Oh, it's a fine 'un, it's fine," Old Mistress Hankens had said of the howling George, and I could not help but think that she would have the same thing to say of this babe.

Still clumsily I felt around until with a smile I ascertained that the babe I held was a girl.

Sarah Elizabeth.

For that was the name that Cyrus had determined we would call a girl baby by, it being named for both his grandmothers. But for the fact that I thought it a most pretty name, I might have had argument with him over it, for it seemed to me that in both these births he had o'erstepped himself in not consulting with me about names. I had done no little of the work involved, after all.

I could not leave the little one naked between my legs forever. I fumbled around again and, gathering the woolen shawl from my head, I managed to wrap it around the little girl and at last draw her out, then pull her to me within my cloak, where she settled quite peacefully. I lay too tired almost to worry.

After a time I felt the afterbirth begin of its own volition to flow through the birth canal. I thought briefly what a mess I must be and then thought once more of Mistress Hankens: "Ye'll be like a old cow a-calvin'." And it seemed I was, nature taking care of all things with no help at all from anyone else, lying in a nest of my own making in the wilderness.

I think I must have slept in spite of all, for I woke with a start, surprised for a minute that I was not in my own bed. And then I felt the pressure of the baby against my bosom and from the regular breathing, I knew her to be secure. I was not sure of myself, though, for the wind was high now and the snow was falling heavy enough that it was lighter than it might otherwise have been. I wondered that help had not yet arrived and begun to worry. Had George arrived safely, and had he been able to remember where to send help? I could not believe that Cyrus himself was not tearing down the forest tree by tree by now, trying to find us. I was uncomfortable and afraid to move lest I rock the babe or make our situation that much worse in the cold night.

I dared not fall asleep, for people froze in the winter when they slept, yet I was tired, my strength so abused, that I thought it impossible that I might stay awake.

"Lord," I whispered. I am not sure wh'er or not it was a prayer or a curse, for at that moment my thinking was fair fuzzy. The babe shifted and whimpered in her sleep, but she did not wake and cry for food at least. Though I listened intently, I could not make out much for the racket that the wind made in the rattling leaves.

I do not know how long I lay there, determined to stay awake, struggling to count the dry leaves that rattled overhead in that effort to stay conscious, an effort that I was beginning to lose. Then in the distance I heard a sound over the racket of the wind and leaves. It was steady and growing louder, and I didn't know wh'er to be afraid or elated. Should I cry out or wait. I thought of the little Bates boy, hidden and too frightened to make himself known, yet I had no assurance that the noise I heard portended sanctuary. I did not even know if it was human or animal, only that it seemed too steady to be one of

54

those various night noises that you can always expect, without ever knowing what causes it.

Caution bade me wait before revealing myself, and I did, the noise growing louder and more persistent until it was obvious that it was an animal and from the regularity of it, finally, a horse being rode.

That was unusual. Almost no one ever rode horseback, unless going a long way, and not always then, for the trails was not that plain and the footing not always sure. I knew at least that it was no neighbor of ours that was abroad a-horseback. So I kept my peace, listening and still, as the sound of the horse come nearer and nearer. I was in a quandary. There was a chance it was help. There was an equal chance that it was a danger.

I had most made up my mind to let the horse and rider go by, lest I find myself landed from the fire into the pot, but when the horse was nigh overhead, I heard a sound little above a whimper, "Mama."

"George! George. Are you there, Son?" I cried.

"Mama!" And from the sound of joy in the small voice, I was certain that we was saved.

"Stay where you are, boy," came a voice that I did not recognize. "The horse won't move with you. Understand?"

"Yes, Sir."

"Brave boy."

And then a figure swung down the embankment, hanging onto sprouts for balance. And such a figure as I had rarely seen. He stood amazing tall, taller even I thought than Reuben Bradene, though slimmer and lighter on his feet. And he called out, "Madam?"

I hardly knowed how to answer, for I don't think I had ever been so called in my life.

"Here," I replied, and he followed the sound to where I lay.

He knelt beside me and in the snowlightened night I could make out his features but dimly, straight and regular and clean-shaved, older than Cyrus by quite some. When he spoke his voice was of such a deep timbre that I was reminded of a drum roll.

"Ye've hurt yerself," he said. "Can ye walk?"

I realized then that he did not know of the baby, nor how could he? I doubt that George, though wise for his age, had made that connection. I was suddenly embarrassed and shamed that a strange man should so find me, wetted and dirtied from the birthing process. I hardly knowed what to say.

"Can ye walk?" he repeated.

I would have give the world to have been able to have said yes to him, but I knowed that I could not. My legs lacked the strength, and the rest of me, too.

"I don't think so," I whispered, and still did not mention the babe.

"Have ye anything broken?" he asked.

"No."

"Then hang on," he said, and without ceremony hoisted me up so quickly that I grabbed hard at the bundle hidden on my bosom beneath the cloak, and he carried us up the side of embankment one careful step after the other.

At the top I saw George, who sat on the saddle of a large horse, the reins secured to a nearby bush.

"Can ye slide back, behind the saddle?" the stranger asked George with gentle solicitude I thought. "Take care, now, good boy, brave lad," he said, and I knowed that I liked this man, so gentle was he with my small son.

"Mama?" sniffed George.

"Are you all right, George?" I whispered and then the man adjusted me to one arm and with unbelievable strength carried us both, all three actually, into the saddle, the babe and I before him and George behind.

"I'm all right, Mama," whispered George but there was tears in his voice, tears of fright and weariness, I supposed, for he was, after all, not yet four years old. It was too much adventure for such a small soldier.

"He will be all right, Madam," said the gentleman holding me, somewhat gruffer in speech.

Clinging tightly with one hand to my precious bundle, I directed him the way and against the warmth of this broad chest and the gentle swaying of the horse as it made its careful way, again I almost slipped into sleep.

We were not yet halfway home when we come suddenly upon Cyrus, who was by then on our trail. For I had left a bloody trail myself, and again I was embarrassed at it, though there had been not a thing that I could do. It was simply that the birthing process was the function of women and ought not to be brought to the attention of men except in extreme emergency. But then, I did not think that there could have been much extremer emergency than this.

Cyrus took George down to relieve the beast of that much burden, and George cried out as Cyrus took him.

"Easy," cautioned the stranger.

Cyrus walked beside as we made our way home and held the door open as the stranger dismounted, carried me into the warm cabin, and lay me on the bed.

Cyrus came up, and I smiled at him. "Look, Cyrus," I said. "I have something for you," and I pulled open my cape and pulled the shawl away from the baby's face. We looked for the first time at the wrinkled face of our daughter.

"Great God!" said the stranger. "The woman's birthed a baby on the river bank."

Cyrus turned to him and extended his hand to the stranger who stood at least a head higher than he. "Sir, I owe you a debt greater than I will ever be able to repay. I am Cyrus Pritchard and this is my wife, Annamanda."

56

The stranger had taken Cyrus's hand, but he still stared incredulously at me and Sarah Elizabeth.

"I am at your service, Madam," he said, letting go of Cyrus's hand and bowing at the waist over me. "My name is Eremus Lodi."

Chapter 4

O'Reilly

Eremus Lodi sat in my house, beside my fire. I could hear his voice, as low as distant thunder rumbling, from behind the curtain where I lay. The curtain was actually a quilt which Cyrus had fastened around the bed, so that I could clean myself and my babe, though it had proved not so necessary, that curtain, as the two men waited outside the cabin for a long time.

Placed on my bed near the warm fire, I had slipped for a time into something like unconsciousness, and I heard but dimly the rustling around within the cabin. I did hear George cry out a time or two, but that quickly quieted. It was that sound, of George fussing, that brought me around finally, and I called to Cyrus to bring me warm water and to hang the quilt. Along with the water, he brought our tiny Sarah Elizabeth. That name was so long and cumbersome for one so small, but it rolled so prettily off the tongue that I could not yet shorten it, as it surely would be so shortened.

I was about asleep again when I heard the men come through the door, and George cried out again and I called to Cyrus. He come and brought me a mug of sugared tea. I advised him not to be hard with George, for though he'd brought us to near disaster, he was no more to blame for them than a puppy is to blame when it chews a ball of yarn.

My wise old granny, years gone, was given to saying that little 'uns are not just small big 'uns. "They ere not big enough to fight in a war or to marry or to vote in office an they should ne'er be treated as if they was. They should only be formed and molded and teached until betime they ere big enough to do all them things, they'll do 'em right."

I said, "He's just little, Cyrus. Don't be hard on him." For I figured that Cyrus's anger might be in part what unsettled the little tad. "Bring him to me," I said. "I'll comfort him."

"He's asleep," said Cyrus shortly. He took the babe from me and said, "You'd better sleep, too." Them was gentle words, but the look upon his face did not match the words, for he wore as grim and hard a look as I thought I had e'er seen him wear.

I would have asked him to remove the curtain, for in truth the side of me that was positioned to the wall was fair cold. I was aware the wind howling outside, and that the reason for it. But it seemed to me unseemly to lie abed in view of a strange man, and so I said nothing.

I drifted in and out of consciousness, hardly noticing anything but the subdued conversation outside the quilt. Had I been more myself I might have remarked the lack of friendly humor in those voices. As it was, it took a sudden, loud oath from Cyrus to bring me around. And I near sat bolt upright in bed, for Cyrus was not given to oaths. I don't think I had ever heard one from him in all the time I knowed him. He could become quite angry, but oaths was not his way, the way they are for some other kinds.

Sometime during the time I had been lying on the edge of sleep, Cyrus had removed the quilt, I suppose so that I could benefit more from the heat of the fireplace. I had been then more asleep than I thought. The two men was so intent in conversation that they did not notice me to be awake, and I was careful not to catch their attention.

Cyrus sat with his face in his hands, George asleep on his pallet in the corner, and Eremus Lodi sat on a low stool before the fire, his long legs drawn up under his chin. He was whittling on a stick of wood, the way some men do rather than to have their hands idle.

The fire was bright, and the light from the falling snow outside brightened the room more than ordinary after nightfall. I could study the faces from my bed more clearly than I might otherwise have. With the hand holding the knife, Eremus Lodi lifted his hat which yet sat a-straddle his head and scratched at his head with the other. And that was just what it was. Head. For there was no hair upon the top of it at all and only a long gray fringe around the edge. I was surprised for a man of otherwise strong and youthful figure and imposing voice to have no hairs upon his head.

Cyrus finally looked up, and the anguish on his face was so extreme that I caught my breath and couldn't let it out even when he cried, "I think I could kill them!"

"Well," drawled Eremus Lodi, "that job's one third done at least, for I saw the shot from my rifle tear through the throat of the one that held the boy's hand in the fire."

So easily did he say it, so casually, that it was a minute registering on me what he had said. "I'd have got the other two had I not been so anxious to rescue the lad. I would give anything I own to have been a few minutes earlier," he added, "fer he's likely to lose much use of that hand I'm afraid, but it could have been far worse." He paused again, and I closed my eyes tight lest the tears give me away, for the terror that was pounding in my head did not escape my lips.

"I would that I had got there a few minutes sooner," he repeated, "before they started to torture the lad, but I might near did not get there at all. Had it not been for my big dog, I never would have gone that way anyway. For he whined and growled and whimpered and insisted that we take that trail. I have had that big black beast long enough to know to follow where he insists. And it is well I did."

"I did not see no big dog," said Cyrus.

"Well, no, he took after those two other scum. He'll turn up; I never worry about Seneca. If there was a confrontation, I'm sure that those two got the worst of it."

George cried out again, but I could see that he only whimpered in his sleep. I also noted the bandage on his hand.

"The laudanum will keep him asleep for a time," said Eremus Lodi, and I had to wonder where he come up with laudanum, as it wasn't the thing that most travelers carried. "But the pain will get worse. And," he added after a short pause, "he may have strange dreams, recall things that seem real but an't. That at least is how laudanum will affect a man. I assume a child might likewise be affected."

"I do not know that I could ever kill a man," said Cyrus, "I have never. . . ," and his voice trailed off.

"Nor have I, Sir. I have never killed a man. But these kinds do not count as men, but rather as dogs, mad dogs, to be dealt with as such. I would dispatch such with the same ease that I would dispatch a copperheaded viper and feel that I had done the rest of the world a turn fer it." The man did not speak with strong feeling. Indeed the very ordinariness of his comment emphasized the fearsomeness of it.

"Forgiveness will come hard," said Cyrus.

"Forgiveness?" frowned Eremus Lodi. "Forgiveness, Sir. I do not know what you mean. Who needs forgiveness and from whom?"

"It is my practice to forgive those that wrong me," said Cyrus.

Eremus Lodi looked at him for a long moment and then announced, "It is a silly practice." And then he added, "Such practices have no place on the border, Sir. For the border is filled with scoundrels, and you'd spend your precious time always forgivin'. In truth, you'd probably not have the time to get to all the forgivin' that needed givin'. Forgiveness does not belong here. It belongs in those civilized areas among churchmen where there's not really so much to be forgiven anyway."

"I am a churchman."

Eremus Lodi looked at Cyrus again for a long time and then spoke with what seemed to be prolonged sigh. "Another of those? I do not know what we have done to merit the multitude of Christians of one sort or another that seem to be overrunning the place."

"Perhaps ye need a balance for the scoundrels?" It was said with a hint of jest.

Eremus only whittled on for a while before he answered. "The scoundrels have a head start, Pastor. Strangely, though," he added with a sly glance toward Cyrus, "it's them that civilization owes some debt, for it's them that

pushes the borders on, do you mind that? It's the sinners and the unregenerates that're always spreadin' out. Civilization," he laughed, "owes a great deal
to such scoundrels. Scoundrels and . . . ," here he paused again, "the lonely
ones," he finished at last.

"I'm not sure what that means?"

"It means greed, Sir, greed. The deadliest of all the deadly sins, for taken
all together, all them sins amounts to is greed in one form or another—
self-serving. Oh, there's always the riffraff, those that needs always flee the
civilized land where the laws and lawmen plague them. But all told, it's greed
that creates new frontiers, plain and simple. Greed and greedy scoundrels.
And," he added, "riffraff and solitaries, and I suppose there's a few fools."
With that he shot Cyrus a long sidewise glance.

"I am not a fool, Sir," said Cyrus, with a surprising amount of grace, I
thought. "I follow the Will of God."

"Well," said Eremus Lodi, rising, "in my mind the one equals the other."

Cyrus did not seem put off as I thought he ought to 'a been, but rather favored Eremus Lodi with that sort of intent stare that usually meant a lengthy
discussion. "You're a rationalist, then, Sir, a Deist, mayhap?" said Cyrus
finally.

Eremus Lodi laughed rather without mirth. "Deist? Rationalist? Is it required that I sport an 'ist' of some sort? No, Sir, I claim no 'ist'. I am rational,
I think, a reader and thoughtful. . ."

"A learned man, then?" Cyrus interrupted.

"Well, now, Sir, you seem intent upon labeling me. No, not learned even,
for that is a term I would reserve for truly thoughtful men, only a handful in
all history. Nor am I a seeker after the truth. I read for my own amusement
and am frequently not amused." At that, Eremus Lodi's expression lost its
sardonic cast, and he peered beyond Cyrus, perhaps beyond even the walls of
the cabin, at some distance I could not explain.

"I have read a great deal, Sir, and yes perhaps I have acquired some
knowledge, enough at least to wonder if there will come a time that we
know too much, will have become sated on the fruit of the tree of knowledge. Knowledge can be a fearsome thing, Pastor, a heavy burden, for it does
not necessarily bring with it wisdom, I think, only terrifying information.
Knowledge will one day even out good and evil, so you can't tell the one from
the other. . . ."

"Ah, certainly not, Master Lodi. That remains God's knowledge."

"God's and Satan's, and can you say that they're not one in the same? Ah,
no, perhaps not, for of the two, evil is far more interesting and poses more
questions. But when the day comes that we have such answers. . ."

"I think not, Sir," said Cyrus, right calmly. "I am consoled that the real
mystery, the essential mystery—the Truth—will always remain a mystery to
the undeveloped reason of mortal man, for he is of too feeble a comprehension to understand the Lord's purpose."

"Indeed," Eremus Lodi as easily as if it were the state of the weather that he discussed, "the mystery is not what we are doin' here or where we come from—the mystery is why we care. The mystery is that men can stare into the vast reaches of the heavens, the myriad twinkling stars and bright planets and think that such puny creatures as they have sole dominion over it and claim importance in the eyes of any deity."

"Indeed," nodded Cyrus. "There's those of us who understand only that, our own puny estate, and admit that all the rest is mystery."

Eremus Lodi cocked his head at that, grinned, and said, "Ah, you're one of them Calvinist Baptists then?" I could not tell what he meant by that observation exactly.

"Well, Pastor," he said rising, "what e'er that may be, you've got a strong and brave son and stalwart woman, for that I honor you. But you'd do well to think of them, and the babe, too. I'd advise you not to stay too close on the river, for the river hosts the worst of the worst, like rats they slide into and out of the water to scavenge, too ignoble even to be called villains."

"I'll think on it, and I thank you fer the advice. But I'll follow the Lord's Call."

"I'm sure you will," said Eremus Lodi. "One last thought, Preacher. It might please you to know that greed has its own pretty punishment—hunger—hunger for what it's lost and can't recover. Remember that. For greed comes in many disguises, and I'd not be surprised if the Lord was one of 'em."

By now it was clear that Eremus Lodi was preparing to leave. He pulled his heavy coat about him. George fussed quietly in his sleep, moaning, and Eremus Lodi and Cyrus both looked at him.

"There is a man of my household who is wondrous gifted of the healing powers. He knows remarkable things of herbs and powders and salves and lotions. I think that he can make the child's suffering considerably less, and I'll send him to you for that purpose."

"I would be grateful," said Cyrus standing. "I already owe you more debt than I can ever satisfy."

"You do and that's certain. But a man that merits a son and wife of the strength and character of your own must do so by some reason. By an' by, you ne'er know, you may be able to pay. But I doubt that I'll need your professional services, else I marry or die, and I have no plans for either at the moment."

Cyrus said nothing.

"O'Reilly is the healer's name," said Eremus. "O'Reilly. He has no other. I am situated south in the New Madrid District, and I'll send him on as soon as I get there. He'll be here sooner than you expect, for he can make more time afoot than most could make a-horseback. Meantime, feed the boy small doses of laudanum, only enough to numb the pain. He's a fine, brave lad, Sir. Take care of him."

And with that Eremus Lodi opened the door and stepped out into the snow. The wind did seem to have ceased, and through the door, I could just make out the soft snowflakes still dropping to the ground.

Beyond the snowflakes and beyond the door was those twinkling stars and bright planets of which Eremus Lodi spoke. When I was a girl, my good granny used to say that the stars was holes in heaven where the light leaked through. I wondered what Eremus Lodi would have said to such observation.

Cyrus closed the door behind him, poked some sticks into the fire, and then sat on the stool before the fire and stared tiredly into it, passing weary all of a sudden, it seemed. I said naught, for I was too weary to comfort him. The spirit was willing but the flesh was weak. Too much had happened to me, and I would have to wait a time of greater strength to comprehend it all fully. And in short order I was asleep.

I woke once only to put the restless babe to my breast and fell to sleep in the midst of that. When I finally did return to full consciousness, it was Mistress Cuthcart whose face I first saw. I was so shocked at that and said so.

"Why," she answered, "ye need help. An't no man alive that can manage when ther's a new birth. Besides," she added with a twinkle, all the while her hands a-busy spoonin' this and wipin' that and adjustin' the other, "I never pass a chance to trade my nine fer someone else's two." And she handed me a plate with some journey cake and mush and a cup of sugared tea. "It an't time fer sassafras," she complained. "That'd get ye on yer feet in short order." And she settled herself on a chair, her short legs not quite reaching to the floor, picked up her needles and commenced to knit, while one dangling foot methodically pushed at the cradle where the babe lay peacefully still. The woman fair twitched with activity; I had ne'er seen the beat of it.

"George?" I suddenly remembered.

"He's sleepin'. And it's best, fer that's as bad a burn he carries on his hand as ever I think I seen." She did not spare me that, and I felt my heart sink.

"Where is Cyrus?"

"Gone. The men gathered this mornin' and ere beatin' the brush and the river bank fer them scum."

"Who's keeping yer little ones?" I asked, and wondered that she would go off and leave them under such terrible circumstances.

"Oh, John Cuthcart is home, and his sister, too, who's a tolerable old maid, but a good hand with young'uns anyway. John Cuthcart would ne'er be much help a-huntin' down and dealin' with them river scum. It just an't his turn. But, now, Brother Amiable Simpson, well, my he'd fair dote on bein' able to track 'em down and extract some tail feathers. Anyway," she went on, "I don't think we got to worry none about bein' bothered, fer the woods is so full of angry men that anybody that an't with 'em best find a hole to crawl into and stay ther fer a while."

"Wher'd ye find that laudanum to dose the young'un with?" she asked presently.

"Why, I suppose it come from Eremus Lodi."

Clara Cuthcart clicked her needles and rocked the cradle in silence for just a moment, but silence was not her customary posture. Sure enough, all at once she said, "Well, I surely do wisht I could've seen him, seen Eremus Lodi. An' what was he like?"

I told her what little I had ascertained, not much considering the conditions under which I observed. For some reason I did neglect to mention that he was bald.

"I've seen him," I said finally, "but all that I know of him is what he looks like." I said it expectantly, for I hoped she would add to that information without my having to ask for it. I had always been shy of engaging in simple gossip, though in truth I do think I relished it as much as anyone and was never shy about listening to it when I got the chance.

"Well, I dunno so much, I guess," she said and then proceeded to prove herself wrong on that matter. "He's apparently one of them that done well under Spanish rule. There's lots you know, them that took great chunks of land. The Spaniards, ye know, give near to five hun'ert acres free to any Americans willing to settle the upper Louisiana, the last ten years or so. That way, it's said they thought to have someone to help ther cause should they get into it with England, which they just about done. So ther's lots of folks hereabouts that come by five hun'ert acres that way. Our own land we bought from just such a one, and methought at a greater price than we should've had to, considerin' how he come by it the first place," she added somewhat indignantly.

"But, then, that's the way of it, says John Cuthcart, that the man benefitted of bein' first. But apparently Eremus Lodi was here long before that and got considerable more acreage than that, and business holdings that go far beyond just wooded land. It's said that he travels this way back and forth to St. Louis and Ste. Genevieve to see to his business. Then ther's others speculates otherwise about his goin's and comin's. I don't know. I only know that, though he lives down toward the New Madrid District, he is spotted with some frequency traveling both north and south along this river. Only," she added with some pique, "I an't never seen him and I'd give the world to."

Well, I wasn't certain that he was all that interesting to see, but I was grateful for whatever it was that brought him past—was it less than a day gone? And I had heard that tale of the 500 acres and the settlers that did bring across the river. And I was all at once 'minded of Eremus Lodi's remark upon the greed of man and its contribution to the pushing back of borders. Mayhap it was an accurate observation?

"Back then," Sister Cuthcart continued her history lesson, "was apparently only the Papist religion that was legal here in this territory, but that never seemed to bother them that brought ther own, fer ther's about one religion fer ever' two families almost, it seems."

I knew she exaggerated, though ther was a fair amount of truth, even so, to what she said.

George fussed, turned, and then cried out sharply. Sister Cuthcart jumped down from her chair, hurried over to him, gently lifted his tortured hand from under him, and placed it carefully out of danger of his lying on it himself. Then she picked up a stick of wood to stoke the fire with.

All at once there was a tapping on the door, which startled both of us. We waited for the tapper to identify himself, Sister Cuthcart standing her full height, a questioning look on her face, the stick of wood still clutched in her hand. When the identification did not come, she cried out, "Who's there? Speak out!" and lifted the stick of wood menacingly. George sat up, even in his groggy state taking care not to lean on his damaged hand.

"Who's there?" I demanded, for incapacitated as I was, I was still the mistress of this house, and quite frankly, despite Clara Cuthcart's assurances, I was not so sure that the river scum might not 'a found us, and us unprotected save Sister Cuthcart's stick of firewood. And when there was still no answer to my question, I begun to search around for some weapon of my own, for did we have to battle 'em off with bread knife and firewood, that's just what we would do.

But before I could drag myself from out the bed, the door swung wide, pushed hard from the outside, and Mistress Cuthcart lifted her stick of wood high and let out something like a little yelp. Standing in the doorway, bent double almost, yet still obscuring all out of doors, stood a gigantic black figure, the biggest man, if indeed it was a man, that I had ever beheld. Bigger than Reuben Bradene and bigger than Eremus Lodi, and even Jacob the riverman and his larger brother. And he was black as a charcoal stump, with as much expression on his face as one.

"Identify yerself, Sir!" demanded Clara Cuthcart, brandishing her stick of wood as though she would force him to make account of himself. I thought her worthy of the task, indeed, though she stood no more than belt high to the bent, black figure.

Though it seemed ages, this all transpired in a matter of seconds. I thought at first it was the devil himself and then not, for I'd always had it in my mind that the devil was passing short, but this black being was tree-top tall, with gray, cropped wool upon his head, for he wore no cap. I thought then it might be one of God's dark angels, for I could not believe that he was of this world.

And then he spoke, in gentle, low tones, rhythmic as the sound that a row boat makes, tied and lapping in the low water at a river bank.

"O'Reilly," was what he said.

He stood still in the doorframe, accustoming his eyesight from the snow-brightness of out of doors to the dimness of the interior of the cabin. Framed as he was against the light, I could study him easily. He wore not the fringed buckskins the woodsmen mostly wore, but rather a farmer's wove cloth breeches and loose blouse, and on his feet, soft boots more like those that the Indians wore than those heavy leather ones of the settlers. He was topped only with a vest against the cold, and slung over his shoulders was an assortment of small leather pouches. He carried no weapon that I could detect, not even a hunting knife.

"You're O'Reilly from Master Eremus Lodi?" I asked quickly, for Clara Cuthcart still clung to the stick of firewood as if she might momentarily attack. As I said, I thought her capable of it, though she mightn't be able to strike this being much over knee high.

O'Reilly nodded slowly, looking around until his snowblinded gaze apparently identified George. For he stepped then immediately toward the boy, and George made not a sound, thinking perhaps this an opium-inspired figure.

"Ye can shut the door," snapped Sister Cuthcart, lowering the stick, for all the world as if she was talking to one of her own young'uns. But O'Reilly did not take notice and advanced to George, his uncommon long legs needing but a step and a half to accomplish that. And with a frown Sister Cuthcart pushed the door closed.

George stood, and the black man knelt without comment and took his injured hand. The boy's eyes got quite wide and he looked at me. "Mama?" he whispered.

In spite of my disability, I pushed back the covers on the bed and would have got out and gone to my boy, but O'Reilly, without looking at me, murmured in them slow and velvet tones, "Stay, Mama." So I sat on the edge of bed and smiled some reassurance at George.

O'Reilly at once unwound the bandages around the wound and without comment tossed them into the fire.

"Here, now," objected Sister Cuthcart. "That's waste. Them can be warshed and used again."

"Be not need dem, Madam," said O'Reilly. He still did not look up from the hand he held. "Need dem water, Madam," he said to Clara Cuthcart. And to me he said, "Mama, look," and brought George to me.

And so I looked at the wound for the first time and bit hard upon my lip to keep from crying out, so wicked looking it was. And I was also suddenly very fearful, for such wounds as that, so deep and angry, could kill. I had seen it happen, seen the gangrene to invade and take, if not the life, at least the limb. All I could do was look helplessly at the big black man before me.

"Brave lad," he said to George, and then he looked beyond the boy and, it seemed to me, beyond the walls of the house. I could not even guess of what he thought, but it did seem that his countenance at last took on some expression, and that expression infinitely sad. But the look lasted only an instant before it passed, and the face was as passive as ever.

"Be not bring back dem gone, Mama," said O'Reilly exhibiting the hand to me. And I could make sense I thought of what he was telling me. Part of

66

the fingers was burned away. There was no bringing them back. I would have cried if I thought it would have helped. But it would only have done the opposite, so I held my peace, daring not to say anything, for fear I give myself away.

George let the black man lead him back to the table. He was still wide-eyed, as if he did not quite trust what was happening to him, and he looked at me again.

"It's all right, George. Mister Eremus Lodi, your friend who gave you the ride on his horse, has sent this man to doctor your hand."

I did not know what else to say, even though I was not at all certain that I wanted the ministrations of this black man. But I had no one else to trust, for we had certain gone to the end of our own knowledge of medicine, and I knowed the consequences should infection set in.

Sister Cuthcart must have sensed my fear for she said rather abruptly, "What is to be, will be." And I knew that to be true. That whatever the Lord's Will, it would be. I must take comfort in that.

Still, I wished my faith a little stronger, for somehow knowing that whatever happened was a part of the Lord's Plan was not as comforting to me as it ought to have been, which proved, of course, that my faith was yet a shallow thing. I wished Cyrus there, for his faith was firm and secure, and he would have comforted me.

"Water, Madam." O'Reilly dragged those syllables out in a low melodic sound, so that they lapped one against the other, and surprisingly Clara Cuthcart did as she was bid without comment.

O'Reilly emptied some powders first from one and then from another of the pouches into his gigantic fist and then he dribbled a little water into the mess and stirred it with his finger until it made a paste, and this he spread carefully all over George's damaged hand. Through it all, the boy made not a sound but stared up wide-eyed into the black face, while I prayed God that I had made the right choice in letting this savage-looking being attend my child.

"Keep 'em wet, brave lad," O'Reilly said at last. "Be keep 'em wet, boy, he your job."

George nodded and tested the wetted paste on his hand gingerly.

"Not hurt," said O'Reilly.

George shook his head.

O'Reilly nodded for the boy to sit and George sat, while the black man carefully restored his pouches to his shoulder and then lowered himself to a seated position on the floor and stared impassively in front of him.

There was no sound. He did not seem interested in speaking nor did he show any inclination to leave. At last Clara, who was never comfortable in silence, asked, "Have you eat, Black man? Ere ye hungry?"

"Be hungry, yes, Madam," said O'Reilly, and again the lapping syllables was drawn out in gentle waves that was most pleasurable.

Sister Cuthcart served up a heaping plate of victuals, and the black man ate them down promptly and shook his head when offered more.

I wondered how he had managed to get past the line of men that was supposed to be out a-beating of the brush, for sure they never would have let him come to the cabin unaccompanied if they had seen him. But I did not ask.

However Clara Cuthcart was not so reserved and satisfied the same curiosity in her customary manner. She asked a direct question.

Then the black man almost smiled. "Need not be noticed, Madam," he said, "would not be noticed."

I wondered about him, for I was not unused to slaves. They was a common enough sight. There was not so many along the border, but as the lands become settled, there would be more for the cultivation of large tracts of land. Such lands as I supposed Eremus Lodi to possess, and I supposed that he probably had many such slaves. But this one, whose speech was so different, did not have the manner of a slave. He bore himself in the quiet dignity of a man possessed of his own spirit, and I could not but wonder at it. And his name, O'Reilly, was another puzzlement.

Clara and I was at some loss to know what to do, for the man did not only not explain what he planned to do, but he did not speak at all, and Clara and I were some constrained in front of him. But in a few minutes, his eyes dropped closed and from his regular breathing, he seemed to be sleeping. Clara went on about her business and I mine, which was resting and gaining strength. But Clara Cuthcart was not capable of going about her business without talking, though she did so circumspectly, commenting on the weather and the likelihood of the men to return to eat and then shortly to point out to me that not only was the black asleep, but that George had slipped down beside him and lay with his head against the long arm, himself asleep.

"Good fer 'em," was Clara's comment.

Sarah woke and fussed, and Sister Cuthcart brought her to me. Just then a shadow seemed to cross over, and we both looked up. The black man stood over us, having risen and moved so quietly that neither of us had been aware of it, and the room so small and cramped, too.

I stiffened and so did Clara, she involuntarily glancing toward the stack of wood and, I suppose, weighing her chances of getting to it. But O'Reilly merely stood there, looking down, a curious and perplexed look upon what had been stoic features, turning his head to one side and then to the other, like a curious jay in summer.

I reached to cover myself as much as possible, but then I realized that it was not I that he gazed at. It was at Sarah that he looked with such strained and curious expression.

"Girl doll?" he asked.

"Yes," I said.

He nodded, looked forlornly at her, and said, "Pretty doll." And then he returned to the corner where George still lay sleeping and sat himself back down in much the same posture that he had been in.

I looked at Sarah. Pretty? Well, certain from my point of view she was. But in truth, being less than one full day old, she was, as most healthy newborns, red and wrinkled and a long way from being pretty. "Be wary the ones that're born pretty," my old granny used to say, "fer it's not healthy and they're like to slip away pretty quick on ye." And I think that that is true, strange though it seems. The redder and uglier, the better. Sister Cuthcart and I looked at each other and then at the black man, but he was apparently asleep again.

By the time Cyrus arrived home, Sister Cuthcart and I had determined that O'Reilly the black man slept as a cat does. For he could be sound asleep and be brought to full, alert consciousness by an untoward sound or movement, then determining all was well, slip right back to sleep again. He had waked up once to George's fussing and immediately lifted the boy's hand and looked at it.

"Keep 'em wet, lad. Be keep 'em wet." And he dribbled water carefully over the hardened paste, patting it gently to uniform wetness.

"A drop of laudanum, Sister Cuthcart," I said.

The black man immediately reacted. "No, Mama. No." He shook his head and frowned, and he seemed almost angry. "No be need dem."

"But Master Eremus Lodi left it with instructions to use a little to keep down the pain," I insisted.

"No be need dem!" O'Reilly snapped with such authority that I immediately put the small bottle away. And in truth, as the day wore on, it seemed that the boy did rest easier and left off crying out in his sleep.

As I had suspected, O'Reilly had come right through the line of men without ever anyone realizing it, and Cyrus when he come into the cabin, stood in some amazement once his vision was cleared enough to see the big black man, who had risen when the door had opened.

To see Cyrus side by side with the black was to realize just how big that man was. But though he nodded his head at Cyrus's arrival and called him "Sir," there was no touch of servility about him.

"Be stay yet," was all O'Reilly said when Cyrus asked his plans. And he seated himself again and commenced to doze.

"I know how far it is to Eremus Lodi's headquarters," said Cyrus once he had removed his coat and stood before the fire, "and I cannot understand how this man has made that trip so quickly."

I reminded him that Eremus Lodi had said that he would make a quicker journey of it than most men a-horseback, and Cyrus only nodded.

"We did not find no trace of them river scum," he said at last. "We did not even find the one that Eremus Lodi claimed to have killed. We did find the fire but no corpse. It is curious that the river scum might come back after one of their own. They are usually not so generous to each other."

"So long as they don't come back here, is all I care," said Clara Cuthcart.

As it turned out, O'Reilly stayed longer than Sister Cuthcart. For all of us mended right rapidly, especially George, and Sarah Elizabeth attested to the strength of her constitution often with loud, hungry squalls.

"It's commencin' to sound like home around here," said Sister Cuthcart. "I may as well go."

Truth was, she really was not so eager to get home to her nine. But that wasn't all of it either. We both was caught up in fascination of watchin' O'Reilly, and Cyrus was, too. For that black man proved to be uncommon gentle, and if George had another sign of pain after the first application of that paste, we did not know it. And he stayed as close upon the heels of O'Reilly as he had before stayed on Cyrus's heels.

And O'Reilly's fascination with Sarah Elizabeth—"Pretty doll" he said to her—was immediately evident, for everytime she whimpered or made a move, his eyes shot open were they closed, or he moved to her were he standing. I'd ne'er be so silly as to say that she recognized him, but she did stop her fussing and seem uncommon alert when he was about. It might 'a been only that he cast such a shadow over her that she wondered what it was that all at once blocked out the daylight.

Twice a day O'Reilly ministered to George's hand, and that hand grew better with each ministration. But it was obvious still that the hand would never be what it was. It had been his stronger hand, the right, and that sorrowed me all the more. In this rugged life, a man needed two hands. The loss of either was grave. O'Reilly showed him how to use the other, fashioned him a ball of twine, and extracted the solemn promise from the boy that he would conscientiously work that ball of twine and squeeze it to strengthen the weaker hand.

I grew stronger myself, much faster than I had reason to expect. Mayhap fearful that O'Reilly might produce some nostrum for my ills, my system exerted itself much more than it might otherwise have.

In other circumstances I might have been alarmed at that giant black presence and the effect that he seemed to have upon my little son. But for banishing that boy's pain, the black man would be ever welcome in our home, though I did have an occasional twinge of concern at the manner in which George attached himself to O'Reilly. I was not jealous, not at all, of the attention the boy afforded the black man. But now and then I was unsettled.

Night and day George stayed close by O'Reilly, or O'Reilly him. I could not say for certain which it was, anymore than I could figure out in what manner they conversed, for they somehow always seemed to be communicating, yet rarely did I detect any actual words to pass between them.

On a bright morning, one of the fine days that mid-winter sometimes affords, I sat outside holding the baby. George and O'Reilly likewise were out taking the welcome warmth, and I watched them. I was too warm and content in my sheltered spot to do aught but contemplate them.

They strolled about the clearing, yet seemed engrossed for all their casual attitude, for their glances met and then the big black's glance would shift to something else—the brown grass, a tree, the sky, things that I could not see—and the boy's glance would follow as if he was following instructions. Yet it was unsettling; it was as if the boy was being instructed by a teacher, yet without words.

Then they disappeared. I looked down at the baby, adjusted her bunting, looked up again, and they was gone. But before I could become seriously alarmed, they reappeared from a dense portion of the woods, each carrying a small forked branch and holding them in identical manner in both hands by each of the branches, the boy in solemn imitation of the man.

It was not the first time I had noted that imitation on George's part. He would hunker before the fire as the black did or fold his arms across his tiny bosom or even attempt to sleep sitting scrunched up, though he generally toppled over after he fell asleep. Such imitation was not unlike the manner in which he copied the elders and deacons and Cyrus himself. I did have to wonder if mayhap the boy was not so bright as we thought, but only a great imitator, like a tiny tree toad that changes its colors to match its situation.

Still and all, it was a curious situation, and curious was it that the boy seemed to show so little discomfort at so great a damage to his hand. Only once, however, was I alarmed at all. O'Reilly and George was hunkered before the little blaze in the fireplace, staring at it, and O'Reilly suddenly had reached, it seemed to me, into the blaze and extracted something and held it out to George.

With sudden intake of breath I was out of my chair. O'Reilly turned slowly toward me, opened his hand, and let the warm ashes drift slowly down. It was no live coal as I had at first feared, but only dead ashes lifted from the edge of the fire. I adjusted myself as best I could as if I had only been rising to see to some business, though I did not think that O'Reilly was fooled. How silly my mind had become—live coals indeed.

Through all of this, Cyrus come and went and only shrugged when I talked of the bond between the black and the boy.

In time, my curiosity overcome my judgment and my good manners, and I decided to ask O'Reilly some questions in hopes of getting some answers. Now had it been Clara Cuthcart, why she would simply have waded in with whate'er was on her mind and no one would 'a thought twice about it. For that was her nature, but it was not mine, and I could think of no way to approach the black man, curious though I was.

One day I chanced upon him, George at his side, standing at the cabin door staring toward the woods, and I heard myself blurting out, "O'Reilly, what do you see?"

He turned slowly toward me, shaking his head from side to side, and then turned back toward the vision—whate'er it was—before him.

"O'Reilly, what is that you teach my son, that he seems to understand?"

O'Reilly once again turned slowly toward me, stared fixedly at me for some time, and then, so quickly that I could not ready myself for it, he reached out his enormous fist and placed it carefully upon my bosom.

Well. I gasped in surprise. George was looking up at me, his expression interested and not at all alarmed. And before I had quite absorbed that, O'Reilly caught my hand, gently formed it into a fist and placed it upon his own chest, and I could feel the slow, rhythmic beat beneath my curled fingers.

I could tell that he meant no harm, that he was in no way taking liberties with my person. "Heart, Mama," he said, staring hard at me. "Heart," he repeated and glanced down at George, then over at the cradle where Sarah Elizabeth slept, and then his glance carried beyond the walls toward the distant horizon.

"Heart," he repeated and then removed his fist from my chest, and I removed mine from his. Perhaps I should have been embarrassed and discomfitted in some manner, but truth to tell, it did seem so normal and natural, I was for an instant so infinitely at peace that I could hardly explain it to myself. I certainly would ne'er have tried to explain it to anyone else.

Heart . . . strange. No telling what he was trying to convey, for the man lacked so many words.

I wanted to ask where he had come from, for he was not a native-born slave, if indeed he was a slave at all—if indeed he was a mortal man and not a spirit come from another world.

Ah. Spirit. Perhaps that is what I had sensed—something spiritual, almost as the communion that the saints was blessed with. Perhaps that was it. And I smiled. Mayhap I had took communion with that black man.

And then one morning he was gone, with no word, at least none to me or to Cyrus.

"He's gone back to Eremus Lodi," said George. "He'll come back in the spring when my hand is healed, to help me work it. It will never be as good as the other'n," he added, as unconcerned as if he was talking of two banty hens and not his own hands. "You've got to learn to accommodate it, is all." And then, "O'Reilly told me."

I hardly could get a complete sentence out of the man, at least a sentence that made much sense, and yet this four-year-old lad had apparently long and knowledgeable conversations with him. In what language, I wondered?

It was a day or two gone that Cyrus commenced to look around for Eremus Lodi's bottle of laudanum, but it was not to be found.

"Where is it gone?" asked Cyrus. "It an't nothing to be left lying around."

I only shook my head and shrugged, after we had satisfied ourselves that it was not nowhere in the cabin. "We'd better to ask George in case he's carried it off somewhere," I said.

When we did, the boy looked at us curiously and answered straight off as if we ought to have known, "Why, O'Reilly took it with him."

Both Cyrus and I looked at each other, hardly knowing what to make of it.

"I suppose," said Cyrus slowly, "that he might just be fetching it back to Eremus Lodi. Is that it, George?"

George shrugged, his thoughts apparently elsewhere. "Mama," he said, "Does the Baptists b'lieve that everything has a heart—the trees and grass and the water and everything, and that evil things try to destroy the heart of the world?"

"That is an interesting thought," answered Cyrus after a pause. "What made you think of it?"

"Oh," said the boy, "I only wondered."

Chapter 5

A First Distress

The promised Christmas Sing was canceled because I was not well enough to leave my bed and Cyrus would not leave me, though two or three did offer to stay in his stead. I did tease him some, though, that it was just an excuse so that he would not have to confront the problem of Patsy Bradene's singing, and, truthfully, he did not deny that.

In addition to regular Sunday meetings, it had been the practice of the deacons and other interested parties to meet mid-week at some home or other to discuss and pray. As Cyrus refused to leave us alone while he went to prayer meetings, then the meetings come to us.

I might have got along myself without those deacons filling up my cabin each week, but Cyrus and George so looked forward to them that I would ne'er have complained, not that I would have anyway, of course. Still, some of them deacons did not always recognize when they'd run out of material to discuss, and we was often late abed those nights.

George would be so still and so intent and, withal, so content, that for that reason I looked forward even to the meetings. While black O'Reilly had attended him, he had seemed hardly touched by his terrible experience, but after O'Reilly was gone, he begun to suffer some, less in body, I think, than in spirit, for he was faithful in using the powders left him by O'Reilly and squeezing the ball, much more reliable than you'd have the right to expect of one so young.

His dreams was troubled and he cried out often, which worried me and unsettled my own sleep. But on prayer meeting night, he was quiet and absorbed, so much so that the deacons often remarked upon it. And he stayed wide awake, no matter how long the discussion went on, which was more than some of the deacons theirselves could do as there was one or two speakers that could not readily be shut down once they started up. And when he did at last sleep, it was a quiet and restful sleep for him and then usually for me, although there was times after long discourse that sleep did not come easy for me, disturbed as I was by the accounts that the brethern gave of their trials and experiences.

Usually the gathered deacons and brethern stuck pretty well to the Scripture and the interpretations of it. But now and again one or another of the brothers would get to reciting his own experience of conversion in awful and lurid detail, which each in turn would feel constrained to match. So that if one brother had fallen forward on his face on the road before a vision of awful and ominous import, the next one would have fallen on his face in the creek before that same vision and so forth.

Still, the descriptions of utter depravity, of a sense of self most vile and humiliated before God, of worthlessness of the basest kind that each had to experience before he could abjectly deliver himself to God and pray for Grace, though knowing himself totally unworthy of it and abysmally fearful of eternal damnation, clouded my own soul terribly. I did wonder if it was possible that I was so hopelessly damned that the Lord God would not even allow me the comfort of total depravity. I could not feel vile for the life of me. And some nights after particularly horrendous revelations by the breathern, I turned and tossed and suffered severe anguish that I had not yet had that experience. But try as I might, I could not worry up a respectable amount of repentance out of my stubborn soul.

At first, Cyrus used to be in charge of opening and closing each meeting with a song, which was to my mind the best part of it all. Maybe I should have been ashamed, and perhaps it was because my faith was yet so shallow, that I had much the same feeling at regular meeting. I could have done with an entire morning of hymns.

And Cyrus did know every hymn that ever was, and all the verses, and eyes would light up when he would slide into some sweet, sad old hymn. "How tedious and tasteless the hours," he would begin and the deacons would one by one, as was their style, pick up the words and join him, sticking with it only long as they knowed the words, as most was versed only as far as two or three, though Cyrus could of course go through them all. Eventually he would be the only one left singing, the rest of us admiring the purity and strength of his voice and praising God that it was.

But Cyrus did not look at it that way. He pondered for a long time on the subject and confessed to me at last that he felt it was a vanity in him and that as long as voices would be lifted in song, he would have a hard time combating that vanity and thought that he would suggest that the singing of hymns during the prayer meetings be set aside. I objected to that immediately.

"No, Annamanda. I have prayed over it and I have studied it and turned the whole matter over and over in my mind, and I can only conclude that this is a vanity of my own, that it is the sound of my own voice that keeps me singing when all others have run out of words. Such vanity which feeds itself off the precious psalms to the Lord has got to be sinful in His Holy Eyes."

It seemed to me that the problem he posed could be solved if everyone else would just learn more verses, and I said as much. But he only give me a long and sorrowful glance.

I thought it a prudent solution and wished he would try it, but I didn't say more, for indeed I had to question my own motive which was more singing and less discussing. And in truth when Cyrus abjectly confessed his vanity, begged forgiveness, and suggested the abolition of the hymns, there was some consternation among those who obviously felt as I did.

But there was a couple, those who talked better than they sang, that nodded agreement at Cyrus's suggestion, and I thought less of them for it, one of those being newly arrived at the Lost River Church, his letter from some place in Tennessee. And when Cyrus confessed to vanity, that man shook his head in agreement most forcefully. His name was Brother Redmon Pitt, and I remarked almost immediately about him that he assiduously combed his spare strands of hair about his head in a manner resembling an ill-made jay's nest, for to cover the bareness of his scalp, such hairs, however, being insufficient to do that job. And I thought of Eremus Lodi's thoroughly bare and honorable pate and wondered that Brother Pitt might thus censure anyone else for vanity.

And when he later remarked that he had heard good opinion already of Elder Cyrus Pritchard, that opinion being that one day the young man was like to be a fine purveyor of the Gospel, well, I thought even less of him. "One day" indeed!

One prayer meeting night in late winter, Brother Cuthcart and Brother Lease arrived together, and both seemed to be under some constraints and agitations.

And without introduction, Brother Cuthcart explained. "Sister Sally Malone, it's said, is ready to bring a distress before the body against Sister Reba Cuthcart." Some might think it peculiar to refer to your own sister as "Sister" but they would be ones who would not understand that in this case Brother Cuthcart's sister was his "sister" in the Lord as well as in the flesh.

Cyrus had not yet had to deal with a distress in the Lost River Church, though he'd handled a few in the past, all quite successfully, well enough indeed that someone—mostly in jest—had speculated that had the Lord not picked him to be a pastor, the devil would sure have got him for a lawyer.

Cyrus did not ask right out what the distress might be, though I was in a stew to know myself, but that would not have been proper, most especially would it not have been proper to have got it from Brother Cuthcart who had family involvement.

"Has Sister Malone followed the tenets of the Word as to filing a distress? Have they met and discussed as has been prescribed?"

"Well, I am not so sure of that. Sister Malone is . . . ," said Brother Cuthcart, and he give Brother Lease a helpless glance, for he did not want to be guilty of saying aught unfavorable about Sister Malone under the circumstances.

"Sister Sally Malone an't always as circumspect as she ought to be. She's inclined to lose her roof at a slighter breeze than most people," said Brother Lease. "None of them Malones," he finished, "is shy about taking offense."

Well, I knowed the Malones. There was a fair amount of 'em about, for as Clara Cuthcart had once opined, they had as a group took the Lord's instructions to go forth and multiply seriously, and had done so copiously and to some minds excessively.

They was bad to argue and, it seemed to me, overly interested in other people's affairs.

It had been a group of Malone children who had cornered George at meeting and teased him to show his damaged hand and to tell all the particulars of the event that caused it. Poor child, so shy with children, had hardly knowed what to do and could not even speak. Some adult Malones was standing by as I come up to rescue the lad. I thought that they ought to have judgment to pull them young'uns off, but they seemed as curious as the children and most put out when I reached for George and said as courteously as I could manage that he didn't like to talk about it yet.

I thought I knowed that if it come to a distress, I'd most like be on the Spinster Cuthcart's side, no matter what the distress. Then I had to chastise myself, as I so often seemed to have to, for that kind of thought, for it was the distress and the evidence of the distress that had to be judged wh'er it be against friend or family. It was not uncommon for someone to have to vote against kith and kin. It had to be done, for that was the way of the Lord. Anyway, not being baptized, I would have no vote of my own, but that didn't deprive me of an opinion still and all.

Cyrus, Brother Lease, and Brother Cuthcart discussed the matter some and then decided to ask Brother Simpson and a delegation from the church to call on Sister Malone and Sister Cuthcart and explain to them both, did they not completely understand, the proper conduct of a distress as laid down in the Holy Scriptures.

Brother Simpson, the day before the next meeting called upon us and reported that the committee had done as it had been directed and had called on both the old sisters, for neither was young. "Sister Cuthcart did understand, but Sister Malone was some stubborn."

"What did she say?"

"Fiddlesticks."

"Fiddlesticks?"

Brother Simpson nodded. "Fiddlesticks, and then the sister took off on a diatribe against Sister Cuthcart as I have ne'er heard. Best be prepared tomorrow for some fireworks," he added.

Well, by the time we arrived at meeting the next day, the air was filled with excitement, for there's nothing like the promise of a lively distress to spark interest and stir attention. Everyone was anxious to know the particulars of the distress. If Cyrus already knowed, which was possible, even though no one but the participants was supposed to know, well, if he knowed he had not apprised me of it, and I had to admit to being as curious as anyone. Probably, it was naught but a misunderstanding, and trifling. I'd heard distresses brought over cows that wandered into gardens or missing hounds or ownership of various berry-picking locations.

But we had to wait through the services for the event. And when at the close of services Sister Malone rose and announced that she wanted to bring a distress before the group, well, all kinds of people sat up and took notice.

"Sister Malone," said Cyrus, holding his Bible open in one hand before him, "have you met the requirements as set forth in the eighteenth chapter of Matthew for the settling of grievances?"

Sister Malone plowed on, ignoring him. "I want Reba Cuthcart throwed clear out of this church and clean into the Mississippi River, if possible. She an't fit to set in Christian company."

"Sister Cuthcart, have you met these requirements?" asked Cyrus, not acknowledging Sister Malone's diatribe.

"No, Sir, we have not," said the Spinster Cuthcart. "Mistress Malone refuses to meet about it."

Sally Malone started to speak, but Cyrus raised his hand and held his Bible aloft and commenced to read in them deep and persuasive tones of his.

"Moreover if thy brother shall trespass against thee, go and tell him his fault between thee and him alone: if he shall hear thee, thou has gained thy brother.

"But if he will not hear thee, then take with thee one or two more, that in the mouth of two or three witnesses every word may be established.

"And if he shall neglect to hear them, tell it unto the church: but if he neglect to hear the church, let him be unto thee as an heathen man and a publican."

Cyrus closed his Bible and said, "The requirements for redress according to our Lord Jesus Christ as reported in the Book of Matthew, chapter eighteen, verses fifteen through seventeen, are plain, and adherence to those is necessary before a distress against a brother or sister can be brought before the church."

Well, Sister Malone stood there all trembly and angry. Instead of sitting down as the Spinster Cuthcart had done already, she suddenly shouted, "Well, I'll not have none of it. That woman don't belong in the house of the Lord fer she's lewd and sinful and did make unseemly advances at my young grandson who was splitting wood fer her."

All this was out before anyone could get to her. Two or three mothers jumped up and gathered up their own children and rushed them out the door and out of hearing, returning quickly theirselves, lest they miss any of the activity.

Sister Cuthcart was on her feet. "That an't so!"

"Oh, an' did ye not request of him that he bare his backside to ye?"

"I did no such of a thing! I don't know what that young 'scallion told ye. I did tell him that I'd take a stick to his bared backside did I ever catch him stealin' from me again."

"Stealin', stealin'!" yelled Sister Malone. "Stealin'!" Cyrus was trying his best to speak and calm things, but they was out of hand, mainly because the congregation itself was so took up in the thing that he could not get anyone's attention.

"Yes, stealin'! The young scalliwag was caught pilferin' of my properties when he thought I wasn't lookin'."

"That's a lie," screamed Mistress Malone, "a lie, fer ever'one knows that yer a liar just as ever'one knows that ye once had a base-born child which ye then drowneded!"

The silence that followed that horrible accusation was immediate and profound. And the look on Cyrus's face was distraught, for he had ne'er let a distress so get away from him. But that was always the danger, that the discussion of a simple disagreement which might be easily settled, did the parties discuss it calmly among theirselves, would degenerate seriously when it was brought before the group, each side so determined to be proved right before the group that sound judgment would not be employed.

Sister Cuthcart sank slowly to her seat and put her face in her hands. Sister Malone, all puffed up, looked around and seeing few friendly eyes, turned and flounced out the door.

"This distress," said Cyrus slowly at last, "having been brought before us prematurely, we must at last judge. But I think it wise that we use all of our persuasion to bring the disagreeing parties together, as it should already have been done, and so to bind the rift, which seems to me to have become more severe than it should have."

At that several heads nodded solemnly, but I did note that there was some people looking around perplexed and I knowed, too, that the more outrageous the accusation, the more likely some people to believe it, unwilling to believe that anyone would make so outrageous an accusation without foundation.

The Spinster Cuthcart sat with bowed head through the benediction and final hymn, nor did she leave her seat until Clara Cuthcart, her sister-in-law, come and got her and led her out the building.

I come upon Cyrus and Brother Cuthcart in earnest conversation and waited quietly. "It is true," Brother Cuthcart was saying, "that my sister did in her extreme youth have a base-born child, a beautiful little girl. And it is true that that little girl was drowneded by accident in her second year. My sister has both grieved and repented ever since, and has made it her business to give of herself to any and all who need it. It was by such Christian and pious acts that she regained her place in the church after having been churched for her transgression." He paused and then announced, "It was a spiteful accusation. Spiteful and hurtful."

"It was said in anger."

"That does not make it the less hurtful."

It was several weeks but the furor did eventually abate. Sister Malone recalled her distress and returned to services, as did the Spinster Cuthcart, though there was some distance and coldness, of course, between them.

The whole thing caused Cyrus no little unhappiness, for even without a distress, people was determined to take sides. Most was in sympathy with the Cuthcarts, but some seemed inclined toward the Malones, mostly those with other little grievances of one sort or another against some who espoused the Cuthcart cause.

I did notice that Brother Redmon Pitt, who combed his hair so askew, had moved himself to the bench where the Malone males sat, so apparently aligning himself with them, though he was so new to the congregation that there was no reason for him to form alliances.

And alliances was what they was. Alliances was what Cyrus feared, for they was what broke up other churches. For there's no need to make alliances unless for purposes of conflict, he liked to say.

It was brought to us by Brother Amiable Simpson that Brother Pitt was noising around that in the church that he had come from in Tennessee there had been quite a spite over the singing of hymns. He said that some was in favor of them and others was opposed, so that eventually they worked a compromise by which the hymns was sung only at the close of the service, so that them that did not care to hear hymns sung could leave.

"Is it what people are saying?" asked Cyrus, who was still tender on the problem of the vanity of his singing, too tender to my mind.

"Well, no. Not most. The Malones have been listening to him, but the Malones these days are looking for reasons to be contrary, I think. Still, ther's lots of Malones. Particularly do you count all ther kin that don't carry that name. And," he added after a pause, "it's been said that Brother Pitt is claiming that he is a candidate for ordination."

"Well, he's not," snapped Cyrus. "He's not even a licentiate."

Well, the whole thing did provoke me, and I said as much later to Cyrus. "Who is this man with the ill-disguised bare scalp who thinks that he can come into this church and cause turmoil?"

But all that Cyrus did was to repeat what he had said before, "Discussion is what keeps the church healthy. Not everyone is like-minded and getting such itches out where they can be scratched is necessary for harmony."

"Well," I said, "I don't think that Redmon Pitt bodes good."

Cyrus smiled and patted my hand. "I will pray for guidance."

I held my tongue at that but could not keep from thinking to myself that I would rather pray for the earth to open up and swallow Brother Redmon Pitt.

Spring did come, surprising us as it always did, just when we had settled ourselves for winter, as if it was to be a permanent thing, and accommodated it. The sun come and the flowers, and the buds grew red on the Judas trees. First the birds' cries and then green one day where brown had been the day before. And we who had filled our lungs all winter with wood smoke could hardly get enough of the sweet, warm air.

On such days I put a comforter on the ground outside the cabin and put Sarah Elizabeth on it. She was a strong, opinionated baby, still not able to crawl. But she could roll herself over and push herself up on her fat backside at will. This was early, I thought, too. But she was an active child and aggressive, more than I remembered George being. And that was strange, for it's usually the boys that are active and always busy, and the girls more quiet and contented.

Though it could be that my memory failed me, because George had become so timid and seemed to be growing more. He stayed close by me or Cyrus and never asked to go play with the boys. He seemed unnaturally fearful, which all things considered was, I guess, natural. But it could be troublesome, for during the daylight hours when I had work enough to keep me plenty occupied and most times Sarah Elizabeth on my hip, George would be hanging about, clinging to my free side, much in the way.

One such afternoon, while Cyrus worked at clearing space for a crop some distance from the cabin, too busy to keep track of George, I put the baby on her pallet under the shadowy, new leaves of the oak in front of the cabin, where she could lie on her back and study those shadows and so amuse herself. Later when she got restless, I sent George to her with a handful of play pretties and instructions to entertain her, for I needed both my hands and was in a stew to get my work complete, for the deacons was due later for prayer and discussion.

But within minutes George was at my side again, whining and fussing and complaining that he did not want to play with the baby, that he didn't even like her, and that we should send her back where she'd come from.

"George," I snapped, "what you're asking for is a nap, for you're grouchy beyond understanding! Get inside and on your pallet this minute."

"Mama," he said.

"George, go!" I'd had enough of that young'un for the time.

"Mama," he said again and tugged at my skirt. The way he said it made me look at him quickly. He was pointing a finger across the way where Sarah sat playing on her comforter.

It took me a moment to ascertain what it was he saw. I had to look beyond the baby toward the edge of the clearing, and still I was not quite sure what it was I saw.

"Mama?" he said again and his voice was fearful. "Mama, is it a dog?"

I caught my breath and held it for an instant. Was it a dog?

That I could not say. The beast that stood at the edge of the clearing was certainly shaped like a dog, but far larger than any dog I had ever seen, and black as tar. He seemed poised for something, his tail high over his back and his ears cocked. I had ne'er seen a wolf in my life, but I had heard fearsome stories of wolves and also fearsome stories of wild dogs. The beast, that stood actually closer to Sarah Elizabeth than we did, could have been either.

"George," I said as carefully and calmly as I could, "you walk easily into the cabin and fetch the rifle. Don't run or hurry in any way that may startle that animal. He is probably perfectly harmless, but should he charge, stay inside the cabin. On no account come out. Otherwise, get Daddy's rifle from the fireplace corner and carry it to me."

The boy had already begun to edge toward the cabin before I got my whole speech said. I was not an uncommon good shot, but I could use the rifle did I have to, though truthfully it was like as not to topple me over if I did not have something to brace against. If nothing else, a shot would bring Cyrus, for a simple yell might not reach him.

At that I reached carefully and slowly into the woodstack and got as heavy a stick as was manageable and begun to walk slow step after slow step toward where the baby, indifferent to any danger, played amongst her pretties, tossing them down and retrieving them and making them contented little noises that babies make.

The beast—wolf or dog—had not moved, but stood alert, watching me. I endeavored to try to catch its eyes for I had heard that a ferocious beast might be tamed sometimes by nothing more than a straightforward stare. But I was too far from him to make that contact and suppressed myself the notion that those eyes when I saw them might be red as hell's fires, for he was black as I imagined the devil himself to be.

The baby, reaching for a pretty, toppled herself over. I looked away from the beast at her, and when I looked back it had advanced a few steps toward her and then stopped as I caught its eyes with my own. They were not red, but they did not blink nor did the beast seem at all discomfited to be so stared at.

I started to move and so did he. I stopped and he did, too. Well. Mayhap I could out-think him for I was certain that I could not move faster than he. I took another step and he advanced just so. I stopped. He stopped. Then very slowly and carefully I lifted one foot and as cautiously as I could took a step. He remained still, his head cocked, his ears upright. Ah. I took another such slow step and another and still he did not move. Indeed, I might have made it all the way to the pallet thus had not the baby righted herself and seeing me, cried out, at which cry the beast suddenly moved and so did I. He jumped at her from one side and I from the other.

"Mama!" cried George.

"Get back!" was all I had time to scream. "Back!"

Sarah had toppled over again from excitement, and I was but a step or two from her and the beast also. That beast would tear me apart before he got my babe of that I was certain. And then I was aware that I also was screaming, shrieking at the beast. He paused, almost with a question in his eyes, but long enough for me to get to the edge of the pallet and position myself for battle.

"Mama, Mama!"

"Seneca!"

The beast without a backward glance turned and trotted back toward the edge of the clearing where that cry had come from. I gathered the baby to me, still clinging to the stick of wood, and looked in the direction he was going.

For a moment I could not see anyone, then I spied Eremus Lodi astride a very black horse, both so still that they might have been statues.

I dropped the stick I was clutching and waved a friendly and relieved greeting. But Eremus Lodi stayed motionless. Though he seemed to stare right at us, and in truth a blind man almost could not 'a missed us, he made no move of recognition.

When the dog arrived expectantly at his feet, Eremus Lodi glanced around, and then with a jerk turned his horse and retreated whence he had come without ever a backward glance.

Well! To be so rudely ignored and after he had earlier gone to so much trouble in our behalf. I was confused and baffled by it and not a little put out. It was the second time I had seen him act thus, and I hardly knowed what to make of it. It seemed somehow more than simple ill-manners. This man was a mystery, indeed.

I continued about my chores, muddling the whole incident around in my mind and coming to no conclusions, finally instructing myself to put it out of my mind. Did that man desire no concourse with us, why then we could certainly do without his peculiarities.

Later, as I stood at the table stirring up some supper, I heard a joyous cry from without. It was George, and I hurried to the door thinking that mayhap Eremus Lodi had changed his mind and returned. But what I saw was George rushing toward the tall, black figure of O'Reilly, pouches slung about his person, striding his long steps toward the boy.

I watched in some bemusement as they greeted, without words yet quite solemn, and then with slow and measured step worked their way across the clearing, engrossed in some silent activity. It almost seemed that they nodded greeting to each thing they passed, as a procession of bishops their subjects. I recalled what George had said—heart—that all things have heart and that evil ones seek to steal that heart. A pagan idea, of course, but interesting the way pagan ideas can sometimes be.

"O'Reilly," I greeted him at last, "you're welcome here."

"Ah, Mama," he replied, "be well, Mama."

It would be an easier feat to describe O'Reilly's speech than to duplicate it, for I had ne'er heard any like it. Those few words he used, it seemed to me, were made up mostly of vowels, though I knowed that couldn't be either, for they was the same words that I used. It was that he give each sound so similar a value that they all seemed to roll together. At the same time, there was strength and command in them tones.

He examined the hand that George held out to him, squeezed it tentatively, and though George grimaced, he did not cry out.

"He can't do many things with it," I answered the question in those black eyes. "He has squeezed the ball faithfully with his good hand and tried some with his bad, but not too successfully." I heard myself explaining all of this to the black giant, for the world as if I was talking to a learned physician.

O'Reilly squeezed the hand again. "Hurt?"

George frowned but he shook his head.

"Brave lad," said O'Reilly, and then he looked at Sarah who had continued her mindless chattering without hardly a pause. O'Reilly leaned toward her and stuck out his giant fist. "Pretty doll," he said.

The baby stopped chattering and eyed him, a little frown between her bright blue eyes, giving him most serious consideration as if perhaps she wondered what dark shadow had confronted her and blocked out the light. And then she laughed. And he greeted that happy laugh with one of his own, or what I took to be a laugh, for it was like low thunder, a sound rolling from the back of his throat, foreshadowing the spark which briefly lighted his eyes.

O'Reilly ate with us that night. He did not sit at the table with us but took his plate and stood in the corner near the fire. That was proper; a slave should not eat at the table. But truth was that I had a hard time thinking of O'Reilly as a slave, for by the man's bearing he did not mark himself a slave. He exhibited great dignity and strength, like a tree in the forest—a tall tree. Nor would Cyrus and I have any notion of what to do with a slave, there being none in either of our families. Here was a man sent by Eremus Lodi for his healing powers. We accepted O'Reilly in that manner only and give no thought to his legal status. It was none of our business.

After supper the brethern begun to arrive, and as it was early enough still to be light, they stood outside the cabin for a time. They did, of course, each of them remark upon O'Reilly, if not out loud then by the startled expression of their eyes.

When a large number had arrived and dusk begun to settle, all but O'Reilly moved inside by the fire, which felt good, as there was still a chill in the air.

Brother Cuthcart rose to speak. "I think, Brothers, that we can safely say that spring is upon us, and to mark that wondrous event, the sign of God's continuing bounty to all mankind," and here he paused and I thought that him and Cyrus exchanged a deep glance, though no one else seemed to notice, "I think it needs a hymn, Brother Pritchard. I am not alone in wishin' that ye lead us in one."

Ah, and there was a gauntlet throwed down. The matter of the hymns, it seemed to me, was probably only the beginning, for there had been rumblings of discontent all winter long. It was time to take a stand. I was a little put out that I had not been forewarned of this, for it was obviously a plan and several of the brothers in on it.

There was nothing to do but object or not, and being apparently taken by surprise, Brother Redmon Pitt held his peace, at least long enough for the hymn to rise. It was one of them sweet old hymns of Mr. Isaac Watts.

84

"How pleasant, how divinely fair," it begun and immediately filled the small cabin, the sound growing richer as each voice was added until full sound was reached. It fair tingled my spine, for it was a favorite of mine and of many others, which was probably why it had been chose.

The song progressed in rich sweetness, and suddenly a shadow filled the door. O'Reilly stood listening, at last entering, bent as he must, and then lowered himself to his knees, probably the better to listen. And he raised his face heavenward, closed his eyes, and though he made no sound, swayed to the melody.

It was a disconcerting sight. I noticed two or three sitting closest him edged theirselves away. But Cyrus took no note, and the hymn wound down as they always did, singers falling away as they run out of words and Cyrus finally finishing up by himself.

Black O'Reilly opened his eyes and stared toward Cyrus. There was no ignoring him. "This man is O'Reilly," said Cyrus. "He is . . . ," and here he paused. I wondered how he would designate the black. "He is a member of the household of Eremus Lodi. He is much skilled in the healing arts and so has been sent by Mister Lodi for the purpose of treating our son's damaged hand."

There was no expression on O'Reilly's face, but immediately Brother Redmon Pitt rose and, hooking his fingers in his belt and looking most solemn, said, "I do think some objection be in order, that we share our meetin' with a savage healer." Well, there was no doubt that Brother Pitt needed to have something to object to, for he always did. Having been temporarily bested in the matter of hymns, he was casting about for objectionable items.

"He is a guest in my house," was all Cyrus said. I was embarrassed that they was not only speaking of O'Reilly like this, but also doing it in his presence as if he wasn't even there, and I looked at my hands clasped tight in my lap. But when I peeked up, O'Reilly was nowhere to be seen.

"Healing is a matter for the Lord. I do not believe in medicine men," announced Redmon Pitt and looked around. I thought he might sit down then, but he was not ready to give ground.

He give a look around, then in dark and low tones said, "It an't no secret to anyone that strange things abound in the presence of Eremus Lodi and his pagan healer, that healer who feasts on milk laced with blood."

"Where come you by such idea?" said Cyrus immediately.

"I have it from a reliable source, ye may be sure of that."

"Why," I interrupted, "I have fed O'Reilly the black numerous meals, and he's eaten what we have eaten!"

"Annamanda," cautioned Cyrus.

"I won't hear of such slander," I said ignoring Cyrus for the moment. "That black man, wh'er pagan or no, is unquestionably a healer, and I must think that if healing be the province of the Lord, then the Lord it is who has blessed O'Reilly!"

Redmon Pitt lowered his eyes and looked right through me as if I had not even spoke and went on himself, "Ye may or may not know that last week Master Jack Sutterfield over west by Canebreak Holler lost a fine bull calf, that calf torn and gutted, his innards strewn about, yet the cow his mother stood near, untouched."

"I do not see the significance in that," said Cyrus.

"Ah," replied Redmon Pitt, puffing himself up a bit more, "ye do not, then? Ye do not mind that evil things seem to follow where'er Eremus Lodi and his various black beings be sighted?"

John Cuthcart, who was slow of talking but often well-thought and wise, shook his head slowly. And Amiable Simpson, who was a little quicker to speak and act, said, "Naw, naw, naw. Eremus Lodi is a lonely man, it's true, and roams afar and always has, fer I been on this side of the river fer a good many years and have seen him coming and going, sometimes alone and sometimes accompanied by them dark companions, but he an't wicked er evil er none of them things. That's witch talk and superstitious, and," here he glanced toward Redmon Pitt, "to be expected of them with a superstitious turn."

"A man that does not ally hisself with any group," spoke up John Cuthcart at last, "that walks the lonely path, why he is oft suspect of them that do not understand that."

"Well," said Redmon Pitt glancing about, "there's quite a lot that I don't understand of this group, and I intended to make some issues come Association."

That night as we lay abed, O'Reilly sitting in the corner by the fire, his knees gathered to his chest, wh'er awake or asleep, I ne'er could tell, I spoke to Cyrus of the possibility of dissension.

"There's always possibility for dissension. Some of it quite honest, for the Scriptures is hard, there's no doubt of that. But then there's always one or two ready for a dissension over trivial points, mainly to make names for theirselves. It's always a problem, and the members needs must address it when it arises and determine which it be, honest or dishonest dissent."

Well, I had no doubt which it was and I said as much.

"Ah, Annamanda, that something may seem perfectly obvious an't always so and needs more considering sometimes than that which is less obvious at the outset."

That didn't make a lot of sense to me. All I could do was try to sleep on it.

However, my sleep that night was restless, the dreams senseless, but by morning light I viewed Redmon Pitt and his various assertions and postures for what they was—silly and intended only to puff himself up before the assembly. That bull calf might 'a been attacked and torn apart by a bear or painter-lion, was a whole lot more likely than that O'Reilly done it.

86

Still, I did catch myself peeking at the big black as he solemnly spooned his breakfast into his mouth. Blood and milk, indeed! Still, I shuddered a little at the thought.

O'Reilly stayed with us for a few days. He worked with George's hand, applying various salves to it. Indeed with each ministering of exercise and salve, the hand did seem to become more limber and flexible. Still, there was little more that could be done. It might get better, but it would ne'er be cured.

Then one day O'Reilly was gone. We woke and he was not there. Nor did George seem particularly concerned or upset over the absence. He merely looked blank when we asked him where O'Reilly had gone, and then shrugged.

Miraculously, George's newfound courage did not disappear with the departure of O'Reilly. He was suddenly sprightly and animated, confident and adventurous in a manner that he had ne'er been, even before his accident. And I was grateful for that.

One warm day I gathered him up for a thorough scrubbing and, pulling his shirt off, I saw a strange thing, an amulet of some sort hanging around his neck.

"O'Reilly give it me," the boy said proudly.

I examined it. It was tied upon a thong that was a common enough kind, but the thing itself was most unusual. I could not make out what it was intended to be, whether a figure or a design. Nor could I recognize what it was carved from, only that it had indeed been carved of something that I did not recognize, some material both extraordinarily hard, shiny, and dark.

"What is it?" I asked.

"I dunno," he answered. "O'Reilly said I should always wear it."

"A good luck charm?"

He only shrugged.

"What else did O'Reilly tell you?"

He studied the question and said at last, "Well, I dunno."

I did not think that he was being evasive. It was just very difficult for a four-year-old child to make sense of such a general question.

"Did he tell you where he comes from?"

"A far place," George said promptly. "A far, far place and he can never, never go there again."

"Oh? What far place is that?"

"Across the wide sea. Far across the wide sea."

"What did he say of that far place?"

"It is beautiful, with hills and grass. It is warm."

"How did he tell you all of this, George? It seems to me that O'Reilly did not speak so much or so well."

The boy looked at me curiously, perhaps wondering why I was asking so many questions, I who had chided him so often about asking questions.

"Well," he said at last, "O'Reilly talks. He does not talk like everybody else, but he talks and I know what he talks about."

"What all else did he tell you?"

Suddenly the boy decided he did not want to talk anymore. I did not know why. But all he would do was shrug, as if tired of that game, even though I asked several other questions.

Later I showed Cyrus the amulet around the boy's neck. He frowned, but finally muttered only that it was a trinket, possibly a savage good luck charm which had no meaning for Christians, but which he thought to be harmless, no more than a toy.

"It is probably better," he frowned, "not to draw attention to it, however. There are those who might like to make a big thing of it."

Chapter 6

Elias Kencaid

Though spring was upon us and favored us with more and more pleasant days, now and again it would turn against us and betray us with an ugly and chill day.

It was such a day that we took us to Sunday meeting, where Cyrus would preach. Though the weather was not actually wet, it was damp and the clouds over-hung, not ominous, but rather dreary and dull. I'd almost rather have hard rain, for at least then there is activity.

The weather seemed to have that effect on Cyrus, for his sermon lacked the warmth and spirit that it usually had, as if he just could not get going, though Cyrus ne'er did preach a sorry sermon, not even at his worst, his worst being better by far than many who took the pulpit. So the congregation was not so conscious of a lacking, I think, as I was.

George beside was fidgeting, which was unusual for him. Sarah Elizabeth was in continual movement when she was not asleep, but George at meeting was usually still and attentive, though I always wondered just how much he could absorb of what he heard.

I give him a little rap with my knuckles on his knee without looking down, yet he still fidgeted. He looked up at me, and I noticed that he was clinging to that amulet that O'Reilly had give him and he wore a tight little frown between his eyes.

"Mama?" he whispered so low that he made almost no sound at all, and then he lifted his head and appeared to be sniffing as if seeking out some odor.

"Mama?" he whispered again, and I shook my head at him and shifted Sarah Elizabeth to my other shoulder, for she was getting most rowdy. I did not want to have to leave the services with her.

"Mama," said George tugging at my elbow, "Mama, does it smell of death?"

Well. I started at that. Death? Whatever in the world? I frowned hard and shook my head at him and put my free arm about him, and I felt him to be trembling. At almost that same moment, I was conscious that Cyrus's tone had picked up, that he had all at once hit his stride and others besides me had perked up, too, listening to him. He was making excellent point after excellent point, spiritedly as if he would brook no argument, his eyes flashing certainty, his gestures controlled, and his voice rising and falling in them beautiful inflections of his. Yet was George beside me clutching his amulet and trembling.

I sensed then some activity behind me and slowly turning was surprised to note that Eremus Lodi leaned against the open doorway, his hat removed, apparently attentive to what was being said. I quickly looked back at Cyrus and give him my careful attention. Though I did not look behind me again, I was certain that Eremus Lodi remained in the doorway or possibly even seated inside, because of the intensity with which Cyrus was preaching. The congregation might not most of them recognize the reason for the sudden inspired preaching, but I thought I did. However, for upwards half an hour or more, the congregation come right spirited itself. There was much in the way of "Amen" and "You tell 'em, Brother" and "God love ye" and that sort of thing.

By the time Cyrus had worked through the final hymn and the last prayer, why the little building fair shook with the electricity of the spirit. Whatever had been frighting George was dispelled, and the color come back to his complexion.

As we filed out the door, I glanced around, but Eremus Lodi was nowhere to be seen. I had that uncanny feeling that mayhap he was indeed not real, but only a spirit flitting from place to place.

And apparently I was not the only one to have that feeling, for I heard a group conversing upon the subject.

"It is said that he hides some secret that makes him traverse the river's edge like a shadow. I an't one to b'lieve in spirits, ne'ermind," said Brother Saucie Malone, "but as the way that man haunts the river and usually follered by that dog and that nigger, both black as Satan's boots, wal, ye do have to wonder."

"Naw," interrupted Redmon Pitt, "it's no ghost or devil he is, but shrewd and cunning."

"How say ye?"

"Ye know how them settlers are, them that come years gone by. They an't so glad to see the federal government take title to these lands. They've had 'em pretty much as they want 'em all these years. Why should they be glad to see American laws and new settlers come pushin' in as we are?"

"And that means . . . ?"

"I don't know. I can't say exactly," said Redmon Pitt, puffing up as if he knowed what he was talking about, though from experience of hearing him, I felt that it was unlikely he did. "I only know t'would be to ther good, to the good of the likes of Eremus Lodi, was these lands back in the hands of the Spanish or the English, particularly the English."

"D'ye then think Eremus Lodi to be treasonous?" asked Saucie Malone.

"Wal," shrugged Brother Pitt, "I'd maybe ne'er go so far as that. But it is a thought. It just does seem strange, don't ye mind, that he glides through these woods and along the banks of the river so constantly and so surreptitiously? And," he added with what seemed a malicious glance in my direction, "that often enough once he's passed is discovered some act of unexplained violence?"

Brother Pitt then turned his glance full upon me. "Brother and Sister Pritchard know more of Eremus Lodi and his dark shadows mayhap than any of the rest of us," he said.

"I know Eremus Lodi to have been generous and helpful," I answered right back, "and I know his man to have saved our child from pain. I am grateful for all that. But that's all I know, for neither of those men is given to allowing his mouth to run on ahead of his brain. It is," I went on with a sharp look at Redmon Pitt, "a characteristic that some of us could benefit in studying." And I turned away.

Cyrus had little to say as we walked home. His only reference to either Redmon Pitt or Eremus Lodi was a casual comment that there was little to be served in arguing with such as Redmon Pitt. I knowed what he meant. He meant that I probably ought to have kept my mouth shut, but he would not criticize me openly. It was not his way. My old granny who had such a wondrous way with words, though, would have said, "H'it takes a fool to argue with a fool."

Neither of us was prepared for what we found when we reached our cabin place—Eremus Lodi seated on the bench list without the door in a protected and sunny spot, his head leaned back as if he was dozing.

But he was not, for he opened his eyes, smiled, and rose in friendly greeting as we approached. I thought that my mouth must have gaped wide, so surprised was I. And I could not keep from wondering to myself if he would turn and quickly disappear as if he had not seen us. But he was apparently waiting for us, for he remained both standing and smiling, that great, black dog that I had seen before seated at his feet.

Cyrus strode forward to meet the guest, though I held back, Sarah struggling on my shoulder and George clinging to my hand. I had both eyes upon that black dog, if indeed it was a dog, for not only was it large and black but its manner was guarded as it glanced up at its master and then back toward us. As Cyrus reached out his hand toward Eremus Lodi, the dog moved almost imperceptibly, alert and poised.

"Seneca!" said Eremus Lodi and the animal relaxed again, but there was none of that obsequiousness of tail flogging and lively panting that friendly dogs are given to.

"Ah, Pastor," said Eremus Lodi, "and Madam," he added inclining toward me.

"Is that animal vicious?" I said. I did not purposely ignore his greeting. I was wary of that dog and needed to know how safe we was around him.

Eremus Lodi cocked an eyebrow at me, an amused expression on his face, though he answered quite solemnly, "Vicious? Seneca? No." And then he paused and after a lengthy stare which discomfited me somewhat, went on, "Viciousness is a human characteristic, Madam. An animal may be dangerous, but it is not vicious. But if you mean, will the dog attack you? No. Not unless you threaten me. His only purpose in life is to protect me. He knows nothing else and would not hesitate, no matter the cost. He is not, however," he added glancing toward George, "a pet. He is not to be played with."

I did not think that George needed to be told that, for he stayed close beside me and kept an eye on the beast, though it made no other movement.

"Ah," said Eremus Lodi, "the babe has growed considerably. A pretty lady, indeed. And you, Madam, you look much more comfortable than the last time I saw you."

Well, I had an answer for that, but I kept it to myself. I would not remind him that he had rode off from us last time without a word or greeting. I would not match him ill-manner for ill-manner.

"Will you take your dinner with us, Sir?" was all I said.

"Thank you, no, Madam. I have my journey yet before me. It was impulse only that led me to pause at your meeting, Pastor, for it's been long years since I've heard a predestinarian preacher. I must congratulate you, for you preach a fairly convincing sermon. I can see why your fame is read abroad. I even found myself almost caught up in it."

"Almost?"

"Well, Sir, indeed we do share certain points of doctrine, if you will. I do believe in the utter depravity of man and of his incapacity to save himself. I do, however, question that there might be any omnipotent being so foolish as to find reason to save any such useless and depraved and corrupt thing."

"That's not so unusual an observation," said Cyrus calmly.

"No, perhaps not."

As Eremus Lodi and Cyrus spoke, George had ceased to be attentive and had wandered away, returning shortly carrying in one hand a stone. He stood studying it and listening to the conversation by turns, the way children will do, finally losing interest in the stone and returning his attention to the conversation.

"What do you have there, Boy?" said Eremus Lodi suddenly.

The boy held out the stone, of a size to fit neatly into his small hand. Eremus Lodi took the stone thus silently proffered him and studied it as solemnly as it had been offered.

"It is warm, lad," he said.

I thought that a curious observation, and perhaps it showed, for Eremus Lodi looked at me with that veiled smile of his and said, "A stone, my lady, originally tossed from out the bowels of the earth, is a hot and lively thing grown cold, which can no longer generate heat from within itself but must depend on warmth from outside sources."

If he thought he had explained himself, he was mistaken, for I was still mystified at the attention thus paid an ordinary stone.

"It was impulse that bade me pause to speak with you," said Eremus Lodi, "and though I appreciate your kind invitation, necessity deems that I move on. Here, lad," he said and he handed the stone back to George, "keep it warm."

George took the stone, and Eremus Lodi retrieved his black horse and called out to his dog, waved, and in short order had disappeared into the woods.

George stood holding the stone. Cyrus looked down at him and said gently, "Put the stone by the door, Son, where the sun will often strike it and warm it."

"Well," I snapped, "and what do you intend to do with it—hatch it?"

"There are people, Annamanda, like that stone, who have lost the capacity to warm theirselves and must depend on outside sources for such warmth." He glanced in the direction that Eremus Lodi had gone and then stepped into the cabin.

The Association had been set for late May. Brother Elias Kencaid arrived on foot a few days before that, having ridden the river as far as he could. He carried with him a portmanteau and asked only for a comforter against the damp ground, brushing aside our offers of a tick inside the cabin.

"This time of year's best for sleeping out of doors," he said. "Ye do yerselves disservice if ye do not try it now and then, before the ground grows awful hard with the dry and the bugs commence to seek entertainment beyond the river."

As I went about my chores, I caught snatches of conversation between Cyrus and Brother Kencaid, enough that I knowed that Cyrus was telling the older man of the situation among the Lost River congregation. Cyrus was troubled. I also could tell from the tone of Brother Kencaid's remarks and the care of his questioning that he was mostly on Cyrus's side.

"Don't be discouraged, Brother," I heard Brother Kencaid say at one point. "These rumors and ruptures are eventually a part of almost every congregation. For various reasons. Now and again it is an honest dispute on point of doctrine, but mostly I'm sorry to say, it is more like a member or two have outgrown their britches and would usurp whatever authority they can for the means of their own aggrandisement. This," he went on and I must admit that I had by then stopped what I was doing and was taking careful note of what Brother Kencaid was saying, "this I am afraid is more and more common, whether the fault of the lowering of standards or simply the distancing from established churches, I cannot say. I only know that there is little splits and dissensions here and there that trouble me considerable."

"Trouble is a good word," said Cyrus.

"Aye, well, trouble is not new to the believers, aye in times past far worse than mere 'trouble'. I am much older, Brother Cyrus, than you are, and I know for a fact that to try to avoid trouble is to court it doublefold. Would ye defeat it, ye must meet it head-on, counter it, turn it aside, or, at worst, drive it off. That last does not always settle things, fer trouble has a way of regrouping and presenting itself again."

That was not too encouraging. I thought that Cyrus must not think so either, for he hung his head and stared unmoved at the ground. Brother Kencaid removed his flat hat and fanned himself with it, for they sat by the side of the house that the sun had just begun to reach. I noted to myself that I had not often seen Brother Kencaid without his hat. I also remarked to myself that that man's hair was spare, too, hardly covering the shiny, pink scalp. But he only combed those few strands in a normal fashion and made no attempt to get them to do more work than they were capable of, as Redmon Pitt always did.

Both men was silent for a time, Brother Kencaid's eyes closed against the brightness and warmth of the spring sun. I studied his face more closely than I ever had. It come to me that the man was quite some older than I had at first realized, not only because of his gray, spare locks, but because of the lines about his eyes and mostly because of the pull of his facial muscles, the flesh drifting away from the bones of his face, as if readying itself for another journey.

"Brother Pritchard," said Brother Kencaid coming back to life, "there is not so many spiritual men these modern days as there once was. I don't know why, unless the greed for land that has overcome us begets greed for power. I do sense, in but few men who profess spirituality, anything approaching a true and profound experience of God. The trivial and false are too much with us." He paused and stared hard at Cyrus. "I do, however, trust your experience, Sir. I trust it and I am profoundly moved by it."

"I do not know," murmured Cyrus. "I truly do not know. I have prayed to God. I have offered myself. But I still do not know."

"Ah, Brother. That's true. That is so, so true. Though I feel confident of ye, of myself I still wonder and after all these years. There are moments that I myself do deeply despair. I wish I could tell ye that with age and experience ye'll no longer experience despair, but, alas, I cannot. What I can tell ye," he went on after a pause, "is that there will be moments, rare—very rare—that will more than make up for that despair, those few moments when ye will sense in all things the glory and the power of the Almighty, sense it in such depth and such surity that it will fair take yer breath away. Those are the moments that I wait for and once or twice, it has been—near perfect, glorious."

They lapsed then into silence. Sarah awoke from her nap and I was forced to busy myself. If they said more on the subject, I missed it. But what little I had heard had moved me tremendously. I wanted to speak with Cyrus about it. But it seemed so powerful a topic that I wondered if I could even broach it, much less understand it.

It was planned that the deacons and churchmen meet at our cabin to make final plans for the Association. I was becoming accustomed to being regularly overrun by these men and, I suppose, proud to be so chosen. Still, it did require a certain amount of extra work for me to make sure that things was reasonably ordered when they arrived. And as the children amused theirselves nearby, I worked around the cabin, sweeping the ground and picking up that variety of litter that always seemed to blow in from the woods nearby. Cyrus was in sight, pulling at the weeds that would take over our garden plot was he less than attentive to them. It was a mild and pleasant afternoon, and I thought more than once how nice it would be to stretch out on the pallet with the children and nap in the warm sunshine. But I had my responsibilities and sleeping was not among them.

"Mama," called George.

"Not now, Son, I've much to do."

"Mama." At the insistence in his voice, I looked up. He was standing, a worried look on his small face. I walked over to him.

"Mama," he said glancing about and speaking quite softly. "Mama, I am watched. There are eyes watching me."

"What eyes, George?"

"Eyes, only eyes."

I looked around and saw nothing untoward and said as much. "What makes you think that you are watched?" I asked that last gently, for I feared the nervousness from which he had suffered was reasserting itself.

"They watch me. I can feel it. I know that they watch me." He spoke with such certainty that I looked around again more carefully. I could see Cyrus moving along the rows of corn, but naught else. I reached down and picked up Sarah and propped her on my hip, for she had become demanding when she saw me.

"Mayhap it's O'Reilly returned?"

"They an't friendly eyes, Mama. They're hurtful eyes." He was hanging onto the amulet around his neck, looking up at me. I did not like that look on his face, for I had hoped that O'Reilly's powerful influence had set those terrors to rest.

"Where are these eyes, George?" I asked calmly.

"I think," he paused, "I think in the brush beyond the near trees." He jerked his head in the direction of the forest closest the cabin.

"Well, I'll just see," I announced, and I started in that direction, the baby riding my hip, her little feet dangling and flopping about my legs.

"Mama. No! No, Mama!" cried George in real alarm.

"Now, George. It's nothing. I'll show you. Daddy's close by and there's naught to fear." I marched directly to the edge of the forest.

"Mama!"

I looked back at George, started to take another step, but was arrested at a sudden, startled movement and the sound of something in the brush. I caught my breath and waited. But I heard nothing else. It was gone whatever it was. A large bird or a small animal? A deer or fawn or even a rabbit or whistle-pig? Was that what he had sensed? I had to admit that he was a most sensitive child, carrying in his being subtle instincts that I could only guess at.

"It was a whistle-pig, George," I said turning to him and announcing it as if it were incontrovertible fact. "A whistle-pig—groundhog. What a racket the fat thing did make," I laughed.

The child only looked at me for a long, searching moment and then said, "It wasn't, Mama. It wasn't a groundhog. I could smell it. But it's gone now," he added fingering the amulet at his neck once more. And then he turned and walked on down the side of the hill toward the garden where Cyrus worked.

I stood at that spot for a time and studied the dark growth where the noise had come from. There was always noises coming from the under-growth, for it teemed with living creatures of all kinds, creatures which could be at times as silent as lurking spirits and at other times noisy as a county fair.

I laughed to myself, kissed the baby on the cheek and murmured, "That boy, Sarah, that boy. Why do I let his little fears unsettle me? Can you tell me that?"

She laughed and patted my lips with her chubby little fingers, and I could do naught but kiss them and laugh again.

The deacons commenced to arrive before sunset. There would be more than the inside of the cabin could accommodate, so we pulled chairs and benches outside, set a small fire a-going and a torch, against both the dark-ness of the night and as a discouragement to whatever bugs might have an urge to join the proceedings.

I saw Brother Redmon Pitt arrive with Brother Saucie Malone, neither of those two being deacons, but of course welcome anyway, welcome in brother-hood, that is. I'd just as leave they stayed away, and I said as much to Cyrus. He only shook his head in mild reprimand and added that it was Brother Kencaid's desire that especially Brother Pitt be present. There was naught else to do but hold my tongue, which I did.

As soon as a goodly number of men had gathered, all chairs filled and the ground around the fire occupied, Brother Kencaid without preface begun the business. He did not open with either song or prayer, but went straight at the business of organizing the Association, asking for volunteers for certain duties, arranging the order of preaching, and setting aside times for church business to be conducted. I stood with George nearby and listened, much impressed with the efficiency of Brother Kencaid's conduct. I had sat through many a meeting of business. They was oft bogged down in detail and long-windedness, as there was always certain of the brothers given to expressing opinions wh'er they was needed or not. Brother Kencaid did not even give such a chance to happen, and I thought perhaps that we might be through and abed at a decent hour. But I was to be disappointed in that, such disappointment coming at the hands of he whom I had been admiring so.

For the subject come up pertaining to the strength of spiritual experience, much the same that Cyrus and Brother Kencaid had been discussing earlier in the day. And when it did, I sighed and hopefully depended on Brother Kencaid to keep such discussion from getting out of hand, for there was nothing that the dear brothers loved more than to relive—at tiresome length—each moment, nay each breath, of their own profound spiritual experience.

Alas, it was Brother Kencaid himself turned treasonous. Yet even he could not resist the chance to tell his own ancient tale. As he begun to speak, I looked around and noted not a few of the brothers looking a little perplexed and worried, for when Brother Kencaid took a deep breath and with a few commonplace remarks begun to talk, it was obvious that he intended to hold that floor for a very long time.

"Oh, I was slow a-coming to the spirit," he laughed. "I dug in my boots and bowed my back and dared the Holy Spirit come my direction. I was of a stubborn, independent turn, determined not to follow meekly after my family and tutors. There was an old brother of family acquaintance who was given to pointing me out with his long and stern finger and allowing that, e're I died, I would be either pilloried or pulpited. And I must confess a large number of folk held with the former and not the latter.

"It is that way with some young folk," he went on, "that they must fight and lash out at all authority, even as they know in their hearts the truth of that authority. I was such a one. Truly, many early church fathers were youthfully so afflicted, as if the Lord occasionally might take pleasure or challenge in the bending of such wills, as certain men do take the most spirited of unbroken horseflesh to be the more valuable, once tamed to their hands.

"I would not like to be so immodest to place myself among such Saints, of course, as Peter and Paul and Augustine, whose youthful barbarity, once tamed, gave full confession and evidence of the Power and Holiness of Almighty God, His wonder and His joy. But I know my experience to have been somewhat the same."

Redmon Pitt, unable to keep to himself any longer, interrupted at Brother Kencaid's pause. "And now how is it that ye invoke the name of a Papist Saint, Sir?"

"Papist Saint? Augustine? Why, Brother Pitt, Augustine was a goodly man of Scriptures, one of the few early on who read them a'right and proclaimed the Grace of God and the elect of Him."

"So? And what know ye of his sin and willfulness then?"

"Why I have read his Confessions, Sir. The Confessions of St. Augustine, as a matter of fact, at one point in my youth had great effect on me."

"I'm afraid that I do not understand," said Brother Pitt, and he looked somewhat smugly about.

"What is it, Sir, that you fail to understand?"

"Why, how you, an Old School pastor, do call upon ancient and classical readings, when we have all been taught and believe in a clergy that is not schooled, but which gets its inspiration, not from books and reading, but from the Holy Spirit, individually."

Redmon Pitt looked right pleased with himself and glanced around at the gathering, having made his point.

Brother Kencaid sighed. "Brother Pitt, I must confess that I am well-schooled. I read Latin and Greek, Sir; I have read the poets, religious as well as profane. I have studied history and I know mathematics. I think indeed that it was such schooling as I had as a boy that made me so reluctant to accept without question the teachings of my family concerning the Will of God. I think also that it was such love of learning, such knowledge, that finally led me to the profound experience of which I was readying to tell you. I know what you speak of, Sir. It is true, I distinctly believe, that those who go to school to be taught to speak for our Lord are much in error, for no man has power to teach such. It is Divine intervention, the Holy Spirit inspiring, that makes a mere man, depraved and defiled, able to speak those words which are Precious to the Lord.

"But I do not think, Sir, that the Lord intended that we dwell in complete ignorance of things secular. I have a great respect for learning, Sir, learning of all kinds."

Redmon Pitt tried to speak again, but to my delight, Brother Kencaid waved him aside and continued speaking. "Indeed, a few years before I was born in Connecticut was passed a law that no man could preach who had not been educated at either Harvard College in Massachusetts or Yale College in Connecticut, or in some theological college abroad. The purpose of that law was to 'weed out' heretical and 'ignorant' preaching. But alas the effect of that law was only to worsen what was already flaccid preaching and strengthen a pompous clergy.

"If you let me digress, I can tell you such a tale." And then without waiting leave, Brother Kencaid went on. "When I was a young man, still struggling with my own experience, vacillating and straining against that inevitable pull of the Spirit, I chanced to pass a few days with a dear cousin in Massachusetts, and though the law did not require that we attend the Congregational church, the good opinion of various neighbors did. I was, as I have said, a very young man, and though stubborn and passing rebellious, I would not have exhibited those characteristics to strangers, and so I attended that church with my cousin and his family.

"Accustomed as I was to regular, Old School Baptist services and the spontaneity and inspiration of such services, I was ill-prepared for the formality of the Congregational services. The pastor issued forth from his Manse, his wife upon his arm, their boy children in a line behind him, their girl children in a line behind her, each line flanked by the colored servants of the appropriate sex, and they marched into the church and up the aisle in formation, the congregation standing until they all was seated.

"As you might expect, I was some startled at the formality of it. Indeed it smacked so of aristocracy that I could hardly believe my eyes. This was, of course, some years before the revolution, so that such monarchism was not so ill thought of as it might now be.

"I sat and listened through the service and found the hymns to be similar to many of those that I did then and do now love." At this point Brother Kencaid glanced at Cyrus and then more covertly toward Brother Pitt. Then he continued without more comment on hymns. "But when the preacher got himself to the pulpit, gowned and perfumed as he was, and passed his hand in blessing over the congregation, I could but wonder if this was the servant of God or God the servant of this."

Here Brother Kencaid paused and there was a chuckle or two at his sally, though Redmon Pitt continued to glare.

"It was when that worthy picked up his pages," Brother Kencaid went on, "and spread them on the pulpit before him, that I realized that unlike what I was accustomed to, this man would speak from a prepared text. I had never had experience of that, knowed that practice to be condemned among the Old Style Baptists of my own persuasion, but the man looked so proud and awesome, standing before that goodly crowd, that I was impressed and eager to hear what he might have to say, thinking undoubtedly that, having spent long hours in earnest prayer and preparation, he would have a sermon of more import than any I had ever heard before."

Brother Kencaid laughed and wiped his eyes. "Please bear in mind that I was then quite young and still struggling to formulate a doctrine. Well, he commenced to read from his script and it become apparent all too quickly that not only was his delivery flaccid and perfunctory, his doctrine was cloudy and his message garbled. I sat in stunned silence and glanced around to see if anyone else might be as outraged as I was. This was no servant of God at all, but only a foolish fop bent on his own self-glorification."

Here it seemed to me that Brother Kencaid did glance side-long at Brother Redmon Pitt, but I might have been mistaken in that. I did note that Cyrus was following every word that the older man was saying, with a look of profound preoccupation on his face.

"But the people around me," Brother Kencaid continued, "did seem most caught up in those anemic words, and I could but conclude that they who listened in so intent a manner, wise and judicious, were neither, but only they that had not ears to hear nor eyes to see.

"Well, I sat for quite a time becoming more and more agitated, hoping that the man would be struck down from on high for such defaming of a pulpit or, at the very least, draw to a merciful close his pointless remarks. But he seemed only to grow stronger as he turned pages, and it struck me that he might well go on forever, which I could not suffer.

"And so I rose suddenly and made my escape, out the door whence I had come, relieved to gasp for the fresh air. But I found myself immediately set upon by a constable wanting to know why I was affecting the peace by rushing out of church mid-service.

"Well, as I have said repeatedly, I was young. It might not be excuse enough for my behavior, but it was the reason. I did not want to be hauled to the pillories for injudicious behavior, so I attempted to look as uncomfortable as I could and whispered to him that I had had to make my escape, lest I defile my person and so the church, and I pointed toward the public privy and danced around in what now seems a most embarrassing manner. And, excused, I dashed toward that privy and waited in there for a good long time."

He paused again to wipe his eyes and then he laughed. "In truth, I think that the doctrine I had heard espoused would give the trots to any thinking man." At that the deacons chuckled and laughed and nodded agreement. All but Cyrus, who was not so inclined to make fun of those he disagreed with.

"But," said Brother Kencaid, "I did digress, for I wanted to talk briefly of my own experience of the Spirit, for it was a most powerful one, wrenched from a reluctant and rebellious youth, so powerful that even to this day I can wake at night sodden with sweat at the dreamy remembrance of it."

Brother Redmon Pitt cleared his throat and, unbidden, interrupted. "Yes, Brother, I too have had such experience." But his voice, following directly after that most effective presence of Brother Kencaid did sound hollow and weak, and miracles of miracles, even he seemed to realize it and retreated into silence.

Brother Kencaid looked around and, apparently satisfying himself that the assembled brothers desired to hear more, continued. George, seated upon my lap, remained alert and attentive, though it was well past his bedtime.

"As I have said, I was a rebellious youth, despaired of by family and friends for my many violent and vain transgressions, which I will not here detail, only to say that they was of the sort that young men are often guilty, and I perhaps no more guilty than most, except that I had been brought up in a home where the Word of the Lord was mighty, where my own father and his brothers were Old Style deacons and elders, and it was expected of me that I would be also.

"It was at that, I suppose, that I most rebelled. To have my destiny spelled out for me before ever I could even taste of any forbidden fruits or even make my own choice. It was indeed very early into my manhood that I determined that if it were true that salvation was preordained, I would prove beyond any doubt that my own damnation was certain. And though both my parents wept and implored me to change my ways, for I was their only surviving son, I turned my back on them and continued my rebellious ways.

"After I returned from my visit to Massachusetts, I went on a spree and squandered my talents in a most profligate manner, daring the Almighty to do anything but damn me. I did not exactly shake my fist at Him, though I might as well have. But for all of my youthful escapades and the certainty in my mind that I was damned and so might as well make the best of it, I was still a most unhappy young person. Unable to determine the source of that unhappiness and disquiet, I lashed out at all who would help me and only redoubled my efforts to prove myself damned.

"Ah, but I was most miserable. I do not think that any mortal could ever have seemed to be enjoying himself and yet be so anguished and unhappy."

Here, I looked around and noted the attentive expressions of the deacons. Some frowned, others nodded, and one or two murmured "Amen" as if they truly understood. I could not myself determine what those profligacies might have been, women of my acquaintance being completely distanced from any such, but apparently many of the deacons had experience of what Brother Kencaid discussed. Even Cyrus stared, almost with a look of guilt, at his boots. Only Redmon Pitt seemed unaffected and fidgeted some in his seat.

"I went on in this manner for several months, sleeping little, eating less, keeping active by some unknown enemy source, terrifying my beloved parents, despairing old friends and acquaintances. My weight was alarmingly down, my countenance drained and dreary, and I had come very close to the conclusion that my days on earth was near termination, that hell was near, and yet I only doubled my efforts at dissipation.

"Then one night I left my parents' home, ignoring their pleas to stay, de-termined on a course of lust and drunkenness, though my strength for either was at that point questionable. I wandered down the road, not really eager to follow the course I had set for myself, yet stubborn in my determination.

"I come at last to an open space, where there was no trees nearby and so the moonlight, which was copious, shined down brightly, without shadow or interference. It was a warm May evening, without breeze or sound, too early for many of the night insects which can make such a caterwauling racket mid-summer nights. I did not intend to stop. I cannot say why I stopped. But when I endeavored to pick up my foot and continue, I could not. It was as if I was held at that spot by some powerful and frightening force. And though the moonlight shined bright all about, I myself seemed to be under a dark and weighty cloud, which I knowed could not be. And yet it was! I felt my limbs begin to weaken, and I reached to clutch what I knowed not, for there was nothing to cling to, nothing to steady me and yet as I reached out and grasped at the air, I felt suddenly strengthened as if indeed I did hold to something. And then came over me such a horror and such a shame and such a feeling of complete defilement and degradation that I know, could I have moved, I would have throwed myself into the river and so ended it all. But I could not move. Gentlemen, I swear it to ye. I could not pull either foot from the ground where both seemed permanently secured.

"I swear that I struggled, I screamed, I prayed, I cursed, all so loudly that methought of a certain that the entire neighborhood must hear and rush out of doors to fall on their knees at the sounds that surely must be coming from all the demons of hell. And yet the kind that rested nearby did not lift their heads or make any movement that would indicate that they was in any manner startled. Yet I could hear my own anguished screams, so loud that I thought my ears would rupture with it.

"And then my knees begun to buckle, my legs to go out from under me, until I found myself at last in a kneeling position in the middle of the road. I tried to move and yet could not, and so I tried then to throw myself forward so as to be on all fours and yet I could not do that, nor could I look down or straight ahead. My face was forced upward as if pulled, though I struggled mightily against the force that tugged at me.

"I need not here remind ye, Brothers, of the experience of Saul of Taurus, his vision on the road to Damascus. But I had no vision. I would never be so presumptuous as to claim one. What I had was an almost unendurable sense of my own vileness, my own depravity and sinfulness. As I have said, had I not been held tight to one spot I might well have done myself grievous harm. And then I swooned.

"When I awoke, I lay in the road, the moonlight giving way to day, the sounds of the early birds filling the air. At first I thought that I lay in a drunken stupor, that it had all been the hallucination of a mind too far gone with drink. Yet withal, I had such contentment that I had never had before in all my life. I had not any of those pains that are the result of debauching, rather I felt a perfect and relaxed sense of peace.

"I pulled myself up, dazed and wondering, and turned back to my parents' house where I found them already up, their own faces alight with joy, for my father, as he related it, and my mother, as she related it, had both wakened at the exact moment from horrific dreams that were exactly identical to the minutest point! Their dreams had been a perfect duplication of the experience that I had had on the road the night before and, as best we could reconstruct, the times of the dream and the incident were one.

"We fell to our knees on the spot and prayed and cried and sang, so profound was our experience. And, Brothers, horrible, fearful, awesome as that experience was, so totally joyful and peaceful was my soul when it passed, that could I just reconstruct it one more time in my lifetime, I would be the most happy of men."

When he had finished, the silence was profound, and I looked around at each man lost in his own deep thoughts and thought me how I did envy those of such wondrous experience.

It was Redmon Pitt who broke that deep silence. "Sir," he said, "such wonderful experience ye've had of evil makes me wonder d'ye have any thoughts on the subject of the two seeds that has of late become a most interesting consideration for many of us?"

"Two-seed? Two-seed-in-the-spirit? Ah, yes. I know of what ye speak. I have given it thought."

He looked around and apparently realizing that there was those of us— for I was not alone—who did not understand what was being spoken of, he explained, "Two-seed-in-the-spirit is a philosophy being passed off in some quarters as predestinarian."

At that I noted that Redmon Pitt flushed some slight amount.

"Nor is it so new an idea, going back in one form all the way to the ancient Persians and even found in the works of Plato the Greek."

"Ah," said Redmon Pitt, with what seemed to me to be a touch of sarcasm, "I had forgot what a learned man ye be."

"Well, I don't know 'learned'," responded Brother Kencaid. "If 'read' is what ye mean, then I am that. Two-Seedism simply put," he went on, "is a duality of good and evil. There are those who suggest that each of us is from either the good seed or the bad seed, the good seed of course the elect for salvation and the bad seed damned eternally. I am not at all convinced of this good and evil, worrying that evil is given equal power with God, and separate from Him, which is not how I read the Scriptures. But," he said with a friendly smile, "I am yet open-minded and willing always to listen to conflicting views."

"Well," said Redmon Pitt ungraciously it seemed to me, "ye may yet have to do that."

At that Amiable Simpson arose and, stifling a yawn, announced, "It has been an inspiring, informative evening, and I for one could sit the whole night through just listening, but, alas, for those of us who must needs arise before the earliest light, pleasure must give way to sleep."

I thought it well put, particular since it put Redmon Pitt in his place.

The deacons then, without either prayer or hymn, commenced to collect theirselves and in groups, for after dark few men would care to walk alone, began to drift homeward.

"Redmon Pitt," announced Brother Kencaid when the last of the groups had departed, "is ignorant and he is vain. It is a combination of characteristics that can cause much difficulty."

"Aye," murmured Cyrus.

George was still by my side, wide awake, but clinging to me most persistently. "Master Kencaid," I said, "I do believe you might be less subject to being wetted by the dew if you slept indoors this night."

He only laughed. "Naw, naw, Mistress. I told ye, this is the time of year to sleep out. I'll sleep like yonder babe," he said nodding toward the cradle where Sarah had spent the night oblivious of the spiritual nature of the conversation about her. So I handed him over a comforter, and he and Cyrus stepped out.

"Mama," said George still clinging to me, so tired and yet so wide awake. "Mama, d'ye think that's what it is that watches me, what eyes? The evil seeded ones?"

"Why, child, what eyes? There is no eyes I told you."

"Mama, they watch me. They do," he insisted clinging to the amulet around his neck.

I sighed at that. That amulet was only making him superstitious. Evil eye, indeed. I thought that the first chance I got, I would see to it that the amulet got lost. It was time, too, that maybe the deacons found themselves another place to meet, for the child was being filled with too much that he could not yet understand—good and evil, two seeds, and so forth.

"There is no eyes, George," I said again firmly.

"They watch me, Mama," he said equally as firmly.

"When do they watch you?"

"They're watching me now," he said. "I can smell it."

Involuntarily I looked around. There was nothing—no odor that I could detect—nothing untoward. "Ah, poor baby, you're just tired," I said. "Climb up on my lap and I'll hold you 'til you sleep, and tomorrow you'll have forgot all about any evil eyes."

The next morning I rose to find Cyrus already up and gone. From the brightness of the day I realized that I had slept over long, I and both babes. I dressed myself and hastened to the fire which was already burning brightly. I glanced outside and saw that Brother Kencaid and Cyrus was involved in earnest conversation, so early in the morning and already at the Scriptures.

I started to the door to wish them good morning and inquire were they ready for tea, but I was arrested at the door by the conversation.

Brother Kencaid was saying, "Was I not such a light sleeper, I probably would not 'a seen him, so circumspectly he approached. But at what little sound, I know not, I was wide awake and caught him full view."

"It was a man, you're sure?" whispered Cyrus.

"Indeed. Shaggy and ill-kempt, but dressed as a man, though ragged, and when I sat up, he made a sound, but not a sound that a normal man makes, rather a gnarled moan, and he clambered away, awkwardly but swiftly."

"You should have waked me."

"I had my pistol close. No need. I just leaned against the door and waited. But he did not return. What d'ye make of it?"

"I truly do not know," said Cyrus. "Someone lost his way or a river scum or even a passing lunatic, for the river is fair alive with all sort of weary folk."

"He did approach this cabin with some certainty. But perhaps yer right, a lost soul of some sort, hungry, looking for something to steal. Most likely long gone on down the river by now."

"It's best I think," said Cyrus, "to make no mention of this. There is no point in making others unnecessarily fearful."

I stepped away from the door, letting my breath come out slowly, unaware that I had even been holding it. I thought of what George had said.

"They watch me, Mama. Them evil eyes watch me."

Chapter 7

A Further Distress

Clara Cuthcart poured more water into the stew pot as I continued to stir. In spite of the earliness of the hour, we both had broke a sweat and had our sleeves rolled up as much as was proper. The camp was begun to come alive, as various people rose from make-shift sleeping—some rolled out from under wagons, others from the pallets they'd laid on the church floor and some others simply rose from the bare ground on which they'd laid their quilts. Although some of the older and more infirm of the brothers and sisters had taken shelter with various families, most of the visitors had made their own sleeping arrangements right around the church.

Such was always the way of Associations. Though there was some loss of comfort and a few who groaned the day long with the stiffness of the previous night's sleep, the joy and pleasure of the Association with kindred spirits in worship of the Lord made all of that discomfort of no particular account.

Clara Cuthcart and I had begun preparations for breakfast for the group before most of them had risen. Indeed it was in part the smoke and smell of our campfire that had begun to arouse the encampment, as much as the coming daylight and the morning sounds from the nearby woods. We would be joined in such preparations by various sisters as they rose.

The ground corn that we poured into the boiling water would not give pause to any appetite, but the fat buck turned on a spit by Reuben and Patsy Bradene give forth aromas that the veriest saint could not've spurned.

Patsy and Reuben had arrived the night before, sometime after dark as the assembly sat around the large fire and sung hymns and visited. No one noted their presence until Cyrus and some of the brothers commenced a sweet hymn—"Grace Triumphant in the Throne," one of those hymns that Cyrus particularly liked and did teach at his singing school lessons—and we was some of us preparing to join in and some of us to to sit back and enjoy. Not three lines into the hymn, a sound rose from the far back that was most remarkable both for its complete lack of musical sense and for its loudness. Though there was some, strangers mostly come from afar, that jumped and turned their heads and craned their necks to see where that raucous sound was coming from, most of us familiar with Patsy Bradene's amazing inability to come anywhere near to the tune of a song only smiled and nodded at one another to know that the Bradenes was once more in our midst.

Though I did shoot a glance at Cyrus who stood before the group and from the frown between his eyes quite aware that Patsy Bradene was making her contribution, I did not know what he thought, but I found myself with the ungentle thought that did Patsy continue to help out with verses and chorus, Brother Redmon Pitt might find himself with a larger number of allies in his contention that the singing of hymns violated the sanctity of the worship.

I looked around but did not see Brother Pitt. I knowed it to be his custom to absent himself along with several of his followers when the brothers and sisters indicated that they would enjoy the fellowship of song. I was some shamed at myself at the relief I felt. Patsy Bradene, so long as one did not count cleanliness next to Godliness, was a dear and beloved sister, no matter that she might have been churched, and she did enjoy the fellowship of music. She just had no ear for it, but of a certainty she was not the only one so afflicted, though most of the others either had the good judgment to keep still or at least not to raise their voices above all others.

Those of us who knowed Patsy and Reuben was happy to see them as they had wintered north at the Saline Creek near to Ste. Genevieve. But with spring and the coming of the spring flood to the river, they was again riding the flood, their boat fined with goods, mostly salt, as was their practice. But they was both of them always welcome, for music was the only area in which their contributions was lacking.

As if to prove that, they had risen from sleep before anyone else, just as the early birds barely commenced to announce morning, left the camp and was back not much after the first light with a fat buck and had it skinned, gutted, and spitted before most of the good brothers and sisters had opened their eyes to the day. It would be a mighty breakfast those good saints would arise to, provided by Patsy and Reuben Bradene and the bounty of the Lord. Sister Cuthcart and I was responsible only for the mush and the coffee and tea.

Three or four of the brothers when they rose came directly to the fire for coffee and, their mugs filled, retired to the shade of a near-by tree and between sips of the hot liquid begun immediate discourse on Scriptures. I could not but remark upon it to Clara Cuthcart, that the experience of the Lord was so great that newly risen and even without breakfast, the saints could not contain theirselves the discussion of it.

"That may be true," she answered, "but never in all my experience have I seen even the most Godly of the saints to discuss nothin' before they had ther coffee in ther hands."

"That may well be true," I laughed, "but still I do wonder at these men that they can put all else aside, when there's like-minded ones around to discuss it with, or even when they are solitary, for more than once I have come upon Cyrus stalled in his work, engaged in studying Scriptures or working out a knotty problem in his own mind. But when there is another about to discuss with, why all else can fall by the wayside, as profound is their regard for the importance of the Truth and the seeking of it. I think that I truly do envy them that, for I don't know that I have ever knowed a sister blessed with such deep regard for the Truth that she would put away all other activities in deference to it."

"No," nodded Clara Cuthcart with something like a deep sigh, "it is truly the province of men to study and pray and seek after the Truth. Women have no talent fer it. The Lord has blessed the men with important considerations and left it fer the women just to do the unimportant. To bear the children and feed the family and other menial things. I do hope," she added with a frown, "that it will be otherwise in the Hereafter. I'd of a truth hate to think that I'd be follered about by nine or more young'uns through eternity." And she sighed again profoundly.

"Only if you're not among the chosen and are eternally damned, I'd say." And we both laughed.

"Ah, Sisters," said Patsy Bradene who had left the spit to Reuben and approached us, "mayhap I kin hep ye here?"

"No, Mistress Bradene," I said, "you've already done aplenty. Sit and rest and drink some coffee or tea. You can have either."

"Wal," she said, "I'll take some coffee and fetch back a mug fer Reuben, too, if ye don't mind."

The preaching commenced almost as soon as breakfast was done. Sister Cuthcart and Reba Cuthcart and Sister Simpson and several Sisters Malone all pitched in to work on the noon-day meal and capture as much of the preaching from a distance as was possible, for it was done out of doors, it being dark and stale inside the building with so many people. I parsed to listen as I could, but could not make out much, though I knowed pretty much by heart the things they would speak of.

"All have sinned and come short of the glory of God," I heard the first Elder cry. The text was a familiar one, and I had remarked to myself more than once of those old texts and how they come out in different voices. Why, that one I had heard of some old brothers "All have sinned" in such a manner that it would fair shiver your innards with terror, whilst others could deliver them same lines with such love and hope than you could wonder that they both come from the same place.

Cyrus was one of those whose voice did offer hope for eventual salvation. For with his gentle, yet firm tones, he could say "all" in such manner that it made you think that it was not that fact of "all" sinning and falling short that was important but something beyond that, something beyond and infinitely hopeful.

I had knowed Cyrus Pritchard on and off for most of my life. When I was a little girl I was nervous of him as of all the other big boys, he being five years beyond my own age. Not over nervous, of course, for I was ne'er that of any person. He, with some of the others, was some rowdy and boisterous, and I do not recall overly spiritual. But we moved away into Kentucky for a few years when I was a good big girl, returning after I was pretty much woman-turned, the land titles in Kentucky being so insecure that my father had lost not one but two pieces of land to bad titles. It disgusted him enough to return to Tennessee, for which I am ever grateful, though I suppose it was all a part of the Lord's Plan anyway.

Cyrus and I immediately caught each other's eyes, and by that time he was settled and not only had experienced the Spirit of the Lord but in so profound a manner that the veriest elder of the Elders took note and offered prayers of thanksgiving. But it was not that spirituality by no means that caught my eyes, for I was no different from any other girl in that manner. And, indeed, we have never had occasion to speak too much of spiritual things, for I have been so slow and dilatory of my own experience.

There's many pastors who do not share of the grace of Cyrus Pritchard's experience, whose texts explode in terror and fear, so that you feel that you must be so vile, sinful, so totally unworthy in all respects to experience the spirit of the Lord that it hardly seems reasonable that the Lord would even want you forever and ever cluttering up Paradise. I remember such kinds of preaching when we lived in Kentucky and have always thought that it colored my own attitude so greatly that I have not been able to overcome it. And though I have approached Cyrus upon occasion about the matter, he concludes that there is nothing that he can do, nor I, but wait the visitation of the Holy Spirit, which I would not hurry except that I have felt so left out.

The mid-day meal did at last come, albeit there was one or two speakers that acted as though that which they fed the flock would be sufficient. After we had fed the multitude, I leaned at last against a tree, for I was most weary, having been at the cooking since before daylight, and I chanced to listen in to the conversation of a near-by group. One old brother was holding forth in particular, his eyes beaming and his voice quivering with excitement.

"Wal," he said, "I listened to Brother Mason when he spoke, and it was so strong, so well thought, so true that I prayed to myself that he would ne'er stop and was most disappointed when he at last yielded to Brother Kencaid. Then that Brother did commence almost where the first had left off and withal, be dimmed, but that I thought I could listen to him for a full day and night and was almost indignant that he at last quit the pulpit."

"Ah," spoke up another that I did not recognize, "wal, if that's the way ye felt, then a treat lies ahead, fer Brother Pritchard will take the pulpit this afternoon, and there's not a soul here that's heard him but will tell ye that ye might be listenin' to the everlastin' angels themselves, so true, so honest and profound does he speak the Truth."

Well, I listened as modestly as I could, but then noted in some annoyance that Brother Pitt was at the edge of that group and at that last did pull himself away and stalk off in another direction to sulk. That man!

And later when Cyrus took the pulpit, I pulled close to listen, though I had heard him many times, and I could not but watch and wonder at the attention accorded him. Cyrus was gentle-spoke for an Old School pastor, starting low, so low that some of the more infirm of hearing was forced to lean nearer and cup ears with hands. But that did not last long, for Cyrus's beautiful voice built quickly with assurance of his message, and all faces, all of course save Redmon Pitt and some of his accomplices, was turned in his direction. Face after face exhibited that wonder and awe and beauty that a true believer, hopeful of Grace and devout in the love of God, does exhibit. There was beauty and joy, loud sighs, and occasional interruptions of ecstasy. "Amen, Brother, Amen. God love ye." "Amazing Grace, Dear Brothers and Sisters, Amazing Grace." That sort of thing. And I was sore proud, though I knowed that I should ought not be for it ill-become me as the pastor's wife.

I felt a little movement at my side and, looking down, beheld George, entranced at his father's sermon. Jeremy Cuthcart, one of the "the boys"—the smallest—that he was wont to associate with, was beside him, but fussing a little and tugging at George as if he would lead him off to play. In truth, most of the children endured only little of the preaching, finding their own childish activities to keep them occupied.

That was all right and would change in its turn. For all these enraptured brothers and sisters had been children and had behaved as children but had in turn put aside childish things, and these would also. In fact, I did often wish that George would behave more like those other children than like the little Baptist he was. But George was having none of the playtime, and Jeremy wandered off. I looked quickly around and found Rachel Cuthcart tending to Sarah, and guiltily determined that I had best relieve her, for she had been without such relief all day, and Sarah was not a child inclined to sleep during the day or even to rest much.

Later in the afternoon, after an elder that I did not know had relieved Cyrus at the pulpit, he searched me out.

"We will take the children and sleep at home tonight," he said without preamble.

"We're not staying for fellowship?" I asked, for I was surprised at that.

"No," he sighed, "not tonight. You've been at this cooking for too many hours and I, well, I need time to myself to think and plan."

I give him a questioning look. But he did not say more. It did not take a great deal of thought to realize that at the heart of his worry stood Redmon Pitt and his group.

As we prepared to make our departure, Patsy and Reuben Bradene approached and said that they would accompany us, and gratefully accepted our invitation to end the night, for Patsy said that the morning next they needs must leave, though they would sore miss the preaching and the fellowship.

We sat that night outside the cabin, for the night was fair and pleasant, and listened to the Bradenes—mainly Patsy, for she did most of the talking—tell of their various adventures upon the river since last we had seen them.

"There was," said Patsy, "a party of surveyors a-goin' up the Mississippi last fall as we was making our own way up the river to the Saline. It was headed by two men," (here Pasty and Reuben conferred and argued some over the names before they finally agreed), "named Mister Clark and Mister Lewis. We come upon them encamped near to the Grand Tower upwards of Cape Girardeau. In some consternation, they was, too, over that tower, fer it takes some skill to navigate around it. Mister Clark, it turns out, was drawin' maps of the river, and they claimed to ha' been sent by Mister Thomas Jefferson hisself from Washington D.C. Mister Clark, fer he's the one we conversed with, claimed they had a mission to go and explore the territory newly purchased by Mister Jefferson, and he said that it was miles and miles and more acres and woods west of the river than they was east of it.

"Wal, a' course that'd be hard to believe, but we was respectful enough not to question it but wisht 'em well. As Mister Clark was makin' a map of the Grand Tower and as we was familiar with the navigation of it, he enlisted our help an' we give it as well we could an' he was most 'preciative of it and fed us a fine meal, and we encamped the night with 'em and listened to ther tales, fer among ther group was several rivermen as well as woodsmen with tales enow to fill a winter's night. And it was a pleasant evenin', though it was November, and headed north, we was always in danger of winter at any time.

"We left 'em the next mornin' fer they was stayin' to finish out ther maps and generally replenish and what-not, and we was in a sweat to get to wher we was headed."

Patsy paused in their story, and I give myself over to wondering that Patsy and Reuben Bradene might offer services to a maker of maps, for I knowed that they like other rivermen did not navigate much by map, relying mainly on some vague landmarks in their heads, and by instinct that let them feel the river and know what it was about at any moment.

"Wal," Patsy continued at last, "we thought no more of it until later in the winter, we took ourselves up the river north to St. Louis—which is a right nice little settlement, ye know, but to my mind will ne'er rival Ste. Gen. We went by foot, fer to pole up the river by ourselves would ha' been too rigorous. We minded to pick up a raft in St. Louis and pole furs and such back down. It is commonly done and profitable.

"Preparin' to start back down, we come upon one of them woodsmen that we had met in the service of Mister Clark, the mapper. And when he learned what we was about, he asked that we take along a Injun. 'He is

Delaware,' he said. 'I have respect fer the Delaware, fer like the Shawnee ther passin' civilized an' honest an' honorable.'

"Now me and Reuben we had to agree, fer that had always been our assessment, too. 'This old feller is sick unto death and he desires nothin' so much as to die among his tribe, but as he has been a follower of Tecumseh and his brother, ther's of course plenty along this river as would as leave slit his throat."

I had heard but vaguely of a Shawnee called Tecumseh who stirred up the Indians of the Indiana Territory. "Wal," Patsy went on, "we got naught agin' the Injun, me an' Reuben, so long's they make no claims to the river. But settlers on the lands is another matter," she added. I could not keep from recalling all our friends and brothers and sisters in Christ slaughtered by rampaging savages at the Old Shawnee Ford, but I said nothing as most everyone on the border could tell a similar tale.

"The woodsman from his own purse give us coin fer the care of the old Injun, and we agreed to it and carried him along with us. And he was no trouble, and when he felt up to it was both entertainin' and informative, fer he was a wise old feller, being conversant in many dialects as well as speaking American language passing well.

"The old feller had traveled with Tecumseh to many tribes in the effort to ally them all together, and the stories he told of his travels was wondrous indeed of the lands beyond the river, though it still be doubtful to me that they are so wondrous as Mister Clark and his band described them to be.

"Now this old feller's name was Chewayewek, an' as I ha' said he was a wondrous storyteller, given to legends and prophecy—in truth the more spiritous liquors he had in him, the more lavish his legends and prophecy. An' would ye like to hear one of his stories?" Patsy said suddenly. It was George she looked at, and it was George who wide-eyed nodded his head solemnly.

"Wal," said Patsy, "as best as I can recall it, this is what he told:

"'Upon a time, so long ago that even the ancient eagles and the wise foxes and brave snakes cannot remember it, the land was fertile and grasses grew and game was plentiful and God's people was happy and content and there was no war and the sun shined always—except when it rained the needed rain (and even then the clouds would pass quickly and the sun return)—and it was never winter and God's people never suffered.

"'But there came upon the land a people that was greedy, that took more than they needed, more than God allowed, and left God's peoples without the necessaries and they suffered and God suffered. And then God grew angry and told His peoples to resist and to take back what had been theirs, but, alas, God's peoples did not understand. They did not understand suffering and they did not understand war, for they had never experienced either and they begun to die and God grew angrier still, and he caused the light of great sorrows to flash across the sky and the earth to tremble and to open wide and the rivers to run backward and mighty boulders to fly through the air and the trees to crash to the ground, and he set the mighty river through the middle of the land separating his peoples on one side of it, and he unleashed upon the land The Beast to consume the hearts of the wicked and the cowards.'"

Here Patsy paused for a moment and then continued, "An' that old Injun, why he told all that in such manner that yer hair'd like to ha' stood on end. An' n'en he said, 'And God was pacified and the earth ceased to tremble and The Beast returned whence it had come. But when God is displeased and when the Greedy attack His peoples once more and they know not how to protect therselves, then God will rise in wrath once more and the light of great sorrow will fly across the sky and the snakes will wake and the earth will tremble and the forest crash and the rivers will run backward—and The Beast, The Beast will be loosed once more and the land will be devastated and God's peoples will suffer and the Greedy will suffer. But it will be God's peoples who suffer most, for he will have no patience left for them, and he will scatter them to every corner of the land where they will suffer in sorrow all their days.'"

I looked at George and found him staring hard at Patsy as if he almost was in a trance, and I thought that I should never have let her tell such a tale just at bedtime. Then he surprised me with a sudden question. "Why would the Injun's God punish them?"

Patsy shrugged and then answered, "I think ther God hates cowardice even more than he hates greed."

"Is the Injuns cowards?"

"Not to my knowledge."

"Do you believe that story?" asked George.

"Wal," Patsy went on with a grin toward Reuben, "now I don't know about it all. The earth might tremble, fer it's done that, and the trees might crash, fer they've done that, but I allow as how we'll be a dimmed sight clos'ter to hell before the river ever runs backwards!"

As promised, the Bradenes left at first light, and we made provision to return to the Association.

Cyrus carried Sarah, for which I was grateful, for she was getting to be a load for my hip, and George walked along beside me. He, too, was uncommon quiet. Glancing at him I thought I detected some apprehension about his expression, and I noted that he clutched the amulet of O'Reilly with one hand and clung to my skirt with the other.

"Mama?" he looked up with worried expression, and I hastily urged him to hurry as we did not want to be tardy. I did want to distract him from his thoughts lest they turn again to all that nonsense about good and evil and evil eyes watching him, all that stuff that Patsy Bradene's story might have roused in him.

112

"The boys will be playing before you get there," I chided him with a gentle smile, but the fearful look, though it abated, did not entirely desert his countenance.

I lost track of him immediately upon arrival and presumed him to have found his friends and to be already lost in play, and Cyrus likewise disappeared for he was swallowed up by groups of brothers and sisters in conference. When the last of the preaching commenced, I pitched in to help clean up and prepare for another noon-day meal, the activity easing the apprehension I felt.

And by the time that meal was concluded I was so busy and tired that I had indeed almost forgot it all, until the call went out for the meeting to come to order and Brother Amiable Simpson, the elected moderator of the Association, took the pulpit. I wiped my hands upon my apron, then took it off and draped it over a branch and took my place on the women's side, where I was welcomed although I was not entitled to a vote. This day I might well greatly regret that I had not come to terms with my own vile corruption.

There was various business of an ordinary nature to be disposed of, and it seemed to me that the whole congregation went at those routine matters with considerably more vehemence than normal, perhaps out of nervousness or perhaps in preparation for more serious considerations to come.

At last there was no putting it off, and Brother Saucie Malone rose and declared that he had a matter to bring before the group. There was a great and collective sigh, I thought, and one or two looked around with more excitement and anticipation than I thought seemly. But then there are always those folk that do love a good fight, particularly be it between others than themselves.

"Well, Brother Malone, yer in order," said Amiable Simpson. "Take yer turn."

"It is," said Saucie Malone without preamble, "the matter of the ordination of Brother Redmon Pitt to preach that concerns some of us."

"I was not aware," said Amiable Simpson, "that Brother Pitt had been a candidate for ordination."

"Wal," said Saucie Malone, "he has spoke of it, asked about it and numbers of us has pleaded his case in the matter of candidacy and has got nowhere, being ignored by them that ought to consider such things."

"Ye cannot seek ordination fer a brother that has not first been licensed and observed in practice and proved to be acceptable. Do ye mean to try to by-step this?" asked Brother Simpson.

"We have tried to seek licensing and have failed to get a fair hearing, and as Brother Pitt is too modest to rise in his own efforts, we who have faith in him and in his teachings feel constrained to do it for him."

"His teachings?" said Brother Kencaid out loud. And Brother Simpson immediately ruled him out of order, which was as it should have been, for one member could not interrupt another member who had already the floor. Brother Kencaid nodded and apologized.

"Brother Malone," said Amiable Simpson, "the rules fer ordination is firm and include examination of the petitioner's Call, a licensing of him to preach for a time, and a final examination of his fitness for ordination, it is a lengthy process, necessary, and all most abide with it."

"There is those of us already secure about Redmon Pitt's Call and his teachings, Brother Simpson," countered Saucie Malone.

At this point, Brother Kencaid rose and asked leave to speak, and the floor was handed over to him.

"Sir," he said to Saucie Malone, "sir" and not "brother". I do not know if I was the only one to note that or not. "Sir," repeated Brother Kencaid, "there is something that needs clarifying, fer ye keep repeating of Redmon Pitt's 'teachings' as if they was his only and not the teachings as set forth in the Holy Scriptures and clarified in the London Articles and Confession of Faith of 1689 which we Old Style Baptists have adhered to for better than a hundred years. Explain to this assembly, do Redmon Pitt's teachings vary in any way from that Confession of Faith?"

At that, Redmon Pitt, who had been sitting most sanctimoniously, his thin strands of hair ill-concealing the shininess of his pate, rose slowly and with spurious dignity turned as if he would address the group.

"Master Pitt," said Amiable Simpson sternly, "the floor is already occupied!"

Redmon Pitt did not pay any attention but went ahead anyway in his pompous manner. "Ever since I joined the congregation, I have been disturbed at certain practices—the singing of copious hymns, for one thing, singing which seems to some of us to be more for entertainment of the assembly and the aggrandisement of certain of the singers than for the glory of God."

"Sir," interrupted Brother Kencaid angrily, "ye've but to read yer Scriptures to find direction from God for the singing of hymns—Ephesians 5:19 or Colossians 3:16, if you will. And the London Confessions do make special mention of that part of the worship service!"

"Mayhap we read the Scriptures differently," said Redmon Pitt calmly.

"Indeed we do," retorted Brother Kencaid. "Some of us apparently reads them upside down and backwards!"

"And besides the misuse of hymns," said the unperturbed Brother Pitt, "there is some of us that has give serious consideration to the deeper implications of the tenet of predestination, and though we have tried to raise speculation on the nature of good and evil, the two seeds of predestination, we have been given ill audience fer it. We think," here he waved aside Brother Kencaid who was giving evidence that he would interrupt and argue, "that there is those so insecure in their faith that they fear to allow the free expression of differing opinions. And we challenge the discussion of those same opinions before this group!"

He said that last in sudden anger and Brother Kencaid responded in kind. "Two-Seedism is idiotic and unwholesome and I have no patience with fools!"

"Then, Sir," snapped Redmon Pitt, "am I to take it that we are split on this matter?" He started to say more, but then he looked puzzled and begun to sway and then to look around as if startled and reached out his hand as if trying to steady himself on something. How peculiar, I thought, and then I looked around and begun to feel myself to reel as if the bench on which I sat would pitch me forward, and I thought, no, it's I who am having a fit. But then I heard people start to yell and children to cry and felt the bench jerk and saw two or three people fall to the ground, and I grasped the edge of the bench and felt myself rolling, as if on a river raft at full flood.

I looked wildly around and tried to rise, and the earth was indeed unsteady under my feet. My children! Cyrus! And as people say of drowning men, whole lifetimes flashing before them, I was recalling the old Indian of the night before. "When the trees crash and the earth trembles and the rivers run backward." But the trees were not crashing and as suddenly as the rolling of the earth had begun, it stopped, and people begun to pick theirselves up and to look around and to ask questions.

Redmon Pitt was dusting himself off and some of his group had gathered around him. Members begun to take headcounts. I found Rachel Cuthcart and took my baby from her, and before I could mount a search for him, George had found me and was clinging to my skirt.

"Where have you been?" I asked.

"Me and Jeremy was playing by the rocks and the earth started to shake and we was scared," he said.

Once the benches was righted and order brought to the proceedings, Brother Amiable Simpson called us to order again.

"It was an earth tremor," he said. "They an't unknown in this country and nothing to be fearful of. The bowels of the earth do in various parts of the world occasionally adjust therselves. And this is one of them parts of the world given to these little quakes. It has happened before," he assured us and since he had been one of the earliest settlers, I was inclined to believe him. But not Redmon Pitt.

Dusting himself and attempting to restore his composure, Redmon Pitt glared at Amiable Simpson. "It do seem that ye have a ready explanation fer this occurrence, glib and ready," he said.

"Mister Pitt, I'd remind ye," said Brother Simpson, "that I am hardly the cause of this 'occurrence' nor could I ha' been ready fer it to such extent as to have an explanation 'glib and ready.' These little quakes is not unknown hereabouts and ha' apparently not been unknown fer a long time as the Indians refer to them as the 'old man earth a-rolling in his sleep.' Ye do seem set to make more of it than could ever ha' been intended."

"The Lord in His Plan has sent a sign," announced Redmon Pitt. "We'll call a vote. The majority will stay and the minority will leave."

There was at that some hasty counsels, both among the elders and deacons as well as the church members, and then the vote was called. I did think that Redmon Pitt had over-estimated his support and that proved to be the case, for when the vote was cast, Redmon Pitt and his followers proved to be too few to carry it, though I was a little surprised that he had as much support as he did.

As soon as the vote was taken, Redmon Pitt and his group begun to gather as to leave. I looked over at Cyrus and Brother Kencaid standing silently side by side, wearing near identical expressions of pain and sorrow. For it was ne'er a good thing to see a congregation rent. I carried Sarah on my hip and held George by the hand and walked over to where Cyrus stood.

"Ye must prepare for this kind of thing, Brother," Elder Kencaid was saying. "As I have said, it does happen and, alas, it seems to be happening more and more. But now, those who are inclined to suffer grievances will have a place to go, and ye'll see a dwindling of yer congregation that way. However," he added with a wry smile, "that does work both ways, as ye lose some from it, ye'll gain from those that'll leave Brother Pitt."

Redmon Pitt at that moment approached and pointed his finger directly in Cyrus's face. "Mark me," he announced gravely, "It's evil days ye've fallen on, Sir. Mark me. Evil!"

Redmon Pitt and his followers had hardly passed from view when Rachel Cuthcart approached looking for her little brother. "Have you seen Jeremy, George?" she asked.

George frowned and answered, "Well, we was playing when the ground begun to shake, and we got afeared and started to run. I an't seen him since." And he pointed through the woods.

Rachel looked a little provoked and sighed. "I just can't keep track of that young'un!"

There was considerable conversation among the remaining members of the congregation, as well as among them of other congregations, over the rift in the church. I listened to some of it and happily discovered most comment to be favorable to the handling of it.

In a few minutes I noticed Rachel Cuthcart back, without Jeremy, and talking to her mother. Clara Cuthcart and Rachel and Brother Cuthcart and two of the older children left the group and went out as if searching for Jeremy. I felt a little uneasy on their account.

I looked down at George and he was staring at them, too, a tiny frown between his eyes. He held the amulet at his throat with his good hand.

"George, do you have any idea what might have come of Jeremy?" I asked.

He only shook his head and stared off into the distance.

Clara Cuthcart returned in a few minutes and joined our group. She was red-faced and puffing. "I can do almost anything anyone else can do but climb," she laughed and fanned herself. "I'll have to let others find that rascal, as it's passing rocky and steep out there." But I noted that she sported that same little frown between her eyes that George did.

In a few minutes Brother Cuthcart was back, concern apparent on his face. "We cannot find sign of that boy," he said. "We have called and searched. Yer sure, Boy," he said to George, "of wher ye saw him last?"

Slowly George nodded his head.

"Well, will ye come an' show us?" asked Brother Cuthcart.

"No!"

I was astounded at that. "No? No, George, no? Whatever in the world did you say no for? Brother Cuthcart needs your assistance. Now go."

"No, Mama. No, please. I'm afeared," he whimpered.

"Why, there's no need to fear, George. The earth belike won't tremble again."

He shook his head violently.

"Now, George, I am right exasperated with you."

"Nevermind, Sister Pritchard," said Brother Cuthcart. "Ye ne'er know what frights these little ones. Don't worry on't. Jeremy is like hidin', fer he's a playful child, or just wandered off. We'll find him."

But they did not.

"Annamanda," said Cyrus coming up to me, a concerned expression upon his face, "the Cuthcarts have need of as many hands as possible to search these grounds. Can you take the children and make your way home? There's little that you can do here. It'd make the search easier if there was not so many young'uns about. Sister Cuthcart is taking hers with her."

"I want to stay with Daddy!" cried George.

"Why, young sir," I said, jerking him to me with my free hand, "you'll do just as you're told, for I'm much put out with you already. Indeed, home and bed without supper might be the best place for one so ill-tempered as you."

I said a word to Clara Cuthcart, who was understandably preoccupied, and with Sarah in my arms and a still reluctant George by the hand, started toward home, leaving behind certain of the utensils, covers, and pots I had brought, for I could not manage those and the children besides. Cyrus would have to bring them.

Though it was growing late, the early summer sun was still high, though in the distance clouds had commenced to gather as they often done of a summer evening, portending possible showers. I glanced up at the sky, assessing that possibility in my mind when an errant cloud, dark but bright-rimmed reached out like a pointy-finger and flicked across the face of the sun, breaking the light in two with a shadow, and a sudden gust of cool breeze passed over and I shivered and then it passed.

By then we had passed into the deeper woods, and the sky and the clouds and sun was lost to our view, and it was passing pleasant walking along that familiar path. I could hear a group ahead of us, though I was not certain who, but knowed that they would most likely take the opposite fork in the path as not many took the same path that we did. And sure enough, when we got to that fork, I could hear their conversation as they veered off the one direction and we the other.

George hung onto my hand so hard that, with the sleeping baby in one arm and his pulling on the other, I commenced to wonder if we would have to stop to rest. I looked down at George and shifted the baby in my arms. George's expression was still uncertain, and he clung to that amulet with his free hand.

"Now, George," I said, "you've got to walk by yourself and let go my hand, for the baby is such a load that betwixt you I can hardly walk."

"Mama?" he said, alarm in his voice. "Mama?"

"Now, Son, don't worry. They'll find Jeremy. He's only got his directions tangled up and wandered off the wrong way. Why, we might stumble across him on our way home."

"No, Mama," said George.

"Why, George," I started to say and looked at him again. He had stopped and clinging to his amulet was staring hard ahead, his eyes wide.

"George, what is it?" I did not know wh'er to be alarmed or angered, and I stopped, too.

"It smells of death, Mama," he said slowly, so softly I had to strain to hear. "It smells of death. Them eyes, Mama, them evil eyes. I'm afeared."

I straightened myself up and looked around. Of course it was childish foolishness. There was no reason to be alarmed. There was no sign of danger. That amulet. It was time that it somehow got lost, and I thought that I would see to it myself.

"It smells of death, Mama."

"Oh, George!" I snatched his hand and dragged him on. The sooner home in bed the better.

We rounded a slight bend in the path, I having to bend low to avoid collision with an over-hanging branch.

"Mama!"

I stopped. On the path ahead was a form. My first thought was "Jeremy," but the form though child-sized was not human.

"Mama," sobbed George clinging to my skirt, "Mama."

It was a dog, and one look confirmed both that it was dead and, I was certain, that it was the remains of that huge black dog of Eremus Lodi.

The dog lay on the trail before us, his teeth bared in death, eyes wide to the sky. I could not imagine how he could have died, so violent and so vicious, his great body mangled and mutilated.

A wild animal, I thought, a bear perhaps. I could not take my eyes from the sight, however, though George continued to sob into my skirt and tremble violently.

The dog's gut was torn open and its innards scattered. So completely had it been gutted, as a matter of fact, that I could identify its various parts. I turned away and then turned slowly back. "Wait, George," I whispered, "Mama needs to examine something."

Why I felt such need, I could not say, only that it was passing important. I knowed enough of the interior workings of four-footed beasts to know what to expect and I was right in what I feared. All that was missing of that dog was its heart and that was nowhere about.

The body of the beast as I hovered over it was soft and pliant, still warm, and as I looked it seemed to twitch, and I thought that it was not so long dead.

I rose and took George's hand and then heard myself speak. "Oh!"

"What is it, Mama?" said George.

"Nothing, Dear," I said as casually as I could. What had finally come to me, what I had been so uncommon slow to realize, was that the dog had been so recent killed that whate'er kind of beast had done it was not too long gone. It still lurked somewhere about, for it could not have got far.

We was out unprotected from whate'er it was—bear or painter or wild beast or man, I could not say. We was out unprotected, and somewhere in them woods, too, was little Jeremy Cuthcart, likewise at the mercy of whate'er might stumble upon him.

"Come, George." I said calmly, taking his hand in mine. "We'd best get on home, for it seems like rain."

We had gone but a few steps when George stopped again "Mama?"

At that, a shadow seemed to hover, the clouds covering the sun, I supposed, though I could not view the sky clearly. And then there was the suggestion of a breeze, though no leaf or branch moved with it, and then the shadow passed and I detected an odor, at once familiar and frightening, yet I could neither describe it or identify it. For just an instant it was almost overpowering and then it was gone.

I looked at George. The frown upon his face slowly dissolved, his figure relaxed, and he took his hand from the amulet and looked up.

"Come on, Mama," he said quite calmly.

The children was asleep when Cyrus come home, and it was nearly dark outside. Still, it was light enough that I could make out his tired form, shoulders sagging, and the weary expression upon his face. It had been a hard day.

"Did you find him?"

He nodded and the spot where my heart ought to have been went hollow. I did not need to ask no more.

"He was broken and crumpled at the foot of a high bluff," said Cyrus, in answer to my unspoken question.

"Did he fall, then?"

"Perhaps."

"Perhaps? How else?"

Cyrus shook his head. "Probably, yes, he fell. Yet," and here he paused most significantly, "and yet, the little body was pitched out several feet from the bottom of the bluff and the incline was not so steep at that point that you might roll so far."

"You think he was throwed?"

He looked sharply at me and then shook his head in doubt. "I don't know."

"Cyrus . . ."

He looked up and I suppose the expression on my face caught his attention. "Cyrus, was he only broken and not torn or otherwise mutilated?"

He shook his head. "He might have just been asleep the way he lay."

"Ah," I sighed and then told him about Eremus Lodi's dog.

"Well," said Cyrus and that was all.

When I woke the next morning, I found Cyrus outside, seated on the bench at the door, from the look of him sleepless all night.

"Cyrus?"

He shot a haggard look at me, and I waited. He turned away and stared out toward the woods and sat for long moments, and then he sighed, almost in anger, and reaching down picked up a stone and flung it hard at the distant trees. I did not say anything, but I observed to myself that the stone he throwed was that same one that Eremus Lodi had remarked upon and that George had laid there for the sun to seek out.

"Annamanda," Cyrus spoke at last, "today I must bury Jeremy Cuthcart, and I have spent the night trying to communicate with my God. There have been times, my dear wife, many times, that I have doubted myself and suffered for it, but this is the first time that I have ever doubted my God." He stopped and stared hard at me. I did not know what to think or what to say.

"I have never questioned His Plan or His Will. But this night I have opened up my heart and I have tried to peer into my own soul and see God. I have never asked for explanation and now I have asked for explanation, but it has not come. I know that I must accept his Holy Will, and yet these long hours, I have doubted it, and I know myself to be sinful and repugnant to God and He to me!"

He buried his face in his hands and I waited trying to think what to say. Even if I had the reason to understand, I would not have the words to explain, for such had not been given me.

And that then is what I said to him at last. "I have neither the reason to understand nor would I have the words to explain did I understand. Such understanding has not been given me. I can only accept each day as it comes, with whatever good or bad, and because it comes, I must consider that it was to be," I said. "I cannot explain that the breeze which cools will turn anon to a wind that uproots, nor the rain that waters the seed will become the flood that washes the seed away. I only know that it happens and so must be—because it is."

Cyrus turned full upon me and looked at me for a long moment, but said nothing. I went on trying to make some sense of the feelings that I had. I thought of my old granny and what she liked to say, "Ye must always do the best ye can by the light ye got." But I did not say that. What I said instead was, "I rise each day and put each foot before me in turn and am grateful when that day ends without pain or commotion. When the day ends badly, I must content myself that it is so and prepare myself for the next day."

My own words did sound so weak and puny that I was a little embarrassed, particularly since Cyrus was staring so hard at me and frowning, and I thought of apologizing for my presumption. And then I thought, "But this is indeed how I do feel, and though it may not be wise or doctrinally sound or well-spoke, it is mine and there's naught I could do about it but accept it."

"I don't know of good, Cyrus, or evil either. I only know of each day piling upon each other day until a lifetime—long or short—is run through, and because it is, it must therefore be." Well, that was more than I had ever in my life had to say on things spiritual, and I was not sure that I had said anything useful. I did know what I was trying to say, but it don't always come out as you mean it.

When Cyrus still did not respond, but only continued looking at me, I finally burst out in something of a passion, "An' anyway, did not the Lord Jesus Christ Himself doubt? Did He not cry out, 'My God, My God, why hast thou forsaken me?'" And as soon as I said it, I clapped my hands over my mouth, for who was I so silly and ignorant to be quoting Scriptures as if I knowed what I was about?

Cyrus reached out his hand and drew me to him and rested his chin upon my head. "Annamanda," was all he said before he turned away and strolled aimlessly toward the garden, his hands locked behind his back, his thoughts elsewhere, and I turned and did as I had been bid.

We wended our way, slow step after slow step, to the meeting house in the early afternoon. We was met on the path by others so headed and, though we exchanged greetings, little else was said, for we was all lost in our thoughts.When we got there, the Cuthcarts with their precious burden was not yet arrived, and we stood about in little groups and talked softly.

Cyrus still stood apart lost in thought it seemed, preoccupied, and no man bothered him, for they knowed his responsibility to be great. Each time one goes to rest in Jesus—whether elderly saint or newborn babe—the words that accompany him, while they will have no effect on the consequences of his hereafter, should lift the burden a little for them that stay behind.

Redmon Pitt and several of his group was present in the crowd and I was again struck by what seemed almost to be a smug look about the man. That was an ungentle thought and I tried to put it from me. No Christian, however ill thought and self-gratified, could take any kind of comfort from so ill a happening.

But I might not have been the only one who noticed him, for I thought that I detected several glances going in his direction, glances that seemed to me to be some of them full of questions. And I thought that it might be true that some of the brothers and sisters might well be willing to give more serious thought to Redmon Pitt's assertions of Two-Seedism. For it did indeed seem that something incredibly evil was lurking amongst us.

At last the Cuthcarts appeared in solemn procession with certain other friends and family, and we all gathered beneath the trees outside the meeting house, for the crowd was too great to go inside, as it numbered not only most of those of the Lost River congregation, but near and far neighbors of other denominations, also. For such a death makes differences of doctrine clear up for a few minutes anyway.

Cyrus led us first in a slow, sweet hymn, which was punctuated by certain sobs of grief, though I noted that Clara Cuthcart stood taller than her stature actually allowed, dry-eyed and stern, her other children in a line beside her, her husband at her right hand.

Cyrus stood and announced his text: "So when this corruptible shall have put on incorruption, and this mortal shall have put on immortality, then shall be brought to pass the saying that is written; death is swallowed up in victory."

Having announced the text, he stood for just a moment and stared out across the congregation, unseeing and still apparently preoccupied, and I felt a little unease at what he might say, for I knowed him to have been sorely troubled.

Cyrus again paused and then begun to speak as was his wont, at first softly, so softly that all but those on the closest row had to strain to hear him, but he builded quickly, so that he spoke firmly and audibly, yet not loudly, for on such occasion was sermons muted and justly so.

"Evil has befallen," he said, "I know that evil walks abroad for it is evil which has struck down this child." I thought that a peculiar way to begin, and I looked around. Others looked perplexed, but I did note that a few of those men who had been at the death scene the day before did glance between theirselves, and the thought come right on me that Cyrus was not the only one who wondered and suspicioned about that fall. I reached my arm around George and tugged him close, suppressing a hard knot of fear that suddenly grasped at my innards.

"And how can we say of evil?" Cyrus was saying. "If God is all, if he ordains all, what is to be said of Divine responsibility?"

Well, at that, a whole raft of folk begun to look around at each other with questions in their eyes. I was certain that I was not the only one who was thinking at that moment of Brother Pitt.

Cyrus waited over-long it seemed to me to resume speaking and stared around over the crowd his expression growing ever more grim. At last he spoke, again quite softly, yet completely audibly.

"I know my God to be merciful," he announced. "I know Him to be just, I know Him to be terrible, I know Him to be at last All-wise and All-knowing, and I know," he paused, and all listened in silence pronounced that it seemed even the birds held their breath. "I know evil to exist in Him and to exist by His permission and in Pursuance of His Plan.

"I know that He has given man leave to choose between Good and Evil. I do not know, nor have I ever heard any man, no matter how wise or well-thought, able to explain why that is. No thinking, searching man that I know would even try to explain why that is so.

"It was by some act of evil that Jeremy Cuthcart fell to his death, that act at last accountable to the Lord God."

There was a general rustling, most especially among them people that was of other persuasions than Old Style and had not been in attendance at Redmon Pitt's declaration of Two-Seedism. Was this then Cyrus's gauntlet thrown at that speculation?

I looked around and my gaze fell upon Brother Kencaid, arrested by the expression on his face, which was filled with excitement and, I thought, something like joy and even happiness, at least with anticipation.

"I know not God's Plan, Brothers and Sisters, no more than does any man living nor any man that ever lived. I could not even presume to specu-late upon it, as others that I have encountered is not always shy about." Here Cyrus glanced about, took a deep breath, and went on.

"I can tell you this, though, that the Word of God records for our assur-ances many examples of evil acts, in evil planned and in evil executed, that in the final analysis was ordained by God for good. When Joseph's brothers sold him into bondage, they intended it for evil, yet it was ordained by God for good. When Christ was crucified, would not anyone say that it was an evil act, and yet what good did come of it for the atonement of them that oth-erwise would not be atoned? When the Disciples was persecuted and drove away into many lands, was that not an act of evil, whose outcome was the spread of Christ's message, and was that not good?"

Cyrus, whose voice had risen in excitement was carrying the group along with him, and there was considerable nodding of heads and frowns of thought. "I cannot say, would not dare to speculate upon the wherefore of God's Plan. It is not for me or for you or for any mortal man to know. I could only say to Brother and Sister Cuthcart that their babe that is asleep in Jesus Christ was not sent by random fate to his death, nor was God otherwise occupied and did not notice, nor was evil triumphant in that act. I can only assure them that in my heart I do know that that babe's going was a part of God's Plan, and I do know that the merciful, just, terrible, all-knowing, and all-wise God is everlastingly, from the beginning to the end, forever and ever, all good and that the Spirit of God is good and God's Plan is good and that evil is only a small part of that Plan.

"There is only one God and that God is good!"

Well, Cyrus's voice fair thundered that out, and the pause that followed it was of such deep silence that again the birds and all the outdoor noises did seemed to have ceased. And then there commenced a certain amount of agreeable nodding.

"I have my faith," said Cyrus, "and I am assured that Brother and Sister Cuthcart are strong in their faith, and to all of you, those who hear my voice with a will to understand, I will affirm and announce that this corruptible Will put on incorruptibility and this mortal Will put on immortality! And for all our days, without question, we can live in the certainty of God's Plan and the goodness thereof."

At that he bowed his head and spoke a short prayer, and when I looked up it seemed to me that the audience did seem less constrained, more relaxed and joyful, than they had been when the service started.

George was looking up at me and he tugged at my arm. "What is incorruptible, Mama, and has Jeremy put it on?"

It was two or three days later that I recalled the pile of utensils and such that I had left behind at the meeting house, and I asked Cyrus to go and fetch them back for me. "If the varmints has not hopelessly scattered them."

And then I added, "You probably will find the remains of that great dog, too. I doubt that anyone has been that way to drag them off the path."

It was not that I was actually telling him to drag them from the path, but I suspected that he would do so, for it would not be pleasant to be stepping over them, as they slowly decayed, each time we walked to meeting.

When Cyrus returned later that day, he carried all of those things that I had left behind, and I was grateful that they had not been scattered by wild critters or even rained upon.

"Ah, thank you, Cyrus."

Cyrus had a curious expression on his face, and I waited for him to speak for I could tell that he had something to say.

"Annamanda," he said, "I did not find the remains of that dog, not anywhere along the path, or from the odor of it, even close to the path."

Well. That was odd. "Betimes, someone come along and done the job for us," I said.

"I don't know. Annamanda," he paused, "Annamanda, I come upon Eremus Lodi—rather he come upon me at the meeting house—while I was out."

"Eremus Lodi?"

Cyrus nodded. "I greeted him, but he only stared vaguely at me, distracted, almost as if he did not know who I was. I made some commonplace observations and still he only looked at me. Finally, I made mention of the loss of his dog."

"Ah, it was he, then, that removed the remains?"

Slowly, Cyrus shook his head and frowned in a most perplexed manner.

"Eremus Lodi only looked at me and finally said, 'Dog? Sir, I have no dog.'"

Ste. Genevieve District
1807

Chapter 8

The Riverman's Story

The summer come and then the fall and another winter, and grief, the way it does, slowly give way to gentle memory.

Shortly after Cyrus had returned from the meeting house where he had seen Eremus Lodi, there come a prolonged rainy spell, ushered in by a violent electrical storm. But though the electricity moved on, the rain remained for several days. And when it at last give way, why, the air was washed clear and clean, the sort of clear and clean that requires that you take a healthy draught of it and praise God that it is so.

Upon the violent death of Jeremy Cuthcart, there had been some muttered and ominous remarks concerning Eremus Lodi and black O'Reilly. "When they pass, ye note," someone said, "that there follers after 'em dark shadows and n'en awful carnage." And there was knowing nods and glances exchanged.

But naught come of it after all, for one reason, neither Eremus Lodi nor O'Reilly was in evidence—from frequent sightings of them to suddenly naught. And it was rumored here and there that they no longer headed north but followed the south'ard path. But Amiable Simpson shook his head and said, "They but gone back whence they come."

"Hell?" said someone.

"Naw. Naw. Eremus Lodi's land runs west a far piece, and I been told, fer I an't seen myself, that he has a household near to them mountains across the great swamp."

"Ah, yes," nodded a settler that I did not know by name. He was not a Baptist. "I have heard of them Injun princesses he pleasures there." And he might have gone on but for a sharp glance from both Cyrus and Amiable Simpson.

"Eremus Lodi and his black come and go," said Amiable Simpson. "I been on this side a' the river fer years now, and I know that this is ther pattern, that they will appear and be conspicuous fer a few months and then they will disappear. It's the way of 'em."

Word got back quickly enough of Redmon Pitt's new ministry. There was a good deal of amusement at the information that they had took to calling theirselves Pittites—Pitties, some of the brothers begun referring to them.

As Brother Kencaid had predicted, some of our members—over one thing or another, mostly puny—took their letters and went over to the Pittites, and some of them returned the favor. One dear old brother, Leonard Samuels, who had give in to his wife's entreaties and gone over, stayed gone but a few weeks before he was back, dragging his chastened wife with him.

"I done two foolish things," he admitted. "I listened to a woman spited and then follered her over. I an't no one to blame but meself. I had but to listen to one service to realize the mistake, but I was prideful enough that I listened through three more before I got my belly full." He glared at his wife, but she was having none of it, looking at the ground, most embarrassed and modest.

"Redmon Pitt an't been Called by nobody, least of all the Lord. Why he don't know a thing about what he speaks. He an't got but a text 'er two to rely on—that 'un about sowing the seed on barren land, y'know—whate're else he needs, why he just makes up.

"But, hard as it is to believe, why ther's them that listens to him fer all the world as if he makes sense. It is," he paused, "an appealing kind of doctrine. Now think on't—if yer a bad seed, ye'd surely know it, wouldn't ye? Why the evil would boil up in ye were ye the seed a' the devil and ye'd know it and so would ever'one else. So if yer certain that ye an't of the bad seed, why then— d'ye foller Brother Pitt's teachings—yer of the good seed an' then ye got nothin' to worry about. Yer saved wh'er ye like it or no."

Less than a year from the time that Jeremy Cuthcart was killed, I give birth once more. This time to a healthy and lively baby boy. Truth was, I had followed the advice of old Mistress Hankens, that midwife that had helped with the birthing of George. I had kept Sarah on the teat, even when she acted like she didn't want it. But somehow that good advice did not seem to hold, and there I was with two small babes and I had my hands full.

But whate're the Lord's Plan for us, it did not include that babe, for he was not quite walking when he come down with the fever. I nursed him night and day and done everything I knowed to do and anything that anyone else suggested. I even had a thought of trying George's curious amulet, though I did not. But naught worked, and in the end death prevailed.

I tried not to think hard on the Lord, though it seemed to me that it had been a kindness not to have give us that pretty babe was we then not allowed to keep him.

Clara Cuthcart on one of the few occasions I had ever heard her make reference to Jeremy, murmured, "I challenged God and dared Him to take one of mine, and so He done it."

I knowed what she meant, and it was not exactly as it sounded. For whate're God had decided had been decided before the world ever was, and puny man—including Sister Cuthcart—could in no way change that, though they challenged God by the hour.

And so we prayed and put that babe away and—sadder—went on about our daily business.

Late summer, when Sarah was nearing the end of her third year, word come to me of my younger sister Martha Elen. Now I already knowed that she had finally married Joseph McCade, that word had already come round-about. The letter I had received from my mother only said that Martha Elen and Joseph McCade had crossed the river, too, and was settled north at Ste. Genevieve.

I presumed them married, of course, aware that a letter to that effect had probably been sent but had not arrived, which was not so uncommon an occurrence on the frontier. It was indeed amazing, I thought, that any letter ever got through, so ill was the post handled.

The letter that come from Ste. Genevieve and Martha Elen had not been so long on the road, actually, though it had been passed by divers folk and was some tattered with it. It was lengthy and rambling, newsy if ill-spelled and ill-writ. I recognized Martha Elen's scrawl, and it brought her image to my mind's eye—impatient, with wild red hair and a temper to match.

What the letter come down to at last was that she was with child and Joseph McCade was gone. I showed the letter to Cyrus, who read it, smiled, and shook his head from side to side and returned it with a shrug, "Ah, she knowed when she married him that it'd take a stout rope to keep him from wandering. He's the son of a longhunter and it's in his blood."

Well, Cyrus had knowed Joseph McCade from boyhood, they being of an age, which put Joseph McCade some years ahead of Martha Elen. That had not deterred her, however, when she set her cap for him, nor had the know-ledge that he had a wanderer's blood, for the longhunters could no more stay at home and tend the crops than a butterfly could make honey. They come and went, gone for long stretches, searching whate'er it was they searched, for they theirselves, often as not, did not know the answer to that, only that there was something beyond the fences that they would seek. Unlike the solitar-ies, the longhunters did return, sometimes with a little extra coin, sometimes their only riches the vivid tales they told.

I pondered the letter for a time and eventually asked Cyrus how far it might be to Ste. Genevieve. He give me a long look and then answered, "Fifty or sixty miles, perhaps, by land, but the trail would not be safe; it'd be safer by water, which upstream is passing hard." He knowed, I was sure, what I was thinking.

It was the arrival of Patsy and Reuben Bradene, headed upstream by keelboat, that prompted me at last to speak to Cyrus about what was on my mind. "I could travel with Brother and Sister Bradene," I said, "for I know

I'd be safe. I cannot bear to think of my little sister, with neither family nor husband, going through her first birth. And if, indeed, Joseph McCade is gone and like to be gone for a long time, why I might bring her back with me. At any rate, if I travel to Ste. Genevieve, I can at least determine how Martha Elen fares, which would ease my mind considerable."

I did not worry how my family would fare without me, for I knowed that under the circumstances, the brothers and sisters would both understand and provide. Nor did I concern myself that Cyrus might deny me, nor did he. He was not eager, of course, to see me travel, but he did understand my mission and approve.

We left early of a morning, when the warm mist was still hanging heavy over the river. The boat we rode was sturdy as it was ungainly, for it looked to be a cross between a flatboat and a keelboat, wider and flatter than the latter but with some of its rounded bottom. It was poled by Patsy and Reuben and the two rivermen that I recognized after a time as that lively riverman Jacob, that loved to spin tales, and his taciturn brother Otto, that only looked out from under his over-hanging eyebrows now and then and left the smiling and idle chatter to his brother.

I sat in the middle as near as possible in the center of the boat, while Patsy and Reuben stood at the two back corners with their poles and with surprising strength pushed against the slow current with some success. Jacob stood in the middle and shifted from side to side as he perceived the need, using a pole or oar. I did know enough of the river to know that there was tricks to the successful poling of it, either with or against the current—knowing the current and knowing the bottom and the shore to such extent that it was not all push-agin'. Still, it did seem a remarkable feat to board the river so easily, as it were, that river with a mind to take everything but one way.

It was cool of a early morning and the birds dashing over and across the river and into the trees at the river's edge was loud with their business. Else, it was so still that the small sound that the barge made against the river was even audible, a soft lapping that was most soothing.

I could, I thought, 'a rode that way for days on end without moving, had not Patsy Bradene decided to take up a tune. I had not counted on that, had even forgot her delight with the sounds that she so ill attacked and so loud. I wondered what hostile Indians hearing those sounds might think, that we was readying for attack maybe or wailing mayhap over our dying?

I looked to Reuben, hoping that having had experience of it, he might have devised some method of dealing with it. But Reuben was poling rhythmically, a rested and peaceful expression on his face, with only a glance now and then toward the area where the noise originated and with a look then of contentment and even pleasure and affection, a look which periodically Patsy Bradene did return him. I was forced to the unmistakable conclusion that Reuben enjoyed the song! Nor did the riverman Jacob seem distressed, but had a look upon his face that was distant and not interested, and Otto did not even look up from the muddy and yellow water that he stared at.

I glanced toward the heavens and wondered would it be out of line to suggest that the Almighty might take a hand in the matter, if only by way of wearing out Patsy's voice. And possibly, then He did, for behold, we come suddenly upon a rough stretch of water, which apparently neither Reuben nor Patsy had been ready for, and we lurched forward and the singing ceased as Patsy and Reuben plied theirselves to their task, and with that, Patsy had seemingly lost track of her song and all was peaceful again but for the lapping of the water and the dying cries of the birds, for it was coming upon that time of day that the activity of the birds dwindles.

The river was still some more active than it had been, and but for the fact that such activity seemed to occupy all of Patsy Bradene's attention, I might have been some alarmed. To pole agin' the current is time consuming, even in the slow water of late summer, and it would be that we would camp out several nights e'er we made our destination. And as the morning give way to noon and then to afternoon, the pleasantness of the adventure begun to be called into question, for I was hot and those parts of me that had been exposed, though they was few, was redder and tenderer by far with the evening than they had been at dawn.

Said Jacob the riverman as the sun begun to go behind the trees against the horizon, "Look alive, Pat, fer ther's a fair place to camp to yer left around that bend yonder." At that the silent Otto looked up and stared a long time at the shore before he bent to his oar again.

Sure enough, we come shortly upon a shallow, and with some effort, but no complaint, Reuben and Jacob and Otto bent their backs, while Patsy guided the craft, and we touched easily upon the shore. I for one was glad to be there. I spread a quilt up on the dry shore and sat down upon it, and then lay back and studied the leaves a-movin' restlessly above me. The breeze off the river was refreshing and I felt comfortably alone, for there is indeed a comfort to honest solitude that there ne'er is to loneliness.

My comfortable solitude did not last long, as Patsy Bradene, having procured some slabs of meat and cold corn dodger, did all at once request that I offer a blessing for our meal. Again, I thought that Reuben looked a little surprised, and I suspected that it was not common practice for those two to bless their meals. But having a pastor's wife aboard, Patsy apparently decided that certain amenities ought be observed. Though in truth, me and Cyrus did not always observe that ritual ourselves, what with two hungry young ones about and the confusion they brought to the table. But I supposed that even cold corn dodger was a blessing after all and ought to be so treated, so I bent my head, prepared to say a brief blessing, when I was startled by a sudden grunt, and glancing up, I saw Otto stalk away from us. All else stood with their heads bowed and took no notice of that ill behavior, so I ducked my head once more and asked a brief blessing of the Lord.

After our simple meal, Reuben pulled out his pipe, found a tree to lean against, and having fussed with the pipe 'til he got it going, leaned back with a sigh and puffed at it, while Jacob took a line, promised fish for breakfast, and disappeared down the shore. Patsy Bradene sat for a while on a near log, fidgeted and sighed and twitched her fingers until at last she jumped up and stomped off to the raft, lifting her skirts high to wade out, rummaged about for a time and came back with her own pipe and, without ever looking at me, lit it up and leaned back with a sigh of contentment

Reuben's eyes was closed and I wondered did he nap. Patsy stared out across the river for a long time, and I enjoyed the silence, broken only occasionally by sluggish summer sounds. All at once Patsy shifted her position and commenced to talk. I could not say why, for I'd have been as happy with silence.

"We been on the river a long time, me and Reuben. Reuben longer'n me, fer he was borned along the Ohio and drifted betimes 'ith his family down it to the Mississippi. I come along later 'ith my own family, a good big girl, found Reuben, and we decided to settle some land together. So we married and done just that.

"But, 'las, we just wasn't meant fer the land I guess. Though we did try. Reuben longed fer the river from the day he left it, an' me, wal, somehow I couldn't get the hang a' bein' a settler's wife, no more n'en he could get the hang a' bein' a settler."

She paused to puff her pipe, but there did not seem to be no reason for me to speak, so I did not.

"Somehow," she sighed, "it didn't seem to matter; we'd find a way to stick our foot in it and get things stirred up."

The memory of Brother Ulysses Kern's jack and that animal's unhappy encounter with Patsy Bradene came back to me, but I would not have mentioned it for the world.

"The land is wide," she commenced again, "and it goes on forever an' I suppose don't never stop. Now the river, it's narrow, an' it goes but one direction. D'ye want to go t'other direction, wal, ye can, but d'ye will yerself to go agin' it, why n'en ye've truly set yerself a task."

I was not sure then just who she talked to or to what purpose, herself or me, or was she just musin'. So I said nothing. Later Patsy and I made our bed aboard our craft while the men took turns keepin' watch. I slept as well that night and those that followed as I have ever slept in my life.

We arrived at the Saline Creek and the nearby salt works past mid-day. The river had give us no trouble, though there had been a few times that three of the crew would go to the shore and pull the boat by rope through some spot or other that was troublesome to navigate, while one stayed on board to steer. It was called "cordelling" and was occasionally necessary. I was pleased not to be called on to help with that chore, though Patsy Bradene did take her turn cheerfully enough.

The trip had been without incident but for the passing of the Grand Tower, some miles north of Cape Girardeau. I had heard of that tower of rock in the river channel but had ne'er seen it and was some impressed by it. Patsy recounted her tale of having helped the mapmaker Master Clark with details of mapping it and explained to me, though I had not the knowledge to understand, the intricacies of navigating around it.

"Since this is yer first trip by," winked Jacob, "tradition has it that ye must afford us sper'ts to drink er ye get th'owed over board." I must have looked alarmed, for they all three laughed, and even the usually glowering Otto looked up with just the hint of amusement in his eyes. "It is the tradition amongst rivermen, that," said Patsy. "But since yer not really a riverman, why we'll let it pass."

The mighty river flowing around and about us, as we cut it, was fascinating to watch. I wondered briefly that I should find myself thus a passenger headed against its current, that I ne'er would have thought myself ever to be. And yet because I was, then it must be that it was planned.

I sighed at that thought and was vexed. The knotty problem, it seemed, followed after me where'er I would go. Truth was, it was such a hard thought, that all things must be, because they was ordained to be. I knowed that it was futile to ponder; I'd heard often enough that mere mortal man could not understand it, but still it vexed me, as it vexed me when I stared into a starry sky and tried to imagine all them stars and where and why they was.

"Yer not meant to know," my old granny had said when I was little. "Don't nobody know, don't nobody need to know."

I knowed her to be right and that thinking upon such things was both useless and probably sinful. Yet my meandering mind would go to those thoughts when it was otherwise unoccupied, and I would find myself wondering at each little sparrow or blade of grass or fallen leaf, wondering was they a part of the Plan, too? And then I knowed that these was the reasons that I had not yet had the experience probably, that I questioned things too much and wondered about things that wasn't none of my business. This was the Will of God and I might as well accept that. I did myself no honor by questioning it.

"D'ye will yerself to go agin' it," Patsy had said of the river, "well, n'en, truly ye've set yerself a task."

Patsy and Reuben was both eager to tour me around the salt works. "Ther's lead mines besides, but we an't got the time to go search them," said Patsy. "But these salt works has been here years and years, an' has put out copious quantities of salt."

So while Otto stayed behind to mind the boat, the rest of us proceeded to take in the sights. I was fair interested in the great vats and drying pans and bushels and bushels of salt. I had ne'er thought to see any one thing ever in such quantity. I dawdled and gawked and finally Patsy and Reuben left me to look while they saw to their business.

Standing near to a building to partake of its shade and listening to the workmen sing, I chanced to look up and catch sight of a slight figure leaning against a stump some distance. He was picking at his teeth with a knife, wiping that then on his greasy buckskins, and I was arrested by something familiar about him, something I could not quite place. Patsy come up then, and we moved away from the salt works and back toward the river.

In time we come up on Reuben and Jacob. "I was tellin' Reuben," said Jacob, "that I plan to stay on at Ste. Gen fer a while an' so an't goin' to accompany ye to St. Louis."

"Ah," said Patsy waggling her finger at him, "an' tell me wh'er not it's a woman has got yer eye, or ye hers, that keeps ye off the river betimes?"

For answer, the riverman Jacob grinned a happy and I thought innocent grin, and I started to say speak, but was interrupted by a loud scream and then sounds of great commotion back toward the salt works.

Patsy, Reuben, and Jacob turned without a word and dashed back in that direction. There was naught for me to do but follow after. I gathered up my skirts and moved as quickly as I modestly could. I had got close enough to see a crowd around one of the vats, when that slight figure I had remarked earlier dashed by me, a crooked grin upon his face, and he looked fair at me, narrowing his eyes some, and then with a look that I could describe only as a sneer, he lifted his cap and inclined at the waist. And then I remarked his ear and how it flopped away from his head, and I knowed then that I knowed him and where. But I had no time to worry about wh'er he knowed me or not, for he passed quickly by, stepping up his tempo until he was trotting toward the river.

When I approached the crowd, Patsy Bradene was among those that knelt about a fallen man who was cursing and groaning. "He's scalded," said someone to me as I arrived, the way people do, speaking to any stranger and giving information in any emergency. "One of them vats of boiling water splashed upon his leg, an' it looks to me he'll lose it, so bad is it burned."

"He says," another voice announced in general, "that it wan't no accident, that it was deliberate done when his back was turned."

I moved in close and watched for a moment. At last I said, "Patsy, you know that Master Eremus Lodi has a black most skilled in the treatment of burns. You might suggest to send for him."

I had thought it a reasonable suggestion, but it was met with a great deal of silence.

"Eremus Lodi's black?" said a voice behind me, and then there was a general muttering.

"No," groaned the suffering man, who unlike most of the workers about the plant, was white and not black. "I'd not have Eremus Lodi nor his black nor all the demons in hell to touch me!" And that ended in such a deep groan of pain that I stepped quickly back.

Others filled the space I had vacated, and in a few minutes I was joined by Patsy and then Reuben and finally Jacob, all shaking their heads and murmuring, and in mostly silence we walked back toward the river and the security of our vessel. Jacob the riverman was most talkative and wondered out loud at the accident and expressed considerable sympathy for that scalded lad.

I made mention, then, of that passing encounter with the floppy-eared one.

"T'would only be Drooly," he said. "An't nothin' to fear a' Drooly, d'ye keep him to yer face. T'wouldn't do to turn yer back on him, though," the riverman added darkly.

"Skeet?" said Patsy, "Was his companion Skeet 'ith him?"

I shook my head. "I saw only one."

"Ah," said Jacob, "ye kin be sure that Skeet was about somewhere, wh'er ye seen him or no, fer simple as Drooly is, Skeet's a sight more simple an' could hardly survive without Drooly to guide him. Was they not so dangerous, they'd be right comical.

"Drooly—wh'er that be his name er just give to him fer that he does drool betimes, the more excited, the more he drools—he comes and goes off the river. He's at home in the woods as well as the river, fer though he's simple enough, he can take care of hisself in water er woods, fer he does survive. An' he shows up betimes here er there, ye ne'er know."

"Ye think he might have aught to do with that scaldin' of the lad back there?" asked Patsy.

"Wal, yes, he's capable. Drooly, he would not ha' minded tippin' over that boilin' water, just fer the sport of it, so long's someone's back was turned. Just fer the sport of it.

"Ther's talk, ye know, of renegades along the river, scum like Drooly, that deals in scalps, that'll scalp ther own fer reward from certain Injuns. I know not the truth on't yet, but someday I will."

"Scalp? How come ye by that?" asked Patsy.

"Ah," answered the riverman, "the river talks, d'ye know how to listen. The river talks. An' sometimes it tells fearsome tales—of man an' beast." He added that last with a long look toward the far shore and the distant trees, and I could not control that small shudder of apprehension that run down my backbone.

Then with a quick laugh, the riverman added, "But fer the most part, ther's naught to fear d'ye keep yer eyes open. Though the scum abounds, ther only seriously dangerous d'ye not watch them close. They'd steal the teat from a babe's mouth, could they get away with it. But what they have most in common besides bein' less than human, yea even less than beast, is that they got no sense fer tomorrow, cain't plan, nor think hardly past the next step they take, an' that's all to our good. Had that lad back there been alert, why he most like would ne'er ha' got scalded."

That recalled me back to that young man's frightened reaction when I mentioned Eremus Lodi's O'Reilly, and I said something of that.

134

"I only mentioned that Eremus Lodi had a man wondrous skilled in medicine," I said to Patsy Bradene. "I was ill prepared for such an assault of words, particularly from one so grievously injured as that man."

"Ah," said Jacob, the young riverman, "those who travel the river have heard many stories, mostly false is my opinion, of Eremus Lodi and O'Reilly the giant black and the dog, for those three do travel in shadow up and down the river appearing and disappearing like shades themselves." Again I held my tongue, not interrupting what appeared to be a story in the making with the telling on the death of that dog. I had not mentioned it to anyone save Cyrus and there seemed no need to bring it up.

"And I have heard it remarked of O'Reilly's gray, cropped hair that it was singed thataway in hell," said the riverman bending over the side of the boat and eyeing the water and then the bank beyond, as if measuring depth or current or some such.

"But I don't believe that to be the truth," he said quite seriously, as if indeed that might be a possibility to be questioned. "I've heard the story of black O'Reilly, how he got his name and so forth. I have heard it and have reason to believe that it's true." He glanced up. "The river carries many stories and when yer practiced of it, why it's easy enough to sort the truth from the error. Would ye like to hear the story of Eremus Lodi's black O'Reilly before he was Eremus Lodi's, and how he come by that name?"

I looked at the man in some curiosity, but it was Patsy Bradene that asked my question for me. "Ye knew black O'Reilly before he come to Eremus Lodi?"

"Wal, not I, but I did know a young man who claimed to know the story and others that did corroborate it. The lad's name was O'Reilly—I an't seen him in many a year on the river. Belike, he's dead fer a riverman will leave the river fer no other reason. Anyhow, this lad claimed that he knowed O'Reilly from the beginning an' that black O'Reilly had that name give him by the lad's old pap."

"Why I never knowed that," said Patsy Bradene.

"Wal, as I said it was a unusual story, but the unusual along the river is the usual, for ther's so much that is strange that goes on that one little story would hardly make a ripple. I'll tell ye about it, though, as we got plenty a' time and nothin' else to do, d'ye want?"

I did try not to look over-curious, but Patsy Bradene did nod her head vigorously, and the riverman commenced his story.

"They was rivermen then, the lad, his pap, and three brothers. I can't say exactly when t' was, only that the boy—by name Frank, Frankie O'Reilly— had to 'a been a good, big boy, able to take his turn, fer no one went along jest fer the ride. His brothers was all older, an' his pap, who was Irish—come as a young man from Ireland and left his folks and was as I said named O'Reilly—and all the rest was big and strong and as a result suffered fewer of the worries that littler men do have to suffer when they travel the river. Oh, they was all—them O'Reillys, father and sons—all good enough in a fight were it brought to their attention, but none too interested in goin' unbid fer one.

"Pap O'Reilly, wal, he's gone, fer sure dead, rest his soul. He come afoul, I heard, a' the river just a point north of the Grand Tower—that we passed, ye recall?" Jacob turned to me and I nodded, for I did remember it.

"Wal," he continued, "Pap O'Reilly, they said, slipped overboard and was warshed away during a rough spell of water, his bones and what's left of him by now most likely warshing some distant shores or riding the crests of some foreign ocean, belike the Indian Ocean, maybe." He stopped and stared hard at the horizon and seemed likely to have mislaid entirely the story he had started.

But Patsy Bradene prodded him. "How say ye then that they come upon O'Reilly the black?"

"Oh, yes, I was sayin' as how all them O'Reillys—big, strappin, lovin' of women and drink, most especially Pap O'Reilly, the last if not the first, but that was not unusual neither, fer if ye travel the river, ye most likely come overdone of one or t'other, ye know?"

"O'Reilly?" said Patsy again, for the riverman could not seem to get himself arrived at the point of the story in which we was most interested.

"They was rivermen," he said, drawing himself up as if to get his thoughts together, "an' they carried whate'er needs be carried by keelboat down the Mississippi at spring flood from Ste. Genevieve to Orleans—sorghum or pelts or sometimes salt from the saline, now and then chicken or pigs, though ye did have to be right desperate to take on either, most especially chickens. Now ridin' a full boat down the river is still much easier than ridin' a empty boat back up, as ye yerselves can see, and sometimes the rivermen will take on passengers or other goods fer the trip back, makin' it tolerable hard work on the 'turn trip.

"They was in New Orleans that trip I speak of, Frankie a right big boy as I said, but wh'er that was his first trip, I don't recollect, only that they had sold ther goods and was preparin' fer the ride back up the river, that bein' so hard and tedious that Pap O'Reilly had spent the day loadin' up on comforts and was in a merry mood, lighthearted and givin' to singin'. And though they got a few hard looks, fer they walked all abreast and was not given to inconveniencin' theirselves in favor of some solitary walker, all they met showed good sense in not accostin' them.

"Movin' back down to the river dock, they chanc't to come upon a large group of citizens and stopped to inspect what they was inspectin', which proved to be a slave auction. Now that was nothin unusual in itself; what was gathering folks' attention was the size of one of the savages, fer they was obviously right off the boat from Africa. He stood towering above everyone, black and shiny as anthracite, chained with enough chain to dock a seagoing vessel, and staring out upon the crowd as if he did not see them nor cared to see them.

"Well, he was an arrestin' sight. Of course, yer right d'ye 'spect that this was Eremus Lodi's O'Reilly, though then of course, he was not Eremus Lodi's. All the men gathered about was talkin' about that big black in some awed and hushed tones, and it wasn't just him bein' big that produced such reaction. For an oversized slave is not so unusual a thing, and by and large they's some prized fer that very strength. But there was about this black man a power and a strength and a dignity that an't usually found in a shackled man. The O'Reillys stood and admired with the rest of the crowd fer a time.

"It become obvious that the auctioneer was not having much success in organizing a bid fer that black giant. 'Come, now, men,' he was sayin', 'we got here fer the price of one, the strength of three. How can ye go wrong?' But he was greeted mainly with a few cat calls and a lot of silence.

"'He needs breakin', Slaver,' called out a voice from the crowd. 'I'd no more take him than I'd call on the devil to send me help.' 'Now, now, Gentlemen,' the slaver was sayin', 'gentle as a kitten, he is. I've not a menacing word or act out of him from the start.' 'Well, now, Slaver, I'd guess not,' cried out someone else, 'but we can hardly keep him shackled with a half-ton of chain as you do.' 'I wonder does he bite or growl?' come another voice, and there followed a general laugh at that. Then there was some comment or other about his privy parts, which of course I can't go into," said the riverman with what looked to me to be a wink in the direction of Patsy Bradene.

"'Well,' called out the auctioneer, 'I'll let ye all look at him and think on't whilst we go to some of these lesser breeds, here,' and he poked a skinny and sick-looking young female with his cane and she whimpered and hung her head, at which the giant black turned his head so slowly and cast such a glance upon the slaver, dignity all mixed up with anger and wrath, controlled and terrifyingly fearsome, and there was a general drawing back of the crowd, though the black man had made not a sound nor even lifted his manacled fists. And even the slaver winced and withdrew the cane he held poked in the girl's back.

"'Slaver,' called out someone in the crowd, 'take him and git him broke, git him good and broke, and bring him back. An't nobody goin' to take him like that.' 'Better to cast him in the river loaded with weights,' called out someone else and there was a general roar of approval at that and some laughter.

"'Ah, naw,' Pap O'Reilly murmured. ''Ah, naw. They'll ne'er break him or drown him, fer he's too fine fer that.' Now bear in mind, ladies," said the riverman, "that Pap O'Reilly was some gone in drink fer one thing and fer another he sported as good a heart as e'er any man ever sported. Rivermen is destined by the good Lord to be poor, no matter, but the O'Reillys might not had been so godawful poor had not Pap O'Reilly give away what he didn't drink away. But that's another story and will have to wait.

"'Why,' cried out Pap O'Reilly before any of us could read his intent, 'I'll take him!'

"'An' what'll ye give fer him?' asked the slaver, quite some startled, but probably almost ready to give the big black away, fer though they could be broke, it was hardly worth it, and truth to tell he wouldn't 'a been the first Africaner to 'a been drowneded out of convenience.

"'Whatever I got in me pocket,' said Pap O'Reilly, an' he turned his pockets out and pulled out bills and coin as he walked up to where the slaver stood.

"'E'god,' moaned the oldest brother O'Reilly, 'an it's a whole trip's pay that goes fer a slave!'

"Whatever it was that Pap O'Reilly turned over in coin and bills fer that slave, it did much, they said, to improve the slaver's humor, and he gratefully turned over the chained and manacled black to Pap O'Reilly, and there they was with the biggest slave in all the Mississippi Valley and maybe even the entire North American continent. And them not slave-holders ever, not even knowin' anybody that had slaves, no place to keep him and nothin' to do with him. An' here come Pap O'Reilly pullin' the monstrous black behind him as if he was a puppy. Though 'puppy' would not dignify that man. An' the crowd fell away and ther was none of them hoots that ye might 'a expected under the circumstances, fer they was five over-big Irishman leadin' probably the biggest man in the Orleans Territory. T'would 'a took a right brave or right foolish man to 'a said nothin' amiss. An' ther was neither apparently in that crowd.

"'Now, Pap,' said one of the brothers, 'what d'ye kin we do with that 'un? We an't slavers.'

"'Wal, first,' said Pap O'Reilly, 'we'll take him to our boat and then we'll eat. No,' he reconsidered, swaying a mite, 'we'll eat and then we'll take him to our boat, fer I'm fair famished and don't think that I could make it all the way to the boat fer victuals.'

"So they stopped shortly at a stall fer bread and sausage and Pap O'Reilly looked at the huge man he still held by chain, and he frowned and said, 'Ere ye hungry, black man?' but ther was of course no answer, fer it was obvious that the black didn't understand the words or if he did had not the words to return in answer. 'Fer shure,' announced Pap O'Reilly, 'he must of a certain be hungry, fer a body that great must need great amounts of fuel regularly,' and he handed over a large loaf of bread and sausage to the man.

"The slave took it and looked gravely at Pap O'Reilly and then inclined his head slightly and slowly broke the bread and sausage, and though he ate quickly, he ate carefully that the O'Reillys, who was stuffin' their mouths with both hands, was give pause and concluded to slow therselves a little. And then Pap O'Reilly located a place that sold sper'ts and restocked himself, fer he had not indeed spent all his money on the slave. Humming to hisself and feeling happy, Pap O'Reilly offered a sip from his jug to the black man, but that man only sniffed and then shook his head slowly from side to side.

"'Ah, me friend,' said Pap suddenly sad, 'it's a wise man ye be. I can tell it about ye, that yer wise and strong and good. Ye know not to sop yer brain in sper'ts that make ye at last vomit and spew. Yer too wise fer that, wiser than we ere and yet look at ye, shackled and tied and we be free. I have ne'er understood,' he said sadly, 'the way that the world works. Ther's them that says that ther is a plan, but be dimmed if I could figger it.' And he cast a long and sorrowful glance at the slave.

"'Hey, O'Reilly,' called out a familiar riverman as they passed, 'what ye got ther on that rope?'

"'Why,' said Pap, 'it's me cousin come all the way over from Ireland. Black Irish,' he said.

"By the time they got to the boat, it was growin' dark, and Pap O'Reilly had near to finished off his comforts. And he immediately sagged by the cabin and stared out across the river, which they would needs begin to navigate once more early in the morning. 'What will we do with him?' said the oldest brother. 'Why, just let him lie,' said Pap O'Reilly, 'he wan't hurt nothin'. An', b'glory, he'll make the trip home easier by half,' he said and then slowly slid down onto the deck, hard asleep.

"They led the slave to the cabin and fastened him to it so that he was sitting down. He had not yet said one word. And then they conversed amongst therselves, cursing the old man fer a fool, something they'd daren't do were he awake or sober, and decided that they would take turns by twos watching over the black by night, with pistols beside them did he decide to rip the cabin up from the deck, which they was sure he could if he wanted.

"But there was naught to worry about, fer he sat, his knees drawed up under his chin, his eyes closed, and seemed to sleep the night through. And when the hot rays of early morning sun struck Pap O'Reilly, he slowly rolled over, groaning and complaining, and at last sat up and stared into the dark and somber face across the way.

"'My God, my God, my God,' moaned Pap, 'it's me dream come to life.' An' he buried his head in his arms and then in a moment peeked out from under them and then ducked them back again and moaned and rolled from side to side. 'It an't a dream?' he asked at last, and peeked again at the black man and announced sadly, 'It an't a dream.'

"But fears of the giant proved unfounded, fer he was tame as could be, not, I'm certain because he was by nature tame, but rather because he knowed the O'Reillys to be well-intentioned toward him. And the old man, recovering his strength as well as his voice, talked almost without ceasing to the black, singing to him, explaining things to him for all the world as if he could understand and even tried without success to teach him a few of the more common blasphemies.

"At last a few days along the river, Pap O'Reilly decided that the black needed a name and set about trying to ascertain if he had one they could use. But Pap could not seem to make hisself understood and finally pointing at hisself and then at the black and back at hisself he kept repeating 'O'Reilly,

O'Reilly' thinking to make the black realize that was his name. Until at last the black said the first word they had heard and that word was 'O'Reilly' in low and deep and altogether beautiful tones.

"Old Pap stopped short and stared at him, a curious and pitiful smile crossing his face. 'Ah, he says it like an Irishman. Me own mither could 'na had said it more beautiful.' And ther was tears in the old man's eyes. 'Fer my money, he could have it his ownself fer a name,' he said. And that was it. From then on he was O'Reilly, and since ther was so many by that name, most folks that had occasion to call them anything of a Christian nature called them by ther given names anyway. An' he become O'Reilly."

Jacob, the riverman, said that last with a certain pride and with a flourish that announced that he was finished with his tale. But we was not satisfied, for Patsy asked, "What of Eremus Lodi? How did O'Reilly come to him?"

"Oh," said the riverman, "it was no great story. They could not keep a slave. They had not the means, and fer all, it was not safe either. Ther are murderous sorts along the river, and many of them was not too grateful to see that giant black amongst them. Sooner or later it would 'a been trouble. An' most nearly was. But that's another story. They come to that conclusion sadly, Pap more so than any of the others, and set about tryin' to sell him and so recover ther monies, but they had less success even than the auctioneer in Orleans had had. Until one day they come up on Eremus Lodi, fer even then, he wandered the river's edge restlessly, and Pap O'Reilly who knowed him moderately well, as well as anyone, accosted him and asked did he know anyone to sell the slave to. And told him the whole story.

"Wal, to make the story short, it was as if Eremus Lodi and black O'Reilly had an immediate and silent understanding, fer Eremus Lodi returned Pap O'Reilly his money and took the slave, unshackled, and left.

"The rest is legend. I don't believe half of what I hear, but many a riverman will swear to ye that ther both in league with the devil or with sper'ts or anything else most awesome that they can think of. That's why that feller, bruised and injured though he was, was in terror of being treated by the big black man."

Later I spoke to Patsy of the riverman's story and she only shook her head slowly, finally commenting, "Jacob loves a good story, y'know, wher the factsis always exact er no. Might be; might not be."

Chapter 9

The Believer

Normally a light sleeper, I slept better than I might have expected on that raft, for it was nosed into the bank and tied to a tree, and the breeze which come from the north and west passed through the small cabin in which I lay, and that breeze, as is not uncommon in the late summer, had turned sudden cool and felt of fall and was nicely refreshing.

At what hour I knowed not, I stirred and was conscious of voices and peered out of the cabin toward the shore. There was a group about the fire there, and from the flames which reached high now and then and danced and sparkled, I could make out that the group included Patsy and Reuben as well as Jacob and Otto and two others, which I took to be likewise rivermen.

Then it come to me what had disturbed my sleep. Patsy was singing—softly for her—but singing one of them hymns that she seemed so partial to. And the others seemed to be unnoticing of the noise that she was producing. Reuben leaned back against a tree and Jacob sat cross-legged, his chin resting in his hand, and Otto and the other two rivermen was sprawled beside the fire.

I detected the reason for their insensitivity soon enough, for it was passed from hand to hand and from mouth to mouth, and though Patsy swigged copiously from the jug, I noted that Reuben did not, for it was passed by him, he only smiling and nodding. Jacob's brother Otto took charge of the jug and held it between his knees, and the others all turned their attention to Patsy, whose singing had been interrupted in the passage of the spirits.

I only sighed and did console myself that we were at least at journey's end, and I would not have to trust myself to their care upon the river in the morning. To give them their due, possibly this was their celebration of that fact, for I had not had no intimations of spirits at all as we traveled up the river.

I lay back and attempted to clear my thoughts for sleep, as I was passing weary, but the rhythms of Patsy's voice nagged at me. I sat up once more and leaned my elbow against the comforter upon which I lay and listened in some perplexity for it was not ordinary conversation that was going on—that much I could tell.

Patsy was up on her knees, both hands outstretched, palms upward, inclining toward the men she was speaking to. From the uncertain list of her body I suspected that having got to her knees, she was as far up as her balance would allow, for she swayed uncertainly even anchored thus on so solid a foundation.

I strained to hear her words, for the rhythms of them was intense and sincere. At last they begun to come clear until I heard distinctly, "An' John the Baptist, don'cha know, he come preachin' in the wilderness."

Lord in Heaven! I sat straight up on my pallet. Patsy Bradene was preaching a sermon!

At least she was attempting to preach a sermon, just as her small congregation was attempting to comprehend the sermon. The three rivermen, theirselves listing in various direction, was inclined in all serious attention toward Patsy, as inclined anyway as their various postures would allow for—except for Reuben who still sat with his back against the tree, and from the small light of the fire I seemed to be able to make out an expression of content and pleasure and even pride as he watched Patsy swaying on her knees like a great heifer trying to rise from the ground.

"All have sinned," boomed Patsy, and both of the strange rivermen jumped. Otto lifted the jug to his mouth and then passed it once more. Again it passed by Reuben Bradene untouched. But Patsy took a heavy draught of it before she passed it on.

"We are all as unclean things," continued Patsy and as if to emphasize her point she paused to scratch here and there. The rivermen continued to watch her intently.

"Brothers," she said, "yer corrupted and vile and stinking and in no ways beautiful in the eyes of the Lord. He can hardly tolerate ye!"

"Ah, Pat," murmured one of the rivermen.

"S'true. Cain't hardly stand ye."

She paused for effect. By this time I was sitting straight up, staring at the solemn scene, unable to restrain a smile. I glanced out over the river, so beautiful in half light, part firelight and part moonlight, calm and still and full of the small noises of the night, and thought that the Lord could not be upset at anything so sincere, no matter the circumstances out of which it came.

"An't yer fault," Patsy went on. "Ye was borned thataway."

"Wal, mebbe," said the other riverman. "Now my ma she was so good it hurt, but my pa, that ol' sot, why he was so mean that the milk'd curdle did he just walk th'u the room."

"Ah, me," sighed the first riverman, "now I never even knowed neither my ma ner my pa. I was raised, what raisin' ther was, by my old grandma and her third husband, and they warned me plenty that I was bound fer hell, didn't I change my ways." And he sighed loudly.

"An't so," said Patsy Bradene. "An't necessarily so. Don't nobody know who's bound fer heaven er who's bound fer hell. Don't nobody know but God and He ain't tellin'. Nothin' ye could do about it, one way er the other. 'Work out yer own salvation 'ith fear er tremblin'." She hiccoughed loudly at that and leaned back against her feet and considered.

I heard a familiar grunt, the one that I had come to associate with Otto. And then I heard him speak, an occurrence that was so rare that it seemed an occasion when he did so. "All's that is is shit," announced Otto with a hiccough of his own.

Ignoring him, the second riverman, listing a little to the right and slurring his words considerably muttered, "Wha's that mean, Pat?"

"What it means," said Patsy Bradene, "is that ye cain't work out yer own salvation. Ye just got to set back and wait an' see what happens."

"Wal," drawled the second riverman, "now that don't seem too bad of a idea, do it?" And he reached over and relieved Jacob of the jug only loosely held. Jacob give him a slow grin, reached as if he would retrieve the jug, and then slowly slipped back against the ground and from his lack of movement, obviously had give up the fight for the night. Reuben still sat against the tree, having moved only so much as to have pulled his knees up.

The breeze continued cool and I lay back myself, wondering what more doctrine Patsy might provide, but too tired to wait up to see. I pulled the quilt up over me, congratulating myself again for the foresight in having brought both comforter and quilt along, for the Bradenes' sleeping arrangements left much to be desired.

Patsy and the two rivermen were passing the jug between them, but their talk had quieted down and Patsy had resumed her seat. If they had more to say of doctrine or anything else, I did not hear it, for I slipped to sleep almost as soon as my head touched the comforter.

Later, I woke again, this time to mostly silence, it probably being that time between night and day when the night creatures have left off their noise and the day creatures have not yet started. I struggled a moment to decide where I was and what I was doing, so soundly had I been sleeping. My first thought was that one of the children had waked me, and then slowly I begun to remember.

I lifted myself on one elbow. The fire had died down to coals, but the light from the moon was such that I could make out various piles of humanity, mostly having dropped to sleep where I had last seen them. Patsy Bradene had apparently made her way to the raft, for she was piled in her accustomed spot, on her ill ticking, her feet drawed up against the cold, for it had turned off right chilly.

I heard a sound and looked about. It had probably been such a sound that had waked me to begin with. And I saw a figure moving carefully among the sleeping bodies. I caught my breath and watched a moment, until in relief I noted that it was only Reuben Bradene, still awake, and moving toward the raft. I watched him in some curiosity.

He stepped carefully onto the raft, balanced himself so as not to jar the

vessel too much, and then tip-toed over to Patsy Bradene. And then I seen
that he carried a cover of some description. He knelt over his sleeping wife
and with great care spread the cover such as it was over her, tucking it in here
and there, gently as a mother covering her child. Then he crept back to the
dying fire. He stirred that some and it blazed up. He threw on some more fuel
and sat there beside it, his hands spread across to ward off the chill.

I lay back again with a sigh and was about to slip off to sleep when I was
arrested by a gentle sound, and I rose once more on my elbow and listened
intently. What I heard was a soft humming, melodious, and then the humming drifted into gentle whistling. It was that same hymn that Patsy Bradene
was wont to attack with such vigor, but this time the melody was true and
beautiful, in no way what Patsy Bradene delivered.

It was Reuben, I realized at last, holding his hands spread over the fire,
humming and whistling alternately, with the true pitch and careful rhythms
of a born musician.

I must have slept again for I was jarred into consciousness by a rocking
of the raft, and I looked up to see Patsy Bradene, carrying the cover, lurch-
ing across the raft and onto the shore. It was by then the first early light of
day. She stepped carefully as she could, which was but awkwardly I noted, to
where Reuben had fallen asleep by the dead fire, his knees drawed up against
the cold, and she carefully spread out the cover and dropped it gently over
him, kneeling to tuck it about him as he had earlier tucked it about her, then
rising, and with a sudden retch, she grabbed her hand for her mouth and
made quickly for the trees.

She was gone a few moments before she come back, wiping her mouth
across her sleeve and looking woeful as a dog, and sick as one, too. She
lurched back onto the raft, jarring it again, and returned to her sleeping spot,
dropped unceremoniously onto it, and within a minute was snoring.

I woke at last to the bright light of early morning to find that Reuben
Bradene for all his lack of sleep was awake before me, tending the coffee pot.
I noted too that the cover was shifted once more to Patsy Bradene, and for
a moment I wondered if I had dreamed the whole thing. No one else of the
party stirred nor looked likely to stir for some time.

Reuben and I drank coffee and breakfasted on cold corndodger. Still,
Patsy had not stirred. I took myself into the cabin and set about to wash myself, for I was uncomfortable of the grime of the trip. But getting myself together proved to be an arduous task under those circumstances. So simple a
chore as washing my face and sundry other parts was so complicated aboard
the raft that I thought I could understand why the river people did give way
before it and accept slovenliness as a way of life.

Ah, no. But there was surely enough water about that great river that
there'd be no excuse for not washing yourself. Did a body want to, he could.
And so I did and felt much better for it.

By noontime, Patsy was abroad but just barely, and from her unhappy demeanor, I could tell she would not be up to the trip out to find Martha Elen for any time soon.

"Reuben," I said in sudden inspiration, "if ye'll show me the way, why I think I'd like to walk around Ste. Genevieve and see the town."

"Why, of a certainty," he said and pointed the way. "It an't far out to wher yer sister is," he added, "that we cain't make the trip when it's cooler." I did not comment on that. I was sure that by the time it was cooler, Patsy Bradene would feel more like moving about. As it was, she just sat forlornly, dangling her feet into the river, and barely lifted her head as I gathered myself together and walked off in the direction Reuben had pointed me.

Well, I had not ever been to any big city in my entire life, and me already in my twenty-third year and the mother of two babes. In truth, I don't suppose that Ste. Genevieve did qualify as a great city, but it was by far the largest I had ever visited.

Jacob had claimed upwards of 2,000 souls—even if you didn't count the blacks—for Ste. Genevieve District. I had had a hard time believing that, but standing on a main thoroughfare, looking about, watching men and women—all strangers to me—going about their business, I had to confess that perhaps he had been accurate of his figures and that a great many of that number did reside in this city proper, for I had ne'er seen such a turmoil of people.

"Remember," Jacob had said, "many of those ye'll see be'nt from here atall, fer the river trade brings folk from far off to business here."

Still, I was impressed and a little frighted as I made my way along the street, and I gathered my skirts close against the dust, held my shawl tightly, for in spite of the summer heat, I felt that modesty forbade my going without such cover, and I walked quickly and alertly along the street, trying not to convey by any manner that I was nervous or at all unaccustomed to such activity, yet heartily wishing me back in the woods which I understood as I could not understand this loud and teeming place.

I slowed to turn a corner and was immediately arrested at the activity within one of the small rooms upon the street. A door stood open and inside upon tables and shelves were copious bonnets of all description and a small lettered sign that proclaimed this to be a milliner's establishment. I stood and stared through the door into the dim interior and watched as two women sewed, attaching ribbon and feathers to bonnets, and it fair took my breath away. I had ne'er owned nothing but a simple country bonnet of the sort that I had on, but I had seen a few of the elegant headgear that others had brought from distant places, made by actual milliners.

It would ne'er do to covet such an article, but I could not see that it would hurt to examine one or two, and I stepped cautiously into the establishment, for a moment right embarrassed at my own forwardness. But I was soon put at ease by the two cheerful women who proved to be mother and daughter

145

and who was quite as open and common as any other women I had met, and they showed me what they was making and some of the forms that they used and told of various customers who ordered from them, for they could obviously tell that there was no sale to be had from me and was most generous with their explanations.

"The most elegant of these is usually fer the kinds of females of which ye probably have no notion, fer they abound in port cities such as this and are the kinds that can oft afford the feathers and furbelows that more modest maids and matrons cannot, though," she added quickly, "we do sell to those, too."

I did not ask for more explanation of that, for I was not as ignorant of the ways of the world as she might have thought. Nor did I remark either to them or myself that their trade should include those ruder elements of society, for I knowed that to be unreasonable, too. I only fingered and admired their work, and they seemed pleased to show it off to me. I at last realized, reluctantly, that I was passing far too much time in such frivolousness, and I bade them good day and stepped back out into the hot afternoon.

As I turned the corner I caught myself just as I nearly stepped right into an oncoming person. I halted and he also and I glanced modestly at the ground and would have let him pass around me, but he accosted me and murmured, "Ah, dear little bird and where d'ye nest?"

I was taken back quite some and looked up at the man before me, for he was quite tall, and then caught my breath in a surprised gasp, for it was Eremus Lodi himself, I was certain, smiling down at me.

"Why, Sir," I began, but he interrupted me with something like a bow and reached for my hand. "Little maid," he said, "an' why is it that I've ne'er seen ye before this?"

Well, I was some constrained for then it occurred to me that Eremus Lodi did not seem to recognize me. But perhaps not thinking to stumble upon the modest wife of a pastor coming out of a milliner's in Ste. Genevieve would be reason enough for such lack of recognition.

"Sir, Master Lodi," I started to say, quite confused about how to approach the subject.

"Ah, an' she knows who I am, this little bird," he smiled, and I stared hard at him then, for he seemed to be talking in a manner that I could not comprehend. "Little bird," indeed. I noted then that he seemed to be under some peculiar humor, for his mouth was twisted, his eyes was glazed under their bushy brows, and he swayed slightly.

I stared hard at him, almost brazenly, so startled was I at his demeanor. His face was pale and he seemed not so strong as I remembered, nor was he entirely coherent. Daft or drunk. I could not be certain which, but whichever I need not have anything to do with him.

Suddenly, he lifted his cap flourishing it and bowed low. "Such a sweet little bird," he murmured again. "Where is your nest? Let us fly to your nest."

"Sir!" I endeavored to step around him, but smiling in a most peculiar fashion, he blocked my path. "Sir!" I repeated. "Let me pass." I had no intention then of identifying myself. I was sorely disappointed and only wanted to be shut of him. But that was not his intention, for he reached and grasped my hand and pulled me toward him before I could even read his intent and circled my waist with his great paw. "Come fly, little bird," he sang. "Come fly."

I did not know what to do. I could scream and alert the milliners, for though others passed, they made no particular motion toward us. I did not want to bring a distress against Eremus Lodi, for I was certain by now that he was drunk and probably would be properly shamed when he come to himself. But I could not allow myself to be so handled in a public place. I could not, public or private, allow myself to be so handled.

"Let go, Sir!" I said pulling hard away from him. "You mistake me and when your sobriety returns you will be most shamed."

"Ah, dear little bird, drunk, drunk, no I an't drunk, not drunk of anything mayhap the loveliness before me. I would have that, my little bird, devil take the cost," he announced, and I commenced to become frightened, for we was being bypassed by various folk as if it were not a strange sight at all for a lady to be so accosted. And then I recalled the words of the milliner and felt my face begin to burn with shame. Was I being so regarded?

I pulled but could not free myself. I took my other hand and attempted to force him to free me, but the shawl that I had been holding slipped when I let go of it and fell to the ground. I tried to reach down to rescue that from the dust, heard a strange, guttural laugh, and suddenly felt myself being hoisted into the air.

"Put me down, Sir! Help!" I cried and yet no one stopped nor did nothing, but a few sniggered into their hands or winked as they passed. What manner of mess was this? "Unhand me, Sir, for I am not what you think, but only a country woman come to town. You do ill use me."

"Ah, little bird, little birdy, birdy, that's what I shall do. Yes, dear, yes, ah yes, yes, I shall ill use ye, and won't it be merry?"

"Unhand me!"

"To my abode, dear bird, to my abode. Ye'll love my nest, fer certain. In my nest ye can flutter and flutter all ye will."

I felt myself being whirled in the air and was ready to screech my head off for there seemed no other recourse, when I sensed more than saw, a great shadow fall across us, and the sudden quiet, like that quiet that sometimes precedes a great storm.

"Mama," came that low and gentle voice that I recognized as O'Reilly's. "Be well, Mama." And I felt myself lifted from Eremus Lodi's great shoulders and set gently upon the ground. I staggered and swept my shawl from the ground where it lay and looked around.

"Ah," sighed Eremus Lodi and unburdened of me began himself to sway and a look of profound sadness seemed to touch his face. I stared full into that face and saw that it was pale and that the eyes was jaundiced, and the little beads of moisture about eyes and forehead was not the honest sweat of toil but of something else.

He grinned a wry and twisted little grin and then murmured, "Ah, my soul, ye've come at last. Dear lady," he nodded toward me, as calm suddenly as he had been distraught, "my dark soul has come. A man is not more than beast without his soul. And as I am without a permanent soul of my own, I keep a spare, which shadows me and comes to me in need. Every man ought have his very own soul, but, alas, there seem to be some of us lacking."

"Be go, Mama," said O'Reilly, holding the swaying and seemingly confused Eremus Lodi with one strong arm, and waving me on with the other. "Be go safe, Mama." He gave me a gentle, sad look, but said nothing more, but that look was enough, for I knowed that black being's countenance to be usually expressionless, and I was therefore considerably took up with that look he give me.

O'Reilly then turned and, lifting the great bulk of his master as if it had been nothing, he carried him in his arms back in the direction that Eremus Lodi had first come and disappeared from view around a corner. I composed myself as well as I could and cast as disdainful a glance as I could manage at the small assembled group and said quite proudly, "Let me pass!"

I had no more stomach for investigating Ste. Genevieve, and I turned back the way I come, passing the milliner's shop without even looking in. It would be hard to tell which was most uncomfortable—that I was hot with anger or burned with shame. I did not even bother to wrap the shawl modestly about me. Did not anyone about seem to care over much for modesty, it seemed to me.

I had not gone but a short ways before I glanced back over my shoulder, though I knowed that I should not, but curiosity got the best of me. A figure was just pulling away from the crowd and with some determination of purpose seemed to be coming after me.

Well. I had not no intention of conversing with anyone. I desired only to get back to the barge and the Bradenes and that in a hurry too. I quickened my steps and hurried on. But I was sensible of steps behind me, wh'er I actually heard them or thought I did, I was not really sure, and it took all my will to keep from turning my head and looking back.

I marched ahead, looking neither here nor there, but only straight ahead of me, but that sense of being followed stayed with me. At last I could not restrain myself from looking back and indeed that figure did seem to be keeping pace with me. I had only a quick glance so could not quite make it out. Did he follow me all the way to the barge, I could tell him he'd regret it.

I determined that I would not hurry any more than usual. It was broad day and I was in no wise afeared of being accosted. I was ready for it this time, modest or no, and he who give me even an inkling of trouble was going to hear about it and hear about it loud! So much had I worked myself into a fury, that at length I did slow my steps a' purpose, thinking that I was in the mood to give what-for to anyone who wanted it.

And indeed the steps then did seem to gain on me, and I strolled on, making my purposeful way back toward the river. When at last the steps were only a few yards behind me, I stopped and turned around to confront whoever it was who was following me.

He stopped, too, grinned at me, spittle running down the thin hairs upon his face, and with unaccountably grubby paw, he lifted his hat and inclined at the waist toward me, his floppy ear thus exposed before the world.

I said nothing, only stared at him, too surprised to be afraid, though truth to tell, in encounter after encounter with this less than human being, I had ne'er really ever felt true fear—a little apprehension, some annoyance, even anger—but no fear.

He scratched at himself, wiped his greasy sleeve across his mouth, hiked up his tattered buckskins, and slapped his ragged cap back on his head, still grinning like a lunatic, the spittle continuing its regular progress down his chin.

"Heh, heh, heh. I know ye. I know ye," he slobbered, mixing spit with words and spraying both at me. I stepped back.

"I know ye, I know ye, pretty lady, pretty lady, I know ye. Ye be from south of Cape Girardeau, now be an't ye?"

"Well, Sir," I said drawing myself up, "I don't know you, nor do I care to know you." And I whirled and stepped briskly along the dusty path.

I could hear him chuckling foolishly behind me. "I know ye. I know ye. I know ye." And I shuddered. Not from fear but more from loathing.

When I got to the raft, I found Patsy up and looking much perkier than she had when I left, and Jacob the riverman also was working about the barge, whistling and generally looking fit for someone who had had such encounter with the spirits as he had had the night before.

To their inquiries, I only said that my tour of the town had been interest-ing, and let it go that. To my mind, it was to everyone's benefit that I forget the entire incident. And thus I made no mention of the rascal Drooly either.

We was making preparations to leave the boat, Reuben and Patsy and me. "Mayhap," said Patsy, "yer sister's husband will be returned by the time we get there?"

"Ah," I sighed, "Joseph McCade being the son of one of them old log-hunters and with the blood of the wanderer in him, who knows when he might return?"

At that Jacob perked up. "A longhunter ye say? Ah, that's too bad," he said sorrowfully, but I could detect the twinkle in his eyes, and I readied myself for the story that was bound to come.

"Ther was a longhunter of my acquaintance when I was young," he drawled, hiking up his britches. "T'was said that he went off an' left his wife an' family fer months an' then fer years at a time. His woman, tolerable stout and hardworkin', did manage to keep the family goin' th'u it all, though it was also said that she commenced to get weary of it.

"Wal, one day he started off an' promised as he always done not to be gone long an' she looked at him most sorrowful an' she says, 'Go, n'en, but when ye come back, ye'll take what ye find an' ask no questions.

"Now it an't recorded what he said to that, but sure enough he was gone one, two, three and more years, so that by the time he come back, why he was near a stranger, but he greeted his woman cheerfully enough an' she him an' he remarked that there was three small young'uns about that he did not know. 'An' who do these belong to?' he asked, an' his woman replied that they belonged to Master Morris that worked the land beyond the creek.

"Wal, that old longhunter then remarked to hisself that them small young'uns not only called his woman 'Ma' but immediately taken to callin' him 'Pa'.

"Then that old longhunter sighed an' hugged his woman an' then he hugged them young young'uns and ne'er a word was said about it, though it's told that he was cured of longhuntin' an' stayed clos't about home ever after."

With that Jacob give me a long, sidewise glance, Otto grunted, Reuben smiled, and Patsy laughed heartily. I only smiled a little smile. For certain, Jacob the riverman did not know Martha Elen McCade, and I did!

"Yer sister, she's settled with a group a' settlers west a' here, but not far," Patsy Bradene said that as we started in the late afternoon, leaving the river behind and following an easy path westward.

"They's four er five cabin together there fer pertection, so even 'ithout her man, she an't in no particular danger, ye'll see. The worse thing about it is the walk. Onct ye get used to ridin' the river, it do come as a inconvenience to have to make yer way by foot over land," she sighed.

But truth to tell, according to my lights, it was hardly no walk at all, and though Patsy Bradene was puffing some by the time we come in view of the little cluster of cabins, I had hardly a hard breath. The cabins, though not uncommon close, was close enough to be well in view of one another, gardens and patches of trees between, and that creek branch that such outposts depended upon meandered among them.

Those cabins was most of them not particularly well put together and they was all new. The one was outsized, however, by any standards. I had ne'er seen a log cabin so big, as a matter of fact, nor so ill put together. And, lo, that was the one that Patsy and Reuben Bradene directed me to. It was a good thing it was summer and that it was dry, because from the looks of that structure, it would ill protect against either cold or wet. But it was big.

The figure I saw standing in the doorway was not what I was expecting either. But coming closer I recognized that wild thatch of red atop her head, though otherwise my little sister Martha Elen, once so slim and light upon her feet, was round as a little gourd. But I knowed better than to comment on it.

We embraced with many squeals and giggles as might have been expected, while Reuben and Patsy stood beaming, and right away Martha Elen would show me about her cabin, that monstrous, leaky affair.

"Joseph McCade," she announced, "don't never go for things in a small way. He's always one to say that either you think big or you think little. An't no in between."

I did not say nothin', but she must have caught my expression as I stared at one of the many gaps in the wall, for she added, "Well, he does have much to finish when he returns, but like he always says, 'You can smooth out the rough when you have the time. But if you aim to have it big, you got to get it thataway from the start, or you'll only be satisfied with what you got.' He has big plans," she said, her chin stuck high into the air. "Big plans. He don't aim to settle for little or naught." And she look at me, her lips tight, her eyes sparkling as if just daring me to say aught about him or her house or anything else.

"Well," I said at last, "in truth it is a big house, and you'll surely have room for as big a family as you want." It was as noncommittal as I could make it.

She stared at me, nodded agreeably, looked around, and then burst into tears. "When I see him again, by the time I get through with him, why that man'll be lucky does he ever father another child!'" she managed to blubber at last, and she sunk down on one of the big stumps that passed for a stool before her fireplace and started to cry again.

"Ah, Martha Elen," I said and looked around, for I did not know what else to say. I knowed from childhood experience that you never knowed how she was like to react to anything you might say. Reuben and Patsy had peeked in the door and, seeing the scene within, had backed quickly out.

Martha Elen jumped up again. "I'll not hear a word against Joseph McCade. Why he's as jolly and sweet as e'er a man could be and loving, too, and would you believe it or not, he's as hard a worker as they come." She'd stuck out her lower lip again, just daring me to say otherwise. "It's just that he can't seem to stick to one chore long enough to get it accomplished, afore he must flit off to somethin' that looks more promisin'. He an't lazy," she said, her arms akimbo. "He just lacks perseverance."

Here she paused again and started to point out other admirable features of her leaky dwelling, the copious loft, for instance, the steps not quite finished, the wood for the cradle, started but lacking rockers, a table but no chairs. "He has all this work laid out for the winter, you see," she said most unconvincingly. And then she stopped in the middle of the room and sighed. "He promised to be back a month gone, an' he still an't home."

And then as if reading my mind, she said, "Naw, an't nothin' happened to him. Nothin' don't never happen to him; he's blessed by charms that get him through thick or thin. He took off toward Booneslick, just at the drop of a hat. He was splittin' wood and plannin' garden, and someone come along and said how fertile the land west was an' it just fer the takin' along the Missouri, and then and there, he dropped his axe and packed his sack and waved me good-bye an' called that he'd be back afore I even knowed he was gone and probably with more land and promises of riches. And he was gone. Like that. And when he gets back," she sniffed, "I plan to snatch the hair clean off his head!"

I had to laugh. I couldn't help it. She glared at me and then seeing me laugh, her own face lit up, for she was like that, her moods flitted, coming and going, the way a bird hops from limb to limb.

We chatted some more and then she pitched in and begun to make a meal for us, and I was relieved to see that she had plenty of supplies. "The neighbors' gardens supply me," she said, "an' Joseph McCade left coin enough for what I need from Ste. Gen. Joseph makes his way, actually, a-trappin', at which he's greatly skilled, an' so he oft has money and he's been generous with it, too, so's our neighbors are forebearin' as most of 'em owes him something, which he probably won't never try to collect neither. Besides," she added with a sigh, "ever'body likes him. He's most likeable and that's a big part of his problem, that nobody can't say no to him. Not even me."

We ate at last, and Reuben and Patsy headed back toward the river while there was still light, promising to return once they had poled their salt-loaded boat north to St. Louis.

"We're safe here as anywhere," Martha Elm had insisted to the Bradenes. "We an't had no trouble of any sort, enough of our neighbors having reputations for fierceness that we are left alone. Else Joseph McCade would ne'er have left me here," she added.

We sat out of doors and chatted and visited well into the evening, and the moon, full and bright as it can sometimes be, eventually come up, illuminating the surroundings. "If you're afeared," said Martha Elen, "we can call upon one or another of the neighbors to sleep the night here."

I shook my head, for I truly was not frightened. I was accustomed to the woods nor did the dark usually fright me. On such a night, when the moon was high, the breeze cool and pleasant and the night sounds calm, it was not hard to sense God's presence and to appreciate His Plan. I stared off toward the horizon, blocked by the tall trees, the shadows playing gently among them. "No," I said, "no, I an't afraid."

I shared the oversized, if somewhat uncertain, bed with Martha Elen and remarked the cool breeze passing over us both from a near window and from the copious cracks all about and thought that pleasant, though it was on a late summer night. I'd not look forward to sleeping there come December.

Martha Elen's breathing was labored, as could be expected, and she groaned and tossed in her sleep so much that I found it hard to sleep myself. At length I rose and stood at the doorway and felt the cool breeze and listened to the various night noises and wondered about my own family and felt a pang of loneliness that life upon the river had shielded me from.

As I stared out toward the line of distant trees, I slowly become aware of a shadow among them that was not of them—a shadow foreign to the surroundings. I watched for a long time, peacefully unalarmed.

I was familiar with the shadow of O'Reilly the black, for he come and went about our house regularly. Sometimes I seen him, sometimes I sensed him, and sometimes I did not even know that he had come and gone until one or the other of the children told me. He was like a dark angel looking over us, particularly over the children, and though he was closest perhaps to George—for they seemed to share a secret awareness—tiny Sarah likewise claimed him for her own, and they two could in some strange manner converse, for she, small babe, had as few words as did the silent black.

I had no way to know that the shadow I saw was O'Reilly, or even that it was human, only my instinct that told me it was protective.

Eventually, I returned to bed and weariness overcome me and I slipped into sleep, dreams overtaking me almost immediately. In my dream I even knowed they was dreams, yet they seemed so real.

I held George in my arms. He was an infant and yet he had that calm expression of aged wisdom that young children often express—wise as forever. And he was reaching out his arm, pointing, seeing something that I could not see, calling my attention to something. Yet all I could make out was a presence, a shadow, and even that I could not be certain of. "It's all right, Mama," said the baby George, gently patting my hand.

With the morning light, I rose, dressed myself and looked around. Martha Elen sat up in bed and yawned. I took the bucket and started for the branch. I had just reached the door when a loud voice, quite unfamiliar, sang out most cheerfully, "Hey, now, an' what's this, an' is it possible I be in the wrong house?"

I whirled around and a person on a pallet in the corner was sitting up. My confusion must have showed, for he laughed and rolled up on his knees. "Marty, me love," he cried for by that time Martha Elen was making for him, arms all outstretched, "an' who's this pretty lady ye sleepin' with whilst I was gone?"

With that he swung Martha Elen to him, and I thought it seemly to go on about my business and took myself on to the branch where I had first started. When I come back with my pail of water, Joseph McCade was seated and Martha Elen was on his knee, and she seemed to have explained my presence to him and he was most cheerful and happy to see me and said as much.

The Joseph McCade from my memory was indeed the same Joseph McCade that faced me, teasing, cheerful, impish, and bright-eyed.

"I comed in the night and stood right over ye," he said "an' nary one of ye fluttered a eye. I could just as easy been a savage Indian and scalped ye in yer sleep an' ye ne'er would a knowed it."

"Well," snapped Martha Elen in some sarcasm, recalling perhaps that she had decided to be put out with him, "you might get your scalp lifted an' not notice, but I for one would suspect something amiss I think, were I being scalped."

He laughed and slapped his thigh.

Now Martha Elen and Joseph McCade commenced to talk and where one left off the other picked up, and sometimes without waiting they interrupted or over-talked one another so that neither a' them nor me could have told what all was being said. I listened until I was quite tired of it and went outside and sat.

Eventually, they moved their conversation outside, but they must have caught up some, for they was by then taking turns talking, but in truth Joseph McCade was holding forth more than his wife. The man was naught if not expansive, for he regaled us with tales of the beauty and wealth of the western lands.

"The soil is so black an' the grass is so green an' the trees so tall an' the water so clear, why it fair makes a man's mind boil. Nor ere the Injuns so bad nor the winters so fierce nor the game so scarce nor the land so dear but what a man could buy an' settle an' make his fortune with less trouble far than in any other place I have ever been. An' south into the Ozarks, wher the Delaware are movin' to, ther's tradin' to be done with them."

"What's an Ozark?" asked Martha Elen suspiciously.

"H'it's French. Aux Arcs—with bows. That's what the French said when they first seen the Injuns with ther bows an' arries. Aux Arcs." And he laughed uproariously as if he had made a fine joke. "Ah, Marty, Marty, me wife, I see a future, a marvelous rich future, ahead fer us."

"Hmmmm," she sniffed in return, "any future you see had better be right here on this spot, for I an't movin' no more!"

"Ah, Marty," Joseph McCade went on as if he had not even heard her objection, "d'ye know the stories that I have heared? Stories of wondrous things beyond the woods and the hills, away beyond the Missouri even.

"Why, they tell of such things that ye cain't even hardly believe. They say ther's wondrous tribes of Injuns—a tribe of white Injuns, fer one, an' fer another Welch Injuns. Imagine that! Welch Injuns!"

"Now, Joseph," began Martha Elen.

"No. I seen the very man, the very person that was on his way to find them an' he swore that it was true, Injuns descended hundreds of years from Welch travelers. An' they told also of a one-eyed Injun tribe an' of a wide inland sea in which no fish can live and no man can drown! Think of it. Oh, Marty, Marty, Marty, now tell me ye don't want to view such wonders?"

"Joseph McCade!"

"An' they say ther's water spouts that shoot high into the air at such

154

regular intervals that ye could set yer timepiece by 'em, an' a wild canyon, so deep that they say h'it's the entrance to hell on earth, an' ther's bears they tell twicet the size of a large man, an' acres and acres an' miles an' miles, 'ithout end almost, of giant bison roaming treeless plains an' a tribe of dwarf Injuns an'. . ."

"Joseph McCade," Martha Elen interrupted indignantly, "Joseph Mc-Cade, do you believe all of that? Do you truly believe such nonsense?"

Joseph McCade, still almost breathless from his tale, paused for a long moment and stared at his wife. "Ah," he sighed slowly with a small smile, "ah, Marty, yes I do believe it. I believe all of it. I believe what I see. I believe what I hear. I believe what I dream, fer I am a believer. I believe that ther's a salt flat that goes almost as far's the eye could see, and beyond that a range of mountains so high that the snow covers ther tops all times a' the year. I believe that ther's gold in the streams an' trees so tall ye cain't see the top an' so wide that a dozen men hands joined an' arms stretched cain't reach around 'em.

"I believe all that, Marty, me love, because I'm a believer, an' I'll believe though I mayn't ne'er see it all in this life. But I desire to try. That's why I'm a believer."

Martha Elen had no answer to that but a long and profound sigh.

When I went to bed (in the over-sized bed, for Joseph McCade had declared that he would stay on the pallet, it not bein' "no fun to sleep with such a bloated woman," for which comment he got his ears boxed—in fun, I think), they was still arguing.

It was yet dark when I was awakened suddenly, for Martha Elen had sat straight up in bed, clutched my arm, and screeched, "Great God in Heaven!" At which I sat up too and looked around in alarm expecting scalping Indians in the least.

"My belly!" she cried and peering over in the corner where her husband lay in a mound, and noting that she had not yet roused him, she screeched again, this time with such force that Joseph McCade come up out of his sleep prepared for a fight.

Well, it did not take too much observation to realize that Martha Elen was in the early throes of childbirth, though not so near as both she and her husband seemed to fear, for they was both trying to give orders at the same time, neither one of them having no experience at all, but not letting that lack stand in their way.

It took some time, but I convinced both that we was still several hours away from the significant event, and they both settled down, a little glumly I thought. But at the earliest light, Joseph McCade was out and making the rounds of the neighbors alerting them as if for all the world this was the first event of its kind ever.

Well, fortunately, people is usually patient and understanding of these things.

Later on in the morning, as was the custom, neighboring ladies begun to join us so that there was quite a crowd about—telling tales, giving advice, and general gossiping, only one other than myself being of any real use, however.

So that in the late afternoon when things begun to get serious, all but the two of us went out to wait the events. By this time, of course, the fun had gone out of the whole thing for Martha Elen, and when she wasn't straining and sweatin' and groaning, she was complaining considerable about the whole affair, not the first woman in the world in that situation to be suggesting that her husband ought not be allowed to get off completely free of pain.

"Oh," laughed Mistress Liggins, an old goodwife of the neighborhood who was marvelous skilled in midwifery, "just consider how much trouble he went to to get you in this condition in the first place. Plumb put hisself out, he did."

But Martha Elen did not see the fun in it, but only gritted her teeth and rolled and groaned, but to her credit never screamed nor carried on the way I had seen women do.

"It does seem about here," said Mistress Liggins finally. "One more good, hard push now, girl. Push! Push!" I did feel for Martha Elen, for I could remember. "Push!" And then miraculously it was accomplished. "A girl," Mistress Liggins announced, handing over the little creature to me, which did seem over small by some, but I held her up for Martha Elen to admire. She only groaned again.

"An't it over?" she said.

At that Mistress Liggins give me a funny look and begun probin' about, as I wiped the babe down and begun to wrap it.

"I do think," Mistress Liggins announced at last, "that ther's another'n in there."

"Another'n?" squalled Martha Elen.

"I do b'lieve."

"Twins?"

"Another'n? Another'n? Joseph McCade!" screamed Martha Elen, and for a minute I thought she was about to jump out of bed and go after him, but she was took with another pain.

And grasping the comforter with both her hands, she grunted and groaned. "Push," cried Mistress Liggins, "Push. Here it comes." And sure enough, out popped a boy.

"Well," smiled Mistress Liggins handin' that one over to me, "ye got one of each kind so now ye can quit. Ye got two fer the price a' one."

But Martha Elen, looking up with glazed eyes, rolled her head slowly from side to side and groaned once more in pain, clutching at the ticking.

In some consternation, Mistress Liggins once more begun to probe, and I come around holding the small babe in hand. "It's not another'n is it?" I asked. "It's not three?"

"I hope that's all," said Mistress Liggins grimly and hardly had she got it out that another'n begun its trip, this time feet first as if to announce its male sex first thing, and we was in a sweat to get it out.

When that was accomplished, Martha Elen give a large sigh that I recognized and relaxed against the pillow.

"I do swear t'ye," said Mistress Liggins, "that I han't ne'er seen nothin the like this in my life before."

All three was by then givin' out lusty cries, and despite their small size, looked in all ways healthy as any other newborn. Martha Elen was breathing hard and not talking, whether taking in what she had experienced or simply tired, I did not know. Mistress Liggins and I in profound silence saw to the afterbirth and the cleaning up and still without a word wrapped the tiny babes—for side 'a side, they truly was wondrous small, miniatures, playthings—and placed them, packed them rather, into the unfinished cradle.

"I think," said Mistress Liggins, "that someone'd better finish this cradle, fer there's about to be a fair amount of rockin' necessary."

The atmosphere, when we announced the births, become festive, with laughing and congratulating, only a few of the crowd, which grew quickly as the news was spread abroad, asking hesitantly after the health of the babes. It was so unusual a circumstance that no one thought much beyond its happening.

Joseph McCade withdrew to visit with his wife and family. Standing close to the door, I heard some commotion within, and I pushed the door a jar and peeked in to make sure all was well.

Martha Elen was sitting up in bed, her face red, her voice loud, giving what-for to Joseph McCade, while he was himself talking and laughing and pointing at the three babies, and I thought that neither one of them was making theirselves understood. And maybe, I thought as I closed the door softly, that was as well.

After a while Joseph come back outside, and he was given cheers and congratulations as if he had indeed done something remarkable, though I could hear Martha Elen through the door still complainin'.

"I always said ye must start big," said Joseph McCade.

"Ah, if this is the way yer goin' to go," allowed some man I did not recognize, "why think on it, man, yer like to have twenty-five or thirty ere yer done."

The women gravitated together as they do, tiptoeing in twos and threes to see the babies, and returning shaking their heads and speaking in hushed tones.

"I hope it an't catching," said one.

"Wal, I wonder what they done to get them?"

"An' don't ye know that!" laughed another.

"I mean different, done different?"

"I didn't know they was but one way," said a third, and everyone laughed.

"Naw," said the first quite seriously, "I knowed a woman back in Carolina had twins onc't and then twice and finally don't ye know a third time, an' she was fair thin of it. Well, her husband, he was that fond of kraut and eggs— now that's different an't it, kraut an' eggs fer breakfast? Wal, she decided somethin' was sure amiss an' that bein' the only thing she could think of, wal, she just cut him off that kraut an' eggs 'til she was p.g. agin', an why that next birth was a single an' so from then on, the only time that man got kraut an' eggs was when she was already pregnant an' he couldn't do no harm, an' she never had no more twins after that!"

The men, too, apparently had some of the same questions, for I come up behind the cabin carryin water from the branch and happened upon a group of men, paying no attention and talking loudly, and I listened in to what they was sayin'. I probably should not have, but I found it amusin'.

"How ye s'pose he got so many on her? I'd love to know, fer I sure don't want to do the same," someone was saying.

"Why, an't no secret to that," laughed a tolerable old man of the group. "Randy as he ere, why he likely does all night what it takes me all night to do." And there was a general laugh at that. Well, for certain I could not make my appearance after that, so I waited, and after a time, the talk drifted on to other things, and I made my way around the corner looking as if I hadn't heard a thing out of the way and excused myself through them.

After the shock had wore off, Martha Elen was quite beside herself with pride, handling one or another of the babes and clucking at them the way you do, the way you just can't keep yourself from doing.

And there seemed to be no question of her havin' enough milk for the three of them, for there was several wives around that was still nursin' or about to give up nursin' that didn't mind pitchin' in, and there they'd sit, three different nurses, them infants growin' practically before your very eyes.

Martha Elen fended off all comments about what lay before her. "Oh, they're fine," she'd say, "they're no trouble."

Well, I didn't want to be around when all three of them young'uns got their legs and commenced to go in three separate directions all at the same time. She'd learn all about that in due time, I thought. She was in for a lesson, truly.

In the meantime, Joseph McCade was full of plans, and miraculously the first thing he did was to construct two more cradles, and he worked quickly and efficiently, albeit all three rocked some awkwardly. But they did rock.

By the time that Reuben and Patsy Bradene surfaced again, I was ready to go home. It had come to me early that with the novelty, Martha Elen would not lack for help for quite a time and I really was not needed. I had been away from my own family long enough and I was ready to go.

So I made my departure both eagerly and sadly, knowing that it was possible that I might not see my sister and her sweet babes again for a long time, did Joseph McCade have his way about removin' to the west.

And Joseph McCade, generous as promised, made offer of coin to Reuben Bradene, grateful for my presence, which coin Reuben of course declined.

It did take some persuasion, too, to get Patsy Bradene to leave them three small young'uns, for she hung over those cradles, clucking of her tongue and smiling foolishly, and at one point asked Martha Elen, "How'd the world ye ever do that?"

"Ah, Pat," drawled Reuben Bradene.

And then we was back on the river, making a quick trip of it going with the current instead of against it. I could not contain myself from thinking how fortunate I was to have Cyrus Pritchard instead of Joseph McCade. For though Cyrus was a believer, too, it was a different sort than Joseph McCade, and Cyrus's believing would not prompt him to drop everything and seek the land beyond the horizon.

New Madrid District
1811

Chapter 10

A Reluctant Conversion

The river was at flood and we was upon it. Mindful again of Lot's Wife, I would not look back, though my spirit was weary with the parting.

The keelboat upon which we rode was commodious, carrying goods and passengers alike with crew aplenty, including Patsy and Reuben Bradene and the riverman Jacob and his brother Otto, as well as other lively rivermen given to singing and chanting and calling out various raucous things to one another. I was busy enough keeping sight of Sarah Elizabeth, who flitted here and there and hung out over the water and asked interminable questions of whoever she come upon, and in the entertaining of Peter, who like most babes was not content to sit a-lap for too great a time and worried and fussed and wiggled until I was sorely wearied of it. Yet I das't not let him loose, for he was of that toddling stage and would have been overboard at the first rough water.

I had little time to worry the whys and wherefores of our destination. Nor did I need to, having had time aplenty to consider as Cyrus had filled appointment after appointment in the New Madrid District with Brother Kencaid, sending back various letters, each one giving more and more certainty of our eventual remove to that southern place.

Cyrus had felt the Call, had heeded it, and though I was not anxious to go, his success and the desperate need of the Lord's people there made him ever certain of the legitimacy of that Call.

So that the visit, which was at first to be but a few weeks, extended over several months. Cyrus's letters, regularly written, were irregularly received, often coming in a bunch all at once, or not at all, for there was times that he made reference to things as if he had written them to me, yet I had not heard of them.

"Brother Gilbert, he who was so generous to me earlier (I had not heard of Brother Gilbert), asked me did I preach duty or doctrine, and I told him that having studied upon the matter, I could hardly see where the one left off and the other begun. He only laughed at that and said that he did agree but that I'd find my benches more likely filled did I stick with doctrine. 'Most of the brothers and sisters I've noted,' he said, 'would ruther hear of doctrine, as that applies to them, than of duty, fer duty y'know is always a trifle of an inconvenience.'"

Cyrus did not try to pretty the picture. He wrote that life in the New Madrid District was passing hard, for the district was filling rapidly with divers folk, many of them of no account at all, and the talk of conflict with British and Indian and even French was constant. And the climate was such that you could almost count on the well and ill being about equal, for the swampy area to the west did seem to breed an almost constant fever in this or the other one.

"Brother Gilbert and his wife have been an uncommon comfort in that, however. Theirs is a blessed marriage of age as each one has already raised a family and lost a spouse. Sister Gilbert is one of those folk—like that black O'Reilly of Eremus Lodi's household—who is talented with the procurement and use of various herbs. 'I can control the fever, I guess, as well as ary man or woman,' she said without seeming immodest in her assertion. Still, it is something we will have to face," he wrote.

"See that feller yonder?" said Patsy and I looked toward where she nodded and saw a pair of male passengers occupying the center of the raft. They had held theirselves aloof, and so I had paid them little mind, only noting that they was both too carefully dressed to be rivermen, the one long and the other short.

"Which?" I said. "I see two."

"Well, both, exactly. The littler one calls hisself a preacher. He's Methodist an' says that he's gain' to New Madrid to save the heatherns and the infidels, as well as the mis-led which he said was Baptist and Universalist and Presbyterian and Campbellite and Fullerite and Newlight and I fergit whatall, as he ticked off a whole string as not being properly saved."

"He's going to save them?" I said.

"What he said."

"Well, then, he does have a great deal more power than any other living man I ever heard of, lest it was Jesus Christ himself."

"What I thought," said Patsy, handing the baby back to me. "Though I did not say nothin', as I seen that his head was nought but a piss-pot fer what it contained."

I could not restrain myself from laughing at that crude observation, but turned the conversation elsewhere, "I'd appreciate did you help me keep an eye on Sarah Elizabeth," I said, "for what she can't think to get into probably can't be thought of. I ne'er worry of George, for he's solemn and dependable, but that girl is a worry wart." I glanced around and sure enough found her, for her tousled and bright red hair always give her presence away. She was a-poking around a bucket that probably was not none of her business, while

162

George stood some paces off, giving her a disapproving stare. It was something he often had occasion to do, as well as the rest of us.

Still, considering that first year of her life, I had to wonder if mayhap some of all that dire excitement did rub off on her and so color her personality. For at not quite seven years of age she was adventurous and plucky as little girls almost never was, as George at eleven years even was not.

George with the passing of years had lost some of that strange instinctiveness of his baby years. It was perhaps his prolonged contact with other children and with his sister that made him more normal in that respect. However, he still was possessed of that amulet that O'Reilly had given him and wore it continually.

That emblem come up lost one day. George missed it and set about searching for it, the thong apparently having broken. I was myself some relieved, I thought, to see it gone, until he begun to take on in a most hysterical manner, and then I commenced to hunt and search, too.

At last it was Sarah who appeared with it, handing it over. "Here," she said. "Here's the ignorant old thing." From the grim manner in which she gave it over, I decided that she was the one who had had it—under her tick, mayhap, or in some hiding place of her own devising.

She marched away, adding in parting, "It don't work, no way."

George was so relieved that he did not challenge her as he otherwise would have, only set to work cutting a thong from a groundhog hide kept dried for that purpose.

The maneuvering of a raft at flood was not always so simple as it might look, for the river was given to spreading out, and it took some skill and knowledge of its habits to keep with the proper channel and not get caught in the low and marshy lands of flood as the current was determined to have its way, to travel at its own speed, and carry whatever was in the river along with it.

The spring freshet was always worrisome, yet necessary, too, for flatboats that depended on the increased speed of the current, yet feared the vagaries of the swollen river. But the spring just passed had been especially wet and wild, and the river reflected that, so the rivermen, which included Patsy Bradene, were wont to jump to action often, all hands, to avert disaster—collision with the trash of the river or the shoreline or any of the normal postures that the river throwed up now and again as if to challenge the attention of those who would use it.

"Look alive!" cried the riverman Jacob, and the rest of the crew swung into action, navigating the raft out of the path of a bouyant object which proved to be a cow or perhaps an ox, for it was bloated out of proportion and could have been either. I shuddered and pulled the baby close to me and called out to Sarah to get away from the side, for she was hanging over, much taken with the bobbing, rolling cow corpse. She was yet young to worry over, but did her proclivities not change direction, I would have wonder later on at her possibilities for courtship.

Cyrus had written of the land around New Madrid as being flat and occasionally marshy, for the great swamp extended almost from Cape Girardeau to there and farther west and north until it hung up with a curious mountain range to the north and west, "Suddenly," he wrote, "as if on purpose it was throwed up as a barrier to the marsh.

"It is as beautiful a mountain range as I have yet to see from a distance, though I'm told it's small and comprised more of groups of peaks than of continuous mountains. And much of the land that lies between belongs, I'm also told, to Eremus Lodi. 'Too beautiful,' claimed my informant Brother Gilbert, 'to be owned by one man.'

"'Ah,'" I replied to him, "'Eremus Lodi may take title of the land, but he can ne'er take title of the view.' And Brother Gilbert nodded and agreed with me."

I had tried to reply to these various letters, but could not tell from the letters I received how many of those I had sent had been received. I wanted to know of the particular living arrangement and the opportunity for school and of the various congregations to be tended, for I knowed by then that there would be more than one. Part of an answer I got back, whether by design or no I could not say.

"There is many professed faiths here and more coming daily and there is infidels enough, wh'er professed or not, I sometimes think, to fill hell and run it over. But I have found all manner of Baptists, New School and Old School both, Free Will and Regular, hungering for truth at the same times bickering severely among theirselves over points of doctrine. But I have said it before— so long as there be Baptists, there will be bickering.

"The prospects for harmony here," Cyrus had written, "is slim, at least for now. Aside from the bickering among the like-minded, there is oft turmoil between groups whose doctrines differ considerably. But I must hasten to assure you, there are hopeful signs.

"Not long gone whilst I was making rounds of congregations—for there is many little Baptist groups comprised of few members, but sincere in their hope and their need—come up a great storm and I was forced to take shelter with a Methodist and his family.

"He could not have been more courteous or kinder, even when he determined that our doctrines were so in conflict. He fed and housed me and in the end sent me on my way, better provisioned than I had come to him.

"We did fall to discussing doctrine and as those things happen, we matched text for text, arguing our cases, and each come away only more convinced of the other's error, and we agreed that the only thing upon which we was agreed was that we did not agree.

"'If yer certain,' laughed my host, 'that a sprinkle does not represent a baptism, only a total immersion, why then ye must think that them Dunkards be three times as baptised as ye.'

"'Perhaps,' I replied with my own laugh, 'but it's not likely that drowning for the cause was what John the Baptist had in mind.'

"I did think that Methodist, mistook though he surely was, was sound in his faith and honorable withal as well as neighborly and Christian. There are professed Baptists that I could not say as much of."

It come to me at last, that letter requesting that I pack up our belongings, bid farewell to our friends and brothers and sisters in Christ, and finally follow him into the wilderness. The letter was delivered by Reuben and Patsy for to make certain it arrived.

Reuben and Patsy would help see to our removal, as Cyrus was near overwhelmed in getting up a cabin for us and by the work of the Lord, which of course always took precedence.

I wrote to my family and to Martha Elen and Joseph McCade, who in spite of periodic promises otherwise, still made their home near Ste. Genevieve, in their commodious if shaky dwelling, with their three children. For as if she had got stubborn over the matter, Martha Elen, having done three times the work at once, steadfastly refused to conceive, though Joseph McCade was most eager to try his hand again and see what wonder he could produce.

"I'll do it when he's willing to give me the credit I deserve," Martha Elen announced to me on my last visit to her. In truth, Joseph McCade did seem willing to assume the entire responsibility for that miraculous birth, going into prolonged and detailed description for any willing to listen—not many at last, for he had about run hisself dry with neighbors both near and far over the matter.

It was to Clara Cuthcart that I clung longest ere we left, for she was as a sister—nay more than sister—to me, and the leaving of her and her lively brood (which had increased by three in the time that mine had increased by two) was harder than I ever thought possible.

But when we was loaded and on board, I set my face to the morrow and ne'er looked back.

The rivermen pulled the raft to an island late in the day, though there was still plenty of light.

"We ere not so far upstream from New Madrid now," said Patsy Bradene, "but too far to float in the dark, and this island is right commodious and comfortable and safe."

"Safe? Safe from what?" I asked.

"Whatever might needs be safe from," said Patsy Bradene reasonably.

Campfires was soon lighted, fish procured, and a meal prepared. Besides the crew there was an elderly couple that kept much to theirselves—mainly I think because neither could hear so well, for they shouted to each other a great deal—as well as the Methodist and his companion and me and my three children.

Peter was a lively enough little feller that he not only kept me occupied, he managed to keep most everyone else occupied until, mercifully, he dropped to sleep on the comforter I had spread. I brushed his hair oft his face and covered him tenderly against the bugs. And then I worried.

We were going into the land of the fever. That was no secret. We had already lost one to the fever, and though I did not want to question the Lord's Will, I found myself doing just that.

After supper we gathered close by the fire, not because we was cold as much as we wanted to keep the bugs and insects at bay. Someone I did not remember who suggested at last that we might sing a few songs to pass the time. But that idea was not greeted enthusiastically by the rivermen.

"Best not to call attention to ourselves, unnecessarily," said one.

"Oh, now," interrupted Jacob the riverman, and I could tell from the twinkle about his eye and his wicked glance toward Patsy and Reuben that he had a story to tell. "Now, singin', why if bein' safe is what yer after, sing, by all means sing, fer haven't ye heard how Patsy Bradene saved us all from a b'ar with her singin'?"

"Ah," said Reuben.

"An't so," said Patsy. "What e'er the scoundrel's got to tell, just an't so."

Undeterred, the riverman went on, "Why we, the three of us, was camped on the shore near to the woods one time and this great b'ar, betimes fishin' er thirsty, come out of the woods and onto the shore, and seein' us, why it give a great growl and started fer us.

"Wal, of a certainty I thought we was dead, fer I could see no escape except the river, and that too far to swim. I thought mayhap I'd try prayin', but before I could get into position, why that b'ar retched out and grabbed up Reuben, and don't ye know, slung him under its arm and started off.

"I supposed then that it was a female, mayhap, and had took a shine to Reuben and that we'd ne'er see him ever agin', er if we did, he'd be follered by cubs, half man and half b'ar." Here the riverman Jacob's face took on a most sorrowful look, and he shook his head from side to side whilst Patsy Bradene murmured, "Not a word a' truth to it, not one word."

"But Patsy knowed what to do, fer ye see she knowed to calm the savage beast took naught but music, so she took in a deep breath and in one mighty blast set sail upon a tune.

"Wal, that b'ar, it stopped dead in its track, stood perfectly still—fer those of you'uns as has heard Patsy Bradene in song, ye certainly must know what the beast was feelin'.

"Now, Pat, sensin' that the beast was becalmed, why she raised her voice a mite louder at the chorus and that b'ar dropped Reuben right on the spot.

166

And by the time Patsy had got to the second verse, the b'ar had disappeared right into the woods, its paws to its ears, and me and Reuben was left to decide t'were it better to let Patsy finish the song an' risk a wholesale desertion of the wood by the wild critters er to stop up her mouth an' risk the return a' that b'ar.

"Fortunate, Patsy took a coughing fit at that point and we was saved of the decision. N'er did the b'ar come back."

"T'ain't no truth atall in it," said Patsy Bradene, while everyone laughed.

I thought it a harmless story, but when I looked at Patsy I noted that there was a hurtful look upon her face, and I left off my own smiling at that. Reuben looked troubled himself and reached over and patted Patsy's hand as if to comfort her.

"Aw, Pat," said the riverman Jacob at last, "tis only a story; don't nobody believe it." But Patsy's hurt expression remained, and the riverman Jacob muttered, "Aw," and kicked at the dirt with his boot. But in short order Patsy's good nature returned and all was well.

As the night commenced to fall, the conversation come sluggish, for everyone was passing weary. But then the Methodist who insisted that he be called The Reverend Mr. Fox (his companion was Master Longene) turned his attention to Reuben Bradene.

"Have ye found Christ?" he asked amiably enough.

Reuben frowned deeply and considered the question.

The Reverend Mr. Fox repeated the question. "Have ye found Christ?"

"Why," answered Reuben Bradene at long last, "I han't ne'er lost Him."

"I mean," said Mr. Fox, "are ye saved?"

"From what?"

"Saved from eternal damnation, of course!"

"Why, Sir, I'd give the world to know."

"You don't know whether or not yer saved?" asked the Reverend Mr. Fox, and Reuben Bradene slowly shook his head from side to side.

"Well, Sir, I know that I am saved. And Mister Longene knows that he is saved. And if ye know it not, why then I feel a deep responsibility to help ye seek salvation fer yer soul."

Reuben frowned and looked at Patsy and she returned his frown.

"Wal, now, Sir," said Reuben at last, "I don't think that's possible. I do not think that ye can save me no more than I can save myself."

"And who, Sir, d'ye think will save ye?"

"Why, Jesus Christ hisself I think will do't or, no, that's not right neither," said Reuben becoming quickly entangled in his theology. "God already done it, 'fore the world was e'er set in motion."

I thought that a right good answer and noted with satisfaction that everyone was listening, except for the old couple, who probably could not understand what was said anyway. They only stared out over the water, the old man commencing to nod off.

"A Calvinist! A Calvinist!" cried out the Reverend Mr. Fox in a voice that suggested he had just caught sight of a many-legged spider.

"Baptist," corrected Patsy Bradene.

"Wal," said the Reverend Mr. Fox, "I surely do have words fer ye, many, many words, for yer misstook and misled and ill-read and wrong." At which he grabbed for his Bible for ammunition.

But it was grown dark enough that he couldn't read it at all, and besides, most everyone else was ready for sleep and made that fact known. I was some relieved at that. For I did not want to see Reuben try to defend his faith; strong though the faith was, the tongue and reason I thought were not.

"On the morrow, Sir, with the light of day," said the Reverend Mr. Fox, "I will fight it out with ye, text to text!" He turned then to his companion Master Longene and sneered, "A Calvinist Baptist is harder shelled than any turtle or terrapin, and when prodded, will pull its head inside its shell and hide until it's safe to come out."

We shoved off early, by the dimmest light of day. The river still ran at flood, the keelboat riding so low in the water that you might easily dangle your feet into the passing river had you the mind to. But I did not, for I was passing uncomfortable in the stomach upon this busy stream and concentrated upon keeping my composure. I held the baby upon my lap and kept a close eye on Sarah Elizabeth.

George stood close by Patsy and Reuben Bradene as they took turns guiding the craft as needed by pole or oar over the runaway water. He wore his flat hat upon his head and held himself so stiff and stern that he did remind me, not for the first time, of a sanctimonious old brother. I did never have to worry about him dangling over the side or throwing sticks into the flood or any of the other many things that Sarah could think of to get into.

The Reverend Mr. Fox, as he was determined to be called, occupied the favored spot in the center of the raft, his companion Master Longene close beside him, the Reverend Mr. Fox short and squat, Master Longene drawn out and rail-thin, a right comical looking pair did you not have to listen to their conversation, which quickly become tedious.

It was along up in the morning that the river commenced to spread out some, and the water slowed to a calmer pace and the men—and Patsy—at their oars and poles relaxed their vigil some and conversation picked up. I was feeling better with the slower water, too.

The Reverend Mr. Fox's name seemed uncommon appropriate, as his face—chin, nose, ears—was all pointy and sharp and his glance cunning. I noted him sidle toward Patsy and Reuben and thought I knowed what he was about, and sure enough he commenced again the disputed doctrine of the night before.

He of course addressed it to Reuben, as men was not accustomed to arguing doctrine with women, though I knowed I could give a lot better than

Reuben Bradene, for though his heart was good, his intentions sound, his faith secure, alas, his tongue was none of those things, and he stumbled and frowned and struggled to make understood the doctrine of predestination and salvation by grace. And of course Patsy was hardly more secure in argumentation of that sort than her husband.

"Now, Sir, Mister Bradene, ye tell me that ye do believe in salvation by grace, in that foul and odiferous and hateful doctrine that come down from Calvin, that limits salvation to just a few chosen? Is that how I understand it, Sir?"

Reuben furrowed his great brow, reached up and fetched off his cap and scratched his head and finally nodded and mumbled, "It is, Sir."

"Ye believe, then, that yer elect and the rest of us damned, then?"

"Wal," said Reuben, a deep furrow plowed across the topmost part of his countenance. "I an't the one to say exactly." He looked at Patsy as if for corroboration, and she matched his furrowed forehead with furrows of her own as well as pursed lips, looking as if she would help if she could.

"But ye say 'what is to be will be', an't that right?" Mr. Fox pressed. "I ask ye, d'ye believe that what is to be will be, and explain it to me why that's so?"

Mr. Fox looked smug, with his Bible tucked up under his elbow, pushing his face right up to Reuben's chest, for his face would go no higher.

"Wal," considered Reuben at last, with a sidelong look toward Patsy, "if ye don't believe that what is to be will be, why then ye must believe the opposite of that—what is to be will not be."

At that logic Patsy's face lit right up, and she turned a proud look at The Reverend Mr. Fox and his long shadow Master Longene.

"What kind of answer is that!" snapped Mr. Fox. "Sir," he said more loudly than I thought necessary, so loud, as a matter of fact, that it brought Sarah from the edge of the boat over to where the group stood, which was all right with me. "Sir, I would have ye explain to me—if ye can—that if ye subscribe to the doctrine of what is to be will be, then how is it that you wear a pistol in your belt against attack by savages or wolves or heathens? If, as ye say, ye think that when yer time comes, it'll come, it's preordained, then it's worthless to carry protection!"

Brother Bradene looked at his belt which did indeed harbor a pistol, and then he looked at Patsy and she looked back at him. Reuben, who most like had never in his life been called upon directly to defend the Faith, looked some concerned and disturbed, and furrowed his brow and rubbed his two hands together and did look altogether as a man lost in deep thought.

At last he looked up brightly, and with a happy smile of inspiration he answered, "Wal, Sir, I think that I carry this pistol in case that I should happen upon a savage or a wolf or a heathern whose time has come."

Patsy Bradene looked so happy and relieved at that, I nearly laughed out loud and did indeed have to turn my face away when she turned upon Mr. Fox and Mr. Longene and give them that grin of hers, lively but exhibiting certain gaps here and there.

The Reverend Mr. Fox commenced to turn colors, first red and then blue and then white, quite patriotic one might have said, but for the fact that he was so angry. And then he started in to sputter and to vilify and blackguard Reuben, startling both that man and his wife, for they both thought his answer appropriate and well-considered.

Mr. Fox, he shook his fist in Reuben's face—rather neck—because Mr. Fox could not quite reach Reuben's face, and commenced to call him certain names so that I objected immediately and strenuously, and he turned upon me and announced, "This doctrine, this that ye call doctrine, an't none of it at all, but ignorant, ill-advised and wicked. Wicked, d'ye hear? And yer hell-bound, all of ye, d'ye not repent yer ways and seek salvation through prayer and good works. Damned to the eternal fires of hell!"

Both Patsy and Reuben stood stock still and stared open-mouthed at the small man's diatribe. But when The Reverend Mr. Fox paused to take a deep breath as if he would continue anew in that manner, Patsy give Reuben a long look and then she frowned and that frown got deeper, so that I reached over and pulled Sarah to me and so out of harm's way, for I had seen Patsy Bradene frown in that manner at other times.

"I would remind you," the Reverend Mr. Fox started, but he got nothing else said, for Patsy Bradene reached out one of her strong arms and caught the little clergyman by his back collar and lifted him high off the floor of the raft, held him struggling and dangling a moment, and then lifted him over the side of the boat above the passing water.

"Naw, naw," she cautioned him, "Don't struggle and wiggle so fer I'd hate to lose ye by chance overboard," at which the man ceased struggling, looked down at the water rapidly passing below him, and back up again into the benign countenance of Patsy Bradene.

"Now, Brother," said Patsy, "I do want that ye tell me again wh'er or no ye believe that salvation is strictly in yer own hands or is it of divine inspiration?"

The man had gone quite pale and his tall companion, confronted by Reuben Bradene, only stood silent and helpless. I glanced about. Both Sarah and George was wide-eyed at the sight, but the other boatmen was bent double with laughter.

"Drop 'im, Pat, drop 'im," one of them called out.

"Naw," she said intently, "this is spiritual business we deal with, and we must deal spiritually with it. Now, Sir, ye say that yer the author of yer own salvation, is that correct? An' that all the baptizin' ye need fer salvation is a little sprinkle?"

"Why, that's how the Scriptures read," he sputtered and Patsy Bradene dipped him a little closer to the water.

"How, Sir? Will ye then work out yer own salvation?"

"Dump 'im, Pat, dump 'im," cried one of the boatmen.

The little man was looking helplessly at the water.

"Sir?" said Patsy dipping him a little lower. "Now d'ye think that what is to be will be or no?"

"Drop 'im, Pat, drop 'im."

The Reverend Mr. Fox looked desperately around but found no face turned toward him in sympathy, even Mr. Longene, too frighted to go to his aid.

"Wal?"

"Yes."

"Yes, what?"

"Yes, what is to be will be."

"And would ye work out yer own salvation?"

"Never."

"Ah, see, it takes but little persuasion fer the truth of the Scriptures to surface." And with that Patsy Bradene leaned far overboard and dipped the little man under the rushing water, exactly as she might rinse the soap from a laundered article of clothing, and pulled him up again and set him sputtering and floundering on the deck.

When he had got his senses back, The Reverend Mr. Fox retreated hastily to the far end of the boat and sat shivering on a keg, his frightened glance hardly leaving Patsy Bradene.

"Now see, George," said Patsy, "that ye don't bother that Mister Fox fer he has just had hisself a profound religious experience."

Chapter 11

The Land at the End of the Ocean

The church to which Cyrus had delivered his letter and to which he ministered one meeting a month was called New Canaan Church and having no meeting house of its own, shared a new-built block house with other faiths on a regular basis—open to all—the block house having been built as a fortress against what was said to be Indians become more hostile as a result of the British posturing in the north.

Indeed, the air was as much filled on those meeting days with talk of politics, Indians, British, Bonaparte, and so forth as with talk of the Holy Spirit and His business. So it had become all along the river and so would remain, it was said, until the British was conquered, the Canadian lands forfeit, and the Indians scattered beyond the boundaries of the country.

Having paid but little attention to that sort of talk, I was ill-informed on the subject and some concerned. But Cyrus bade me not worry, as he did not feel that the Indians near offered any serious threat. Still, our cabin was built close by several others, so that in case of such emergency we could all gather quickly.

"There is greater turmoil to be feared," he said, "from the various groups of professed Christian. They be not life-threatening as the Indian might be—though," and here he paused as if he wondered where to proceed or not, "I have upon occasion been set upon by an angry Protestant who, unable to convince by strength of argument, determined to persuade by strength of body. But I am prepared to defend not only myself, but also my faith." Well I knowed that to be true.

"No," he went on, "what troubles me is the hostility of them many others toward the word of the Old and Faithful Baptist, Armenians that would work out their own salvation, a salvation they consider conditional upon their own merit and are distressed at the promise of unconditional salvation, though it be writ yet most obviously in the Holy Word.

"They are mistook, of course, but I do think I understand their reasoning. They are as a breed self-sufficient and confident nor would they be here was they not, and working out their earthly salvation as they are, they are determined therefore that they can work out their eternal salvation."

We had hardly set up housekeeping but that the brothers and sisters started calling. One of the first, Jonah Smith, an old gentleman who identified himself as a sometime preacher of the Gospel, sat himself right down and made himself at home, and immediately begun to advise Cyrus on matters of the church—who to take seriously, who not to, odds and ends of gossip, things in the main of little importance.

"One of the problems ye'll face soon," he said finally, "will be from the Sisters Leretta and Berdetta Morphew."

When Cyrus failed to respond to that, Brother Smith went on, "Them old sisters, though secure in ther faith an' honorable withal, is both unmarried an' a little on the peculiar side. Ther father Master Thomas Morphew owns a fair tract of land, an' though he's passing aged, keeps a firm halt upon his daughters.

"They, in turn, are possessed of three slaves, two brothers and a sister, that they would have baptized into the church, but fer ther father, who is Deist or infidel or some such, an' does protest that action, an' has threatened to call the law on anyone who dunks his property in the creek with a mind to ther salvation."

I looked at Cyrus and he at me.

"The Sisters Leretta and Berdetta has tried every little thing to get ther slaves properly baptized, but so far no one will go agin' the old man's wishes. It's something," he added, "that ye will a' probably have to attend to right off." He seemed right satisfied with himself having told Cyrus all of that.

"When the time comes," said Cyrus at last, "we'll attend to what we have to attend to."

There was some more idle conversation after that, and shortly the old brother rose as if to take his leave.

"Brother Pritchard," he said, "ye've a fine reputation, and the congregation is eager to listen to ye, so yer bound to have full houses fer a time, but these people I'm sad to say ere a little fickle of their pastors and ther interest is easily diverted.

"Ye know by now, I'm certain, that the territory is filling rapidly with all kinds of folk—some Methodist, some Presbyterian, some Universalist, and Deist, and New School, and Congregationalist, a smattering of Quaker as well as Campbellite, Fullerite, Pittite, Newlight, not to mention atheist and infidel and Papist.

"Fer them as ere not hard-rock firm in some foundation, why the choices is wide, very wide indeed. So while I'd not try to tell ye yer business," which of course he went right on and did, "I would suggest that ye be very wary of what ye teach and how ye teach it, so's to draw the greatest crowd."

"In what manner would you suggest wariness?" asked Cyrus.

"Why, Sir, I'd not teach hard doctrine nor strict duty neither."

"Hard doctrine?"

"Why, election and predestination, special redemption and unconditional salvation. Mind ye, I'm not sayin' that ther not true, that the Scriptures don't teach them. I'm only cautionin' ye to soften them so's not to drive away the shaky to the less firm ground of Methodism or Congregationalism or Universalism."

"Well, then, what would ye have me teach, Brother Smith?" asked Cyrus calmly.

"Why just some of this and some of that, ye know, some love, a little duty, touch upon election, if ye like, but include some Armenianism and don't be too haughty on the subject of full immersion baptism, as some folk don't care to get therselves all wet," said the old man cheerfully. "What needs is that ye spread a table full of choices, so that the congregation may pick and choose and satisfy therselves, and of course ye may do the same," he added.

"I do not understand you, Sir. Would you spread a table with pleasing and appetizing victuals, which yet would offer no nourishment and would leave the feaster at last hungrier than when he come to the table?"

The old man with a solemn shake of his head, though still friendly and cheerful, said, "Brother Pritchard, ye'll do what ye want, of course. But do ye want to be popular and fill yer benches and make yer mark, well, ye'd best heed my suggestion some."

"It is not my intent to be popular or even to leave my mark, Brother Smith," said Cyrus sternly. "It is my intent to preach the Gospel as it is written. Are there those that cannot tolerate that, they had best find theirselves another place to listen."

"Well," said the old man, "what ye will."

"Indeed," said Cyrus.

The next visitors we had was Brother and Sister Gilbert, that old couple arriving by foot one Saturday afternoon and making theirselves acquainted to me.

They was, as Cyrus had promised, a dear and pleasant old couple, married to each other for only a few years. Brother Gilbert was round and jolly and frankly admitted his love of the various victuals that made it so. His wife, on the other hand, was dry as a leafless limb in wintertime, that kind of limb that looks dead until you bend it and find it still supple and lively withal.

"When my times comes," said Mistress Gilbert, at one point in the conversation, "it'll come. I'll not worry on't. We have been put on this earth for a reason. Of that much I am certain." Her husband nodded.

Those two affirmed what Brother Smith had told us of the Sisters Berdetta and Leretta.

"It's true," said Brother Gilbert, "that those two, who are as strong in ther Old School faith as any ye'll e'er see, are determined that those three slaves, who similarly profess belief—though I can't say how much of that is from ther own need and how much from the prodding of ther mistresses—should be properly baptized. Of course, ther's a few in the congregation that objects some to the idea of slaves being so baptized. But, to my mind, that only tells much about the strength of their own predestinarian beliefs."

Sister Gilbert interrupted, "Old Master Morphew is truly not so bad as he'd like people to think. He only likes to poke fun at believers."

They left before dark, and I was some comforted to know them, for they was well-grounded in the faith and sturdy and hopeful, and I found myself less lonely because of that.

We was not long in discovering the two sisters, Berdetta and Leretta Morphew, that we had heard so much of. The very first meeting that I attended with Cyrus, they come into the room—marched might be a more apt description—followed by two black boys and between the sisters, a young black girl.

I tried hard not to stare, but I did peek at intervals at the group, for they would have stood out on any occasion. The sisters, not so young as they once was, was as alike almost as you could ask for—twins I supposed, but though their gowns and bonnets (uncommonly pretty) was identical in make and design, they was opposite to each other in color. Where the one was pink, the other was yellow, and where the other was light, the one was dark. And when they gestured, the one did so with the right hand and the other the left hand.

They seated theirselves upon a bench, the girl between them and the boys behind, and stared straight ahead. The black boys was in truth most boy, for they played and poked one another when they thought no one was looking, just as almost any boys would do in a like situation, but the girl, their sister, sat silently between Sisters Berdetta and Leretta, her elbows resting on her knees and her chin upon her fists.

Now and again one sister or the other directed a remark to the girl, and she nodded and repeated that remark to the other sister. Otherwise they was as silent and as stern as death itself.

It was not until Cyrus struck up a hymn that the two sisters come to life, for they picked up the song right with him and raised voices true and beautiful, and in perfect harmony, one taking the melody and the other the parts! No one else seemed particularly startled by that. The girl between them did not look up, but remained chin upon her fists.

After the service I stood waiting for Cyrus as he talked with this or that brother or sister. In time, the sisters Leretta and Berdetta come up and waited until he was free. The slave girl still stood between them.

"Suh," said the girl, "I name is Anna an' we'd lack to talk to you. We'd lack you to baptize us—me an' my brothers, Tim and Jim."

"Well," said Cyrus casting me a glance that suggested this might more comfortably be a private conversation, "there's of course certain procedures. . ."

At that point I left Cyrus to the sisters and joined a nearby group until he was through.

Brother Enos Ray who rode the river often, sometimes south through the Orleans Territory and sometimes north to Ste. Genevieve or even all the way to St. Louis, was holding forth considerable, having of course more recent news than anyone else.

"Well, the talk's confused." He was answering a question put to him by Brother Curtis Layman. "Bonaparte's mixed up in some of it, dependin' on who ye listen to, or the British up in Canada, and of course the Injuns. Trouble is in Washington, D.C., Mister Madison and Mister Monroe ere a-playin' games with Napoleon and the British on the seas, an' not givin' the western frontier no consideration at all."

"It's them shopkeepers in the east," nodded Brother Layman. "They want the trade with Europe and don't care a feather what comes of us out here at the mercy of the Injuns. Would that the President and the Congress concern therselves with the west and settle our western frontier, so's we could add Canada and ship all the Injuns west out of the boundaries of our country. Fer they say that beyond is large stretches of land fer them to hunt and live ther savage lives, as fer as the western ocean," and the speaker waved his arm in an expansive manner to the west.

I looked down to see Sarah Elizabeth a-frowning and then shading her eyes in that direction. Then she tugged on my skirt and whispered, "Is there a ocean out that way, Mama?"

"Yes, Dear," I answered.

"I an't sure," said Enos Ray solemnly, "that we got that much time. Fer what I'm told is that the Indians is organizin', that Tecumseh and his brother The Prophet has done what no Indians has ever managed to do—ally themselves with one another. Would ye believe," he paused significantly, "that Tecumseh single-handed has sobered up the Indians, convinced them to avoid whiskey. Why, who'd a thought that, whoever would have expected it?"

"Would not a sober Indian be safer than a drunk one?" ventured a voice that I did not recognize.

There was a long pause at that, and then Curtis Layman answered darkly. "More dangerous, fer ther mind's not muddled with drink an' they can think clearer and plan with more certainty. Drink's one true way to keep the Injun disadvantaged is the truth."

"That's up north, of course," added Brother Ray, "but it is drifting southward, and truthfully westward and eastward, for Tecumseh and The Prophet ere a-reachin' into all kinds of Injun tribes. To my mind, we could not get the whole mess settled in the west fast enough, far enough west that we'd ne'er ever have need to go that far."

"Indeed we would not, especially did we have the Canadian lands to settle. Run the Brits out of Canada, I say," cried a voice. "Run the Brits out of Canada and chase the Injuns all the way to the western ocean."

"What d'ye suppose gives them Injuns the strength an' wisdom to unite?" asked someone.

"Why," said Curtis Layman, "the British encourage them, give them promises, an'," here he paused, frowned and glanced around, softening his voice some, "an' truth of it is, that ther's regular settlers here, Americans they call therselves, that an't so happy with the westward expansion. Them as has been here a long time an' had things the way they liked 'em. Content with the Injuns, livin' in peace with French and Spaniards and Papists and what not. To the mind a' many, ther's treasonous folk abroad that give comfort to the Indian and to the British, that would be as happy to see us all gone to hell and things the way they was before President Jefferson bought and opened these lands to American farmers."

No voice had said "Eremus Lodi," yet that name come to my mind, for though Eremus Lodi had ne'er been accused, there'd been hints aplenty. Were he not allied with the devil, then for certain, it had been suggested, he was allied with the British, or with Napoleon, or with the Indians, no one having any clear indictment.

Though Eremus Lodi's name come up often, I had not actually seen him again since the day he had accosted me in Ste. Genevieve, though black O'Reilly continued to make his sudden appearances, come and gone sometimes so quickly that you'd question wh'er you actually had seen him or no. But the children took him for granted, and accepted his comings and goings as they accepted the rain in the summer and the snow in the winter. I had ne'er quite been able to shrug off the feeling that he watched over us, though I'd ne'er have tried to explain that feeling to anyone.

In a few minutes Cyrus joined the group and we gathered up our own and started for home. All he said of his visit with Berdetta and Leretta was that he had promised to visit with them and with their old father at some distant date.

"It is a peculiar situation," he added.

A few days after that, I come upon Sarah and George in front of the cabin a-bickering and shook my head from side to side, for it seemed one or the other of them was always at odds about something. And I thought to myself that in truth there was Baptist blood in 'em both, that it was just in 'em to bicker.

It took but little to set them off. Sarah was quick and temperamental and George slower and more careful and thoughtful. Sarah could handle a charcoal with unusual skill for one so young and make all her letters and numbers and spell certain words, while George yet struggled, for the charcoal was hard for him to manage with his damaged right hand and his left hand would not do easily what it was bid, that his letters and numbers oft looked ill and confused to the great delight of his little sister. Nor was she slow to point out her superiority, at which her brother might argue or sulk or stalk off.

And much as I tried to explain to the girl that George's affliction was the cause of his ill handling of the charcoal, she would have none of it, insisting that it simply attested to her own superiority.

This morning they were engaged in lively dispute, and I could tell that for a change Sarah was catching the worst of it. I thought I would just slip away before I was seen and let them work it out. But I did not get away quickly enough, for Sarah called out to me.

"Mama! George says that girls are not well regarded in the Bible." She was most indignant of that. "That they're not important. They are, an't they?"

"Well, I'd think. How do you mean 'not well regarded'?"

George intent on pressing his advantage answered quickly, "Well, girls are not important in the Bible, Mama. You know that. They an't but hand-maidens and wives and sisters and such. They an't warriors or prophets or disciples. They an't a single girl disciple."

"Mama!" wailed Sarah Elizabeth. I did recall, when I was a little girl, similar sorts of discussions. Children don't never change. I searched my mind for me of the arguments of my childhood.

"Well," I said at last, "you must remember Mary was a girl, George."

"Oh, Mama, she was a mother! Mothers don't count. Everybody has a mother. There's nothing important about a mother."

I was a little took back at that, but I knew what he meant and I could see that he was not making connection with everybody's mother and his own mother. I started to laugh and say that I thought the conversation was not going to satisfy anyone, but George interrupted.

"Anyway, even if you count Mary, you've also got to count all the girls that were foolish or troublemakers."

"Who?" snapped Sarah.

"Well, there was Delilah and Salome and Eve, don't forget Eve," said George. "Eve brought down sin and shame and everything on us all, and we're degraded and vile and corrupted ever more."

"You said mothers don't count," said Sarah. "Eve was a mother."

"Oh, but that was after."

"After what?"

"Oh—just after," said George archly.

"Mama!" wailed Sarah again.

"Oh, Sarah, there are important girls in the Bible."

"Who?"

"Oh, I always liked the story of Queen Esther," I said and then I told them the story of how Esther had saved her people by convincing her hus-band the king that they should be saved. And then I told her the story of Ruth and the alien corn.

George's answer to that was a sarcastic, "Oh, that's something, it really is. What did I tell you—just wives."

178

"Mama!"

"Ah, Sarah, indeed I'll find us a hero and a warrior," I said for I had remembered the story of Deborah. I went and found Cyrus's Bible and had to hunt the story out, for I could not remember it in detail. I found it, however, and set out to read it and to explain it to the children, forgetting how violent it got. And when I got to the part where Jael, the wife of the Heber the Kenite, slew the enemy Sisera by driving a tent stake through his temple while he slept, Sarah's eyes was shining.

"See," she turned to her brother, "we could be brave warriors."

"Ah, you couldn't never," retorted her brother. "I'd like to see you drive a tent stake through someone's head. I'd just like to see you."

"Well, I could. I'd do it, too. I'd save Mama and Daddy and I might even save you, too. I might."

I left them then, still arguing. But the story of Deborah and Jael must have caught both their fancies. For several days thereafter, they played at the story with Sarah always being either Deborah or Jael, relegating her brother to be the wicked Sisera or Heber the Kenite.

The game at last broke off on the day that George insisted that it was only fair, since he had played a supporting role, that it was Sarah's turn to be a handmaiden or a concubine.

"What's a concubine?" asked Sarah.

"I don't know," replied George. "But it's a girl and every king has one. I'll be King David. So you've got to be a handmaiden or a concubine. It's fair."

"Well, I never will!" snapped Sarah, and she flounced off.

Of course, I hastened to Cyrus with the story, and though we both had a laugh over it, he agreed with me that it was time he took George aside and explained certain things to him, things that other boys seemed to learn from each other, but that George in his solitude and his preference for the company of elders seemed slow in picking up.

"We'd be hard pressed to explain," Cyrus laughed, "did George suggest to some girl other than Sarah that she be his concubine."

It was some weeks later on a hot afternoon when I missed Sarah. Cyrus was gone for the day, having at last, reluctantly I thought, made his promised visit to the Morphew household to discuss the baptism of Leretta and Berdetta's slaves.

I had been caught up in the washing and had set George to entertain Peter, which George did object to as being girl's work, but in truth he was much more reliable than Sarah, being older and being of a sterner disposition.

Sarah was just as like as not to jump up and chase off after a butterfly and leave the baby unattended. It was a flaw of character that I hoped she would one day outgrow. And it was that character flaw that left me unalarmed when I could not find her. Nor did George seem to have any idea where she was.

I waited awhile, going on about my business, but keeping my eyes open, and when she did not reappear after a time, I got some worried. She was not given to staying out of sight. She might be adventurous, but even the most adventurous of pioneer children understood the dangers of solitary movement. Or at least I thought that Sarah was too wise to wander away.

She was most like lost in playing a make-believe game somewhere out of sound, for I had called to her, or lost in her play, just did not hear.

"George," I said, "you stay with Peter and, mind you, don't leave. I am going to go out and find that girl, and when I do, I'll leave some stripes upon her bared legs, let me tell you." Truth was, I was annoyed, but also a little frighted.

Having satisfied myself that she was not anywhere close by the cabin, I followed the path toward the trace as being the most likely way a little girl would go. As I walked, I alternately struggled with the lump of fear in my throat and promised myself what I would do to that girl once I got a hold on her.

There was cabins near enough that, most like, that was the way she headed. Brother and Sister Mayhew had a pair of little girls close on her age, and though she had orders not to go a-visiting without consent, that did not mean that she would not in a moment of inspiration do so. Still, it troubled me, for she never had done that, never had just gone off a-visiting without consent, nor had the little Mayhew girls ever done so either.

And then it embarrassed me. To think that I would have to go to my neighbors seeking my child, as if I could not keep her home. I would attend that girl!

But when I got to the Mayhews, Sister Mayhew had not seen Sarah but offered to send one of her big boys along to help look. I thanked her for her kind offer but assured her that by the time I got back home, Sarah most like would have surfaced.

"Wal, now, Sister Pritchard, don't tarry, y'hear? Do ye not find her soon, we'll needs all turn out to look. Between the wild Injuns an' the beasts an' the river an' all, t'ain't good atall fer a young'un to be loose." She said that right cheerfully, but that observation hardly lifted my spirits none.

I went back the way I come and when I come to the place where two paths joined, I stopped and considered. Should I hurry back home where George and Peter were and hope Sarah had wandered back, or should I track this path before me aways? I knew that the path led through the woods, separated again, the one path going on to Master Eli Thomas's cabin and the other going off in a direction I had ne'er been. Master and Mistress Thomas, who was practicing Methodists, had no children, but was good neighbors and friendly. It was possible that the girl had gone that direction. It would take but a few minutes to make that detour, so I turned down the path toward the Thomases', taking care to gather my skirts close against the brambles that lined the narrow way.

When I got to the Thomases' cabin, I did not find nobody home. I was left once more in a quandry, to go on or back. One path that left the Thomas's cabin circled back toward the Mayhews and the other path led deeper into the woods toward the south and west. I had been gone away from my house too long as it was. If Sarah had not turned up by the time I got back, we'd needs send out searchers. There was no point my going further.

I had turned toward the path to make my return journey when I thought I heard some unusual noise. I stopped, held my breath and listened. There was indeed a noise, steady in the distance down the other path. The Thomases returning? I waited, not seriously alarmed for whate'er it was that was making that racket was not being stealthy about it.

Then it come to me that it was the sound of a horse passing along the trace, and I stood stock still, certain before I even saw what I was going to see, and I felt my color rise and my breathing come hard.

And indeed it was—Eremus Lodi a-horseback and before him on the saddle, that rascally little girl, a-chattering a mile a minute. I saw them before they saw me, and I took note of the look of mild amusement on Eremus Lodi's face.

I was frankly both relieved and humiliated. Only twice in the years I had been a mother had I ever let a young'un get completely away from me, and both times it had been Eremus Lodi who had fetched them back! What would the man think of me for such carelessness, for he could not but think my children wandered free and unfettered at their own will? Oh, I would leave my mark on that wandering girl!

"Why, Madam," said Eremus Lodi, drawing close and reining in, "have ye lost something?" It was said still with mild amusement, and I felt my treacherous complexion go red, and in vexation I said, "Indeed, Sir, I have and when I get that girl home, I shall make sure she remembers not to leave home on her own again."

"I would not be so hard on her, Madam," he said. "She tells me that she was on her way to the ocean," he added.

"The ocean!"

"Indeed. I did myself think it odd to head that direction to find an ocean, but she assures me that there is one right out there, and truthfully she described it wondrously well and if there is indeed such a beautiful body of water out there, why I might go along myself to see."

"Well, there'll be no oceans today, young lady," I said. "Now dismount this moment and let Master Lodi be about his business."

But it was Eremus Lodi who dismounted, leaving the wide-eyed girl alone on the horse. "Let her ride, Madam, for she has been telling me wondrous tales of her plans to be a warrior-lady and that she would need to have such a horse some day. Hang on tight, now, Girl," he said to Sarah.

Sarah, who could talk the bark from a tree on a good day, was strangely silent, only the sparkling of her eyes giving away her excitement.

"May I walk with ye, my Lady," said Eremus Lodi, "to yer cabin and let the girl ride? It is no inconvenience, I assure ye."

I was not a little flustered. Being unaccustomed to being addressed as anything much but "Sister," the "my lady" was a little discomfitting. I did not reply. I knowed what George would do did he see his sister ride up on a fine horse whilst he had been left at home to mind the baby, but I did not know how to object. Eremus Lodi read my indecision correctly, for he added, "I would look in on George anyway and allow him his turn on the beast, lest he be put out."

"You do understand children right well, Master Lodi."

"Nah. I understand human nature right well, and children are possessed of human nature in like amounts as everyone else, only they have less experience in covering it up, is all."

I waved toward the path that led away from the Thomases' cabin toward our own. "That way," I said, for he was standing beside me hanging onto the reins. "The path is narrow," I added.

He smiled a slow smile and murmured, "I know the path to your cabin well, Madam."

"Oh?"

"I keep informed. I know of your comings and goings. I feel somehow a-kin to you and yours, fer we've survived a few experiences together."

When last I had seen this man he had been completely irrational, and before that Cyrus had found him vague and odd. Yet, there before me he was courteous, friendly, and helpful as any neighbor could be. I hardly knowed what to think.

"This is an ill place fer settling, Madam. The fever is too common and the land itself uncertain, given to earth tremors as it is. Yer better off north er back east."

"West?" I could not keep from saying.

"Settlement has already gone too far west, to my mind. West is fer the Indians."

"The Indians?"

"Ther's a natural boundary here with the river, Madam. Were I believer in the Will of God, I would have to say that he ordained that this river be set here for the white man to have one side of the continent and the red man the other side. But will of God or no, it strikes me as an equitable distribution of resources."

I did not say more on the subject, but I could not keep from thinking of those rumors and suspicions concerning Eremus Lodi's sympathy for the British and Indian cause. And I was made some uncomfortable on account of it.

We walked along without comment for a time, and I become aware in the closeness of the narrow path of the bigness of the man and the masculine odors of him—of leather and horse and tobacco and sweat. It was not an unpleasant sensation, them things, for they spoke of security and strength.

I glanced up at the tall man and was some discomfitted to find him staring down at me in a curious manner.

"Yer husband is off on his appointments," he said abruptly, and then continued quickly without giving me time to question how he come to know that. "I wonder that he would leave ye to fend fer yerselves in these unsettled times?"

"We're well situated," I said. "Before anyone would get to us, they would have to get by our neighbors. Besides, when he's gone fer a long time, one or another of the young men of the neighborhood come of an evening to stay."

"Ah," was all he said at that.

When we got to the cabin, Eremus Lodi fended George off so easily that I was amazed. "Yer sister insisted that we bring this horse fer ye to check out," he said to the boy. "She said that ye had plans yerself one day to have such a one, and she was sure ye'd like to see this one and give him a ride fer comparison."

George's eyes was wide, along with his mouth, and he did not even make any effort to complain. Eremus Lodi helped him up on the horse and, truth to tell, I was surprised at how well the boy managed the beast.

"Why," said Eremus Lodi in honest admiration, "I do think that yer a natural horseman, George."

After George had ridden for a time, Eremus Lodi bade him tether the horse to a nearby tree, which George did, and joined us where we sat on a bench beneath the shade of a big tree. Sarah had already positioned herself on the bench beside Eremus Lodi, and he had packed his pipe and was preparing to smoke it, while I wondered at the propriety of inviting him to sup.

"Yer sister set out to find the ocean, George," said Eremus Lodi much to my consternation, for I thought that George would immediately begin to laugh and tease, but to my surprise he did not, only looked interested.

"At meeting last they said there was a ocean thataway," said Sarah, pointing in a westerly direction. "I thought to find it."

"Did you?" asked George quickly.

"No. I got tired first."

"How far is it?" asked George.

"Why, George," I said, "there is a western ocean, at least so I've heard, but it's so far that I don't know a single soul that's ever seen it."

"Oh," said George with real disappointment in his voice. "Have you seen it, Master Lodi?" he asked.

"Well, no, Boy, not the western ocean. I have seen oceans, fer ther's one south, just beyond New Orleans."

Both children brightened. "Can we go?" asked Sarah. "I want to see the golden sand and the blue water and the white waves and the fisherboys that dive into them."

"Well, my word, Children," I said quite perplexed at this sudden interest in oceans, "wherever have you heard of oceans before?"

"Why, O'Reilly told us. He told us of the oceans and the waves and the sand, for he comes from the land at the end of the ocean," said Sarah.

"O'Reilly?" I looked at Eremus Lodi whose expression was as inquisitive as my own. "An' did O'Reilly himself tell you that he comes from the land at the end of the ocean?" I asked, for though I knowed that the black man did communicate more with the children than with others, still I did not know that he had the language to describe so much.

"Well," answered George, "not directly. O'Reilly tells us stories. That's how we know it."

"Stories?" said Eremus Lodi, and I could tell he was as interested as I.

"Yes," said Sarah. "He tells us stories of the happy warriors, strong and brave, in the land at the end of the ocean."

"Oh?" said Eremus Lodi.

"Yes," said George. "At the end of the ocean he says is a beautiful land, with tall, strong people, and the land goes to the ocean."

"Upon a time," prodded Sarah.

"Yes, 'upon a time was a strong warrior who lived in peace and worked hard and was blessed. His cows give milk and he drove them to the grass and sometimes he went all the way to the ocean for to trade and sometimes he went to the mountains and sometimes to the water, for his land was fertile.'"

"Remember the babe," prompted Sarah Elizabeth.

"I'm getting to that; don't hurry it," retorted her brother. "'And the warrior was happy. And then the happy warrior took a beautiful princess to be his wife. And again he was blessed. His wife gave him a son and the son grew tall and strong. And then his wife gave him a baby, a girl.'"

"'Pretty doll,'" interrupted Sarah.

"Mama! Make her let me tell it," complained her brother.

"You'd have forgot that part," said Sarah.

"No, I wouldn't either!"

"Children," I interrupted, "stop that bickering. George, get on with your story." In truth I was quite anxious to have him finish.

"'The warrior asked no more but to care for his family and bring them milk and trade for pretty things.'" George paused and Sarah broke in.

"'One day,'" she said, and George snapped, "Just wait, I'll tell; you can't get it right."

"'One day,'" he went on, "'the warrior was driving his cattle and he sat down to rest and he fell asleep and many wicked men sneaked up and as he slept they tied him with ropes and chains and though he struggled, they hung him like a painter-lion from a pole and carried him away and threw him at last upon a ship and sailed him away from his princess and his children evermore.'"

I waited. "Is that the story?" I asked finally. "Is that all?"

"Well," said Sarah quickly lest George get to tell it all, "not quite. Only that the warrior was sad for all his days that he would never see his princess or his children ever again and that they could never know what happened to him and must mourn him forever, not knowing if he was killed by a beast or drowneded or attacked by enemy."

"And this is O'Reilly?" I asked. "Is this O'Reilly's story?"

"I guess," said George. "He didn't say."

"What other stories does he tell?"

"Oh many. But we like it best when he tells of the ocean because it's beautiful, don't we, George?"

I started to ask about the amulet that George wore around his neck, but then thought better of it. I did not like to call attention to it to no purpose, for it somehow unsettled me.

"Is this how you understand O'Reilly's story?" I asked Eremus Lodi who had listened as intently as I.

"It is news to me. He has ne'er spoke of it to me."

"Not? Why that surprises me. An' have you asked him of it?"

He looked at me curiously for a long time it seemed, until I felt the color rise once more. At last he said, "It is a lesson hard learned and must be, it seems, learned over and over. That which one does not readily tell ye, ye need not know."

A smile that did not touch his mouth danced and played about his eyes under the heavy growth of brow, and I was embarrassed and flushed again.

He did not sup with us, but left shortly thereafter, regretting he said that he had other pressing matters and could not tarry. And I believed him, at least about regretting that he could not tarry.

I watched him go, lost to woods within seconds almost, and pondered. That we could know so much more of black O'Reilly, so distant come, so silent and alone, than of our country man Eremus Lodi seemed peculiar.

"Mama?" It was George.

"What, Dear?"

"What are you thinkin' so seriously of?"

"Oh, naught, Son, naught."

"That which one does not readily tell ye, ye need not know." I would give a lot to know as much of Eremus Lodi as I knew of his silent slave.

It was late evening when Cyrus at last returned from his visit to the Morphews. He had but little to say of it. "The old man was not at home. I talked some to Anna as the sisters listened. The best I can determine, the old man is only a typical old rationalist, one who delights in being perverse on the subject of religion."

"He claims that they are his slaves and therefore cannot be baptized without his consent?" I asked.

Cyrus nodded and then with a sigh said, "You may enslave a man's body, but no one can take title to a soul."

Chapter 12

Smoke and Fire

I stood just out the door to the cabin, damp from my efforts in the noonday sun, trying to keep my attention both at the candles I was dipping and Peter who played close by. I needed either Sarah or George to keep watch over the babe, so that I could give my full attention to my task and get it done with, for it was not one of my favorite activities.

It seemed to me that the children had had ample time to get to the spring house and back, even counting the inevitable time needed for dawdling. George at least was certainly old enough to know to get right back.

I reached up to wipe the moisture from my forehead and looked quickly at the babe and turned once more toward my work. But I was arrested at a sudden loud scream, followed by crying which I knew to be Sarah. Nor was it the kind of disagreeable whimpering which children are wont to indulge in when they bicker or desire attention. It was a full out scream of fright!

I whirled, started in the direction of the racket, remembered the baby and swept him up on my hip, and gathering my skirts about me, moved as quickly as I could toward the sound which seemed to be coming from just beyond the garden where Cyrus had been clearing away brush and forest most recently.

My heart thudding in my mouth, I made it to the top of the rise and caught sight of the children, Sarah still screeching at George—who held aloft the metal hoe from the garden and was menacing her with it!

That was beyond me. What was he doing tormenting the girl like that? I would put some stripes to his legs, and I called out to him, but he didn't seem to hear, which was not surprising considering the volume of noise coming from his sister. I walked swiftly toward them, getting madder with each step. I had better things to do than to referee such bickering.

"George! Sarah!" I called out. "George. . ." I started to call again but the name died in my throat for George suddenly with a mighty swing brought down the hoe, and Sarah's noise stopped abruptly as my own voice went absolutely dead. He would not, he could not, never, no matter how angry he had become with his sister.

"George!" I managed at last, "George! Put down that hoe," for he had lifted it once more over his head and I could not see Sarah at all. "George!" But he either did not hear me or he ignored me, for the hoe came down hard again, and I shrieked as loud as I could, so loud that Peter begun to cry.

At that George turned to face me, leaning on the hoe and smiling broadly. "Mama, Mama, hurry, come see," he called and then I saw Sarah, she was bent low, intent on something on the ground. She looked up and called, "Hurry, Mama." My legs had near gone to rubber, but I moved toward them quickly as I could and was but a few, steps from them when I saw the snake, still thrashing on the ground, its head nearly severed from its huge body. Even from a distance I could tell that it was a copperheaded snake and as big a one as I think I had ever seen in my life.

"She was messing around the brush pile," said George. "I told her not to. I told her there was likely snakes in it, but she wouldn't listen."

"You never either," said Sarah. "He never, Mama. Anyway I just poked a stick into it as I thought I seen a skink a-sunning itself."

My strength was coming back and I stared in horror at the writhing serpent, its huge copper body muscled and glistening struggling in its death throes. The children, even Peter, was stooped over watching it, quite interested and excited, but I could only shudder and had a hard time even looking at it. I had no affection for snakes of any kind, particularly not big ones and most particularly not venomous ones.

I had thought on other occasions that it seemed most strange to me that Eve would have allowed herself to be tempted by a serpent. Had it been me, why the human race might still be in Eden, for I most like would have took a stick to the thing, apple or no.

"You know now why Daddy said to stay away from these brush piles," I said at last. She was lucky that it was a copperhead and not a cottonmouth, for a copperhead is shy and slow to attack, not like other poisonous vipers that will attack with little or no provocation.

I wished that Cyrus would burn them brush piles away, but I knowed that he'd save the burning of them for fall when the daylight hours would be short and he would work late by the light of the burning brush. He was not alone in that, but because he had to mend much time away from home preaching, he often had to work later and longer than others who spent all their time in the clearing of the land and the planting of it.

"Leave the thing alone, George," I said for he was prodding and poking at it. Though it was most certainly dead, it twitched and shuddered with the poking. "Come on now. I need you to watch Peter while I finish my candles. And don't mess around the pile anymore. Where there's one copperhead, there's another." I said that last in certainty for I knowed it to be true. Not all snakes traveled in pairs, but copperheaded ones seemed to. If you killed one, you needed to be on the lookout for its mate.

Reluctantly, the children left the snake. "I saved you," said George to Sarah. "That snake would have swallered you whole had I not killed it."

"Would it, Mama?" asked the little girl in some alarm, and then she snorted her own answer. "Oh, it would not. Anyway, I could have killed it. You never give me a chance."

"Ha! You could not. You'd still be standing there screaming if I had not saved you. That's the way girls are."

"Mama!"

"Stop your bickering," I said. "I've no mind to listen to it."

Both was quiet for a few moments, and then Sarah stopped and, suddenly remembering, announced, "I saw a Indian."

"What! Where?"

"Back at the spring. I saw a Indian looking at us. George never seen it."

"George?"

"Oh, Mama, she never. She tried to tell me she saw a Indian, but all I could see was trees and that's all she seen, too."

"I did see a Indian. He wore no shirt and he stood with his hands on his hips like this," and she stopped, her arms akimbo, her lower lip stuck way out and a serious frown upon her small face.

"He never."

"Mama!"

"If you seen a Indian, why didn't he run up and scalp us?"

"Well, I don't know. He didn't look fierce. He just looked at us and then I blinked my eyes and then I didn't see him no more. He just disappeared."

"Ha!"

"Mama!"

When Cyrus came in late in the afternoon—for he had been away on church business, as he too often was to my mind—the children was immediately after him on account of the snake and would not rest until he went with them to inspect it. I had seen all that I care to of snakes and so did not go along.

When they come back, the children were still full of the snake, and most of the evening's conversation centered around the killing of it, with no mention of Sarah's Indian sighting.

"Why is it that you cannot fire the brush piles close to the house?" I asked Cyrus. "They harbor snakes and other kinds of varmints."

"It is the wrong season for such fires. It's too dry and windy. You don't want to set a fire under such conditions unless you've got a goodly number of hands about to contain it. Even then, it's chancey."

"Well, I see smoke from such fires all the time," I said.

Cyrus only shook his head slowly from side to side. "That may be," he said at last, "but that does not make it any the less of a risk."

When the children was at last abed I brought up the matter of Sarah's Indian. In the excitement over the snake, she had forgotten it again, but I had not. Sarah was a matter-of-fact child, not given to fantasies, or even caring for them. I was certain that she had good reason to think that she had seen an Indian.

"Is it possible that she actually saw an Indian?" I asked.

"Well, possible, certainly. There's Indians about. The Delawares in particular cross back and forth across the river. There is a band which regularly encamps across the river on the Tennessee side, as a matter of fact."

"Are they dangerous?" I asked recalling the conversation at meeting last concerning the growing restlessness of the savages, and at such talk my thoughts was never very far from the memory of all our brothers and sisters and neighbors at the Old Shawnee Ford, so carelessly slaughtered by marauding Indians.

"I think not. Not these. Farther north they are perhaps more restless."

"It's just that I hear rumors," I said, "rumors of the disaffection of the red men who would band together and drive the white man back across the eastern mountains."

"Not entirely rumors, I think," said Cyrus. "It is no secret that Tecumseh, the great Shawnee, does travel far and wide attempting to gather great forces of Indians to stem the tide of the white man."

"It sometimes seems, doesn't it, that the Indian does have some just claim," I said, "for they have lived and hunted this land forever, I guess, and been content, and now the white settlers come and take the land, and game is scarce for either food or fur. I cannot say that I blame the savages so much."

On Sunday next we visited the Elm Creek Church, where Elder Joshua Murdock pastored the flock. Our walk to Elm Creek took us about four miles from our cabin, a distance near nine miles from the New Canaan Church. Cyrus was wanted there for the ordination of a brother to preach, it taking at least two elders to accomplish the ceremony of laying on of hands, that ceremony ordained by church law.

"Do you know Elder Murdock?" I asked Cyrus, for I did not.

"No, I have heard of him, but I have not met him yet. I have made a pass or two at visiting with him and his flock, but," and here Cyrus paused and frowned before he went on, "in truth he did not seem over eager to have me in attendance, for he sent back somewhat flimsy excuses to my entreaties."

"That seems a most peculiar way for a Baptist to behave," I said, as Baptists is usually congenial to one another and anxious to meet and discuss, indeed Baptists meeting one another is like to fall to discussion of doctrine almost before they exchange names.

"Well, he may have his reasons."

"Such as?"

Cyrus, who was carrying Peter, stopped long enough to shift the weight of the child to his other arm and then said in a noncomittal manner, "I am not one to listen to tales and rumors and gossip too seriously, no matter how reliable the bearer, 'tis always better to withold judgment until you've had the chance to evaluate situations on your own."

"Situations?"

But Cyrus only shook his head slightly. I knowed then that he'd have no more to say on the subject and I might as well save my breath. Apparently he did know what he was getting into, however, and did not seem overly alarmed, so there was no point my getting in a stew over it. We would see what would come of it. That was all.

And, in truth, unless we was greeted with outright hostility, I was eager to meet and get to know others of our Association, for though I had some new acquaintances, I was yet without those kinds of friends—brothers and sisters—that we had left behind.

We was greeted by several of the Baptist members outside the meeting house with the customary friendliness of such. Indeed, the group which was large, and growing, did seem of an uncommon good humor, joking and laughing and greeting one another as if it was a party they attended and not a worship service.

And one couple singled us out in particular and made themselves acquainted, he being Nathan Dalton and his wife Obediance Dalton. They looked to be close upon our own ages and pointed out a number of children playing in the clearing, claiming them as their own and Obediance—"call me Biddy" she insisted—took George and Sarah in hand and introduced them to those children, for which I was grateful, at least on George's account. Sarah had no need of help and would have made her own acquaintance with the group in short order. But her brother would have hung back and clung to the adults, were he not pushed toward the children.

But both children seemed immediately accepted, and in the manner of children was almost immediately at play with all the others.

"This is certainly a large and friendly group you've got here," I said to Biddy Dalton.

She nodded, but I noted the suggestion of a frown between her eyes when she said, "Brother Murdock does attract goodly numbers to meeting, many from other persuasions and even some non-believers and infidels."

"Well," I said, "that certainly would seem to speak well for Brother Murdock's meetings."

"You'll want to be the judge of that, I suppose," was all she said, less enthusiastic it seemed to me than I might have expected under the circumstances.

"We've heard a lot of yer preachin', Brother Pritchard," I heard Nathan Dalton say to Cyrus. "And those of us who've been practicin' Old School Baptists have been eager to hear ye. Why, I've thought onc't or twice even of travelin' to New Canaan to hear ye, but given that idea up since I did not want to stir things up here any more."

I glanced at Cyrus to see if I could tell what he made of that, but his expression did not change. I had the feeling that he understood what Brother Dalton was talking about. And I thought I did too. We had probably walked into a nest of bickering Baptists, nor was that hard to do. It was harder betimes to keep them from bickering than to bicker right along with them.

The brother who came up and introduced himself at last as Elder Joshua Murdock was of the sort that, had you not knowed him, you would but had to look at him to have said to yourself that here was a Baptist preacher. Not only was his countenance stern, his words measured, his look unflinching, but his back had that rigid straightness that I had even noted at times in Cyrus—mainly at meeting—that made him look taller than he actually was.

But there was about the man a certain coldness, it seemed to me, when he took our hands and addressed us, a coldness that I had not noted when he come up and greeted those standing about and was greeted by them.

About all he said to Cyrus was that they would have the ceremony of the laying on of hands after the morning service, and then after dinner the newly ordained brother, Plesance Bryan, would preach his first sermon as an ordained Elder. He made no plea, as was ordinarily the custom among Old School Baptists, to Cyrus to preach. Indeed, he only nodded toward the open door and then in a perfunctory manner led the way inside.

The service was conducted in the manner that we was familiar with. The men sat on one side of the room and the women on the other. I sat at the end of a bench with Sarah beween me and George, so I could keep up with her. Of late as we sat thus, I caught myself glancing at George in the knowledge that he would not be seated beside me for much longer, that he would probably sooner than most boys and young men take his place on the other side of the room.

A deacon rose, announced a hymn, and promptly slid into the first verse of it, others joining in slowly until the joyful noise was at full tide. I glanced over at Cyrus, and I could tell that he was being careful not to overwhelm the singers and I could not contain a smile. If Cyrus Pritchard had a prideful flaw, it was in the singing of hymns. I was fairly certain that that pride would soon overcome and, sure enough, by the chorus his rich, full voice carried over all, and not a few heads was turned and admiring glances shot his way.

At the conclusion of the hymn, Brother Nathan Dalton rose and said, "Elder Pritchard who is visiting us from the New Canaan Church is obviously possessed of a remarkable singing ability. I for one would hope that he would bless us by leading us in a song. Am I alone in that?" he asked, and it was obvious by the exclamations and general nodding that he was not.

I looked at where Elder Murdock sat near to the pulpit, his head bent over his Bible as if he were studying his text for the morning, but I could not help but note a most disagreeable expression upon his face.

Cyrus could no more have turned down such an invitation than he could have flown, but he did make some attempt to seem reluctant before he at last rose and went before the group and called up a familiar and beloved old hymn.

On Jordan's stormy banks I stand,
And cast a wistful eye,
To Canaan's fair and happy land,
Where my possessions lie.

I noticed happily—for I was a little prideful myself on Cyrus's gift, though I knowed that we neither one should have been, as it was God's Will that he should sing so for the Glorification of the Almighty—that others in the congregation was slow to take up the song, being more eager to listen to Cyrus than to themselves.

But through all the verses, Elder Murdock did not lift his face from his Bible nor was the frown of disapproval at all softened. At the close of the hymn, as Cyrus made his way to his seat, Biddy Dalton bent over in my direction and said, "My, I don't know when I've heard nothin' so pleasin'." Though she intended it as a whisper, it carried through the small building, and I thought I saw Elder Murdock actually jerk.

Brother Murdock at last rose and with little preliminary begun his discourse. I had to admit that he had a right nice voice and delivery, and I was almost immediately caught up in what he was saying. The text he chose was ordinary—ordinary in that it was in common use and I had heard it preached often. Romans 8:30, "Moreover whom he did predestinate, them he also called: and whom he called, them he also justified: and whom he justified, them he also glorified."

And in short order it was obvious that Elder Murdock preached doctrine over duty. His voice rose and fell and he thumped betimes his Bible or the pulpit, his eyes flashing or beseeching, whispering and shouting, but once I got used to his delivery, it come to me that what he preached was pretty ordinary and routine and, but for his excellent delivery, nothing to get overly excited about.

I thought that Cyrus must be thinking the same thing, for once when I glanced his direction, I thought I caught him a-sighing. And I noted Sister Biddy a-picking at her skirt in a disinterested sort of way and a-glancing around and in general not paying over much attention. While some of the congregation did seem caught up in what the Elder was saying, others by various means suggested that they was not.

Such was Brother Murdock's performance that I thought I could almost predict about when he would commence to wind down, and sure enough at about the point I might have expected it, he come to a halt.

Immediately after the prayer, he called upon Cyrus and Brother Plesance Bryan to come up, and the ceremony of ordination was held. Brother Bryan was a comely young man, serious of expression, and a little on the gangling side. And for just one minute I had what amounted to a vision of George one day in exactly that same spot and posture. For if anything was predetermined, it was to my mind that George would one day fill a pulpit. I did hope that by the time he did so, I would myself have gone through the experience. At that thought, I sighed out loud, loud enough that two or three around glanced over at me, and I was immediately embarrassed and fussed with smoothing my skirt and such.

We broke off for dinner as soon as the ordination was over, a table spread out under the trees. I spread what I had carried, as did everyone else, and what amounted to a goodly feast resulted. After we had eaten, we visited. And in time the newly ordained Elder, Brother Plesance Bryan—several referred to him as Brother Ples, I noted—come up and commenced to speak with Cyrus, being anxious it seemed that Cyrus stay to hear him preach his first sermon as an ordained pastor. Cyrus reassured the young man on that point.

"I do appreciate it, Brother Pritchard," he said. "I have heard naught but good words about yer abilities, and I would be grateful did ye listen and offer any word of instruction that ye might have."

I thought that a very modest and refreshing speech from the young man, especially considering the attitude that Brother Murdock had been exhibiting.

And in short order we begun to move back into the church. "I surely hope he don't speak too long," I heard someone in back of me say. "I come mostly fer the fireworks. I've had about as much doctrine fer one day as I could absorb."

Fireworks? Well, I did wonder what he meant by that.

Elder Joshua Murdock rose abruptly and dispensed with any singing of hymns on the grounds of time, which I could tell from several startled expressions was not the way things was usually done. A body did not have to be too deep to realize that Brother Murdock was not eager to give Cyrus any recognition and that the reason was most likely simple jealousy. Nor was that unheard of, of course. But still it was disappointing wherever it occurred.

However, I did have to consider that wise of Brother Murdock, for Cyrus could have preached circles around him and, like enough, he knowed it.

Brother Ples rose, obviously quite nervous, for he stuttered and stumbled some getting his text off, which he took from Luke, the 12th chapter which included a favorite verse of mine, "The life is more than meat, and the body is more than raiment." And though he stammered considerable and did have some awkward moments, Brother Ples took off after duty as well as doctrine, especially duty, which to my mind was a courageous thing. And Cyrus seemed to think so, too, for he was bent over, his elbows resting on his knees, his hands clasped before him quite intent on the young speaker.

I was pleased to note that, fireworks or no, most of the people assembled give Brother Ples their interested attention, though Brother Murdock sitting on the front bench did seem to wear something of a smug expression at the young brother's awkwardness.

I concentrated for a time on trying not to have hard thoughts on Brother Joshua Murdock.

As soon as Brother Ples had come to his final amen, Brother Murdock rose and said, "Well, now Brothers and Sisters, I do believe that we have here in Brother Plesance Bryan promise of a goodly future. Before we take up the business of the church, let us recess a few moments so that we can congratulate that brother and bid farewell to Brother and Sister Pritchard who have a long walk yet ahead of them."

I looked at Cyrus and he looked as surprised as I felt. I had the distinct impression that we was being asked to leave before the business of the church was run. Not that I would have minded, for sometimes such business could run on awful long to no real purpose. Still, I was not pleased at being throwed out as it were.

But once in the yard, where small groups gathered here and there, Brother and Sister Dalton come up, and Brother Dalton without preface said, "D'ye need to be on yer way, of course, we'd understand. But the truth of it is, ther's several of us as would like fer ye to stay and set in on the business."

"I do not think," drawled Cyrus, "that Brother Murdock is among those several, is he?"

Brother Dalton only grinned and repeated, "Ye'd be welcomed by mostly everyone here."

Something then occured to me, and I asked, "Did you not say that some of this group is of other persuasions and even infidels and unbelievers?"

Brother Dalton nodded, "Yes, quite a few."

"And will they be staying for church business?" For I had not seen anyone at all make any move to leave.

"In truth," snapped Biddy Dalton, "that's why most of them are here. We do have the most entertainin' business of any group about." Nor could she entirely contain the sarcasm in her voice.

Looking around, I could tell that the groups that had gathered was involved in more spirited conversation than one might ordinarily expect. There was intense expressions, some laughter, and wild gesticulations amongst the groups, some obviously right serious, others in a merry, almost county fair attitude.

"We'd be most excited to have ye stay," repeated Nathan Dalton grimly.

"We'd have to leave in plenty of time to get us home before dark," said Cyrus. "but the day is young. We can listen for a time."

Brother Dalton smiled and nodded.

It seemed to me that we tarried over-long out of doors, and it must have seemed so to others also, as there was some looking around and some milling and general readiness. At last Elder Murdock called the meeting to convene inside, and though he didn't say anything contrary to us, it was obvious that he was not happy that we was still there.

Nevertheless, we followed everyone else into the building. The crowd was still goodly in spite of the afternoon heat which invaded the interior of the small building. I hoped that the meeting would not last long, but in truth I had no great hope in that matter for I heard someone laugh and sing out to Brother Murdock as he passed by, "Hey, Brother, let's git on with it n'en," as if it were a game that was commencing.

Brother Murdock called the meeting to order with only one quick glance toward where we was sitting and, with almost a shrug, addressed himself to the rest of the group which was by and large waiting eagerly.

First he called upon the minutes to be read, and an elderly deacon stood and opened his book and started to read. I sat and tried to appear attentive, but the longer the minutes went on, the less I had to work at being attentive, for I thought that I had ne'er in my life heard any such rigamarole. They began routinely enough.

"On May 1, 1811, we the members of the Old School Baptist Church of Elm Creek met to set in a church way to do the things that is wanting in God's house. The following items was considered on that day.

—Agreed that our sacrament meetings to be on the meeting day in May and September.

—Agreed for the church to find a tablecloth.

—Made up fifteen shillings for the use of the church.

—Agreed Brother Plesance Bryan have license to preach.

—The church took up accusation against Brother Daniel Moore for having a hurt against Brother Joel Mason. Postponed until next meeting.

—Whereas there has been a report circulating through the country, took up the distress against Brother James Buckner for drinking too much spiritous liquor, postponed it till next meeting.

—Took up the distress against Brother Thomas Brazendine for telling falsities and after laboring with Brother Brazendine laid him under the censure of the church and referred the matter till next meeting.

—Put Joshua Driskell under the censure of the church for getting in a passion.

—Nathan Fry came forward and made confession that he had done wrong in shooting a gun for whiskey—and the church forgave him for same.

—Took up a distress against Joel Mason and excommunicated him, this church considers, for taking unlawful interest and for selling of a cow to Brother Charles Kelly for a good milk cow and said cow proven in the church to not be such a cow as he said Mason represented her to be.

—Sally Kelly brought in an allegation against Sister Rody Phillips for drinking too much spiritous liquors. And has dismissed Sister Phillips for drinking too much from under the watch care of this church.

—Took up the case of Thomas Brazendine and Bedance Mason and excluded them from us for going and joining Clay Creek Church which we consider to be in disorder.

Well, the brother who was reading so seriously, stopping from time to time to catch his breath and clear his throat, had not even got half way though the list before I was looking around in amazement. I had ne'er before, even among the most contentious of Baptists, heard such a list as this.

Cyrus did not look so amazed, only grim, and Brother and Sister Dalton looked both to be annoyed and embarrassed, while a part of the crowd looked properly serious and another part to be enjoying theirselves no end with it. Elder Murdock stood throughout the recitation nodding his head and looking important.

The list went on some minutes longer, filled mostly with piddling little matters that was either naught but simple gossip or else very minor matters. I could not isolate a single grievance that seemed worth bringing before the body of the church. I just wondered how some of them named would take it all. Had it been me, I'd have been mad as spit.

When the minutes was finished and the meeting opened for comment, there was a spate of hands a-waving in the air, and Brother Murdock's eyes fair danced in anticipation, as did those of several others around me.

"Phillips, yer in order," announced the preacher.

"I'd like to ask this body," began the tall brother who stood up, "just why it is that they can exclude my wife from this group on grounds only of malicious gossip, and yet time after time let Dan Moore get away with owing me debt that the rascal has no intent of paying?"

"Now, just a minute here!" came an angry voice that I took to be Dan Moore's.

"Why," said Elder Murdock, "in business, ye needs proceed slower than in matters of moral turpitude. Now Master Moore disputes this debt, while we have it on several accounts that Sister Phillips has been seen under the influence of spiritous liquors."

Heads was craned about. "Tell me whose account besides Sally Kelly's who ever'one knows always has a spite agin' someone?"

"Master Phillips is out of order," yelled a voice from the back, and heads was again craned in that direction.

"Now, Brother Kelly, in time, in time," said Brother Murdock cheerfully, and I couldn't keep from noticing the happy anticipation of many of the audience.

"Wal," came another voice, "I do have to agree with Brother Phillips that this group does seem to take upon itself much that an't rightly its business, or even true atall."

"Now ye'll have yer say in time, Brother Buckner. Just wait yer turn."

A woman sitting near me jumped to her feet and, without waiting to be noticed, said, "Brother Buckner and Sister Phillips has been reported to be drunk. And if they recall our ordinances, they did agree to submit themselves to the disciplines of this church as part of Christ's visible kingdom, agreeing that we will all act toward one another as brethern in Christ."

She sat down, and with a smile Brother Murdock recognized a man who stood and said right reasonable, "Now, we could argue these charges over and over to no account. It seems to me that we ought to appoint a committee to look into the charges and report back."

Well, after a good deal more conversation on the matter, charges and counter charges, that course of action was finally voted upon.

Elder Murdock then recognized another man who was identified as Joel Mason who talked long and round about, at last admitting that he might have been guilty of taking a mite more interest of a brother on a loan than he should have, but insisting with a great deal of fire that the cow that he sold to Brother Charles Kelly was as good as he stated.

And then there was much conversation on that account, until after considerable wrangling and questioning, it was admitted that the cow had indeed calved and give a full bucket of milk morning and night in addition to what it fed the calf, which was good enough to get Brother Mason reinstated in good faith with the church.

Such business went on all afternoon long until I was fairly dizzy with it. This one complained and that one defended and the other criticized, and through it all the good Elder just nodded and smiled while they jumped from topic to topic, complaint to complaint, nothing accomplished of most of them but to defer them to another time so that I could see that did this happen each month, why they'd have such a store of gossip and gripes that that's all there'd even be to the church.

The afternoon had dragged on over-long when a brother identified as Joshua Driskell rose to defend himself against charges that he had got in a passion. George leaned over and whispered to me, "Mama, is such distresses as these the real and proper concern of the church you think?"

The question was asked in all seriousness for he had been taking it all in the way he always took in spiritual things. Peter and Sarah Elizabeth had both long before fallen asleep against me. As luck would have it, George managed to bend and ask his question just at one of those moments when all other sound was suspended, and his brisk-pitched little voice carried distinctly.

I looked at Cyrus. He had stiffened. Sister Biddy had her hand over her mouth and it was obvious she was trying to stifle a smile. Someone else near-by snickered. But Elder Murdock's face had got red and angry and I thought his breath had entirely suspended it was that quiet. Then he spoke out and, looking straight toward Cyrus, said, "In our meeting house we think that it is best fer children to be seen and not heard."

There was another snicker at that, and I thought that would then end it, but to my great surprise, Cyrus quietly rose and turned so that he addressed the greater part of the group.

"What I have witnessed here this afternoon," he began, "is just as it has been represented to me. I had been warned that this was a congregation of more smoke than fire, and now I know that to be true. I am sorely saddened that the Elm Creek Church has seen fit to fall to brawling and bickering for the apparent entertainment of them that have not even the right to sit in on church business."

197

Brother Murdock started to say something, but Cyrus waved him aside abruptly. His voice was heavy with anger, and in truth there was many there that, like children chastened by an angry father, hung their heads and looked shamed.

"To become the laughing stock, the entertainment center for the community, seems to my mind to put the entire church at distress. To allow such shallow things to come to the attention of the entire congregation—things that should have been handled individually, or if brought before the body, treated in an orderly manner—is serious enough, but then to invite the neighbors in to witness the family a-bickering is inexcusable."

Brother Murdock was by this time huffing and puffing and attempting to speak.

"Amen," come a voice from the back.

"That's been long a-coming," said another, and there was a general rustling as if everyone would get in on it, but Cyrus interrupted again.

"You'd do well not to fall a-bickering over this matter, Brothers and Sisters, but consider your own selves in distress and speak to that without inviting the neighbors in.

"I am not a member of your church. You have not petitioned my interference. Nor had I intended to say aught to the matter and perhaps have spoken out of turn. That's for you to decide. Should you need the help of the Association in interfering in the matter, you have but to call on us."

At that he nodded toward me and, shaking poor Sarah awake, I lifted Peter and flung him over my shoulder, rose with Sarah by the hand, and followed Cyrus out of the church.

"I'm sorry that George spoke out, Cyrus. I don't think he meant harm," I said as we walked back the way we had come, Cyrus having mercifully relieved me of Peter, the poor tired blessed babe still sleeping soundly.

"Perhaps it was the Lord's Way," smiled Cyrus. "If ever a house needed setting in order, that one does. There are too many of those preachers around," he went on as much to himself as to me, "who put on a showtime for to attract people to their entertainments. The Baptists have usually managed to avoid that, but I fear with the great number of strange and new persuasions sifting into the frontier, we'll see more and more of that." He sighed. And we walked on some time in silence.

We walked briskly, and it hardly seemed no time at all that we begun to see familiar landmarks. It had been a long, hard day. And I was thinking to myself that mayhap the next time Cyrus was wanted to visit another church, he'd have to go by himself, when he stopped short on the trail and lifted his head, looking around and then sniffing.

I did the same. "What is it, Cyrus?" I asked.

"Do you smell smoke?"

Well, I think I had been smelling smoke for quite some time, but it hadn't really come to my attention. The smell of smoke was not so uncommon. But when I though on't, I realized that the air was fuller of it than was usual. My eyes had begun to sting some with it and the smell was probably stronger than it ought to be. We had come up on someone a-burning of a big brush pile, I guessed.

"Why," I said, "now who do you suppose would be burning brush on a Sunday?"

And then even before Cyrus could respond, the answer to that question come to me.

Nobody.

Nobody would be a-burning brush on a Sunday. All that smoke was something else.

"A house, Cyrus?"

He shook his head. "It don't smell like that. It smells like brush, like a brush fire that's got out of hand. Hurry. We need to find the source."

I knowed that to be true, for if there's anything scarier than a fire gone wild, I don't know what it is.

Chapter 13

Copperhead

I was not relieved in my mind until we left the trace, followed the path and come out of the woods, and I saw that our cabin stood firm, no sign of fire anywhere close, though the smell of smoke was fierce enough now that it clogged our noses and made our eyes to water.

"It's over yonder." Cyrus pointed to the west. "Beyond the Mayhew cabin, I think. No one would let a brush fire get that big a-purpose. I think it's a brush or grass fire got away."

"Will it burn us, Daddy?" asked Sarah Elizabeth.

"Well, I don't know about that, Sally," said Cyrus using her pet name. "We don't aim to let it burn us. The wind is going away from us, and depending on the conditions and circumstances, we are probably not in no danger."

He turned to me. "I'd best go on over there and see what's happening. I'll stay to help if I'm needed. Should there be any indication that the blaze is serious enough to affect us here, why, I'll return and tell you."

"Can I go, Daddy?" asked George.

"Well, Son," Cyrus answered quite seriously, "one of us needs to stay here. Which one do you think that ought to be?"

George only frowned but didn't say nothin', knowing he'd been outmaneuvered.

"Annamanda, gather everyone in before dark and keep a watch, a careful watch. If there is a bad fire, the critters will know it and they'll be on the move, large and small. They have a sense for that kind of danger and will move away from it toward the river. Don't go out in the dark whatever you do. Mayhap, though, I'll be right back, for the fire will proven to be naught," he added patting my arm.

I watched him walk toward the path which led to the Mayhew's. I fanned the air a bit with my hand. The smoke was in truth not so bad, no worse than being trapped by the winter in a cabin with a leaky fireplace. It was just a little annoying, but nothing you couldn't get used to.

I set in to spread a little supper for the children, and then I gathered some wood, and having fed and washed the children, I pushed the chunk against the door, protecting from intruders, yet letting in the night air, and readied the children for sleep, telling them not to worry, for I'd stay up and wait for Daddy and keep an eye out for sparks and such.

Peter, who was an uncommon good babe, did not struggle but fell quickly off to sleep.

"I will stay up and help you watch, Mama," announced George.

"Well, if George is to stay up, I will, too," said Sarah Elizabeth.

"Daddy told me that I had to stay and help," said George indignantly. "You go to sleep."

"Mama!"

"Well, you both may sit up and help watch, though there's nothing much to watch for."

"Varmints and critters," said George casting an evil glance toward his sister.

"Mama!"

"George. Mind yourself or you can go to bed."

They bickered awhile longer, but it was just as I had knowed it would be. First Sarah and then George, weary from too long a day, slipped off to sleep, Sarah on her own tick and George against my bed.

Cyrus had been gone by then long enough that he could easily have been back so I had to assume that there was indeed a serious enough fire to keep him so long occupied.

At intervals, I rose and stood at the door and listened and sniffed the air, which remained smokey, and looked in the distance, but I could not make out anything untoward. The only glow in the west was the one that the sun leaves behind when it retreats for the night, and the only sounds were those night noises that you can always expect, neither louder nor more insistent.

The critters did not seem to be on the move to any degree. I had to think that the blaze was probably not so serious, though the smoke in the air was still pronounced. But it was smoke and not necessarily fire, for the smoke could linger long after the blaze was gone.

I stood thus for a while and then moved back and sat at the table with my mending and knitting to keep me occupied. There being no one to talk to, the silence was telling, and after a time I rose and stood once more at the door, mindful of what Cyrus had said about going out.

I glanced back at the mantle over which Cyrus had hung his rifle, ball and powder already loaded in it. Should a bear or painter menace, I thought with a little shudder, or an Indian. . .

I had not thought of Sarah's Indian all the week long, but in the dark night it come back to me, and I run my hand involuntarily over my scalp and then had to laugh quietly at myself. There is just something about the dark and still of the night that seems to make things seem greater and more menacing than they are.

I sat again, took up my sewing without enthusiasm, glanced over at the sleeping children, and then without hardly realizing, nodded off myself. Nor did I know how long I sat a-dozing, but when I jerked awake, why, my neck was stiff and my shoulders sore. I looked longingly at my own bed, but when I rose I wandered back to the door to look out.

The glow in the west remained, but this time I knowed that it could not be what was left of the sunset, nor could it be moonlight or sunrise. The smell of smoke was still strong in the air, perhaps stronger, it was hard to determine.

I listened for a time, but still the night noises was not unusual. Indeed, it was upon that hour that they diminish before the day noises commence. And the air was still, no wind or even breeze at all. I concluded that there was not any significant danger from the fire or from wandering critters or no more from Indians than would normally have been.

I was so tired and sleepy I decided, heading toward my bed, that did the Indians decide to attack, well, they was just going to have to take my scalp as I slept. And so I did.

I could not have slept long for when I woke, still heavy of eye and dull of head, day had just begun to break and the sun was not yet up. I stretched and looked at the children, all sleeping as children do, careless of everything, and thought how pleasant it was, how tired I felt and yet how comfortable, cool with the breeze a blowing steadily through the open door, in spite of the smell of smoke it carried. And I slipped off to sleep again.

I do not know what waked me the next time, but I woke with a start and sat straight up in bed, the sun already high. My first thought was: breeze!

That pleasantly strong breeze coming through the door was coming from the west and carried with it not only smoke but possible sparks and fire. I shot up out of bed, stumbling over George as I did so, and he stirred and straightened in a groggy manner.

"Mama?"

"Go on back to sleep awhile if you want, George. There's nothing to be alarmed of."

I still thought that to be so, for had Cyrus not said that if there was danger to us, he would return? I stood at the door for a long time and stared toward the west. The air was heavy with smoke and it was carried on the breeze from the southwest. I wished that Cyrus would return with news. I was not comfortable in not knowing what was happening.

By the time the children had risen and I had fed and dressed them, the breeze had picked up considerable and the smoke was heavier. Well, Cyrus or no, it was time to get prepared.

I gathered all the old rags and cloths and comforters that I could find. In truth that was not so many, and not so old that I would like to sacrifice them to the fire. And probably I would not, but I would be ready in any case.

I removed the chunk at last from the doorway and went out and checked the rain barrel, which was a little over half filled. I would send George to the spring with the bucket to bring up more water. I turned back toward the house, looked up for a moment, and caught sight of a deer a-standing at the edge of the clearing to the west. It was late of a morning to see such, for the deer should have all fed and taken cover by that hour.

"Mama," cried George, "I think the critters is moving. Look at the birds."

I looked up and indeed the birds which generally flitted about here and there was all moving toward the east, and I looked back for the deer to find it gone, to what direction I could not say.

Where was Cyrus?

"Well, I still see no danger, George," I said at last as matter of factly as I could manage. "I suspect they are just fleeing the smoke, and who could blame them for that."

As the morning wore on, though, it become obvious that the varmints and critters was on the move. As in a line for the ark they come, skittering through the forest, rabbits, squirrels, chipmunks and whistle-pigs, skunks and foxes, night critters that should be already holed up for the day. I thought of bears and painters.

"Mama," cried Sarah, "fire!"

It was not actually fire she'd found, but a hot ash carried on the breeze and I knowed it was time to act. I dragged out all the quilts and comforters and rags I had gathered and I begun to soak them in the rain barrel.

Someone would have to go to the roof to spread them. "Sarah!"

She was light and nimble afoot and more dexterous than George, and we hoisted her up with many a heave and scramble. I had other need of George anyway.

"You take the bucket down to the spring and bring back water for the barrel," I directed. "Make as many trips as you need. But keep a watch for the critters. I don't think any'd bother you lest you stumbled right on top of one."

He went off in something of a pique I could tell, that he had to carry water while his sister played on the roof. I handed the dripping rags to Sarah, straining as high as I could as she knelt and reached down as far as she could, both of us getting thoroughly wetted in the process. She carried the cloths and spread them about the roof at my direction to guard against errant sparks and hot ash that might ignite it.

Such effort lowered the water in the barrel considerably, and George grumbled a little when he poured the first bucketful into it and realized he'd have several trips to make.

"Why can't Sarah take turns?" he complained.

"Sarah's too little to carry heavy buckets of water. You know that."

He did know that, too. He only wanted to grumble, I was sure, and get a little attention. "Hurry on," I said. "We may need all the water we can get."

I went back in the house, found some pretties for Peter to keep him occupied, gathered up some more cloths and stepped back outside. I started around the corner of the cabin and stopped abruptly mid-step, for before me on the path, slithering slowly along, for all the world as if it were on a leisurely stroll was a very large copperhead snake, headed east.

It stopped as I stopped, and though I can't say we actually stared at each other, we both took in the situation, and though I could not speak for the snake, for myself I was wondering wh'er to flee or to attack.

Was this the mate of that great snake killed the week before?

The thing with its head lifted seemed uncertain, as was I. I could dash for the hoe which was some steps away, but I did not want to lose sight of the snake for fear it might in some way make its way into the cabin where Peter played or down the path to the spring where George would pass. So I waited and stared, and it did the same.

What was it thinking? Was it wondering at the force which drove it from its secure place, where it minded its own business and lived its life as nature directed, unmolesting unless first molested?

What a strange thought to have. There was I faced with a forest fire on the one side and a deadly viper on the other, and I was having philosophical thoughts on the subject. I laughed to myself and moved a bit and the snake, as if taking polite leave, dipped its head and suddenly moved on down the path and into the brush, and with relief I noted that it was not going in the direction of the spring.

I went back and commenced to soak rags. They lapped up the water much as thirsty kine might. Where was George? He'd need make many trips, and yet he dawdled, probably in a snit still over his ill fortune against his sister's great fortune. The wetted comforters was heavy and it was quite a struggle to get one up to Sarah. She managed to get a corner and by dint of pulling and dragging got it finally on the roof.

"I'm tired, Mama," she complained.

"Well, would you rather take the bucket to the spring and let George on the roof?"

She thought about that for a minute and then without comment dragged the comforter across the roof. "Step carefully, now," I admonished not for the first time. Then I sighed and deciding that I would at least have to call to George to hurry him on, I turned toward the spring path and had taken but a few steps down it when I saw George approaching slowly, bucket in hand— and an Indian at his back!

Did he know that the Indian followed? Should I yell or turn quickly back to the cabin and secure the rifle from over the mantle? George was struggling with the bucket, and I could not tell if he saw me or if the Indian had seen me. I backed a quiet step backward and then another, and would perhaps have stepped thus quickly backward all the way to the door of the cabin had I not noticed that the Indian was followed by another Indian and that one another, so that by the time I had waited a few moments, a whole line of

Indians—mayhap ten or twelve altogether, warriors all by the look of them—stepped one by one from the forest, led by George, a-struggling yet with the heavy bucket.

Well. What to do now? There was a forest fire to one side of me, a poisonous viper to another side of me, a line of savage Indians before me and the Mississippi River behind me and three children to protect, and naught to protect 'em with. And where was Cyrus?

A dread thought hung in my mind and caused me to tremble. Was the presence of these Indians the reason for his delay? Could he have come afoul of these and lie somewhere in the forest bereft of life and scalp?

Such thoughts scampered through my mind in just an instant's time, and before I could make up my mind what action to take, much less take such action, I realized that the Indians had seen me, for they stopped, gathered, and looked at me all in uncanny silence.

I held out my arms to George, who stopped and shifted his bucket to his free hand. "I'm a-hurryin' as fast as I can," he grumbled, and from the way he said it I knowed that he had not the faintest notion that he was followed by a line of Indians. He kept a-comin', I kept my arms out, and the Indians stayed put.

All manner of queer thoughts tumbled through my head, memories of stories I had heard, particularly as a child in Kentucky, of the way of savages, who might attack and scalp, turn and leave, take prisoners or what not, so unpredictable was they.

"George," I managed to speak at last. "George, put down your bucket quietly and just walk over here by me." I was as calm as I could be but he stopped and looked questioningly at me, accurately reading the alarm in my eyes.

"Mama?"

"Do not run, George, or scream. And do not look backward. There are Indians behind you."

At that his face first flushed and then went pale, but wise lad that he was, he carefully did just as I said, and I kept my eyes on the Indians.

They was mostly young, I thought, but for one who even at a distance showed gray in his hair and lines upon his face. He must have been their chief, for even in my fear, I could not but note that this was a magnificent looking man, savage or no.

And then it come to me that they did not wear paint. The stories that I had always heard of savage Indians had included their wild and piercing screams and the copious paint upon their bodies and the flailing of their tomahawks and knives and such. There was no evidence of any of that. Though they had knives in their belts and some had what looked to be tomahawks over their shoulders, they did not menace with them but only stared at me.

I took George firmly by the hand, gathered my skirts in my hand, started

to turn back toward the cabin, changed my mind, and instead walked directly toward where the Indians stood at the edge of the forest. I glanced down
at George, whose eyes was wide as cups and whispered to him, "You go back
to the cabin and get Sarah from the roof, and Peter, and get you in the cabin
and get down Daddy's rifle. Go now."

"It is not necessary," said that magnificent Indian, startling me with his
careful English, his voice low but powerful, and he pointed back toward the
cabin. I looked back.

In the time that I had been standing confronting the Indians, the air had
filled with sparks and burning debris for the wind had picked up and what
had simply been precautions now seemed critically necessary. The fire was
upon us. I whirled and ran back to the cabin.

The danger from the Indians now seemed less than the danger from the
fire, for I knowed not what the Indians might do, but I did know what the fire
would do. Sarah was yet on the roof of the cabin and Peter was inside.

"Mama, there's fire," cried George and sure enough, little flames was lap-
pin' slowly across an open space.

"Wet some rags, George. We have to beat them out before they burn out
of control." And I wetted a heavy cloth and carried it dripping toward where
the flames was creeping across the grass which mercifully was not tall but
stubby. I began methodically beating at them with the wetted cloth, holding
my skirts back. And in an instant George was beside me doing the same.

Such would do for a small grass fire, but would certainly not put out a
conflagration.

"Mama!" It was Sarah. I had forgot about her. She still stood on the roof.
I turned and looked. She was standing on the roof, the morning sun glinting
off her red hair, her skirts whipping in the breeze.

"Mama! Look!" She pointed toward something that she only could see
from her vantage. "Look! It's Daddy," she cried, "and O'Reilly!"

My first thought was relief, my second fear. I remembered the Indians
and looked around to find them. Several of them had helped themselves
to rags and cloths, wetted them and was themselves at work beating at the
flames, which as the bare space spread wide, so they spread, nibbling on the
low grass which fed them, not grown big enough to attack trees and undergrowth. But beyond them to the west, the smoke billowed black and high
enough, that I understood those flames to be only scouts for a much hungrier
force.

I realized, too, that the Indians was as much at the mercy of the flames as
we and so they beat at them, all but that tall and handsome leader, who stood
apart without expression on his face, his bare chest glistening copper brown,
his arms crossed over his chest.

Then I seen Cyrus and indeed black O'Reilly did tower behind him, and
with them four neighbor men, and in a rush of relief, I gathered up my skirts
and ran to them.

Cyrus and O'Reilly stopped abruptly, and I was close enough to see that Cyrus's mouth had fallen open at the sight of the Indians, though O'Reilly's expression did not change.

"My Gawd," exclaimed one of the men whom I recognized as an older Mayhew boy, "Injuns!"

I explained the best way I could and ended by pointing out the Indian leader standing apart near the edge of the forest.

"He speaks English," I said.

Cyrus started for him stepping along quickly, and O'Reilly followed after. I noticed that the other white men hung back. I had to rush to keep up. A few steps from the Indian, Cyrus stopped and spoke. "I am grateful that you help us, Brother," he said.

The Indian said nothing, but his glance traveled to O'Reilly standing so tall and proud, and it come to me that the two of them was of an age, not old but older. It would be hard to judge exactly. And looking between the two of them I wondered—it almost seemed that a flicker of recognition passed between them, an almost imperceptible nod. I could not be sure. Else, their two expressions did not change. Cyrus waited.

At last the Indian spoke, his words something of an accusation. "The fire comes," he said, "at times. It comes from the sky or from the devil or," and here he paused significantly, "it comes from the careless white man, who destroys God's growth and scars His earth."

Cyrus's gaze was as firm and unflinching as the red man's, and he repeated, "We are grateful. We thank you."

But the Indian remained silent. Cyrus turned to me, "The fire has got almost completely out of hand. It was started by some new settlers south of Master Thomas's place. They did not know what they was at and left the fire under the care of two small boys who wandered off to play."

I had to sigh at that.

"The fire was checked at the creek before it got the Thomases' cabin. So far," he said, looking around grimly, "no cabins has been destroyed."

I did not like the sound of that—"so far," he'd said.

"Mama!" the cry from the roof interrupted my thoughts. We'd forgot the little girl atop the roof. "Mama! Daddy!"

Sarah was standing on the roof, her face smudged, a wet cloth hanging limply at her side. Ah, poor thing, she had worked hard for one so little.

"She's got to get off that roof," said Cyrus. "I think it likely that we will lose the cabin, for the fire gathers strength. We must rescue as much as we can from it and take it beyond the spring where perhaps the fire will not cross."

"Copperhead."

"What?" I said. "Where?" I looked around frantically. It was the Indian who had spoken, but he was not looking toward the ground where one might reasonably expect to find a snake, but at the roof where Sarah stood.

"Copperhead," he repeated. His stoic face had taken on something of a surprised look. Then I realized what he was remarking upon—Sarah's hair which sparkled in the early morning sunlight, bright as a new penny indeed.

Copperhead.

Cyrus turned to the red man and said again, "We are grateful that you help, but I do not think we can hold the fire back. We would move our belongings from the cabin."

The red man was still for so long that I thought perhaps he did not hear. He was still looking at the roof where Sarah stood, her long red curls escaping the plait I had put them in.

"No." The Indian spoke so unexpectedly that I almost jumped. "No," he repeated. "Will not burn. The tears of God will water the earth. Soon."

George had come up and had taken his father's hand and was watching the red man. "He thinks it will rain soon, Mama."

Well. I suppose that was it. Trust a child to understand, for the Indians often spoke as children. "Tears of God". I thought that I would remember that expression for the rest of my life.

"Cyrus? Do you think he's right? Do you think it will rain and put out the fire?"

He looked around shaking his head. "It does not seem rainy, but the Indians is uncanny in such matters of weather and natural things. We could take the chance." He was smudged and blackened, and looking closely at him, I could tell that he was also very tired. "We can try for a while and see what happens. The fire is at least predictable. You can see it coming and you can predict where it will go. It will not cross this bare ground until the conflagration has got great."

He turned to me. "Someone else has got to go on that roof and guard from sparks. Someone light." He looked at George.

"No," I said, "I'll go up. I'd as leave Sarah stayed there, for there we can keep track of her. But if you set both her and George to the same task, they'll spend all their time bickering and lose sight of what they're to do."

So I was hoisted up, struggling in the process to retain my modesty, and Sarah and I, armed with wetted rags, patrolled the rooftop looking for errant sparks, cautious, as the wetted rags had left damp spots here and there upon the shingles making them hazardous.

It was not so bad a way to fight a fire, for the breeze was pleasant up there, the view good, and the heat of the fire not yet arrived. But there was sparks a-plenty to keep us busy. And through the smoke in the distance, I could begin to make out the tall flames licking as if whetting their appetites for what was to come. I wondered how long we ought to wait for rain.

The Indian held his ground, looking impassively as the others worked—although 'worked' was perhaps an ill term, for that was not what the Indian force did. They played. They attacked the little flames aggressively now and then, whooping and hollering and dancing about and shouting to one another. Suddenly one might yelp and and hop around, apparently having stepped on a hot place, and others around him would stop and fall to laughing at him.

They seemed to make a game of it, rushing from place to place, racing each other in mad dashes to get to a spot where the flames presented more of a challenge.

I turned away from watching them and got back to my job. Sarah had stopped to look. "Mama!" she yelled. "Mama! Peter!"

I looked around, following the direction she pointed. And Peter, who had I thought been napping inside, had toddled out, and dragging a wet rag behind him, had appeared among the Indians. There was no telling how long he had been at the cabin door watching the activity before deciding to join in. He was laughing and swatting at the ground in imitation of the Indians, and they had in a group gathered around, pointing at him and laughing.

One of the Indians picked him up, and I stiffened, uncertain as to his intentions, but a sharp word from their chief and the Indian put the baby down again.

"Cyrus," I called. "Cyrus—the baby!"

He saw immediately, came over, and picked the child up and carried him to the tree beside the cabin where we kept a rope for that purpose, and he tied the babe to the tree, allowing him a little freedom. It was not a new experience for Peter, for there was times when no one was about to watch him closely that he had to be so tied for his own safety, but he never liked it and squalled his head off, as he was then doing to the great joy of the Indians, who had to be encouraged back to their jobs with another sharp word from their chief.

I could only tell of the passing time by the rising sun which had got uncomfortable for Sarah and me upon the roof without shade or breeze. Breeze! The breeze had died, and of a sudden it had become uncommon still, and as a result the sparks on the roof was fewer.

I tried to see beyond the heavy smoke for to detect clouds mayhap portending rain, but I could see naught but smoke and haze. But I thought the stillness and the heaviness of the air a good sign. I realized that I had uncommon faith in the Indian's prediction. I was expecting rain.

And within the hour, I was not disappointed. It come up suddenly, with the lightning and the thunder upon us almost without warning, and Sarah and I had to scramble to get off the roof, a roof being no place to be, I thought, during electrical weather.

At first the raindrops come slow and soft, disappointing, and then perhaps God got considerably more worked up, for at last the rain come down hard, in buckets, sizzling the hot ground, and we all stood right out in it, braving the lightning, for we was relieved. But, at last, even our relief was not enough to keep us out of doors.

We slipped into the cabin, shaking ourselves like so many pups. "Call the Indians," I said, "and O'Reilly." But when Cyrus looked out they was gone, all of them. "Well," I said.

By late afternoon, the rain was gone, and the neighbors, too—strangely making little comment on the appearance of the Indians—but not the smoke for it steamed yet in the distance. Cyrus went out and come back some time later to confirm that the blaze was gone, drowned in a torrent. He suggested that we pray our thanks to God, and I concurred, and we knelt right down on the floor and Cyrus prayed and give thanks.

I for one could not keep from thinking, as Cyrus spoke, of God on high blubbering out copious tears over all. I just could not keep myself from thinking such errant thoughts. I was bad about that. I supposed that there was no help for me.

"The Indians is back, Daddy," whispered George. And sure enough we looked out the door and there they was in a group in the cabin clearing. I glanced toward the rifle, but truly could find no fear in my heart, nor apparently could Cyrus, for he rose—not forgetting to excuse himself to God with a quick "Amen"—and stepped quickly out to meet the Indians.

By the time that we had joined the group, me with Peter securely in my arms, Cyrus had concluded his thanks once more, and much to my distress was offering to feed them!

Mercifully, the leader declined. I do not know what I would have done, tired as I was, if I had had to work up a meal for such a group.

"The fire is gone," announced the Indian, as if that were why they had returned.

Cyrus nodded. "We have give thanks for that." He started to say something else when Sarah interrupted with a loud squeal.

"Stop that!" she snapped.

One of the Indian braves had moved around behind her and had lifted her hair and was letting it run through his fingers. "Stop that!" she squealed again, and jerked her hair away and whirled to face the young Indian.

She pointed a little finger at him, her other hand stern upon her hip, and snapped again, "You stop that, hear! That's my scalp and you'll be pleased to keep your hands from it." Her little eyes was giving off angry flashes and her face was flushed to where the freckles across her nose stood at attention.

The guilty brave stepped back, startled, and the others broke down laughing and pointing at him and pushing him. He strutted some, looking discomfitted, and at last stalked off and stood with his back to the group.

"Copperhead," said the chief once more.

I pulled Sarah to me and chastized her gently. "They come to help, remember. And he meant no harm, I'm sure. He was only curious of the color."

"Well, he could just keep his hands off my scalp," she repeated.

210

"Hair," I corrected. "Scalp," indeed. I did not say to her the thought that crossed my mind, that hair was not a scalp to the Indians until it left your head.

Tired as we was, Cyrus and I stayed up late, though the children after only a little fussing collapsed in unwashed heaps upon their beds.

"Where did you get O'Reilly?" I finally thought to ask.

"He just arrived," said Cyrus. "You could see the smoke for miles. I suppose that's what alerted him."

"Where did he go and when?"

"That I don't know. I looked up after the rain started and he was gone. As silent as an Indian himself."

"And what was them Indians doing here anyway?" I went on.

"My, you're just filled with questions, aren't you?"

"Well, you're not filled with answers, are you?" I retorted.

"No," he frowned, "no, I am not and would that I were."

The next morning was bright and clear, the way days can be after a hard rain. The smoke was gone, but the smell of the burned forest was still strong. We needed water from the spring house, but I had no intention of sending George off by himself, so I bundled up Peter and Sarah, and all of us made an excursion of it.

I did not expect to find trouble nor did we. We come back up to the cabin without incident, and I set out to clean all our smoke-covered things, a chore that I was not looking forward to.

I had been at my task for quite some time when Sarah appeared at the door. I had all but forgot the children, who could, it then occured to me, be of some help. I started to say as much, but Sarah interrupted. "Mama, come see what we found."

Her expression was curious enough that I asked no questions but put aside my scrubbing and followed after her down the path toward the garden. Peter and George was stopped just off the path a few feet before the garden started, staring at something on the ground.

It was not until I was right on top of them that I could make out what it was they was looking at. A snake. Long dead.

"Copperhead, Mama," said George.

I nodded. It was not the copperhead that was of so much interest so much as the manner of its death. For it was split wide, lengthwise.

A tomahawk, its handle apparently broken upon impact, was still imbedded in the giant viper's flesh.

Chapter 14

The Blockhouse

It was late summer when word come that the Bradenes, Patsy and Reuben, was arrived and unloading their raft and planned to be with us as soon as they finished.

Eli Thomas, the Methodist, brought us that word, for he had been to business in New Madrid that had took him down to the river. "They said to tell ye that they'd drift on down toward us and prob'ly be here no later than sunset tomorrow."

The children was immediately excited, recalling their own adventures some months earlier upon that same river. "Can we go down tomorrow to the river to meet them?" asked George.

To my surprise, Cyrus did not tell them no. "Mayhap we'll all walk down," he said instead, for along our stretch of the river, there was only one place secure enough to land and it was not so great a walk, at that.

That was enough for the children. They could hardly be got to bed that night for excitement and was up early the next morning with it.

In truth, I was a little excited, too. Except for our trips to meeting, we never had nowhere else to go. We did not even go into New Madrid itself, for it was with divers folk—most, they said, of a rough disposition—and recalling my own adventures in Ste. Genevieve, I was loathe, I suppose, to tackle a city again, though New Madrid yet was not so great a city as Ste. Genevieve.

Therefore, an excursion to the river for the day seemed a most pleasant diversion. I would carry our dinner in my basket and we would make a day of it.

We got an earlier start than I had anticipated, for the children could not be contained. Before it turned abruptly east, our path took us through some of the area that had been burned by the forest fire. It was amazing to see in how short a time the growth reclaimed the ground, inevitable and undeterred, indeed greener and fresher looking than ever against the fading charcoal of the ground. And for no good reason that I could think of, I was reminded of that saying I had once heard that after a great natural event: all things must start over again.

Ours was not a lonely walk for there was many cabins between us and the river, and each one we passed, wh'er we was known or not, the residents poured out to talk and bid us welcome and importune us to take a meal with them, which we politely declined. And thus we made some new acquaintances, for some of these cabins was only newly raised by recent settlers.

Cyrus did not inquire as to the doctrines of any of these, for which I was most certainly glad, for had they been Baptists of the Old School, why, he certain would have fell to immediate discussion, and had they been of some other persuasion, why, there would possibly be some argument, depending on the strength of the other's convictions. I knowed the strength of Cyrus's convictions.

Our leisurely walk took us to the river by early afternoon, and we spread our quilt and had our dinner right there at the river's edge. At that point the river spread wide and flowed in a leisurely manner, and the bank sloped down to it gradually and it was a right pleasant setting.

After dinner, Peter slept and Sarah and George took off their shoes and gathered their clothes about them and waded and lashed about in play.

"I should teach George to swim," said Cyrus abruptly. Then after a time he said, "No time like the present." He called George over, and the two of them left us there on the shore while they went to search out a place private enough for swimming.

"Mama, why can't I learn to swim?" asked Sarah, most annoyed.

"Well, girls don't need to know to swim," I said and when that answer apparently didn't suit her, I added, "You'd have to take off all or near all your clothes, would you swim. Think about that."

"Is George going to take off all his clothes?"

"I suspect so," I answered and thought, but did not add, that so would his father, it being to my mind the lure of a swim for himself that had encouraged him to give George a swimming lesson.

In time they returned, damp and refreshed and bright of eye, for George it seemed had proved to be a most natural swimmer, catching onto it quickly and enthusiastically. Sarah at that intelligence turned her back and marched off by herself and would have nothin' to do with George when he approached.

"It an't fair," she said later. "Daddy should teach me to swim, too." No amount of reasoning could dissuade her from that strange idea either, so I just give it up.

It was just after mid-afternoon that the Bradene's raft, a smaller one than I had seen them on before, drifted into view and with much oaring and poling was prodded to shore, some downstream of against a steeper bank.

We all scrambled over to that bank and waited eagerly for them to climb off the raft. It would have been better had they come in to the bank where we was, for it would be an awkward climb up this bank.

Patsy was talking mile a minute, even before we was close enough to understand. Reuben had waded ashore and tied the raft to a near tree, and then he and Patsy maneuvered it around and positioned it hard against the bank.

"Watch yer step, Pat," said Reuben, but Patsy was talking and apparently not paying attention, for she took a step toward the bank, misjudged, and the raft not so securely positioned, perhaps, as they had thought, jerked away from the bank and Patsy took a tumble, right into the water, several feet from shore.

She commenced to thrash around, weighted down as she was by her heavy skirts, and squawking and hollering. Before anyone else could react Reuben yelled, "She cain't swim!" and was right in the water after her, and they was both a-thrashing around, while we waited for him to pull her out.

We waited a few moments, and it come to me that Reuben wasn't making no headway. Indeed, he seemed as much the problem as the solution, for they two was wallering around, first one and then the other on top, making much noise and confusion, but little progress.

"Cyrus?"

But by the time I spoke, he already had his shoes off and quickly slipped into the water and commenced to wade out, waiting for the bottom to drop off. But curiously it never did. Until he was right up on the thrashing couple, standing in water up to his shoulder but no farther, and him considerably shorter than either of the Bradenes.

He took a hold of the first one that surfaced and then the other, and said something to them both, and with sheepish confusion on their faces, they let their feet down and realized that no one was in danger of drowneding in that shallow water.

They all three, soaking wet, waded out.

"She cain't swim," said Reuben.

"Well, hell, neither can you!" snapped Patsy, who was not always careful of her language.

"You mean you jumped in the water after her and you couldn't swim either?" I asked.

"But she cain't swim," he repeated stubbornly.

It was fortunate that there was day and sun enough left to dry the three of them out. And though I'd ne'er have said nothing, I couldn't help from thinking that a dunk in the river would ne'er hurt the Bradenes and might possibly have divested Patsy of any fleas she might have harbored. It was not a kind thought, but it was true that she seemed to attract those bugs in uncommon amounts, while they ne'er seemed to discomfort Brother Bradene at all.

We wrung out the wet clothes we could, draped all but what was necessary for modesty and decency across the bushes to dry, and visited there on the shore, the Bradenes bringing us up on a variety of news.

"Sister Cuthcart sends her best wishes," said Patsy, "and says to tell ye that ye are missed."

"Ah," I said, "and I hope that Sister Cuthcart and her familiy are all prosperous."

"Well, I don't know about that, but she said to tell ye that about the first of the year she has plans to bless Brother Cuthcart with yet another mouth to feed and that will make a total of thirteen, d'ye count that'un that they lost."

"Thirteen!" I couldn't imagine. "Well," I laughed, "did John Cuthcart make money as he makes babes, I think he'd be a wealthy man by now. Still," I added, "thirteen is an awful many. It seems to me that he's about to run it in the ground."

"T'would seem to me that that's what he ought to do with it. Run it in the ground and give Sister Cuthcart a rest," answered Patsy Bradene bluntly.

Well, there was no answer to that!

"We have brought ye a letter from Brother Kencaid," she went on and then added proudly, "and we have brought our letters from Lost Creek Church to present to ye at New Caanan, fer I have gone before the brothers and sisters and pleaded my case and was accepted conditionally back under the watchcare of the church."

"Well, Patsy, this is wonderful news." And I truly meant it. And I started to say more, but Patsy was suddenly up on all fours, with a startled look upon her face.

"Mama! Daddy!" It was Sarah at my back. "I'm going to fall in the water," she screamed, and I turned just in time to see that wretched girl actually jump into the river, at a spot that looked deep.

It was Cyrus, in the water, almost as quick as she was, that caught up with her and dragged her sputtering and flailing her arms, and deposited her near at my feet, him once more soaked through.

"Sarah Elizabeth! What did you do that for? I've a mind to thrash you good, Girl."

"I fell in," she said.

"You jumped in."

"I fell in," she insisted, her lower lip out a-pouting. "I fell in and nobody cares if I was drowneded or not. Girls," she said with a sly, sidewise look at Cyrus, "can drown, you know, just as easy as boys can."

Cyrus was once more wringing himself out and did not answer directly, but from the look upon his face, I suspected that one day soon, the girl would have her swimming lesson.

The Bradenes was traveling mainly between New Madrid and New Orleans. "It winters too cold north beyond here," complained Patsy. They raised theirselves a tiny cabin near to the river for to pass the time when they was not actually on it, and Patsy even threatened to make a garden, yet I thought we'd be lucky ever to see it.

The letter from Brother Kencaid to Cyrus was both welcome and generous. He told of various activities around the Association of churches founded and members baptized.

"Yet, withal," he wrote, "we miss you and the sweet words of grace that you blessed us regularly with.

"Redmon Pitt and his Pittites has grown considerable, though I've yet to get a clear understanding of just what it is that he teaches. Other denominations has grown, some others has splintered off as the Pitties done, so that the variety of those that profess to be Christians is just astonishing. As is the variety of interpretations that they try to make of what is plain, uncomplicated Scriptures.

"And there is almost constant fighting and bickering amongst all the various sects. I try to remain aloof from such, but it comes increasing hard, as most all of them denominations is determined to take a-holt the Old School doctrine as a dog a old sock and thus growl at it and snarl and shake it, all noise and commotion and naught of substance."

And he had words to say of Reuben and Patsy, too.

"We have sent Brother and Sister Bradene to live under your watch-care, but truth of it is, unless your congregation be broad of mind as well as understanding of spirit, you could well have your hands full in short order, a-keeping of the peace."

The very next meeting was eventful for two reasons. First of all, Brother and Sister Dalton of the Elm Creek Congregation appeared for services and brought with them four or five other couples.

"We have decided to move our letters here, if ye'll have us," said Brother Dalton. "It's a considerable more walk, but we think it worth the effort, though we do expect a good deal of fireworks from Elder Murdock and his followers on the matter. He's a most jealous and self-centered critter an' cannot abide that someone else might be thought equal, or even better, than he is."

That excitement had hardly died down when Sister Leretta and Sister Berdetta Morphew's three blacks presented theirselves for baptism.

When Cyrus called for mourners to approach the bench, well, them three blacks rose as one, obviously planning it, and come forward. There was a little uncertain rustling about and some whispering, and I noted that although Cyrus had give an uncommon good sermon, the sort that usually produced quite a few mourners, none else but the slaves approached.

I glanced at the sisters and they sat up at attention watching the proceedings, that space usually occupied by the black Anna still wide between them. I had ne'er heard them speak to one another nor to anyone else. But they did sing and sing very well, so they was not deaf and dumb.

Cyrus most likely was in on the plot himself, for he proceeded without hesitation his examination of the applicants and truth to tell, they give good account of theirselves, especially Anna.

When Cyrus asked her why she sought admittance, she considered only a moment and then turned toward the congregation and answered firmly, "Ah desire a chu'ch home fer m'self, suh, an' fer m'bruthers, a chu'ch home an' hope of salvation."

I was suspicious that them coloreds had been carefully coached, especially the boys, but withal, their answers was thoughtful and sincere, as much as any other applicants usually was.

And after several of the deacons had questioned them to their satisfaction, the church voted on them and they was accepted for baptism. There was always some folks uncomfortable of darkies in the congregation, but it was not unheard of. There had been other blacks baptized, for the Lord had ne'er specified the color of his saints.

When the slaves nodded that they did have a change of clothes, Cyrus announced the baptism would be immediate. Well, I did have to wonder what old Master Morphew would have to say about that, but I had to trust that Cyrus had thought it through.

And Anna and her brothers Tim and Jim was baptized in the nearby stream, and their bright black eyes and happy grins give good testament to their joy. As the last one was pulled up from the water, Sister Leretta and Sister Berdetta at once broke into a joyful hymn, and all else followed them along that tune.

As we walked home late in the afternoon, I asked Cyrus if he expected trouble from the slaves' owner, Master Morphew.

Cyrus shook his head, shrugged and said, "We'll have to wait and see."

It was not long after the baptizing of the Morphew slaves that Cyrus come home from a Saturday afternoon meeting of the deacons, preoccupied and serious. When I asked him how his meeting had gone, he looked at me, pursed his lips and sighed. I waited and, as I had suspected, in short order he opened up to tell me what concerned him.

"We have," he said, "uncovered an odd alliance set on making mischief for the Old School Baptists. Redmon Pitt has arrived at New Madrid with some of his followers, and he has apparently joined with Elder Murdock of the Elm Creek Church, those two being none too happy with us, and they have got together with Morris Mundy the Fullerite and a littler feller that calls himself the Reverend Mister Fox, a Methodist."

Well. I did not recognize the name of Morris Mundy, but I certainly did recognize all them others, and I laughed out loud at the mention of the Reverend Mr. Fox. I reminded Cyrus of the reluctant conversion of Mr. Fox at the hands of Patsy Bradene, and he likewise laughed, not having connected the man with that event.

And them other two, Brother Pitt and Brother Murdock, was to my mind cut from the same cloth, and it a raggedy and ill-wove one at that.

"They have, the four of them, been scurrying around, rounding up support among the various persuasions and have proposed a meeting at the blockhouse for to take up certain "housekeeping matters," which is naught but a thin disguise to oust the New Caanan congregation from that building so that we will have no place to worship."

"You don't aim to allow that," I said indignantly.

"We'll have to wait and see. All we know for certain is that whate'er happens will be the Will of the Lord."

"Mama," cried Sarah one afternoon, "Daddy, Mama, a rider a-horseback!"

I felt my heart pound a little. Eremus Lodi, I thought. But that proved not to be. The rider who stepped his horse up to our door and glanced down at us was a tolerable old man, a thatch of white hair upon his head and in no way resembling Eremus Lodi. He was a stranger to me and apparently to Cyrus. Cyrus invited him to step down and refresh himself with water or tea.

But the old man shook off those suggestions, nor did he dismount.

He looked down and said, "Mister Pritchard, I am Morphew!"

I could not help thinking that if Almighty Jehovah come down and announced his presence, it would likely be in such manner. "I am God!"

"Master Morphew," said Cyrus sounding much calmer than I felt, "you're most welcome. We'd be happy to have you in for some refreshment."

I sighed. I didn't know what sort of refreshment Cyrus had in mind, but I did know who would be charged with preparing it. But the old man shook his head again.

"It has come to me that ye have baptized three of my blacks, contrary to my expressed wish in the matter."

"How come you by that information?" Cyrus asked, surprising me. I would have expected him to have admitted the baptizing right off.

"Why, one of yer fellers, that preacher from Elm Creek Church come to me with it," said the old man.

Ah, I thought, and braced myself for the onslought. I looked around for the children, thinking at least to send them out of earshot.

"Sir," said the old man, looking sternly down at Cyrus, "if that indeed is the case, why, I have come here to ask that ye come down to my place and baptize the rest of my blacks, fer them two young rascals Tim and Jim, that could be most sly and dilatory, has since the time of that baptizing been so conscientious and so prompt and hardworking that I have wondered what had come over them." At that, he laughed loudly.

"Well, Master Morphew," said Cyrus, "I am indeed happy to hear that."

"Sir," boomed the old man again, and I detected then the suggestion of a twinkle in his eyes, "indeed, I have an old ram in my barnyard that is a menace and a scoundrel, and I am wondering do I send him to ye, could ye then baptize him and perhaps cure him of some of his hazardous and unhappy ways?"

I didn't think that was necessary, but Cyrus only smiled, and the old man with no other word turned and trotted his horse down the trail toward the woods.

"I suppose that's the end of it," said Cyrus.

Another week passed, and then it was announced that a meeting of Christians was to be held at the blockhouse on the coming Friday, the meeting planned to meet through that night and on into the next day.

"It will be necessary to carry equipment to sleep and eat out," said Cyrus.

That thought did not please me, to carry all the necessaries as well as the children with us, for I was determined to go along.

At last I hit upon a solution, and I went to Mistress Thomas, the Methodist, and explained my problem and asked that she watch my children overnight. Well, that was presumptuous of me, I suppose, except that I knowed that good woman, Methodist or no, without no children of her own, did dearly love to have temporary custody of other's children when that was possible.

Nor did Master Thomas mind at all. Nor the children, for that old couple was good to them and give them attention of the sort that grandparents usually give, playing with them, making them toys and dolls and telling stories and stirring up molasses candy. It seemed an ideal solution, nor was the children at all put out when I suggested it.

George, serious turned as he was, made some motion toward accompanying us, claiming age and interest, but he was easily dissuaded because, age or no, he did enjoy them same attentions from the Thomases that the other children did.

And so it was set, and but for the serious nature of the meeting, I would have been as excited as the children, to have such occasion to get away without them and enjoy the company of adults.

There was little strategy for Cyrus to plot. Some of the deacons come by to talk of it as well as Brother Dalton, but they come away with naught of a conclusive nature.

"It's hard to battle spite," said Brother Dalton, "fer there's no logic to it."

By Friday afternoon we was ready, our few things packed away, for in truth it took but little to camp outdoors overnight in such pleasant weather.

I gathered the children together, to instruct them as to behavior and such, and found Peter unconcerned as babes can be and Sarah, indeed, quite excited with it, so excited that I feared she might just chatter her way out of a place to sleep and eat for the night.

It was George who was suddenly quiet and sulking. "I do not want to stay with the Thomases," he said.

"Why, George?"

"I'm afeared. I do not want to stay with them, and I do not want Sarah and Peter to stay with them. I'm afeared," he repeated.

I looked hard at him and saw in his eyes that distant expression that I sometimes saw, that expression that seemed to look beyond me and to see things that I could ne'er see, sometimes urgently, sometimes curiously, sometimes fearfully. In truth, as he had growed he had possessed such expressions less than in his early childhood, but he could still turn his eyes upon you so that you wondered at the wisdom in them. And so he was doing.

"Mama," he said, "I will not go to stay at the Thomases. I do not know why, but I will not. Nor Sally nor Peter," he added.

There was no dissuading him. Cyrus come right provoked with him, upset as he was, and come close to making threatening gestures toward the boy. At that point, I intervened.

"There is no meeting so important as to destroy the harmony of the family," I said. "You go, Cyrus, and I will stay behind with the children."

"No!" cried George. "I want Daddy to stay with us or we to go with him."

"Ah, George."

"We cannot stay alone," he said.

I looked at Cyrus and could tell that he was as provoked as I and still as concerned.

"Why are you afraid, son?" he said at last.

George shook his head. "I don't know."

"Cyrus, leave the boy. You know how he can be."

It was finally determined that Cyrus, on his way to the meeting, would go out of his way so far as the Bradenes small cabin near the river and send them back to stay with us, or not being able to find them, to send one of Brother Gilbert's sons or Brother Mayhew's.

It was aggravating, but in truth we both had respect for the boy's instinctive side and was concerned.

It was Patsy and Reuben who arrived later, eager to be of help. In my heart I was gladder to see them than I might have been one of them big, silent boys.

By the time Patsy and Reuben arrived, George was over his fit and did not seem to be bothered of anything.

I was still unhappy at not being able to attend the meeting, and seeing George all at once happy and unconcerned left me wondering at the wisdom of giving in to the boy's entreaties. Like as much we was only spoiling him. Still, the Bradenes' presence done much to cheer me up, for they could be entertaining, often wh'er they intended or not.

"Last week," Patsy said winding into a story, "we heard that our neighbor Old Uncle Tom Hawkins's wife had died—she was his second wife and they had not been wed at that fer too long. So we set out to pay our respects to the old feller, who's tol'able crippled up with the rheumatism. Wal, we got ther an' found the old woman, dead fer some hours, still seated in her chair, already froze in that position, an' d'ye believe, her kin was ther, makin' no attempt to right that situation, but had already took the ring from her finger an' the shoes from her feet an' was carryin' out furniture and clothes and pots an' poor ol' Uncle Tom a-hobblin' about protestin'.

"'Why, that spinnin' wheel an' that butter churn,' he cried, 'they was my first woman's!' But them rascals was payin' no mind, but was apparently intent upon strippin' ever'thing out of that house as if it belonged to them."

Patsy paused for a moment and then said calmly, "Me an' Reuben we righted things, though."

I laughed and commented then upon the number of scoundrels there did seem to be. I could not keep from thinking of Elder Murdock and Redmon Pitt.

"Ah," said Patsy, "s'true. An' more comin' all the time. Recall them scum Drooly an' Skeet?" she said. "We seen them just north of here on the river awhile back. Indeed, we ha' seen a motley collection of scum an' slime of late, as if they was all collectin' to some purpose. Mayhap, though," she added, "h'its only the comin' cold that drives them south like the fowl."

Our supper was accomplished before dark, and we sat out in the cool of the early evening, remarking the sense of autumn in the air. "It can come on so quickly this time of year," I said.

"Mama," interrupted Sarah Elizabeth. "What's wrong with George?"

I looked where she pointed. The boy stood in an almost frozen posture, staring before him. I could not see the expression on his face.

"George," I called out, but he did not answer directly. "What do you see out there?"

At last he turned toward me, and I saw that look upon his face, that distant look that always worried me. "Nothin', Mama. Nothin'," he said at last and then turned back to stare toward the woods once more. He stood thus for a time without moving.

"H'its the age," said Patsy. "Young'uns that age always commence to act unnatural," she added.

At last, though, he turned and come and sat on the ground before us, though he still wore a perplexed expression.

The gloom was settling in and the night noises starting. Had there been anything untoward about, why them noises was the first to be stilled or reduced considerable. The sound of them was reassuring. And I thought that them critters that sung their songs so carelessly in the warm night had best enjoy the concert while they could, for the cold would anon still the sounds and drive them that survived it under the ground.

"Mama!" It was Sarah, her face turned like a saucer toward the sky. "Mama! Look!"

Moving across the sky between the little stars just becoming visible there was a bright light.

"A shootin' star," murmured Patsy. "It's late fer them. In August is when they shower down in great quantities. On the river," she started to say and then stopped.

"I don't b'lieve," said Reuben, "that I ever seen a shootin' star quite like that'un."

We watched for a long time, craning our necks toward the heavens, waiting for the star to burn out, but that one did not. That was indeed peculiar, for them falling stars was given to flashing like a lighted lucifer for only an instant before they was gone. Indeed, in August when they seemed more plentiful than any other time, they often flashed and popped like fireworks or early spring fireflies.

"Mama," said George, "look. It's got a tail, an't it?"

The burning star or light or whate'er it was, did indeed seem to be tailed by a shimmering light

"Is it forked?" asked Patsy. "It is forked, ain't it? Look the light is split like the wake of a boat. I don't hardly know what to make of that," she announced. "I an't ne'er seen nothin' like it before. D'ye s'pose it's the judgment?" she asked.

I felt a little shudder of fear as I watched the light proceed in a leisurely way through the heavens. It was curiously beautiful.

"Mama," said Sarah, "I don't want it to be the judgment, as I haven't had my birthday yet."

"I'm afeared," said George softly.

"Of the judgment?" asked Sarah.

"No. I don't know. I'm just afeared."

"Wal," said Patsy after a while, "it don't seem in no hurry to disappear. Seems like if it was the judgment, we'd hear the trumpets of the Lord an' the walls would come tumblin' down an' such."

I saw Sarah look nervously at the cabin walls. I laughed. "It an't the judgment," I said. "Strange things happen now and then, things for which there is no explanation, that you accept as a part of God's world and let it go. I don't know what it is, but it an't the judgment."

I don't know why I was so certain of that, but I was. It just didn't feel like judgment. For one thing the night critters still sung and the air was clear and the breeze cool. But for that light spreading across the sky, there was nothing else amiss.

"We'll go to sleep," I said finally, "and in the morning, it will be gone."

We did sleep that night, Patsy and Reuben on pallets spread before the door, in spite of my entreaties that they come within. George slept restlessly. I could hear him and my own sleep was troubled. I dreamed of critters moving—I could not tell if it was two by two—through the night, headed for some mysterious destination, still and quiet as death.

It was the sort of dream that you're relieved to wake from. At early dawn I peered outside and scanned the sky. There was no trace of that peculiar light. All else was normal as could be.

It was mid-afternoon, the sun still high, when Cyrus returned. He had but little to say of the meeting, only that as he had suspected, there was a serious move afoot to oust the Old School Baptists, though there was also considerable support for them from some unexpected sources.

"That old Methodist, Master Nelson, that was so kind to me when I first removed to this district, was in attendance. It is the first time that I have seen him since and he spoke right up, accusing his own of lacking Christian Charity, and holding out that in these troublesome times, all thinking Christians ought to be working together and not bickering over small points of doctrine and allowing theirselves to be moved by other persons' spite and jealousy."

Well. That was an encouraging thing it seemed to me, and I said as much.

"Yes," said Cyrus, "yes, I suppose so. The meeting got out of hand after that, however, as certain of them in attendance then wanted to talk of unrest and danger and tell stories of Indian and British atrocities and all manner of other wild tale. In the end, a committee of the various groups represented was appointed to look into certain accusations—vague by any standards— and another meeting set for a month hence. So we're very much where we was, except," he sighed, "that now there will be political maneuverings among the various persuasions to influence the committee to their thinking. That's what committees are good for," he added.

"Perhaps it's as well that I did not attend," I said, and Cyrus nodded and glanced toward George.

The boy stood staring hard at his father, as if working out a knotty problem.

"What is it, George? Do you have a question?"

"Daddy, did you not see nothin' amiss?" asked the boy.

"Amiss? Where?"

"I don't know. I feel a heavy feeling. It has bothered me for a day an' I cannot shake it. There is somethin' wrong, somethin' that bothers me. I have the feelin' that somethin' is amiss. Daddy, there is a sense of death in the air."

I looked at Cyrus and he at me. "George," I said, "mayhap you're coming down with something, the fever or an ague or something. You ought to go to bed and let me tend you."

He shook his head and stared at the ground.

We was at supper, Patsy and Reuben already departed, when Brother Mayhew and two of his big boys and Brother Gilbert and his married son and Brother Enos Ray and several others that I did not recognize, that I was certain was not Baptists, arrived in our clearing and signaled Cyrus to come out.

Well, I just followed right along after him, for I did not like the look of the thing, and the children trailed me. Brother Gilbert, almost always of a pleasant and jolly turn, was grim-faced as was every other member of that group.

"Brother Pritchard," said Brother Enos Ray without preface or greeting, "Master and Mistress Thomas, yer neighbors, has been found massacred in a most bloody fashion."

I felt my knees go weak. "Massacred?"

"They was found by them two." Brother Gilbert nodded toward the two big Mayhew boys. "They had been dead fer a good long time, them both stiffed up, and the blood and gore dried and dulled."

"Who?" I whispered.

All eyes was suddenly upon me. "Sister Pritchard," said Brother Mayhew, "you and yours was here last night, did ye hear naught?"

I shook my head. "There was nothing," I said, "nothing untoward, for I remarked to myself the chattering and loud noises of the night. There was naught abroad that stifled any of them."

Sarah was leaning against me and George had gone quite pale, but he said nothing, and I thought it best not to make mention of his restlessness and fears of the night before. I was too unsettled by it all to think clearly.

"Most like, a passing band of Injuns," said Brother Ray, and he give me a queer look. "You was close enough," he added, "that it's a wonder that they left ye intact."

I was not so addled that I didn't catch his meaning. We was known to have had some friendly relation with that suspicious band of Indians that had appeared and disappeared so suddenly during the grass fire a few weeks earlier. Had I not been so stunned, I might have had some words for Brother Ray.

It was Brother Gilbert who intervened. "Now, now, remember, Brother Ray, that Brother Mayhew's cabin is if anything even closer to the Thomas cabin, and the Mayhews was not molested. An' truth, it might not necessarily ha' been Injuns. The river scum has been knowed to rob an' kill an' try to leave evidence that it was done by Injuns."

"Ah," said Brother Mayhew, shaking his head, "I have not ever seen such savagery. It's hard to believe that it was not Injuns, fer not only was the scalps took and the corpses savagely torn and mutilated, but the very hearts of that good old man and old woman had been torn from ther chests and was nowhere in evidence."

I could not contain a glance at George, and I found him to be trembling violently.

"Brother Pritchard," said Brother Gilbert's married son, "we'll not ask that ye join us in our hunt—we're lookin' fer whate'er evidence we might find, and we also intend to alert as many settlers as possible to the danger. We know that ye need to stay close to yer family. We could do mayhap with some prayers," he added, with just the trace of a mirthless grin.

Cyrus nodded. He had been strangely silent. After the group had gone, he turned to George. "Is this what you sensed, George?"

The boy shook his head. He was very close to tears.

"You think it was Indians, Cyrus? Do you think it might have been Sarah's Indians?"

"I would that I knowed," he said.

"But there was no sign last night, nothing untoward."

224

"Mama," interrupted Sarah, "there was that light in the sky."

"Cyrus, did you see the bright light last night?"

"Light?"

"In the sky, a bright light, vivid, like a falling star that refused to fall. It lighted up the sky for quite a long time. Did you not see it?"

"We was in the blockhouse bickering until quite late, Annamanda, and besides, the blockhouse is heavily shaded. It would have been easy not to have noticed."

"Well, it was spectacular."

"We thought the walls was goin' to tumble down," said Sarah.

"The judgment?" laughed Cyrus. "Naw, Sal, I don't hardly think that the judgment is upon us yet. I suspect an explanation. We'll wait and see if the light appears again this night."

Sarah shivered but there was a look of eager expectation on her face nevertheless.

"Cyrus, do you think we need to protect against Indians—or whatever?" I added somewhat awkwardly.

"It somehow does not have the sound of Indians, but you never can tell about them. They are unpredictable as wounded bears, and about as dangerous. I will plan to stay awake this night, I think. But, truth, whate'er we're dealing with will likely not strike again so soon." He said that last with a stern and distant look upon him, and I wondered what he was thinking of.

We sat in the darkening night and watched the skies. The children was anxious and chattering about the possibility of sighting that light once more.

"It had a tail, Daddy," said Sarah.

"An' the tail was split, forked like the devil's," added George with a wicked look toward his sister.

"Mama!"

"Now, George none of that teasing." He was obviously feeling much better, since he was prepared to torment his sister again. Did that mean the danger past, I wondered?

"Look!" It was George, his face turned to the heavens.

"There it is!" cried Sarah.

"Ah," said Cyrus. He watched it for a long the. It had come from the same direction and followed the same course as the night before, and the same forked light trailed it.

"It must be a comet," said Cyrus at last.

"A comet?"

"What's a comet, Daddy?" asked Sarah.

"Well, I don't know exactly, only that it's like an extended shooting star and appears in the sky regularly every night for some time and then disappears. It usually has a tail."

I had heard something of comets but had no idea exactly what they was. But Cyrus knowed much that I did not, and I was proud of him for it. And, truth, I was also some relieved to know that the light had some kind of natural explanation.

I started to say as much to Cyrus, but my attention was caught by what I thought was a movement in them long shadows, and I strained to see. I saw it again, a movement, deliberate, I thought.

I didn't want to say anything, yet I could feel my scalp commence to itch. There had been entirely too much talk of Indians and such.

"Cyrus," I said, "I think I see something in the woods beyond the cabin. Do you see anything?"

Both children was staring wide-eyed at me, afraid, I think, to look any other direction. Cyrus was still and quiet, and we both strained to see in front of us.

"Yes," said Cyrus, "yes, there is something."

But by the time he spoke, I had seen the shadow moving, and with something like relief in my heart, for it was too big a shadow to be Indians.

The only being that tall in the whole district was O'Reilly, and O'Reilly it was who came out of the shadows. But around his neck, almost like a muffler against the cold, hung a human form—limp and unconscious. Unconscious or dead. And as O'Reilly advanced slowly, we all recognized that limp form.

It was Eremus Lodi, dangling from the black's shoulders like new-killed game.

226

Chapter 15

Wrestle the Devil

I struggled up the path with the pail of water, George a few steps ahead of me. It was our last trip from the spring and we had the water barrel filled. Sloshing the water up the hill from the spring was to my mind the hardest part of a washday, and after three trips I did not need encouragement to pause for rest.

I put my pail down and shook my skirts which had become damp from the sloshing water. George, bless him, plodded determinedly ahead, more accustomed to carrying water up the hill than I. With something of a sad sigh, I noted to myself that he was growing bigger and stronger, too.

I reached for my bucket again, but a rustling in the damp leaves by the side of the path caught my attention. Upon inspection I discovered an old terrapin, his scarred and over large shell giving testimony to great age. Poor feller was upon his back, feet in the air, struggling now and then to no effect. Soundless, uncomplaining, he waved his feet for a time and then waited, not wondering perhaps at what fate had toppled him thus, only waiting patiently for whatever fate would aright him.

Well, I guessed I was it, and with the toe of my shoe I give him a little flip. And without either a thank-you or even a backward glance, with measured and purposeful step, he set out on whatever journey had been interrupted.

George struggled ahead. I thought it perhaps fortunate that he had not been attracted by the terrapin, for he undoubtedly would have stopped and played with it and begged to take it home for a pet.

Cyrus had moved my buckets from the lean-to attached to the cabin and had already set up the black pot to boil. That lean-to now housed O'Reilly and Eremus Lodi, the one nursing and the other unconscious from coma or stupor or fever—we did not know.

The lean-to, where we often cooked on hot summer days and would store wood in the winter, was hardly a commodius place for a sick man, but O'Reilly had simply made a bed for Eremus Lodi there and ignored any suggestion that he be bedded in the cabin.

My first thought was of serious illness. Cyrus had no such concern apparently, for he went straight 'way to the sick man and begun to help O'Reilly prepare him a bed. "Does Master Lodi suffer from some contagion that is dangerous?" I asked. Perhaps it was not Christian of me, but I had to think of my children exposed to the smallpox or the fever or whate'er else the sufferer might carry.

"No, Mama," O'Reilly answered my question thus simply. I did not know what I might have done had the answer been yes—chased them away? Not likely.

"Does he need bandages or medicine?"

"No, Mama. Be him need rest is all."

The nest that O'Reilly and Cyrus finally constructed for the sick man was reasonably comfortable, did we not have an attack of weather, and it probably was better to house those two big men thus, rather than to try to crowd all of us in the cabin.

The sudden appearance of O'Reilly and Eremus Lodi right on the heels of the hideous murder of that good old couple Master and Mistress Thomas crossed my mind frequently, no matter how much I tried to put it away.

I slept that night fitfully, waking at odd times. Two or three times I noted the light from the comet, and I was likewise aware of sounds and moans coming from the lean-to which was connected to the house at that wall against which I slept. There was some activity in that lean-to through the night, but I had no way to know what it was.

Remembering that O'Reilly was much skilled in the medicinal arts, I wondered did he minister thus to Eremus Lodi, and then with a shiver I had an imperfect vision of some savage rituals performed around the pallet upon which Eremus Lodi lay. But I shook that off as unworthy.

I woke from my restless sleep with the morning light. I was not well rested, but that made no difference. The day would not wait for me to catch up with my sleep, nor would my chores or children.

When I peeked into the lean-to, O'Reilly was alseep in his accustomed manner, seated his back against the wall and his knees drawed up to his chin. Eremus Lodi lay sprawled across the pallet, and though I could not make him out in detail, he breathed uncommon hard and tossed about on his bed and then lay deathly still. O'Reilly lifted his head, glanced for a long moment at the still form, and then tucked his chin back down upon his knee. Were he not alarmed, then it would not do for me to be alarmed.

Cyrus, who had been up at first light with his axe to attack the brush and the forest, came in for breakfast and paused to look into the lean-to.

He seated himself at the table without saying anything, and I supposed would have eaten and gone back to work without comment, had I been able to contain myself.

"What think you? About Eremus Lodi? What is wrong with him and why did O'Reilly bring him here?"

228

Cyrus shook his head and replied, "All I can say is that Master Lodi needs help. We would do ourselves no merit did we not extend such help, much as we owe him."

I thought for a moment of telling Cyrus of Eremus Lodi's strange behavior in Ste. Genevieve and how O'Reilly had rescued him there with such sadness upon his face. I had it in my mind that Eremus Lodi was given to immoderate use of spiritous liquors, and I wondered if such might not now be the problem. But to thrust him in that condition upon us?

Eremus Lodi would certainly not be the first man to be felled by strong drink, which could be slept off and often was in any old place. Mayhap it was just that O'Reilly was uncommon careful of his master. Whatever the case, it was more than I could think through, and so I stopped trying to and went on about my business.

I brought food for O'Reilly, who at my step uncurled his long form and stood, accepting gracefully the plate I offered him. I asked him did he think that Master Lodi would need food and he only shook his head, holding the plate carefully, obviously not intending to eat until I was gone.

I got a good look at Eremus Lodi when I turned to leave. He lay upon his back, his arms and legs almost randomly flung about, his color pale and gray, his visage haggard, his breathing shallow. He did not look like a man who was long for this world.

"Will he be all right?" I murmured.

O'Reilly nodded. "One day, Mama."

At that I sighed and left O'Reilly to his meal.

To the children I simply said that Eremus Lodi was ill, and that certainly seemed to be the truth.

But as the day wore on, it become more and more obvious that he was not simply sleeping off a condition caused by intemperate application of spirits. For he thrashed wildly about, now and then shouting incoherently, sitting up wild-eyed upon his pallet before then falling back exhausted or unconscious.

Passing by the lean-to in the afternoon, I was arrested at a sudden scream. I stopped. It was Eremus Lodi, and his words, which had mostly been garbled screams, come out clear and loud.

"I damn God and I damn God's god!"

At them awful words I could not keep from turning to stare into that small space. Eremus Lodi, sitting straight up, suddenly fell back upon his pallet, and O'Reilly sat cross-legged and impassive. I glanced around, hoping that the children had not heard. But they was nowhere in sight.

I burned suddenly with anger of such arrogant blasphemy. God might damn man, but no man could damn God!

Through that night and the next day and night, he suffered so. At one point, Cyrus and I were both roused from our sleep and sat upright at a shriek from the other side of the wall. A shriek and then silence. The children sleeping in the kitchen made no stir, either not hearing the noise or absorbing it into their dreams.

Through the ordeal, O'Reilly helped himself to water, carrying some of it into the lean-to with him. I saw him prop Eremus Lodi up and gently tender water to him, but that was all. I saw no evidence of potions or savage ritual, though in truth I did not often peek into the room.

"How long will this go on, Cyrus?" I asked one night as we readied for sleep.

He shook his head slowly. "I don't know. I suppose until he's recovered or dead. That's the usual course of illness."

I thought that sort of a flippant answer, but I suppose there was no other.

But that night we slept through without interruption and rose considerably refreshed. When I took O'Reilly breakfast, I glanced at Eremus Lodi and thought that his color was better and his breathing more relaxed.

"Is he better?"

O'Reilly considered the patient, giving him a long stare, and then murmured, "Cannot know, Mama."

And then that night at what hour I could not say, only that it seemed close to morning light, I was wakened by a soft conversation beyond the wall. I might not have heard it had I not been turned in that direction. Cyrus, facing the opposite way, slept soundly through it.

I could not make out what it was all about, only that it seemed to have a sense of urgency about it, and though it was whispered, I was aware of two separate voices, those of Eremus Lodi and O'Reilly, I was certain. I tried to make out what was said but could not and slowly drifted back to sleep.

The next morning O'Reilly was gone. I took his plate of food into the lean-to and was surprised to find him not there. I glanced at Eremus Lodi, who seemed to be sleeping much more comfortably. I took the plate back to the kitchen and waited awhile, checked again, and the black was still not back. That was most unlike him, for he had hardly quitted Eremus Lodi's side the last several days. I did not know quite how to proceed. Had we been left the care of him? With no notion of what ailed him?

It was indeed curious how O'Reilly come and went, like a dark spirit, first here and then gone.

Through the day, Cyrus and I alternated in checking on the sleeping man, but he did not wake nor did we try to rouse him.

"I suppose if he does not wake by nightfall, we'd best rouse him and get him at least some water," I said at last and Cyrus agreed.

Late in the afternoon I went into the lean-to. The southern breeze had cooled the room pleasantly. I looked at Eremus Lodi, resting on his side. He still seemed to be comfortably sleeping, so I turned away and stood pondering the situation for a moment—whether or not it was time to try to wake the man.

All at once I suffered a peculiar sensation, the sort of sensation that comes of having someone watching you covertly. I tensed and listened.

"My lady?" The whisper came from the pallet, and I turned slowly. Eremus Lodi was up on his elbow. He was clear eyed, though uncommonly pale of color, gaunt and haggard, with a scraggly growth of beard on his face, and the long hair that fell from the side of his otherwise bald scalp was matted and greasy.

He had a curious expression on his face, as if he was trying to recall something, as one struggles sometimes upon waking to reconstruct a dream, its shape but a vague outline and a remembered sensation.

"Might I get you a drink of water?" It was the easiest thing I could think of to say.

He sighed and nodded weakly and immediately fell back on the pallet. But when I returned with the water, he had risen again and was propped against the wall of the lean-to.

He took the cup I offered, his eyes ne'er leaving my face, almost as if the answers he sought might be found there. It was some disturbing to be so stared at. He drank down the water and handed the cup back, hardly taking his eyes from my face.

"You have danced in and out of my dreams, Madam," he said.

I was took back at that and struggled for some remark, but it proved unnecessary, for he lay back on the pallet once more and immediately drifted off to sleep.

Eremus Lodi mended slowly. Cyrus took him in hand at first, helping him to wash and clean himself, dressing him in his own clothes, while I washed the others. Cyrus's shirt hung from Eremus Lodi's gaunt frame, but his trousers were shy of the ankles by several inches, those inches having to be made up by stockings.

Nor did Eremus Lodi eat as I would have had him do, but nibbled and poked at his food. Throughout, he watched me. Did I turn suddenly to face him, I would find his gaze fastened on my person, a curious, almost pained expression on his face. At such times, he would greet me with a slight nod and a crooked, wry smile. It was always disconcerting, and though I tried to make idle conversation, he rarely committed himself, though he was always gentle-spoke and friendly toward the children.

Now and then, he would make odd remarks, remarks that I could make little sense of.

"Time after time," he said at one point, "I have stood at the precipice. Each time, some will that I cannot account for, pulls me back. But that will grows ever weaker."

"You must eat for your strength, Master Lodi," I said when he did not show what I thought was serious interest in his food.

"Ah, now, must I, my lady?" he might remark with a cocked eyebrow and gentle amusement in his eyes.

I wished that he would not call me "my lady", for it was disturbing, possessive almost.

In one of those strange and distant moods one afternoon, he sat in dark silence, grim and glum, in some strange way frightening even. He spoke at last, to me I supposed, as I was the only one near. "Have ye e'er seen a cockfight?" he asked, and then realizing perhaps who it was he spoke to, he answered himself. "Nay, no, ye ne'er have, of course." And he inclined slightly in my direction.

I might have passed on about my work, but his deep sunk eyes under shaggy brows was intimidating, and I paused, for I knowed he'd speak again and he did. "I am not a gaming man, Madam," he began. "I have little use fer either frivolous use of time or for games of chance. Indeed I have little use for chance at all. Yet happening upon such a fight recently, I paused to watch.

"A cockfight is a bloody event, Madam. It is not intended that both combatants survive. Indeed, if both should perish, the winner staggering and expiring once his game is won, why the gamers would not be happier. Those cocks are bred to fight; they will fight to the death unless separated. It is their nature. Nor would the gamers separate them, fer that is their nature.

"Yet watching that hateful display, a cock, his feathers ruffled, his talons sharp, his eye bloody fer battle, I was confounded by a question that had ne'er occurred to me. Did he fight to save his own life or to take another or simply because it was just in him? I ne'er knew the answer to that, and yet it was so basic and simple a question that it ought to have an answer. That question troubles me yet, Madam, that set upon each other, or simply chancing upon each other, them cocks will tear each other apart, fighting to kill, urged on by some force that I cannot understand."

Eremus Lodi was by then staring into the distance, not asking my opinion nor did I give one. I left him thus, and I did not think that he even noticed.

At last, he begun to gain strength, almost in spite of himself, it seemed to me. The days was warm but headed toward fall, and he often sat, almost asleep, on the bench outside the door, absorbing the warm rays from the sun. At other times he would conduct court, as it were, for the children, talking to them, listening to them—most especially Sarah, who was always more inclined to deliver than to receive when it came to conversations.

Through it all, there was no sign or word from O'Reilly, and though I tried to introduce that subject, any such questions or observations were gently turned away, almost as if Eremus Lodi did not want to think of O'Reilly at all, as if O'Reilly had not ever been in attendance upon him.

With Cyrus, Eremus Lodi conversed on general topics, now and then touching upon doctrine and theology. And though what was said was general and casual, Eremus Lodi's observations was often wry and, I was sad to see, touched with disbelief.

When I mentioned such to Cyrus, he only shrugged and once commented himself that such ideas were not all uncommon, particularly among the modern thinkers, as they tended to rationalism and Deism, which lent theirselves to agnosticism.

"Deism? Is Eremus Lodi a Deist?"

"I don't know. I don't think he really espouses any doctrine, and even Deism is a doctrine."

Well, I had heard of Deists all my life, but truth to tell, I was but vague as to what that doctrine included and had always thought that Diests was little more than infidels, and I said as much to Cyrus.

"No," he said, "Deists are not atheists. They do believe in God. But they believe in a natural order of things, that God having set the world in motion by means of natural laws does not concern himself with its day to day workings."

I thought about that. Finally, I could not keep from observing that I could not see that much difference between Deism and predestinarianism then, as in both God had predetermined how the world would go.

Cyrus looked at me for a long moment and then laughed and said, "Ah, perhaps you've a point, Annamanda. Perhaps you have indeed. But," he added before I had a chance to savor my intellectual observation, "it is more complicated actually than I have represented it." And then he left me. I was a little annoyed, to be put off with an answer such as you give a child.

One afternoon Cyrus and Eremus Lodi sat talking on the bench outside the door while I worked at my baking just inside and listened. Their conversation ranged more than it had heretofore, Eremus Lodi apparently being more disposed to conversation.

To be truthful, I did dally at my work, kneading more than was probably necessary, just so that I could have excuse to listen. The conversation had got around to the Indians, as it almost always done them days, the border becoming more and more restless, and the threat from the British and the Indians being to everyone's mind very real.

I already knowed of course that Eremus Lodi's sentiments was mostly with the Indian, in so much as he opposed their being removed from their land. I supposed that he did not favor their violence.

"Would you retard our westward growth, Master Lodi?" I heard Cyrus ask.

"I could as easily hold back the river at flood," said Eremus Lodi after a pause, and then he added a curious comment to that answer. "Beyond the wilderness lies the future. Perhaps that is what I would retard—would stop altogether—time itself."

"Ah," said Cyrus, "it is to be."

"You are perhaps right, Pastor Pritchard. And," he added, "the westwarders'll take you and yer like with 'em, to bless ther greed and carnage just thus—because it is happening, it must be intended."

The conversation had taken such a serious turn that I stood listening, my hands stuck up in the dough yet not working it.

"It is, I think, the nature of the race of man to move with the sun," said Cyrus at last.

"There is little, Sir, that I care to say of that race, for to me it is puny, sickly, withal, an evil thing. Not a blessing, but a curse perpetrated upon this planet by whatever force—God or Satan or only the mindless order of the universe."

That last by Eremus Lodi, when I finally absorbed it, caused a chill to touch my heart. But if Cyrus was shaken, it did not show.

"Ah, Master Lodi," he said quite calmly, "you do perceive then evil to be the greater force than good?"

"Good, Sir, I do not recognize good!"

"You believe not in good?"

"It is not perhaps that I do not believe in good, so much as that I do not separate the two. In my mind they belong together as the breathing in and the breathing out belong together. They are as the positives and the negatives of the poles. But good is the negative force, Sir, the absence of evil. And as such, is it then not possible, only an ideal? All that I would recognize is an innocence of evil, as ye find in dumb animals or children or certain lunatics, of which kind I think that Jesus the Nazarene must have been. But now yer St. Paul, why he was as wise and crafty and ambitious as Old Scratch himself."

I caught my breath at that and stood almost paralyzed, so fearful was those words, yet spoke casually, almost cheerfully. I commenced to pound and whack that dough, finally putting it in the oven and raking the hot coals over it. It was by then too hot to remain in the cabin, and so I stood wiping my hands at the doorway, catching the fresh air and attempting to control my quivering heart and hands.

I must have made a sound or movement, though I was unaware of it, for both men turned abruptly toward me. It has always been a burden to me that I possess that kind of face that cannot keep a secret. Whate'er I think is mirrored on my face, and Eremus Lodi read it easily.

"Ah, Madam," he said, "you do not agree with my assessment of this evil race?"

"I know naught of good or evil, but I do take it hard to hear my Lord Jesus referred to as a lunatic," I snapped so quickly that even I was surprised, and both Cyrus and Eremus Lodi looked startled.

"Ah, Madam," said Eremus Lodi, "I do most humbly apologize. I would not for the world cause ye grief or offense." He said that with such a look upon his face, gentle and tender, that I was some disconcerted and did not reply right off.

"Truth is, Madam, in my own defense, yer husband and I are not so far apart in our assessment of the evil within mankind. Our major difference is of hope, which he has and I have not."

There was nothing I could add to that conversation for it was too thoughtful for my limited capacities, so I did not reply.

"Madam," said Eremus Lodi, as if he were prompting me, "have ye ne'er done nothin' that ye was ashamed of?"

"Well, no," I said quickly.

"Nothin'?"

"Shamed is a harsh word, Sir. I've ne'er been shamed. I've done things I wished that I had not, and said things, but I'm ne'er ashamed."

"And yer without evil deed or thought?"

I started to reply but had to stop and think about it. I did not know that you could be censured for what you thought, but only for what you did. Mayhap that was the problem that I was having in achieving that experience that others seemed to achieve so easily, to recognize their vileness and depravity. Did my thinking have to be as pure as my actions, well truly there'd be days that I'd fair be in for it.

I did not say anything, for there seemed nothing to say, and Cyrus, his two hands clasped, frowned at them as was his style when he worried a thought. Eremus Lodi stared straight forward, a gentle look, almost a wistful one, upon his face, still hollowed and worn from his recent illness. And it was Eremus Lodi who at last spoke and that softly and without glancing away from the horizon at which he stared so intently.

"Ah, perhaps it is true that each step is predetermined by whatever fate determines things. Had there been other choices, though, would I have taken them and what would have been different? I apologize once more, my lady," he turned so abruptly toward me that I was caught off guard, staring at him. "I am sorry to have troubled you with useless profundities." He laughed softly and murmured, "Perhaps each man must face that which he fears or run away. I have to wrestle my own devil withal, now don't I?"

If he expected an answer to that strange question, I did not have it, and I excused myself back to my baking.

Later in the afternoon I watched as Cyrus paused at his work, put aside his axe, took up his Bible, and sat upon a near stump to study. I had often seen him thus, as he worked worrying a thought or a text, stopping to take up the Bible and study it, poring over the problem area, verse by verse, line by line.

Some pastors insisted that whate'er they taught was so plain and so clear that anyone who argued against such doctrine was either a fool or just determined to be fractious. But not Cyrus. He studied the Word hard, turning it and reasoning the words at every angle, often spending hours on just one text. I wondered what it was that bothered him this day and assumed that it in some way dealt with the earlier conversation with Eremus Lodi.

Eremus Lodi seated in warm and pleasant place had apparently fallen asleep, for his head nodded over and he was quite still.

"Mama?"

It was Sarah. She had come up behind me, and though she spoke softly enough, I jerked in surprise.

"Mama," she said, her lips pursed and a frown of question between her eyes, "why does Master Eremus Lodi stare so much at you all the time?"

"What, Sarah? Why, I don't know what you mean."

"He does. He is always lookin' at you. Just looks and looks and looks."

I laughed. "Well, now, I don't know. I hadn't noticed. Mayhap I'm just always wanderin' into his line of vision."

"Well," she shrugged and flitted away.

Then one morning almost a fortnight after O'Reilly had carried Eremus Lodi to our cabin, we woke to find him gone. He disappeared in the night just as O'Reilly had. Albeit to do him justice, the night earlier he had hinted at that. He thanked us for our kindness to him.

"It's only part payment for the debt we owe," Cyrus had insisted. "And you know you're always welcome here."

"Ah," was all that Eremus Lodi answered, but that sigh had such a forlorn kind of sound to it that I heard myself asking, "Master Lodi, do you have family anywhere?"

Well, it was none of my business, but the question which had bothered me for some time slipped out before I could reason with myself. Had he ignored it, I of a certainty would ne'er have minded, but strangely, he answered.

"No, Mistress, I have no family. None. Unless ye count certain of those in my household upon whom I depend and whom I trust. But they are few and in truth not kin. I came an orphan of a early age and largely raised myself, with only a little help, but that made the difference. However, it's a long story. I'd not bore ye with it."

Well, I wanted to tell him that I certainly wouldn't be bored, but I sensed that he had told me all he intended to, and I could not think of any way to pry. So, all my question had done was raise more questions.

But after a moment he added, musing almost as if to himself, "I wonder, my lady, had I been brought up in such a home as this, what would have been the difference?"

"Such a home as this?"

"An atmosphere such as this," he answered, "wherein a full and hard and honest day's toil is respected and holy."

"Holy?" But he said no more, lapsing into a distant stare that precluded me. What a curious thing was that observation. Holy?

"Why do they do that?" I asked Cyrus in some vexation when we realized that Eremus Lodi was indeed gone. "Why do they just vanish without a word, when taking a polite leave would be so little trouble?"

Of course Cyrus had no answer to that any more than I did.

It was near a week after that Cyrus returned from his meeting at the blockhouse. He was glum and out of sorts.

"They have indeed taken a vote and ousted the New Canaan congregation."

"Why that's not fair. We was here first!"

"Fair has naught to do with it, Annamanda. The problem mainly is that they perceive our friendliness with Eremus Lodi as a danger." He paused and then added solemnly, "The killing of the Thomases has hardened feelings against that man, just or not."

"Eremus Lodi?"

"That he has been here so long is known abroad. But worse, the news has come that O'Reilly was seen in the company of Indians over across the river, those Delaware that do camp there. And rumor has it that he was seen heading south with several Indians."

"Why, there's no truth to it."

"Now, Annamanda, you don't know that. O'Reilly would not be easy to mistake. There has always been divers rumors concerning Eremus Lodi, and he is feared by a great many, for what good reason I can't say. At any rate, Redmon Pitt brings disquieting news from Cape Girardeau and north. Rumors of serious Indian war abounds. Redmon Pitt insists apparently that it is the Indians north of the Ohio River that are most malcontent, and that they are enlisting the aid of southern Indians, who have been more content."

"Is all of that reason enough to turn us out?"

"It seems to be."

"Well, what are we to do about it?"

"For the moment, nothing."

"Nothing!"

"Now, my dear, rushing off ranting and raving and carrying on is usually futile. We will wait and see how things progress. In the meantime, until cold weather, we can meet out of doors. Brother Gilbert has a nice space around his house which he has offered."

"It is not just."

"No. It is not just."

September had give way to October when Patsy and Reuben Bradene, along with the riverman Jacob, walked home with us for dinner after a Sunday meeting at Brother Gilbert's.

Jacob, after long years, had at last his own flatboat, which, with his brother Otto, he planned to float the Mississippi, carrying goods of this or that sort. "What e'er will turn a profit," he said in his good-natured way. He was much filled with his new enterprise, as was Patsy and Reuben, as proud as they could be of the young man. And the children, even Peter, remembered the riverman from the spring earlier and our own adventures on the river, and they would hardly leave him in peace. And in truth, he seemed as much taken with them as they with him.

Though Patsy and Reuben had curtailed their river activities, Jacob insisted that he would run the length of it year around, "dodgin' Injuns er ice floes as is necessary."

"Ah, I dunno," said Reuben shaking his head.

"'Til the British is settled," added Patsy, "the Injuns won't be settled. They say h'it'll take war with the both of 'em, and I fer one would ruther float the river south wher the Injuns is tamer than them northern 'uns."

"Wal, might be," said the riverman Jacob, "but the stories is that Tecumseh hisself is right now in this very area, stirrin' up things as he does so well, so that them tame Injuns may right soon be not so tame. I've heard," he added, scratching himself along his ankle with a sharp pointed stick, "that he claims that the sky lights is a warnin', that the Great Spirit is angered at both red an' white, an' will one day soon destroy all them that has had a hand in disturbin' his great hunting grounds."

"The sky lights?" said Sarah, who had been amazingly still for an amazing length of time.

"The comet," said Cyrus.

"Wal, yes," drawled Jacob, "if it is a comet," he added. "The newspapers in Cincinnati and St. Louis an' such is sayin' of course that that's what it be, but ther's plenty of folks—red an' white an' black, fer that matter—that question it. Ye'd be surprised, I bet, the stories about it that abound up an' down the river. I b'lieve ther's a sight of sinners a-givin' the whole thing some thought," he added with a laugh. "An't that right, Brother Pritchard?"

Cyrus answered with a smile and said, "There have of late been a few suspect souls at the mourners bench, in my church as well as others, I've heard."

"Mayhap," said the riverman, "they's some that fears time has come to rassle ther devils."

"Wrestle their devils?" I said. It was that same phrase that Eremus Lodi had used that I had found so strange.

"It's a river sayin', Ma'am," said the riverman Jacob, perceiving, I suppose, my ignorance.

"What does it mean?" asked the matter-of-fact Sarah.

Jacob frowned and thought for a moment and then said, "Wal, I cain't quite say. Like many of such sayin's it means what the speaker means it to mean."

Sarah looked at me and I returned her stare, for I was quite as perplexed as she was.

"It comes from a story," said Jacob. "An old story, that has about as many versions as some of them river songs, an' some as rude, too," he added with a glance toward us.

"A story?" cried Sarah. He had found her weakness. "Will you tell it?"

"Wal," hesitated the riverman and then drawed himself up as he would do when he commenced a long story. She had found his weakness.

"Wal," he began, "the story about the devil an' Ben Blough that I always liked best goes like this."

238

"Ben Blough? Who was that?" interrupted Sarah.

"Shhhh, Sarah," I said, "how can he tell the story if you interrupt?"

"Time'll tell, girl," said Jacob. "Be patient."

Well, I wasn't going to bother to point out that, of all the things Sarah might be, patient was not one of them. We all just settled back and listened to the story.

"Now Ben Blough, they tell, was a riverman away back, probably before we was any of us borned. Whether he really was or wasn't, I cain't say, of course. All I know is that the story says he was, so I'll b'lieve that once on the river there was a Ben Blough an' he did get hisself in a pickle of his own making an' ended up having to rassle the devil.

"So that's mayhap what the expression means, to get yer own self in trouble an' have to work yer way out of it. Anyways, Ben, they said, was as big as he was mean, an' as ugly as he was big, an' as strong as he was ugly. An' he loved to rassle.

"He had a black beard, they said, that come clean-to his belt, an' he wore moccasins an' a shirt of bear skin that they claim he rassled off the bear itself. I don't know fer I warnt ther. But they said he'd rassle on any pretext at all er none if that's what it taken. Drunk er sober—him er them er both—he'd rassle 'em down.

"Wal, finally got so's nobody was willin' to rassle, drunk er sober, fer no one no more ever got that drunk, an' though Ben Blough thumped a considerable number around an' bounced them from tree to tree, an' left some bones broken an' heads busted, he ne'er could get a real rasslin' match. So that all he could do was brag and boast.

"Wal, one night as they set about a fire, drinking sper'ts an' telling the kinds a' tales that gets told under them circumstances, Ben Blough commenced to get all sad an' teary an' to tell of the days before, when he could rassle any single man er any group of men er any combination of bear an' painter-lion an' Injun an' black an' white man an' come out on top.

"'Why,' he stood up and shouted, his voice thundering along the river an' through the woods, 'they an't nothin' on this earth or beyond that I cain't lick, devil take me, one hand behind me.'

"Wal, now, almost anybody ought to know better than to issue a challenge like that, wouldn't ye say?" And he looked at Sarah, and she, with her eyes wide and big, nodded vigorously, for she as well as the rest of us all knowed about what was coming.

"Now, I cain't say fer sure that it thundered or that the earth opened wide an' smoke an' fire an' brimstone—as well as a little coal an' rocks and such—an' boiling water an' liquid electricity come fuming out through them fissures, but it has been told by a great many that that's just what did happen." The riverman's voice was low, and he bent slightly at the waist and asked Sarah and George in whisper, "D'ye know what happened then?"

Neither said nothing, but Sarah nodded vigorously again.

"Wal, nothin' much," said Jacob leaning back. Both Sarah and George, as well as Reuben and Patsy, I think, looked disappointed, and Jacob laughed and then said, "Nothin' much right away, so ever'body kindly set down an' arranged therselves and sniffed the air an' watched the steam an' smoke an' such an' didn't have nothin' to say.

"Finally, Ben Blough, who knowed a challenge when he seen one, stood up and bellowed, 'I kin lick the devil, an' that's fer sure.'

"Wal, you better believe that ther was several of them revelers that would have cut from ther in a hurry but fer the fact that they was surrounded by smoke an' brimstone an' deep holes an' piles of coal an' such.

"Then they heard somethin' a-comin' th'u the woods, an' two or three of them rascals, they said, went an' got religion right ther on the spot, but it was too late. Fer out into the light of the fire stepped a little feller, a-brushin' his jacket, an' pattin' some sparks on his pants leg an' dancin' along on little neat feet.

"They tell that in truth he didn't look like much, an' prob'ly nobody would have b'lieved it when he introduced hisself as the devil but fer the smell of brimstone about him an' eyes that was like rivers of fire. They tell that he was quiet-spoke in an uninteresting voice, an' altogether looked weak as a willow reed at the river's edge. But in truth ye know yerselves that looks like that are deceivin', especially in the case of willow reeds.

"Wal, now who can say, maybe Ben Blough was drunk er foolish er both, er mayhap he b'lieved what he said, that he could lick the devil hisself, fer he right ther issued up the challenge agin, an' the devil nodded precisely, took off his coat an' brushed hisself over agin, an' said that all he wanted was Ben's soul, an' Ben said he'd have to take it an' the devil said that he would.

"'The hell ye say!' shouted Ben an' the devil nodded. 'Ere ye prepared to fight fer it!' said Ben.

"'Indeed,' said the devil.

"Wal, then and there they commenced to fightin', an' they fought an' rolled an' rassled and tore an' gouged, an' wher they rolled, they tell that the trees snapped off like broom straws an' the valleys sunk down an' the hills rose up.

"They th'owed one another agin' the ground, an' it rolled an' shifted. They waded in the river, it's said, an' fought an' rolled an' splashed until the river itself commenced to run backward.

"They fought by day an' they fought by night, an' part of them a-watchin' they slept by day an' the other part by night, so that the whole thing could be witnessed in its entirety.

"Wal, the devil give as good as he got an' so did Ben Blough, an' some felt like the devil was pretty surprised at that. But Ben Blough was as nimble as he was mean, an' as quick as he was ugly, an' as fast as he was big, an' then of course he was strong as he was strong.

"Now on the seventh day that they rassled, while they was rollin' around

240

on the ground uprootin' trees an' destroyin' forests, the river, which had been muddied an' mistreated considerable, up an' changed its course. Wher it had been opened up a giant fissure in the ground with steam and brimstone an' such escapin' and right then an' there with a mighty push fer such a little critter, the devil pushed old Ben Blough in an' went right in after him, an' don't ye know that fissure closed plumb up to wher you couldn't see it, an' the steam and the smoke an' the brimstone and coal an' boilin' water all disappeared with it.

"But they tell it fer the truth that deep in the bowels of the earth, they could still hear that old devil an' Ben Blough a-rasslin', rollin' an' thrashin' an' growlin' an' even today, sometimes, ye can feel the earth move an' hear that noise way down deep, an' it's Ben an' the devil, still fightin' an' rasslin'."

At that Jacob caught his breath and stopped, for he had been talking loud and fast and was fair winded. Both Sarah and George was wide-eyed with the story, and truth to tell, I had enjoyed it, too.

"Now, Jacob," said Patsy Bradene, "ye've left some out of that story that I recall."

"Ah, Pat," cautioned Reuben and Jacob laughed.

"Remember, Pat," he said, "we're amongst gentle company here."

That night after our company had gone, as I put Sarah and Peter to bed, Sarah asked, "Mama, do you believe that about Master Ben Blough and the devil?"

"Oh, Sarah, it's only a tale, an entertaining tale."

"But there's stories about the devil in the Bible. Are they tales, entertaining tales only?"

"Sarah!"

"I mean, I don't see the difference."

"Sarah, you ne'er question the Word of God, ever! Mind me."

"Well . . . I bet I could wrestle the devil"

I could not keep from smiling. "Indeed, I'd wager you could."

Chapter 16

A Time of Extraordinaries

It begun to seem that commonplace times had gone forever, for when people met, there was so much to think about and discuss that there was no time for that idle conversation and gossip that mostly made up such meetings. Indeed it was a true wonder that we got any worship done at all on meeting days, for both before and after services, the groups would form, this one to talk politics, that one to talk Indians, the other to talk the dissension amongst the various congregations.

And too often to my mind, the name of Eremus Lodi come up in those discussions, and also too often it seemed to me that there was glances cast toward Cyrus and me when talk got around to Eremus Lodi or to Indians. Whene'er I got a chance and could do so in a modest and seemly manner, I'd right such conversations with the truth. But not everyone, of course, was interested in accepting the truth, for truth ne'er is so interesting as the other.

"I have just this week heard terrible rumors," said Enos Ray to one such group gathered after Sunday service, "of carnage and killing east of the river, on the Tennessee side. Wanton slaughter, of the sort perpetrated upon Master and Mistress Thomas." At that point I felt two or three glances cast in my direction, but I stared ahead of me, as if I had not noticed.

"Injuns," murmured one.

"Wal," said Brother Ray, "possibly, though ther's reports that some of that group of Injuns—for it does appear always to be the same group—is not red, but white."

"White? White men?" said a young sister nearby.

"It's not unheard of," interrupted Brother Mayhew. "White renegades disguised as Injuns, killing as Injuns. It's not unheard of," he repeated.

"Whoever they are," said Brother Enos Ray, "they apparently scoot back and forth across the river. They strike and then lose themselves in that great swamp that surrounds Eremus Lodi's land like a fence."

"Ah, Eremus Lodi," I heard and there was a general rustling at the mention of that name and some knowing nods.

I saw one brother nudge another and, straining just a bit, I made out his remark. "Seems to me that someone ought to discuss Eremus Lodi and his curious behavior with regards to the settlers with the proper authorities." The other looked solemn and nodded. I sighed. Would they ne'er be done with Eremus Lodi?

"Wal," said Brother Gilbert, "it's a mercy, the conversation and the confusion of these days. Ther's war talk to the one side and comet talk to t'other side and Injun talk to the east side an' judgment talk to the west side. If ye don't find one conversation to suit you, why ye can just move around and betimes ye'll find one that will."

Brother Curtis Layman laughed and said, "An' I have heard of an old sister, just south of Cape Girardeau, so convinced that the judgment is at hand that she dresses herself all in white each morning and climbs a tree so as to be nearer to heaven when the Lord calls."

"An' does she come down at night?" asked someone else.

"Indeed, she says that the Lord has promised a 'day of judgment,' so most certainly He will not come at night." There was a general laugh at that.

"Wal," said Biddy Dalton at that, "ye must wonder then if that comet portends good or evil. That determined, I suppose, on wh'er yer ready fer the judgment or not."

"'For God shall bring every work into judgment, with every secret thing, whether it be good, or whether it be evil,'" recited Brother Gilbert, catching everyone by surprise with his verse. "It's Ecclesiastes," he added, for apparently I was not the only one unfamiliar with it. There was some more nodding at that, though I was not quite certain just what was meant.

"There's much good," said Brother Layman, "but ther's also much evil. And, truth, ther is much that is passing strange goin' on. The comet is not the only strange thing, for the atmosphere is peculiar, heavy and colored, the way I've ne'er seen it colored, and the various animals is even acting strange."

"My old milk cow," said Biddy Dalton, "all of a sudden she will not go in one area of the enclosure, even though there is still good grass ther fer her to eat. I cannot drive her to it even, for she stalls and balks. I have ne'er seen a cow that wouldn't trample anything in its path to get to good grass."

"The river is up, unusual this time of year," said Sister Gilbert suddenly, "and the fever—a most severe ague—is passing serious in some areas, and the catarrah as bad as I have seen it. I have been called to several cabins, especially those near the river, and I have used up much of my medicine and have had to go forth and gather more, not easy," she added, "this time of year with my lumbago as it is."

I was not the only one that took the talk of the fever and the ague more seriously than the talk of judgment. We did not quite know what to expect of the judgment, but we did know what to expect of the fever.

Winter was a-knocking at our door, but we was prepared. Indeed Cyrus and George had stacked us enough wood, I thought, for a year of winters. In addition we had roots in the root cellar and game all salted down and jerked. If I did not look forward to winter, neither did I dread it.

By the end of November, rumors of a pitched battle to the north between Indian and American begun to drift down the river, most insistent, yet vague still. I paid little heed even so, for rumors was a way of life along the river.

One night I woke with a start and sat straight up. It was, as might have been expected, a sudden cry from Peter that roused me. I waited, snuggling back under the warm comforter, hoping that whatever bad dream or pain had roused him was over and he had gone back to sleep. But that was not to be. He whimpered and cried out again, and with a sigh I forced myself out of my comfortable nest and hurried over to him lest his noise wake the others.

I felt his face, but it was not hot, and though he murmured something, I knowed that he was mostly asleep, and sure enough after a few moments of rocking and patting, he was gone again. But I was by then wide awake. That is the way of children. He most likely was only a little lonely in the dark and wanted company. Alas, I would not slip easily back to sleep, I feared.

I did not know the hour. I could guess at it, for though there was usually signs about that give indication of the time, of late they had not been so reliable. Things was not as they ought to have been. Little things always so natural seemed a little out of kilter, even the air around us seemed unnaturally heavy and dense, and the atmosphere beyond, so that oft times even at midday the sun was obscured in a haze, like a red ball, as at sunset.

Of course, as Cyrus said, it was probably a most natural condition, some normal atmospheric presence that, were it not for the ominous presence of the comet nightly, folks would only shrug off simply as "conditions."

I listened for sounds of morning, but only caught a rustling noise in the trees, though it did not seem particularly windy without. I glanced out through the window and, despite the rustling which was still evident, the stubborn old oak leaves that might have been rattling in a slight breeze was theirselves quite still, as was the branches.

I was staring at them to no purpose, when beyond, toward the distant horizon, I detected a sudden light, but not in the direction that it might have been the comet, unless that celestial body had changed course overnight. Lightning in winter was of course not unheard of, but it was unusal. Perhaps an electrical storm was brewing.

But the light did not flash as distant lightning is wont to do. It rather glowed brighter and brighter until, in a mighty rush, faster than I could hardly comprehend, two vast columns, bright as lightning but otherwise not similar, shot from the horizon, terrifyingly bright and rapid, straight up and not down as is customary of electrical activities. They hovered only an instant and then disappeared, all of that so fast that I could not have wakened Cyrus and alerted him had I sought to.

I stood there for several minutes, shivering unaware in the cold, staring at that spot where the phenonenon had occured, but it did not repeat itself. Mayhap it had indeed been only an unusual blast of lightning, too distant for the thunder from it to be heard. Yet I was sensible of a peculiar heaviness about me in the air, as if a fog had been given body and circled around us dancing with distant ghosts.

I smiled to myself at such nonsense, yet quickly returned to the warmth of my spot beside the sleeping Cyrus and snuggled close to gather warmth and cheer from him. Such was night thoughts, and I wondered if I had seen what I had seen.

The very next day, word come to us of two wondrous electrical shocks that had been seen by several early risers, and I knowed that I had not imagined it. But Cyrus put down them stories with other portentous claims as being exaggerations of the times, and so I did not mention to him my own sighting.

"Mama," said Sarah one morning, "I could hardly sleep at all for the lights a-dancing through the window at me."

I knowed that not to be the truth, for I knowed myself that she had slept hard as a rock. Probably she had waked once to the comet light, but hardly more than that.

"Well, it's naught to trouble over. It's only a natural thing, not even serious as thunder and lightning. It's only little more than a falling star that's just takin' its time in the fall, is all."

"Missy Gilbert said that her brother said that he heard that it was a sign from God that he intends shortly to rend the earth to pieces." She announced all of that most matter-of-factly, almost as if she could not wait for the excitement.

"Well, let's hope that Missy Gilbert's brother misunderstood what was represented him."

"I should like to stay up one night and watch it again, for I have forgot what it was like," she said.

So that was what was behind all of this. "Why, Sally, you may stay up long as you can tonight then."

She was so took back at my easy agreement, mayhap all prepared to argue her case, that she was at a loss for speech, an unusual situation for her.

Truth was, I had no fear that she would be able to stay up much past her normal bedtime. Sleep would catch her and trip her, as it always done.

Alas, I reckoned without Sarah's determination, for her bedtime come and went, and apparently perceiving herself to be sleepy, she set out to talk herself awake, and I had ample reason to regret my decision.

She asked questions. She wanted to know the why of it, the where of it, the what of it, all the things about comets that we didn't know anyway and that she could have asked during daylight hours now occurred to her—repeatedly—until we was all, including George, passing weary of it.

When she wasn't asking questions, she was darting to door or window to stare out. "When will it come?" she would cry, apparently unable to recall that not having known a minute or two earlier, we still did not have that information.

"Close the door," I warned her, "you let in the cold air. Peek out the window."

Not five minutes later, she was back at the door, swinging it wide, and staring out. "Close the door, Sarah!" I said, but instead she stepped right outside.

"There's people comin'," she announced.

"What people?"

"Why, a group of people," she said, shading her eyes with her had so as to distinguish them better.

Indians!

I shouted at her, "Sarah, get in the house," and I jumped for the door. Cyrus was already reaching for his rifle. But instead of heeding me, Sarah danced on down the path.

"Sarah!" I cried stepping out after her. And shading my own eyes, I could indeed make out the figures of three men a-greeting Sarah, two of whom I recognized with considerable relief: Reuben Bradene by his peculiar sloping height and Jacob the riverman by his bandy-legged sailor's gait. It wasn't until they was within the circle of light around the cabin that I recognized the third.

"Ah, an it's the Pritchard family, now isn't it?" said Joseph McCade.

Well, the first question I had for Joseph McCade once they was within the cabin concerned the whereabouts and welfare of my sister Martha Elen and her three babes.

"Why, they're sound as can be with Patsy Bradene. We floated the river with Jacob here, even struggling through the darkened water, as we was close to our destination. But the babes could go no farther, so they stayed at the river with Patsy, and we come on to let ye know our situation."

"What is your situation?" asked Cyrus.

"Well, we escaped just ahead of the Injuns with as much of our belongings as we could carry aboard."

"What Indians?" asked Cyrus.

"You have not heard, then, that the Injuns is on the warpath, massacring settlers and devastating the lands, intent on chasing all the settlers back beyond the eastern mountains and," here his voice lowered ominously, "mayhap even into the sea whence they come."

At our looks of incredulousness, he went on, "There was pitched battle, it's said, between the warriors of Tecumseh the Shawnee and the troops of Governor Harrison, on the banks of the Wabash at Tippecanoe, and Governor Harrison's troops was badly defeated and that the victorious Injuns is gathering strength and preparing for a great onslaught." He paused for breath at that, and Cyrus turned to Jacob the riverman.

"Have you heard aught of this?"

Jacob frowned and murmured, "That is the rumor along the river, but it's vague. Ther's reports of such battle, but the reports of the outcome is insecure enough that I'd not feel safe to go one way er t'other."

"Well, it come to me from enough reliable sources that I wasn't willing to risk staying north. To my way of thinking," Joseph went on answering the question that was in my mind, "the Injun is going to concentrate on goin' east and north, recovering them lands already confiscate, so that its safe enough to go west."

"You think to go west?" said Cyrus. I could tell he was startled at that idea.

"The Injuns, y'see, they have always been less menace to the trading man, the white man in the wilderness to meet their needs. It's only when you try to move them from their lands in concentrated effort, as the American government has been doing, that they become fractious. An' I have heard," he added with a look of bright anticipation about him, "that the lands west of here, beyond the swamp and into the mountain of the Aux Arcs, is as beautiful as any lands ther be, with timber and grass and the greatest boiling springs of clear and cold water that ye kin imagine. They tell of great lakes beyond, and creeks and rivers made up of naught but purest spring water."

"What does my sister say to all of this?" I asked finally, and he only shrugged his shoulders, though there was the suggestion of a grin about his lips, and that told me all I needed by way of answer. I could imagine, then, Martha Elen arguing and complaining while her husband waxed eloquent and persuasive, both at the same time, becoming each one louder in the effort to over-ride the other, as was the style of their domestic discussions.

"I plan to travel west and choose a place and return fer them."

"Return for them?" said Cyrus.

"I want to leave them here, wher they'll be safe, with kin," he said and Cyrus, who was usually equal to most any situation, turned to me, unable, I think, to know how to respond to that.

"I'll get them a cabin up, fer certain, before I leave. It'll be but temporary, but I know that you an't got the space to winter four more," said Joseph Mc-Cade, glancing around our tight little cabin. "But I'll want them close by. So's their need can be seen to. I'll buy what ground I need and, of course, make payment in gold to someone to help see after them. An' then I'll be off and hope to be back fer them before the Injuns destroys all in ther paths."

He said that last so cheerfully that the suspicious thought passed through my mind that he had only taken such rumors of war as excuse to relocate, as his nature did not permit him to stay for long in one place.

I think that he was genuinely startled when Cyrus pointed out to him that there had indeed been massacres in our neighborhood, and those real and not just rumors.

"Rumor, it is though, links them to Eremus Lodi," interrupted Jacob the riverman.

"You've heard those rumors?" said Cyrus.

"When aught strange goes on, ye kin count on rumors to include Master Lodi," said Reuben Bradene. All was silence for a moment, less I think because of what was said but because it was Reuben who said it, so rare was his contribution to any conversation.

"That's so," concurred Jacob.

"Well," said Joseph McCade, "I have heard much of that man, of his comings and goings and various associations, and not much of it good, and that he does have unnatural association with the Injun."

"It's true," said the riverman, "that Eremus Lodi keeps questionable company at times, both north an' south, fer he's roamed the river's edge fer as long as I can recall, back an' forth as a caged animal. An' he's been known to haunt some of them places in Orleans an' in St. Louis that, well, that'd make Sodom an' Gomorrhy to be a grammar school picnic."

"It is not the place to tell of all that," said Cyrus glancing toward me and the children, though in truth, Sarah had long given up the battle and leaned sleeping against me. I looked up and sure enough the light from the comet was streaking the night sky, and I wondered if I should wake her but thought better of it. Another night. No one could say just when that light would disappear from the skies, but from the look of it, I had begun to think it might last forever.

"No. No I suppose it's not," said Jacob finally, "but one day I'll tell ye all that I know of that man, which is both better an' worse than ye might expect."

"How d'ye come by such accurate information?" asked Joseph.

"Ah, I've said it before. The river talks. D'ye listen, ye learn to separate fact from fancy an' who to listen to and who not to, an' if yer of an inquisitive nature, as I most certainly do be, ye learn to add up fact an' rumor an' how to ask yer questions. It's a skill," he said proudly, "an' not many are so skilled as I be at seekin' an' findin' information."

Well, I already knew that to be truth. I was also most anxious to know the story of Eremus Lodi, but could think of no seemly way to ask. Sometimes to be a respectable woman was most inconvenient.

True to his word, Joseph McCade did indeed erect a cabin on a small plot of land purchased at greater than its worth from Brother Mayhew, and having contracted with Brother Mayhew and Brother Mayhew's two big sons to help look out for Martha Elen and her three babes, within a fortnight was gone, cheerful and optimistic as ever.

"We'll never see you again, for the Indians will take your scalp and hack you into little pieces and feed you to the crows," Martha Elen called out to his departing figure, and he turned and gave her a cheery wave in return.

The rumor of death and destruction at the hands of the victorious Indians that had spurred Joseph McCade's westward interest was slow a-dying, though the truth was knowed in short order. A military commander on his way to New Orleans, pausing for business in New Madrid, had given solemn assurances that it had not been the Americans that had been bested and routed but the Indian.

"I have follered that rumor downstream all the way from St. Louis," he had sighed, "a-stomping at it all the way. But once started, such a story is mighty hard to beat down."

And though the Battle of Tippecanoe, as it come to be called, was a thorough defeat for the plans of Tecumseh the Shawnee, there was still them that refused to believe but what they had heard first, and even some of those who admitted the truth, shrugged it off with comment that it meant nothing, as Tecumseh was still at large and at his mischief.

I did not understand much of it but was willing to take the word of those of official position who traveled the river, even if others was not.

The cabin that Joseph McCade had built for his family was some tighter than the one I had first encountered in Ste. Genevieve, but of a certainty it was not meant to withstand many winters. It would provide shelter, but little more, although this one, as that last one, was large and commodious, so large that it was the talk of all those men who had helped to erect it at Joseph's direction.

Happy as I was to have my sister near once more, the added responsibility was great and tiresome as well, for her three babes–Robert, Janie, and John—was alike in all ways, from their ability to find mischief to get into to the bright copper-colored hair of their heads. They was younger by some than Sarah and could not begin to out-talk her, but otherwise they constituted a handful for everyone, and some was heard to comment out loud that no wonder Joseph McCade bolted for high ground.

It did not help that Martha Elen did not seem to notice or care that they was continually at odds with the world around them.

"Mama," said George, one day home from the school room where they all attended, "they are an embarrassment. Janie today was showin' her petticoats abroad and her brothers was eggin' her on.

"Not only that, but Robert and John spend more time in the corners of the room, with their faces to the wall, than they do on the benches, for if one is not in trouble, the other is or they both are."

"Now, George, you must be patient They are quite little yet to be at books, seems to me, and only trying to attract some attention."

Though Sarah did not seem to be discomfitted by her cousins, she now and then found herself at odds with them, her to one side and they to the other, for they never split, and you would either be with them or not.

One night, not long after Joseph McCade's precipitious departure, Martha Elen arrived at our cabin after we was all abed and sleeping, pounding on our door and crying out. By the time I had let her in, Cyrus was already into his trousers and pulling his blouse over his head.

"They're gone," cried Martha Elen. "My babies are gone, the Indians have got them. I hope that Joseph McCade may rest in hell for this. Oh, help me."

We was some minutes getting her coherent enough to tell her story, but at last she got it told. She put them to bed and gone on herself, after bolting them all in. She had waked just a few minutes earlier by the draft of wind through the rooms and discovered the children gone.

"They're scalped. They're dead," she cried.

"How could anyone get the door opened from the outside without calling your attention to it?" asked Cyrus, pulling his boots on and reaching for his coat.

"Oh, I don't know. But they're dead, I know, dead and scalped. Oh, my merciful God," she wailed.

"Mama?" It was George. "Mama," he repeated somewhat insistently, and I turned to him.

"George, what is it?" I asked impatiently.

"Mama, where is Sarah?"

In that moment my heart flopped over and took up residence in my mouth. "She is not in her bed?" I finally managed to ask and he shook his head.

Cyrus was already headed to the door. "Cyrus! Indians?"

He shook his head. "There have been no Indians in this cabin nor, I suspect, in Martha Elen's either. I think," he said grimly, "that the children have all sneaked out together for some activity of their own devising." With that, he stalked from the cabin.

I pulled my own clothes on and, with Martha Elen behind me, stepped out into the clearing. The night was bright, for the comet was in full flower, and you could easily make out its twin tails. The air about was diffuse with light. I had not for weeks paid much mind to that strange sight, but I was at that moment drawed up short at it and could not keep from standing and staring into the heavens wondering at that sight.

"Mama," called George, "Daddy has found them."

Sure enough, just beyond the garden in an open space atop a slight rise, there they sat the four of them, all wrapped in Sarah's comforter.

"They come out to watch the comet," said Cyrus, his voice strained in anger.

"Oh, Mama," cried Sarah, "it's so beautiful, and they say that one day it will fall on the ground and split it open and that will be the end of everything. Do you think that's so, Mama?"

"I think that you ought to be in bed."

"Oh, it's wondrous," said Robert, or it might have been John, for truth of it was, I could not always keep them apart. "Do you know that all the animals are out a-lookin' at it, too?" he added.

"There are always animals out at night," replied his mother none too patiently.

"Not bears. We seen a bear," said Janie.

"You did not see a bear," said Martha Elen. "It is not the time of year for bears. They are all safely asleep in the mountains. Bears do not run about in the winter."

"No," said Sarah, "we did see a bear. He walked out of the woods, and he wandered back and forth and back and forth and stood up and then sat down. We thought he would eat us," she added. "And squirrels, we saw lots and lots of squirrels running through the trees."

I did not say anything more. I was too tired to argue with these active imaginations. Cyrus walked home with Martha Elen, and I could hear her yet a-giving it to her children long after they was out of sight.

I put Sarah back to bed and stood still dressed by the door to wait for Cyrus. The light was still bright, and in spite of myself, I felt its pull and stepped quietly outside to look up and watch. It was an uncanny display. I caught myself wondering if the thing could fall from the sky, and if it did, what would happen to the earth? I was as bad as a child.

As I stood staring, I begun to hear the noises of the night, noises that our talking and running about had temporarily silenced. In the winter such noises on a still night are few, not as they are on a summer night, or should have been, but there was—it finally come to me—an unaccountable lot of rustling.

My first thought was of the bear that the children had spoken of, and then of Indians, for my mind seemed more and more to dwell on that thought, but truth was, neither bear nor Indian would make that kind of sustained rustling. Looking up, I caught a glimpse of something moving in the trees and I watched. No bird would be abroad at such an hour. But the movement continued and I stared hard at it. Squirrels. It was squirrels. Not one but many, moving through the trees. I had never seen anything like that before.

Perhaps it was a kind of moon-madness, I thought, brought on by the light of the comet that made not only men but animals act in strange and restless fashion. And I thought of the old sister, dressed all in white, sitting in a tree, awaiting the judgment.

I looked up again and watched the receding comet and wondered where it was going, making such a strange and determined journey through the sky. It was part of God's Plan, in truth, and though I might understand certain superstitious people's fear of that beautiful sight, I could not believe that the Lord God would hang so wondrous a weapon of destruction over the planet, threatening and menacing. That He would one day smite the land and lead the saved across, I had no doubt. But I could not think that He would tease and taunt as He did it.

With a sigh, I turned back toward the cabin, for it was passing cold without, and as I looked up, a dark shadow blocked the light from the open door. I started for only a moment, for I recognized that shadow even without seeing its form. No person or thing, I was sure, cast such a shadow as O'Reilly, the black.

Sure enough, that form pushed its shadow from the light and replaced it and stood waiting.

"Ah, O'Reilly. You're back," I said, and he followed me into the lighted room.

Even in the irregular light of the candles, however, I could tell that the figure of O'Reilly was not the same that I was accustomed to, for he was gaunt and worn, and he drooped in near exhaustion, but the voice when he spoke at last was the same gentle sound that I remembered so fondly.

"Ah, Mama, be well," he said.

"Sit, O'Reilly," I said quickly, pointing the corner by the fire where I knowed he would sit, for I feared that if he did not soon sit, he would surely fall, so unsteady had he become.

"Ah, Mama," he sighed, and without else did as I had bid, yet that so silent that he did not disturb the children, except George, who raised himself up on one elbow and watched the silent black slip into sleep, if that was what it was.

When Cyrus returned, he listened to my explanation and then frowned and shook his head slightly. If he knowed anymore what to make of it than I did, he did not say. His only comment was that the black, from the manner in which he slept, seemed more exhausted than ill.

Well, it had occurred to me that he might have come down with whatever it had been that had felled Eremus Lodi earlier. But staring at him, I too decided that even in the flickering light of fire and candle, his face did not have that ravaged and pale look that Eremus Lodi's had had, nor was his sleep so restless and labored.

Though gaunt and tired, he rested as was his style, crouched rather than stretched, more as a man who is weary rather than ill.

Neither Cyrus nor I had ever said what was in both our minds, I think, that Eremus and his slave were allied in some manner or other with the Indian Tecumseh. Nor had neither of us conjectured aloud that it might have been Tecumseh and his band who had helped to fight our fire. Sarah's Indians.

Now, with the Indian defeat at Tippecanoe and Tecumseh's whereabouts unknown, this black man's stealthy comings and goings were to my mind worrisome. Especially in the light of nearby massacres by Indians, or at least what passed for Indians. Staring at the man so beloved by my children, I felt a fearful hollow in my stomach, as if feeling had left it and naught remained but mystery.

The next morning, discovering the silent slave at the fireplace corner, after first excitement, the children was strangely subdued, as if some instinct that I could not quite understand were at work. But as the day wore on, both black and children became more communicative.

"O'Reilly," said Sarah at length, "have you seen the comet and an't it pretty?"

O'Reilly looked blank.

"The star," explained Sarah, "the falling star that does not really fall but runs across the sky at night?"

"Ah," said O'Reilly, "ah, see him, yah, be great light of big sorrow dragging broken feather."

Big light of sorrow? Broken feather? Both were peculiarly Indian ways of expression. But sorrow? Big light of sorrow? Indeed that was what he meant, for the expression upon his face and the distance in his eyes testified to it.

O'Reilly went out of doors but circumspectly that day and indeed slept over much. But each time he wakened, for he wakened as usual with any little untoward sound or movement, he seemed that much more rested. And each time he ate, for I pushed food upon him every chance I got, he seemed that much more strengthened.

By nightfall, he was restless, and Cyrus and I felt certain that he would be gone by day. But this time he did not slip away as he had before. He waited until it had been dark for some time, Peter and Sarah fast asleep. Sarah, after her adventure of the night before, could not, though she tried mightily, put off sleep, and Peter was ne'er one to refuse a nap.

George accompanied the black out the door, and the two of them stood and communed in that fashion peculiar to them. Of what they spoke I could not say, or even that they did speak. Only as I watched through the window, I saw O'Reilly reach over and free the amulet that George wore yet beneath his blouse. Then a moment later, the slave stepped forward and threw his head back and stared long at the sky and then commenced to pace back and forth.

He stopped and held his hands out, palms up as if he were testing for raindrops. And then, suddenly, he dropped to the ground on all fours and stared hard at it, rocking gently back and forth, and with a word or gesture, I could not tell which, invited the boy to join him.

I wondered what foolish supplication that was, what pagan gods O'Reilly might be calling on, but I could hear nothing, nor have any indication that any words was spoken.

I saw O'Reilly gesture toward the tree and then toward the sky, perhaps seeking the comet, for it had not yet made its nightly appearance. George rocked back on his heels and followed the black's gestures.

In time, the two rose. Cyrus was standing behind me. I did not know how long he had watched nor could I tell his thoughts, for his expression gave nothing away.

I started to speak, but then O'Reilly, without backward glance, stepped forward so effortlessly and quickly that had we not had our eyes right on him, we would ne'er have seen him go. In a moment George returned, a little frown of concern between his eyes.

I wanted to ask questions but did not know how. It was Cyrus, who was not normally given to asking questions, who broke the silence. "Do you know why O'Reilly calls the comet 'the great light of big sorrow,' George?"

"The light has brought much sorrow," he answered simply, "and will bring much more."

"What kind of sorrow, Son?"

George, fingering the amulet under his blouse, shook his head. "All is unsettled, and the light splits in two as it passes. The beginning and the end."

I looked at Cyrus who shrugged, "It sounds the superstition of savages only. And, surprising as it seems, remember that O'Reilly is a savage, too."

We bedded down shortly after that, but while George and Cyrus seemed to slip quickly into unconsciousness, I found sleep hard come by. My errant thoughts just would not settle theirselves down. By and by, I detected that light, at first a general diffusion and finally beautifully bright through the window.

I got up and pulled my shawl about me, opened the door and stepped out. It was cold, but not freezing. My stockinged feet would not take too long out of doors, however. That same rustling noise of the night before, as well as a variety of noises not usual in the wintertime, was apparent. Sometimes it seemed to me that the night was more alive than the day, perhaps because that was the time that I watched instead of participated.

In the trees and the growth there was a commotion—moon-madness—as the critters wandered in something like confusion, mayhap thinking it daylight they saw or early sunrise.

I watched the brilliant star, shooting across the sky, dragging its twin tails behind, too beautiful to be the precursor of sorrow. Indeed, it was said that the comet would hold until after the Christmas season, and there were others who calmly maintained that, like the star that first proclaimed the birth of the Savior, this one was harbinger of the Second Coming.

If true, was that cause for sorrow?

I slipped quickly back into the house, for inspiring as the sight of the comet was, my feet was still rooted to the cold earth and not too happy withal about it.

A few days after, Sarah rushed into the cabin in some agitation. "Mama," she announced, "there are snakes all over!"

"Snakes?" I looked at her. Curious as things had become, I was certain that they had not become that serious. Bears and snakes, indeed. Mid-winter at that.

"Sarah, there an't snakes out there. I don't know what you've seen or thought you've seen, but you have not seen snakes."

"But, Mama."

"No more. You have not seen snakes, or bears either for that matter. It's winter. In the winter, snakes sleep and bears and a variety of other animal. That is the way it is."

"But, Mama, it was snakes, spread about all over the snow, froze stiff, too."

"Sarah, you've seen some sticks or such that's all. Snakes in the snow, indeed!"

"Mama! I know what I saw."

I was just about to become exasperated with the girl when George come in, a deep frown upon his face.

"Mama, come and see what Sarah has found," he said. "It looks like snakes."

"See," said Sarah triumphantly.

"Oh, George, you, too? You know there an't snakes in the winter."

"I don't know what it is, then, Mama. Come and look."

I did have better things to occupy me, but for the sake of peace, I followed the children out to the edge of our clearing. Before we had even got to our destination, I could indeed make out strange and twisted forms, grotesque forms, like a handful of fishing worms.

I bent over and examined them and felt a chill descend upon me. It was snakes, it looked like a large nest of copperheads had crawled out of the ground and froze.

"See," said Sarah again.

I couldn't even speak I was so surprised. I did not care that the child had bested me in an argument. What concerned me was the sight of one more thing that should ne'er have been. Frozen snakes and comets and strange lights and agitated squirrels and stubborn milk cows and a foreboding atmosphere.

When Cyrus returned, I showed the sight to him, and he stared at it in silence for a long time.

"What do you make of it?" I asked.

He shook his head. "It is truly a time of extraordinaries," he said.

Chapter 17

The Bear

"Mama," said Sarah as I tucked her into her pallet for the night, "what if Daddy does not get back for my birthday tomorrow?"

"Well, he promised he would," I said more cheerfully than I felt, for though Sarah might be anxious, I was myself concerned and distressed in a way that I could not quite explain.

"How far is Little Prairie?" she asked for not the first time, and for not the first time I replied that it was near to 30 miles down river. It would be by horseback better than a day's journey.

"The services should have been over this afternoon," I said reassuring her, "and Daddy should be on his way home now. He will most certainly be here tomorrow."

I had not been happy that Cyrus had accepted the appointment from the group at Little Prairie. Brother Ples Bryan had called upon him and persuaded Cyrus to accompany him south, offering him the use of a horse for the trip.

Of course, Cyrus could not turn away from such an appointment and made plans to accompany Brother Bryan, even against my arguments about the cold and the danger, for the talk of Indian depredations was still much in the air.

"We will stay only long as we must," Cyrus answered. "We should be back by Tuesday or Wednesday next."

"Daddy," Sarah had objected, "my own birthday is on Monday next. Will you not be home for that!"

"Ah," smiled Cyrus, "I could ne'er miss so important an event as that. I shall be home by Monday then, do I have to ride the entire night long to make it."

For me, that depression that had been building in me for a long time had become exceedingly oppressive, for I was not given to that kind of lowering of spirit and hardly knew how to react to it. It was only by the greatest effort that I managed to keep my countenance clear of the distress that I felt.

The children slept, yet I turned and tossed and stared into the darkness, the only light that from the dying flames in the fireplace. I would add exhaustion to my distressed mental state, did I not fall soon to sleep. Yet sleep eluded me. Though the room was becoming more chilled, I had by my restlessness managed to overheat myself, and so I kicked the comforter from me and stared hard and accusingly at the small window.

One of Brother Mayhew's big boys I had thought would pass the night with us, but he had not appeared. By the time I realized that he was probably not coming, it was too late to go after him. Our signals most like had got crossed up. Nevermind, I was not so frightened to stay alone. I did not expect Indians or any other marauder on a cold winter night.

I did not know the hour, but I assumed that the comet must make its nightly pass some time soon, and I found myself waiting that and listening for the night noises that over the past weeks had been unusual in occurrence.

At length, the hour took its toll and I begun to feel drowsy and my eyes drooped closed. I had not yet fallen into deep sleep when I was startled to attention. George was beside me, tapping gently and whispering.

"Mama, Mama? Hear that noise? What is it?"

I sat up and listened. There was indeed a strange noise, almost as if a great breeze was rattling those dry leaves yet clinging to certain trees, but it was not quite that sound.

I threw back my comforter and looked out the window, peering into the darkness, my eyes quickly adjusting to that darkness outside. Behind me, the fire on the hearth was near extinguished. Shadows charged through the trees, ominously, great and small, like nothing I had ever seen or heard of, rustling the leaves and whirring the air. It was—I could determine finally birds— great flocks of birds, of all kinds and sizes, though I could not in the darkness identify them, all moving through the trees and rising into the sky, headed near the same direction.

"Look, Mama," whispered George, and I followed his gaze to the ground and made out all kinds of small critters and varmints moving across the open ground, as a mismatched and ragtag army on the move.

"What's happening, Mama?" asked George.

Watching in fascination, I only shook my head. "Mayhap," I said at last, "it is the comet or some other odd alignment of the skies that confuses the birds and beasts." And even as I said it, I thought that it had a Biblical sound to it—the beasts of the field and the birds of the air, a-fleeing something, or a-marching to it. The picture of that old sister dressed in white waiting on the judgment come to me, only it did not seem so amusing, and I caught myself hoping that she was right, that judgment day would not happen in the night.

I could feel George trembling beside me, and my own feet had commenced to get cold. "We'd best back to bed, George, lest we freeze. Tomorrow in the light it will certainly make more sense than it does now."

I lay in my bed and George in his, and neither of us slept. I sat up and sniffed at the air, thinking all at once that it might be fire that drove those critters ahead of it, but I could not detect any such evidence. Then I thought of rising water, yet there was no reason to expect that, though each of those ideas was a possibility. I wondered how long until daylight, for I would not feel comfortable until I could see what was happening.

I lay for a long time, listening, until at last the sounds of the migrating animals had begun to diminish, and I felt sleep begin to assert itself again. Surely it could not be so long until daylight. I sighed and pulled the comforter up around my chin. Day would undoubtedly solve the riddle, and I closed my eyes.

"Mama!"

I sat straight up in bed, still groggy from the sleep I had fallen into.

"Mama, listen." It was George again. "Listen!"

I listened, and in the distance I heard thunder, rolling, deep, ominous. Yet instead of diminishing, the sound grew until I knowed that it was not thunder, at least not any thunder that I had ever heard, for it rolled and rumbled and picked up sound, until it was loud enough that Sarah cried out and then Peter.

"What is it, Mama?" cried George.

"The comet has hit the ground," cried Sarah. "The comet has fallen and the earth is rent!"

The baby was crying and Sarah was screaming. I jumped out of bed and went over to them. "Shhhh, Sarah, it's only loud thunder," I said not believing it. A wall of water, I thought. I had heard of such. A wall of water was upon us and I could not see it, had no place to flee. "Climb in bed with me," I said as calmly as I could. I picked up Peter and carried him with me. "George sit upon the bed with us," I directed, holding the other two close to me.

We had no more than positioned ourselves but a great shattering noise was upon us, and the bed begun to pitch and buck as a wild horse might. Sarah screeched again, "The earth is rent!"

"Shut up, Sarah," said George remarkably calm over the rising noise. But the bed continued to pitch until I thought we should all be throwed from it, and I waited for the splash of water that I was certain would hit. But it did not. Without was a great shattering and splintering sound, combined with another-worldly roar, so that we must surely be caught up inside a great thunder bolt.

There was a buckling of the cabin floor, and I heard a rumbling crash nearby and could make out the chimney slowly toppling to the floor, the stones striking the spot where moments earlier Sarah and Peter had slept. Still there was no water.

What there was, was smoke or dust, suddenly and in such quantity, that we all begun to cough. And with the dust and smoke and smell of something that I could not recognize remained that mighty noise. It was most assuredly the Judgment. The earth was being rent, and we would all have to face our Maker, and where was Cyrus?

I clutched the children to me and waited. The rumbling had slacked off, but still there was the sound of snapping and cracking as a thousand buggy whips were put into play at one time.

"Mama," said George, his voice high against the noise, but otherwise calm, "Mama, is it an earthquake?"

Earthquake. Ah, in my panic I had forgot that this was indeed unstable land given to quakes, and this was indeed a similar feeling to that one years gone which saw the death of little Jeremy Cuthcart.

And then the rumble subsided and but for continued sounds of toppling outside, which could only be trees a-falling, there come an eerie silence.

We sat clinging to one another, waiting, for several moments.

"What shall we do, Mama? Where is Daddy?" wailed Sarah.

"We had best just wait, don't you think, Mama?" Again it was George so calm for one so young.

"I think mayhap we'd best just wait here until daylight, so we can see what's transpired and then," I started to say but was interrupted by another sudden shock, and the floor buckled again and more of the stones from the fireplace tumbled and a log from the roof collapsed right at the foot of the bed.

When that shock subsided, I said to George, "Gather up shoes and comforters, George. We'd best sit outside in the clearing lest this house tumble right down on us."

The door had been throwed ajar, and I carried Peter out and cautiously stepped away from the cabin. It was light enough that I could see just before me, but beyond the landscape seemed strange. It was moments before I realized that much of the forest around us was collapsed and that I could make out sky where once I could see only trees. I stood and stared at that for a long time, hardly able to comprehend, and then the rumble from the earth once more signalled a tremor.

"Get to clear ground, away from the trees, George," I said, and we scrambled as the earth begun to rock gently under our feet, that it was not unlike trying to walk across a small boat anchored in choppy water.

When that tremor had ceased, we searched out what seemed to be the clearest piece of ground. What trees there had been nearby seemed to have been snapped right off, still shuddering and trembling, dry leaves rattling, many of the stumps visible, others hidden in the brush.

I spread a comforter on the ground and we sat, I holding Peter on my lap, with George to one side and Sarah leaning against the other side. I wrapped all in comforters and there we sat.

I tried to make light of our situation. "It's like camping out of doors," I said. The words had hardly escaped my lips when another light tremor rocked us and then another, as if they might ne'er cease. I thought again of riding a small boat upon a flood.

"Mama," said Sarah suddenly, "is it Master Ben Blough and the devil a-wrestlin'?"

I laughed. "That mayhap is just what it is," I said.

"Really."

"Ah, no, dear. But I'll bet there's those that do think that, don't you?"

She said nothing, but I think nodded her head.

There was another light tremor. None of these tremors had the noise and the odors of those two first ones, and I could assume that they was subsiding and it was all over. But I was mistaken in that, for in only a few minutes time that roar commenced again, a low rumbling in the bowels of the earth and then a gigantic heave that, seated as we was on the ground, we could feel lifting the earth below us and rolling it around and settling it again, and along with it great quantities of dust and dirt. And we was set once more to coughing fits.

Then it was quiet again, uncommon still against the commotion. We sat, not saying anything any of us for a long time. Sarah and Peter begun to wilt and then to sleep, for it is a blessing of babes that they will have their sleep no matter what.

I stared ahead at the unfamiliar landscape, wondering when dawn would come and with it what sights would be revealed to us. I worried first about Cyrus and then about Martha Elen, but there was naught we could do until light, for no telling what lay between us and the others.

Seated on the ground for a time, all I could hear was the regular breathing of my children and George a-tapping absentmindedly against the ground with a stick. The rustling sounds of the fleeing beasts and birds was no more, and I could but wonder how they had sensed the coming devastation, what instinct had warned them to flee, and had it done them any good after all? I pondered that. Would the shocks have rent the air as well as the land and pulled the birds to earth, too?

Suddenly I detected a moan nearby, so unexpected that I jumped.

"George?"

"What is it, Mama? What is that noise? Is it someone?"

"I don't know."

We both sat and strained at the silence, and in time heard the sound again, a low and muffled groan. I was glad that Sarah slept, for she'd be sure that it was the devil himself, so weird did it sound.

"What is it?" repeated George. I shook my head, for I certainly didn't know. "Should we speak out?" he asked.

After that came a slight rustling, and as we strained to listen, another low and painful groan, a cry of some sort. We had not been silent. Whoever or whatever it was must surely be aware of our presence, unless it was deaf or unconscious. Were it a person a-suffering, we could not simply sit by.

"Hallo," I called out. "Hallo. Ere you hurt?"

There was no response, and I started to call again, but we was shaken once more by another tremor, so hard that I clutched the sleeping children and braced myself against the ground. "George," I said, "crawl around and get on the other side of me against Sarah, so we can all reinforce one another."

There followed another shock and then a moan and then silence. Though I called out two or three times, there was no response. There was naught to do but sit and wait. As the night wore on, we was shaken by small tremors over and over and now and then we heard the moaning sound.

"I think I hear breathing, Mama," said George after one hard shock, and I listened, too. There did seem to be heavy and labored breathing nearby and then a moan.

"I think it's an animal, George," I said, "an animal in distress. We must be still and wait the daylight."

I did not believe that any night could be so long, for we sat, warmed by each other and the comforters, enduring almost endless rocking of the earth, so that we lost count of the shocks. Some seemed to run together and there was several that was hard, preceded by the rumbling of the earth. Mercifully, Peter and Sarah slept, stirring and fussing with the harder jolts, but otherwise unconscious of our precarious situation.

I had heard of earthquakes, of the earth opening wide and swallowing whate'er was upon it. But our spot of ground at least held firm, and I was too fearful to try even to surmise about the ground around us. We heard no human voice in all that time but our own, and the unearthly moaning, which now and then rose nearby, sometimes loud and sometimes soft.

In time, I was aware that George had not spoken in some time. And I bent around trying to see him, realizing not only that he, too, had fallen asleep, but that I was uncommon stiff and tired myself. The moaning now was soft, but almost constant. Mayhap it was some natural phenomenon only. A tree limb pressing and rubbing against something, startling us only because of the dark. But that was idle thought, for the other sound was too much like labored breathing to be so simple a thing as a tree limb.

The dawn did rise, slowly lighting the distant horizon, lifting the dark, yet leaving the landscape obscured as if in a heavy fog. I waited, straining my eyes, looking for landmarks. Behind us, the cabin still stood, its chimney toppled, but no other outward sign of damage. We would have fared all right to have stayed within. The rest of the scene, as I could carefully make it out, was one of unbelievable devastation. Tall trees was everywhere toppled, broken like broomstraws, lying criscrossed over one another, as if an errant woodsman had gone berserk in the night. In the light shocks, the branches and leaves quivered as if they had just fallen. Indeed the land was cleared away as if a great scythe had mowed it down irregularly, some stumps standing high, others broken at the ground, but to my relief I could make out what I took to be the Mayhew cabin in the distance, still standing.

I eased myself, and George suddenly sat up and then Sarah. I looked down, and Peter upon my lap was staring wide-eyed around him, awake for no telling how long. Carefully we stood and looked around us. There was no sea of fire, no devils dancing, no smoke or gaping chasms or horrendous screaming. All was still at dawn, for there was no sound of birds cries either.

And then there was the moan. George and I looked at each other. "What was that, Mama?" asked Sarah clutching at my hand.

"It come from over there, Mama," said George. "In the brush."

"George and Sarah, sit upon the pallet with the baby. I will look. Be very still," I cautioned, but I need not have, for I do think that all three was holding their breaths, as I was my own.

I walked carefully, picking my way around the fallen debris, small trees and broken limbs, holding my skirts close about me. A large tree, with many big branches obscured the path, and I climbed up on the trunk and looked around. Beyond was another tangle of trees and branches, and it was from those that the moaning came.

I crawled over a large trunk and stopped short in my tracks, for there lying pinned beneath one of those monstrous old trees was a great bear. Blood was both caked and flowing from his mouth, and the animal's legs looked both to be crushed beneath the fallen tree.

He saw me, for he opened his eyes and looked at me. Wh'er the look he give me was pain or fright or anger or what, I could not know, for a wild beast's face and eyes do not speak the way a person's or even a dog's will speak. He moaned again softly, in pain I knowed, yet he did not struggle, accepting his plight as if it was meant to be as a terrapin turned on its back, waiting what would come.

There was another tremor, and I grabbed at a near branch and stood against the swaying ground, and a great groan was wrenched from that mighty beast and he opened his eyes wide again and stared at me.

Carefully, once the rolling had subsided, I made my way back to where the children sat. "It is a bear," I said. "He is hopelessly trapped and in great pain. George, can you go back into the cabin—carefully, now—and find Daddy's rifle and bring it to me?"

"Are you going to shoot the bear, Mama?" asked Sarah.

"It is suffering, Sarah. It may be beast, but it knows terror and pain. It would die soon enough, I think, but with great suffering."

George brought the rifle, pulling it behind him, barrel down. Wise boy.

"Can you shoot it by yourself, Mama?" he asked.

"I don't know." I had shot it before but never very accurately, and it usually knocked me six ways from Sunday in the process.

"I'll help you, Mama," he said simply.

We climbed back over the trees to where the bear lay. I heard George breathe hard when he saw the animal, but otherwise he said nothing. The beast looked up at us, without menace or strength even.

"He is beautiful, isn't he, Mama?" sighed George at last.

I would ne'er have thought of a bear as beautiful—fearsome, mayhap, frightening, but not beautiful. Yet as I stared at that animal, lying panting slowly in and out, its face seemed wise as forever, no grimace of pain crossed it. Nor, I thought, would e'er a look of envy or spite or malice, no sneer of impertinence or stupidity, mar that expression. Rage, perhaps, were the teeth bared and the claws raised, or surprise, or perhaps curiosity or playfulness. But those baser expressions which cross human countenances a thousand times would always be missing from this beast. Even pain and fear seemed lacking, yet surely the animal suffered those.

"Yes, George," I answered at last, "it is beautiful."

We positioned the rifle in the crotch of a fallen branch and steadied it, George holding the stock hard with both hands, while my fingers sought the trigger.

Calmly, the beast watched, his groans silenced. Did he know what we intended? Did he understand? Ah, how could a beast understand? We would take his life, the only one allowed him, but that only to ease his suffering. Yet in his great bulk, was he not also one of God's mighty creations? I suddenly felt a tremendous awe at that.

Once more we was shaken. "Mama, hurry," said George once the tremor had subsided.

I looked at the bear and in my heart commended him to God and pulled the trigger. The explosion from the gun threw both George and me backward, harder than any of the tremors we had so far experienced. But when we pulled ourselves together and looked at the bear, we discovered that the rifle had done its merciful job, for the beast was slumped peacefully against the tree that pinioned him, and there he would have to lie.

We gathered up comforters and carried them back into the cabin. Regularly, like a drunken person with the dry heaves, the earth rolled and hiccoughed until we had to stop where we was and sway with the land.

It was not safe to stay by ourselves, for safety was dictated by number, and we started toward the Mayhew's cabin, only to be met part way by one of the Mayhew's big boys on his way to look for us. He carried his rifle, having heard the report from our own. I was glad to see him, for we needed all the help we could get in order to navigate our way through the fallen forest.

"Watch for critters," I murmured. I could only wonder what those tremors might have unearthed, what sleeping beasts had been driven forth and what others forever buried by the unsteady ground.

The Mayhew boy assured that Martha Elen and her three babes was safe, though one of the little boys had suffered a bad bruise to the head, having tripped and fallen. It was a relief to know that they was safe. Would that I could have knowed the same about Cyrus.

We could make out Martha Elen talking before we caught sight of her. Like us, the Mayhews had left their house in fear of its falling, and they, large brood that they was, along with Martha Elen and hers, made quite a crowd in the clearing outside their cabin. That cabin stood, but stood somewhat askew with its chimney likewise toppled.

"We have to eat," announced Sister Mayhew. "Judgment or no, I an't ready to join the saints on a empty stomach." And she set about to prepare a meal, sending this or that one into the cabin to bring out whatever was necessary. The smokehouse near by seemed untouched by the shakes, and the foodstuffs within quite safe.

The tremors which had gone on almost without let-up had finally ceased, and Brother Mayhew announced that he thought we was over it and wondered out loud at how the rest of the neighborhood had fared.

"We'll go after breakfast and look to them," he said to his big boys. "Ther'll doubtless be cabins in need of rebuildin' and we'd best get to it, fer winter an't goin' to wait our convenience." He must have thought that last a merry thought for he chuckled at it, and it almost seemed that chuckle signalled the earth again, for we all stopped short at the sound of the rumble beneath us, as loud as any of those had been, and from our experience through the night, we knowed what to expect and was not disappointed, for the earth was convulsed in a mighty shaking and rocking and rolling, to such extent that we could hardly keep our feet.

"Fall to your hands and knees," cried Brother Mayhew as the earth pitched and rolled. In the distance, trees that had survived the night were snapped as little boys snap twigs between their fingers, and the Mayhew's cabin trembled and sighed and slowly, log by log, begun to settle to the earth before our eyes. I waited for gaping, yawning chasms, expecting them momentarily, but there were none, and then the earth's spasm was apparently run and it was over. Most of us simply sat and stared around us.

"Lord have mercy," sobbed Martha Elen, "when will this be over?"

"That was most likely it," said Brother Mayhew.

But he was wrong, for the tremors continued on and off, and the Mayhew boys dispatched to ascertain the damage to the rest of the area, returned each with harrowing tales.

"They say," said the one, "that ther's no tree left standin' within miles and that the banks of the river has collapsed and that the whole of New Madrid is in danger of sinking into it."

"All kinds of houses and cabins ere damaged, and a few like our'n collapsed," said another. "Folks ere repairin' to the open ground away from the river and settin' up tents and such, reasonin' that if a tent collapses on ye t'won't do the damage as a log roof would."

It was also ascertained that no one was seriously injured, though one of the Mayhew boys claimed to have heard that a black had been drowneded in a sinkhole caused by the earthquake.

Slowly, our neighbors come together through the morning. We suffered another hard shock and then several more shallow ones. Eventually it was agreed that sleeping indoors would not be safe until all sign of tremors was long gone and cabins repaired and shored up as needed.

"We're best off together," suggested Brother Gilbert, "and in truth the safest ground is that high ground where others have gone to set tents. I suggest that we do likewise."

"Are we goin' to sleep in a tent, Mama?" asked John McCade, for by his bandaged head I could now identify him with certainty.

"It would seem so," Martha Elen answered, and then added, "I hope that Joseph McCade has not fallen into a bottomless abyss where'er he is."

On Tiwappity Hill, seven or eight miles distant from the river, the tent city grew through the day, tents being erected of all kinds of material, from quilts and comforters to heavy canvas, our own being of that last kind and belonging to Joseph McCade. He had left behind enough tenting material indeed to make us quite more comfortable than many of those around us.

Though it was passing chilly without, there was fires enough around and about that the discomfort was not great, and we carried with us provsions of all kinds. Indeed was the conditions different, it would have been like a great outdoor meeting, a revival, or association. But the tremors which continued through the day kept us all aware that the occasion was not joyous.

"This is my birthday," announced Sarah glumly, "and my daddy an't here."

I had refrained from saying anything about that, only watching each group that arrived, waiting for him to appear and fearing what might have happened to him. All through that long afternoon I waited and watched, and yet he did not arrive.

Nor was there any sign of him the next day or the next, though various stories and rumors run though the camp like the plague, most of them terrifying, if true, though many of them were suspect from the beginning.

One old gentleman regularly collected a crowd with his explanation of the connection between the comet and the persistent quakes. "That ere comet," he'd begin anew with each fresh batch of tenters, "has toppled the earth over on its side an' the far mountains has slid into the sea, an' the earth now struggles to right itself an' if it don't," and here he would pause most ominously and stare at the heaven, for he was a fine dramatic sort, "if it don't, well, the rest of the earth will slide into the sea an' all the human race with it."

That idea did startle Sarah some when she heard it, until I pointed out to her the difficulty of the earth a-sliding into its own ocean. She frowned and thought about it, apparently satisfied.

Other stories was not so comical. One exhausted group of marchers, claiming to have come twenty miles from the south, told of terrible devastation, and the shocks they described was even more terrible than the ones we had suffered. "The water has come up and is floatin' all things away," said one man. "I seen my own cow just up and drift away into the channel—backward!"

Indeed, he was not the only one to claim to have seen the great river flowing backward, and it was Patsy Bradene who reminded me of the old

Indian's prophecy years back, claiming the forests would be flattened and the river flow backward. And it was also Patsy Bradene who recalled the riverman's tale of Ben Blough.

Patsy and Reuben had joined the settlers in the tent city, though they said that their cabin had not suffered great injury, but the river was in great turmoil, rising and falling, and the shocks, great and small, was devastating the banks and sending them crashing down, sometimes crushing boats tied under them.

"I an't ne'er seen the like—ever," announced Patsy with as grim a look upon her face as e'er I had seen. "Ther's no way to know the number lost upon the water, fer it does not behave in any manner the way it's supposed to." Reuben had reached out his hand and taken his wife's hand at that, and a glance passed between them, anxious and tender at the same time.

Two more days passed, and though I inquired of all persons coming from the south, I had no news of Cyrus, though several claimed that the small community of Little Prairie had been destroyed. That information did little to ease my mind.

"I fear that we'll spend Christmas here, Sister," said Brother Gilbert, whose family had likewise joined us.

We had begun to separate between God-fearing and infidel, for there was a goodly number of those unregenerate who likewise eschewed cabins and riverbank to rise to high ground. And they brought their unregenerate ways with them, so that the earthquakes was not the only things we had to fear.

Two afternoons after the first day of the quakes, Master Morris Mundy, the Fullerite, come to me with his hat in his hand. "Mistress," he began quite kindly, "we have heard that yer husband is not yet found, and we are heartsick over it and grieve with ye. We will be holdin' a prayer vigil this night to pray his safe deliverance."

I thanked the man and agreed that I would attend. I thought it of little matter to pick doctrine at this point. Prayer would ne'er alter God's plan—what would be, would be. Still prayer and fellowship, be it Fullerite or Methodist or whatnot, would be a comfort to us all,

The small tremors had by that time become so regular a part of our routine that, for most of them, we hardly paused in our business. Come one moderately sharp shock as I stood without our tent, and I braced my feet and stared at the ground waiting for it to pass. When I looked up again, I was staring into the face of Eremus Lodi.

"Why, Sir," I said recovering my composure, "we're right glad to see that you've weathered the earthquakes." It seemed an awkward thing to say, yet I could think of no other.

His response was terse. "I have come especially to remove you and yours to the hills, for it is safer there, as the shocks do not devastate so much."

"Why," I said quite lamely, "my husband is missing and I must wait for him here."

"I have heard that, Madam. You can leave him word. In the meantime, you and your children will be far safer there than here. Not only is the earth here insecure and the river, but some of the company is not the safest either."

Before I could respond, another of those shakes struck without warning, and we was forced to ride it out.

"Well," I said as calmly as I could with the earth yet a-rocking under me, "these tremors will certainly cease soon. They cannot go on forever."

"Madam, no one can tell how long they will go on, but the nature of earthquakes suggests that yer far safer in the hills than in the valleys, fer the tremors tend to run along the valleys whilst the hills, particularly those rugged and ancient hills to the west, absorb more of the shock. You and your family must remove yerselves at least temporarily to the hills, and to that end I offer my home, which has withstood these shakes in great fashion. D'ye intend to stay in this part of the district, then ye'd best plan to remove yerself permanently to those hills," he added with a grim smile.

"Why, Master Lodi, this will probably ne'er happen again."

"Madam," he said patiently as he was talking to a child, "Madam, these shocks are not new to this area. There are certain parts of the world unsteady and unstable and given to earthquakes, and this is one of them. It is not a whim of an angry or petulant God; it is a natural phenomenon likely to oc- cur again and again."

"And are you gifted with prophecy, like that Shawnee warrior, Sir?" I said with more tartness than was my usual nature, stung perhaps at the conde- scending note in his voice. Yet I knowed Eremus Lodi to be well read and learned, and certainly he did know more of natural things than I.

"The shakes are not new to this area. They have happened before, many times I'd wager. Some lighter shocks have been recorded in the near past, but there are enough stories that suggest earthquakes in Indian lore, that there must certainly have been earthquakes of this severity in earlier times.

"The Indians," he went on quite seriously, "do not keep history in the manner that the white men keep history, with facts and dates and proper names. They keep their history mingled with their legends and stories, so that it is hard to separate what is fact and what fancy.

"Yet a catclysmic event or an overpowering personality will surface enough times in legend to attest to its reality. And the Indians in this area, yea, in almost all of the North American continent, have various tales that suggest at least one great earthquake and perhaps many others."

Perhaps I looked disbelieving, for he said, "There are, for instance, vari- ous stories along the river of wrestling with the devil. Have ye heard any of those?"

I must have flushed bright, for I detected a twinkle playing about Eremus Lodi's eyes, which happily did not make it to his lips.

"Well, such stories have been around in one form or another for a long time," he went on, "and probably were borrowed from the Indian stories and adjusted some to our own tastes in folklore. Mind me? But the Indians seem to me more sensible in their legends," he added, again with the suspicion of a twinkle in his eyes.

I nodded again for what he was saying made great sense.

"Have such earthquakes happened before, they will happen again. Count on that. In a day, a month, a year, a century, nay, two centuries gone, there's no tellin'."

He stared so straight and hard at me that I felt compelled to respond. "Well, no matter, I guess, for after this won't no one want to settle here and it'll be left to the varmint and the Indian, I 'spect."

"Ah, my dear lady" he said, and reached over and took my hand, and that so quickly and easily that I did not know what to do and so just let him hold onto me thus.

"My lady," he repeated, "don't ye know the human race better than that? They are foolish and greedy and will only pick right up where they left off. Why, parts of New Madrid have been regularly falling into the river since the town was first set here, and yet they keep on a-buildin' it right back near to the same place, fer the river to eventually reach out and grab. So it will be with all this land.

"The earthquakes when they cease will be so quickly forgot, it will almost be as if they never was. And with the Indian effectively pushed beyond the river, the settlers will then pour in here. One day, Madam, if ye will fergive my exercising once more my gift of prophecy, ther'll be tens of thousands, yea, hundreds of thousands in the Ohio and Mississippi valleys, with cities and acres and acres of masonry homes and buildings and crowded streets, all of which is what gives rise to casualties in such natural disasters."

"Well," I said at last, "that will not likely be tomorrow or the next day or the day after that. So I must wait for Cyrus, for I know that he will make his way back to us here."

It might have been that Eremus Lodi sighed, but all he said was, "As ye will, Madam, but I hope ye will not object do I stay near to ye until he comes, fer ther's as many villains made homeless by this disaster as ther are saints."

It was Christmas Eve when Cyrus at last arrived. I heard of his coming before I saw him. Near to one hundred souls had marched from Little Prairie, where the water as we had been told had risen and claimed most everything. They had walked that distance, slowly covering the ground, which had become marshy, the trail lost. They were a most tired and woebegone lot.

It was Sarah who led Cyrus to our tent. She held him by the hand an' announced in an annoyed voice, "He's here, but he's late."

We was all so relieved and happy to see him, and we had so much to catch up on, that it was quite some time before I recalled Eremus Lodi and told Cyrus of his protective presence.

But when we set out to find the man, he was not to be found.

"Someone said that they seen him leave, Mama," said George coming in from his own search. "They said it was right after the group from Little Prairie arrived that he secured his horse and rode away to the west."

Well.

Chapter 18

Lively Stones

I rose on Christmas morning more thankful, I think, than any Christmas I had ere spent, for Cyrus was safe with us again, and though we was passing uncomfortable and stiff with the temporary accomodations, it was enough that we was all safe in such rickety times. The only way it could have been made better had Joseph McCade been there with us.

Although Martha Elen had been almost as jubilant as I with the safe return of Cyrus, I could tell from the frown and distant look she wore later that her thoughts were even more with her missing man.

I had explained to her what Eremus Lodi had told me—that the mountains to the west muted the shocks, thus danger was far less. Joseph McCade would most certainly not suffer the hardships that Cyrus and his band had suffered, struggling through the newly created marshy lands, forced to make out their own trail.

But on the other hand, Joseph McCade was by himself among what could be hostile Indians, for there was no telling how savages would react to the great shocks from the earthquake. Indians was bad to look around and try to find someone to blame for such natural events.

Martha Elen must also have realized that. We did not speak of it. Instead we listened to the various brothers a-talking, including Cyrus.

"The land has sunk in spots and is dangerously flooded," he was saying. "It was the fear of the water more than anything that drove the people from the vicinity of Little Prairie."

Here he paused to consider. "So much land is gone. It is so hard to believe that what once was good land for farming is now naught but marsh. That a man might lose house or livestock by flood or fire is understandable, but to have the very land taken. . . ."

Enos Ray nodded. "It is that way all about," he said. "All around here great chunks of what was once good land is sunk into the marsh. There was swampy land enough as it was, but now, well, as ye say, many good farms are no more. I do not know what people are to do."

We repaired early to Christmas services. All practicing Christians of whatever persuasion had made plans to meet together to praise God and glorify the birth of His Son.

We was all grateful that the day was passing fair, chilly but neither damp nor windy, for we would meet out of doors—benches, logs and spread comforters our pews and the vaulted sky our cathedral, for there was no other. The disputed blockhouse was no more. It was one of the few structures completely and irrevocably brought down. Had I been of some persuasion other than predestinarian Baptist, I might have suspected the Lord in His Infinite Wisdom of having flicked the annoying structure over.

Indeed, it was surprising how many structures still did stand, albeit some unsteadily, considering the number and variety of shocks we most continually absorbed.

"Them log buildings," Eremus Lodi had explained, "are most resilient. They will bend, like willow trees, but remain upright at last, where masonry buildings will collapse."

The plans for Christmas services was sketchy. The several pastors of one sort or another would have words to say and hymns would be sung. There was no provision in such insecure times for any more elaborate worship or any Christmas celebration beyond that. That there had been few human casualties in so extraordinary times was enough.

The group gathered was large, spread out at the foot of a slight rise, which would act as podium and pulpit. I was amazed to see folk there that I had not realized was among us. Near the entire congregation from Elm Creek was in attendance, led by Elder Joshua Murdock, Elder Ples Bryan, of course, having accompanied Cyrus on his adventures. Obediance and Nathan Dalton was there also, as was a number of them fractious Baptists whose names I had forgot.

"We had to give it up," said Biddy Dalton, a look of infinite weariness about her. "We tried to stay with our farm, fer we put so much into it, but much of it is sunk into mud and the other covered over with fallen timber and our cabin damaged beyond hope. If I did not have faith in the Lord's Plan. . . ," but her tired voice just drifted off.

Of course, most of the New Caanan congregation was in attendance, anxious for Cyrus to speak. They was scattered some amongst the large gathering, but slowly most made their ways to where we waited, among them the sisters Berdetta and Leretta and their three slaves. The sisters wore long, dejected looks, but it was Anna, the slave girl, who explained their troubles.

"We has lost ol' Marster Morphew," she said. "He was upon the river bound fer New Orleans on bid'ness," Anna went on. "Word come to us that his was one of dem boats caught tied on the riverbank 'ith the first of dem earthquakes an' was crushed beneath the bank and sunk and ever livin' thing upon it."

She paused, and the sisters cast a forlorn look at Cyrus, yet said not a word. The five made altogether a most unhappy and solemn picture, though in truth the boys, Tim and Jim, could not long sustain that solemnity without breaking into their puppyish playfulness.

Both Cyrus and I give the sisters our condolences, and Cyrus assured them that bereft as they was, they still did have their church home and their brothers and sisters in Christ, and they would be looked after as family.

He started to say more but was summoned to join the other gathered pastors and deacons as they took their places in front of the multitudes. I could not keep from wondering if it was just such a sea of hopefully upturned faces that Jesus the Nazarene had looked upon on that day that he fed the hungry with fishes. We might, I could not keep from thinking to myself, have need of some of them miraculous fishes before this winter was done.

I was not surprised when Cyrus rose to attend the hymns. Nor was I surprised that the singing lasted a good long time, for as them sweet old songs of praise and glory rung out over the land, why you could almost see the weary and frightened and hopeless expressions begin to relax and the fellowship of the crowd commence to exert itself.

Them old psalms was of course common property, nor did they belong to one persuasion over the next. Though some might be prized more by this group or that, they was all well known, and it did seem that by common consent the assembled Christians could not get enough of them. Voices was raised wh'er cracked or ill-tuned or weak or strong. It give my heart such a pull that I could not but sit up straighter and raise my own voice that much surer.

I looked out over the crowd which had swelled, I thought, to several hundred, spread out over the slope and beyond, all voices, or almost all voices, raised in glorious song. I could tell that there was among the group a goodly number of faces that had probably not graced a Christian service in a good long time—river people, scoundrels, gamers, and assorted licentious folk—wh'er drawn by the sound or by the general fear of the times, it would be hard to say.

The singing was given over reluctantly at last, and the various pastors rose to speak. Nor was there any of that exhortation that might be expected, the using of the occasion to stress individual differences in doctrine. Redmon Pitt spoke, but spoke only of love and God and of Jesus Christ, his only begotten son. He said naught of two seeds or good or evil, though he made mention of the Will of God and our need to accept it.

That strain indeed ran through all of speeches given that morning, for they did not quite qualify as sermons, but only words of comfort and thanksgiving and love, as was meet on such a day in such a situation.

The Reverend Mr. Fox spoke along them same lines, and I could not keep from looking around and locating Patsy and Reuben who was of course likewise in attendance. But if they recognized the little clergyman or even cared, it did not show. What did show was that Patsy in particular had been mightily affected by the service, for she sniffed and wiped her nose across her sleeve, and Reuben reached over to touch her hand.

Then Brother Ples Bryan was give a turn, and Morris Mundy, the Fullerite, and Brother Murdock, and a Presbyterian that I recognized but did not recall by name, and two or three others that I did not know at all, and finally Cyrus. I was a little nervous lest they did not intend to give him a turn, but they did, and his talk run along the same lines as all else—God's Plan and our but puny understanding of it. And then there was more hymns, the whole congregation having sat upon the ground or on benches through several hours but still being most reluctant to give up the comfort of them songs and words.

But the human body was ne'er designed to absorb as much of the spirit as the human soul. Eventually, earthly considerations commenced to intrude.

"I'm hungry, Mama," announced Sarah to the considerable annoyance of her brother, who was caught up in the service. "Shhhh," he hissed at her.

But she was apparently not alone in that, and so the service eventually wound down to a final prayer delivered by Cyrus, and we rose stiffly to visit and wend our ways back to our tents.

As Martha Elen and I set out our simple meal, Sarah and her cousins played nearby, and I left Cyrus to keep an eye on Peter who was given to going off on his own at any opportunity. Both Cyrus and George was quiet and thoughtful. It was George who broke the quiet.

"Daddy," he said quite seriously, "I keep hearing it said that the Lord has sent these earthquakes as punishment for our sinful estate? Do you think that's true?"

Cyrus waited a moment before he answered. "My son," he said finally, "our God does not rule by whim. He does not rise up each day as a pagan ruler dispatching pain or pleasure as it suits the moment. Our Lord rules by Divine Plan, and if there is any confusion, it is that we are as ill-equipped to understand that Plan as is a speck of dust its place in nourishing the root of a great tree."

George nodded at that, and they continued both to sit quietly for a time. In a bit, I noticed that George had got up and got a Bible and was seated again studying it. My reaction to that was mixed. I was pleased to see such interest in the word of God but sad to see my son turn away from childhood toward manhood.

Later that evening Reuben and Patsy arrived at our campfire and was welcomed. It was immediately apparent that they had something serious to speak of.

"Brother Pritchard," said Patsy at last, "can ye speak to us of grace?"

"Grace, Sister?"

"God's Grace and salvation. I am a wretched sinner, Brother, and so is Reuben. Just wretched, the both of us." Reuben nodded gravely at that.

"But we have always believed as we was taught that, though we ought to try to be good and do right, even if we couldn't manage, no matter how hard we try, that we still had a chance to be saved through the Grace of God and unconditional salvation?"

"Are you fearful, Sister?"

"I am," Patsy answered. "I am not so certain that the judgment ain't at hand, and I know that I am a poor, wretched sinner, unworthy as I can be of God's love and mercy. And Reuben is, too." At that Reuben again nodded.

"So are we all, Sister Bradene," said Cyrus and he stared for a time at the fire and then he begun to speak, softly at first, and then with more strength, yet never leaving his seated position. But his words carried so strongly that a crowd begun to gather, people standing or squatting within the firelight, listening to what amounted to a brief sermon, yet delivered quietly and simply.

"God is a holy and spiritual sovereign," he begun, "and His law, which is an expression of His mind and will, is also holy and spiritual, and justly requires of all His creatures a complete, perpetual, and uniform obedience to all its commands, in thought, word, and deed."

He paused a moment and looked at Patsy and Reuben, and then continued gently.

"All men are continual transgressors of the holy judgments upon them. In the day of God's power, the spiritual law shines in the sinner's heart and makes him sensible of his depravity and poverty, and his lack of both will and power to do anything in the great matter of salvation—that he cannot make himself spiritually alive, or remove the burden of guilt from his conscience, or cleanse his heart from pollution, or keep the law, or act faithfully in the Lord Jesus, or comply with any conditions of salvation, or make hay stubble answer for lively stones in the spiritual temple built by God.

"He becomes thoroughly convinced that nothing but omnipotence can deliver him—none but Christ can do him any good. To such laboring and heavy-laden sinners, we proclaim the glad tidings of a free and full salvation through the Lord Jesus Christ, who has perfectly fulfilled all the law for you, who has atoned, in the bloody, dying agonies of Calvary, for all your sins and wrought out a spotless and everlasting righteousness for you, who has accomplished all the prophecies of the Old Testament in your behalf, who is the grand source of all spiritual life, in whom all fullness dwells, and all grace is deposited, who is the foundation on which His church is built, who has all power in Heaven and earth, and is able to save to the uttermost all that come to God by Him, seeing He ever lives to make intercession for them, whose blood cleanseth from all sin, with whom is fullness of redemption, so that God can justify a sinner through Christ without infringing on His law or impeaching His justice."

In the firelight, Cyrus's eyes glowed bright, and naught could be heard but his voice and his silences.

"Ye hungry and thirsty souls, ye poor, lame, halt and blind, come to the gospel supper, the feast of fat things, and take wine and milk without money or price; look to Jesus, from whom all saving virtue flows; view Him on the cross as the great atonement for sin; view Him rising triumphant over death, and ascending to Heaven, to give repentance and remission of sin. Put all your confidence, repose all your trust in Him alone."

I looked around and thought the fearful expressions of the last weeks relaxed as the gathered listened to Cyrus's quiet talk.

"When enabled thus to believe in Him, be buried with Him in baptism and arise with Him to newness and true holiness of life. Identify yourselves with His poor, despised people; follow Him through evil as well as through good report; feed upon the sincere milk of the Word, that ye may grow thereby. Exalt the great Jehovah above the Heaven of Heavens, and consider all His creatures, in competition with Him, as less than nothing and vanity.

"Walk humbly with Him all the days of your life. Regard Christ as the prophet, priest, and king of His church, the sum and substance of the gospel, the unfailing surety of the eternal salvation of all His people. Live in loving compliance with all His holy and blessed commands, and thus manifest the glory of your Father in Heaven."

As that last faded into the dark silence, there seemed to be something like a sigh, in unison, from all those gathered and no word else. As silently as they had assembled, so they disappeared.

I glanced at Patsy and Reuben. They was clasping hands, and there seemed to be a look of profound sadness playing about Patsy's face, though in the dancing firelight, nothing was certain.

The rumors and the tremors continued both with great regularity, though the tremors was more reliable at that. You at least knowed what they stood for.

Here and there, small groups gathered to speculate about the final days before the judgment. One story circulated claimed that once the epiphany was run through, the comet would then disintegrate and fall to earth in several places and signal the rising of the saints and the coming of the Lord. I did not take great stock in it myself.

On the other hand, while some held hands and prayed and waited, others picked up their axes and went to work, going back to their land, beginning the hard work of clearing away the fallen timber, and patching up cabins.

"I have put up my smoke chimney three times," grumbled one of them new neighbors of ours, "and three times it has been knocked loose."

The tent ground settled into a kind of routine. Each day many of the men went forth to hack at the fallen forest with their axes and Cyrus was among them. Nathan Dalton and one of his big boys returned to their farm and come back most gloomy, saying that there was not enough plowable land left for to make one decent crop. Similar stories abounded.

Martha Elen remained in a gloom for we had heard naught of Joseph Mc-

Cade. Indeed, almost no one come from that direction, and there was reports that the great swamp between us and the St. Francis River was uncommon high and in some cases impassable from the repeated shocks, and the wildlife therein greatly agitated and dangerous.

Carefully, as if to spare us, Cyrus unfolded his tale of the happenings at Little Prairie. He told of tremendous shakes and great fissures opening up and filling with water, of sand and black rock throwed high and of water spouts and finally the flooding that engulfed the little community so quickly, the water unnaturally warm in spite of winter weather, taking both his and Brother Bryan's horses. The destruction there, he assured us, was much greater and more violent than what we had experienced.

Still, we waited for the continuing shocks to abate. I become finally quite depressed of spirit with it. It was as if one was caught in a fit of hiccoughing, holding your breathing until it seems you have conquered it, only to have it suddenly spit out again, that much harder, rocking your innards and frustrating your hopes.

The river traffic was almost stalled, for they said that the channel remained hazardous and was in many places all changed, with large islands completely disappeared. "Them Injuns that camped east of the river," came the story, "is gone without a trace, and the campground where they was is covered with water and more rushing in by the hour until a great lake lies where once was cyprus forest." That story was repeated often enough and by respectable enough sources that it was little reason to doubt.

With every new story, each more harrowing than the last, the harshness of our own situation seemed to grow. We was pitiful small and puny, even so large a group as us, to withstand the devastation that was being reported. And too many well-thought folk had commenced to express concern that the continuing shocks was not a sign of the dwindling earthquake activity, but exactly the opposite. The sudden disappearance of the comet from the night sky was to some a confirmation of that notion and to others a sign that the Lord was no longer angry and the shocks would soon disappear.

However, when I gave to Cyrus the warning of Eremus Lodi that we seek higher mountainous ground, he only muttered ominously, "It may come at last to that."

"I am of a mind," said Cyrus one day, "to return us to our cabin, for I have shored it up and reubilt the chimney, and I do feel we might be safe there, though we might inhabit the lean-to at night, just to be safe, for its collapsing would not pose the threat that the cabin's would.

Well, though the earthquakes had if anything become more intense, it would be a relief to get away from these crowded conditions, where I had not only to worry about the divers rough folk, but also the constant threat of fever and ague from so many folk crammed together. So we made plans in that direction.

With Sarah and Peter that afternoon out walking, we come upon Patsy

Bradene. Reuben, she said, had gone to talk to some other rivermen with a view to making plans to start out upon the water again.

"That's dangerous, Patsy, until the quakes cease," I said.

She shrugged. "Ye've got to get on 'ith yer lives," she said. "Ye cannot forever live in fear. The worst is over, anyway." She announced that as incontrovertible fact, nor did I try to dissaude her of it, her opinion being, I was certain, every bit as good as my own.

I started to speak, but noted suddenly that Patsy had a strange and distant expression upon her face. I turned to look in the direction she was looking. She seemed to be gazing at a sorry looking group of rivermen, of the sort that I tried to stay away from.

I stared at the group for a moment, started to turn away, and then looked again. A small man standing with his back toward us had turned, and I did not need to see the ear covered by a cap to recognize him, for the ragged beard with the spittle coursing through it was all too familiar. Drooly.

He did not seem to notice us and I turned quickly away. "There," I said quite calmly, "is reason enough, I think, to go elsewhere." And Patsy Bradene nodded grimly.

We was still some weeks getting our cabin shored up enough that we felt safe in returning to it. At last, however, Cyrus determined that we was ready and we packed our goods together. Most everything we had was strapped away, and Cyrus was preparing to fold the tent down, when we heard the first awful rumbling, too loud, too strong to be ignored. We had but a few seconds warning before the shocks come, each successively stronger, until you could actually see the ground rising and swelling, leaving a wake almost as a boat upon the river leaves a wake.

"Fall to the ground," cried Cyrus. "Cover your heads with your arms." I had pulled Peter to me and threwed my own body upon his, protecting him from what I did not know. There was perhaps more danger from the earth a-falling away from us than from anything falling on us.

But I was mistaken in that. As the roar increased, so did the screams from the varied tenters, and the commotion was awful. The ground rocked and shook, and the noise was deafening. Accustomed as we had become to the tremors, we was still unprepared for the severity of this one.

"Mama!" I heard Sarah scream. I looked up. Cyrus had drawed the girl to him, protecting her body with his, and George lay with his head covered hard against the two of them.

"Hang on," yelled Cyrus. Calmly, I caught myself thinking. "Hang on? To what?"

Peter was crying beneath me, and I realized I was indeed hanging on, at least I was trying to grasp the very earth as it rolled and pummeled us. I felt my face hit the ground and my teeth was jarred. We was rolled and bucked until I thought we would be hurtled across space.

And then I was struck by something and then something else. I was afeared to lift my eyes to see what it was about. Something was raining down upon us, dust and stone, for I could begin to see it hit the ground, like little black lumps of hail and fine silt, and I thought I heard a hiss, as steam from a kettle.

Ah. At last was the judgment come. All them people had been right. The Lord had come to claim His saints, and the old sister, was she yet perched hopefully in her tree? I hoped not for she'd surely be crashed to earth and crushed if she was.

And then it was silent.

So suddenly did the silence descend, that you could yet hear the small black stones rolling against one another. I realized that I felt sick, as if I would vomit, the way I felt when I stayed too long afloat in rough water.

Cautiously I looked up. Cyrus and George was both looking up, too, and Sarah had commenced to talk, giving testimony to her safety. There was smoke and dust all around. Then I realized that it was not smoke, but steam, for it was vaporous and warm. We sat up and then stood up, the earth still quaking a little but the awful roar gone.

Beyond our tent a few yards was a gaping hole, all surrounded by sand and charcoaled rock, with steam still rising from it.

I did not want to get close to it, for I feared to stare down into it. Cyrus started over to inspect it, but I did not move.

"Mama," said Sarah slowly, "is it the devil or the Lord?"

I wished that I knowed.

That earthquake of January 23rd come to be knowed as the large shaker. Wh'er it was actually bigger than the big quake of December, no one really could tell, for that first one come as such a big surprise, with naught to measure it by, that most people could not recall it well enough for comparison.

But as this most recent one had brought down many more structures and left rifts in the ground and sand blows of great round craters, most people figured that it must be the greater earthquake of the two. Cyrus observed that the earthquake might not have been any greater, only that we might be just nearer to it, for our experience was now similar to the one they had suffered in December at Little Prairie.

I did not know. I only knowed that I was finally afeared, nor was I the only one.

I had come to believe that indeed we must be nearing the end as prophesied in the Bible. Nor was I the only one of that concern. However, I did note that the saints about did not seem to be as enthusiastic as might have been expected at the possible arrival of our Lord and their eventual removal to paradise. Indeed, everyone was considerably glum at the prospect.

It did not help that one old brother, having thought things through carefully, announced to everyone that it was obvious to him that the Judgment had already arrived elsewhere and the saints removed and that we was already damned, having been led here for the purpose of being delivered to the devil, who was only just a little dilatory in picking us up.

Others of more Armenian beliefs insisted that the Judgment was indeed at hand, but the Lord was giving us ample warning to mend our ways.

One afternoon, we come upon Sarah down on her knees in fervent prayer. She explained to us that, though she realized that she had been either saved or damned before the world ever began, still she didn't think it would hurt to pray a little about the matter.

"I think, Sally," said her father with a smile, "that you are probably not alone in such precautions."

Though we could still smile some, fear was never very far away, for the spasms of the earth did not abate but, if anything, were getting stronger. Day after day we suffered tremors of varying degrees, though mercifully they was not any accompanied by that awful roar which preceded only the truly monstrous quakes. We was all of us becoming quite expert in the matter of earthquakes, as a matter of fact, and could estimate the duration and strength of a tremor almost within seconds of its beginning. But it was not a skill which I hoped to use often.

Except for Master Morphew, we did not know of any loss of life. There had been numerous stories of great waves upsetting boats in the river and of banks crushing those tied to them and of great sucks whirling around and around and pulling vessels down into them, but those was the kinds of stories that everyone seemed to have heard about instead of actually seen. Did the earthquakes continue, as they seemed determined to do, we could not expect to continue free of casualties. I did not speak of that, but neither could I shake the fear of it.

As if the shakes was not enough, the winter weather had set in seriously, the wind whipping our tent about and the threat of snow hanging over us.

Cyrus went back to our cabin and returned with the intelligence that it still stood and, but for the chimney which once more needed shoring up, was sturdy as ever.

"We might as well take our chances there," he said, "for we could freeze to death here."

We determined that the lean-to would be better protection from the wind than our tent and knowing the ways of earthquakes, we would be safe in the cabin during the day, for we would have warning of the approach of a dangerous quake.

Nor was we the only ones to make that decision. Others, however, such as Sister Obedience and Brother Nathan was not in position to make such a choice, for not only was their cabin destroyed but their land also sunk into a slough. I could not think what they was going to do.

I was considerably relieved to get back to my home, though the barren landscape where trees had once been was depressing, even though Cyrus had made considerable progress in clearing out the mess of broken trees.

The cabin was crowded with Martha Elen and her brood along, but we would ne'er have thought leaving them behind in the tent. Oddly, their own ill-made and leaning structure still stood, but in no way could the thing be safe for them to return to.

The lean-to we protected as well as we could, and spread pallets and straw ticks upon the ground, piled them high, filling the small space with bed, "a good old Baptist bed" as was a common expression. We would be warm and snug from the north wind at any rate, though I hoped to myself that a painter-lion or some such did not decide to ride with us in the night.

And thus we stayed for nearly a week, spending our waking hours in the cabin, but for safety's sake sleeping in the lean-to, our heads to the outside wall, away from the heavy timbers of the cabin. Still, the tremors continued, a recognized part of our daily lives. Yet I could not escape that hollow fear that attacked my innards and clung like a dull ache.

Cyrus returned to the cabin one afternoon from visiting with some brothers and sisters still camping at the tent ground. The expression on his face was tight and grim. Nor was he slow to tell us the cause.

"A family by the name of North that returned to their cabin before the great shake has been found murdered and scalped. The whole of them."

"Oh, Cyrus." I did not know the family in question, but I did not need to know them.

"Those wise to the way of the Indians do not think it an Indian raiding party, but more like a bunch of renegades, mayhap composed as much of white as red, possibly the same that has been harrassing settlers for some months now on either side of the river."

"Cyrus!"

"I don't know. But," he sighed, "I think that it best that we abandon our cabin and return to the group. We have too many little ones to protect," he added, that argument stronger than any other he could have presented.

I was not eager to go back to the crowded, often muddy and stinking camp. But I was also not eager to take leave of my scalp. Was there raiders about, we was safer within the group, however crowded and uncomfortable.

We made our plans, then, that early on the morrow we would gather together our equipment once more and return to the camp. The children was not so unhappy at that prospect as I was, for there was many others for them to play with, and indeed discomfort is always something that children take lightly.

"Annamanda, I think to stay wakeful tonight," said Cyrus as we repaired to our snug sleeping quarters. He had his rifle loaded and ready. "If I get too sleepy, I will wake you while I catch a quick nap. At any untoward sign, wake me immediately."

I could not know the time, only that it was dark and cold when Cyrus shook me awake gently and whispered, "Let me sleep only a little while, just enough that I can carry on until daylight. In truth," he added placing my hand on the cold metal of the rifle barrel, "I do not expect any marauders to brave the dark and cold to attack. Still, keep a wary eye and listen keenly."

I pulled myself up and leaned against the wall, wrapping my comforter about me. Having been pulled abruptly from a sound sleep, I had a struggle to keep me from returning to it. In truth, I was too sleepy to worry about my scalp or anything else. I immediately fell to dozing in spite of my best efforts.

I do not know what it was that brought me to full wakeful attention, nor how long I had dozed. But my eyes shot wide open and I was suddenly alert. I listened hard and stared out into the darkness. There was nothing, no sound, no shadow, only the dimmest silhouette of the disfigured horizon. I held my breath, my muscles taut, and wondered if I should wake Cyrus, whose heavy breathing nearby testified to the depth of his sleep.

The breathing of the sleepers around me was the only sound I could make out, try as I would. Yet something disturbed me, mayhap only my guilty conscience for having slept at my post.

But that was not it. It was not fear either, fear of attack, for I was too calmly alert for that, my senses straining in ways that I did not realize they could strain, almost as I might assume animal senses to strain.

It was the eternal silence and the closeness to the earth that made me to sense rather than to hear that approaching roar, to know brief instants before it sounded that it was coming, to realize that the tremor was upon us and that wild things sense such events, so in the dark and still of the night did I. But not quickly enough to alert the sleepers.

With a cry only, just ahead of the roar that preceded only by an instant the lurch of the ground under us, I threw myself across the sleeping children.

And then the full roar was upon us, and almost as quickly, the ground heaved and swelled and groaned beneath us, and we was tossed as if on a mighty wild river. I could only make out above the awesome, loud thunder of the striving earth the puny sound of our cabin collapsing around us, the still hot dust of the fire scattering over us, and the distant snap of the few trees that had survived various other quakes.

There was no sound from the sleepers. They had come awake soundlessly, mayhap still in their dreams, trying to make sense of what was happening. And just as I thought it was over, it started again, the dull roar growing ever louder until it enveloped us as a noisy cloud, and the earth beneath us give way altogether, and we was tumbled and rolled and bumped.

The children, one after the other, begun to cry out, and I heard Martha Elen calling to her children even as I tried to call to my own. And still we was buffeted and battered against the ground, and I thought for certain it would cave in upon us and we would be suffocated.

And then we was jostled and pitched again, so hard that my bones ached with it and my head was jarred. I was clinging to some figure, but I could not in the commotion make out who it was, only that from the crying and thrashing about, we must all still be close together.

"Is it God?" I heard Sarah cry out.

"No!" I snapped. No, it was not God, nor was it the Judgment. This thing was of the earth only, the bowels of the earth adjusting theirselves, as an old man's after a full and satisfactory meal, or maybe the old man earth had a crick in his back and was trying to work it out.

For a minute we lay back still. The quiet had descended, the only noise in the background the crashing of a few trees to the ground and a distant unidentified rumbling and rolling, as if great boulders was being knocked together and the smell in the air of dust and something sulphurous. No, I thought to myself, it was not the Judgment, indeed, nor had the devil come for us.

Eremus Lodi had said it, and Cyrus, too. This was a potential of the earth from the beginning of time, not no whim of an angry and petulant God. It was a part of the Plan just as we was, only we could not see it or understand it. We had only to endure it. I was not looking to see the devil no more than I was looking to see Ben Blough.

I commenced to call out, to check the roll. The only one not to answer immediately was Cyrus. I called out to him again and at last from a few feet away I heard him groan.

"Cyrus. Are you hurt? Are you all right?"

"I don't think I am hurt," he answered, though his voice was tight. "But I am pinned to the ground by a great weight across my legs. I can't tell what it is."

I started to crawl cautiously toward the sound of his voice. "Where are you?"

"Take care, Annamanda," he whispered and then he called out, "Martha Elen, children, stay where you are and don't move. It is too dark to tell what precarious position we might be in."

When I reached him, I ascertained that he lay pinned beneath a large and heavy timber from the cabin. "No," he said, when I tried to tug on it, "don't. Let it be until daylight. I am not in pain. No telling what you might bring down on us if you try to dislodge it. We must wait it out."

"Mama," whispered Sarah, a few feet away. "Don't shoot Daddy."

Don't shoot Daddy? What on earth? And then I recalled that bear of that first quake. It seemed so long gone, yet still I could in my mind hear the labored breathing and groaning of that dumb animal, and in memory I could detect the level look of understanding almost that he had give me seconds before I took his life.

"No, Sarah. I will not shoot Daddy. He is not suffering. He is only trapped there, and at daylight we can see how to free him."

Slowly and cautiously we drawed together, gathering up what we could easily find of comforters and wrapping ourselves and hugging each other. I covered Cyrus as best I could and we waited, my every instinct tuned toward the earth. But it did not move.

One by one the children drifted off into some kind of sleep, and I think

Martha Elen and perhaps even Cyrus did, too, for it was suddenly quiet, not a rustle of a leaf or any night noise at all.

I stared hard into the dark, trying to cut it away so that I could see, but what little I could make out made no sense. I was in complete disarray, my directions uncertain. I had the feeling that we had been turned upside down and inside out.

And then I become conscious of a noise—mayhap the rushing of my own blood to my brain—a gurgling, lapping sound as slowly rising water. I listened, straining toward the sound, yet uncertain of where it might be. And I begun to entertain all kinds of ideas, none of them pleasant. Was there water rising all about us? Was we to be slowly washed away or pulled into a stream?

I did not wake anyone; I only listened. But the sound of something splashing did not subside, nor did it get any stronger. I pulled the comforter tighter around me and reached out to touch the baby who lay beside me. What would be, would be.

The light did come, slowly as a candle sputtering to life. I sat with my eyes to the horizon, still uncertain as to our predicament, until at last I could make out forms and figures. Cyrus, his eyes closed, did indeed lie beneath one of the great timbers that had held our cabin, but the rest of the cabin was not in evidence. Nor was anything else that I could recognize, for we seemed to have slipped down a hill, but no hill that I knowed.

I did not move until the light was sufficient to make things out clearly. Then I rose and looked about. Cyrus was only pinned beneath that timber. He did not seem himself seriously damaged. But it would take more than one person to lift that log from him.

There was a gash in the land and we rested in it. It was not, as I had feared, a fissure. Only it looked almost as if the land had been lifted and then throwed down, for there was great boulders, not rounded by the continuous play of the elements upon them, but jagged as if freshly crushed and broken.

I stretched my cramped muscles and looked slowly all around at the devastation, the very land itself having been rearranged in unbelievable fashion.

"Almighty God," I murmured softly. "Almighty God."

In the dark I had felt in control, unafraid, certain that the origin of the noise and confusion was not supernatural. But in the bright light of day, with the landscape and all we knowed throwed about in the confusion of a few moments, I felt my own puny estate and the wondrous power of the Almighty that such could happen. That the placid earth had within it such power for its own eruption and devastation was all at once testimony to that Being that made it so.

We was unable to free Cyrus, the log being too heavy for us. We tried to prize it off by means of another log, but we had not enough weight among us, nor did we have the strength in our arms to lift it, George, who might have had such strength, hampered in the lifting process by his damaged and mostly useless hand.

At last we determined that I should go in search of help and that George would accompany me. Indeed, I hardly knowed which way to go, so turned about was everything. "Just walk to the sun and make certain to keep it always at your right shoulder," Cyrus directed, "for we can at least count on the sun not to have been disturbed in all of this."

Well, I was not even certain of that, but I held my tongue.

"Just don't go where you think you ought to go, for if your landmarks are gone, you'll surely get lost."

It was possible that we might have to make our way all the way to the tent city outside of New Madrid, for I did not know what of those cabins between might be occupied. I did know that the Mayhew cabin was not, for it had been destroyed completely in that first great earthquake. But there was other cabins in between.

We did not find those, however. Whether we passed them by, so completely destroyed as to escape notice altogether, or whether we just missed them in the confusion of the landscape, I did not know.

What was distressing was the sudden marshy condition of the land in between, for the water that I had detected was indeed running in rivulets from what source I could not tell. Only if I had not been so certain that I was headed east, I would have suspected that we had stumbled into the great swamp.

George had little to say, and without Sarah along to provide a little comforting chatter, it almost seemed lonesome. I begun to worry finally that we might indeed have lost our way, when I heard some voices ahead, and coming into view, I seen the tenting ground, or what was left of it.

Tents was everywhere fallen or askew, and people wandered among them aimlessly. The silence was uncanny, the voices I had heard suddenly stifled, as if perhaps I had imagined them.

Eventually we found Brother Dalton, and he rounded up two or three others. We made our way back as we had come, those brothers as awed by the general devastation as we had been.

"I had not thought," murmured Brother Dalton, "that it was possible to harm the land no more than was already done. Will it stop only when the land is no more?"

With so many hands to help, lifting the log from Cyrus proved to be a slight chore, and he was soon freed, limping but otherwise unhurt.

In mostly silence, we searched out as much of our scattered goods— clothes and food—as we could find, and still mostly in silence, returned us once again to that tent city upon Tiwappity Hill.

It was two days after, the cold and the gloom settled in almost to our very bones, that Jacob the riverman found us. I would have been excited to see that old friend had it not been for the expression on his face.

That usually cheerful and happy face told us clearly that he was come to give us news that we probably did not want to have, which proved to be exactly true.

"I've come," he said abruptly after greetings had been exchanged, "to tell ye what I d'ruther not. Patsy and Reuben Bradene," he said without pause, "is dead. Drownded in the Mississippi near a month gone. I have been so long in the coming because both Otto and I needed to recuperate, and we had to travel over rough territory and," here he paused again, "mayhap I was just reluctant to have to tell my tale."

Shock was the seed sowed that grief would anon sprout from. For the moment, we all of us just sat and listened to the riverman's tale.

"Otto an' me," he commenced, "we joined Patsy an' Reuben on a calm day when the river seemed less in turmoil and determined that we would float a ways downstream as to assess the damage and decide our course of action. Fer river people off the river is like a dog balanced on only one hind leg—uncomfortable and unbalanced.

"Wal, I can tell ye that what we seen on that trip downstream was not so comfortin', fer the bank was collapsed in many places, an' landmarks we depended upon fer navigation was gone or otherwise displaced, so that we determined that it'uz best not to go no further, but to put ashore at some place that seemed safe from damage and return to New Madrid overland, fer goin' upstream seemed at that point almost impossible.

"That then was what we done. We was wise enough not to tie the boat under any bluff or overhang that might collapse on it, but found a spot wher the river run right up to the bank on the level, an' we camped ther', thinkin' that on the next day we would drag the boat ashore as far as we could, in hopes that it would be safe until we could return fer it.

"We bedded ourselves, I takin' the first watch, an' then Reuben an' finally Otto, the last. It was a bright, clear, moonlit night, an' that ol' comet was still makin' itself knowed, an' the way it can be on such a winter night it was tol'able cold, but we done the best we could makin' a nice big fire and gatherin' around it.

"I passed my watch and turned it over at last to Reuben, who must then have at last turned it over to Otto, for when I come awake, startled into a sudden alertness, it was Otto I seen, leaning agin' a tree, the fire still bright and shadows dancing around it.

"I stared at Otto, for there was something unnatural about the way he sat. At first I thought that he had fallen asleep at his post, most unlike him withal. An' then I realized that he slumped sidewise because there was a tomahawk imbedded in his back.

"Reuben, who must have waked at the same sound that waked me, was suddenly upon his feet, scrambling for his weapons, but the Injuns was already upon us, before I could get myself up off the ground."

Here the riverman paused and sighed a profound sigh and stared into the distance. I was not certain wh'er he was searching for the right details or perhaps trying to put the whole scene from his mind. But presently he continued.

"It might well ha' been bright daylight," he said, "betwixt the firelight and the moonlight. I could not know what time of night it was exactly, only that it was probably close upon dawn, for the moonlight cast bright ribbons across the river in uneven streamers.

"The Injuns, I couldn't say how many exactly, a large group, however, was painted all over and was intent on massacrin' us all. My brother Otto slumped over agin' the tree, and a Injun reached down and grasped him by the hair and pulled his head back, and then I realized that Otto was not yet dead. And so, too, apparently did Patsy, fer she lunged at the Injun and with the barrel of her rifle struck him so hard a blow to the neck that he staggered and fell.

"But two or three others was immediately at Patsy, and Rueben with such a scream as I have ne'er heard before, startling the Injuns, too, hurled himself at them, knocking Injuns sideways and backward and end over end. But," he sighed, "even Reuben, so great and strong as he was, was not a match fer so many savages, an' though Patsy managed to retreat, Reuben was forced backward, until at last he was at the river's edge, and with a great shriek of glee, one of them Injuns hurled his tomahawk and caught Reuben directly in the face, and soundlessly he tumbled backward into the water and was caught immediately in the current and pulled toward the middle of the river.

"'Reuben,' cried Patsy—I heard her," said the riverman solemnly, staring hard at the earth, "'Reuben, ye cain't swim; ye cain't swim!' An' with that she dashed across the open ground and threw herself headlong into the water, after Reuben, who was most like even then dead, an' she thrashed about fer a minute before she, too, sunk below the water.

"That was when I looked up an' realized, though, that one of them painted heathens was advancing toward me with tomahawk raised high over his hidiously painted face, an' I lost interest in watching wher Reuben an' Patsy had gone. I was certain, too, that he was not a true Injun. Fer the rest of the Injuns was poised at river's edge. The sight of a person giving up his life in favor of another, y'see, is to the savage mind a sign that they ere both favored of God, an' they ere always impressed and awed by such a sight.

"But the grinning savage bearing down on me was obviously not impressed but only intent upon my scalp. I would wager a great deal that he was not a red man, white or black, but not red."

"What did he look like?" I heard myself asking.

Jacob shook his head and grinned slightly. "I did not give too much thought to his countenance, fer y'know when ther is a tomahawk aloft o'er ye and menacin' ye, ye tend to give most of yer attention to that one thing, which is what I done.

"I done that an' I tried to recall some effective prayer I might ha' heard sometime, fer I was feelin' the need of such. I was up on my knees and prepared to struggle, but I had no weapon near an' could not make any coherent plan, an' truth, hoped that Providence might intervene."

Here he sighed and shook his head once more. "I know what ye think yerselves of Providence interferin' in the affairs of man, but truth, this next I tell ye, I'll just leave fer ye to figger your own selves.

"I knelt before the savage, my arms raised fer pertection, preparin' myself fer the feel of that cold stone upon my head, when I heard a sudden, terrified screech, felt the earth roll as it does so often these days, but not so bad withal. However, the savage menacin' me jumped back and darted toward his companions.

"The Injuns was in a terrible turmoil an' I looked wher they looked. There was a awful, rattling, crashing sound upon the river and overhead was smoke and sparks enough to light up the river. Wal, fer a minute I thought that the judgment was fer certain right upon us. An' then I decided that the comet had finally fell into the Mississippi.

"I don't know what the Injuns thought, only that they didn't like it, fer without lookin' back, an' in a headlong rush, they deserted the place, an' I took the opportunity to roll into the brush an' hide.

"After a time, I decided that the Injuns was gone, an' so timidly I roused myself up an' stared at the river. Smoke and sparks still hung above it, an' that awful racket was comin' clos'ter. Then I heard a moan and recalled that Otto still lay agin' the tree, an' so I rushed over to him an' found him in great pain, but not mortally wounded.

"An' then all at once, that racket was upon us, an' around the bend in the river come them sparks an' that smoke, an' it was a boat."

"A boat?" said George. "What kind of boat?"

"Wal, it nearly took my breath away, but I finally realized that it was a steamboat."

"A steamboat? What's a steamboat?"

"A steamboat, wal, h'it's a boat run by fire. I have heard that they was used some back on the eastern rivers, but I had ne'er seen one in the west before. It was monstrous thing, with a great wheel aft that displaced gallons an' gallons of water an' a smoke stack that fired sparks into the air, an' the whole contraption rattled and banged an' made such a racket that no wonder the Injuns was terrified."

"A steamboat?" mused Cyrus. "A steamboat upon the Mississippi?"

"In truth," said the riverman, "I don't think that ye'll see many such, fer it was such ragtag affair an' such an affront to the quiet of the river, wal, I cain't b'lieve that rivermen will ever put up with it. But truth, I have to be grateful that it come when it did, an' sad, too, that it could not have arrived a few minutes earlier."

Ah, for a moment in the excitement of hearing about the steamboat, I had forgot about Reuben and Patsy, and then the grief that I had been holding at bay washed over me and I supposed it showed, for Jacob said quite gently, "The steamboat rolled right over wher Patsy and Reuben went down and mayhap give them a little shove on down the river. They ere a part of the river now an' they'll go with it where'er it goes, making calls at ports they ne'er dreamed of before."

The Lord wills certain miracles to be, it seems. In the entire district, only one structure stood, hardly damaged at all by the convolution of the earth, and that was Joseph McCade's ill-made and wobbly cabin. But for cracked clay and sticks of the chimney and a door awry—in truth it might always have been so awry—it stood much as it stood the day that Jospeh McCade wandered off into the wilderness.

Beyond Tiwappity Bottom
1812

Chapter 19

McCade's Refuge

For days after that last great shock in early February, a persistent mist and fog, mixed with dust and ash, hung over all and with it, a gloom that pervaded everything and everyone. There was little conversation and depression was wide spread.

That gloomy weather had hardly lifted when it commenced to rain and then to freeze and then to snow, and we was confined to our make-shift shelters. The simple making of fire, collecting water and wood and foodstuffs in such trying situations was all the occupation we had—indeed, all the occupation we needed.

We was among the fortunate, withal, for we had salvaged roots and smoked meat from our cabin and root cellar, once we located what was left of them. But for others, simple nourishment had become a trial, as finding game and fish proved much harder than it had been before the earthquakes had destroyed the forests and disturbed the waters.

Those of us with provisions did what we could to share, making up copious soups and stews of what we had, yet still being on the lookout for the unscrupulous, who would even steal that. That the licentious could want for food as much as the veriest saint seemed to me a curious idea, until I thought about it for a while.

We was, it seemed, at bottom, creatures of identical need, no matter our persuasion or doctrine or lack of that. Did that, I wondered, in the end extend to spiritual nourishment as well?

The winter was harsh and our situation without comfort, yet it seemed that few people suffered those serious illnessess—fevers and agues—that might be associated with such physical deprivation. Indeed, certain folk seemed to thrive withal, and my own children, that worried me considerable, and their McCade cousins was rosy of cheek and all things considered—for children—happy of disposition withal.

But gloom is not a normal human condition and it did not hang on. Spirits slowly rose and after a time, religious services each evening was instituted, though no particular doctrine prevailed.

When the weather was fit enough, the saints among us (as well, I think, as a number of sinners) gathered in a less-scarred field for hymns and prayers of thanksgiving that we had been spared in the tortuous rending of the earth. There was a general feeling, though certainly no proof, that the worst of the quakes was over, that the damage was done and—according to some of our Armenian brothers and sisters—we had been forewarned.

The talk become ever more optimistic as the winter started to give way to spring, yet there was a little hesitancy on some accounts when talk come round to the spring floods. There was no way to predict what would happen, for the river was uncertain, banks was still rumbling away, and land that had once resisted the freshet was now sunk so low that it, too, would likewise flood. The Lord's Plan, it seemed, was far reaching yet.

In early spring, rumors started to circulate of severe eathquakes in other parts of the world. Travelers returning from Orleans confirmed that.

"The tales," they said, "that they ere tellin' on the docks, the sailors arrivin' from the south, ere horrendous and terrifyin' of damage and death in South America. They ere tellin' of thousands dead in Venezuela, fer the shocks struck great an' crowded cities. It was on a Holy Thursday," they added and paused for that last to make its effect, "an' many of them killed was killed right in church."

Thousands dead. I had to think of that. That was indeed a great many people. "It is in the crowded cities and masonry buildings that casualties from such catastrophes occur," Eremus Lodi had said. These crowded Venzuelean cities, with people praying in church—ah, it was hard thought, a terrible thought.

I tried to think sympathetically, for I knowed what it was to suffer the earth tremors and to fear for the lives of your children. But I could not even think where Venezuela was located—somewhere in South America, they said—the home of brown-skinned people. Yet did not brown-skinned people suffer equally as much as white-skinned people? Was their pains not as much and their grief? Yet the distance was so great. Perhaps that was the reason that, though I could think the sympathy, it still did not seem real, but rather like a story told.

There was confirmation, too, of what we had been hearing of the extravagance of our own earthquakes, that we had not suffered them alone. We had heard such stories—that the shocks from them quakes had not been confined only to our side of the river, but had indeed, as Eremus Lodi said, run through the Mississippi and Ohio valleys all the way to Washington, D.C., and much of the eastern coast.

"Wal," Brother Gilbert was heard to say, "mayhap them congressmen and Boston merchants will wake up now and realize that ther's somethin' out west to think of."

"They was not felt so much in New Orleans," someone commented, "though Natchez, they said, did rock quite well with it. And between here and ther, the damage along the banks is most fearsome and the river frighteningly disfigured. Miles and miles of timbered banks has caved in, all the way almost to the fourth Chickasaw Bluff, so that great trees stand in the river, as if they was living and growing ther, and obstruct it. Such planters and sawyers has always been a part of the river, but now, why, ther's great forests of them, wher none used to be. Times, we had to get out and cordell up the river with ropes, an' that ain't never fun.

"An' the channel is so uncertain now that many a good navigator has had to throw up his hands in despair of ever findin' the true channel again."

The spring floods come upon us and was just about as bad as the worst prediction. The swollen river reached out and took what little was left of the town of New Madrid, and then overlapped and spilled into areas that it had ne'er reached before.

The men went out each day and come back glummer with each outing, telling of quagmires where once was plowable land. "When the river recedes," said Brother Nathan Dalton, who had give up all hope of salvaging any of his land, "it'll leave behind enough sloughs and stagnant pools to extend the great swamp by at least twice its present area. Won't be fit fer naught but muskrats and waterfowl."

I hoped that in his gloom he was being more depressed about it than necessary. But Cyrus also seemed to concur. Cyrus was not one to be put off by much. He could usually get himself up and go out in the direst of circumstances, and yet he, too, was gloomy at the prospects.

"What an't covered by water," he said, "is crushed under heavy fallen timber, and sometimes both water and fallen timber, and there now stand sand blows of various sizes and great racks and chasms where fine meadows for grazing once was.

"I measured the crater of one of them blows, and it was by rough calculation about as round as it was deep and that about twenty feet in both instances, with sand continually seeping into it. I do hardly see what we will be able to salvage of this," he ended glumly.

Yet the tremors continued, though abated by quite some. Instead of dozens a day as had at first been, there was usually no more than one or two or three at the most, and them little more than ugly grumbles, so that we was of a mind to move us all back into Joseph McCade's cabin and away from the muddy, filthy mess that our campground was becoming. But still, I could not get that last great earthquake to quit my memory, nor could few other people.

We had become that watchful, that with each little tremor or suggestion of a tremor, we stopped, held our ground, and searched with our eyes for loved ones. Our numbers dwindled as settler after settler simply deserted the ruined land, most heading back across the river.

Still there was no word of Joseph McCade, and though Martha Elen made only irregular reference to him, I could tell from her worried glances at new arrivals and her sometimes distant westward stare that he held a regular part of her mind's attention.

At last come trouble with the rowdies and the river scum. During the heavy earthquake activity, they had held their peace, perhaps as afeared of the judgment as the rest—indeed more afeared, as they did have just reason to be. But with the cessation of that activity, their bravado started to reassert itself, and as we was all more or less camped out together, the situation quickly become strained.

At first, it was merely wild talk and raucous comments, most particularly directed at the ladies. Violence between the groups was confined to a fist fight or two. Brother Mayhew's oldest son, Bradley, a right strapping young man, busted open the head of one of them rascals for his injudicious use of language in the presence of Bradley's younger sister. As was the custom, of course, there was apparently considerable scrapping among the licentious with one another.

One evening, however, a young girl, out taking her comforts alone, as she should have knowed not to do, was set upon by two or three of them rowdies. Though Cyrus would not tell me the details, I did get them at last from some of the neighboring ladies who said that she had had her clothes torn from her and was right badly abused and left for dead.

Well, she did not die, though badly beaten, but she was not able to identify her attackers. And though there was some, most notably the girl's family, ready to take rifles and clean out the entire nest of rascals, cooler heads did prevail, among them Cyrus.

"You cannot punish those guilty only by association," he said, "even though they be quite capable of committing such offenses."

With that, the rascals seemed to become more flagrant in their behavior, which still consisted mainly of ugly talk and thievery, for goods of all kinds especially foodstuffs was in short supply and like to get shorter, as the river traffic remained slow. Martha Elen and I kept our children close by at all times, and none of us was ever very far from the group, and rifles was kept loaded.

One afternoon carrying water back from the only decent spring left flowing, Sarah and George with me, I heard a sound behind us, too familiar to ignore. I stopped and looked back over my shoulder.

"Heh, heh, heh, Mistress, good day," said Drooly, lifting his stained cap slightly, only enough to expose his floppy ear, pausing, and then moving away.

"Who was that, Mama?" asked George.

"A river scum, I suppose," was all I answered.

"He did not look nice," added Sarah, and I shook my head.

"No, he does not look nice. Avoid him if you ever see him again. Avoid anyone of that sort," I added.

If all of that was not enough, Redmon Pitt begun to spread around his spurious doctrine of predestination, using our own situation—Christian and scum—as example of the good seed and the bad seed.

Well, Redmon Pitt, like a burr on a sock, could be hard to dislodge. And of a sudden, the mistrust of predestinarians was in the air once again.

We had all of us put aside doctrinal disputes in coping with the disasters about us. It had not been done by any suggestion but as common assent. At the time, earthly salvation had seemed to take precedence over points of doctrine.

But here we was, of a sudden bickering again, and all on account of Redmon Pitt. Inevitably the like-minded drifted together—those that favored sprinkling over full immersion baptism, and those that was in favor of missionary societies, and those that insisted that you had to work your way into heaven or not get there at all, those that espoused sanctification or seventh day meetings or music or no music or the Trinity or No Trinity and on and on, all opposed to various predestinarians, of which of course the Old School Regular Baptists was one.

The various groups, of varying sizes, splintered off, and each carried on its own worship. Well, I never would have said, of course, but it did seem to me that in the face of the awesome display of the work of the Almighty God that we had witnessed and been a part of, such little differences did seem puny. But that's the way it was. And again, it was the Old School Baptists that seemed to alarm all them others the most.

We collected a right fair congregation, however. Several from the Elm Creek Church joined us, including of course Nathan and Biddy Dalton and Elder Ples Bryan, as well as some of those surviviors from Little Prairie. Many of all persuasions was gone, some back across the river, or up or down, searching out kin and friends, loathe to stay anymore on this unsteady land. Others continually talked of escape but was afeared to go off by theirselves, either because of the Indian threat or the continued tremors or the instability of the river.

So Cyrus gathered ours about us—Brother Mayhew's family, Brother and Sister Gilbert, who though elderly was strong in faith if infirm of body, them silent Morphew sisters, and their three young slaves.

The talk in our group, when it was not of a spiritual nature, usually centered around what we would do to adjust ourselves to the situation. The suggestions ranged from everything to staying where we was to going off into the far western wilderness, that last a wild idea that not too many seemed to favor. Not a few was in favor of going back north to the Salt Creek Association of Elder Kencaid, that area though damaged apparently not so seriously as our own.

The problem was of course land, for we none of us had much left in either land or goods to trade, and there was little land back toward Ste. Genevieve available, any worth having, anyway.

"I don't see why the goverment don't do something to help us," grumbled Brother Mayhew.

"Wal, now, why would the government want to do that?" countered Brother Gilbert.

"Why it ain't our fault that the land was sucked out from under us and rent and tore," said Brother Mayhew.

"Wal, it ain't the government's fault neither," said Brother Gilbert. Brother Mayhew just left it at that and did not respond.

At last the waters of the freshet receded and left behind what it would— cracked and torn land and ponds and sloughs, much of the tortured surface of the land holding stagnant pools of water. It was not a wholesome sight. And still the population was dwindling, as settlers determined ways to escape and did. There seemed to be few and fewer Christians and more and more unregenerates.

George and I was out scouting berries one day when we chanced upon a nice thicket that was heavy with fruit. That was such a relief, for there was few left and those considerably picked over. We set about immediately to fill our baskets, George on one side of the thicket and I on the other. The wild berries—poor man's fruit I'd often heard them called—was tasty and passing plump and would make a welcome addition to our meals, but it was an addition justly earned, for what skin the brambles did not tear at, why the copious insects attacked. And it was hot work, withal.

We worked quickly and silently and was almost finished when some instinct made me pause and listen. I think I knowed what I would see before I turned to look, for the skin of my shoulders prickled uncomfortably. Drooly stood watching me from a short distance, a simple-minded grin upon his face. He hiked up his trousers and ambled toward me, grinning all the way.

"I know ye, Mistress," he slobbered. "I know ye, heh, heh, heh."

At that there was a sudden rustling of the briars, and George appeared, an uncommon stern look upon his face. Nor did he look so much like a child, for he was growed taller than me, though boyhood's gentle marks was still upon his face.

He did not say naught, but only stared hard at Drooly, and that man, still giggling in his simple manner, commenced to back off until he reached some near brush and fallen timber and disappeared into it.

"I do not think he meant no good, Mama," said George.

"No. I suspect you're right. He meant no good. We'd best take our fruit and get back to camp," I added.

We gathered up our things then and took a more direct route back toward camp, not bothering to look for more berries. We had not gone far when George stopped and frowned, shifting his basket of berries from his good hand to his damaged hand and staring around in a curious manner.

"Did you hear nothin', Mama?" he asked.

We both listened and indeed, I did hear something, as a moan of distress in the brush. Maybe we both thought of the bear of that earliest earthquake, but neither of us mentioned it. Nor did it sound as if it was an animal.

"I think it's someone, Mama," said George, and I nodded, for I did too.

We stepped carefully through the weeds and almost stepped us into a slough of water but avoided it and went around, George a few steps ahead. I heard the moan again, quite close, and then George stopped abruptly and bent down.

"Don't look, Mama," he said urgently. Well, if he could look, I most certainly could, too, child that he was.

What he had happened upon was a man, a stranger to me, at least I thought so, for though he apparently lived, his head was bereft of its scalp and the blood that covered his face still ran fresh. "Lord God," I heard myself saying, "does he live, George?" For answer, there was another moan.

"Oh, Mama," cried George, "what'll we do?"

That I could be so calm in the face of such a horror surprised me. I had ne'er seen a scalped person and it was no pleasant thing, but my mind was not absorbing the horror of the thing so much as it was running ahead to think of what to do.

Drooly was about, that we knowed. But we did not know who else might be with him. Wh'er Indians had done this thing or Drooly himself or what? There was naught to do but go for help and leave that poor soul in the Lord's care until we could get help from earthly source.

When I told that to George, he objected and complained that he ought to stay to watch over the sufferer, but I would not hear of it. "You can't be of no help to him, and I'll not risk the loss of your scalp."

We was very quick getting back to camp and in dispatching help, but not quick enough, for by the time Cyrus and the other men arrived, armed and ready, at the site of the scalping, the poor, unidentified soul—apparently one of them solitaries—was gone to his reward.

The men come back grim and quiet, and that night, after the scalping victim had been laid to his final rest in Christian manner, was called together a meeting of our dwindling neighbors, their various doctrines left behind as the general fear and need dictated.

The agreement among all parties was that we was betwixt a rock and a hard place, no doubt.

"The war," said one of the Fullerites, "is declared, ye know?"

Well, we did, or at least that had been the minor, but it seemed so distant and truth of it only incidental to the horrendous calamities we had been faced with, and still was faced with, that most of us just accepted the announcement of war and didn't think much beyond that.

"What that will likely mean," continued the Fullerite, "if it drags on for long, is that the river will become mightily involved. Should the English and the Spanish take the river, why then we're cut off. Just us and the Injuns," he added, unnecessarily I thought.

"The problem now, however," interrupted Brother Gilbert, who was always thoughtful and well-spoke, "is that we here ere caught face up with dwindling supplies and ravenous heathens and what to do about it."

Well, after discussions of some length, the only agreement reached was on the nature of the problem. Obviously, quite a number of folk still intended to desert the area as quickly as they could, leaving what was left of their land, for there was certain not to be no buyers any time in the future.

During the discussion, I had reason to recall Eremus Lodi's assertion that when the earthquakes was over, the land would be settled once more as if they'd ne'er been. Well, I'd not like to dispute Master Lodi, but seemed to me that such land would likely ne'er again be settled, for it was as useless as if it had been sowed with salt.

The upshot of our meeting, at last, was that Cyrus announced that we would return to Joseph McCade's cabin, which continued to withstand our daily shocks, and that anyone who would like to join us there to camp out was welcomed to do so. "You must cut your shirt from the cloth you have," said Cyrus.

Quite a number of our own congregation at last decided upon that, and on a day, we all trekked out there. Brother Mayhew did sigh long and hard as he surveyed the land that he had sold to Joseph McCade at greater, he thought, than its value, for he had managed to sell off the only piece of land within miles, apparently, largely unaffected by the terrible earth tremors.

Our little fortification, for quite frankly that's all you could call it, growed until it numbered more than two dozen families, many of them driving ox-pulled wagons across the spoilt land, and was appropriately called McCade's Refuge. And in no time we was settled in and far more comfortable than we had reason to hope.

Then one day, as we all went about our various tasks, come a small tremor. We paused as was our custom and waited for it to pass, which it did, and we went on about our business.

It was at that moment that Sister Gilbert, who sat upon a bench a-mending, looked up and quietly said but one word, but that was a word that stopped each of us in our tracks.

"Injun."

Indeed, there was a solitary Indian approaching, crossing the clearing with measured steps and expressionless face. There was always two or three men about, armed, so that we all felt safe to keep our spots.

The Indian, neither quickly nor slowly, walked directly up to Martha Elen, who stood just at the door to the cabin, and without a word extended her a piece of rolled and tied paper. In silence, both his and ours, he turned then and, with the same measured step, retraced his path and walked back down the trail.

Martha Elen stared at the paper and then still silent, carefully unrolled it.

"Why, it's from Joseph McCade," she said, glancing quickly over it. And then without a word but with the excitement about her eyes and face suggesting a maiden with a love missal, she read slowly through the paper, while we all stood and waited none too patiently.

That paper was so ill-treated, rumpled, and dirty, that I suspected it must have been long upon the trail, but when Martha Elen spoke at last with a happy and relieved sigh she contradicted that.

"It was writ but only a few weeks ago," she said, "in June of this year, for so it's dated." And then as if to answer our unspoken questions, she said, "He writes that he is sending it by Indian messenger, which may mean a short or a long transit, for it's ne'er certain. Well, that much can even be said for the United States Post," she added.

"I'll not tell you all that it says," she went on demurely, as that same blushing maid, "only that which pertains to us all."

And she begun to read.

"'I have come across Tiwappity Bottom, through the big swamp, and to mountains more beautfilul than any I have e'er seen in my life, and so to them great springs that I had been so oft told of. Ye'd not believe it did ye not see them, fer they're like lakes, lakes of the purest and coldest water, with fish just swimmin' to the surface and requestin' that ye catch them.

"'And the game is likewise as accommodatin', more big bucks and fat does than could feed whole tribes of Injuns, which ther is in like measure, too. And I have been welcomed here, fer the Injun would like nothin' more than tradin' posts fer the trinkets they afford, and I guess, too, the spiritous liquors.

"'From the springs I traveled for months across them mountains Aux Arcs until I come finally to flatter lands. The Injuns told of even flatter lands, great rolling lands of tall grass, covered with acres and acres of bison, and then great mountains beyond that, mountains so tall that they sported snow at ther tops all the year 'round.

"'Wal, much as I did desire to go on, I knowed my duty, and I could not erase the memory of them glorious springs and mountains, and so I have returned.

"'I have heard of the recent shakes ye've suffered, though but for a little unsteady ground here and ther, we in the west hardly noticed it. But I've come to fear fer yer safety since my return from the west, having at last heard great tales of mighty earthquakes and awful damage. Ye ne'er know how much stock to put in Injun reports, of course, but truth t'tell, the Injuns do seem some put out about it all.

"'My immediate business being about done here, I will start back east fer ye soon with plans to return us all to this place fer settlin'.'"

Martha Elen at that stopped reading aloud but continued silently to herself, with a slight frown about her eyes. Then foldin' the paper carefully, she only sighed and shook her head. I could just imagine the kind of gentle conversation Martha Elen and Joseph McCade was like to have over the prospects of moving west into the wilderness. But Martha Elen had married the son of a longhunter. I wondered if she remembered that.

I was surprised at the stir that Joseph McCade's letter made, of the serious consideration given it, for I knowed Joseph McCade, knowed him to be wildly enthusiastic of plan. All the same, his talk of the west had piqued interest, and at last I had to remember that these was westering souls, perhaps not much less intemperate in that than Joseph McCade.

"You recall what is said, that it be an ill wind that blows no good?" said Cyrus one day. "I have talked with some of them Fullerites, and they tell me that Redmon Pitt has taken his Pittites and gone on back east of the river to read his curious doctrine there."

"Ah," said Brother Gilbert, "that leaves fewer to be terrorized by the river scum."

Cyrus nodded, but then added, "The river scum, even, seems to be dwindling, too. The whole population is drifting elsewhere. We have," he added solemnly, "but a few months to prepare for another winter. It is a sobering thought."

I caught myself mulling that thought as I went about my tasks. If all this was the Lord's Plan, why was we charged with the preparation of it? If it was the Lord's Plan that the earth rock and split wide, why did we have to suffer the consequences of it? Why would a merciful and just God put the likes of river scum upon the earth to pester us like fleas in the first place? Was I to ask that aloud, I'd only be reminded of the mysterious workings of the Lord. Well, I certainly knowed that to be true. I, for one, of a certain couldn't figure it out.

In the midst of these considerations, I come up on George and the two black slaves, Tim and Jim, intent in quiet conversation. They did not see me, and so I stepped back and wondered what to do. I had a good idea of the sort of conversation they might be having, for I was not so innocent of the kinds of things that boys liked to talk of. Nor, I thought, was I likely to change that situation, even if I did barge in, tongue-lashing all three of them. Still, I couldn't keep from straining some, out of curiosity, and was surprised to realize that they was not talking about those things I supposed them to be.

"Ah dunno," the round one was saying. "Ah don' think ah'd lack to go across Tiwappity Bottom an' dem swamps."

"Yah, dey says," said the other, "dat dey's Injuns and turr'ble critters in dem swamps."

"There's always Indians," said George quite calmly. "If we was afeared of Indians, we wouldn't be here. We'd be in a far city, hiding behind a house."

"Ah don' lack Injuns," said Tim or Jim, grabbing his own hair and stretching it back from his forehead, "dey takes yer scalps," he said. "But dat's not what's so fearsome. Dey's critters, turr'ble critters, dat'll cut off yer feets whilst you sleep," and he rolled his eyes back and shuddered deliciously.

"An' yer haid!" added the other.

"An' yer pecker!" added the other.

They was just boys, after all, though probably three or four years older than George. "They're good workers," Cyrus had said of them, "if you can keep them at a task. In truth, they start with great enthusiasm, but their attention wanders and sooner or later, so do they, and you have to go after them."

"Dey's good boys," I had heard Anna say, confirming Cyrus's opinion of them. "But dey will wander away. D'ye need somethin' finished right up, why ye needs to stand right over 'em."

"Well," said George quite seriously, "you cannot run away from evil, for it's a part of God's Plan, too." And after a pause he added, reaching as he spoke for the amulet around his neck, "And anyway, I have heard it said that all things have heart that the evil will suck out given the chance and that you can seek out the evil or let the evil seek you out. Which would you rather?" he asked cheerfully.

To their credit Tim and Jim just looked at him, undoubtedly wondering just as I was why he would make so peculiar an observation.

Well, I had to think that sometimes George did sound like a small and pompous Redmon Pitt. Such talk of evil anyway. What did a lad not quite thirteen know of evil?

News of the war come irregularly to us, but it was fought at such a distance that we could not concern ourselves much with it. The Americans was apparently intent upon taking Canada, and the British and the Indians defended it. Why anyone would want such a cold and distant land was beyond me. Still, the gloomier souls about was given to pointing out what would happen was the war to reach the river, but I could not see what the war could do to us that God had not already done.

The earth continued to tremble, but each day the shocks seemed to grow slighter.

We ate communally, for that arrangement made the most sense. We cooked mostly outside and set tables of logs and rough timber, and then battled the flying insects for our food. Their world having not been disturbed at all by the mighty upheaval of the earth, they went about their business as efficiently as ever, which business was to interfere with our business wherever possible.

At the appointed time one afternoon, the tables all laid and the aroma from the cooking pots wafting across the clearing, we assembled all, washed and prepared, and Cyrus give up his customary blessing, that being as usual lengthy. We stood thus with our eyes closed and listened through it.

Cyrus had not yet come to his final amen when I detected a rustling and looked up, for I sat at the table with the children. All three of the McCade children was stirring, and I glanced toward where their mother ought to be but she was not there.

"Papa!" With that cry, the McCade children, careless of benches and tables and skinned shins even, went dashing across the clearing, and the daily blessing was effectively rent, for there indeed at the edge of the clearing, much as he was when he had left months earlier, stood a grinning and happy Joseph McCade holding Martha Elen close and reaching for his scrambling children.

Well, things was indeed in an uproar over that, and we was some time getting us back to our meal, but there was no question of getting us back to our regular routine, though we did manage to clear the tables and clean the plates.

Everyone was anxious to hear what tales that Joseph McCade had to tell. He was not loathe to tell them and being, withal, a talented storyteller, we spent an entertaining afternoon.

He affirmed all that he had writ of his adventures and added wondrous detail. "Ther's heavy growth of timber, mostly hardwood and nut," he said, "lush growth, nor any barren or marshy land at all that I seen. And the spring—the big spring wher I propose to settle us, why ye'd think me crazy did I try to do it justice fer beauty and quantity. Wild muskrat and beaver to be had fer the askin', as well as possum galore, skunk, and raccoon."

"What of the Injun?" someone asked.

"Why, they ere there, odd collections of 'em, mostly new settlers as ourselves will be. Delaware and Shawnee, anxious to hunt and trade—fer the Injun to my mind won't ne'er make a farmer."

"An' won't they resist ye, d'ye try to settle there, as the Injun to the east has resisted?"

"Ah, naw, ther's so much space, of such variety, that unless the white settlers come in droves, they'd hardly run into one another."

"They an't wild, then?"

"Wal, no wilder I suppose than anybody else. These are Shawnee and Delaware, many of them, an' they build houses and work the soil. There's wild ones of course, but. . . ," and here his voice trailed off and he made a vague gesture, finally adding, "not so wild er unsafe as some of the scum and slime that hugs this river. If it's a thoroughly safe and snug nest ye seek, wal, yer in fer disappointment, fer from my experience I feel safe to say that such does not exist—nowhere—this side of Glory. All y'uns," he said with sudden characteristic expansiveness, "all y'uns, come along, the whole bunch an' leave this land that God has forsook—fer I've ne'er seen such a mess in all my days—an' come on with me. Westerin', we'll go westerin', as my daddy before me and his before him. Ye wouldn't be here, any of y'uns, were not the westerin' in yer blood anyway. What choice of land have ye got here er east er north fer that matter?"

I looked around and could see the glow of interest that crossed some faces, as well as the distrust and anxiety that crossed several others. Cyrus's expression remained impassive, and I wondered what he was thinking.

"Wal," said Jacob the riverman cheerfully, "me fer one, I'll take the river, even ill-used as it now is, to the possibility of Injun and painter-lion as the westerers'll have to face."

"Ah," murmured Joseph, and he started to say more, but was interrupted by a dull roar and immmediately the tremor and rattle of our daily shake, moderately heavy by the standards we had come to be used to, and we sat with some apprehension, quietly, and waited for it to pass.

When it was gone and the ground stilled, there was something like a common sigh, and then Joseph McCade laughed out loud and cried, "Wal, now, that's what I'd call 'fear and tremblin'."

Before anyone could respond to that, of a sudden come another hard and quick shock that took us by surprise. And then there was a crack and a moan, and looking up, we watched as a timber that supported the cabin begun to sag, and the roof over it, too, and then the walls, as if that one timber was all that held the structure, and once damaged, would bring the entire thing down. Which is just what it done.

"I think," said Joseph McCade as we silently watched the dust settle over McCade's Refuge, "I think that our future lies across Tiwappity Bottom."

Chapter 20

The Lord's Plan

The arguments against westering was simple and boiled down at last to one thing, and that was the knowledge of our precarious position upon the unsteady land around the river, as opposed to the uncertainty of a future situation elsewhere. In truth, it was no new argument, for most every move, particularly every move west, come down at last to that one thing.

Measured against that was the promise of the first choice of stable and beautiful land, abundant game and tall, undamaged hardwood timber.

"Or ye could go on back to the east or the north or the south wher civilization is already established," said Joseph McCade.

To any suggestion of danger, he only shrugged and repeated, "Anywher ye draw yer breath, city or frontier, ye face danger. Danger an't to be avoided in this life."

From the time Joseph McCade first suggested the westering, maybe even before that time, perhaps when he sent home his letter extolling the virtues of that western land, it was obvious that the westering spirit had struck several of our group. Nor was that so unusual, for as Joseph McCade had pointed out, it was in our blood, or at least in the blood of our men.

There are just them kinds of men that are ne'er content unless they are a-putting one foot before the other. Be it greed or just the itch to see what's behind the mountain, I'd not always be able to say. A little of both, I'd guess. And truth to tell, Cyrus Pritchard did seem to be one of that kind, but he had a name for his especial itch—the Lord's Call.

Well, it was not the Almighty Lord that had to pack up His belongings in an ox wagon and then walk across Tiwappity Bottom with a young'un on His hip. But I said naught of that. Because it was happening, it must then be, for as Reuben Bradene had said, "Ye cannot say that what is to be will not be, can ye?"

Joseph McCade was not in no great hurry and had plans to ride the river to Orleans to pick up supplies for his trade post, but once the decision was made for a large group to go west, it become obvious that haste was in order, for we'd either winter there or we'd winter where we was, and where we was certainly did not bode well for wintering.

Three or four families fell away from us upon our decision. One of those, Brother Enos Ray, opined that he and his needed to visit kin in Tennessee through the winter and then would join us in the spring. Well, I said naught of that neither, but it did seem to me that Brother Enos Ray intended to eat both ways on his spoon, wintering comfortably in Tennessee and joining us after the harder work of new settling was done.

Those who chose to go along included old Brother and Sister Gilbert and two of their grown sons. The old brother, who was noted for his capacity to store victuals, explained that he figured the venison and squirrel to be fatter in them western lands, which was reason enough to go. He was a jolly sort and, when teased about the quantities of food he ate frequently, explained with a twinkle that not being overly fond of milk and honey, he needed to store up provisions against Paradise.

Of course Biddy and Nathan Dalton, who had little to leave behind but swampland, and their young'uns planned to come along, and Brother and Sister Mayhew. To my surprise, the Sisters Morphew approached and stood by, while their black girl Anna explained that they, too, along with the two black boys, would like to be included in the group.

The two sisters still did not speak, but waited patiently as Anna did their talking for them, the one, either Berdetta or Leretta, for I could not tell which, stood with her hands clasped before her and the other with her hands clasped behind her.

"We h'ain't got no place else to go," was Anna's simple explanation.

By final count, our group, all Old School Baptist ("We'll get there first and let them Armenians beg fer room," said one of the brothers), numbered a dozen families with a dozen wagons, oxen, several cows, a bunch of old hens, and a rooster. From previous experience of trying to move chickens by wagon through the wilderness, I did have some misgivings about the success of that venture. But there not being very many chickens left after the severity of our winter, we might as well bring them along as leave them for the river scum to feast on. Better the beasts of the swamp than those.

The first concern of almost everyone was the wilderness that we would pass through.

"Well, it an't so bad," said Joseph McCade, "if we cross north at Tiwap-pity Bottom, especially this time of year when things is naturally more dried out, fer south of there all the way to the Arkansas is often all but impassable most any time of year. Still, t'won't be easy, but not impossible. Ther's paths and traces, fer ther's been mining across that bottom fer years, and trapping and hunting. T'would indeed be easier without the wagon and ox, but I don't know how'd ye go a-westerin' without 'em."

It was determined that Jacob the riverman would float south to Natchez or beyond, if necessary, and procure provisions for us and for Joseph Mc-

Cade's proposed trading post. We made up money for that purpose, what we could scrape together, for there was not much among us, and we commenced to wonder if we had money enough for our venture, for by the time Joseph McCade had ordered provisions for his post, he had but little gold left.

Succor came from the Sisters Morphew. Anna presented herself to Cyrus one evening and handed over a bag of gold, with the explanation that it was their contribution for our removal to Canaan Land.

"Canaan?" said Cyrus. "Brother Gilbert, are you aware that we're bound for Canaan? You know that will mean milk and honey instead of fat deer?" There was a general laugh at that, but still we thanked the Lord for this timely assistance.

Jacob left early one morning, thinking that he could be returned in about 30 days, and it was arranged that he would be met at that time by wagon and oxen. "And armed guards," said Brother Dalton, "fer yer cargo is like to attract some attention."

"There are some other settlers already out wher we go," said Joseph Mc-Cade, prior to our departure, "and some of them could use a little religion."

A removal through the wilderness by oxen and wagon is not a thing to be hurried. It is understood that wagons will mire down or wheels will come off, that rainstorms will soak and that progress in general will be slow and some days all but nonexistent. But with cheerful company of the like-minded, all of that can be borne, for that is the way of the westerers.

However, we started at a disadvantage, for simply to get out of our own neighborhood, negotiating sinks and fallen forests and treacherous ground, might prove to be the hardest part of the trip.

As there was few left to bid farewell, there was little need for ceremony, and on a day with wagons packed and securely tied, we set off on our slow pace, along the trace where we could or working out a path as needed through the tortured land.

The sights of the havoc was wondrous indeed, especially that we was leaving it all behind. We paused by a great mound of sand surrounded by water, and Brother Gilbert insisted that it had once been a pond and that the rending of the earth had forced the very bottom of the pond up through the water so that the water run off it and pooled at the edge. I did not have reason to doubt Brother Gilbert, for it was indeed like no sight I had ever seen.

But it was the crashed timber, mile upon mile of it, that near amazed me. We would go through stretches of prairie land and meadow and then come upon one of them stricken forests, nearly every tree uprooted or crashed in tangled heaps. Sometimes it was not even possible to pass through, and so we'd have to work our way around, careful not to lose our way.

Nor did we come upon any houses or cabins. Had there been any before, they was no more, though Joseph McCade did say that the farther west we moved, the fewer people and settlements we'd find.

We was one full day a-gettin' one of the wagons unstuck from a fissure. It was the lead wagon, and the small chasm into which the wheel wandered had been effectively hidden by brush and sand. From then on, a man afoot went ahead with a staff and poked carefully at the trail ahead of the first ox cart.

At night we camped near water, which was ne'er hard to find, for it bubbled up in odd places, though we did have to take care that it was good water and not tainted.

Joseph McCade had been right that much of the marshy land dried out during the long summer months, for you could tell by the cracked land where water had stood. Yet there was still bayou and stagnant water enough so that you could not lose sight of the kind of land you was crossing.

"Why it an't near so bad as the land south of here, which is both insalubrious and gloomy most times of the year," Brother Gilbert affirmed optimistically.

He was not, however, able to give us any positive suggestions concerning the insects, which both by day and night feasted upon our fresh flesh and darted around our faces and tangled in our hair. It was a bother, but thinking about it, I had to admit that the insects was at home, that they had not come to us, but we to them, and we had perhaps rather curse our own judgment than to curse them as they went about their normal routine.

For the first few nights that we camped, we was too tired to do naught but feed ourselves and fend off the insects so that we could sleep, that last being accomplished mainly by building up smokey fires and enduring that to the insects. There was some concern that the smoke thus generated might alert unfriendly Indians or bandits to our location, but the bugs was so pernicious that bandits or Indians was to be preferred to 'em.

It seemed amazing that the night sky was not in any way disturbed, that it escaped entirely the depredations of the land. It was that time of year that the falling stars showered the night, and the first of those that I discovered brought me up sharp, thinking of the comet that had first appeared near a year gone and what travail it had portended. But it was not a comet. It was only what it appeared to be, a great star a-falling, gone in only an instant's time, with neither tail nor trace.

In surprising short order, we accommodated ourselves to our new living conditions; perhaps having been camped out for so long had helped to prepare us. Whatever it was, we begun to find ourselves reasonably rested, so that after our supper we had time to visit and to have evening devotions.

Them devotions expanded each night, until one night, it was suggested that we include the singing of hymns. Well, perhaps it was foolhardy to thus call attention to ourselves in that wilderness with both smoke and noise, but the spirit was upon us and Cyrus led us into some singing.

In the clear night air, under stars so bright that they seemed almost to have been lighted one by one with a taper, it was the sweet sounds of Cyrus singing and the sisters Leretta and Berdetta joining in that put us all in touch with the heavens above. No one was willing to add their voices to what was already exquisitely pure, though I did note that the two boys, Tim and Jim, was scuffling some in the shadows behind where the sisters sat. The scuffling did stop abruptly, however, when Anna glanced over her shoulder and shot them a hard look.

The two sisters sat as usual upon a log, Anna expressionless between them. I had remarked to Biddy Dalton earlier that I did believe them two sisters to carry a log with them for the purpose of sitting, for it seemed no matter where we was, they managed to find one to share, the three of them.

At length Cyrus begun his devotions quietly and we sat through them, and at the end, after a prayer, he offered up another hymn. Not a single voice other than his and the sisters' was lifted, however, and we sat in the complete and pacific joy that only the purest harmony can produce. And in near silence we took ourselves to sleep, all but those charged with standing a watch.

Eventually the land we come upon could only be called swampland, in spite of Joseph McCade's assurances that it was not near so bad as that which lay south of us. It was gloomy and damp and desolate altogether, but beyond, when we broke into the open, we could see mountains of magnificent grandeur towering in the distance. Peaks and domes and jagged rock stood not in continuous run, but in groups, detached—disdainful, it almost seemed, of the gloomy mess at their feet.

"I've seen some of this sight before," said Cyrus, and then he remarked to Brother Gilbert, "Do you recall that when I first arrived in this district we rode out this way and viewed these mountains from a distance, and you told me that much of the land was claimed by Eremus Lodi?"

"Ah," replied Brother Gilbert nodding, "indeed, the land but not the view?" And he laughed.

"Yes. The view is as much ours as anyone's, though there don't seem to be nothing else about to appreciate it but swamp things."

"You'd be surprised," said Joseph McCade.

I looked at him and waited for him to explain, but he did not.

In time we was forced to make extended camp on a dry place while various of the men searched out the safest and easiest path across the swamp for us. "We better not just blunder on and hope fer the best," said Joseph McCade. "We got too many young'uns with us."

That evening as we stirred around the fires, putting together a meal, I was aware of a sudden intake of breath and Biddy Dalton's muttered, "Wal! We got company."

I looked in the direction she was looking and, sure enough, at the edge of the clearing stood a man, a stranger to me, and I suppose to everyone else. Neither young nor old, tall nor short, and dressed in fringed buckskins with a powderhorn slung over his shoulder, he leaned ever so slightly on his long rifle and stared at us, and we at him.

Joseph McCade rose up and walked over and greeted him. It was not an animated conversation and was brief. By his gestures I could tell that Joseph McCade was inviting him to sup with us, but the stranger's barely perceptible shake of his head indicated that he would not. And then, almost before our eyes, he was gone, disappeared into the gloom whence he had come.

"It's a solitary," said Joseph McCade, returning.

"What's a solitary, Papa?" one of the triplets, Robert, I thought. I still had to catch a glimpse of their foreheads to ascertain the scarred one to tell the difference between the two boys, they was so alike.

"A solitary, well, it's a woodsman, a lone hunter, that lives and hunts and trades all by hisself in the deep wood."

"Well. Why would he want to do that?"

"All kinds of reasons, I suppose," said Joseph McCade. "Some men are just solitary kinds, that do not care for company, for whatever reason, I couldn't say. There are more of them about than ye might expect."

"Where do they live?" asked Sarah.

"Why, who knows? Some have small cabins, others live in caves, when they need, or under a tree when the weather's fair. They won't hurt ye," he added to my relief. "Ther fer the most part timid and shy as the other wild creatures around here. Least that's been my own experience of them, though," he added quite unnecessarily I thought, considering the impressionable children listening to him, "they tell of one such solitary, neither man nor beast, they say that haunts these swamps, that is most frightful to see and terrifying withal. But I myself think that it's only a story and no truth to it."

The scouts was back by the next afternoon with a mapped route they assured would carry us through the swamp, and the next morning by early light we set out again. And in surprising time, we come out of the swamp, and before us lay a small mountain, a rocky path leading around it. With relief, we started up that mountainside in short order, becoming so much a part of it ourselves that we was hardly aware that we was on a mountainside.

We had made good time on that much firmer ground, and I was feeling calmer and more confident, when we was overtook by a thunderstorm, both fast and fierce.

Well, that first clap of thunder that I heard near jarred me out of my boots, as near did it sound to an earthquake rumble, and for just a moment I reacted as if that was indeed what it was. I was not the only one so mistaken, and there was some hilarity about that, so used had we become to them shakes.

"Ah," said Joseph McCade, "if you think yer afeared of them, ye ought to've seen the Injuns. They near clean come apart with 'em."

"I thought," said Brother Mayhew, "that ye said ye couldn't feel them shocks here?"

"Well, here, yes. Why, the swampland did tremble considerable, which

308

is one reason we had more of a time finding our path, fer parts of it has been destroyed, it looks like. I did not feel them shocks so much to the west, but the Injuns felt them here and some in the mountains, too." And he gestured toward the mountains on the horizon.

"The Injuns was right terrified of them and put them off to all kinds of reasons, mostly dealing with God's displeasure, ye know? The Injuns ere not so different from others in thinking theirselves so important that their god would tear the very earth asunder, did they displeaure him. The few settlers and trappers and solitaries around did walk on tippie-toe fer a while, as some of them Injuns was inclined to look fer someone to blame ever'time the earth rocked."

I wondered to myself then why Joseph McCade had kept such intelligence to himself before we set out on this journey. There was no guarantee that the earth would not shake again hard enough to unsettle the Indians. It was a sobering thought.

"Them Injuns has been nervous and skitterish fer years, anyway, going near crazy amongst theirselves trying to purify theirselves and all around them, apparently convinced that their losing battle with the white man was due to their unhappy god."

"Joseph McCade!" said Martha Elen, and from the look on her face, I could tell that she had been thinking along the same lines that I had been. "Joseph McCade, how come you didn't tell us none of this before we cut loose from the river?"

"Why," he said, "whatever fer?"

The rain introduced by that large thunderbolt set in for serious, and it was one of them warm rains, of the kind that leaves you feeling wet wh'er you're sheltered or not, close and damp as the air becomes.

Whate'er trail our scouts had mapped turned teacherous, and we was forced to make our camp once more on the side of the mountain. And there we sat, waiting out the storm, which did stay around long enough to leave everything sodden and rivulets where none had been before and land too dangerous to trust. Thus we was stalled, our path washed out and the thunderstorm giving away to serious rain, soft and drizzling.

Were it not for the rain, the place we paused would be a pretty place for camping, far pleasanter than any place we had been for a long time, for there was a meadow and a right pretty stream running through it. When the sun came out we could dry ourselves nicely.

But for that moment I had ne'er felt so wet and sticky and gummy, I thought, in all my life, nor my children remarkably dirty, for it was impossible to keep clean under the circumstances.

The scouts went out once more and come back with the warning that we had best wait out the rain.

Well, I was considerably weary of it but held my tongue, for complaining would benefit no one.

I chanced to look up in the evening and catch Martha Elen and Joseph McCade in serious conversation, the looks on their faces exceptionally grim.

When Joseph eventually left, I wandered over to where my sister still stood with a clouded expression, and I was not long in finding out the trouble.

"John is sick," she announced without preface. "Very sick with the fever. He come down with it uncommon quickly, too. One minute he was rousting around with his brother as usual and the next minute he was down and burning up with fever."

"Have you poulticed him?"

She nodded.

"Well, give it time," I said sounding more confident than I felt. The fever was not what we needed, yet the amazing thing was that this was the first case of it that we had had, having passed so many days and nights in fever country.

The fever made me nervous. I had seen near whole families wiped out with it overnight, while others might suffer its effects for months and then either get well or expire. It could run its course quickly or hang on forever. I had lost one babe to it. I held it in great respect, as one respects a merciless and unpredictable enemy.

The next morning two more children was down, and we knowed what we was against. Old Sister Gilbert produced a small bag of dried herbs. "I have fought that fever fer a lifetime," she said. "These weeds will do as good as nothin else, weeds with very hot tea. Seems the more ye boil the tea water, the better the cure and," she added, "make the well young'uns drink that boiled tea, too."

I did not know if she knowed what she was talking of, but I was not of a mind to argue with her. I would take any offered cure that I could find. And we set about immediately making hot tea from them dried roots and leaves, and dosing the young'uns with it.

It was not a day until John McCade was sitting up, his fever broke, complaining loudly that he wanted to play, though he looked peaked and wrung out. Martha Elen had all she could do to make him stay abed lest he break down again.

And then without warning, Robert McCade come down with it and his sister Janie, both felled so quickly that nobody was expecting it.

"That's the way young'uns is," said Sister Gilbert, digging deep into her bag of roots and herbs again. "They will go under and then pop right out again," she paused before she added, "or not."

I begun to fear for Martha Elen, for she was looking drawn and peaked herself. "I just ain't slept enough," was all she said, but it did seem to me that she was sweating more than the surrounding air, which had cooled considerable, would merit.

I watched my own children and made them stay by our own tent and not play with any of the others. When they complained, all I said was that the fever would not run its course did we keep spreading it around amongst ourselves.

Still, the fever did not abate, and it swept through our encampment, the way that it can do, felling the children first and the infirm and finally striking even the healthier adults. Had it not been for Sister Gilbert's weeds, I think that we might have lost more than we did.

As it was, we had to bury one of Sister Gilbert's own grandchildren, a sweet baby boy, and there was signs that we might have to bury more before the fever run its course. That Sister Gilbert's remedies could not help her own was just one of them mysteries that the Lord keeps to Himself.

"It is hard," said Cyrus, "hard, but it is the Will of the Lord, and nothing we can do about it but bow before it."

Maybe that was the hardest part right there, that there was naught to do but wait. The entire McCade family was at last taken with the fever. As the children seemed to mend, Martha Elen come down and then Joseph Mc-Cade, that man complaining loudly that this was happening to him. "Man n'er boy, I an't ne'er been sick," he moaned over and over, the moisture from his over-heated body soaking through his clothes.

Martha Elen bore her condition with a good deal more calm than her husband did, but that was not so uncommon either. Women have an understanding of the human body and its workings that somehow men do not. Knowing its ways, its possibilities and its dangers, a woman will respect her body more than a man who expects it to do its work no manner how ill-treated and then expresses surprise when it gives out.

Though few tents was left untouched by the fever, the blacks of the Sisters Morphew was none of them apparently affected, which was a blessing, for they all three give free of their time, carrying water and cooking as was needed, nursing and tending.

I made mention of that to Anna at one point, and she sighed. "We 'uz all put upon this earth to help one another," she said, "de well to tend de ill an' de strong to help de weak."

The Sisters Morphew was both ill, she said, but she did not think them to be seriously so. Tim and Jim, she said, was fine, as she was herself.

I had to wonder if there was some special aura about the blacks that made them so healthy and give them healing powers. Perhaps that thought showed upon my face, for Anna pulled a small bag from under her shirt. It was attached by a thong to her neck. "Ah got mah pertection," she said. "I tried to git dem boys to wear ders, too, but dey won' do it, but jis' th'ow 'em away fas' as I fix 'em. Ah don' know what pertect's dem—de Lawd—I s'pect He got udder plans fer 'em."

We was among the last to experience the fever, but our turn come at last. Peter, my sweet, happy babe, looked up at me with a soft cry, his eyes suddenly gone yellow and his skin pale and damp. I knowed what I'd find before I ever put my hand to his small face. It was hot and fevered. Was the Lord goin' to take this one from me, too? Then I thought, "Well, not without a fight, He an't—what is to be or no!"

I wiped his face with a cool cloth and then wrapped him against the hard chills that all at once wracked his little body. Then I went in search of Sister Gilbert, who shook out the last of her weeds. "Ah," she sighed, "I an't so familiar with this kinds of land, but I needs get out and search fer more weeds, fer we're about all used up."

I looked at her as she spoke and was struck by the distant look upon her face. "We're all used up, ye know?" she muttered again as if she had not just said it. It come to me, then, that she herself had begun to look peaked, and I said as much and allowed that she should keep some of her weeds for herself.

"Ah, me, no," she said. "I'm a tough old boot that has survived many years and plan to survive many more. It's the babes we got to worry over. They're the ones hardest hit by these fevers and agues." That last struck a chill to my heart, and I clutched the little handful of weeds tighter. "The young'uns, Mistress," she continued, her breath coming in short bursts of air, and the color of her old skin seemed to fade right before my eyes, "the young'uns to my mind is why we're here. Let all the brothers talk of Paradise and the Will of God and all of that, but a woman knows her mission, ner does she need nobody, not God Hisself, to explain it to her, fer it rests agin' her heart and suckles from her bosom. An't nothin' else that matters, do it, Mistress?"

I shook my head slowly. "No, Ma'am."

I took the weeds back to my fire and boiled them and strained them carefully. I thought briefly of O'Reilly, then. He would know where were more such weeds, most like he would have them in hand already. He had nursed Eremus Lodi through grave illness, could he not save us all? I wondered where we could dispatch a man to find him? But then I thought that there was no telling indeed where he was, on which side of the river or up or down it. To beat around in the brush searching for O'Reilly would probably be more futile than trying to search out the weeds for ourselves.

Though I nursed the babe through the night and the next day, I could not tell that he was any better, only that he was perhaps even worse, for he whimpered most uncharacteristically and cried when I left him and only slept restlessly, soaking his bedding through with the moisture of his heated body.

Then Sarah come down with it, dropped almost at my feet with great shaking and vomiting. I wrapped her against the ague and dispatched Cyrus to Sister Gilbert's tent in hopes that that old sister did have more cure about her.

Cyrus returned shortly, a grim look upon his face. "Sister Gilbert is gravely ill herself," he said, "and has not even enough powders left for her own self. I will return to sit with her, for I fear that she will cross Jordan this very night."

I sat right down hard on the pallet between my sick babes and rested my elbow on my knee and sat thus for a long time, patting one or the other of my children as they tossed in turn upon their sick beds. My mind was in something of a turmoil, for I was both tired and afeared for my children, but I could not get out of my head that Sister Gilbert, that dear old sister, would leave us. "I fear that she will cross Jordan this very night," Cyrus had said. And what was it about that which bothered me, nagged at my mind? To "fear" crossing Jordan? And should we not be happy at that prospect? Was not the crossing over Jordan to that happy land where the blessed spirits already dwelled occasion for rejoicing?

Truth was, it was not. In the end, we didn't want to go; we did not want our loved ones to go there neither. Well, I was obviously not of the proper disposition. I truly did not understand the ways of the Lord. Surely there would be a time—in the far, far distant future I hoped—that I would be grateful and happy in Jordan's Fair Land. I hoped.

Cyrus did not return that night. It was near to daylight when he joined me between our sleeping babes.

"Old Sister Gilbert?" I asked.

He answered simply, "She went to sleep in Jesus not an hour gone."

"And you stayed the night at her bed?"

He nodded.

"Ah, Cyrus, that must have been a great comfort to her."

He give me a strange look, both tired and gentle, and with a slight smile, he slowly shook his head from side to side. "No," he said at last, "it was a greater comfort to me, Annamanda, for. . . ," and here he paused and stared hard at his two hands clasped. Then he looked up, a sparkle come suddenly to his eyes. "For this night," he said, "with that old sister as intermediary, I think that I have come as close to God as e'er I shall again in this life."

It was so startling a statement that I could not think of a response, but that didn't matter, for all at once he was so full of his experience that he just run over with talk. There was naught to do but listen and so I did.

"The old sister was lying abed when I come in but was awake and alert, and so I said a few words and offered a prayer and give up a hymn at her request. And then for a time, we all just sat there. But at last she begun to speak, to talk as the dying often do—especially the old a-dying.

"'Brother,' she commenced, 'dying don't come so hard as some folk might think, I believe, when yer ready fer it and got yer mind prepared, which is why I think to linger thus on this side of the brink be preferred to going sudden and unexpected.

"'I know that not to be the customary wisdom, that most folks would tell ye that they'd prefer to go in ther sleep unawares and so not have to face the awful end. To go sudden and simply sink from living to dead. Such as my first old man done.

"'He walked from the house, as far we knowed with years yet ahead of

313

him, and I watched him go as far as the wild pear, and of a sudden he stopped short and turned back to look at me in puzzlement and then slumped to the earth, dead I think e're he ever struck it.

"'First here and then gone. 'Tis not my way. Though I'd not like to suffer through to the end, and in truth, I have not. It is curious this fever, fer it strikes some low and leaves their minds weak and confused, while others remain clear-headed.' Here she paused for a brief moment, as if to consider that thought before she went on.

"'But I consider it a blessing to lie abed and take stock of what has been. In truth, it's been a good life, but hard. I'd ask no other.

"'Yet as I look back on it, first it seems to have passed so swiftly as to have been over almost before it begun, and then as I look again, why it passes event upon event, day upon day, the motion slowed, stepping as a early spring terrapin across the garden, almost as if what I look back on is some other life, a life led by someone else.'"

Cyrus stopped talking, and I couldn't keep from observing, "Well, she did seem most talkative for one a-dying."

"Oh, it was not all said at once," said Cyrus, "but come in fits and starts between rests of various lengths lasting the whole night long. But I do not think that she slept, though she rested sometimes at long intervals; her mind and memory was much engrossed."

"'I mind the Injuns,' she said at one point, 'fer, a young wife, I traveled into Kentucky and eventually lost my first husband and a married daughter and first-born grandchildren to the Injuns, which was fair bad them days.'

"'Have ye e'er seen a corpse without its scalp, Brother?' she asked me at one point, and I said to her that I had. And she went on, "'A corpse that used to be a loved 'un, without its hair covering, staring its deathly stare. It's hard. Hard. Yet ye know that corpse, that body, to be naught but the paring of a nail, so far as God's concerned.'

"She lapsed into a long silence after that, but her changing expressions give testimony to the multitude of her thoughts and memories.

"'Brother Pritchard,' she said suddenly, well into the early morning hours, 'I can see ye. I can see ye clearly. Oh, I'd naught be able to call the color of yer hair or eyes or to measure yer height, or naught such. But the blind do see, y'know? The blind do see. I can see ye as clear as I can see God, though of a truth, I could ne'er describe God no more'n I could describe ye.'" Cyrus paused, and then went on, "That was the first I knowed that the sight had left that sister's eyes," he said. "But though her sight was gone, her observations was yet acute."

"'When I was but a girl, long before our westerin', I heard that wondrous old preacher Jonathan Edwards speak—several times—and I remember, a little girl, a-thinkin' then that I could see God Hisself so wondrously did that old brother call Him up.'

"'Well, it's been a long time, I guess. A long time, so many tunes and so many verses,' and here her old voice trailed off, and she remained silent for a time.

314

"Finally, she lifted herself up some on the pillow and said, 'In the looking back on it, it's as if a story told, an't it? And yet I'm sure, just as certain as can be, that it could not e'er have been lived no other way. That I stepped each step as it had been written, and so not a single one of them can I therefore e'er regret.'

"She was then silent for a long time, her eyes closed and her breathing a gentle rattle that we recognized for what it was. At last she opened her old eyes, so glazed and filmed and sightless, and with a sigh and a smile she said, 'Truly I can see God, just as I seen him a'fore as he was represented to me long years gone.'

"And with her voice grown so weak, we had to bend near to hear, and she said, 'In truth, Brothers, I see God.'

"Brother Gilbert said at last, 'I would that I might sicken and die so that she might not have to cross that river alone.' And then he bade me leave him to his grief."

Cyrus, being tired, eventually slipped off to sleep himself, and I sat for a long time and thought on it, deciding at last that it was well and good that Sister Gilbert, who was old and who had passed a good, long life, might be prepared for Glory, but I was not—not for myself or for my children.

Brother Gilbert did not sicken and die, and we quietly buried his old wife. "If it is not the Lord's Will that I go," said the old brother, "I will not go, for He in His Wisdom then has some else fer me in His Plan."

Still, the fever did not abate, and one day turned into two and then into three, and Cyrus come down with it. He tried for a time to hide the fact, but at last could not and lay him down beside the babes, his own breathing labored as theirs. And truth of it was, I didn't feel so well myself. I was overheated and had a hard time concentrating. Only George seemed completely unaffected. He was concerned but in no way touched by the sickness.

Nor was I surprised at that, for from the time that his hand had been damaged by the river scum and he had been ministered to by O'Reilly the black, he had ne'er had a day of sickness nor so much as a runny nose or a loose bowel, that last being so common an occurrence itself amongst the settlers as to be almost normal it seemed. The thought come to me that, though he did not have the bag around his neck that black Anna did, he did have his amulet, the pagan charm, given to him by O'Reilly.

Well, I did have neither, but there was naught I could do. I could not get sick. The McCades was still down and needed help, and precious few souls about the encampment was not touched one way or another by it. I drank great quantities of water and tea and wiped my heated face and then as quickly was forced to wrap myself tight against the chills that shook me.

Well, I did not feel well, that was certain. But I was not sick. I would not be sick.

"Mama," said George, "don't you think you'd do well to rest?"

"Yes, George," I said carefully, for it seemed suddenly hard to make the sounds navigate around my tongue. "I am tired. I need some rest and that's all."

I lay for along time after it had grown dark. Mayhap I slept, for I had that dulled feeling that comes of interrrupted sleep. When I opened my eyes, I could see George, silhouetted by the dimming campfire. His head was pillowed on his arms and he seemed to sleep. I was hot and cold by turns. Peter cried out at my side. Or was it Jamie? No, Jamie was dead, dead of the fever long years gone.

I had not gone for O'Reilly and Jamie had died. O'Reilly could have saved him. I sat up. I needed to find O'Reilly lest we all die, even George. There was no power against the sickness except O'Reilly. For the Lord was not paying no attention. I lay back again, for I was dizzy with the effort of sitting up.

My thoughts was confused. O'Reilly was not here. We could not call him. Someone would have to go for him, wherever he was. Probably to the Indian Ocean. He was at the Indian Ocean, with the fisherboys and the golden sand. Patsy and Reuben was there, too. And Jacob. Someone had to go to the Indian Ocean, to the land at the end of the ocean.

It could not be so far. Hadn't they said that there was an ocean to the west, where the Indians would go? I sat up, the night air was cool upon my face. I wondered how my clothes had got so wet. Had we been rained on? Someone had to find O'Reilly, but everyone was afraid of him, for he drank milk mixed with blood. But I was not afraid of him. I could find him. He would come back with me, and with his amulets and powders and weeds, he would cure us all. The babes. It was the babes that had to be saved for that was our purpose. That was the Lord's Plan.

When I got back from the Indian Ocean, I would tell that to Cyrus. Wouldn't he be surprised that I had discovered the secret, the wondrous secret of life, the Lord's Plan?

First, I must find O'Reilly. I stood unsteadily, my head strangely light. The ground seemed unsteady under my feet. An earthquake? Well, I was not troubled by earthquakes. I had suffered enough of those to know that I was beyond their reach.

"George," I heard my voice as if from a barrel, "I won't be gone long. I'm goin' to the Indian ocean to get O'Reilly, and Patsy and Reuben, too." The sleeping boy did not stir.

Cautiously, I stepped from the circle of light. Which way to the Indian Ocean, I wondered. Well, straight ahead, of course. I lurched ahead, angered at the ground. Why would it not hold still? I staggered along, descending, I thought until I felt water sloshing about my feet, but I knowed I was not yet to the Ocean.

"It's down the mountain and then straight ahead and to the right," I heard myself saying. It could not be so far. I was chilled again and forced to stop and shiver, my knees weak, and I sank down upon the damp ground and sat awhile.

316

The woods around was dense. I remembered that all the trees had fallen, had crashed and thundered to the ground, roaring, growling and snapping. What was these doing standing? Unsteadily and unaccountably thirsty, I struggled up and was immediately caught up in a great spider web, for I could feel more than see it. I whacked impatiently at it. I was in a hurry and had not the time to dawdle with spiders.

What light shone from the night sky illuminated but slightly the shadows, and they would not hold still. Well, neither would I, and I pushed ahead, straight ahead and to the right, straight ahead and to the right. I sloshed through another pond, impatiently, pulling my skirts behind me, careless of snags and rents.

Took with a fit of coughing, I seized upon a tree and then commenced to puke until I thought I could ne'er stop. Dizzy with the effort, tired and unsteady, I leaned against the tree and stared out into the night. It was uncommon quiet, hardly the rustle of a leaf. I found myself listening then intently. Something bothered me. There was something I was listening for, a sound, a snap, a twitch, I did not know. Something was about. Was it O'Reilly? I called out. "O'Reilly, here!" But my voice only croaked and didn't even make no sense to me.

I knowed he was there. I could see his shadow. I could almost hear his shallow breathing. "O'Reilly," I croaked again and listened. Nothing. Then a snap, as a footfall, yet quiet withal.

It might not be O'Reilly. If not O'Reilly, then who?

"Who are you?" I called. Still nothing.

Well, I'd find out. Pulling my skirts about me, I started toward the shadows, but my feet and legs turned traitor on me. They went weak and light, as my head commenced to grow heavy and burdensome. I thought I would puke again, and then the lights begun to come on in my head, and I reeled and sagged and grasped for I know not what. But naught was there, and the earth reached out for me. "Who are you?" I cried, but the sound did not reach my voice, and the deepest darkness came over me and still for one instant I could hear the breathing close at hand.

Chapter 21

The Solitary

The heavy burden of dark lifted briefly and I was thinking, "I know the Plan, I know the Lord's Plan. I have to tell it to Cyrus for it has troubled him so much. The Lord's mysterious Plan."

But as I searched my memory for the Plan, it would not come. Elusive as an early spring firefly or a late night dream, it danced right outside my understanding. The Plan? I had it, I knowed it. It would take a moment but I would recall it. I had only to relax and wait, for I knowed that I understood it. Well, it was most annoying to have it right in your grasp, yet out again.

I opened my eyes, but it was still dark. I thought about rising, but it did not seem important. I turned my head and thought I made out daylight drifting through an opening, a window? Yet there was the smell of ground all about. I reached out my hand and tried to touch. I did not encounter the earth but, what, leaves? I lay in a nest of some sort, yet could smell the damp ground.

I looked up and thought that I seen a shadow hovering over me. I closed my eyes again and thought about it and opened them once more. The shadow was closer. That was curious. It blocked out all the light, and I detected the breathing close at hand.

"A drink of water, Ma'am?" come the soft voice right at my shoulder, yet it seemed so natural a part of the place that I was not startled. I knowed it was not O'Reilly. Mayhap it was God? I nodded my head, or tried to. I was thirsty.

I felt my head raised and a gourd placed to my mouth, and I drank down wondrously cool and tasty water. I could have drunk and drunk and drunk. But the gourd was pulled away at last, and I was laid back and I sighed and the deep darkness descended once more.

I did not know where I was, not the Indian Ocean. Mayhap a tree? I was sitting in a tree and I was dressed in white and I was searching the horizon, looking for what? My children, where was my children? I could not go without them. I realized God's Plan. Now what was it?

The earth shook the tree that I clung to and then unaccountably I was standing by the river. Where was George and Sarah? I could not never keep track of them young'uns. They was probably off in the garden playing with snakes or Indians. We had to go to meeting for Cyrus was going to baptize O'Reilly and I needed to tell him about God's Plan.

There was a sound and the smell of the damp earth come upon me, and I opened my eyes. A figure still hovered over me. I closed my eyes again. It was only the devil, come to wrestle, come to wrestle on little neat feet.

"Patsy!" I tried to call out. Patsy would put him in his place, yet though I called out, I could not hear my voice. It was most annoying. The bear? Where had that bear gone to? I had tipped him over on his feet and he had crawled away.

The Lord's Plan! Well, what was it? Where had it gone? Why could I not keep track of things? I needed to remember. I'd remember it on the morrow. Then the deep darkness descended again, the troubled dreams faded.

I woke shaking and coughing, gasping for breath, and the figure kneeled by me again offering the gourd of water. I shook my head. "A quilt?" I said, "Have you a quilt?" For answer, I was immediately draped in something heavy that smelled of earth and man. What could be more suitable, I thought, and drifted off to sleep again.

My eyes come wide open again, and I caught the figure illuminated by the opening. I was in a cave. And the figure, bearded and buckskinned. It was the Solitary. How curious.

My dreams continued confused, pulling image upon image, sensation upon sensation. I knowed I was hot and cold by turns, and I sensed that I cried out, yet I could not tell what was real and what was dream. And then I felt lifted and carried. I tried to open my eyes, but it was too much trouble. I thought I heard voices, but it might only have been my troubled mind deceiving me. And for a time I sensed a rhythm and the smell of horse and of leather and smoke, the odors of man and sanctuary. I slept then.

When I woke the light was not so bright, and by degress I made my eyes to stay open. My body did not want to move so at peace was it. I was clear-headed. The smells that lingered in the air were of wood smoke and fresh linen. I looked around slowly. I was indeed in a large bed, covered over with a fluffy comforter. I could make out a little fire dancing upon the hearth. The light was filtering through the windows. I wiggled my toes most comfortably.

My toes! Where was my shoes?

I felt around, passed my hands over my person. I lifted the comforter and looked. I was dressed not in my worn and muddied skirts, but seemed to be in a loose linen nightgown, so clean that it still smelled of the out of doors. I run my hand over my face and through my hair, which was not tangled as it ought to have been, and come away with some kind of powder, as if my hair had been dry-brushed and cleaned. I tried to remember what had happened, how had I got to this place, wherever this place was? Where was my family? I tried to sit up but found myself uncommon weak, so that even that much effort was near impossible.

I was not frightened but I was confused. I had a memory of the Solitary. Was that a part of the dream I had dreamed?

The room I was in was commodious, made of logs, but tight and clean. It had a substantial look to it, as if it had been there a long time. There was a heavy door, with a bolt, though it was not bolted, and I thought of rising and peeking out, yet realized that I did not have that strength.

Beside the bed was a small table and upon it a pitcher and a glass. I rose up on one elbow, poured water from the pitcher into the glass, and drank it down. It was cool and refreshing. With that much effort, however, I was tired clear out. I lay back and in an instant, almost, I slept again, dreamless I supposed, for when I woke again I did not recall anything of the sleep, though the day had obviously begun to give over to night.

The door was open and I looked quickly around. Someone stood by the fire poking sticks into it. It was a woman, and when she turned to me, I realized that it was an old Indian woman. Her long gray braids was wound around her ears and she wore a soft buckskin dress, beaded and fringed.

Without expression, as if she stared only at an unmade bed, she padded out again, leaving the door still wide. Well. I did not know quite what to think or what to do. I was thinking to swing myself out of the bed when another shadow darkened the door.

"Ah, now, my lady, yer at last fully awake?" said Eremus Lodi.

I was too confused to be able to think of anything to say and so only stupidly nodded my head. The old woman followed him into the room and went about lighting various candles against the deepening gloom. What a waste that was, I found myself thinking, to light so many candles with such a bright fire upon the hearth.

Then suddenly, a voice from my memory announced, "We'll away to my nest, little bird," and I found myself blushing.

"Are you well?" asked Eremus Lodi.

"Oh, indeed, thank you," I answered quickly. "I am much better."

"Well," he smiled, "you watched over me and nursed me through ill health, and so now I have returned that favor. Shall we call ourselves quit, then?" But he smiled gently as he said it.

"My family, the fever," I started, but he seated himself on the side of the bed and nodded.

"Ye've been our guest here fer several days already, Madam. And O'Reilly was dispatched immediately to aid yer fellow sufferers. I am assured that everyone is convalescing satisfactorily, and I have sent word to yer husband that you will soon be returned to him."

"Where did you find me?" I asked.

"Well, word come to me, as it often does, for I am in touch with a busy network. Ye'd been found in the swamp and transported to a cave."

"The Solitary?"

"Well, yes. One of them solitary woodsmen. There are a number of them through the swamps and mountains. They ere, for the most part, harmless fellows, skittish as frightened deer. This'un was most nervous and distressed and hardly knowed what to do and sent me word."

"You could have returned me to my husband," I said, feeling guilty that I was so comfortably disposed while the rest of our suffering group was forced to camp in the weather.

He looked at me for a long moment, and I was suddenly uncomfortable that he was seated so close. "Yes," he said at last, "I could have."

The old woman padded into the room again, this time bearing with her a tray with a bowl and a cup, and I realized that I was hungry.

Eremus Lodi rose and backed away and stood by the fire as she arranged the tray on the table by the bed. Her expression still impassive, she looked up at me. She was indeed old, her skin dried and wrinkled as parchment, and the flesh of her neck withered as a turkey gobbler's. But withal, her eyes was bright, and I wondered uncomfortably could they see right into my heart. But they was blue. Them eyes was blue, very blue. Though not the blue of an October day, they was more the blue of old ice. I thought all Indians to be brown-eyed.

"This is Hannah," said Eremus Lodi. He give no further explanation, and Hannah padded silently out of the room again.

I recalled stories of Eremus Lodi, stories that hinted of wanton behavior, of Indian maidens and slave girls. Well, I thought that surely he could do better than this cold-eyed, ancient Indian woman. If this was what give rise to such stories, I'd have to question that.

"I'll leave ye to eat and rest, Madam," he said at last. "Yer likely to mend quickly now. I could not," he added, "return ye to yer camp until yer fully recovered."

He left before I could begin to frame arguments. Well, no matter, it was late and I could not go tonight, but I could not stay in such comfort, with a servant to wait on me, while my family camped on damp and swampy ground and recuperated.

I woke in the night, a single candle and the small fire only to illuminate the room. Hannah stood beside my bed, staring down at me. How long she had stood thus I could not say. Nor did she flinch or glance away when I returned her stare, only turning at last without word or expression and padding back to the fire. She slowly lowered herself in the manner of the old, stiffly and awkwardly, upon a mat before the fire and, using her bent arm for a pillow, she laid herself down to sleep. I watched for a while and then drifted back into my own dreams.

I had intended to rise the next morning and insist upon being returned to my group, but I found that, while the spirit might be willing, the flesh was still uncommon weak. Merely standing and walking a few steps proved to be as much exertion as I was capable of.

"See, yer not so strong as ye thought," said Eremus Lodi from the open door—and me in my nightgown! I plopped back down on the bed and pulled the bedcovers over me, flushing bright in spite of all my efforts.

"It will not be so long, Madam. Don't be in such haste. And yer family are doing fine without ye. Don't worry about them."

Indeed, it was two more days before I had the strength to rise and dress myself in my cleaned clothes and present myself to the next room. Eremus Lodi was not about when I come in, and I was very weak and tired with the simple effort of dressing. I must indeed have been very sick. Hannah moved in and out of the room, which was large, with a nice fireplace and some very large commodious furniture, including two very sturdy rockers by the fire. Along the walls was cases filled with books. And beyond was another room, which was apparently the kitchen. I might have investigated that, but I was left with the impression that Hannah was not interested in having me so investigate.

I took my seat beside the fire and rested for a while, and then rose and wandered around the room. Cyrus had a few books—his Bible, *A Pilgrim's Progress*, a primer, and some pamphlets and tracts and printed sermons, all of which he guarded carefully, for they was valuable and hard to replace. He had managed to rescue them from our fallen cabin, and he carried them with him in his own pack.

But here was more books than I had ever supposed was in all the world. A school would not have so many, a university even. In curiosity, I started to count them, but a sound from behind me made me turn. Hannah stood in the door to the kitchen and stared at me. I was embarrassed to have been found counting the master's books and immediately returned to the seat at the fire. I wondered did Hannah speak any English, and so I spoke to her.

"Where has Master Lodi gone?"

She stared at me, neither shrugged nor answered nor in any way indicated that she had heard. Well. Perhaps she was deaf, hard of hearing, or mayhap just simple. Whatever it was, she disappeared back into the kitchen and left me with my curiosity.

I did wonder how in the world a man could get so many books removed so far inland. I sat in the rocker and faced the fire and looked into it. But I was not comfortable. I found it unsettling to be seated with all them books at my back—as if I was being watched by so many strangers.

It was another full day and night before Eremus Lodi presented himself. Silently Hannah prepared the evening meal and laid two places at the sturdy table and Eremus Lodi, neatly combed and dressed in cotton blouse instead of them buckskins I was accustomed to, strode into the room and smiled at me. He give no indication where he had been but only asked after my health, and I immediately importuned him to take me to my family.

"If you've not the time to spare, then just point me the way, for I'm strong enough to walk I know," I said.

At which he smiled a curiously twisted smile and answered quietly, "Ah, my lady, the swampland is filled with strange critters. Yer well off that ye was found first by that gentle solitary, fer ye could have been discovered by worse. The shaking of the land seems to have aroused all manner of strange beast and left them dangerously unsettled. Ye might not fare so well again," he added.

I waited for him to say more, but he remained silent. At last, to make conversation mainly, I said, "That solitary, an't it strange to live so in these wild places?" And then I wondered if he thought the same thought that immediately crossed my own mind—that Eremus Lodi himself was something of a solitary.

But all he did was shrug, "Yes, by most lights, such solitary life seems strange."

"By most lights?"

"There is something to be said for the solitary life, Madam. It can be lonely, of course, but the solitary is less like to suffer greed and envy and malice and self-aggrandizement, as it is the group that fosters such."

I thought about that for a moment before I answered. "Perhaps that's true," I said, "but the solitary must bear total responsibility for himself. If you're a part of the group, you expect to help and be helped."

"Wisely spoken, Madam," said Eremus Lodi, staring hard into the flames.

I could not think of nothing else to say but was saved the awkwardness of that by Hannah, who silently delivered our meal. We repaired to the table and ate in silence. And afterward, still in silence, we repaired us to the two rockers before the fire.

I sat in the rocker quietly rocking, though I had to stretch my toes some to reach the floor, for that chair, like the other furniture in the room, seemed to be oversized by some.

Eremus Lodi had nothing to say, and I was at last uncomfortable at the silence and murmured some observation about the number of books the room held.

"The books, Madam?" said Eremus Lodi. "Why, indeed, they are most important to me. For it is only through those that a lonely man might hold conversation with the dead."

He fell silent again and rocked slowly, as I did, and we both stared into those copious flames. It seemed so strange a comment that I had to mull it over for a while.

The soft light of the fire and the candles was kind to Eremus Lodi, softening his expression and returning some of his youth to him. Though his top scalp was mostly bare, his side hair hung almost to his shoulders, and he was clean-shaved.

Of the times that I had seen Eremus Lodi, each one he seemed to be a different man—gentle, fierce, crazed, violent, but now at this moment more gloomy than anything. The look on his face as he stared into the fire was distant, his eyes near closed, and I wondered did he sleep.

"I wonder," I mused aloud, thinking that perhaps he might or might not hear me, "that a man as you might need to seek conversation with the dead. There's surely wise and perceptive souls a-living to converse with."

The silence was profound, and I thought for a moment that indeed he had not heard me, but finally, with a slight shrug, he turned them near closed eyes in my direction.

"Ah, yes, Madam, there are indeed wise and thoughtful men abroad, but their wisdom is clothed with flesh and all the iniquity that implies, their wisdom tainted by that flesh."

Well, what a peculiar idea. "Does that mean," I said at last, "that those dead thinkers was without taint, then, and that's why you would converse with them?"

"Were not? No. Are not is more to the point." He sat up and his eyes come open. "They were flesh, they were mortal, they were tainted. But—that flesh is gone and all that remains are ideas in pure form."

I just sat still and watched him, for I had no idea what he was talking about, and as he went on, I did think that he was not talking to me anyway, only talking.

"'The evil that men do lives after them, but the good is oft interred with their bones.' I would not necessarily take issue with Master Shakespeare, but truth to tell, I do not think that necessarily true, at least not true of the written word, fer some of the greatest beauty is within such words and comes from apparent scurrulous types. But their character no longer has any bearing and only words remain. Does that make sense to you, my lady?"

I did not know what to say, so I sat and rocked slowly and stared into the flame. But his eyebrows was cocked and his smile was expectant, so finally I said, "I'm ne'er comfortable just talking, for I'm not well spoke at all. Indeed, I'm most out of place just sitting before the fire. Do you suppose you might have a sock or something that I could mend and so keep occupied?"

He sat bolt upright and laughed and then looked stern. "Madam, I would speak of lofty things and probe for rich answers and praise the words of wise ones long gone, and you—you would mend a sock!"

"Well, I told you I'm not well spoke, nor more am I well thought. I do what needs be done and have not the time to probe and think. That's men's concerns. Brother Kencaid could talk so with you, and Cyrus, but not I. I can cook and mend and mind the children, spin and make butter. But I cannot converse with the dead!" I said that last some testily, for I thought him perhaps to be making sport of me. And I rose and strode around, he watching me and rocking slowly still.

"Mistress," he said at last, "my pipe and pouch is at yer hand. Would ye bring them to me?"

I started at that, but looking down, did note them both to be on the sideboard where I stood. It was little enough to do, considering all he had done for me, so I picked them up and carried them the few steps to him and offered them.

He reached for them with one hand and suddenly grasped my other wrist with his free hand and held me there, thus loosely gripped. I was startled but not afeared. He only looked quizzically up at me without a word, and thus we was for a moment. I made no move to pull free. He sighed and smiled his slow smile and finally let go my wrist, and I went back to the rocker and sat. And so we sat in silence for some long time, I growing more and more tired, rocking and staring into the flames.

Eremus Lodi did likewise, only holding his pipe and occasionally putting it to his mouth and puffing thoughtfully at it.

"My dear," he said at length, "I am only curious. I know you and your husband to be devout and serious in your religion." He paused at that and I sighed. I did not feel either the inclination nor the ability to argue the Old School doctrine that night, nor with such as he, especially. But what he said next so startled me that I stopped rocking and sat bolt upright.

"I have often wondered why the devout do believe the Bible to be the foundation of God's word any more than any other collection of ancient myths?"

"Why," I answered when I caught my breath, "why you ought to take that up with the brothers who are more capable than I to discuss them things." I could hardly believe what he had asked. To question that basic Truth in any way seemed to me to be completely mad. That there was difference of interpretation I knowed, but to question the whole thing—well!

"I would not discuss it with them because I am not interested in what they have to say," he said with that curious half smile playing about his lips. Was he making sport of me again? "I am interested in what you have to say."

I took a deep breath and thought of ignoring him, but it did not seem that simple to ignore a direct question.

"I've told you before, I am neither well spoke nor well thought. It an't my duty to be. But some things I do know. I do know that the spring will come betimes and the summer, the fall, and the winter, each in its turn, that the grass will grow and the moon will wax and wane. I trust that them things will happen, nor will I question that they are and that they will be forever and ever. There are some things that cannot be explained, yet I do trust them to be forever and ever. The Holy Word of God is one of those things!"

I thought about going further, of telling him that Cyrus or Brother Kencaid could cite chapter and verse, could give him full measure of learned argument that I could not. But I thought better of it. He had asked me and I had said what was in my heart and that would have to do.

He smiled slowly and nodded. "What ye've described is faith of the simplest and sincerest form—honorable and direct. I could not argue with that even if I would."

I said nothing and we rocked some more. I felt myself growing more and more sleepy, mesmerized by the warm flames. I may have dozed for a moment for Eremus Lodi rose and said, "Madam, I think it is perhaps time that you went to bed."

I shook my head. "Really," I said, "I am not tired. I will be fine sitting by the fire. You may go if you like." I was suddenly unsettled at the thought of going to bed in the same house with a man not my husband. It had not seemed a problem while I was ill, but all at once I was both embarrassed and shy.

"As you will, Madam," he said, but continued himself to sit by the fire rocking and smoking.

I clasped my hands and looked into the flames and then away, and thought of what I could concentrate upon to keep my eyes open, for in spite of my best efforts, it seemed my drooping eyelids would turn traitorous. I blinked and rocked and tried to think of my babes and Cyrus and of all the things that I must do ere we would be permanently settled.

But I must have dozed for I jerked awake to find Eremus Lodi standing over me, gazing down. "You'd rest better, my dear," he said, "in a proper bed. The fire is warm in that room, and it's quite safe," he added with a smile.

"No. Truly. I am not so tired. Go on to your rest, Master Lodi. I will be fine right here before the fire. I am quite comfortable."

He inclined slightly at the waist, turned, and quitted the room. I sighed, content that I was to be left by myself, indulged my heavy eyelids, and must have immediately fallen quite hard asleep.

My dreams at first more half-conscious thought than dreams, at last settled into them irrelevant connections as dreams mostly are, though I could not ever recall them once I was awake, try as I might. And in my dream I seemed to feel myself weightless and at once comforted and safe. And I sensed the smell of leather of the sort that I associated with Cyrus when I rested my head against his chest, and then I caught the unmistakable aroma of tobacco and my eyes flew open.

I was indeed borne aloft, but not in sweet dreams, rather in the arms of Eremus Lodi, my face resting hard against his chest, and the leathery smell that I associated with Cyrus was fused with that smell of tobacco which was not associated with Cyrus. Eremus Lodi did not seem aware that I was awake, and I did not struggle, for strangely I was still ne'er afeared of this man.

Gently, I was borne into the bed chamber and just as gently was I lowered to the bed. I kept my eyes closed and my wits about me, and I breathed deeply and regularly, though my heart had begun to pound with some insistence. And then after what seemed an over-long pause I felt the weight of a comforter settle over me, patted and tucked about me as a mother might bed her child. The male presence hovered over me some moments longer, and then I heard the steps retreat and the door pulled closed. I sighed again, opened my eyes, and could dimly make out the objects in the comfortable room, for the fire in the fireplace did indeed blaze brightly. It was cozy and warm, and I was—between waking and sleeping—suddenly most content in that selfish kind of comfort that begrudges any interruption, and I was almost conscious of drifting off to sleep.

I come awake groggy in the night sometime, but not so groggy that I was not aware that a form stood over me, nor could it be other than Eremus Lodi. Something suggested to me that I keep my peace. I fluttered my eyes but briefly, as if only disturbed in my sleep and closed them again.

I know not how long I lay thus, feigning sleep. The odors of man were all about him, the heavy odors of the out of doors, of smoke and horse and tobacco and leather.

I dared not open my eyes again. In a while, I heard him move away, the boards creaking lightly beneath his feet. I waited and then flickered my eyes once more. He stood with his back to me, leaning against the fireplace mantle. By his manner, he seemed to be staring into the fire, though I could not be certain. Still not daring to move, I watched him. The time, if it was passing, was passing with mighty slowness, it seemed to me.

After a while, he stooped and hunkered before the fire, spreading his hands wide before the flickering flame. Then he reached and caught up a small stick and poked it into the fire and watched as the greedy flame snatched at the morsel thus fed it.

I was myself aching to turn, and becoming miserable with it. I could not understand that a man could hunker thus long without suffering acute pains of stiffening joints, but Eremus Lodi did it.

Mayhap, I thought, I should rise on my elbow and inquire as to his purpose, for it was not seemly that he stay thus in my room and me bedded down. Still, I was hesitant to do that, to call attention to myself. He seemed to be engrossed so in thought. He had undoubtedly only come in to stoke the fire and, staring at it, got lost in his thoughts. Fires can do that to you.

I had come to that point that I thought I should have to move or shout with the discomfort of my position, when he rose abruptly, with amazing agility for anyone in such uncomfortable position, much less a man of his years. Still facing the fire, he rested his head for a long time against his arm on the mantle, and as carefully and gingerly as I could, I flexed my own aching muscles and made every effort to stare down a persistent itch upon my chin.

Suddenly, he faced sharply about, and I closed my eyes hard.

"Madam," he said roughly, quite apparently aware that I was not sleeping, "I am going out now. There is a heavy bolt upon that door. When I have gone, close it hard. It will not give, I promise you." And with that, he lurched toward the door and slammed it hard behind him, and I unstiffened my aching muscles and darted to the door to do as I had been told.

When I woke again, the room was flooded with morning light and the fire had near died completely down. I could feel the chill upon my face, but the rest of me was right warm under the down comforter.

The smell of coffee boiling was heavy in the air and of food being pre-pared. This would not do—to lie abed while breakfast was cooked. I stood up and smoothed my clothes and my hair and looked around for my shoes, but they was not in the room, removed in the next room most likely while I slept. I smoothed the bed and read the comforter over it and started for the door, but before I could get there, there was a gentle knock. I slid the bolt back and slowly pulled open the door, expecting Eremus Lodi.

It was not Eremus Lodi I confronted, but rather the large, dark form of O'Reilly. I'm sure my mouth fell open, so surprised was I. Where had he come from? How long had he been around? He carried a small wooden table, upon which was arranged coffee, mush, and a large pile of eggs. He inclined slightly at the waist, carried the table directly to the fire, and set it down. He stirred up the fire without comment, laying logs upon it, and giving it life in a few deft movements.

He rose and looked at me. "Eat, Mama," he said.

"Where is Master Lodi?"

"Be him gone, Mama."

"Gone?"

"Be him rode to de dark, Mama. Eat, Mama," he added.

"Where is Hannah?" I asked. But, though he looked straight at me and most certainly must have heard the question, O'Reilly made no response, either by word or gesture. Had I dreamed her?

It was O'Reilly who returned me to my family.

The rainy weather had give way to bright fall, and the foliage upon the distant trees was like a patchwork quilt, the weather yet warm and the sky most brilliant blue.

As promised by Eremus Lodi, our group had mended most satisfacto-rily, a total loss to death being but four. It was sad but true that under such circumstances such a loss was slight, except of course for those families most directly affected.

"We have sanctified this ground with our dead," said Cyrus.

In the evening before our devotions, the group met to discuss our future. Several was in weakened condition from the fever, and all was tired and wea-ried of the trip.

"We an't so far from the big spring, indeed were we without wagon and ox, the footpath would carry us there in under an hour," said Joseph McCade, himself well recovered from the fever. "By wagon trail down the mountain, it's another day's journey yet, do we have no trouble with ox and wagon, and still we'll have time to throw up cabins and bed us down 'fore the winter snow falls."

Nor was the decision to proceed so difficult, for we ne'er could go back that was certain.

"What's wrong with this land?" Brother Curtis Layman asked, waving his hand to indicate the land around us.

328

"Wal," said Joseph McCade, "the worst thing wrong with it is that it belongs to Eremus Lodi, and though he might not mind do we squat here, he might take a longer look do we try to build on this spot."

We was still a few days getting ready to move on, though three of our party went on ahead to the spring and returned with the intelligence that it was just as Joseph McCade had promised, beautiful and firm land.

In that time that we was camped out on Eremus Lodi's land, we thought we detected a couple of tremors, slight though they was. We was all experienced enough of them that we understood what we felt, like pain recalled.

"If ther this strong on this mountainside," said Brother Mayhew, "ye can 'spect that same innards along the Mississippi was fair shook."

The good October weather was on our side, and we was able to lay things out to dry and to wash what could be washed in that stream, which was in truth so frigid that it pained.

"It's fed by that spring and the water up from the bowels of the earth, is why it's cold," explained Joseph McCade, and I had to wonder at what a busy place the bowels of the earth must be.

By the time we was packed and ready to proceed, we was all rested and everything was fresh once more, and it was almost as if we was starting out at the beginning again.

I had to reflect as we made our slow way along the narrow trail that we was a long way gone from Tennessee where we had started, and our heads did seem to be determinedly set to the west. And I couldn't keep from thinking that there was a great amount of west out there, and I hoped that we would not see the need to chew up too much more of it.

Our way wound along the side of the mountain, though in truth now that we was on it, it did not seem so peculiar as it had seemed from a distance.

"These mountains," said Joseph McCade, "is unusual in the way they spring up in groups here and there."

Someone asked him again about the Indians, for it did seem strange that we was right atop the area that he planned to service with his trading post and we had yet to seen an Indian.

"Wal," he said slowly in answer, "to tell the truth I'd have expected to see some by now. Ther not all that spooked by white men, fer ther in the main hunters and fishers and not fighters. But," and here he paused over-long it seemed to me, "ther are some scatterings of outlaw Injuns, them that's been drove out of ther tribes back east. And," again he paused as if weighing his words, "fer some time amongst the Shawnees and the Delaware, ther's been some upheaval, rites of purification, wildness, and fury."

"Wal, now," said Brother Mayhew's oldest boy, "I thought you said there weren't no danger from the Injun?"

"Oh, they an't been a threat to no one but therselves, don't worry. People that have watched ther behavior is at a loss to explain it, but it's been goin' on fer a time, ordeals and trial by fire and executions—but all amongst themselves. In truth, though, the shakin' of the ground has not done much to settle ther nerves."

"Ere we then walkin' into danger from the Injun?" a voice demanded.

"Naw, as I said, naw, savages is savages, but these an't been bad to scalp white settlers or burn them out or nothin' like they done so many years in Kentucky." Joseph McCade was ever his happy and optimistic self, but I noted more than one frown and a good deal of silence after that.

We come at last upon the spring, and it was every bit what it had been represented, beautiful and friendly and bubbling a body of water you could ne'er imagine. For though it churned and frothed like a great river at flood, it fell into a quiet pool, large as a lake, surrounded by land, the leaves of autumn drifting placidly down upon it, a beautiful and clear river at last carrying some of the water away.

I had become used to the busy waters of the Mississippi at flood, dark, carrying with it debris of all kinds, the castoffs of civilization as well as what it could grab from the earth, that I had come to think of all waters that way. To find so great a body of water contained and sparkling and clear seemed so unusual that I found myself staring deeply at it, wondering if it might pitch something out, some wild thing drawn from the innards of the earth. But of course it did not. Everything about it was predictable, and you quickly got used to it. It did only what you expected it to do, cold and clear and uncommonly beautiful. The seasons would produce what they would produce with little effect on the great spring, for it did not rise or fall very much. As with some people, it was an inward and solitary thing, going about its own business, unaffected by the world around it.

We set up our camp close upon the spring, and Joseph McCade showed us around where he planned his own trading post. He described it in wondrous detail, more lavish you knowed than was needful, but that was just how Joseph McCade was. Then the heads of the various families set out to mark land for their own cabins, which was prudently to be located close together. We would needs barter for more land and perhaps one day, when civilization was more secure, the families would be housed upon their own farms. At that moment no one felt so secure.

Our own tent was set up close to the woods on one side, at the edge of the crystal clear stream beneath a wondrous old sycamore tree that, as it was coming hard upon fall, was giving up its giant leaves, and they sailed into the stream like so many little vessels.

It was that time of year that you think you can be forever content, that it seems impossible that it might ever change, and I stood over the boiling wash pot, transferring the boiled clothes to the stream, which nicely rinsed away the soap. I reminded myself to suggest that our cabin go up within easy reach of the stream, for it did make washday easy.

"Mama," said Sarah, "what's George doing?" She was sitting on a bench close by under orders to watch Peter, lest he wander too close to the boiling pot.

"Why, he should be gathering fallen limbs," I answered. "That's what I sent him to do."

"Well, I don't think he is," said his sister. "He is just standing there. He's been standing there like that for a long time. What's he looking at?"

I looked in the direction she pointed and sure enough, the boy stood still as a small and wiry statue, staring into the woods.

"George," I called. When he didn't answer, I raised my voice. "George! Get about your business. Don't dawdle. Get into them woods and find me branches before my fire gives out on me."

He turned and looked at me, and then instead of moving off toward the woods, he commenced to step backward toward me, slowly, his face still turned toward the wooded hill.

"Watch the baby," I said to Sarah. And I marched over to where he had paused.

"George, young man, just what do you think you're about?"

"Mama. . . ," he said and then his voice just trailed off.

"George, what is it? What's troubling you?"

He turned then, ever so slowly.

"I don't know, Mama," he said, reaching for the amulet around his neck. "Something watches. Something watches us."

Chapter 22

A Feast of Fat Things

No one else was awake. I sat upon a bench outside the tent, watching the tidy little flames lick at the kindling. The mist rose from the spring lake in the distance and followed the stream like smoke through the valley. It was still; only occasional leaves drifted down.

On the opposite shore stood a perfect doe, come down to drink. Upwind, perhaps she did not notice us, or if she did, understood the ways of man enough to know that, most like, everyone still lay asleep. Whatever it was, she was most unconcerned, dipping her nose into the water, lifting it once more to sniff around. I sat still and could see the tiny ears flick and the tail. She was uncommon beautiful and so perfect a part of the scene that it might have been a painted picture.

I should have roused Cyrus. She was fat going into winter and would make some nice meat. Yet I did not move, only watched her. To shoot her would destroy the peace, would bring down the busy world on this other worldly scene, and I could not bring myself to do it. You could, I thought, as soon down the great sycamore over us or wring dry the spring lake itself, as to destroy that still and simple beast, natural was they all to one another.

Well, I was not usually given to such impractical imaginings. Meat was meat and we would want a lot of it, smoked, before the winter was gone. I turned my head toward the tent with a thought to whisper to Cyrus, and when I looked back, the gentle critter was gone, disappeared as if enveloped into the rising mist and carried beyond. It was uncanny that she had been at once before me and was as suddenly gone, no sound, no trace. I sighed once for what was lost and then the morning was upon me.

As predicted, the cabins had gone up quickly, ours the very last one, for we all pitched in to get the walls and roof and chimney done, leaving the finishing and the chinking to each family. Though it did seem to pain him some, even Joseph McCade made do with a modest cabin to get him through the winter, promising much more commodious quarters come the spring.

As it was, we raced the winter, but providence was kind and the fall weather gentle.

Withal, we had not seen a single Indian. O'Reilly arrived one day, carrying a fat turkey. He offered it to me and I was glad to have it. Yet when I dressed it out, I could find no wound of any sort upon it, only its neck broken. Was it possible that O'Reilly had simply marched up to one and wrung its neck, as you would an old rooster's? Well, this was no old rooster; it was a young, fat tom, which roasted would be tasty. I thought to ask O'Reilly the manner of the kill, but he had disappeared again.

Three of our men left, as soon as the last cabin had been raised, to go back to New Madrid to meet Jacob the riverman and his cargo. But for the fever and the loss of life we had suffered as a result, everything seemed to be going as planned, and I could have been right content had it not been for George. His behavior had become passing strange. Always quiet for a boy, he had become distant and thoughtful, so that sometimes you had to speak to him a second or third time to get his attention.

Had that been Sarah, I'd not have thought much of it, for she was of so flighty a temperament that you sometimes all but had to put your knee upon her back to keep her still enough to talk to her. But George, dear serious boy that he was, was usually more attentive and anxious to help.

He did not seem afeared as I might have thought, though now and then he did hang onto that amulet, and when he did a curious expression, more questioning than fearful, might cross his face.

I spoke to Cyrus, but he did not make much of it. "He's growing, Annamanda. His boy's thoughts are giving way to man's thoughts."

Well. That did not seem so sensible an answer. Was a man's thoughts so much deeper than a woman's thoughts that he must be forever pining and pensive? I did not think so.

Then all at once such self-centeredness give way to something more frightening. He commenced to lose his appetite and his eyes was sometimes fearful, sometimes angry, but always distant. His clothes, already too short about the ankle and wrist, begun to hang upon him, that gangling appearance adding to his general distraught appearance. But though I touched his forehead frequently and inquired after his health, he did not seem to be ailing in any way that I could understand.

And when I questioned him or importuned him to eat, he would only look sad or distracted or some other mix of expressions. He might mumble something about not being hungry or being tired, or he might not even acknowledge that I had spoken.

Sarah, on the other hand, took up the slack. I did wonder that any human being could think of as many things to talk about.

One of the first things that we had done when we encamped had been to establish a time and place for the children to take lessons. Biddy Dalton conducted those both for her own children and any others who was sent. Each morning for two hours, all the children trooped down to Biddy's cabin, and she instructed them out of doors. When winter come, we would likely discontinue them lessons, at least until we had constructed a meeting house large enough to hold them in, for our cabins was too modest in size for all them young'uns.

If there was one thing Baptists could do well, it seemed, they could produce young'uns. And there was a passel of them to be taught.

George was one of the older school children, for several of the young men, who in truth might have benefitted a little more reading and ciphering, would have none of it. So George and one of the older Mayhew girls become sort of assistant school teachers, apparently quite successfully, though Sarah was given to complaining of his authority.

"He's a quiet, well-thought young man," said Biddy Dalton. "I do wonder sometimes what he thinks of, though, for he can become most distract."

Well. I wasn't the only one to notice.

"Cyrus says it is because he is growing up and that his boy's thoughts is giving way to man's thoughts," I said to Biddy.

At which she laughed and winked and said, "Wal, I know what young men's thoughts most generally is about, an' ye can tell Brother Pritchard fer me that the sort of behavior them thoughts produce an't quiet an' thoughtful by a fer piece."

When I told that to Cyrus, instead of laughing or smiling as I had expected, he only shook his head slowly from side to side and murmured, "Ah, Annamanda," in such way that said quite plainly to me that I did not understand nor was there any hope that I would ever understand. And that pricked me considerable, so that I went around with my mouth tight and a frown between my eyes all the rest of that day. But precious good it done me. Nobody noticed. Thus I went to sleep feeling very sorry for myself and put upon.

One afternoon, I come upon George staring pensively out aross the stream. He was leaning against that sycamore and tossing little bits of its bark out upon the water, watching in a disinterested way as the water carried each little bark away.

"George," I said, "there's wood to be got."

"Ah, Mama . . . ," he started.

"George. We need wood." I turned away from him. I was in no mood to pamper him, all his man's yearnings being what they was would not keep us warmer nor cook our food.

"Mama, Mama, Mama," he cried, and I turned back to look at him for his voice was choked with some kind of emotion that I truly did not understand. He stood looking at me, his expression wild almost, frightened and pained at the same time, distraught, you might have said. "Mama!" he cried, clinching both his fists, crushing the sycamore bark in one. "Mama. I am so evil. There is such evil in my heart," he stuttered at last.

Oh. That.

Well, it was something of a relief after all. He was only leaking Baptist experience.

That was probably what Cyrus had reference to, with all his mysterious sighing. I just did not understand it, I guessed, that them men could so lose themselves, their direction and their appetite, over such.

"George, I know. We're all evil, from the fall," I said. "We're depraved and vile, as corrupt in spirit as in body, in original sin. You know that. You've always heard that explained. I thought you understood."

"Ah, Mama. I tried. Indeed I did try. But I did not believe it, Mama. In my heart I did not truly believe it. I could not keep from thinking of myself as one of the elect, all of us Baptists, I was certain was elect. But I did not know of evil then, Mama. Now I do."

"Well, Son," I said, "that's perhaps a part of the necessary experience."

But George was not listening. His glance was distant and the pain upon his young face was so apparent that I thought I might feel it if I put my hand to his face, like a raging fever.

"Mama, Mama! I have a memory of evil, such a memory of evil has come over me that I cannot eat or sleep for thinking of it. A long, long time ago that evil crept into my heart, that worm is there. I have remembered it. I tried to kill it, to escape it, but it found its way in. In distant memory I see the blood of evil and the flame, and I am afraid." He said all of that wild-eyed and passionate, and with his damaged hand he clung to O'Reilly's amulet, unaware I think that he did so.

"What do you remember, George?" I asked softly.

"Flame and hate and fear and blood and dark, the dark, dark of night, and pain," he added.

Well, I did not need to be a learned doctor to understand the memory he had and to understand that it was like a dream to him. Yet I wondered how to explain it to him. It did not seem wise somehow to try to destroy his parable.

"I tried to kill it, Mama, to fight it. But I could not, and the worm crawled into my innards and found its way to my heart and there has hidden all the rest of my life. Now, the memory is there. I remember that evil, and I suffer from it and know myself to be more hateful and vile and hopeless than any sinner that ever was."

I seen the tears rise in his eyes. With a sudden sniff, he turned away. He was man enough, at least, that he would not allow me to see his tears. Or perhaps not yet man enough—for Cyrus had ne'er spared me his pain and his tears.

"We still need wood, George." If there is any solace for pain of the spirit, it is work.

"We plan a feast of thanksgiving," said Cyrus one day. "A feast of fat things, a feast such as our fathers in Christ who first inhabited these lands provided so many years gone."

Since winter could be upon us at any time, that feast was planned for the nearest Sunday, with the morning give over to preaching and the afternoon to feasting and then more preaching, not unlike an Association, with Cyrus and Brother Ples Bryan to preach.

And in spite of the work involved, it was an exciting prospect. For nearly a full year we had been racked and buffeted first by the tumultuous ground and then by the remove west and the fever and the building of a new settlement. We was all of us ready for some serious rejoicing.

A day before the feast the hunters come back with a pair of bucks and a doe, as well as an assortment of small fowl and lesser game. I watched for a while as they set about to clean the animals, my attention drawn to the beautiful doe in her stillness. But for the slash of red across her throat, she might yet be living, so perfect was her poise and soft her body. I sighed and moved away. I hoped somehow that it was not that same doe that I had once espied drinking from the stream in the early morning. Again I was struck by the silliness of that. The beast of the field and the fish of the water and the fowl of the air had been put here by the Lord God to provide for us, not for us to become sentimental over.

Later that same day, O'Reilly appeared once more, this time with a brace of fat turkeys, and I invited him to stay over and to feast with us.

"Ah, Mama," he said slowly and then after a long pause, "No, Mama." That last with no explanation. Sister Leretta and Sister Berdetta's slaves would feast with us, for they was in truth a part of the membership and treated so. I did not see that it would be unseemly to invite Eremus Lodi's slave to likewise feast. But he apparently did. So I did not press the subject.

When I glanced up from my baking some minutes after that, I saw George and O'Reilly in earnest conversation. At least George was and O'Reilly was bent low over him intent upon what the boy was saying.

I went back to my work, but when some time later I went looking for George, he was not to be found.

"He went off with O'Reilly," said Sarah.

Well. I could not worry that, after all. Mayhap O'Reilly would teach the boy to capture and kill the wild turkey as efficiently as he could do. Or perhaps they was just off watching the preparations for our feast, for the air was most festive and the weather generally appropriate for such actitivities.

Whatever, it would not do to worry, for I had much to do.

After some time, however, the afternoon shadows grown long, it come to me that George was still absent. It was unusual for that boy to absent himself for so great a time. He was always good about reporting to me. I put my apron aside and determined to go looking for him.

I did not find George and O'Reilly, but what I did find was great deal of excitement around the pit where the general roasting of the meat was in progress, for the first of the wagons from the river had arrived and with it Jacob the riverman.

Well. I do think I would have been less suprised to have found the Angel Gabriel himself a-sitting upon that wagon as to have found that riverman. It did ne'er occur to me that he would ever get so far away from his beloved water. But he had explanation for that.

"Ah," he said, "I did think that it was time fer me to travel." But then he added with considerable more seriousness and therefore probably more truth, "I an't ne'er goin' to desert that river fer long, but fer the time, we're considerable weary of it, fer them earthquakes and tremors and shakes still continues almost daily. Ye ne'er know when the bank will cave in on ye or wher the channel is like to be from day to day or what obstruction ye'll find that wasn't ther when ye passed afore. I just think to rest from the river fer the winter."

There was a large crowd gathered, and it was more temptation than the riverman could manage. He singled out Robert and John McCade, who was staring their identical wide-eyed stare at him anyway, and he asked them in all seriousness, "Ye do know what caused all them earthquakes, now don't ye?"

As one, the two little boys shook their heads and, from long acquaintance with that riverman, I sensed a story a-coming on.

"Injuns," he said. "Injuns caused it."

"How do you know that?" prompted Sarah.

"Wal, they said so therselves. They take all the credit—er blame, whichever." And without waiting any comment, he sailed right into his story.

"Said ther was a very arrogant chief of the Chickasaws that lived on the east side of the river. Now this Chickasaw chief had a game leg, a bad foot, ye know? So they called him Chief Reelfoot, fer the way he kindly reeled when he walked.

"Wal, one day he come upon a beautiful Choctaw princess and decided right there that he would have her fer his wife, but, of course, she was already promised, and ther wasn't real good blood between the tribes anyway.

"But that Chief Reelfoot, wal, he didn't care. He was used to havin' his way, an' so he made plans to steal the princess away from her tribe.

"Wal, it come to him in a dream that the Great Spirit would be angry if he done that, an' would smite him an' his people an' cause the earth to tremble.

"D'ye think that made any difference to old Chief Reelfoot?" said Jacob to the wide-eyed children, who shook their heads in unison, knowing of course what was going to happen, yet anticipating it anyway.

"No Sir, it never. An' he fallered th'u on his plans an' he stole that beautiful princess. That were a mistake, weren't it?"

Again the children nodded.

"It surely were," he answered his own question. "Fer right in the middle of the wedding ceremony, the ground commenced to shake an' the river commenced to run backward an' it flooded over that Chickasaw camp and drowneded ever last one of them Injuns. An' not content of that, it stayed an' made a lake over the land, so that couldn't never nobody ever live on that spot of ground again!"

There was a general chuckle at that, and Jacob said right seriously, "D'ye believe that? Wal, if ye don't, them Injuns has another story, fer ther bound to claim them earthquakes as ther own doin's.

"Said that the Shawnee Tecumseh was a-visitin' a tribe way east of the river tryin' to enlist ther aid agin' the white settlers. Wal, the old chief that he was tryin' to convince, he took the gifts that Tecumseh offered, an' he listened politely, but Tecumseh in his heart knowed that the old chief did not believe in him, did not believe that the Great Spirit had sent him and that the old chief didn't have no intention of follerin' Tecumseh into battle.

"An' Tecumseh told him as much and Tecumseh was angry. An' he said to the Old Chief, 'Old Chief, when I leave here, I go back to Fort Detroit, an' when I get ther I will show ye the power of the Great Spirit, fer he will cause me to stamp my feet hard upon the ground, and it will bring down ever' house in yer camp!'

"Wal, it wan't but a few weeks an' one night the Old Chief an' all his people was wakened by the rollin' of the ground, an' sure enough, ever' single house in the camp was felled, an' next mornin'—after considerable prayer an' apologies to the Great Spirit—the chief an' his warriors took up ther weapons and prepared fer war."

At that Jacob the riverman paused for breath and looked around in a satisfied manner.

"Where do the stories come from?" asked Janie McCade, who was a matter-of-fact kind of child. She tossed her bright red curls, identical in color to her brothers' and Sarah's, but she had a concerned expression upon her face.

Jacob looked at her for a moment and then throwed back his head and laughed, at last admitting, "Ah, Miss, they come to me on the river, carried along as debris from a great flood. Each spring the river brings enough tales to me to keep me goin' th'u the winter."

By then the next wagon had arrived, and again there was much excitement. This wagon was handled by Jacob's silent brother Otto, his presence as big a surprise as Jacob's had been.

"Did ye see any Injuns?" someone asked.

"Oh, a sight," said Jacob. "We seen all kinds of Injuns. Seemed uncommon interested in our mission, though they did ne'er menace us in any way. Still, I felt fer my scalp with some regularity."

"Why," said Brother Mayhew, expressing the surprise of the rest of us, "we have yet to see our first Injun."

At that one of Brother Gilbert's older sons that had accompanied Jacob and the wagons back spoke up. "We did come further north and missed a part of the swamp and crossed the St. Francis at more accommodating spot where the land is more agreeable, and the river, too, and there was numbers of Injuns camped along that river. They seemed peaceable enough," he added.

"How come ye to come so far north?" asked Joseph McCade.

"We couldn't land at New Madrid. It an't safe no more," said Jacob, "so we had to go all the way up to Bird Creek, below Cape Girardeau afore we found a safe landing spot. It was then a easy march over to the St. Francis River."

"True," said Bradley Mayhew, "and it's the way we ought to 'a come the first place, fer the swampland is much less and the path easier."

"Ah," said Joseph McCade with a wave of his hand, "why that'd been forty or fifty miles out of the way. Why go so far to avoid a little swamp?" Well, Joseph McCade was ne'er one to be put off by a little common sense, that was certain.

"Ye ne'er can tell about Injuns," said Brother Gilbert deliberately. "It don't do to take them lightly."

At that I felt a little shiver go down my spine, and I turned and glanced over my shoulder, but saw nothing except the stream and the valley and the woods beyond.

"Fer an unsettled land," said Jacob the riverman, "this is most uncommonly populated. Not only is ther great numbers of Injuns, but truth t'tell, all manner of settlers is headed this way already. An' then we come upon strange, solitary critters, too," he added with a frown.

"The solitary? Wal, yes," said someone, "ye do find them in advance of any civilization."

"That," said Brother Gilbert's son, "that, yes, but, well," and here he paused, frowned, and carefully formed his sentence. "Ther's somethin' else out ther, somethin' that don't qualify as settler or Injun or solitary. Somethin' we sensed more than seen, a shadow or presence or spirit or somethin' that seemed near to us most of the way. It was," he laughed, "a little spooky."

You could feel a little sagging of spirits at that, and I glanced back over my shoulder once again and immediately started, for there was shadows at the edge of the wood, shadows that moved at us. And then I laughed. The shadows that emerged, like ghosts, where naught had been before, was only George and O'Reilly.

George come forward, but O'Reilly paused and waited, and then as that doe at dawn had done, he disappeared almost as we watched.

"George, where have you been?"

"In the meadow."

"The meadow? Whatever for?" I looked at him, aware as he sometimes made me that he had grown bigger than I. His face was as if new washed, clear and untroubled, where only hours before it had been tired and drawn and worried, and the shoulders that had sagged then were suddenly squared and the harried eyes was sparkling and clear.

"The meadow of the dead," he said.

Well, I didn't need to hear that kind of thing. "George."

"That meadow where we was, that we left sanctified with our dead. O'Reilly took me there."

"So far?"

"Oh, it's not so far, Mama, do you cross over the mountain by deer path and not round it by wagon trail."

"What did you do there?"

"Well," he said, "we prayed." Prayed? Yet he said it uncertainly, a little frown between his eyes.

"George, you've hurt yourself," I said, noticing a spot of dried blood on his forehead just below his hairline.

He flushed and brushed at his forehead self-consciously and that was when I noticed a red welt about that wrist, for it was his bad hand, which he did not much use. He must have caught me staring at it, for again with self-conscious and hasty gesture, he disposed of it behind his back.

I did not ask no more questions, for though much doubt and uncertainty assailed me, I did not in truth know what manner of question to frame.

We come to meeting early, the new morning smells enriched by the smoke from our feast and though we approached serious worship, still the air was festive. Cyrus would deliver our morning sermon and Brother Ples, the evening one. Them two did take turn-about in that matter, for Cyrus was not one to try to hog the pulpit, as was some that I could have named.

We took our places beneath the trees, close upon the spring lake, seated on the new-hewn benches, benches that we planned would one day serve in our own meeting house, and we entered immediately into songs of praise and rejoicing. The singing of the Psalms was always a time of special communion, and we all joined in, lifting our voices almost for the sheer pleasure of lifting them.

But now and then at parts of special beauty, we would all, as one, fall away and listen as Cyrus and Berdetta and Leretta carried through, the leavening of their pure, sweet sounds lifting spirits and raising them to might-nigh explosion, they was so beautiful.

The benches was filled, and there was indeed faces in the crowd that I did not recognize. Jacob had been right that settlers was drifting into this area, escaping the trembles along the river or fearful that the war to the northeast would be expanded or just among them that share the need to press ever westward, settling for a time and moving on. Word of a church, sometimes it didn't matter which kind, would bring them out for fellowship, nor was any ever turned away.

Jacob and his silent brother sat toward the back. It was not the first time that Jacob had joined us for worship, though in truth he did not ever seem affected much one way or another. I was curious just how his brother might react to our doctrine, however, as I was always curious about that when strangers come to listen. I had seen too many come in hostility only to remain in curiosity, and oft times renounce what other persuasion they had professed to join us. Cyrus in particular had that effect, for he could make the doctrine to sound so reasonable and true.

Cyrus rose at last, prayed for guidance, and read his text which was lengthy. He read from Isaiah, the 25th chapter.

"'And on this mountain,'" he began, "'shall the Lord of Hosts make unto all people a feast of fat things. . .'"

Well, I knowed of course the text did not actually refer to real fat things, in spite of the smell of roasting meat upon the autumn air, but of a spiritual feast of fat things, such a feast as Cyrus would likely provide us in preparation for that other one waiting us.

Now there's all kinds and manner of preaching. I have heard of some pastors who prepare lengthy sermons, practice them, and present them at last, having carefully determined the style of their presentation. Nor is that the way of the Old School Baptists, for they depend on and are certain of inspiration to carry them through. They know that the Holy Spirit will fill them to overflowing and give them the words to speak. Although it did seem curious that the Holy Spirit did fill some more generously than others. And Cyrus was such a one.

And truth, Cyrus insisted that it was not him, but the Holy Spirit speaking through him, guiding his voice, when he sang or preached. Well, whoever it was played that voice like a fine musical instrument, appropriate to the occasion, and Cyrus spoke what must have been three hours, for the sun moved in its course to the near top of the sky before he was finished, yet it hardly seemed that he had begun.

To say that we was awash with love and hope at the conclusion of his sermon would not even do justice to the power of it. I did not think that I had ever heard him preach so, but in truth I often thought that and so did others, so powerful could he be. We had been transported by the Holy Spirit to the depths of our souls where love dwelled, and had the very stones ears, they could not have failed to have been moved. It was a feast of fat things, and at the conclusion, there was tears and hugs aplenty, for the hope of salvation and more important for the faith in God's Holy Plan as it would one day be revealed unto us.

And then come our own feast of fat things, and we dug into it with the good appetite of the full heart, and of course, the empty belly, for we was but clay after all. All but Cyrus, who sat quietly at a distance, washed out and drained from his preaching. He was affected differently by certain sermons. Sometimes he would hardly seem to be finished and would continue his discourse with interested brothers—there was always them. Other times he would be excited and elated, and still others he would be quiet and pensive and lost into himself as he then. I knowed to let him be at such times, for the Holy Spirit was still leaking out of him.

I could not keep from noticing that George, who had been so silent and ill for so long, was all at once happy and jovial, excited, laughing and pushing with the other children.

After a time I looked over where Cyrus still sat and noticed that he had not eaten, and that Jacob's large and silent brother Otto had gone over to him and they was engaged in quiet conversation.

It was too much curiosity for me. I filled a plate with victuals and carried it over to Cyrus, as much, I'm sure, in curiosity of what was going on between them two as in concern over Cyrus's lack of food.

When I offered Cyrus the plate, he reached out and took it, rested it on his knee, and then proceeded to ignore it, intent on the conversation. So I stepped back but waited within ear-shot. Had Cyrus looked at me to suggest that the conversation was private, why, I most certainly would have moved away. But he didn't, so I didn't. In a moment, I was conscious of George at my side, also, but when I looked at him, why, he was engrossed in listening to the two men talk, as was I. And so we stood.

"I an't ne'er been one to think on things like this, Sir," the big riverman was saying. "We was taught some of our verses when we was young'uns, of course. But I suppose that if I thought of it at all, I thought that were there a choice fer me, why, it'd certain be hell an' not heaven, fer I've been less than perfect in my lifetime. Under such circumstances, it's easy not to think on the hereafter. But what ye say of salvation, how pure an' honorable it sounds, an' how hopeful, why I cain't hardly to believe that that's possible."

"It's how the Scriptures read, Sir, that God's eternal family is already chosen."

"Ah, but that don't seem right somehow, much as I'd like to believe. It don't seem right that ye might do as ye wish an' sin an' blaspheme an' all them things, an' still be the elect of God. How d'ye know?"

Cyrus smiled. "You don't. I know that I cannot speak for God and His plan, nor do I think that anyone else can, Pope or bishop or pastor. But," Cyrus added "d'you want to be a part of God's visible kingdom on earth, to join us in brotherhood and fellowship, you do have to strive to be good by our lights. As for your eternal disposition, I cannot say. I can hope for you only so much as I hope for myself. God's plan remains a mystery to us."

"Ah, but Brother, ye don't understand," sighed the big riverman, "I have been a bad man, I am a bad man. I have cursed an' blasphemed an' consorted with wanton women an' drunk whiskey until my mind was gone soft. I have fought an' raged. Though I have not killed, I have tried to. Fer certain the evil in me goes clean on down to my shoetops. So that when the earth rolled an' rattled so, when the fiery comet was overhead an' the river in constant turmoil, did I think that the judgment was at hand and Satan on his way fer me. An' then, a Injun blade in my back, providence er somethin' intervened to save me. I have to think that I ha' been spared as ye say to some purpose. I'd like to do somethin', but to be so good an' perfect just an't possible fer me."

"Or for anyone else," said Cyrus, "for we, being mortal, are sinful. We can only strive to be less sinful."

The big riverman lifted his head, for he had been staring at his offending shoetops, and stared at Cyrus. "I must think on it, fer in truth what ye say offers me more hope than anything else that I have heard on the matter."

I felt George move at my side, and looking over, I noted that he was smiling gently, his air distracted but in a quiet and altogether gentle manner, all the stress and strain and wildness of past days no longer in evidence. Mayhap he had got the worm out of his system.

"I'll think on it," muttered Otto, the riverman, rising and walking slowly away. I did not think that he even noticed that George and I was standing there. I glanced over, and indeed George had likewise walked away.

I turned back to Cyrus. "Eat," I commanded, "your victuals are getting cold."

"Oh," he said.

Mid-afternoon, we all commenced to gather once more. The shadows had already begun to lengthen, as the days was growing shorter. Elder Ples Bryan took the pulpit after songs and prayers.

Well, it was the kind of situation that many preachers does not relish, for it takes an uncommon good sermon to compete with contentedly full stomachs and minds that might be refreshed with napping. But Brother Ples proved to be equal to the task.

For one thing he had the judgment to keep his remarks short, and he did not try to compete with Cyrus. His remarks did not soar with great flights of spirit, but remained calm, and he spoke more of duty than of either doctrine or Holy Spirit.

At the end of his remarks, he did give the customary call to any mourners who might like to present themselves at the mourners bench, but no one expected that call yet to be answered, for though there was a few strangers in attendance, there did not seem to be any serious candidates for baptism.

At his call, however, there was a rustling in the back of the group that indicated someone was coming forward. Well, heads was immediately turned to that direction, my own among them, and I suspect I was not the only one startled to note that the large figure making his slow and deliberate way to the front was Jacob the riverman's silent brother, Otto.

Otto affirmed that, after much pondering, he did seek inclusion in our hopeful band. He was of course questioned by the deacons about his experience and the sincerity of it, and he struggled to make it clear.

He was awkward and ill-spoke and slow, but he stumbled through his explanation, much the same sort of thing he had talked to Cyrus about earlier. He spoke of his sinful ways and his feeling of hopelessness, his knowledge that he didn't think he could ever be good enough to be saved.

"But," he said, "when I listened to the brother this morning an' begun to think about it, I realized that mayhap all was not lost, that mayhap I was not doomed."

His answers was right satisfactory, and I could tell that Brother Ples Bryan was well pleased, and it seemed an exceptional way to close what had been a fine feast day. As an afterthought almost, Brother Bryan called out for anyone else who might like to make known his experience, and there was a quick movement and a small figure marched straight up to where Brother Ples and Otto stood.

It was George, standing tall and straight, yet looking mighty slight and puny next to the giant riverman. I felt a knot climb up into my throat as I looked at him. I glanced over to where Cyrus sat among the deacons, but I could not decipher the look upon his face, for it was very mixed.

I wondered if he might be envious that Brother Ples was the recipient of these mourners' pleas, or that George had chose Brother Ples over his father. Then I immediately realized that such a small thought did not do justice to Cyrus. Brother Ples, to my way of thinking, was only reaping the benefit of Cyrus's earlier sermon anyway.

Gently, Brother Ples spoke to George, and I was proud of the way the boy answered, for though his voice was not always true and did turn traitor on him now and then, the way a boy's voice will do betimes, he give extraordinary good account of himself, I thought, and so, too, did various of the brothers and sisters, for I could see them nodding their heads and smiling in appreciation.

"I have only recently become aware of my evil and depraved nature," said George in answer to a question. "In spite of my Baptist upbringing, when I was a child I thought that I could be good enough to merit salvation on my accord. I know, at last, that not to be the case, that I am helpless on my own to be good, that should God suffer to save me, it will be through His divine grace and not of my own doing.

"I would seek to join with likeminded brothers and sisters, and I would beg that they would teach me and guide me, and when I do wrong that they will gently tell me and help me to be better than I could be by myself, and I promise that I will do the same, struggling to overcome my awful nature and support others in that same struggle, for only by helping one another do we have any hope of improving our miserable natures."

Well, if there was anyone who had doubted that Cyrus Pritchard's son would one day be a preacher, that speech surely convinced them. But I was, I think, as sad as I was proud, for with that speech my babe had come to be his own man. I glanced down at Sarah who sat beside me and she was staring curiously at her brother, this boy that she had bickered and played with all her life, who now stood tall and solemn, speaking as a man speaks. She said nothing, but I knowed that she had to be thinking a great deal about it.

Our meeting was adjourned then, baptism to take place immediately in the stream that ran through our valley. Well, I did not envy anyone who had to be baptized in that cold, crisp water.

344

"I'll go get your change of clothes, George," I said, "and a sturdy comforter, too."

"No, Mama," he answered. "I do not plan to be baptized this day in these waters."

That showed remarkable judgment I thought, but I didn't say so. "Why not?" I asked, for I knowed that it was not the cold that held him back.

"I will wait that day that we can all go over the mountain to the land of the dead. For life and death are one and should be celebrated together."

I couldn't answer that, but somehow I knowed that idea was not original with him, that he had got it elsewhere. Absently, he fiddled with the amulet at his neck, and my attention thus drawn to it, I realized that it was not the same one that had worn so long. It was of an entirely different design, not new and shiny neither, but roughcut and with a patina of age upon it.

I started to make mention of that, but the exaltant expression that suddenly crossed the boy's face directed my attention to where he stared. O'Reilly stood near, appearing suddenly from the shadows like the eternal shade he almost seemed to be.

"Good boy," he muttered and inclining his head toward me, he added, "Ah, Mama."

I spoke greetings without hardly hearing myself speak, for I was looking at that black forehead and the fresh scar it bore, remarkaby like the one upon George's forehead.

"Good day to you, O'Reilly," I said. "I hope you're well this day." The amulet hanging around the black's neck was that very one that George had worn for so many years.

Chapter 23

The Beast and Redmon Pitt

In the end it was the ease of the winter contrasted with the hardness of the preceding winter which was the most remarkable part of our remove.

True, the wind come out of the north and the temperature dropped and there was some ice and snow, but we was all snug in our cabins by then, with firewood aplenty and meat. If we lacked for anything, it was for roots and fruits, those things destroyed by the rocking earth that we had not had a chance to replenish. We did have flour and corn, but in slight supply, and must wait patiently for early spring for the others.

Dock and lambsquarter and wild mustard was prized as much for their earliness as for their green. Indeed many settlers, low on provisions, depended on those at last for early spring and survival. For it's true that you do not live on bread alone, or for the matter, meat alone. The body craves and needs them green things and roots and fruits and suffers without them. So we was surprised and pleased that the greens come on early that spring.

The Indians, timidly at first, begun to arrive in small groups to trade with Joseph McCade. They was familiar enough with him, though they seemed to ignore the rest of us. It did seem at last that things was falling easily into place.

Jacob and Otto, to no one's surprise, lasted only a few weeks in the woodland until they made excuses to return to the river, for rivermen they was and rivermen they would always stay.

And Eremus Lodi come down from his mountain upon several occasions, apparently just to visit. Nor did any of our companions seem to find that of any concern. The war was far away, and if anyone recalled the rumors of Eremus Lodi's possible connection with that war and with the Indians, they never brought it up. Indeed, they may have forgotten the whole thing, as we had begun our lives so completely anew. There was also the matter of gratitude, for it had been Eremus Lodi's O'Reilly who had brought so many through the fever. And Eremus Lodi himself had quietly contributed certain provisions for the benefit of certain of the settlers who would have suffered considerable without them. And through the winter, Eremus Lodi moved in and out of the settlement easily and naturally, calm, with none of the strangenesses about him that had earlier characterized his actions.

All in all, it commenced to look as if the turmoil was all behind us.

And then Redmon Pitt arrived, without warning or apology, and settled himself right down with a small group of Pittites on ground to the west of our settlement. Well. Was there ever a rose without thorns or an Eden without serpents?

Word come to us round-about that it was the general westering of the population that had brought the Pittites into our country. That was reasonable, but I had my own theory and that was that the Pittites' strange and fragile doctrine of two seeds could not survive on its own, but like a wild shoot from a tree, depended upon the original roots for sustenance. That spurious doctrine made no sense without resort to its origin.

Well, we could not expect forever to keep that beautiful land to ourselves. There was already few Papists as they had been the original settlers, and there would anon be Methodist and Campbellite and Universalist and what-not following our tracks.

Eremus Lodi confirmed that, commenting upon occasion at the arrival of new settlers. He showed up without warning now and then, riding into our settlement on one of his great, dark horses. It did seem a wonder that he always rode, when for most everyone else the only sure method of transport was afoot. I asked him about it one day, just how it was that he could find trails for his horse to carry him over.

He laughed and replied, "Why, ther's trails aplenty, do you know wher to look. And I do know wher to look. I've traveled this lonely land for many years, Madam, and I can find my way anywher I want. And I go where'er I want," he added.

Seated by our fire one cold and damp evening in conversation with Cyrus, Eremus Lodi was moved to speak of Redmon Pitt and his Pittites. I was nearby at work on my mending and was surprised at how knowledgeable he was about that puny doctrine.

"That parable of the sower," he said, "wherein the seed that is cast upon rock and barren land does not bear, or bears in ill-manner, provides Christian text for the premise of the bad seed, that some of us was damned by chance, when the seed was sowed. It is an interesting metaphor."

There it was. I was ne'er comfortable when Eremus Lodi spoke thus, for I knowed him to be a non-believer. Though he was always courteous in his arguments and I knowed that the Lord would not strike us all down for blasphemy, it still made me nervous to hear him talk so.

At another time he spoke of the Indians. "I do not think that the settlers coming in have much to fear of the Indian," he said quite seriously, "for I think that the Indian's back is broke, that like a pack of wounded dogs they have turned upon themselves."

"In what way?" asked Cyrus.

"Why for some time now, ther has been a good deal of upheaval amongst them. If ye'd allow me and not take it amiss, I'd say that it was a fervent religious revival, a purging of therselves for sins that they can only ill-define. Them sins they think to be what has brought the wrath of the Great Spirit upon them, for like Job they feel that they have been sore tried by the plague of white settlers taking ther lands and ruining ther souls with whiskey and destroying ther manliness, withal.

"At any rate, they have committed great atrocities amongst therselves in the name of spiritual purging, excessively so, many of them."

I recalled that Joseph McCade had said much the same thing earlier. We was quiet for a while thinking about it. Then Eremus Lodi laughed in a mirthless kind of way and said, "Indeed, it is something that I cannot understand. I am a rational man. I do not believe in the mysteries and the unexplainable, for I am of the mind that all things have their rational explanation, do we just find it. But," here he sighed somewhat sadly I thought, "that philosophy does not explain the power of the irrational. Only metaphor does that.

"O'Reilly comes closer than I to it and the wild Indians and Redmon Pitt, and, Master Pritchard, you and yours likewise."

I waited for Cyrus to say something. He had a bemused expression on his face and said naught, but seemed to be waiting for Eremus Lodi to continue.

"The wild savage resorts to violence and pain in explanation of the unexplainable, or to curious ritual. Yet is that ritual so much more curious than Christian doctrine that passes as rational?

"Ther is no beast, Sir, upon this planet more vicious and ugly than one of them great snapping turtles, nor is ther beast more primitive. Do you throw a patchwork quilt around one and package him up prettily, yet that neat package still does not change the primitive beast within, and given time, it will tear through the covering and make itself known."

Cyrus with pursed lips said nothing for a time and then only quietly answered, "There's a good deal of truth in your parable, Sir. The church provides the quilt that keeps that beast inside and strives ever to keep the quilt strong enough to hold it there.

"Armenians," he added after a pause, "will try to tell you that the beast can change itself into a harmless terrapin, but we know better. We know that only the perseverence of the saints can keep that beast bundled and harmless."

"There's a stranger coming, Mama," cried Sarah one day. She was outside and I was in. I poked my head out the door to see what she was talking about, and had I not seen him with my own eyes, I would ne'er have believed it.

T'was no stranger at all that approached but Brother Amiable Simpson from Lost River.

348

I greeted him as if he had turned up from the dead, though had I speculated upon it, I might have been surprised to realize that we was not so many
months gone from Lost River ourselves. For it had passed only slightly more
than a year and a half, but with all that had happened in that time, it did
indeed seem two or three lifetimes gone.

And if I was surprised to see him, I was completely confounded at his
mission.

"The earthquakes that tore up your land was not kind to our own," he
said. "And though the devastation is apparently not as great as was yours, still
much of the land, and most of the timber, is rent and unstable, and still the
tremors and quakes persist. Even though there is talk that the United States
government is considering some kind of restitution fer the land that was thus
battered, there is considerable nervousness toward the continuing tremors,
and many settlers have moved on—quite a number toward Booneslick on the
Missouri and others back across the Mississippi into the Indiana Territory,
but that's where the war is.

"Wal, those of us left at Lost River Church considered all our choices, and
hearing that you and others of our brethern had settled in this land, we made
up our minds to follow and join ye in fellowship."

It was true, for Brother Simpson proved to be the first scout and was followed within a few hours by the several wagons of the rest of his group.

I went forward to meet them, stepping very quickly, eager to set eyes on
my old friends. And sure enough, right near the front, marching with sure
and quick steps was Clara Cuthcart—round as ever mayhap rounder even—
followed by a succession of young'uns, John Cuthcart leading the ox team of
a wagon.

I do not know that I was ever a' happy to see anyone as I was to see Clara
Cuthcart, and I throwed myself at her and hugged her neck, and we both
cried and laughed all at the same time. I could not wait to get my two friends
together, Clara Cuthcart and Biddy Dalton. And when I did, why we all three
laughed heartily, for Biddy and Clara might have exchanged names, each
bearing a name more appropriate for the other, Biddy being uncommon long
and strung out for a woman and Clara, round as an India rubber ball.

I observed later to Cyrus that the Lord did indeed have a way of evening
things out. Having visited Redmon Pitt upon us, He had then balanced that
out by sending us our dear friends from Lost River.

"Well," said Cyrus with a smile, "that is the way of the Lord, it seems. All
things are in balance. The summer has its winter, the sweet has its sour, the
good has its ill, and," here he paused with a distant and serious expression on
his face, "the living has its dead."

I speculated upon that for a while and then dismissed it as simply the
preacher in him. No matter how frivolous the observation, he would always
have to slip his message in.

The caravan bringing the folks from Lost River included the Simpsons
and the Cuthcarts and Thomas Lease and his family, as well as a couple of

Malones who had deserted Redmon Pitt's movement and also old Brother and Sister Samuels. That last Brother was some put out when he found out that Redmon Pitt was in the neighborhood, for he had been the one who had been most incensed at that doctrine and had returned in a hurry to the true church at Lost River.

That group had crossed at the northern-most edge of Tiwappity Bottom, near to the base of the mountains, and affirmed that they, too, had seen a number of Indian encampments, but there had been no particular threat to them.

Well, they was hardly settled in and begun to construct residences when Brother Enos Ray, as promised, arrived from Tennessee, having started he said in late winter, and with him he brought several other settlers, some Baptist and some not, and things begun to get crowded.

"The war shows me signs of driftin' south," he told. "The Creek Injuns is stirred up. Some say that Tecumseh is amongst them yet, others claim he's up to Canada. And meantime, the earth along the lower Mississippi continues to erupt and tremble at regular intervals, though there an't been so great a earthquake as them of last winter. The word is," he added, "that general settlement to the west is only a matter of time, and so it's well that we got here first."

He said that right smugly, and no one pointed out to him that he hadn't got here first, that he had waited until there was something to come to before he came. When I made that observation to Cyrus, he only sighed.

"Ah, Annamanda, sometimes you're so cut and dried in your opinion, as most people are. Indeed, had we not been driven from our river lands, we'd yet be there. As it was, we followed Joseph McCade here ourselves, and before him was Eremus Lodi and a few papist traders, and before them the Indian. And did not the saints from Lost River follow us here, also. Don't be so hard on Enos Ray. He's a good man."

Well. Maybe Cyrus was right. I made every effort not to think so hard of Brother Ray after that. Still, he had avoided coming with us when he could have. I thought about it. I guessed maybe I was a little hard-headed sometimes about things like that.

Sister Berdetta and Sister Leretta and Anna appeared at our door one afternoon. There was concern on all three faces. Anna asked to speak with Cyrus. As he and George was up on the hillside clearing land, I sent Sarah to fetch him and asked the three women to come inside and sit, but Anna declined that for them and said that they would wait without.

I went inside then to bring out some chairs and upon turning back toward the door, I heard a peculiar sound, like a generalized humming. I peered carefully through the open door and realized that Sister Berdetta was speaking to Anna, only it was not speech as I, or anyone else I knowed, practiced it, for she was actually singing softly into the black girl's ear, and the girl was inclined, listening intently.

I made a sound and Berdetta stopped short, but with no sign of discomfort about her. I carried out two chairs and in a moment Cyrus presented himself.

"Mister Pritchard," said Anna, "dem boys has run off agin' an' lef us."

"Tim and Jim?"

"Dey sometimes wanders away, y'know. But dey been gone a long time now, an', well, dey has now an' den talked of runnin' away to find dey fo'tune. Dey ain't bad, Mister Pritchard, dey's jis' boys. An' ah don' think that even did dey think to run away, dey'd really stay gone long. Dey jis' ain't got no common sense. But dey knows we needs 'em. I cain't think dat dey'd really desert us."

After some general questioning, Cyrus said that about all he could do was to send out a message among the various settlers and solitaries and traders in hopes that they had been seen.

"We only wants 'em back," said Anna. "We don' want 'em hurt. Lack I said, dey an't bad. Dey jis don' got no common sense."

"Mama," said Sarah, a day or so after Anna had reported her brothers missing, "Mama, you remember that Indian that called me copperhead that time our house near burned down?"

"Yes, I recall."

"Well, do you remember, then, the one that run his hands through my hair and made me so angry?"

I nodded.

"Well, I thought I seen him today. We was playing outside of the trading post, me and Robert and John and Janie, and a group of Indians that had been inside trading come out, and they stopped and stared at us and pointed and one of them run his hands over his own hair and they jabbered to one another and laughed, and I thought that one of them was one of those Indians that helped to fight our fire." She said all of that on one breath and finally had to pause so that I could slip a word in.

"Well, Sally, now that was a long time ago and much has happened since then. I wonder that you could remember a particular Indian. I have very serious doubts that you have seen what you think you have."

"Well, maybe," she said at last, and as was her wont, scampered suddenly away, her attention caught by something else.

I worked around the cabin for a while and worried the idea until I at last took Peter by the hand and walked toward Joseph McCade's trading post. The trading post was located centrally to our encampment, while our own cabin lay to the outer edge. Still it was not a great walk, and it was pleasant, for spring was seriously coming on.

As I approached, I noted that there was indeed Indians about the clearing. But that was not so strange; for the past months their various visits had become more and more frequent so that there was often Indians in and

351

about, though always in very small groups. Where they lived and in what numbers, I did not know.

I had seen Indians all my life, again, however never in very large numbers. To me they was just Indians, and I never paid no attention to them individually. Some was built sturdier or slighter, taller or shorter, much as other people was, but their individual expressions never made no impression, no more than does the expressions of any crowd of people that you meet or wander through.

Still, as I walked carefully toward the trading post, I glanced at these Indians, fewer than a dozen, and I noted that they all seemed to be young, for the younger braves could be playful as kittens. I made some effort to recognize any of them, but truth was, I could not. Even had I stopped and stared hard into their individual faces, I don't think I could have recognized any of them. And if I could not, I did not see how Sarah Elizabeth could have.

I walked into the store and found Martha Elen there, and we stood visiting for a while. It was remarkable what a store of provisions that Joseph McCade had managed to accumulate, most of it of course brought overland by the brothers Deiterbeck. I had been in such trading posts before, and they was often ill-stocked mainly, with only the sorts of things that the Indians prized: whiskey, brightly colored cloth, beads, trinkets, and such.

But Joseph McCade made plain his intention to establish a permanent trading store for both white and red, and to that end, he had stored a goodly stock of items—none frivolous, of course. But the necessaries was all there.

Martha Elen found a stick of sugar for Peter and broke him off a piece and offered me tea, but of course, I declined. It was mid-day and I had work to do. I could not idle my time away drinking tea.

"We only come for a short walk, as Peter was fretful," I said, laying the blame on the blameless boy and hoping that the Lord would not hold it against me. Truth was, I was not quite sure why I had come to look at the Indians, some little uncertain fear plaguing me.

I had turned to leave, when Anna come into the dim building and said that they had run low on tea and would buy some.

"Have ye heard naught of your brothers, Anna?" I asked.

She shook her head, a glum expression on her face. "I's worried about 'em, too. Dey cain't take care of deyselves. Dey ain't but boys." She stared for a moment and then blurted out, "I have to think fer dem and to talk fer de old sisters!"

I was trying to think of some discreet way to pry into the situation, when Martha Elen done it for me, and none too discreetly neither.

"I don't see how come," she said, "that them two sisters can sing like angels and indeed seems to love to do it and yet will not speak out a single word of conversation?"

"Cain't," said Anna. "Dey cain't really talk, fer dey both stammers and stutters when dey tries dat ye cain't make out atall what dey tryin' to say.

It's so hard on dem dat dey give up tryin' long time ago, long befo' I was big enough to work fo' 'em."

It was as a dam broke. Once Anna begun to talk about it, she held nothin' back, and we listened in some amazement.

"Dey's twin, y'know. So alike dat ye cain't make out one from de other, been dat-a-way from birth, an dat was de way dey ol' papa wanted 'em. Two of a kind, dat he could brag on. Dey ol' momma died when dey's borned, y'see, she bein' too old to have first young'uns dat-a-way.

"Dis is de story dat 'us told me anyhow. Dat dey was like as two peas in a pod, 'cept dat as dey begun to grow dey done everthin' back'ard to one another. One used her left hand fo' ever'thin', an' de udder used her right, lack dat. One has a high sweet voice an' de udder a low, rich voice, you noted dat, din't you?"

Without waiting for an answer the girl went on, "Well, dey ol' papa din't lack dat. He wanted 'em just alack. He wanted fer people to be continually confused over 'em, lack dey was pets an' not little girls. An' he pushed at 'em hard an' confused de little things much dat dey got so's dey couldn't get nothin' said fer stammerin', an' of course dat made dey ol' papa mad so's he jis' push at 'em dat much harder.

"Wal, dem girls finally got so's dey couldn't talk to nobody not even one another until one day dey discovered dat dey could sing to one another without stutterin'. Wal, dey ol' papa foun' dat out an' about had a hissy fit over it, told 'em if dey couldn't talk right, dey couldn't talk at all, an' dem bein' good little girls, tryin' to please de ole feller, wal, dey jis' stop talkin' altagedder. Only thing dey do is to sing an' if dey got somethin' 'portant to say, dey'll sing it to me, udderwise dey keeps dey mouf shet.

"Seems to me," she added solemnly, "dat dey'd ben a sight better off dey ol' papa die when dey's borned instead of dey ol' momma."

What a curious story that was. Martha Elen nor I could either one think of anything to say, and Martha Elen fetched the tea for Anna without comment.

"I dunno what we gwine do," said Anna as she prepared to leave, "if we don' git dem boys back. We cain't git on by our ownselves alone."

"I wouldn't let that worry you, Anna," I said. "I know that the brothers will not let you want for help. Be assured of that."

The girl only gave me another mournful glance and then went slowly out the door.

It was late in the afternoon when a messenger came for Cyrus. It was one of the Mayhew boys, breathless with news.

"We found Redmon Pitt, raving and screaming, his clothes shredded and deep scratches about his person. He is wild-eyed as a lunatic, and whimpers and rages by turns. His only sense is that he would see you, Brother Pritchard."

"Where?" said Cyrus.

"He is at the traders post with quite a crowd about him," replied the lad.

"I'll be back," Cyrus muttered to me and immediately took up his hat and left.

Well, I wandered about a bit, but curiosity overcome me, and I called the children and told them that we would wander down to the post where they could play with their cousins. That was of course good enough for them.

We got nigh the post and there did seem to be a goodly crowd about. "You'uns stay outside," I said, "for there's serious business within. On no account go anywhere else, but stay right in front."

I did not worry that either, for there was several children of assorted ages in front of the Joseph McCade's store, so I knowed they would not have reason to wander.

I peeked in the door and found the room fair crowded, but looking around, I noted several women in the crowd, among them Martha Elen and Biddy Dalton, so I did not feel uncomfortable in slipping in beside them.

Indeed, Redmon Pitt sat in a chair in the midst of the crowd and though his wounds had been washed and tended to, his face still was puffed up with swelling and battered considerable. Cyrus sat in a chair beside him and inclined in his direction.

Redmon Pitt was speaking softly. "I have come upon evil, Brother," he whimpered, "the very beast itself." The look upon his face was not that look that we had come to expect of Redmon Pitt, not superior or disdainful or fretful or pouting. It was a look of fear, the kind of fear that many of us had learned to recognize when we lived for so long with earthquakes, terror of the unknown, the fear that comes of having no defense.

"The Beast, Sir?" said Cyrus gently and Redmon Pitt could only shake his head vigorously, for he did not even seem to be able to put anything else into words.

Joseph McCade appeared from a back room with a cup, and I was fair certain the cup did not contain tea. Redmon Pitt sipped at it, coughed, and sipped some more. There was some general murmuring around, but I could not make out any particular strain to the whispering.

"Evil, Sir, pure Evil—the worm, the serpent, the fiend. I have seen it and I am afraid!" Redmon Pitt cried out so suddenly that several actually jumped in surprise. And then putting the cup aside, he buried his head in his arms and commenced to sob. No one else spoke, and I felt my own skin begin to tingle with it and thought that mayhap I should quit the room and gather my children and go elsewhere.

But curiosity, fearful though it was, held me, and everyone else, for we waited the man to speak again.

At last, he looked up, his wild eyes some calmed, the spirits from the cup having taken effect, and he told his story, with many pauses and stops and starts.

"I was working timber upon my land this afternoon, as is my wont,

354

considering the ways of the Lord as I worked my axe and my saw. But as I worked, it come to me that my axe had dulled so much that it was not doing its duty properly, and in my haste to be at my work, I had managed to leave my cabin without the stone to sharpen it.

"I was much provoked at myself for as ye all know, every hour of daylight is precious when ye work the land and need to clear a space in time to get yer crop planted. But ther was naught to do but go after the stone.

"Instead of going as I had come, I determined to take a route that would get me there quicker, I thought, over the hill instead of around it by trail. It seemed an easy path, but as those things betimes will happen, in just a few moments I was turned clear around in heavy timber and uncertain of my path and extremely provoked at my ill-luck.

"After a time of wandering around, I come to a clear enough space that I could check the sky and determined that I had been going not in the direction that I thought, but in a circular fashion, and I studied the sky for a time and determined the path I thought I ought to take and set out.

"I had not gone far when I become aware of a foul odor which growed stronger as I walked. It was as something dead; some large animal only would give up such a smell. Going along thinking that the day had certainly gone from ill to worse and considerably annoyed with it all, I pushed through some brush, snagged myself, and let fly an oath, though I'm much ashamed to admit my temper. It was a loud oath, and in the silence that followed it, I felt unaccountably uncomfortable.

"The stench had got almost unbearable and there was about me a heaviness of spirit that could only be called frightening. I had an overpowering sense of danger then, though I could see nothing. My entire being told me to back off, to leave, to quit that place in haste.

"I stepped back only a step or two, looking around and telling myself that it was the irrational fear of a small child in a lonely place, that there was naught to be afeared of, yet I could not rid myself of that pervasive dread.

"Of a sudden, without thinking beforehand, I cried out, 'Who is there!' There was not a sound. The regular noises of a busy forest was not in evidence, and my own breath had of its own volition ceased, though the pounding of my heart sounded like cannonshot in my ears.

"Then I heard a rustling off to the side, slight like a small animal, a rabbit or whistle-pig. Instead of following my instincts which told me loudly and clearly to go quickly elsewhere, I determined to assuage my curiosity and pulled aside some heavy growth and found myself peering into a small clearing."

At that Redmon Pitt suddenly stopped, caught his breath in a sob, and for several moments sat with bowed head and shaking shoulders before he could continue. There was not a sound to be heard other than his sobs.

"Before me, horridly disposed, lay the bloated forms of some blacks—I could not tell how many, only that it was more than one, for limbs had been torn from the bodies and randomly distributed about. Huddled over one of those torsos was a gigantic, living form. I would not call it human, for I do not believe that it was, though upon its body was remnants of human clothing. Whatever it was, was making a meal of them remains.

"I gasped, unable to quell the sound that escaped me, and the wild thing, The Beast, the fiend looked up. Its face was hair covered on one side, the other little more than scar, the claws upon its hands so long that they curled around. Nor could I tell how much of that stench was from the corruption of the dead and how much from that living being. His eyes was fire, pure fire, and the bellow of rage that escaped his twisted mouth, set my feet to flight as no other sound has e'er done.

"I heard him crashing after me, but I did not look back. I ran as the devil was on my heels, and in truth, I am certain that he was. Most of the damage done me was done as I crashed headlong through the forest, in my terror running agin' trees and falling and sliding. In perfect terror I run until at last I stumbled upon a path and was found by them hunters there." He nodded toward the two boys who had come upon him. Then he muttered almost to himself, "An' I lost my good axe in the process."

For a time there was perfect stillness and then a random shuffling, as no one knowed quite what to say or do.

"Brother," cried Redmon Pitt, "I have come upon the purest of evil and I am afraid." It was said so piteously that even I could feel sorry for the trembling wretch. He who had been so smug about his good and evil was not nearly so smug when faced with the reality of evil.

"Could them be those missing darkies?" said Brother Dalton at last.

"Whatever it is," replied Cyrus, "we do have to go out and look for ourselves."

The group slowly left the room, and small groups commenced to form outside, and there was much subdued conversation.

"It is possible," said Brother Enos Ray, "that Redmon Pitt has let go his senses and just imagined all of this."

"Possibly," said someone else, "but I don't see that we can just fergit it. We better find out fer sure what's happenin'."

It was decided after some more general discussion that the coming darkness prevented any immediate action, and a group volunteered to go out directly at daybreak next to search out what Redmon Pitt had said.

George standing near to Cyrus spoke up. "Is it The Beast, Daddy?"

"The Beast, Son?"

There was no look of concern upon George's face, only interest. "The swamp beast, the evil thing," he answered, and I noticed that he toyed with that new amulet at his throat, as if his former terror had been replaced by nothing more serious than curiosity.

Cyrus looked at the boy for a moment and then shrugged, "We don't know what it is, Son, if anything. Do not bother yourself with it. We'll find out tomorrow," he added, somewhat grimly I thought.

Cyrus rose early the next day, pulled on his boots, and took only some cold biscuit for his breakfast. "We will make as short work of this as we can, Annamanda. But we do have to put this story to rest, whatever it is."

With that he pulled open the door, paused with a surprised expression upon his face and murmured, "Well," and stepped out.

I peeked through the open door. Eremus Lodi was seated on a bench waiting.

"I thought, Sir, to join your search," he said.

Well. I did not ask how he had found out about the mission. I knowed he had a network of sources, and I didn't suppose there was any point in trying to unravel it.

"Well, Master Lodi, you're certainly welcome to come. We don't have no idea what, if anything, we're like to find. But Redmon Pitt is some determined that there is something supernatural out there."

"It is possible," said Eremus Lodi, his eyes narrowing. "You ne'er know what strange and frightful things the swamp will disgorge now and then. I know of some of them myself," he added.

I waited for him to explain himself. He did not, but I did not care for the expression upon his face. For of late he had been a pleasant and relaxed companion, seemingly at home with us and ours. At that moment, however, his expression had hardened, and it come to me that this was the expression that I had long associated with the man, and it was a little frightening.

"I want to go along, Daddy," said George suddenly at my elbow. I had thought him still sleeping.

It was Eremus Lodi who answered that request. "No," he said. He didn't give no explanation and that expression upon his face suggested that it'd be better not to ask for explanation either.

"I an't afeared," said George so sternly that I looked at him quickly, with a mind to suggest that he look to his manners.

"No, George," said Cyrus gently, "you're not afraid. But Master Lodi is probably right. You had better stay here." Cyrus gave no explanation either, but he glanced at Eremus Lodi almost as if they had some kind of understanding.

George accepted the decision with surprising grace and returned to the cabin and, I supposed, to bed. The early spring air, though right fresh, was brisk and cool yet, with mist rising from the water into the cold air like so much smoke.

The morning sunlight, barely rising above the ridge, filtered through the lacy leaves, still the tender green of early spring, their fragile look belying the strength that would hold them through all manner of tempest until they was ready to give up the ghost theirselves, when their time had run its course.

I liked the early spring, but not so much as I liked the fall. Belike I was just lazy. But spring heralded the coming busy season, long and hard days, and hot nights alive with hungry insects. Winter, when the larder was comfortably filled and the woodpile well stocked, was an easy time for sewing and mending and studying letters with the children and deep, warm, snug sleep at night.

I sighed, knowing that my opinion of the various seasons did differ from most others, and were I a wild animal forced to fend for life during deep snows, I might not feel so kindly toward the wind when it come out of the north and sent down snow to cover what little there was to eat.

It was in such a frame of mind that I glanced up and across the clear little stream. On the other side, almost at that same spot where I had months earlier espied the pretty doe drinking at about this hour stood a woman. It was Hannah. Hannah, the Indian woman from Eremus Lodi's household.

She stood ever' bit as still as that doe had stood, tensed in much the same way, watchful. Had she come with Eremus Lodi? If so, why had he not mentioned that?

She stood staring at me, so I knowed she seen me, yet she made no motion toward me, only continually staring as she had done when I mended under her care months gone.

The log that crossed the stream was some yards up the valley, and I was the one who made that trip and stepped carefully across and at last faced the old woman.

"Are you come for some reason?" I asked without preface, still uncertain wh'er or no she could hear or talk, for she'd ne'er given no sign of either.

She ducked her head quickly and then as quickly looked up again fixing the hard, cold blue of her eyes on me and holding me thus in her vision for a long moment.

"I come a-purpose," she said at last. Her voice was old, yet like the rest of her, firm in its agedness. What was most curious about it was that it was not the voice of an Indian. I could have closed my eyes and thought that one of the old sisters was talking to me.

I nodded ever so slightly but said naught. I would wait for her to commit herself. In truth, I had no way to know were her mission friendly or no, for she'd ne'er given me any hint of her disposition toward me, or toward anyone else for that matter.

"The message I have is fer you," she said at last in her strong, yet raspy voice, "it is fer you. Keep yer eye on yer children."

My children? "Why?" I asked.

Her ice-blue eyes met mine, and the cold from them bored its way clear down into my heart and left it chilled. "Watch yer children," she repeated. "Watch yer red-headed young'uns."

"Why? What will happen?" I whispered, the strength of my own voice giving way to the urgency of the situation.

"Watch 'em close."

With that she turned and walked away, back, I supposed, in the direction she had come. She walked with the stiff back of the aged, but she was not slow. I did not try to run after her and importune her to tell me what she meant, for I knowed that she had said all that she would say. There was naught I could do but await the return of Eremits Lodi and see if he could make sense of it.

But that thought gave me little comfort, and after breakfast, I gathered up the children and trudged to the traders post. "The red-headed children." Well, I had but one, the only others were Martha Elen's three, all copperheaded as could be. Yet I was loathe to raise any alarm on the basis of what had happened. Cyrus would know how to proceed, and Eremus Lodi.

I left George and Sarah then at Biddy Dalton's with the other children to study their lessons and led Peter, who had become far too heavy to hoist, to the traders store, only commenting that Redmon Pitt's story had me unsettled and I would wait for the men to return.

It was not yet noon when the group returned, but they was without Eremus Lodi. Immediately, a group gathered, men who should have been in the fields, apparently waiting near to hear what had been found out. The story that Cyrus told, corroborated by the others in the party, was grim.

"We found the remains of the two blacks," he said. "They are most assuredly the ones belonging to the Morphew sisters, and someone will have to go to them and tell them," he added, for they was not there. Indeed, it was not certain that they had even been informed of Redmon Pitt's tale.

"They had been as Redmon Pitt described, dismembered, bits and pieces of them flung at random about, as if they had been gnawed on by wild animals."

"Could Redmon Pitt have come upon a large bear and mistook that fer a man?" Brother Mayhew asked.

"It is hard to mistake a bear for a man," said Cyrus slowly after a long pause, "unless of course you're far gone in drink or fear."

There was some nodding at that.

"Ye ne'er found no sign of the kind of beast described by Redmon Pitt?" asked Brother Gilbert.

"There was somethin' about," said Brother Mayhew's oldest son Bradley. "Somethin'. We all sensed it, maybe even heard it or smelled it. 'Twas not anythin' that ye could put yer finger right on. But we was wary."

"Might only have been some nervousness resulting from Redmon Pitt's story," said Cyrus vaguely, yet his expression was such, his glance so distant and his mouth so firm, that I knowed he was sorely bothered on some account.

"Where is Redmon Pitt?" someone asked. I had been wondering that myself.

"Some of his group come for him early this morning," said Joseph McCade, "with the intent of settin' up an all-day prayer meeting to counteract the evil they presumed to be at large."

"Ah," sighed Cyrus.

"We must find that beast," said Enos Ray suddenly, "fer any beast, wh'er devil or animal, that kills men is too dangerous to be abroad."

"No beast was it that killed them two boys," said Cyrus abruptly.

"How d'ye know that?" asked Enos Ray.

"A beast does not take a scalp with a knife," was the answer he got.

Chapter 24

Hannah

I rose again at dawn the next morning. My rest had been broken by strange dreams and periods of wakefulness through the night. It was not that I was anxious to view the dawn that I rose stiffly into the cool morning, but rather that I did not feel well.

Quickly and quietly I dressed and stepped outside where the misty morning air was refreshing, and I sat upon the bench at the door and stared across the stream at the hillside where only the morning before I had encountered Hannah.

I had finally told that story to Cyrus who was as perplexed as I.

"I was planning to speak to Eremus Lodi of it," I had said, "but he did not return with you as I had expected him to."

Cyrus had bit his lip and frowned. "I don't know," he'd said finally and paused before he continued, "but there is something about Eremus Lodi that troubles me much. Bradley Mayhew was right—there was some presence, some spirit abroad that we could not confirm. It was," and here he paused long again, twisting the fingers of his two hands together and then abruptly finished his sentence, "a spirit that I think I saw reflected in Eremus Lodi's eyes. I would be hard pressed to explain that sensation, of course, for it is not rational."

I had sat waiting for him to continue, and after a time he went on, as much to his own self as to me. "That Eremus Lodi is a distant and solitary man, we know, and we can also suspect that he carries secrets, mayhap secrets that we're better off not knowing. Yet," he paused, looking up, "yet I trust him." I nodded, for I knowed what he meant. In spite of the man's strange and solitary ways, there was about him that honorableness that other honorable men recognize.

Still, I knowed more of that man's peculiarities than did Cyrus, for I had encountered him in divers situations, at least one of which was in no way honorable. None of that had I ever spoken to Cyrus of, and truth to tell, I did not even feel guilty over that omission, as a good wife probably ought. It was a private matter, that once I forgot would ne'er have been.

"I am troubled, Annamanda, not only by your story of Hannah and the red-haired children, but about the strangeness of the Indians, their wariness. I am troubled at the senseless murder and wanton dismembering of them innocent blacks and of the manner of their deaths and of Eremus Lodi's reaction to it. For when we spoke of Indians, he only murmured, almost as if to himself, 'The red man does not lift the black man's scalp.'"

"Well, if not the red man, then who? The Beast?"

Cyrus shook his head. "I wish I knowed," he said.

Thus I waited on the bench outside the cabin door, waiting for the ill feeling to pass, breathing deeply of the fresh air. The tenderness I had been feeling in my breasts, coupled with a rising illness in the morning, piqued my suspicions.

I did not conceive easily as other women did, as Biddy Dalton and Clara Cuthcart did. I was nearing thirty years of age with only four births to my credit and three living children. Well, there was plenty of women who'd have thought me blessed in that, like Clara Cuthcart, mayhap, that conceived near ever'time John Cuthcart passed across the threshold. But I could not help feeling sometimes that I was not keeping up my own end.

Though it was up to the Lord, of course, and His Plan, but still, did I have that house full of young'uns once prophesied by old Mistress Hankens, the midwife, why I'd best get on with it.

I had kept my suspicion to myself. There was no reason to trouble Cyrus with it one way or t'other until I was certain. But of late I had been some uncomfortable upon rising, and as I sat upon that bench, I was right down troubled in my stomach to the extent that I feared I might not keep from puking up all that it held.

At length the feeling subsided, and after I took a little hard bread, I begun to feel normal and roused up both Cyrus and the children. It was strange that Cyrus slept late, for he was usually up early and out with his axe by the earliest light, but though he made no excuse, I suspected that he—like me— had had a troubled sleep, for his eyes was circled dark, as I suspected my own was.

I walked the children to school that morning, stopping by the store to pick up the McCade children, again making no reference to Hannah's peculiar warning. It had been so quick that I still could not in truth quite give the whole thing credence. I only determined that I would, as warned, keep a sharp eye on them for a time, until I could talk with Eremus Lodi who might shed some light upon it all.

It was well into the morning, and as Peter played by, I worked in the garden space. I was in a sweat to get a piece of it ready for potatoes, for the moon was right and I needed to get them planted. I heard something behind me, and looking up, I noted that George was making his way along the edge of the stream, dawdling as boys would do.

I stood up, stiffly, for I had been at my hoeing for some time. "Why, George," I called, "why an't you at your lessons yet?"

"Mistress Dalton let us go early," he called, "for she said she did not feel well and needed to lie down."

"Where's Sarah?"

"She and the McCades thought to play awhile. I told her she'd best come home, but you know how she is," he sighed.

I started to laugh and agree, and then it come over me that I did not want them four red-haired young'uns unsupervised even for a few minutes. And I sighed. There was naught to do but tell Joseph McCade and Martha Elen what I had heard, and so I laid by my hoe and said to George, "You watch Peter, George. I think to go find that girl and have a chat with your aunt, for I don't want them young'uns playing about by theirselves."

I stepped off the distance to the trading store quickly and found Martha Elen at her chores and asked after the children.

"Why, I an't seen them. An't they at their lessons?"

I went on and explained why they were not and then, taking a deep breath, told her also of Hannah's warning. It was hard to make her understand, for it required that I explain Hannah herself, which was not so easy to do.

I could tell when she at last begun to understand, for her face went quite pale.

"I don't think it's much to worry over," I said, "but it won't hurt to keep an eye on them."

By that time, Martha Elen had taken off her apron and was headed to the door. "Well, let's go find them," she said.

We headed back toward Biddy Dalton's cabin, but though we saw other children, excited at the unexpected freedom, we did not find the red-haired cousins among them. Upon inquiry, we was told that they had been seen headed toward the upper end of the the stream—that would've been Sarah's idea, as she knowed to stay as far from home as possible, did she want to idle away her time in uninterrupted play.

I could tell that Martha Elen was getting excited, but that was to be expected because she was of an excitable nature. I would have preferred a calmer companion under the circumstances, as I did not need no encouragement myself to imagine the worst.

Nor did we find them where we had been directed, and we stopped and looked at one another, perplexed and not a little frightened. We had started to turn back when we heard someone comin' through the brush, and we turned and waited. It was George.

"Where's Peter?"

"I left him with Mistress Cuthcart, as I had an idea where the children might be playing, and sure enough I found them. There's a small cave back beyond the stream about twenty rods yonder," and he pointed. "They're comin'," he added.

In just a few minutes they appeared, muddy and damp and altogether disreputable looking and not a little sheepish. I did not have to say nothing to Sarah, for Martha Elen give enough tongue lashing to do for her own and mayhap a dozen others. Indeed, she scolded them young'uns all the way back to the store.

I felt both relieved and a little foolish of my own fears, and only admonished Sarah not to get out of sight of adults in her play.

"Mama?" said George suddenly, as he and I sat quartering potatoes for planting and Sarah kept watch over Peter playing at the stream's edge, piling little stones to no good purpose as youngsters will do betimes.

"What, George?"

"How was my hand damaged?"

I looked up from my work to find him staring intently at me. Well. That was a curious question after all these years. I had often wondered what he remembered, for he had ne'er said a word of it at all.

"Well," I answered slowly, "don't you remember any of it at all?"

"I have a memory, Mama. But I have always been afeared of that memory, and I have likewise been afeared to ask after it, for it is as a dream to me, and," he stopped and stared again intently into my face, "I think mayhap I have been afeared that you would tell me that the memory I have, which is most horrible and frightening, was no dream at all. Was it a dream, Mama?"

I didn't answer directly, and so he prodded me, "I am old enough, Mama, and I am no longer afeared. I have become a man and put away childish fears. I would know the answer."

It was a reasonable question, and so I recounted the story to him, nor did he seem in any way alarmed. He was attentive, a slight frown between his eyes, nodding his head at some regularity. When I spoke of Eremus Lodi and of his firing the shot at the wicked river scum that held the baby hand over the flame, the boy's frown deepened considerably.

"And is that your dream, George?" I asked gently at the conclusion of the story, which included O'Reilly's arrival with his medicinal weeds and powders and potions.

He frowned again. "Well," he said, "in part but not quite. My memory differs some. I do remember that Eremus Lodi rescued me from the fire and that I was terrified of that fire and that we rode upon a horse and, dimly, I remember O'Reilly, for I thought at first he was the devil after me again."

"Again?"

"I was running along the river, Mama, and it was snowy and dark, and I was looking for my daddy because you had told me, and you were hurt. I was frightened, for I had fallen in the water and broken through the ice. I remember that.

"A great figure loomed up in front of me in the dark, and I could not make it out. It grabbed me. I was so frightened, Mama, to this day I am frightened of that memory. I thought at first that it was a bear that had me, for it growled and snarled and the odor from it was fierce.

"I thought that it would eat me, and I cried, but it only stuffed me under one of its great arms and carried me thus, how long I don't know. But we come at last in sight of a fire, I remember, and a figure was seated at the fire, and a horse was nearby, and we crashed through the brush and into the fire-light, and the figure by the fire stood up, and I looked up then into the face of my captor and it was more hideous than I could have imagined. For it was hairy on one side, but horribly scarred on the other, and its eyes was wild and its hair matted, but it was not an animal, for it was clothed in bits and pieces as a man is clothed.

"Seeing the figure by the fire, The Beast—for that's how I remember it— shrieked a loud and terrifying sound and, lifting me high in the air, hurled me toward that figure beyond the fire. But I landed in the fire, my hand hard in the livid coals, burned before I could roll away.

"I thought that it was a pair of devils and that they would cook me and eat me, but The Beast fled then, crashing through the undergrowth, and Eremus Lodi rescued me—for I know now that it was Eremus Lodi resting by that fire—and buried my burning hand in the snow, numbing the pain from it."

"When did Eremus Lodi shoot The Beast in the throat?" I asked.

"There was no shot, Mama. I recall no shot. I am certain there was none, for my memory of Eremus Lodi standing stock still by the fire is clear. I can see him staring at The Beast, the two confronting each other across the circle of light, and then the beast flinging me, as if he flung me at Eremus Lodi himself. But there was no shot."

I said nothing, for I could think of nothing to say.

"But," I said, "wasn't there two others with him, two of the river scum?"

He give me a perplexed look and shook his head.

Ah. I could think of naught to say.

"All these years I have feared that dream, for it was too real and would not quit my memory as other dreams do. But at last I have crossed that stream of remembrance which is manhood, and I no longer fear the memo-ries of childhood."

He said that right seriously. It was a strange thing to say. I had ne'er heard nothin' like it before. It had to do, I was convinced, of some rite betwixt him and the black O'Reilly. Might be a primitive and pagan rite, but somehow I could not find censure of it in my heart, for the decency and honorableness of O'Reilly was of a universal kind, and I knowed that the Lord's chosen saints did not necessarily need to be white and Christian.

That evening after the children were bedded, I spoke to Cyrus of it and told him George's story and asked him what he thought of it.

After considerable silence he answered, "Well, a small child's memories might be tinged with dream and confusion. It's hard to say. Yet, as I have said before, there is something about Eremus Lodi that troubles me, something beyond his solitary ways and his emphasis upon reason as the only guide for living. There is something deep within the man, like the rent in the earth that presages them earthquakes, a rent in the man's soul, a rent that he holds compressed only by the greatest effort."

We sat thus in silence for a while, each busy with our own thoughts, and at last took us to bed. I thought to speak to Cyrus of my ill condition but put it off again. Time enough.

The fire twinkled on the hearth. I could see the forms of the children upon their pallets near to that fire. Cyrus and I slept in the small room off the kitchen, and the thought that carried me to sleep, curiously, was not the strange confessions of George or the excitements of recent days, but rather the thought that were another babe on its way, we was going to have to find a way to enlarge our room, as we could not continue to pack young'uns into the kitchen indefinitely. A loft, mayhap, I thought, and then I slept.

I did not know what waked me. A sound, perhaps. I turned upon my bed. The fire on the hearth was dimmed to just a few live coals, and a sudden rush of cold blew across my face. Reluctantly I raised me on one elbow and noticed the door ajar, a shadowy figure poised in the dim light. Cyrus, I thought sleepily, going out to take his comforts, and laid me back down and drifted off to sleep. I woke again, abruptly, for the room was fair cold, and I sat up. Cyrus was beside me in the bed, and the door was still ajar.

George. Had George gone out to relieve himself and left the door open? That was what I wanted to think, yet the chill that struck me was more than just the chill of the night air. Cautiously, I crept from my bed and made my way across the cold floor and into the kitchen, where my children was piled on their pallets.

Two of the pallets was occupied with sleeping children. It was Sarah's that was empty, and the comforter which should have been on it was missing, too.

I stood with my heart beating wildly and then calming myself, I thought, "There is an explanation. She has slipped out as she and her cousins slipped out before to watch for the comet."

The figure I had seen poised in the door had not been Sarah's, however, for it had been too tall and too masculine. I woke Cyrus and he was up immediately. He had not gone out, he said. We woke George who insisted that he had not left his bed either.

"Oh, Cyrus," I cried, "where is she?"

"I'll find that out soon enough," he said grimly, already in his pants and pulling his boots on.

He went outside, calling loudly. There was no answer. In my heart I had knowed there would be none. In a few minutes Cyrus was back in the cabin. He pulled down both rifles and handed one to George. "I am going to the store," he said. "I'll take a gun with me. George, build up the fire and sit here with this other gun and be ready. I don't know that there's danger, but neither do I know that there isn't danger."

I dressed and built up the fire and lighted a candle, too. George, taking his instructions quite seriously, sat upon a chair with the rifle upon his knee, staring hard at the closed and bolted door, as if just waiting for someone to push it open.

Cyrus returned shortly with the information that I most feared. The triplets was gone, too, apparently carried out through a window.

"Could the four of them be out foolin' around, Cyrus?" I asked. "You know how foolish young'uns can be sometimes," I added with little hope.

"There's copious disturbance and footprints around that window," he said grimly. "Heavy footprints in the mud, but moccasined, not hob-nailed prints. There was more than one and they was most certainly Indian."

With the first dim light of morning, we went out and scoured around our cabin but could find little evidence of footprints, as the space around our cabin was fair rocky and hard. Yet we was certain that whate'er had happened to the McCade children had likewise happened to Sarah Elizabeth.

In short order, all the citizens around was amassed and several plans of action was discussed.

"I know the Injun," said Joseph McCade, "an' if they took the trouble to kidnap only an' not to scalp all of us in our sleep, why the chances are that they only want ransom." He said all that in most casual and off-hand manner, as if he was discussing just a minor point, but still the expression about his face was grim and frightening.

It was decided eventually to send out inquiries amongst various friendly Indians and to load up a wagon with the sorts of items that Indians might barter for—the colored cloth and trinkets, "And," said Joseph McCade right grimly, "whiskey, do we have to."

By early afternoon, intelligence arrived that give us to believe that the children was amongst some Indians encamped upon the St. Francis River, and all able-bodied men gathered with the wagon full of goods but also with rifle and shot. "Fer," said Enos Ray, "if we cannot ransom, why, we'll fight."

Well. I had at that point to take back all the ill thoughts that I had had of Enos Ray, for when the time come to string beads or not, he proved himself a stringer after all.

Not only was Enos Ray among the group but also Saucie Malone, who had followed Redmon Pitt for so long, and also a couple of Methodist recently arrived in the area. Where the welfare of children was concerned, why differences of doctrine was apparently secondary.

"I'll go, too, Daddy," said George resolutely, but Cyrus shook his head.

"We must take only grown and experienced men, son," he said. "Besides, we have to leave behind someone to help keep watch here. Bradley Mayhew is staying and several others. Your mother needs you," he added gently.

George, good lad that he was, said naught else, though the look of disappointment upon his face was plain.

"Time enough, George," said Cyrus.

Though they would send scouts ahead to bargain with the Indians, still, with the wagon and all to pull, the trip to the St. Francis and back would take several days. I did wonder if my quaking heart could tolerate that wait.

I heard Martha Elen giving Joseph McCade what-for before the wagon pulled out. "If we had stayed on where we was at Ste. Genevieve," she cried, "instead of wandering all over the savage wilderness after you, my babes would still be safe at home with me."

Whatever answer she got, I could not hear nor did I try to.

Immediately after the caravan left, winding up the mountain trail, Martha Elen took herself to bed and vowed not to get up until her children was back safe with her. I wished that I could do the same and fall unconscious, and so not to have to live each slow minute.

But things had to be done, and the only way to pass the time without shrieking in madness was to do them. I busied myself at my various tasks and tried to amuse Peter who was restless and seemed to realize that all was not well.

I was a time noticing that George was gone and when I finally did, the bottom near fell right out of my stomach. Had he gone off after the men after all? Surely he would not summarily disobey his father. He never had before. Yet though I looked high and low for him, I could not find him. And there, I had one more worry that I did not need.

I went to Clara Cuthcart with my story, for I had a mind to leave Peter with her and go in search of the boy myself. "Naw, naw. Just wait. He's a boy. Have faith that he'll return unharmed," she said.

"Leave the babe here," said Clara, "and go get your things and come stay with us until the men come back. Don't worry about George. What is to be, will be," she added unnecessarily. I truly did not care knowing that whatever happened would happen wh'er I liked it or no.

I left Peter then and walked back to the cabin in a confused state of mind. I was much surprised and relieved to find George there waiting when I got back. I was indeed too relieved to scold.

"You give me a fright, Son," was all I said.

"Mama," he said urgently, "Mama, I have found them. I know where they are."

"What do you mean? Who?"

"Why Sarah and John and Robert and Janie. I know where they are. They an't at all where Daddy and Uncle Joseph and them thinks they are. They are just over the mountain. Mama, we have to hurry," he said, "fer they are held captive by a band of Indians and they are about to get scalped."

Lord have mercy. My legs might have give right out from under me, but for the fact that I needed them.

"How do you know that, George? What are you talking about?" In my confusion I could not even ask a straight question. George turned his head and I followed his gaze and then saw the Solitary standing in the shadows of the trees. Ah. I went toward him. Trying to think of what to do, I said to George, "Run and get the rifle and shot."

"You," I said to the Solitary, who immediately ducked his head in shyness, but I was of no mind to be gentle, "can you find the men and the wagon? They have been gone for several hours, but they cannot be too far."

For answer, he nodded his head.

"Can you direct them to where the children are held?" I asked, and again he nodded, still staring steadfastly at the ground.

"Go then!" Ah, how much I must have sounded like an imperial majesty, but I neither thought about it or would have cared had I thought of it.

Without argument, he disappeared into the shadows so quickly that I might have marveled at it, had I not other thought on my mind.

George appeared with the rifle, the powderhorn slung over his arm, the rifle longer than the boy who carried it.

I had no idea and no plan. Frantic as I was, however, I tried to think things through. If George was right, and I could not risk questioning that, there was no time to try to arrange another ransom, nor was there men enough to storm whatever encampment we might find.

The Solitary would find Cyrus and bring them back, but that would take time. It remained for George and me to find that extra time by some means. I thought then of Eremus Lodi and O'Reilly, and wondered should I perhaps have sent the Solitary in that direction first, but, no, there was no way ever of knowing where them two might be and precious time could not be spent in search.

"Let's go, George," I said grimly. It would be just we two, for I could not spare the time to argue the matter with Brother Gilbert and Bradley Mayhew and them others who would probably insist on arming theirselves and going along.

George headed directly up the hill from the stream along a narrow path and I followed, pulling my skirts tight around me. In my mind I cursed them skirts, and that not for the first time in my life. But for them I might have relieved George of his rifle, an awkward load that slowed the nimble lad down.

In a few minutes I realized that we was going straight up, and then when I thought I'd give completely out with it, the ground flattened, though the timber and brush was heavy. Still, there was a path, or what might pass for a path, for it was not man-made but only natural breaks here and there in the undergrowth, that George seemed to know existed, for he did not have to pause to find his direction.

I could not have said how long we had been afoot—only that it was probably not the eternity I thought it was—when George halted and, leaning upon the long gun, pointed silently ahead. All I could make out was a break in the timber, as if it might be a clearing ahead.

George nodded his head and, lifting the rifle, moved forward with great care, and I did likewise. As we approached the clearing, I begun to notice familiar things about it, but it was not until I saw the clear, little stream running across the otherwise unbroken meadow did I realize that this was that same clearing where we had camped that last time, where we had been fever-ravaged, where the graves of our dead showed as ugly gashes upon the early greening grass of the meadow.

We was well hid by the heavy growth, and following George's careful lead, we stepped lightly along the edge of the meadow, until at last we come in sight of a camp of Indians. It was not a permanent camp, or as permanent as Indians made camp, for there was naught but a few campfires, around which was gathered a large group of braves. There might have been twenty or possibly thirty. I was not in no mood to count

"There, Mama," muttered George so softly that I almost could not make it out. Seated on the ground, cross-legged but not tied or otherwise hindered was the four red-headed cousins, Sarah the tallest among them, her bright thatch of hair sparkling in the early afternoon sun. They might have been at play, rolling stones, so casually did they sit.

The Indians indeed was not even paying close attention to them, for they seemed to be agitated in another direction. It seemed to me best just to wait and see. All we could do was mark them until Cyrus and his band arrived.

I watched for a time, but could not make out what the commotion was.

"Mama!" whispered George urgently.

A young Indian had broken off from the crowd and, with knife drawn, strutted over to where the children sat, reached down, grabbed up Sarah Elizabeth by the hair and pulled her up. My hand shot to my mouth to suppress the cry that was trying to get out.

But Sarah jerked herself away and stood with hands upon her hips, and, I could tell, though I could not hear, just give that Indian what-for in the strongest terms. There was some general laughing at that, but not from that young brave whose ugly expression was clear even from that direction.

He yelled something and shook his fist, and give Sarah a sudden hard push backward and then reached for her hair again, and her kicking and screaming the while.

Looking around I spied a sturdy tree, with about a boy-sized crotch. "George, secure your rifle in the crotch of that tree. I am going into that camp. I will tell them that much ransom is on the way and will stall them in any way that I can. But if any of them should try to attack any of them young'uns, you're to shoot. It don't matter if you hit anything or not, just shoot and distract them, drop your gun and lose yourself then in the brush and head for home as fast as you can. There's naught else you can do, so don't stay around. In the confusion, mayhap we can lose ourselves. Don't," I cautioned, "don't shoot without very good cause. You understand?"

"Yes, Ma'am," he said already moving quickly to the tree I had pointed him to.

I took a deep breath, cast a glance to heaven, and then gathering my skirts close about me, I stepped into the clearing and marched directly to where the Indians was gathered. Looking neither to the right nor the left, I marched right up to where the young'uns was, as if I was naught but a mother out lookin' for her dawdling children.

"Sarah," I said, "where have you been? I need you."

The Indian countenance will not ever show much—anger or rage and sometimes playfulness—but in the main, whate'er thoughts lie behind their faces remain hidden. My sudden appearance, however, was so startling that not only was no move made toward me but several jaws went slack, including Sarah Elizabeth's before she jumped to my arms. And then I was surrounded by Indians.

I didn't know what to expect and, for an instant, half expected to feel the sting of a tomahawk across my neck.

"Heh, heh, heh," I heard at my back and I whirled around. I did not have to look to know that the rascal Drooly was behind me. "Mama," said Sarah loudly. "It's him, it's that scum from the river."

"Scum, heh, heh, heh, scum, is it, pretty lady? Wal, red-haired scalps is prized, is highly prized, pretty lady. Bright red-haired scalps, heh, heh."

Of a sudden was a loud command and reluctantly the young braves fell back, and I was faced by the tall Indian that I did recognize, for it was he who had led them Indians who had helped to fight our fire not even two years gone.

Was this the great Shawnee leader Tecumseh that I was looking at? I had always had that suspicion ne'er voiced to anyone. But if this were Tecumseh, why was he here and not involved in that war beyond the river?

I had hardly time to consider that thought before he shouted another loud command, and the group of Indians behind him fell away and exposed two familiar figures.

Eremus Lodi and Hannah.

They stood apparently unharmed and unfettered among the Indians, and a look of anger momentarily crossed Eremus Lodi's face when he saw me.

Well, I did not care that he was angered at my presence. This was my child and there was no stronger consideration than that. But still, I was most perplexed to see the two of them side by side, apparently a part of this group.

"Pewannee!" cried Eremus Lodi and the Indian chief, for that was what I took him to be, turned toward Eremus Lodi. Pewannee. That must have been his name. That was not Tecumseh, then. I had been mistaken in that.

Eremus Lodi spoke quickly and firmly, rattling off I knew not what, for he spoke the Indian dialect without hesitation or discomfiture. He spoke several sharp sentences and then stopped. Hannah, beside him, held her hands clasped before her and her gaze level at the Indian chief. She said nothing.

The chief Pewannee did not answer. Instead one of them younger braves stepped forward and proceeded loudly and angrily to talk. Still, I had no idea what he was talking about, only that he was angry, and his speech alternated between the chief and Eremus Lodi. He gestured wildly, raised his voice, pointed back in the direction of the children, and then apparently appealed to those other braves around him. Drooly, the river scum, come then and stood at the young warrior's back and grinned, the spittle forever running down his chin. Then I recognized the companion he had with him—Skeet, the name come to me suddenly as I stared at the vicious smirk upon his stupid face.

I gathered all four children close, and I stood as straight and firm as I could, trying not to show the terror that was building in me. Drooly and his companion spoke to each other and then laughed rudely, Drooly scratching at his private parts and then wiping his damp chin. "Pretty lady," I heard him mutter to his disreputable companion.

Eremus Lodi, ignoring the two white men, interrupted the angry brave at that point, but managed only a few words before the brave shrieked and menaced him with his tomahawk.

"Kuleeniah!" came the sharp rebuke from the chief, who turned his full and stern gaze upon the raging warrior, it was then that I noticed for the first time that those lidded eyes beneath the shaggy brow was icy blue, as icy blue as the old woman Hannah's. That color which had so startled me in her, now startled me in him.

Quickly and forcefully, Pewannee spoke to the angry brave before him— Kuleeniah, by name, I was certain. Whatever Pewannee said did nothing to temper the other's anger, however, for he waved his tomahawk in the air and argued and flashed angry gestures and words toward Eremus Lodi and Hannah and then back toward the children and me. Then, menacingly, he took a step toward us but was stopped by another sharp word from his chief.

Sullenly, he stepped back, yet he was poised and anxious. I could not know for what exactly, but the possibilities was not comforting. I pulled the children closer in the circle of my arms, for they was what he eyed with such menace.

There was some amount of stillness broken only by the occasional stupid giggles of Drooly. Pewannee's eyes, cold and expressionless, held the angry brave in check, and then they looked up, and there was just a suggestion of expression in them. I followed his gaze. Beyond the clearing and at the edge just removed from the shadows, I seen what he was gazing at.

O'Reilly, still as one of them oaks, was poised at the edge of the clearing, and in relief I realized that he stood close to the spot where I had left George. He made no move and, but for only the flicker of recognition from Pewannee, no one else seemed to have seen him. I looked quickly back at Eremus Lodi whose own gaze was fastened upon Chief Pewannee's face.

There was much deliberation about that Indian, as if he had been called upon to make a decision, and indeed I was certain he had been. At length he spoke, slowly and carefully. But his remarks was not addressed to Eremus Lodi or to the angry brave Kuleeniah, but to the woman at Eremus Lodi's side, Hannah.

"Old woman," Pewannee said slowly in careful English, "this one appeal I must grant. No more. That you might die one day at peace in your sleep is my prayer to the Great Father, but never come here no more. Go down the mountain, and take your white blood with you. Go!"

Hannah's level gaze did not waver nor was there any expression upon her face. She stepped two steps backward, never taking her eyes from the chief's face, turned slowly, and in the stiff gait of the elderly, she stepped without haste down the trail. Pewannee gazed after her. Suddenly, the warrior Kuleeniah shrieked out something and then spat violently in her direction. She did not look back.

"Eremus Lodi," said Chief Pewannee at last, "take the copperheads with you and go in safety. The debt must be paid. But," he paused and crossed his arms over his bare chest, "come no more in brotherhood, for that tie is broken."

The warrior Kuleeniah stepped up and protested, again gesturing wildly, arguing and pointing an accusing finger at Eremus Lodi, who had not yet moved. The chief heard the brave through his lengthy speech, a speech that was punctuated with loud growls and cries and appeals to heaven. Had the circumstances been otherwise, I might indeed have admired the oratorical ability of the savage, for even without being able to understand the words, his meaning was full clear.

He wanted us dead, all of us, particularly Eremus Lodi, and even that old woman who had disappeared so quickly from view. Carefully, cautiously I let my gaze travel to where I had seen O'Reilly. He was still there, but were you not looking for him, you'd had a hard time discovering him. I was some comforted in that knowledge.

"Mama," Sarah started to speak, but I clapped my hand over her mouth, lest she draw attention to herself.

At last the angry brave run down and stopped as abruptly as he had started. And then he waited.

The chief's gaze remained level and certain. He spoke slowly and deliberately in that dialect that I could not understand. But, though the words was unknown, the intent was clear. The chief having made his decision would stand by it.

Kuleeniah commenced to argue again, but his chief cut him off with a sharp word. Their glances crossed and held, Kuleeniah's eventually wavering. He turned and looked around at the crowd of Indians, then strode off to the side and deliberately turned his back on them. And as I watched, one by one several of them young braves broke away and went over and joined him, as did Drooly and his companion. I did not like the look of that.

The group around Kuleeniah, numbering perhaps ten, likewise turned their bare backs to the rest of the group, and Pewannee stared at them for just a moment and then turned again to Eremus Lodi.

"Go," was all he said.

Eremus Lodi with a deep breath, walked over to me, and with only a nod, indicated that I should follow him, and in a line with the four children between us, we turned and walked across the clearing toward where O'Reilly had stood, for he was no longer there, at least not in view. Eremus Lodi did not hurry, nor did I. "We'll see ye agin, pretty lady, heh, heh, agin, y'hear?" Drooly called after us, but I did not turn my head or in any way give evidence that I had heard him.

"Mama," said Sarah.

"Shhhhh," I murmured.

"But, Mama, that Indian wanted to cut my hair off," she said.

We walked without speaking, past where I had left George, but he was not there. I felt comfortable that he had gone with O'Reilly. Back we went along that same natural path that George and I had followed coming, Eremus Lodi navigating from open space to open space as easily as had George.

We had got clear back to the trace when we encountered Cyrus and a group of men hurrying behind the Solitary. There was no describing the joy upon Cyrus's face when he beheld us. And when we got home to our cabin, we found George there ahead of us, though there was no sign of the black O'Reilly.

Well, by the time we had delivered the triplets to the McCades and suffered through that confusion, it had been a full day and dark was upon us. Curiously, Eremus Lodi stayed by us, though I half expected him to go the way of O'Reilly and just disappear as they two often done.

"It's late," Cyrus said to him at last. "Won't you stay the night with us?"

"I am not afraid of the dark," said Eremus Lodi in a slightly mocking tone. "But," he added, "I owe you explanation, I think, and I am prepared to give it."

Well. At last!

"The story is long," he said, "and goes a ways back. But I will start with Hannah who is a white woman and mother of the Chief Pewannee and grandmother of Kuleeniah, who is the son of Pewannee."

Here he paused and finally murmured, "And also the mother of the woman who was my own wife. And so I am brother-in-law of Chief Pewannee."

Hardly had I time to absorb that startling information until he added, "Regrets is a poor salad of low nourishment, Madam, yet do I feed regularly upon it."

Chapter 25

Eremus Lodi's Story

We sat before the fire, Eremus Lodi focusing intently on the flames. It was warm enough out of doors that we could have got on without a fire on the hearth, but the situation seemed to call for one. For the warmth of a crackling fire draws ones together and gives a point at which to focus, and something to do in the occasional tending of it. When matters of import need be shared, a fire can be an important part of the setting.

Peter and Sarah was already asleep. I could but wonder that the girl could fall easily to sleep after her ordeal, but she was that way, able to absorb the most momentuous things as easily as she absorbed the inconsequential. George, however, was in full attention, nor did it seem to us inappropriate that he be included.

Eremus Lodi told his story with few interruptions, as if he had planned in detail for a long time how he would proceed, what details he would include, how his story would begin, and how it would end.

"I come west a long time ago, a lad of nineteen, orphaned many years earlier and raised by an old rationalist who encouraged me in my westering.

"I brought with me a new wife, and along the trail she bore a baby boy. But both died before we crossed the river, brought down by the fever. It has been a long, long time gone. I could not now call up her face or her voice or even her form with any great accuracy. I laid them both east of the river, at the foot of a great tree.

"I did not see any warning in that. I grieved, but considered it only ill-fortune, always to be expected, ere ye humankind. It was greed that moved me, greed for the kind of land and fortune that I could ne'er expect to acquire in the settled eastern lands.

"This was even before the Spanish encouraged both Christian and Indian across the river and into their territory, knowing that once settled with land, both might be counted upon to resist any other kind of dominion that might jeopardize that.

"It was not until later that the Spanish offered land as incentive to settlement and carefully avoided enforcement of their anti-Protestant stand. Still, that did not keep either Protestant or anyone else with the courage to come across from doin' so. Indeed there was a few Spaniards that they could no way hold back them settlers, nor keep them from taking whate'er land they could.

"These lands back then was especially unsettled; few Christians dared much beyond the river. There was some traders and of course the Indians. So that when, as a normal and healthy man needs must, I took me another wife, she was Indian, rather she was a half-breed Indian, her mother being completely white." He stopped, nodded, "Hannah," he said.

"Nor was Hannah's story altogether unusual. The Indians then, as now, could ne'er be trusted. They might kill most wantonly and then turn around and take prisoner, killing some of those or turning them into slaves or, often in the case of children, adopting them into the tribe. Such was Hannah's story, a prisoner of the Indians, adopted, and then wed, so completely assimilated into the tribe it was virtually impossible for her or for anyone else to tell that she was not Indian.

"To my knowledge she bore only two children before her warrior husband was killed in battle with the white. Her son Pewannee, who grew tall and proud, led a group of outlawed Indians across the river into Spanish lands.

"There was some murmuring against Hannah after her beautiful daughter, much coveted by certain of the warriors, was wed to a white man, but so long as she had the sanctuary of her son, she was in no danger."

Eremus Lodi paused at that point and stared into the flames, and for a moment I was afeared that he would cease his story, for I was much taken with it and anxious for him to continue. As if he read my apprehension, he looked directly at me and then started speaking again.

"My own position with the Indian was tenuous. I was the brother-in-law of the chief and so enjoyed certain privileges usually denied white men—at least for a time. And my beautiful wife bore me yet another son, this one surviving and growing tall and handsome, in blood more white than red, but in bearing more red than white."

Eremus Lodi stopped to think, again staring into the fire. I glanced at Cyrus, wondering if this confession from Eremus Lodi had taken him by as much surprise as it had me. But Cyrus remained expressionless.

"The Indian," he went on, "can be wild and terrible, capable of a consuming rage and riotous and irrational behavior. He can be most horrible.

"Yet I did not, nor do I, hold that against him, for it has been his nature and his religion for eons and should we expect a little exposure to Christianity, especially as it has been practiced against him, to erase all of those pagan centuries, most especially when Christians exposed to 1800 years of Christianity are themselves guilty of some of the same kinds of rage and horrible behavior?"

He looked up at Cyrus, but it was not possible to read the expression upon his face. He went on.

376

"Upon two occasions I have felt the concerted force of that Indian barbarity, yet I accept it as their nature, though occasionally the bitterness of it will rise in me," he added.

"The Indian cause is lost. It has been lost for better than a hundred years, indeed ye can argue that the loss was inevitable from the very moment that the white man stepped upon this continent. Tecumseh the Shawnee, brave and brilliant as he is, has come too late. The Indian Savior does not signal the beginning of his reign, as the Christian Savior, but rather the end of it. And the Indian, I think, is futiley and angrily aware of it."

He stopped talking, and I heard my own voice break the silence, speaking out, as I sometimes did, without realizing that I was going to. "That may be, Master Lodi, that the Indian cause is lost, but surely the Indian an't lost. He will needs only be absorbed into the culture, learn to farm and govern as the white man does, give up war and accept the inevitable. Mayhap he does not want to, but he will have to, an' then he will be safe."

Cyrus and Eremus Lodi looked at each other, and I intercepted that look and was some provoked, for it said most clear, "Ah, poor weak-minded woman, how little she understands!"

"Well!" I snapped.

"Ah, my dear lady," said Eremus Lodi at last, "did everyone think as you do, then there would be no problem. But history is not writ that way, nor do I see any reason to expect history to suddenly change its manner. The only thing, Madam, that will be beat into plowshares is the vanquished. It is part of the prize of the victor, defeat and humiliation of the vanquished."

Embarrassed, I looked again at Cyrus, finding myself once more provoked that his expression would give away so little of what he thought, while my own blabbered every secret I had.

"For several years," Eremus Lodi went on at last, "as I have mentioned earlier, there has been much wild tribal purifying, appeasement of the angry Great Spirit, such purification rites directed largely within. Wanton and merciless executions for no real reason that is apparent from without."

Here he paused again with a sardonic expression upon his face. "I wonder," he mused at last, "how much different the savage has been in that as the Christian over the ages? That is to say such behavior," he went on, "has not been confined altogether to the unenlightened of the world."

He stopped and stared at his shoetops and then again at the useful flames. George was the only one who moved and he shifted in his chair. I chided myself for having interrupted Eremus Lodi's train of thought and was now afraid that, having suffered us some tantalizing information, he would of a sudden back off. Then I tried to chide myself for curiosity over that which was none of my business.

Truth to tell, I was relieved when he commenced to speak again. "I can say that for a brief time I was a happy man, which is a condition that since early childhood I have had little familiarity with. I had a fine son and a loving wife, and no man, Sir," he said this directly to Cyrus, "should ever ask more of this life." Cyrus ducked his head, and I could not catch his expression.

"But happiness is not ever a constant condition. Perhaps it is grace that I should have strived for."

"Grace?" said George. I had all but forgotten his presence still had he been.

"Grace, boy," said Eremus Lodi, "an't happiness, but only the closest state ye can really come to permanent happiness. It is a condition that I have observed not only in predestinarian Baptists, but in assorted folk of all persuasions, including in some cases the pagan and infidel."

To George's questioning look, he explained, "Grace, lad, as I've seen it evidenced in all of you and in your group and have studied it and thought upon it a good deal since I've knowed you, is that capacity to rest when ye sleep, to be filled when ye eat, the honest reward of a day of labor. Indeed," he added slowly, "the past few months I have come as close to the Kingdom of Heaven as I ever dare hope, its satisfaction and peace. If there is such a thing as sin, Sir and Madam, it must be in departing from the group," he added after a pause.

"But for that brief respite some years gone, I have been an aimless drifter, wandering back and forth along the river's edge, as a fenced animal its cage—the cage of my being that holds my soul. What would you do, Sir," he turned abruptly to Cyrus, "how would you think did you look at that horizon and know in your soul that there was naught beyond but more of the same forever and ever unto infinity?"

The conversation had taken a strange and unsettling turn. In some alarm I looked at Cyrus, but he quite calmly and quietly answered the question that had been put to him, "Why if I truly thought that, Sir, I'd be empty and hollow, a pitiful shell."

"Ah," said Eremus Lodi.

The silence then was profound, and again I heard myself speaking, this time quite calm, saying what I could ne'er have foretold, but speaking because the moment insisted that I speak. I knowed in some instinctive way that the time had come.

"Sir," I said to Eremus Lodi, "you erred in your story long ago, did you not?"

"How is that, Madam?"

"When George's hand was so wickedly burned, it was not an ordinary river scum simply torturing the boy, was it? It was some greater evil of which you knowed. Mindlessly it throwed the little boy at you, and the babe landed in the flame. An't that right? Nor did you lift a hand toward it, much less fire your pistol at it?"

Well. That got their attention.

"Mama?" murmured George, his face gone pale, but not so pale as Eremus Lodi's.

378

"Madam," said Eremus Lodi slowly, regaining something of his composure, "where came you by your information?"

I did not answer and after a pause George spoke up, "I remembered it, Sir, from the dream-memory of childhood it come back to me."

"Ah," said Eremus Lodi. He made no denial but looked steadfastly into the flames without blinking or moving for a long moment. At last he murmured, "The Grace of God is denied me perhaps forever, but at least in this life. Madam and Sir," he sighed, "now you needs must have all the story, and I shall tell it."

With something like a deep breath he began again. "I shall continue with my Indian connection and then go a way back beyond that.

"As I told you, I was happily married and fathered, but after a time, I commenced to notice small but alarming changes in the savages toward therselves and toward me. It seemed a kind of frustration, and of a sudden, almost overnight, there seemed an unusual pagan religious frenzy, which grew and seemed to feed upon itself.

"It was about that time—fate seems ne'er happier than when bashing you upon the head at the most inconvenient of moments—that my beloved wife took ill with one of those sicknesses that you can neither diagnose nor treat. She faded and at last died, leaving both son and husband bereft.

"My son, at that rebellious age, very early manhood, on a whim betook himself to his Indian family and deserted me. There, after only a few months, he fell into an argument with his cousin, Kuleeniah. They fought. It was an honest fight, I was told, but in the end, my only son lay dead.

"Wh'er it was guilt or pity or anger over his sister's death, or the sudden violent religious fervor, I know not, but Pewannee not only sided with his son but cast me out and away from them, citing only my white blood. And in short order, again from what source, I know not, but do suspect the same religious fervor, drove away his old mother, who would have chosen death had I not come to her aid. I do not know that she has ever forgiven me that, the fact that she still lives, but being human and feeble, she cannot will her own death and so is sentenced by her weakness to live."

I could not contain a tear, and I turned away, wh'er the tear was for Eremus Lodi, his son, his wife, or for old Hannah, I could not say.

"For most people," he went on, "to be driven from the group is death, the end, for the group is the meaning of life. Good and evil, Sir," Eremus Lodi turned toward Cyrus, "are the province of the group, for the solitary, they have little meaning. The fruit from the tree of knowledge is the understanding that you're not a part of the body of God, that you are separate. Knowledge, Sir, is sorrow and sorrow is pain."

Abruptly then, he returned to his story. "The pagan religious revival of which I spoke was most markedly increased with the coming of the comet last season and then the earthquakes. It cannot be hard to imagine the reaction of the pagan mind to those.

"In the hard mountains they was not so much felt, but many Indians was killed or disappeared in the basins both south and east of here, and the news traveled through all the tribes and encampments that the Great Spirit was mightily angered over the white encroachments of Indian lands and would destroy both the whites for so doing and the Indians for letting them." He bit his lip and considered for a while, shrugged then, and went on.

"I think that Kuleeniah, now grown and ambitious, either believes all of that or at least makes use of it for his own purposes. It is he who is adamant that the Indians purge themselves, most especially he. For he afflicts himself with most horrendous scars and fasts and travails for to purge that white blood within himself. Withal, he is three part Indian to one part white, while my own son was three part white to one part Indian. It may well have been Kuleeniah's influence that drove his old grandmother away. For it has always seemed to me that Pewannee was a reasonable and sensible man, only caught up in the frenzy of the day.

"I do not know why I did not think myself of the danger to your red-haired children, for that red scalp, the color of blood, is the prize of the frenzy. How Hannah found out that there were red-haired children, I know not, for her ways are yet the Indian ways, ways that are not even comprehensible to those who have studied the Indian for a long time."

I looked at Cyrus and he looked at me, and our alarm must have been apparent, for Eremus Lodi said gently, "Fear not. Pewannee has freed them; they are under his protection and safe. This much he did in the name of family, at his own mother's request and mine, for I called in the debt of a son, and he paid it."

He rose then, pulled out his pipe, and struggled with it until he got it lighted. Cyrus likewise rose and fetched an armload of wood from outside and stoked the fire again, for night was proceeding in its accustomed manner, and the cooler air was replacing the warmer.

At last Eremus Lodi sat again and studied the tidy flames and commenced to speak again.

"And now," he said, "I must speak of great and real evil, for the Indians is not evil. As all groups must to survive, they live by a code, wh'er that code seems evil or not depends on wh'er or not ye subscribe to it," he added.

"What I must speak of is that mindless evil, raging nature, or that which laughs at us through our own eyes."

The stillness then was broken only by the sputtering of the fire, for some of the wood must have been damp or green.

"I told ye that I would speak of a time a ways back, and so I shall," said Eremus Lodi at last. "I was the child of westerers, a father whose big eye beheld the virgin land and coveted it. There was brothers and sisters, for I was born about the middle of the brood, as well as aunts, uncles, and cousins, all westerers.

"We followed the sun, crossing Carolina to that far western part which would eventually become the state of Franklin and later Tennessee.

"As a child I knowed naught else, was not taught, for we was all un-learned, though mightily skilled in the way of the woods, as we had to be to survive. The Indian was always a threat, but then so too was chills and fevers and agues, not to mention hunger and cold. They was all one that we accept-ed because we knowed no other way.

"We stayed close, cabins near enough for protection and comfort, but withal there was none else but our little group within several miles of us. Still, with brothers, sisters, and cousins we was not lonely, indeed, I remem-ber it as a pleasant, exciting childhood.

"One such cousin was Barnaby Burris, the son of my father's sister. Barnaby was perhaps a year or maybe two older, but we was both big for our ages and developed a strong bond. It was, I think, the kind of bond that sometimes comes between dissimilar types, for though skilled enough of the woods, I was even then of a more in-looking temperament, given to solitary ways and deep thought, or at least such deep thought as an unlettered boy can entertain." At this point Eremus Lodi paused long enough to reload his pipe and then continued.

"Perhaps it was not even deep thought so much as questions that I was too innocent to be able to form. Barnaby, however, was of just the opposite turn. For he would act before he would think, impulsive and excitable, ne'er given to thinking things through, and indeed, being a little the older, he was the one most inclined to get us into the mischief that betimes we got into.

"At any rate, Barnaby and me, as boys will do, played, fought, played some more, explored, and passed on much misinformation about the myster-ies that haunted us, as boys have always done and always will do. And so we might have grown to manhood thus, as any pioneer boys, and that would be all of the story, but for the event which overtook us and over which we had no control." He paused again and then said gruffly, "I shall tell it or not, for it an't pretty?"

I looked at Cyrus, who finally said quietly, "I think you've gone too far, Sir, not to go on."

Eremus Lodi nodded and then began talking. "I have ne'er told this story in its entirety to any other living soul, though it has lived with me night and day since that afternoon of my late boyhood. I will tell it simply as I can.

"Barnaby and I had been out all afternoon, for it was early fall, and though we had orders to bring in wood, we had not let them orders get in the way of our pleasure, and we had roamed far and wide and knowed as the af-ternoon waned that we was probably both due and like to get a caning. Being boys, I suppose we felt the pleasure worth the price.

"The way that our trail wound would take us by my cabin before we got to Barnaby's, and we approached quietly, in some apprehension, I suppose, over how we expected to be greeted. The apprehension proved to be our sal-vation—or mine at least." Eremus Lodi stopped, stared at the fire, and took a deep breath and then went on.

"As we approached, I think we both sensed that all was not well. For one thing, it was most unnaturally silent, and for another, I seem to recall—though memory may be faulty in this—an odor that I have since identified as blood, the same smell, I think, that ye find at hog butchering time, of blood and singed hair and boiling water.

"Barnaby and I paused and looked at each other without speaking. I think we both sensed the same thing, fer we was children of the deep woods, and we relied upon our senses, as all the woodseys did, for survival.

"Cautiously, slowly we approached the clearing and seen the first bloody body, one of the smaller girls, though in truth, it was in such condition that it was hard to tell which one. The sight was grisly and ghastly, the small head unrecognizable, its hair gone, the rest of it naught but blood and gore. Perhaps that was our salvation, for we could not feel for that mess and run in sympathy and grief to it. It shocked us into total silence. And thus we stood, as still as oak trees, for I could not say how long.

"At length, a lone Indian appeared from the front of the cabin, looked around, yawned, and staggered about the clearing until he settled in a drunken pile against side of the cabin.

"Still we waited. At last it come to us, that he was the only one, most likely as events proved, a guard left or simply too drunk to follow the rest, for the silence all around give us to know that there was no one else there—at least no one living.

"I was a stiff from terror that I was a long time in arriving at any rational thought, and when I finally did, I begun to hope that small child that lay butchered before us was the only one and that somehow the rest of the family had escaped and run for help.

"I was to be disappointed in that."

He stopped once more, almost overcome, it seemed. "I told you," he murmured at last, "that I have ne'er spoke any of this aloud in all them intervening years. The words come harder than I might have thought they would."

We waited, for I could not think of any word of comfort, and mayhap, neither could Cyrus. George, in his boy's way, was much intent upon the story, and though I knowed him to be deeper than most boys his age, still he was a boy and had not the experience of mature emotion to comprehend the acute horror of it.

"It was Barnaby who at last begun to move, motioning me after him, and I followed dumbly not knowing, I suppose, what else to do. We circled the clearing, keeping to the heavy growth, quiet as fear could make us, for we could make our way through the woods almost as stealthily as any Indian.

"The sight that greeted us when at last arrived at the front of the cabin, was more horrible than I could have dreamed in any nightmare. I froze with it and so did Barnaby, though I remember that at last, I tried to call out, but Barnaby clapped his hands over my mouth, and there we stood and stared at what was left of my family.

"I tried to count them, but they lay in dismembered heaps, without scalps. My two older sisters and my mother I recognized only by the clothes, even though those had been torn, mostly, from their bodies.

"'Don't look, turn away,' muttered Barnaby, yet I could not no more than could he, for our eyes was riveted upon that terrible sight.

"My father—whom I could recognize only by his size, for he was far and away the biggest man I knowed—had been flayed and scalped. My mother and my sisters, I knowed, had been most terribly mistreated." He stopped again and stared at the floor. "In all the years that I have gone over and over the details of that sight, I have tried for something that would tell me that they was all dead before such depredations was laid upon them. But there was no such evidence. I have ne'er, not a single conscious night of my existence, failed to dream of them and recall all their agonies and take them for my own.

"It was not a single Indian that done all that, we knowed. The one left, for whate'er reason, lay in drunken sleep, but there was others, and we had no way to know where they was. That was a hard, clear fact, that more real to us at that moment than the reality of them corpses. It was the reality of the corpses that would overcome me later.

"I might have stood there until I took root had it not been for Barnaby. I heard him cursing and then, with a sudden movement, he whipped out his knife and dashed so quickly and so silently across the clearing that I was a moment understanding his purpose.

"By the time that I understood and dashed after him, the drunken Indian was already dead, Barnaby kneeling over him, slashing repeatedly at the quivering body, mutilating it, covered with the Indian's gore. I dragged him at last away. His eyes was wild, yet he made not a single sound that I remember. I can only remember them raging eyes.

"We slipped back into the woods, then sat and got ourselves together. If there was danger to us, there was danger to everyone else, for there was several cabins around, and we determined that we needed to sound the warning, even as I think, deep inside us, we knowed the futility of it.

"You ne'er could know what them Indians would do. They might strike and leave and ne'er be seen again or they might systematically destroy everything and everybody they could find. That they had left behind one of their own suggested to that they had not simply struck and then disappeared into the forest. I think we knowed the odds of what awaited at them other cabins. Still, quietly and stealthily, we made our way through the woods toward Barnaby's cabin."

Eremus Lodi lapsed into silence once more. I was by then so stiff with terror that my very arms ached with it, and yet the events he chronicled had took place many years gone by.

"What we found at Barnaby's cabin was even more horrendous, if possible, than what we had found at mine, for the Indians was still there, still involved in their atrocities, so far gone in drink that they was in no way careful, but was making drunken noise and revelry as if they was at a party; indeed, by ther lights perhaps they was.

"It was growing dark by that time, but the cabin having been torched and a great bonfire resulting illuminated the scene. There was scalped bodies all about, and the Indians, mayhap a dozen of them, making great sport over them.

"I heard the hard intake of breath beside me and a hiss, like I might imagine volcanic steam, released from Barnaby. I grabbed at his arm and attempted to pull him back, realizing, I think, what was like to happen. I might indeed have succeeded, but at that moment the Indians' attention was all drawed to a tree with a form hanging from it. In the torchlight, we could see it all too well. It was naked and it was a woman, the gray hair—for it still retained its scalp—giving testimony to its identity. My aunt, Barnaby's mother."

I gasped. I looked at Cyrus and then at George. Their expressions was stern as they stared at Eremus Lodi.

"I could tell at a glance that she was dead, her soul mercifully departed. The Indians was only making sport of the corpse, stripping flesh from the bones, to what purpose who could say, for they was far gone in drunkeness. I tried to pull Barnaby away. I remember whispering urgently that we needed to get away, that they was too drunk to notice. But Barnaby didn't hear. He was breathing hard as a winded horse, stiff in rage.

"'Barn,' I remember whispering, 'Barn, let's go, let's go!' But either he did not hear me or did not heed me, for with a sudden loud shriek, his knife out and poised, he darted in among the Indians, flailing away at them. I stayed where I was only long enough to realize that they had him down, and then I tore through the brush, dashing wildly as if the devil was on my heels.

"But I did not get away fast enough to keep from hearing his final screams, shrieks of pain and terror in the night.

"I lay that night, finally, in exhaustion, deep in the woods, waiting daylight and what it would bring. Even after the day turned bright, I did not leave my spot. I stayed hidden through most of the day. I knowed the manner of Indians well enough to realize that they would surely be gone by then, and so I slipped back toward the cabin. I cannot say why I went, or what drawed me. Remember, I was but a boy and a very frightened boy at that.

"The stench of death was all over by then, permeating everything. I felt it attach itself to me and cling to me. I approached the clearing where the cabin still smouldered, and the Indians was indeed gone, the mutilated forms lying much as I recalled them.

"And I saw Barnaby, then, lying near to the tree where his mother's carcass still hung. There was horrible gashes all over him, his face torn. I could not bring myself to go to any of them, but I had the feeling that Bamaby was not yet dead, for his form was not stiff as the others was.

"I went for help. But I was a long time finding any, for the Indians had been systematic, and the scene at the other three cabins that comprised our group was similar to what I had left behind.

"In time I did find my way to another such settlement that I knowed existed, and back we went, a large party of armed men with me. We buried our dead. But," here Eremus Lodi looked up at, "Barnaby Burris was not among them. His body was not there. Nor to my knowledge was it ever found."

He fussed again with his pipe. "Eventually I found a home with an old solitary, an old rationlist who was a solitary for reasons of his own that I ne'er inquired into. But he was a man of learning, had books aplenty, and took my education in hand.

"He did not ask after my experience, nor did I offer him any explanation. Yet I can't but think that he knowed it all, for he encouraged me in rational thought, in understanding that there are things over which we have no control, and that guilt over such is ne'er warranted. I think that he tried to instill in me the realization that what I had done was the only sensible, rational thing to do, that Barnaby's rashness was only that, as there was no way that his act could change anything.

"Yet," here he sighed, "I am haunted, and I think that term not undue, by pain and memory. And," he looked up at each of us in turn, his expression strange and distant, "I have been followed for many years by that strange critter, that beast ye speak of. It tracks me. I cannot explain it. I only know that it comes and goes. It rises regularly out of the swampland to meet me, ever accusing and angry, and then disappears for a while."

The silence then was overpowering. I was afeared even to look up, and I heard a small sigh escape George. It was Cyrus at last that asked the question that troubled us all. "You think then that the beast is what is left of Barnaby Burris?"

Eremus Lodi did not answer forthwith, but fussed with his pipe and stared hard into the fire. Finally, he spoke with a smile that held little actual mirth, "Ah, that hardly seems probable, does it? Barnaby Burris, when I last seen him, was far east of the river, mortally wounded. How over the years could he have made his way to the river and beyond just to haunt me?

"For The Beast an't a ghost. Too many have seen him and know him to be all too real. No, though in the dark night I may sweat and swear, in the daylight I know such idea is not rational. That The Beast is likely only one of them solitaries betimes attacked by a bear or painter, lost his reason. The solitary life has bred lunatics before, you know."

"Do you believe that?" asked Cyrus abruptly.

"Yes, Sir, I do believe that. It is only that in those dark nights, or during living dreams brought on by a sick mind—such dreams and such sickness as I would not detail you—that I think I know The Beast and he is me."

"Sir?"

"Ah, that is no rational thought, is it? No. But there are times that I think my soul escapes me and runs amok and that The Beast is my own evil, made carnate, that I am without a soul."

At that my own memory come to life, and I recalled just such words— where? "It is my own dark soul, Madam. A man is not more than beast without his soul. And as I am without a permanent soul of my own, I keep a spare, which shadows me and comes to me in need." O'Reilly? Where did I remember it from? Before I could chase down that elusive memory, however, Eremus Lodi begun to speak again.

"Ah, Sir and Madam, I speak methaphorically, of course. I am a rational man—except of course when I am irrational," he added with that twisted grin of his.

"Your memories, Sir, are frightening," said Cyrus at last, "yet I am sure they are true. Such stories of Indian butchery and barbarity, especially in the early days before the Revolution, were not so uncommon. And yet, still you champion the red man?"

Eremus Lodi seemed to consider that apparent contradiction for a while, and then he answered, "In truth I do. For their cause is just. I have said to you before that the Indian is the product of eons of his own religion and rules and conscience, and he is mostly honorable in the light of that conscience. Nor would it be rational to condemn an entire race because of the violences of a few drunken, young bucks.

"I have knowed the Indian for a long time, as much as any outsider can know him. I respect him, I respect his ways, even though his ways have cost me much. Perhaps I respect him more for that I can foresee his decline, which though unfair, seems inevitable."

It was growing late by then, but I knowed that I would not sleep after such a tale, so we might as well sit and talk.

"I cannot but wonder," said Cyrus at last, "at why this sudden attack upon us by the Indians, as they have been generally non-threatening?"

"That concerns me, too, Sir," said Eremus Lodi at last. "I have no doubt that Kuleeniah was anxious to take some scalps. I do not understand why, unless it is simply an extension of the purification rites that I have told you of. But those have been so far solely within the tribes. Indeed there has been little of the violence perpetrated against the settler as you had east of the river in days gone."

"Sir?" I said, recalling that I did have a question, "can you explain why them river scum, Drooly and that other, would be amongst them Indians? What is their purpose?"

"Madam," replied Eremus Lodi, "I would give worlds to understand that, for them two are wicked and evil as can be, mindless, too. Whate'er the Indian is, he an't mindless, and he can certainly recognize the filthy nature of such as Drooly. I simply do not know. What I do know is that it is not ac- cident, that there is reason for it. It is," he added grimly, "my suspicion that it was them white scum that took the scalps of them murdered blacks, fer The Beast does not take scalps. It is only a scavenger, nor will the Indian generally take the scalp of a black."

It was right late before we all bedded down, and much as I would have doubted it, sleep come right away and I woke abruptly at early morning, strangely refreshed after a most frightening experience.

Chapter 26

Kuleeniah

So we went about our business, a little more cautious perhaps than we had been, but our routine was set, and we kept to it as the busy days of spring commenced to run into summer.

Eremus Lodi, far from disappearing after his strange confession, was wont to come and go, sometimes staying to sup or sleep, at other times watching for a time in near silence from his black horse and then disappearing as he had come.

O'Reilly the black was strangely absent during those summer months.

The men was extra busy as they had to help the Morphew sisters with their crop, the question of buying more slaves a ticklish one, for there was none in the area that we knowed of, and most of us was not comfortable with that idea anyway.

The crops was good, the weather hot but fine, and the summer danced by, and with its passing many of our cares seemed to lift. We saw little of the Indians but those come to the trading post, in the main the older braves, fewer than in the early spring, but as far as I was concerned that was good enough.

There was no sign of The Beast, and Redmon Pitt seemed to recover himself without ill effect, though I suspected that he was not given to wandering far abroad by himself any more.

Accustomed as we was to living on the rugged edge of the world, we was all able to absorb all the excitements and put them aside, just as we had done the earthquakes. It was indeed amazing to think that them earthquakes—which still occasionally troubled—was nearing two years from the first of them.

And I was content. Each passing day the babe within me seemed to grow, and it was of course not long until even the slowest sort could figure it out. I was teased some about my condition, which was usual, though a little more gentle than might have been with someone who give birth more easily than I did. Everyone was happy, most especially Cyrus and Sarah, who I think looked forward to having a new toy to play with. Alas, how soon she would learn!

One morning early on a fall day as I was busy about my chores, something caused me to look up, and I beheld a-walking down the path to the house, casual and big as life, Jacob the riverman, a big grin upon his face.

Well. Here he was come overland again, and I greeted him enthusiastically and he me. Yet there was an apprehension about me, for Jabob was not fond of traveling any path but the river. And he come alone, afoot, without any provisions.

The riverman Jacob proved to be his own cheerful self, full of winks for the children and merry tales for all. "The earth still shakes," he said, "but don't nobody pay much mind to it now. Of course, an't not a lot of people left to notice. But them that's left consider that the Lord missed as good a chance as he e'er had to sink the wretched and so they don't worry no more.

"Now the river still's a mess and betimes will stay thataway, but don't think that keeps the traffic from it at all. But it'll sure give ye a merry ride all the way to the fourth Chickasaw Bluff and beyond."

Jacob settled himself in such manner, yet I knowed and so did Cyrus that something of import had to have brought him all the way from the river, for he affirmed that the travel had been passing hard, as that land that had been dry in the summer was with the sudden fall rains sodden and impassable in spots. It was not for idle gossip and conversation that he was come.

"Otto," he laughed at one point, "is a changed man, fer it's as a load was lifted an' as glum as he was betimes, he is now so cheerful that them that has always knowed him is givin' to peekin' over ther shoulders to see if it's real."

Jacob, being a good and willing worker, throwed himself into activities where'er he was needed, joking and storying as was his wont. Yet I knowed that there was something behind it all, and I wondered that he could not seem to bring himself to tell it.

At last I could wait no longer, and of a early evening, after we'd supped and the children played, chasing and tagging one another the way children do, I spoke up abruptly. "Jacob," I said, "have you come here a-purpose to tell us something or not?"

He did not answer directly, but I could tell from the way he frowned and studied the ground and twisted his two hands in front of him that he was seriously considering the question and that told me that the question had not been frivolous.

"Ma'am," he said at last, "an', Sir, in truth I an't much of a serious person. I learn't a long time ago that ye fare far better d'ye not let nobody take ye serious. Still, I watch and listen, and though I an't the skill to write me own name ner read it, ther's other things I read right well and absorb and understand, things that learned doctors and preachers and such ne'er could, no matter how well writ er spoke they is."

He paused at that and we waited, for Cyrus was as much curious of what the riverman would have to tell us as I was.

"Fer the most part, I just keep what I know to meself, because fer the most part, it don't make no difference one way or t'other. But," and here he sighed an uncharacteristic sad sigh, "I've now learn't too much to keep to meself and find that it needs must overrun, like the spring freshet does the river."

He stopped and then with some frowning and fidgeting he at last went on. "I come to speak to ye of Eremus Lodi an' to tell ye things of which I've hinted before, things that I knowed and things that I suspicioned then and now know to be true—things that I told ye onct was both better and worse than ye might expect."

He sighed again, and I started to speak up and tell him that we had already got Eremus Lodi's story and that from the source itself, but I caught myself. As I could not know what the riverman had to say, would he only confirm what we already knowed or would he add something to it, I held my peace.

"Eremus Lodi, ye know, has been a dark legend up and down the river fer as long as I have memory, how much longer than that I cain't say. I only know that they said then as now that some dark spirit follered in his tracks, that the devil was ne'er far behind him.

"In truth, it did seem that strange and sometimes horrible things would occur before or after he passed. But I always considered much of that simple witchery. D'ye know what I mean by witchery?" he asked suddenly.

I shook my head.

"Folks is given to claimin' witchery fer any strange or unhappy or unexplainable event. An' ther like to pick out some person to blame that witchery on, y'know."

I nodded at that, for I was aware that such had been and still was sometimes the case.

"Wal, when ye live on the border on the hard edge of the wilderness, ther's no end of the things that can go wrong with no help from the devil or witches at all. Any sensible persons should know that. So that was how I explained to meself much of the stories about Eremus Lodi.

"In truth, however," he said frowning some, "Eremus Lodi did comport hisself in such manner sometimes as to draw such accusation down upon him. Fer as long as I have been on the river and old enough to know of such things, I have knowed that Eremus Lodi wandered the western bank, north to south, and that betimes he could be found haunting places of too vile a nature to be explained.

"Don't ask how I know of that, fer I care not to talk of it, only to tell ye that ther are places along the river that traffic in the kinds of things that ye'd best remain ignorant of and which Eremus Lodi betimes availed himself of in copious quantities.

"Fer he was given to sper'ts and opiates from the east and all the ruinous activities that accompany those." Looking up, the riverman pinned Cyrus with his eyes and announced coldly, "I doubt that ther is any vile thing that the man has not participated in."

Cyrus nodded slightly, but that was all.

"However," Jacob continued, "as I said afore, Eremus Lodi is both better and worse than ye think. It is clear that he does not want the settlers to cross the river into the lands that he alone claims fer the Indians. But of that I'll have more to say anon.

"But the settlers will come and have come. Once on his side of the river, those settlers, ere they deservin' of it, at least, fall under the protection of the man. Ther's many a family survived barren winters because Eremus Lodi took it upon hisself to furnish food or medicine. An' ther's many river scum that now feed the fishies because that man chose to rid the land of them. I know that." He stopped again, leaving me to speculate upon what he had said.

I realized suddenly that my heart was tight in my chest and my innards was heavy and I held my two hands tighter than they ought to be held.

"But it is the Injuns that Eremus Lodi has seemed to take under his special pertection, in a way that don't make no sense to me, that is strange and unnatural. I have heard certain rumors of him, of his Injun wife and son, but that don't go to explain it all. Now, ther's them that puts it to greed, that claims that Eremus Lodi sides with the Injun to protect these lands agin' settlers. Ah, but the Eremus Lodi that I think I know an't greedy in that way, though truth of it is, any man has his own kind of greed, fer sure." He looked up at that as if to see did we agree with him, and again Cyrus returned him a slight nod.

"Now," he went on, "is the problem. Ther's plenty of us has suspected all along that Eremus Lodi's sympathies in this war was not with the Americans, and probably not with the British either, but with the Injun. Wal, the way it stacks up, d'ye sympathize with the Injun, ye must therefore champion the British cause, too. Fer the Injun and the British an' likewise Eremus Lodi have that same goal, which is retarding the westward settling.

"Wal," said the riverman, "it's now time to get to the meat of me story. The rumors that has had Eremus Lodi givin' aid and comfort to the enemy has at last been confirmed, at least, they say, confirmed to the satisfaction of the American officials, and they say that warrant fer his arrest is made or bein' made."

The riverman made that announcement casually and with so little excitement that it took a moment for the full realization of it to hit me.

"Arrest?" I heard my voice made hollow, I suspect, from the void that had suddenly hit my midsection.

The riverman nodded. "I come away as fast as I could onct I heard that. I don't know Eremus Lodi to speak to him, to warn him, but I knowed that ye was clos't to him and so I brung ye the information to use as ye see fit. That's all."

After a long silence in which images and ideas rattled around my brain, I heard Cyrus calmly ask, "What details do you bring?"

"Wal," answered the riverman, "from listenin' to this and that information over several years, I feel safe to tell ye that Eremus Lodi has indeed been in contact with both the British and with the eastern Injun, most particularly the Shawnee Tecumseh. Don't no one know, of course, exactly what that contact was all about, only that it was frequent and friendly.

"Eremus Lodi upon his frequent trips up and down the river has been knowed to meet with various trappers and Injuns that worked with the British, and that black O'Reilly has trekked several times to meet with Tecumseh, here or there, fer as ye probably know, that Injun's travels has took him to all parts of this country and, indeed, beyond.

"It an't so easy," he added quietly, "to foller the tracks of O'Reilly, but big and black as he is, it an't possible fer him to remain perfectly hidden neither. Wal, this bit of information and that bit—some only gossip, some fact—will add up d'ye have the 'sperience to winnow th'u it."

He sighed and then went on, "Most recent ere the several stories of the black headed north. Wh'er he got so far as Moraviantown, wal, I an't heard that," he added.

"Moraviantown?" said Cyrus.

"Ah," said Jacob, "ye an't heard? I thought prob'ly not. The news has drifted down the river, true it seems to be, that a battle fought at Moraviantown in Canada, between the Injuns and the British on the one side and the Americans on the other, has resulted in a great loss fer the British cause. Very great indeed. Tecumseh the Shawnee is dead."

No one spoke for a moment, all three, I suspect, trying to absorb that fact, even Jacob who had brought it. The Shawnee Tecumseh had been a part of frontier lore for so long almost as I could recall, his legend growing so great that at times it seemed almost impossible that he could be a simple mortal. He was, many people had said time after time, the Indian Cause. Without him there could be no Cause.

But that O'Reilly, that honorable black, and Eremus Lodi might be a part of that conspiracy between Indian and British was so startling that my whole heart and mind wanted desperately to reject it. But I had too much experience of Jacob the riverman's reliability in such matters, his ability to sift through all manners of gossip and idle conversation to find the truth.

At last Cyrus spoke. "Eremus Lodi, then, is wanted by the United States government for treasonous acts? What of O'Reilly?"

"Ah, I don' know that. It's some legal problem, him bein' a slave and bound to his master's instructions. Truth is, I an't heard him mentioned in that connection. Far as I know, Eremus Lodi is who they want."

"What's he to do?" I cried.

"Wal," shrugged the riverman, "he can give up or be captured and likely hung, or he can turn outlaw and lose hisself into the wilderness. That last makes most sense, of course, as ther's a sight more wilderness than ther is Americans to search it, an' Eremus Lodi is certain a woodsman of good account and could survive as them solitaries survives. I an't," he said slowly, "about to try to tell Eremus Lodi his business, ner would I get caught up meself with the American government, but lack I've said, though I cain't read me own name er write it, why, the lessons of the river have taught me much more I think than lessons from a book could ever. Among them things I think I understand is the nature of various human kinds.

"What I ere tryin' to say, I think," he sighed, rubbing his calloused fingers together, "is that Eremus Lodi be an honorable man, fer honorableness has to be called by the circumstances yer in. By his own lights he done as he done, an' I cain't find it in me heart to fault him fer it. But," he added, looking hard at Cyrus, "he needs must be warned, an' it's possible that he an't heard yet of the fate of the Shawnee, which to my mind is likewise the fate of the Injun Cause."

Jacob did not stay out the week. "I cain't stay so long from the river," he said, "fer winter might catch me here, an' truth t'tell, a winter in the woods, with none but Baptists to converse with—to beg yer pardon—would leave me lunatic fer sure."

Well, I knowed he joked in that, but, still, he was ne'er comfortable away from the river and having done what he set out to do, he left us with it.

I waited for Cyrus to speak, but he went on about his business, nothing about him to suggest what he might be thinking, but a frown between his eyes.

What thought he worried was not clear until Brother Ray come to him and asked would he be available on the next day to help burn the brush upon the Sisters Morphew's place, for the brothers all planned to gather and be done with it in one or two days, as the bright fall days would not last much longer.

Cyrus, to my surprise and I'm certain to Brother Ray's, shook his head, his only explanation that he was called away on business. Brother Ray waited expectantly for a moment and then when no explanation was forthcoming, nodded and shortly took his leave.

"You're going to Eremus Lodi," I said. It was no question. "What think you of charges of treason?" I asked.

He only looked hard at me and then murmured, "There are things that are the proper business only of a man and his God."

"But," I said, "Eremus Lodi claims no god."

"I was not speaking of Eremus Lodi," was his answer.

Before daylight, Cyrus left, headed toward the cabin occupied by Eremus Lodi, though there could ne'er any certainty that he would be there. "I shall tell him but briefly of the speculation I have heard and leave the rest with him. What he chooses to do is his own matter."

When the sun rose at last, I was relieved to find that we had been delivered a fine, bright day. Cyrus could make his trip easily and mayhap be back before the day was out, the brothers would have an excellent day for brush burning, and the sisters would all gather at the fire near the Cuthcart's new cabin to turn our collected grease into soap. I would, I decided, send George out with the brothers to take his father's place. Had it not been for the burden that Jacob's news had laid on my heart, I would have thought it a fine day indeed, a day for accomplishment.

When I suggested to George that he go on ahead so he could join the brothers headed for the plot of land that the Morphew sisters was cultitvating, he did seem some reluctant. Well, that surprised me, and I thought that it must be his age. For he was at that age that was sometimes adult and other times child. And though he was not one to shirk his jobs, still, that there was other children about for playing with probably had something to do with his reluctance.

"Now go on, George. You're needed more by the brothers than the sisters."

"But, Mama," he started slowly. There was the trace of a frown about his forehead. "I don't think that I ought to leave you," he started, but I would not let him finish, for I knowed that he could string out a puny excuse and make it sound far more weighty than it actually was. I thought that was probably the preacher in him.

"Shame, boy," I said. "Now get you to the fields where you belong. You're too big for women's work." He started to speak again, but I just ignored that and pointed him the direction I wanted him to go. Still sporting that curious frown, he went.

And so it was that we gathered after our chores was done in front of the Cuthcart's cabin, where several big black pots had already been set up, the fires already stoked under them, several of the Cuthcart children responsible for that, I suspected. Upon a large plank table, various pieces of fat had been dumped and I added mine to that collection and joined the sisters already cleaning and chunking and sorting.

We had lye and we also had potash, so that we would have both hard and soft soap. The best part of the tallow, each of us had saved to use for candles. In short order we had the various pots a-boiling with crackling pieces of fat. And there was a steady stream of warnings and directions toward the smaller children about the danger of getting near to them pots.

That was the nice thing about a community soapmaking. It got it all over with quickly and lessened the danger of young'uns getting scalded by the fat.

And there was a copious quantity of young'uns about, of all sizes and denominations. Them that had not chores assigned them was off in various groups thinking up games or gossiping or playing. I looked at them and thought with a sigh how numbered them days was for outdoor play, and I hoped that they'd get much of the activity out of their systems, though I knowed that they probably would not, for there's nothing quite like a tiny cabin in bitter cold to make young'uns think that they need to wrestle around and fight and so forth. And then I thought me with a smile how soon, maphap six or eight weeks, we'd have another young'un of our own to winter through.

Well, it was a pleasant time. The air was crisp enough that the fires was appreciated, yet there was breeze enough that the smoke blew gently away so that we could get ahead of it and not have to suffer burning eyes and such. Nor was the work tedious, which I was grateful for, for I was at that stage of childbearing that is both awkward and tiring. There was many of us, and we did have opportunity to visit and gossip, that last some impeded by the presence of old Brother Gilbert whose gout and lumbago had kept him behind.

He didn't seem to mind and enjoyed the various attentions of the sisters. Still, with a man about, even a passing old and harmless man, we could not be as free as we otherwise might have.

Biddy Dalton and I was in charge of one of the pots, and we laughed and chatted and stirred. The Morphew sisters was seated upon a log again, and we was chuckling and giggling about that, them so neat and prim while poor Anna done twice the work to make up for it.

"Wher's my mama?" said a little voice right at my elbow. I was so startled I liked to 'a dropped my paddle right in the bubbling fat. It was one of the little Cuthcart girls. I was embarrassed that she'd got so close without my noticing.

"Well, I don't know," I said glancing around and then I seen her. She was off at the far edge of the clearing, moving quickly and quietly amongst the groups of young'uns, and one by one them young'uns broke away and made their several ways back toward the cabin.

How like a little banty hen Clara Cuthcart was. I couldn't figure why she'd be gathering them young'uns in. It wasn't close to feeding time. Myself, I'd preferred to 'a had them as far from the boiling pots as possible.

"What do you suppose she's up to?" Biddy Dalton muttered to me. So she had noticed, too.

Clara was walking back toward the cabin herself by then. She stopped to speak to Brother Gilbert, who was seated off by himself. He'd probably been dozing. That old feller got right up, at least got right up as fast as his infirmities would allow, his expression suddenly serious and watchful. I looked at Biddy and she looked back at me.

Clara marched right up to where we was and said just loud enough that all those around could understand, "Ther's somethin' not right. I went back behind the cabin a few minutes ago and the old goose was all ruffled up and squawkin', but all the other birds was still. I don't know what it is, but I sense that somethin' an't right, an' I think we better gather in the young'uns and take stock of what's goin' on."

Well. Clara Cuthcart had lived on the border all her life. Nor was she one to lose her direction over nothing slight. Was she concerned, then the rest of us ought to be, too. Brother Gilbert had already gone into the cabin, and I knowed he was taking down the long guns.

"Have we got all the young'uns in?" whispered Biddy Dalton, and by her manner of nodding her head, I could tell she was ticking off her own. I commenced to look around for mine. Peter was playing with a group of the little children watched over by a big Dalton girl and a big Cuthcart girl. But I did not immediately see Sarah.

Then I remembered that Martha Elen, having contributed the lye for the hard soap, had stayed then to mind the store and that Sarah was there with her three cousins.

"What do you think it is?" said Biddy Dalton to Clara Cuthcart.

"Well," said Clara, "could be a painter or a bear nearby, or mayhap nothin' more'n a skunk or whistle-pig. That old goose don't know a cyclone from a spring breeze. But," she added, "wan't do to take no chances."

We'd all got moderately quiet, even the young'uns, all sensing danger. Nor was it simply the disposition of a cranky old goose or even the sudden stillness of the woodland that bothered us. There's sharp senses when you live in the woods amidst all kinds of potential danger. Mayhap, even them that lives in safer climes do have that art of sense. I did not know, for I had always lived with the danger on the border and had knowed from the time I was myself a young'un that the sparrow that did not heed each crackling twig and hovering shadow was the sparrow that did not long survive. We did not just spook to no particular purpose.

We was all trading glances then and I knowed what we was all thinking. Wasn't a one of us but what could picture The Beast snatching up a young'un in its teeth and running away with it.

"I think to go to the store and stay with Martha Elen or bring her back here," I said.

"Ye prob'ly ought not," said Biddy Dalton slowly. "But. . . ," and then she paused and frowned.

"Someone needs to go to her," said Brother Gilbert from the cabin door. He leaned against a long gun.

"Probably it's nothing to worry about," I laughed, but Brother Gilbert looked grim.

"I'll go 'ith ye," he said at last. "Ther's two more rifle in ther. . . ."

"No," said Clara, "let's all go. I'd ruther leave the boilin' taller to The Beast as to try to defend all ourselves in that one cabin—did the need arise," she added.

There was several quick nods at that. Was there a serious problem—I knowed that we was then thinking about Indians, too—the trading post was a more secure refuge, for it had been designed in that manner, like a block house. Likewise, there was shot and powder and more rifles there.

"Like as much, we'll laugh at ourselves 'fore this day's out," said Biddy

Dalton, but I noticed that she wasn't close to laughing then, nor was any other of our group.

"Fetch the guns," said Clara to her two big girls, for there was not big boys in attendance, they all being gone with the men to burn the brush. The two girls slipped into the cabin.

"I think . . . ," Brother Gilbert started to speak but was interrupted by a sound in the distance, a loud sound, distressful. "It's Martha Elen," I said, and started in an awkward run in the direction the noise had come from, for I perceived it to be a cry for help.

"Wait!" screamed Clara Cuthcart. She must have seen the Indian at the same moment I did.

He come from the woods behind the cabin, menacing in paint, with up-raised tomahawk. I stopped. From the opposite direction, we could hear the clatter of someone crashing through the brush. I held my breath.

In an instant one of the triplets, John or Robert, I couldn't tell which, broke into view and behind him the other two, with Martha Elen right after and a pair of painted savages in pursuit of them.

Sarah! I didn't see Sarah.

One of the Indians pushed past Martha Elen and she fell, screaming. The Indian was after the red-haired triplets, and he reached them, easily grasping one of the boys and his sister, the other boy scampering ahead out of reach.

Martha Elen was up and with a shriek, she threw herself at the Indian who held her children, scratching and clawing at him. Both children tore away from him, only to be caught up by the other brave.

Martha Elen was still fighting and kicking. The Indian backed off from her and then pulling his tomahawk stepped toward her. She stepped back and he raised his weapon, pulled his arm back, and I heard my own voice as if from an empty barrel, screaming something that I could not even under-stand. But the sound of my scream and all else was drowned in a loud explo-sion and the brave paused, tomahawk still upraised, and then slid slowly to the ground.

Brother Gilbert, the smoking long gun still poised, let out a satisfied sigh.

"Run, Martha Elen, run!" I cried.

But she did not. She turned her attention to the brave who was struggling with her two children, those two giving him full measure of difficulty. Well, I could have told him that they was a handful, had he asked me. Their mother, scratching, kicking, and pushing added considerable to the commotion, enough so that he, too, pulled away and drew his tomahawk, only to be felled by another shot.

Well, that shot could not have come from Brother Gilbert, for he had not the time to reload, had he the means, and I was not certain that he had. I looked toward the cabin. Biddy Dalton was armed with a rifle, as was Clara Cuthcart, but Biddy's rifle appeared to be the one that had been shot.

All of that had transpired in so short a time that I had not even moved, but stood poised as I had been. "Look out!" cried Biddy suddenly, and I whirled about. But I was not the one she was warning, but Brother Gilbert.

In the confusion we had forgotten the first Indian, that one that had appeared at the edge of the forest on the opposite side, and it was he who stood face to face with Brother Gilbert, menacing that old feller with his tomahawk.

Brother Gilbert backed slowly away, for in truth, the old man was so crippled up with the lumbago and gout and other infirmities of age that he could not have moved no faster, no matter what.

I waited for the shot from Clara Cuthcart's rifle to fell the Indian, but that shot did not come in time. For with one quick and powerful thrust, the Indian landed a blow upon Brother Gilbert's neck that near severed the head from the body, and the old man was dead before he struck the ground.

And then the Indian turned toward me, for I was nearest to him, the only one who stood between him and Martha Elen and her children. And I was unarmed.

Except for the pots of boiling fat.

I positioned myself behind one of them pots. I could not think of any way to make use of it, save to keep it between me and that Indian, which is what I done, dancing and darting from pot to pot and fire to fire, praying that Clara would get her rifle working, whate'er the trouble of it was.

Then I seen Clara coming, her rifle in her hand, but not in the manner that rifles is usually carried, for she held it by its barrel as if it was a club and seeing her intention, I started screaming at the savage, taunting him, darting and dancing and keeping him occupied.

I do not know if this savage was just inexperienced of warfare or was drunk, which was always likely, but whate'er it was, he did not use his head but allowed me to vex him and make him lose his caution.

When Clara was almost upon him, I stopped short, behind one of the big boiling pots and with a shriek of triumph, the savage raised his tomahawk and lunged around the boiling pot toward me. Had Clara's blow come at an instant later, it would have been too late. But the Lord's Plan favored us and putting all of her weight behind it, Clara swung the rifle butt as high as she could and caught the savage full in the side of his head, and off balance anyway, he started to fall, but it was Clara who administered the shove that landed him head first in the pot of boiling fat.

I would like to think that he was dead or unconscious before he hit that oil, but I could not say. I only knowed that he fell so hard, that he submerged fully into the bubbling cauldron, and I remember remarking so calmly how he sizzled much as a chuck of fresh fat would sizzle. I was almost curious even to see how he would shrivel as a crackling. No horror overcome me the way it should. I was completely calm, matter-of-fact about it.

"Come, hurry," shouted Clara, "ther may be more." It was then that I noticed that the stock of her long gun was broken, and we was one gun less.

Martha Elen and her triplets had reached sanctuary by that time, and it was Biddy Dalton, her rifle poked through the window, that guarded the clearing.

"Where is Sarah?" I cried when I'd got my breath. "Where is she!"

Martha Elen's face was white and she had no control over her voice. She tried to speak but could not. All she could do was shake her head.

I turned to the children. "Have you seen Sarah? Where is she?"

"She was with us," said Robert. "We saw the Injuns and we all started to run. That's all I know," he added.

"They've got her!" I cried. "My baby, them savages have got my baby!"

"Someone will have to go for the men," said Biddy. "They'll have to track the Injuns and find her. Maybe," she added without conviction, "she be in hiding and they an't found her."

"I'll go," I heard myself saying.

"No," interrupted Clara Cuthcart. "No. Nobody can go. It an't safe. We'll just have to wait it out here and hope that the Injuns don't try to rush us."

"Someone needs to warn the men," said Biddy. "The Injuns could catch them out in the open, without warnin', and massacre them!"

"It an't safe," said Clara again. "What good's it goin' to do if that someone gets kilt on the way—won't nobody be warned then."

Clara Cuthcart I knowed to be practical, of a turn of mind that added credits and subtracted debits. Biddy Dalton was not of that temperament.

"Someone's got to go," she insisted.

Clara shook her head firmly and started to speak but was herself interrupted by a curious sound. Someone was singing pitch, humming the way they done at church when they wanted to get started right off.

We turned, almost all of us of one mind, to where Leretta and Berdetta sat, hands prim in their laps, humming their perfect pitch.

"What're you doin'?" snapped Clara.

The two sisters looked at each other, their perplexed frowns matching and after something of a struggle, Berdetta opened her mouth and, grimly struggling to get the word out, at last managed to say, "Anna," so that we could understand.

"Anna!" I looked around. The black girl was nowhere in sight. Ruffled as I was, I got it in my mind that she, too, had been taken by the Indians, but Clara Cuthcart, not so easily untracked as I was, snapped, "Anna? Has that girl gone to warn the men?"

Both women, looking relieved, nodded their heads vigorously.

"Ah," murmured Clara Cuthcart. "Wal, now, all's we got to do is wait."

We had gathered all the children close to the cabin where we could dive in at a moment's notice. We had two rifles and powder and shot piled up.

After a time Clara said, "I don't think that they'll be back or they would have been back by now."

I kept my mouth closed. It would do no good to moan. But where was my child? Where was Sarah? I paced back and forth in front of the cabin. The dead Indian still sizzled in the pot of oil, but Clara had gone out with an old quilt and gently covered the remains of Brother Gilbert.

That dear old brother. It come to me then that upon the occasion of his old wife's death, when he had mourned and wondered out loud why the Lord had not seen fit to take him also, he had at last opined that he could not question the Lord's Plan and that had the Lord not wanted to take him then, He must be saving him for something else. And was this then it?

My pacing grew more frantic as my thoughts commenced to race. What would they do with Sarah? They wanted her scalp, that was it. But what had happened? We had the protection of the old chief—what was his name, I could not recall. Maybe she was hiding. Maybe they had not caught her. Sarah was quick and bright. She could have got away and having got away, she would be smart enough to hide.

Hide? The old cave. Ah. That was it. She had got away and she was hiding in that cave. In absolute certainty, I snapped upon that explanation. I would entertain no other. The more I thought of it, the more I believed it.

I paced further and further, widening my circle. "Sit down, Annamanda," said Biddy Dalton. "It won't help to wear yerself out."

Ah, but she didn't know. I did. Then I decided that I would go fetch my child. I knew the way. I'd be back before I was missed.

It proved uncommon easy to make my way to the back of the cabin and slip into the woods. Once out of sight, I knowed that they would not come after me, no more'n they had gone after Anna. I would take a roundabout way to the cave, find Sarah, and lead her back. I could not be comfortable until I had her safe.

Though the path was fairly even and without obstacle, still I tired quickly, my breath coming in heaves and sobs. I was not in no condition to be marching through the woods, no matter how fine the trail. But I needed to find my babe. The path would take me right by the trading post. I did not even try to be careful. I was in a hurry.

Still, I had to stop several times to catch my breath, and when I got to the trading post I could see signs that the Indians had been there and that there had been more than three of them, for there was numerous footprints and a great deal of damage done the building, though it had not been burned. But I was certain what whiskey and weapons had been there was no more.

The cave I was after, I knowed to be several yards beyond the trading post, through some woods. Truth of it was, I was not just certain exactly where it was, only that George had mentioned its whereabouts to me. I paused long enough to tell myself at last that it was not bright to walk into that forest with wild Indians about. And then I remembered what Clara had said, that the Indians must be gone, otherwise they'd have attacked. It was certainly safe enough, and I had to know if Sarah was there.

The trail through the woods was not as plain as the other had been. It was mostly just open spaces between trees, and in a short time I commenced to become nervous that I might not be going in the right direction. I thought perhaps to turn back. But the thought of Sarah alone and frightened kept me headed in what I presumed to be the right direction. I stopped to listen, knowing that there would be a little stream near to where the cave was.

I thought about calling out, but quickly decided against that. The faint sound of water running become apparent, and I struck out immediately in the direction that I perceived it coming from, turning abruptly, and of a sudden finding a well-trod path. Ah, this was it, for the children played here often.

I followed the path a few steps until it turned into a thicket. I stopped, took a deep breath, and marched ahead, only to be stopped short after only a few steps.

On the path before me lay an unmistakable form, the head bereft of scalp detached from the body, the black of the skin already turning gray in death, the slave girl's blood soaked into the leafy soil.

I felt myself begin to tremble, and I started to back away stifling a cry. Anna, I thought, ah, dear Anna, to have gone the same way as her brothers. I stopped, knowing that the way to the cave lay beyond that mutilated corpse. Had that girl been headed toward that cave herself?

Where was Sarah?

I wondered if there might be another path, decided to search one out, and turned. Behind me was not one but several Indians, their hideous paint giving testimony to their intentions. I stood as stone, knowing that I could not escape. Leisurely, one of the Indians stepped up to me and took my elbow roughly, but he did not menace me in any way, nor did he speak either to me or to anyone else. With a jerk, he pulled me along, and I trotted to keep up.

Well. I had made a mess of it.

It was awkward going through the brush, for I was being pulled along, my breath coming in short gasps, stumbling occasionally, struggling to keep my feet.

I could not say how long we marched, it was probably not long as it seemed, but at last we come into a clearing where there was several more Indians. It was obviously not a camp, for there was no fire or anything else to give it any permanence. There was a group of Indians gathered in something that resembled a circle, and in the middle of that sat Sarah, unharmed as far as I could tell.

"Mama!" she cried, and before they could stop her, she had darted to me and pressed her face into my skirt. I brushed her hair and spoke as sooth-ingly as I could.

There was a burst of chatter from the Indians. I could not say what it amounted to, only that one of the braves at last detached himself from the group and stood before me, and my heart sunk. It was the young brave, Ku-leeniah, the wild one.

He stared at me for a long time and then snapped something. One of the other braves released his tomahawk from his belt and quickly stepped up, and at a command he lifted it up over me. Well, I thought, what is to be will be. And I said nothing, only held my child tight against me. Whate'er it was, I did not want her to witness it.

There was a sudden sound behind me, and a voice vaguely familiar spoke in the Indian tongue, rapidly. Kuleeniah seemed to consider and then spoke sharply, and the brave menacing me with his tomahawk slowly lowered it. I peeked over my shoulder to see who my savior had been.

"Heh, heh, heh, pretty lady."

Drooly. From his belt, caked with blood, the unmistakable scalp of a black hung. I thought that perhaps I might have been better off if the Indian had gone ahead and used his tomahawk. Drooly confirmed that.

"Heh, heh, heh, pretty lady," he slobbered, and so suddenly that I did not see it coming, he punched me lightly in my protruding stomach. I stepped back.

"Heh, heh, heh. Brand new baby scalp," he said. "Copperhead scalp and baby scalp."

Chapter 27

The Beast

I was not blessed with the leisure to ponder Drooly's threat, for the Indians was obviously in a sweat to be gone before the men returned from the fields, and with good reason. The Indians numbered no more than a dozen, I would have said, though I had neither the time nor the presence of mind to take actual count.

And in spite of what I had seen at the trading post, they did not seem to carry rifle or shot. They was armed primarily with their knives and tomahawks.

Neither me nor Sarah was tied. Indeed we seemed not to be much noticed at all, but I was certain that any untoward movement on either of our parts would have brought down attention aplenty.

I would have spoke with Kuleeniah, but I could not catch his eye, and I was afeared to try to go to him. Besides, I could not be certain that he would even understand what I had to say, though I suspected that he would.

If I had entertained any hopes that they might not burden themselves with us, them hopes was immediately dashed, for as soon as they was ready to move, a brave, at a word from Kuleeniah, prodded me lightly with his tomahawk, and I decided it best to do what he wanted.

We was under the protection of the older chief, what was his name—one of them names that will not stay put in your memory. Strange that Kuleeniah would be so easily recalled and the other not. But it would come. The more you worry such things, the more difficult they become, so I let that be.

I had heard that chief promise, and Eremus Lodi had repeated that promise. Once the chief seen that we was captured again, why, he was most certain to be angry and to free us. These young bucks would be most sorry.

Still, that thought was not as comforting as it ought to have been, for the chief was not present; Kuleeniah was present and did not seem in the mood to listen to reason and argument.

We was prodded along, the braves moving quickly with uncanny lightness of foot. I made no effort to walk lightly and managed to step on any twig I could and leave footprints upon any damp ground we come to, though truth of it was ther wasn't much such, for the path we took wound mainly through hard and rocky ground, and led quickly uphill.

Sarah clung to me as she could, though the narrowness of the trail forced us to walk single-file upon occasion. Nor did she seem tired nor winded, as I quickly become, but then she was not burdened as I was.

It come to me that I could ill afford to tire and stumble or give evidence of weakness, lest I be left behind in the manner of the slave Anna. I glanced heavenward. Whate'er the Lord's Plan, of course, I would have to abide it. Then that old sayin' "The Lord helps them that help theirselves" popped into my mind. Well, did the opportunity arise, I'd certainly take advantage of it and not wait for the Lord to intervene, that was certain.

But it did not appear that any such opportunity would present itself. We walked silently and quickly through the forest, and in no time, I was turned completely around. I looked heavenward again, but this time it was not for help but for information, but I could tell nothin' from the position of the sun. For one thing it was passing cloudy and for another, I just didn't have that kind of ability, the kind my old father had and George, to know directions and to sense the condition of the weather and such.

Except to prod us on when we slowed, the Indians paid scant attention to us, and I was ever mindful of any chance to dart to safety, though I knowed that possibility to be unlikely.

I could not think where we might be going, but from the way we traveled, I had to think it was quite some distance. The Indians did not pause, but moved as if they had a precise destination. I looked back over my shoulder now and then, always hoping that Drooly and his menacing-looking companion were gone. But they stayed right with us. They was apparently an accepted part of the group.

"Mama," whispered Sarah from time to time, "I'm tired" or "I'm thirsty" or such. I could only shush her, warning her mainly by my expression or by a quick press of her hand that it was not safe for us to converse.

I do not know what I wondered about more—how tired I was or how I managed to keep walking. Eventually, however, the shadows lengthened enough that I realized dark was approaching, and in the fall of the year when dark descends, it does rapidly.

Abruptly, we pulled up, probably at a signal from Kuleeniah, though I could not see him. I was immediately apprehensive of what was goin' to happen to us, but though Drooly passed by and give us a sidewise and stupid grin, otherwise we was left alone.

No fire was built, but one of the braves passed us a string of jerked meat. Though I was hungry, I hesitated over the meat. You never knowed. I'd heard stories of how the Indians ate dog and I wasn't too eager to eat jerked dog, but Sarah had no such reservations and tore hungrily into the meat and seemed to relish it. So I did, too.

After we had finished that, the same brave motioned us to follow him, and he led us to a small stream and indicated that we drink. There's nothin' quite like jerked meat to make a body thirsty, so we fell to our knees and savored the water, the first I realized that I had had since morning.

The brave then made much of turning his back on us. My first thought was that he wanted us to try to run away, and then I realized that he was giving us privacy to take our comforts. Well. That seemed an uncommon civilized thing to do.

They was apparently not intent on taking our scalps or otherwise misusing us, at least not immediately, or they would not have been so concerned over our welfare. I felt some relief.

It turned out that, except for the cold, a fire was not needed, for the clouds had give way, and the beginnings of that big October moon rose and shined down. It would be a few days before that moon was perfectly round, but it was big enough to cast a nice light, and by that light I made out Kuleeniah standing apart, staring into the dark woods.

I took a deep breath, rose and walked toward him. "Kuleeniah," I said in my most reasonable voice, "you have no right to take us prisoner. Your father. . . ," I paused and then the way it will happen that elusive name popped onto my tongue, "Pewannee has give us protection. I heard him myself. He give it in the name of his mother Hannah, and he paid the debt of a son to Eremus Lodi."

If the Indian understood a word I said, he give no notice, and only motioned one of the Indians nearby, and that Indian took me roughly by the elbow and steered me back to Sarah.

"Heh, heh, mistress," Drooly pressed close and hiked up his pants and giggled. "Heh, heh, an't no good—Pewannee, an't no good. Dead," he said and, as if to emphasize that, drawed his hand across his throat. "Dead," he repeated and jerked his head toward Kuleeniah. "No good, no good, no good," the scum sing-songed, "dead, dead, dead. Heh, heh."

I looked quickly at Kuleeniah, and I caught him staring right hard at me with a look so cold and vicious that I was surprised that it did not bore clear and clean through me and bounce off the tree at my back.

Well. Here was a problem, indeed. Was that Indian chief dead, then he took his promises with him. Still, I had no way to know wh'er Drooly knowed what he was talking about or no. I'd certain ne'er trust him on his word alone.

The night did pass, and though it was probably not any longer'n any other such night, it did seem to drag considerable. I could not say that I actually slept, only that I dozed and woke and nodded and come awake with a start at regular intervals. Each time I did, I saw an Indian or two wide awake and watchful. Sarah slept against me, snoring lightly, so tired was she, and the babe in my belly, too, for it was passing quiet as if tired out.

Almost before the first light of morning, we was roused up and without ceremony prodded to start moving. I was aching with discomfort, stiff and sore and my bladder heavy, yet not allowed to stop, I was at last unable to keep myself from dribbling, which was not much relief and both annoying and shameful. But my body was not concerned of shame, only of need.

Trees and bushes slowly grew out of the dim light, and I made out the rocky trail ahead of us, winding up, and I wondered vaguely how far we had walked. My tired feet told me that it had been a far piece.

At length we stopped in a slight clearing. Kuleeniah and two or three braves were locked in quiet, intent conversation, and I felt my palms begin to sweat and my breath come short. What was they up to?

They was looking around, over their shoulders suspiciously. Perhaps we was followed. Certainly the brothers would be on our trail by now and Cyrus, perhaps Eremus Lodi. But how close could they be?

Suddenly we was motioned ahead and roughly pushed forward. Two of the Indians, however, stayed back, and looking quickly over my shoulder, I could see that they was headed back the way we come, darting soundlessly through the woods, tomahawks clutched in their hands. I did not know what they was after, but my heart sent out a silent warning that my voice could not.

We descended for a time. The trail grew rockier and narrower, enclosed by large boulders of a variety that I had ne'er seen before. It was like a tunnel, and we emerged from it several yards beyond into another clearing, covered over with a deep carpet of molder'n leaves and ringed by heavy fern. The trees and fern was so heavy that little light was admitted, though I knowed that high overhead the sun was bright. Here we stopped and waited in perfect silence.

I could almost hear the beat of each single heart so still was it. My own breathing sounded loud as a drum and I tried to hold it back, yet it would escape me. Sarah stood at my side, clutching my skirt, so silent that it would hardly seem to be the same little girl.

I did not think that I would be able to contain myself, so powerful was that silence. I thought for certain that I would have to shriek, for my voice was pushing so hard at my throat that it hurt. I clutched at my own skirt and clinched my fist tight and could feel the fingernails pressing at the flesh through the several thicknesses of skirt and petticoat.

Then, abruptly, there come the sound of shuffling feet, and the braves at the edge of the tunnel fell away, showing no alarm. But it was not one of the Indians that come through that tunnel. I caught my breath so hard, it sounded like a rainstorm.

It was Hannah and she was followed by George!

And directly behind her come one of the two Indians that had darted so soundlessly away. He was clutching a terrible trophy, and at the sight of it, the rest of the Indians let out a loud whoop of delight.

The Indian held aloft a bleeding and gory head, a head freshly detached from its body, and the Indian threw it down and pulling out his knife commenced to hack at the scalp. Before I could turn away from that grisly sight, I recognized that dead and contorted face.

The Solitary. That shy and timid solitary. There was so many questions in me that I could not begin to sort them out. George? The Solitary? Hannah? What was they doing here? How had they got here?

"George!" I cried. He saw me and started to run to me, but one of the braves reached out a stong arm and grasped him and pulled him back. There was naught I could do but watch.

Hannah had marched right up to Kuleeniah and stood before him. He sniffed and turned away dismissing her with a wave of his hand.

"Kuleeniah!" she cried. "Hear me! For I come from your dead father and I bring you his message." She spoke in English, her aged voice firm and strong.

And Kuleeniah turned back toward her. I could not describe the expression on his face, wh'er fear or hate or both. It was terrible to see, but the old woman held her ground, her voice suddenly mocking. "Ye have betrayed yer blood," spat out the old lady. "Yer red blood and yer white blood, ner will the god of neither find place fer ye in the hereafter!"

Still she spoke in English, and I was certain that Kuleeniah understood her words, for he reacted to them as if shot. The rest of the Indians seemed more puzzled than anything, yet they sensed the confrontation, for even those hacking at the solitary's scalp fell away from their work and stood to listen and stare.

Kuleeniah shouted out a command in his own dialect, but Hannah only sneered at him.

"Yer a woman!" she cried. "Yer a dog butcher," she shrieked. "Yer scorned of the gods!"

Again the Indian shouted a command, pulling his tomahawk and menacing her with it.

"Ye take no scalps in battle. Ye purchase them from scavengers," and she jerked her head toward Drooly and his companion, they two standing close by, grinning and scratching, for all the world as if it was a cockfight or shoe-throw that they watched.

Hannah pointed her finger at Kuleeniah and jerked her head toward Drooly again, "Taker of father's scalp," she hissed. "He took yer father's scalp."

Drooly was suddenly serious, pale under his scraggly beard, and he shook his head violently from side to side.

"Ye eat dog vomit!" cried Hannah. "Ye scavenge like a possum in the night."

The shadows that danced upon the Indian's face was terrible to see, and suddenly, he dropped his tomahawk and tore his knife from its sheath and with an unearthly cry, raised it high over his head.

"It was white milk that suckled ye," hissed the old woman, and deliberately she tore open her buckskin gown to reveal withered dugs, as white as my own.

We stood poised in silence, and then in the background I heard a soft, "Heh, heh, heh," and then a cry of animal rage, and Kuleeniah brought down the knife, plunging it deep into the target thus exposed.

There was no sound from the old woman, but she held out her wrinkled hand toward her attacker and then crumpled at last to the ground, her sightless eyes wide toward the heavens, the blood spreading evenly over her flesh and soaking into the soft buckskin of her gown.

Kuleeniah stood with his dripping knife held high, his own eyes wide, a frightful grimace on his face. I could not take my eyes from him. Thus we stood still, not so long probably as it seemed.

Suddenly, Drooly's stupid companion let out a yelp, as a boy at play, and pulling his own knife, fell upon the body of the old woman, grasping her by the hair and pulling her up. He was going to scalp her!

Well. I think even I would have knowed better than that. If I had time to think about it, I would have knowed that no Indian would let a scum such as that defile his own flesh, no matter that he might himself have killed her.

With a swift move, Kuleeniah jerked up that scum, and in the instant before the knife was sunk into his chest, a look of comprehension crossed that stupid face. But it was too late, for Kuleeniah plunged the knife, still dripping his own grandmother's blood, into the throat of the scum, and the blood so unexpectedly released shot forward in a hard stream.

I looked at Drooly. His mouth had fallen open. He started to complain and then, perhaps thinking better of it, commenced to back off. But Kuleeniah, with a sudden, almost impatient sigh, picked up his fallen tomahawk and, much as flicking at a pesky insect, smashed it down on Drooly's forehead with such force that the miserable wretch's face was cleaved in two and I could see into his wicked brain as he sunk to earth.

I held Sarah to me, her face buried in my skirt. George on the far side of the clearing stared at the three fallen bodies, his own face gone pale. Calmly, I found myself wondering if the blood-letting had just begun, and would we all we left piled together in this darkened forest?

But Kuleeniah suddenly grunted something, retrieved his tomahawk, and waved off a brave who ventured up as if he would take these two new scalps.

Kuleeniah muttered something, and then he turned full to me and said in quite pure and distinct English, "The Beast will feast this night." And then he turned away, giving a quick command to his braves. Had I attempted to translate what he said, I would have said that he simply ordered them to go on, for obviously our journey was not yet done.

One of the braves took George roughly by the arm and pushed him ahead, and another paused behind Sarah and me and nodded us forward.

Another brave all at once said something sharp, and everyone stopped and looked around. A puzzled, annoyed look passed across Kuleeniah's face, and he surveyed his men with a frown. It come to me then that we was missing one. Two had gone off and only one had returned with Hannah and George and what was left of the solitary.

Kuleeniah muttered something, with a wave dispatched another brave back the way they had come, and then motioned the rest of the group on.

We was not through walking it seemed, for we stepped quickly ahead, the trail winding ever upward. My thoughts was all a-jumble, so much so that I think I could not even comprehend the discomfort and pain. Even Sarah remained uncommon silent.

Our skirts snagged on this or that limb or bramble, tore and rent. We stumbled now and then, yet the Indians only prodded us on, they seemingly tireless in the face of the increasing steepness of the trail. My own breath was becoming more and more labored, and I commenced to worry. Did I fall, unable to go on, I had no doubt I would be left dead and scalped, mayhap my infant with me, for I recalled what Drooly had said.

I could not dwell on my painful weariness. I had to put my mind to something else. It was necessary to think clearly and to plan, in such way as I could plan. I had to look back, think things through, and thoroughly engage my mind, so that little was left to think on my painful condition.

I had two, no three, young'uns to think of. That we might on our own account escape such dire circumstances seemed wholly impossible. Short of having our captors felled in some incomprehensible manner, our only hope of salvation lay in being rescued. So that the one thing that was important was time. We had to dawdle for time.

The unsettling thing was the question of what was going on. Was it simply a matter of wanting a particular scalp—Sarah's red one for instance—we would have been dispatched already as easily as Hannah and Anna and the solitary and Drooly and that other. There was some purpose at work that I could not comprehend, nor did I feel that whate'er it was could be to our advantage.

I was deep in such thoughts when we come to a halt. I was surprised but relieved, and both Sarah and me sunk down upon the ground, ready for a rest. I could not make out the reason for our stopping at first, and then as the Indians commenced to mill about, I noticed that we had come right up on a large boulder across the trail, from the look of the trail it had made down the side of the mountain, I could tell that it had fairly recently dislodged.

Well, I was used to dislodged boulders and supposed that this one might well have been sent tumbling down the mountain by one or another of them earth tremors, for though you could not always feel them, they did occasionally rattle hard enough to dislodge trees and stones, even upon such rugged mountains as this.

The Indians was some time in searching out a different route around the boulder, for we was in deep and rugged country, and paths, even for Indians, was not easy to find. I did not mind the chance to rest, nor the time thus wasted. George was still too far distant for me to talk with, but we regularly exchanged glances, his own I could tell was attempting to tell me to be brave and that he would, too, for he nodded his head and attempted to look cheerful. Sarah was not near so cheerful. She was as a matter of fact right down glum in the mouth.

In time we was prodded up again and around the boulder, down the mountain and around through some tolerable rugged land. I held my skirts tight with one hand and grasped at trees and saplings for support, as did Sarah.

In time we started back up the steep incline, and even the Indians, I noted, was breathing heavy with it. I set my weight and put one foot before me, trying not to think of nothing else, only that single move each time. Still, by the time we got back upon what seemed to be a regular trail, I was so winded that had I been called upon to speak, I never could have.

I could not have told the time by then, for I could not even guess at how much had passed, only that my empty belly suggested that we had passed through several meals. Yet we was prodded on, and I commenced to wonder did Indians have not the same need of nourishment as other people.

We marched on, higher and higher, hardwood trees giving way to needled trees, hour after hour, until at last the evening shadows could not be denied, and yet we walked, hurrying more it seemed to me. Nor did the falling dark slow the Indians. They was in a hurry to get where'er it was they was headed.

It did seem to me that the slope had lightened some and that the ground was clearer, the path more secure, which was a blessing, was you in the mood to look for blessings, for it was dark enough that movement on a less clear trail would have been might nigh impossible.

At last we and the moon seemed to come out at the same time upon a wide, flat clearing, high atop a mountain. I looked around and to the east of us, for the moon was near perfectly round and bright as a hundred candles. I could make out hills and mountains, gently rolling, and across the way, a ridge, bare as the one we was on, as if the Lord had placed stepping stones at some intervals across the mountains. The light was so shining and clear that I could near make out single trees and bushes from that distance.

Had the circumstances been other than they were, I might have stood and admired and contemplated in awe the wonders of the Lord's world. But I could not long admire such view, for my attention was brought back to reality roughly, as one of the Indians shoved me forward into the clearing.

George and Sarah, too, was thus encircled, and we stood and watched. What we seen brought chills all down my person, and I reached for each of my children and held their hands tight.

The area we was in had been illuminated by torches and fire so that with the light from the moon it was almost like daylight. In the center of the clearing stood a large flat rock, stained with the brown of dried blood, and round about several poles was hung with various scalps, dried and pitiful-looking things. I looked away. I did not want to examine them, but I could be certain, I thought, that they contained the wooly scalps of Anna and Tim and Jim.

I could not help myself. I looked back at them. There was all kinds, pig-tailed, gray and blonde, black, and Indian. And I could feel certain that some of them scalps had been raised at that very altar before us, for altar was the only term I could think of to describe it. I could not contain the shiver that ran down my back.

What manner of place was this? A butchery? What was the purpose of all them scalps and where had they come from?

Then it come to me, the memory of Hannah's last moments. "Ye take no scalps in battle," she'd cried, "ye purchase from scavengers." Was that it? Was it Drooly and his kind that had furnished them scalps?

At a sudden command from Kuleeniah, the Indians fell away, leaving the three of us in the circle alone. I braced myself, but we was ignored and left standing there. Kuleeniah threw his hands high over his head and throwed back his face to the sky and commenced to chant, though of course I could not make nothin' of it.

After a time, he lowered his hands and turned to us, the look upon his face serene, and he spoke carefully, distinctly in our direction for all the world, as if we could understand his dialect, which of course we couldn't. He seemed to be explaining something, and from his general behavior and attitude I was just as glad not to be able to understand.

He stepped back, threw his hands and head high once more, and then turned. Deliberately stepping to the fire near the altar, he spread wide the fingers of his left hand and stuck the whole thing into the flame. He pulled the hand from the flame and held it triumphantly high.

Well. He may have burned it and he may not have, but the expression on his face give no hint. Then with a quick movement, he stripped the loin cloth from his waist and stood perfectly naked before us. I turned Sarah quickly to me and buried her face in my skirt and stared at the ground myself.

The Indians did not take no notice of us but commenced to chant again. Kuleeniah cried out, pointed at two of the braves, and they broke away and disappeared into the woods on some errand I could not understand. Then he fell to his knees before the altar and commenced to chant softly. I ducked my head once more to keep from staring at that naked copper form.

I stood that way for some time, at last peeking up once more. The naked Indian still prayed before his altar, and I looked away, staring hard across to the far mountain, just in time to catch sight of a moving figure. I strained and stared. Then I looked quickly away lest I be noticed. I was not wrong. On the far ridge, his long legs eating up the distance, silhouetted in the moon-light was the figure of O'Reilly the black. I knowed it. Even at that distance, I could not mistake them stretched out legs.

"Mama," murmured George.

"Shhhh," I poked him.

Kuleeniah rose at last, and I glanced away from his exposed manhood. He was calling out something. His tone was annoyed. Indians commenced to looking at one another.

"Mama," muttered George again, "Mama, he wants to know where them other Indians is? The ones that just left."

I knowed that George could not exactly understand them savages, but that he did have a keen general understanding and could likely figure out what was going on.

Then it come to me that we was now four Indians short, for them other two, the ones left behind where Hannah had been slain, they had not yet arrived neither. That was peculiar. The group had definitely dwindled, what with four Indians and Drooly and his companion all gone.

Kuleeniah snapped out a command, and one more Indian broke away and slipped into the forest after the first two. I wondered what their mission was.

"Mama," said George, "whate'er it is they got in mind will be done at sunrise."

Well. So we had the whole night through then. "Whate'er it is they got in mind." I had a pretty good idea what that might be, and that idea give me no comfort. But O'Reilly was in the vicinity. And then I thought that perhaps I'd been mistaken. Being tired, I could have been confused and not seen what I thought I'd seen. Yet the shadow of that figure flying across the distant ridge had seemed so real I could not doubt it. Indeed, there was no need to doubt it, for it was the only hope we had.

Kuleeniah called out another command, and the Indians at once rose and commenced to mill around, and one of them brought out pouches and passed them around, and they all commenced to drink from them. Spiritous liquors would be my guess, whiskey. With Indians and whiskey, you ne'er could know what to expect. We might make it to daylight and we might not.

I thought that we was being ignored, and it come to me that, did they get drunk enough, we might be able to slip away in the dark. But even that hope was denied us at last, for with a word from Kuleeniah, we was seized and each of us loosely bound to one of them stakes so gruesomely decorated with scalps. We was able to slip down and sit, which was a comfort, but not much of one, for we did have but to look up to confront the hideous specter of our immediate future.

And so the night passed minute by minute, hour by hour, and the Indians, all but Kuleeniah, continued to partake of the contents of them pouches, but instead of them getting drunker with it, they seemed only to become more excited and danced and chanted, and periodically one or another would break away and dance around us and menace. It was altogether quite uncomfortable.

"Mama," whispered George at one point, "them Indians an't come back."

He had a worried frown upon his face, and I noted that the amulet at his neck seemed to glitter in an unusual manner, perhaps catching the light of the dancing fires.

I had noted them Indians missing myself and only nodded. The revelers seemed not to have noticed, and Kuleeniah was involved in some sort of ceremony which involved much naked posturing, kneeling, praying—I supposed—and things of that sort. He had danced around so much in his nakedness that, truth to tell, I give up trying not to watch him, for once you got used to it, it didn't seem to matter so much, for one naked man an't so very different from the next, except that I wished that I could keep Sarah from noticing him.

Late in the night, Kuleeniah called a council to him, and in the light of the fire, he offered his knife to one of the braves and then made much of turning his bare back upon that brave who then, with great ceremony, drew that knife in two long stripes down the bared back, and the red blood oozed slowly from the wounds.

"Mama!" hissed Sarah, "What'd he do that for?"

I could only shake my head and make some effort to keep from wishing that the brave had cut quite a bit deeper, for that was no Christian thought.

"He's purging himself," whispered George.

"Why?" said Sarah.

"Trying to make himself clean."

All in all, it did not sound so good for us. While the Indians was thus occupied, I suddenly thought to ask George a question that had been bothering me. "George," I whispered, "how come you were with Hannah and that solitary?"

"Me and the solitary was following your tracks, Mama. Between us, we was quite good at tracking," he said with just a trace of pride. "We come upon Hannah. She seemed certain that she knowed where you was, and me and the solitary was prepared to go back for help, but we was set upon by them Indians," he added.

We was silent then for a moment and suddenly George whispered urgently,

"Mama!"

"What is it, George?"

"I don't know, Mama. Something. I don't know. There is something about that troubles me."

Well. It was not O'Reilly, I thought, that would cause him to reach for that amulet. I might have worried about it some, was I not about worried out.

I was passing uncomfortable, but I did not want to wish for the night to pass quickly. The longer we sat unmolested, the better. I started to turn toward Sarah when I was arrested at an uncommon terrifying shriek, and straining, I managed to twist myself in its direction.

Staggering into the lighted clearing was an Indian, or what was left of one, for he was near hacked to pieces, dragging parts of himself, blood flowing copiously. He did not make it even to the center of the circle before he collapsed, and then I could see no more, for the Indians closed immediately about him.

We was left unattended and the silence then was fearful.

"Mama."

I turned toward George, but he was looking curiously about him.

"Mama. Be still, Mama," came the hissed instructions from nearby. It was O'Reilly edging close on hands and knees, his knife between his teeth. The occupied Indians did not see him, and in an instant he was upon us, and with one swift move he slashed the cord that bound George and then me and then Sarah.

George darted quickly to the underbrush and Sarah, but stiff and over-burdened as I was, I could not move so quickly. O'Reilly give me his hand and pulled, but just as I rose an Indian turned, seen us, and shrieked the alarm.

"Run!" I cried to the black, "run to the children!"

But whate'er the reason, perhaps to help me, perhaps to give the children time to hide, he paused over-long, and when he at last turned to dart away, he was cut off. He certainly had the size and the strength to run right through them Indians, which is what he tried to do and might have succeeded, but that one Indian managed a telling blow with the blunt edge of his tomahawk, and the black was felled, yet not mortally.

I squeezed my eyes shut tight, for I could not stand to see what I thought was about to happen. There was no sound but the murmuring and grunting of the Indians, no noise of death. At last I opened my eyes. O'Reilly still lay on the ground, knocked senseless.

I wondered then that perhaps they would not kill him, for they danced about the giant form, and I thought that he, having been their ally, perhaps he would be spared. I would that had been the case, for what they had in mind was a slow and painful death, for it come to me at last as the Indians danced about and held aloft their dead comrade that it was O'Reilly who was blamed for that. And hard as it was for me to think of the black as violent enough for such, I had to believe that indeed he had been the one.

I was bound immediately again, and several Indians dashed into the woods in search of Sarah and George. Well, they was not long in finding them, for the children was not skilled in hiding and was easily found.

Two Indians come dragging them back, calling out into the wilderness, apparently alerting their fellows of the capture. George was dragged back to his post, and I noted that he was clinging with his good hand to that amulet around his neck. One of the Indians apparently noticed that, too, fer he reached as if he would take it, and George, mild and shy George, snarled at him and slapped the hand away, clinging hard to his token. It was not a smart thing to do, for the Indian with an angry grimace grabbed George's good hand, which held the amulet tight, and twisted it so hard that even I heard the crack of the bone in the boy's wrist, and I cried out.

George sank, an anguished expression upon his face, holding the broken wrist, and the Indian reached down and triumphantly jerked at the amulet. But try as he would he could not break the cord upon which it hung. I thought that he would strangle George with it, but a sharp cry from Kuleeniah turned the brave away from the boy.

They had strung O'Reilly from two trees by his arms and was taking turns torturing him. I saw a flicker of the big black's eyes, but no more. He made no sound, though he was burned with hot coals and slashed with sharp knives, his head pulled back and his scalp menaced.

At length, Kuleeniah called the braves together, started to say something and then looked around, some perplexed. He looked back at the gathered Indians, said something, and the other Indians began to look around.

It was not hard to determine what they were talking of, for the group of Indians, who with Drooly and his companion, had numbered fourteen or fifteen were no more than eight, not counting the butchered one at their feet.

I looked to O'Reilly hanging limply from the tree. Was he the reason for such decimation of their ranks? Then it come to me with a start that some of them Indians that had gone after Sarah and George when they run off, after O'Reilly was captured, had not come back neither.

We was losing Indians right and left to something.

Whate'er it was left them savages some distressed, and like a mess of ants when their hole is destroyed, they milled around in some confusion.

"Mama," whispered George, "Mama, day's comin' on, but ther's no birds' sounds or anything you'd expect." He had not been tied, but left in a pile upon the ground, and he was holding onto his broken wrist, as if trying to brace it. I could see the red welt about his neck where the savage had tugged at the amulet, but that token still hung there.

"Mama," whispered George again. "Mama, it's something. I don't know. It's something. . . ."

George had hardly got that much said when sudden silence descended and the Indians become intent, and we at last heard a commotion as if something, a bear, mayhap, something large withal, was crashing through the woods.

"Eeiiiiiii," came the skriek of one of them savages, and then I seen it, tall and terrible, in its hand a bloody axe, tearing in a horrible fury, screaming such an anguished scream that my very blood run cold with it.

"The Beast, Mama," said George, suddenly very quiet and calm, as if he had been waiting for it, and mayhap he had, for all these long years, to see it once again in the flesh, or whate'er it was, for I was not entirely certain that it was of this world.

The Indians was wild with fright and I could tell why, for the thing was much as it had always been described to me, wild and hairy, clothed in bits

415

of human clothing, scarred red across the face, nails or claws curled long, its odor preceding it by quite some, for it smelled of death.

The thing, The Beast, come among us so quickly that not a single Indian thought to run. It swung that axe, a most normal-looking axe—Redmon Pitt's lost axe, ah—in wide circles, catching this Indian and that. I seen a head go flying across the clearing, and the blood and gore was frightful. Savages was scampering all ways.

George had managed to find a knife and cut through my bonds and Sarah's, and we turned to run. "O'Reilly!" cried George and dashed toward where the black hung limp, yet eyes wide and alert. "O'Reilly!"

At that Kuleeniah turned, and with awful scream he hurled himself at me, tomahawk upraised, and I felt the impact of his weapon, a dull, awful blow to the side of my head. I fell to the ground, surprised I think that I still lived. Over me towered the savage, the tomahawk menacing me again. I raised my hand to ward off the blow and saw his hideous mouth opened wide, and I waited for the shriek that would follow, but the sound was lost in the loud explosion of a rifle, and the Indian, turning slowly, grasped his middle, sighed, tried to speak—a curse I supposed—but that died on his lips, and he sank to the ground face forward in his own gore.

Through the mists of my dazed brain, I made out, standing at the edge of the clearing, his gun still smoking, Eremus Lodi and at his side Cyrus. Cyrus had aimed his own weapon at The Beast, but with a cry of rage, that animal, for that's all you could call it, hurled the axe clear across the clearing, and it caught Eremus Lodi in the side, and he fell sidewise into Cyrus. I tried to rise, but my brain somehow could not send the proper signal for it.

Cyrus struggled to regain his feet, but The Beast was upon him, growling in hideous fury. He tore the rifle from Cyrus's hands and lifted him bodily high into the air and slammed him to the ground and was upon him in a minute, and reaching for a huge rock at his side, he lifted it high over his head and prepared to bring it down upon Cyrus's head.

"Sarah!" I heard George scream out his sister's name, not in the anger of playmates, but fiercely, in command, and groggy as I was, I managed to lift my head and focus my eyes in the direction of the sound.

George had retrieved his father's rifle and stood bracing the barrel wedged in the crotch of a small tree, Sarah Elizabeth beside him. My vision clearing, I looked in the direction the gun was pointing. The Beast on one knee was poised over the prone figure of Cyrus Pritchard, the rock upraised for to bash in my husband's skull. I struggled to rise, up on all fours, but I was yet dizzy from the blow I had taken.

"Sarah, here!" I heard George again, just as The Beast did, and that shaggy, evil creature, noting the weapon pointed at him by the boy, tossed his wild mane, and still holding the rock, slowly rose, like a giant bear—no more human than that—his filthy rags hanging about him, his matted beard and hair adding to the impression of wild ferocity.

And though George had the gun aimed at his father's tormentor, he could not manage the trigger I knew. For his good hand hung useless from the broken wrist and the mangled fingers of his right hand could no more manage the manipulation of a trigger than they had been able to manage the manipulation of a charcoal for making his letters.

Sarah Elizabeth stepped quickly in front of her brother, stood high on her toes, and slipped one tiny finger around the trigger.

"Both!" yelled George quite excited, bracing the long rifle with all his slight weight.

The Beast stood tall without moving, as if he did not believe what he was seeing—two children holding a weapon on him. I did not know if Cyrus lived or no, or Eremus Lodi either, though black O'Reilly had ceased his struggles against the bonds that held him to the tree, his breathing undoubtedly suspended as was mine, for between all of us and certain death stood only my children, and had they been twice more, they would have been no match for that evil giant they faced. I could not have screamed had I wanted to, for the roar that filled my head was not the shriek of monstrous evil that one might expect, but my own terror giving itself the voice in my brain that it could not give in my throat. For The Beast had made no sound, though his presence was louder in my heart than any noise could ever have been. Then calmly, I almost heard myself saying, "What is to be, will be."

"Now!" cried George. "Both fingers. Pull!" Still The Beast had not moved, nor did he move after the explosion that followed. For Sarah standing on her tip toes, doing as her brother had bade, squeezed both her eyes and the trigger tight at the same moment, her brother steadying the rifle, which when it did explode, sent both children flying backward, tumbling over each other.

The Beast stood still and then took a slow step forward. My children! I struggled up, my hand closing on a stick nearby. Before he would attack my children, he would have to trample me. I swayed and staggered, clutching my skirt in one hand and the stick in the other.

But The Beast stopped and stood still as a stone for an instant, and then he begun to sway, imperceptibly at first, like a giant tree cut nearly through by the axman, struggling to stay attached to its roots, shuddering and then swaying, and finally tumbling slowly to earth.

I did not know. Had he been hit or only shocked from the nearby explosion of the powder? I clung to my stick and watched. Through the brush on his face, I seemed to be able to recognize a look of foolish confusion, and then behind him I saw Cyrus begin to rise, swaying himself, pushing as I had, first to his all fours, then to an almost erect position, and then flinging himself, pitching forward against the giant. The Beast fell, slowly, like that same tree, and rolled, for the incline was most steep. Cyrus was on his feet. His face bloody and his posture insecure, he steadied himself against trees and saplings and made his way down the incline and was gone a moment before he returned, and I knowed from his expression that The Beast would trouble no more.

And then there was a sound behind me, unreal and uncanny, a sound as a wail, triumphant and anguished at once. It was such a sound as could have come only from O'Reilly. I could have called it a howl, almost, and meant no disrespect, for we owed our lives to that battered black. And to his master.

"Eremus Lodi," I cried, remembering, and I picked up my skirts and ran across the clearing toward where he lay, for I had already seen Sarah and George disentangling themselves, and I knowed them to be safe.

Eremus Lodi grinned at me, wryly as he always did, but the color of his face was too gray and he was soaked in his own blood, his large hand still not large enough to entirely cover the gaping wound in his chest, though he tried.

And I started to tremble for I knowed that all O'Reilly's many powders and potions would likely be of no use here.

"Annamanda," he sighed, his deep voice no more than a whisper, "would ye touch my face?"

It was an odd request, but I would never deny it, though the face I touched was clammy and cold, but I ran my hand over his face and stroked the scalp where the hair had ceased long before to grow, and he closed his eyes against my ministrations.

O'Reilly knelt beside me. Cyrus must have freed him. Had I not been struggling with horror and grief, I might have wondered that the slave could still be upright after the torture he had endured. His battered face was as expressionless as always as he bent over his master. I could not make out what he said, for he had slipped into that savage dialect, the remnant of his former life that he shared only with George and Sarah. It might have been an incantation; it might have been a prayer. Eremus Lodi's mildly mocking tones come back to me from some distant memory. "Whatever god that black man worships, he has faith in, and I honor that faith."

I looked up at Cyrus as much as to say out loud, "He is beyond prayer."

Cyrus knelt and took the dying man's hand. "Ah, Brother Pritchard, at last I think I have need of yer services." His reference was clear. How long ago that had been, Sarah but newly born, that he had said that preachers were useful only for marriages and funerals, and as he had no plan to wed again, he'd have to wait his funeral to call on Cyrus.

There was nothing to say. Sarah Elizabeth and George approached timidly and stood just without the circle. Eremus saw them and motioned them close.

O' Reilly continued his strange muttering, but softly.

"Sarah, my dear, that was a fine shot," said Eremus, as if complimenting the child for some small task successfully performed, "and you, too, George. Good shot. You've saved us all. Or most of us, that is," he said.

"O'Reilly," he went on, "I would lie in the meadow. Just below that spot where the preacher—Brother Pritchard," he corrected with a wan smile, "where Brother Pritchard and his group lay their dead, in that meadow."

418

Cyrus and I lowered our eyes, for we both recognized that Eremus, who had disdained both Elder and Brother as titles, had at last consented. On his deathbed, of course.

Ah, but I was premature in that. For then he looked up at us, for we were now all standing but O'Reilly, and murmured, "Sister and Brother, I truly do think that if the Lord has faith in You and keeps Your Counsel, He cannot fail in this fearsome life."

Well, I thought for a moment that in his desperate straits he had got it mixed up, but when I glanced at Cyrus I had to but note the wry smile on his lips to realize that it was yet another of Eremus Lodi's gentle barbs.

I did not yet understand that man's theology, or lack of theology, but I did not think now that it mattered. For the Lord knows His saints and who they are wh'er they recognize theirselves or no, and He would take them Home. Many of them, I thought, would be quite surprised, too.

We did indeed bury Eremus Lodi in the pasture meadow as he had requested, not far from where our meeting house was planned and near to where Sister Gilbert and them lay. The crowd was great and the tears many.

O'Reilly stood tall and quiet as a tree throughout the ceremonies, for he had already made his own. George had followed the big black the night before down to this very meadow, whilst the rest of us sat in unutterable sadness with the earthly remains of Eremus Lodi. George had stood patient, he said, for what he thought was hours at the edge of the meadow within the trees, while O'Reilly, on his knees near to where Eremus would lie, carried on what must have been his own devotions. At last he had risen and, facing east, had thrown back his head. In that posture he had stood for several moments, at last turning and making straight for the spot where George had thought himself concealed. O'Reilly had taken the boy's hand, and they had walked without words back to the cabin.

At last we was able to piece together all of the events that had come to pass. George had left the brothers burning the brush and trees of Berdetta's and Leretta's land because he was still troubled and, having arrived at the carnage around the Cuthcart cabin and heard the story, he had gone searching for me and quickly ascertained my predicament. I could not even try to guess at how he sensed such things, but did. Nor could I have guessed at how he could search out the solitary, but he did that, too. And the two of them set out upon our trail. It was then, of course, that they found Hannah.

"I don't know that she realized that you'd been captured, Mama," said George. "She was wild-eyed and angry, saying only that her only son had been murdered most wantonly. Mama," he added, "I think that I knowed, too, that The Beast was prowling. Somehow, I have always knowed when The Beast was about. I do not understand it either."

Well, I certainly didn't understand it.

Then Cyrus told his story.

"I went to Eremus Lodi. I have to wonder did the Lord plan it thus, for I found him with no trouble and immediately told him my mission. Nor did he in any way deny the treasonous charges. He only sighed at length and sat pondering for a long time.

"I waited a decent interval and then said, 'You owe me no explanation, Sir. I have come as a friend and to repay those debts that we justly owe.'

"At that he laughed, and asked a most curious question. 'Sir,' he said, 'd'ye know why that the gods lift certain men so much higher than all ther fellows?'

"I shook my head, for I did not understand what he was saying.

"'Why, it is,' he said in that wry manner of his, 'so that they can take better aim.'

"At that he lapsed once more into silence and I rose to take my leave.

"'Ah, Master Pritchard, wait. I'll saddle up my horse and carry you back to your place, for I would see yer little family one last time.'

"Well, I did not know quite what to make of that, but that is what we done, and of course when we arrived, we found all of you gone.

"Whate'er else Eremus Lodi was, he was most certain a wilderness man. Between the two of us, we was able to track you. Truth to tell, however, it was not after a while a difficuit thing to do, for between the Indians and The Beast, there was a string of corpses. We come first upon Anna and Hannah and Drooly and then, one after another, a string of dismembered Indians.

"I think we both knowed that we was on the trail of The Beast, but Eremus Lodi did not speak of it, only one time to mutter almost to himself, 'I will meet him, then.'"

Cyrus did go no further, and we all sat and pondered the various stories.

For several days thereafter we recuperated, I more slowly than the rest. At first I thought that what troubled me was not only pain and grief but that depression that sometimes come in the weeks before a babe is born, though I ought to have been much relieved, for the fluttering within my womb proved that the babe, too, had survived the ordeal that we had endured together.

Still, as the others recovered their strength as well as their spirits, my own did aught but sink lower. I felt betimes that I could not lift one foot high enough to put it before the other, as if all the muds of spring weighed down upon my very soles.

I thought upon all that had happened to us and wondered and weighed, but still I could not understand it. I knowed that what I questioned was the Lord's Plan. I could not understand why so many good people, honest and abiding, each by his own lights, should be made to suffer and die while others, scum and reprobates and thieves and murderers even, continued to live and to thrive.

I had seen good and evil rewarded as one. I had seen evil destroy itself but also destroy everything in its path.

I considered all of that for a long time, becoming more and more distressed of it, and thought upon that scripture that tells us that it rains on the just and the unjust alike. But did that answer? Ah, at last I had to think that we are the just—each of us—and the unjust, too, and so it rains upon us equally as we are.

I was filled not with pain so much as a sadness that approached remorse. I noted that the others all looked now and then askance at me, but none said aught.

At last nearly a week past the burial of Eremus Lodi, I took myself slowly down the path to the edge of the cheerful little river. I lowered myself slowly to a log and sat long and still. Though the day was bright and the birds made sweet noise, my own spirit was so afflicted that it might as well 'a been the darkest hour of the wintriest night.

George walked down the path toward me, concern upon his face. "Mama?" he said.

"Ah, George, son," I answered, "I am sore afflicted. I feel as I have ne'er felt in all my life, and I wonder that I am allowed to occupy space upon this earth, so unworthy am I and so depraved. I am a vile, impure, corrupted, and loathesome wretch."

"I know," cried George, his eyes brightening and the light spilling across his face. "And an't it grand, Mama?"

I was baptized the following spring, Brother Kencaid coming from Salt Creek to do the job. My babe was born in the meantime, a bright happy little girl, and I was pleased with the neatness of it, two of each kind. George chose to be baptized with me, we both of us choosing the cool, clear stream in that meadow sanctified by our dead. Cyrus stood on the bank with Sarah Elizabeth, O'Reilly a few paces behind.

And I myself felt so strong and so certain, certain at least, except for a moment or two when Brother Kencaid bent me backward and so under the cold water, and for just a minute I thought he liked to drowneded me. But then he lifted me up to many amens and loud clapping. And Berdetta and Leretta immediately broke into song, which everyone else joined in.

I gathered my wet garment about me and slipped quickly into the woods to retrieve my dry clothes. In passing I heard George, he standing yet soaking wet, and Sarah, bickering again. George was saying, "You cannot be baptized until yer ready to declare yerself the worst and awfullest sinner that ever was."

"Well," snapped Sarah Elizabeth, "I bet I shan't do that anytime soon." And she flounced off.

Dried once more but for my hair, I returned to the group, and passing Martha Elen and Joseph McCade, noted them to be in lively conversation.

Though I did not a-purpose try to hear what they was saying, I could not avoid all of it.

"Joseph McCade," Martha Elen was saying, her hands planted firmly upon her hips, "you'll not, you understand, you'll not go—we'll not go. We've gone as far as needs and here we'll stay!"

"Ah, Marty, Marty, but d'ye know what's beyond the hills? We've seen what's here an' what's to our rear, an' you interested in what's to our face? There's wonders, Marty, wonders. Ye can't just sit down in one spot when miracles lie before ye an' beckon."

Well, I did not stay to listen more on the conversation for it was likely to become livelier.

When I returned to Cyrus's side, he was engaged in conversation with a stranger. It was quickly evident that they were discussing O'Reilly.

"He is one of the finest specimens I have ever seen," said the stranger who had a look of prosperity about him. "I would give a lot to add him to my stable. Name a price."

"Why," said Cyrus, "that is not possible. He is dear beyond price."

"Ah, now, I cannot believe that. Name a price. As high as you like."

"I cannot name a price," said Cyrus. "He is not mine to sell."

"Well, then, who do I bargain with? Who does he belong to?"

"He belongs to no man," said Cyrus. "He belongs only to God."

And at that I nodded my head vigorously, and I added under my breath that it was certainly true and not only that, God was lucky to have him.

Afterword

The thousands of earthquakes which racked and devastated a large area around the Missouri "bootheel" in 1811 and 1812 included the most powerful quakes ever witnessed in North America—an estimated 8.4, 8.7, and 8.8 on the Richter Scale.

Events have not stood still in the nearly 200 years since.

For years after, earthquakes continued with less severity in that area, and the United States government, after making a sizeable contribution for earthquake relief in Venezuela, eventually made the same efforts to help its own, efforts which largely failed. Congress proposed to trade equal parcels of good land for ruined land, but it was the speculators who profited, buying up the worthless land before the settlers realized what was happening. Litigation went on for years.

Meriwether Lewis and William Clark completed their explorations and drifted into history, one of those famed duos remembered by their combined last names. Settlers poured across the river so rapidly that within ten years of those earthquakes, Missouri was granted statehood.

The Indians were eventually removed west; those who did not drift willingly in that direction were forcibly marched, most notably on the infamous "Trail of Tears" in the 1830s, when thousands of Indians died on the way to what would become Oklahoma. When oil was discovered in that state many years later, some of the descendents of those Indians became wealthy. Most did not.

The Old School Baptists—the original Hardshell Baptists—survived the protestant explosions of the 19th century which saw the splintering of established churches and resultant innumerable protestant sects.

Nearly 1,800 Old School Baptist congregations still go about their quiet ways from New Jersey to California. Generally now, they call themselves Primitive Baptists or simply The Old Baptists, their doctrine of predestination and unconditional salvation largely unchanged. There remain only a few Two- Seed-in-the-Spirit Predestinarian Baptist congregations, those mostly in the south, and not to be confused with Redmon Pitt's Pittites, which is a fictional creation.

Cities have grown up along the lower Mississippi, including the village of St. Louis which eventually outdistanced both Ste. Genevieve and Cape Girardeau, in area and population, if not in charm. That river landmark, the Fourth Chickasaw Bluff was ceded to the United States by the Chickasaws in 1818, and Fort Pickering was established. Fort Pickering eventually gave way to Memphis.

Steamboat traffic on the Mississippi River, ushered in by Nicholas Roosevelt on earthquake-churned waters in December 1811 went on to become the stuff of legends. And the split-tailed comet Flaugergues, visible in North America from September 1811 to January 1812, eventually went on its predetermined path, not to pass this way again for another 3,000 years.

The swamplands in southeast Missouri have largely been drained and developed into fertile farmland. The most visible reminder of those great earthquakes is Reelfoot Lake, a fisherman's paradise in northwestern Tennessee. Born of earthquake turbulence and once covering an estimated 40,000 square acres, that lake was doomed at its origin, cut off from any source of refreshing water by the very violence which created it. But civilization has hurried its demise, and scientists predict that in little more than 50 years, it will be nothing but swampland and bogs.

The big spring country of southern Missouri, on the other hand, has managed to stave off pollution of the many springs, some of the largest and most beautiful in the United States.

The little community of New Madrid was eventually rebuilt, still astride the fault that bears its name. The visitor who goes there can tour the small earthquake museum and purchase a tee shirt that says *Visit New Madrid While It's Still Here.*

What is to be, will be.